CAT'S CRADLE

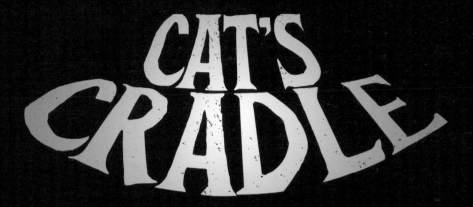

THE MOLE KING'S LAIR

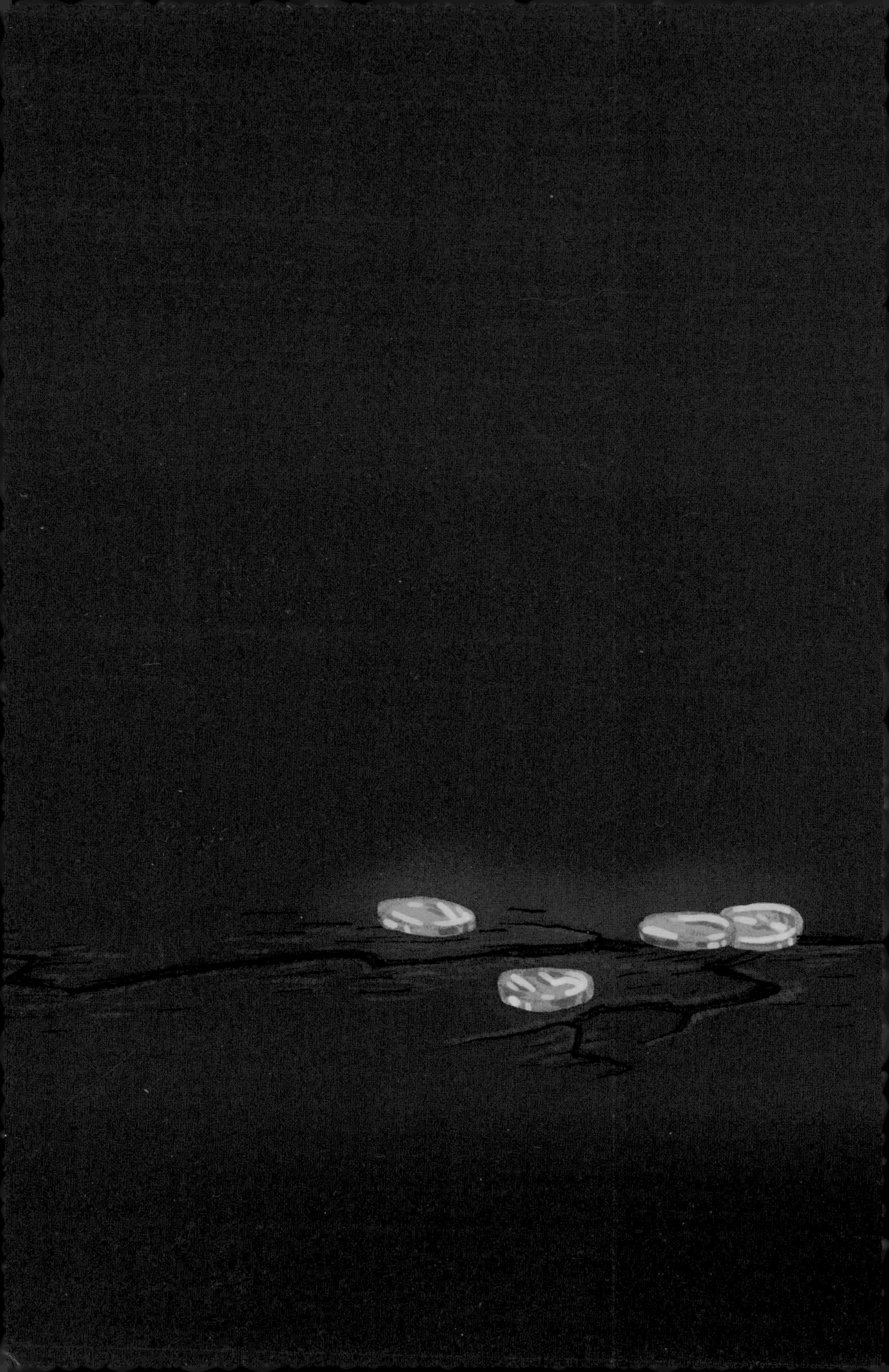

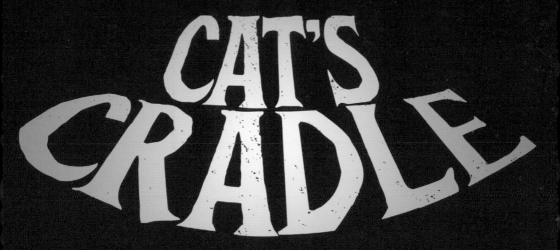

CAT'S CRADLE

THE MOLE KING'S LAIR

JO RIOUX

:01

First Second
NEW YORK

TO KEITH—FOR HELPING ME
THROUGH THIS MONSTER OF A BOOK!

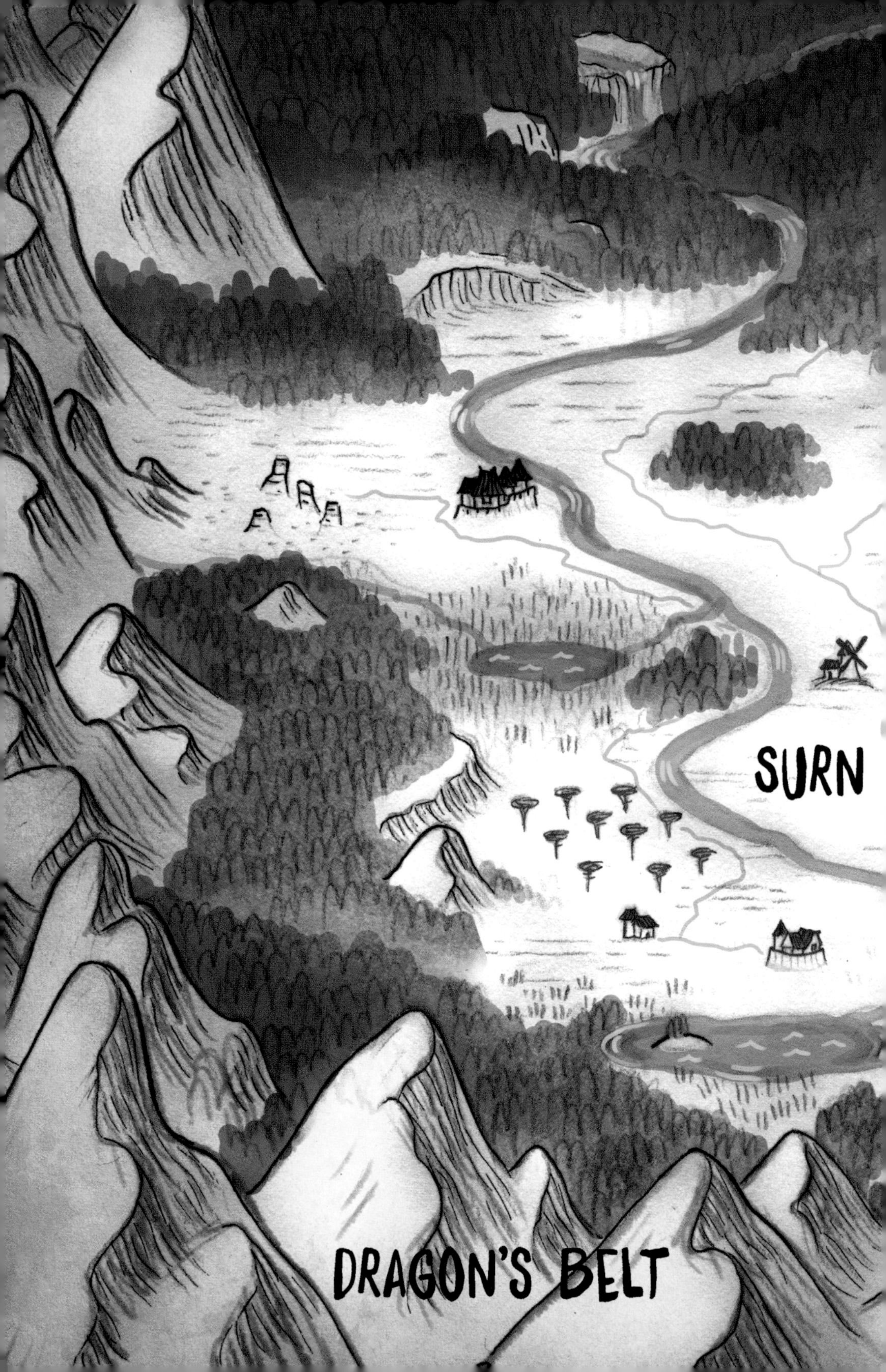
SURN
DRAGON'S BELT

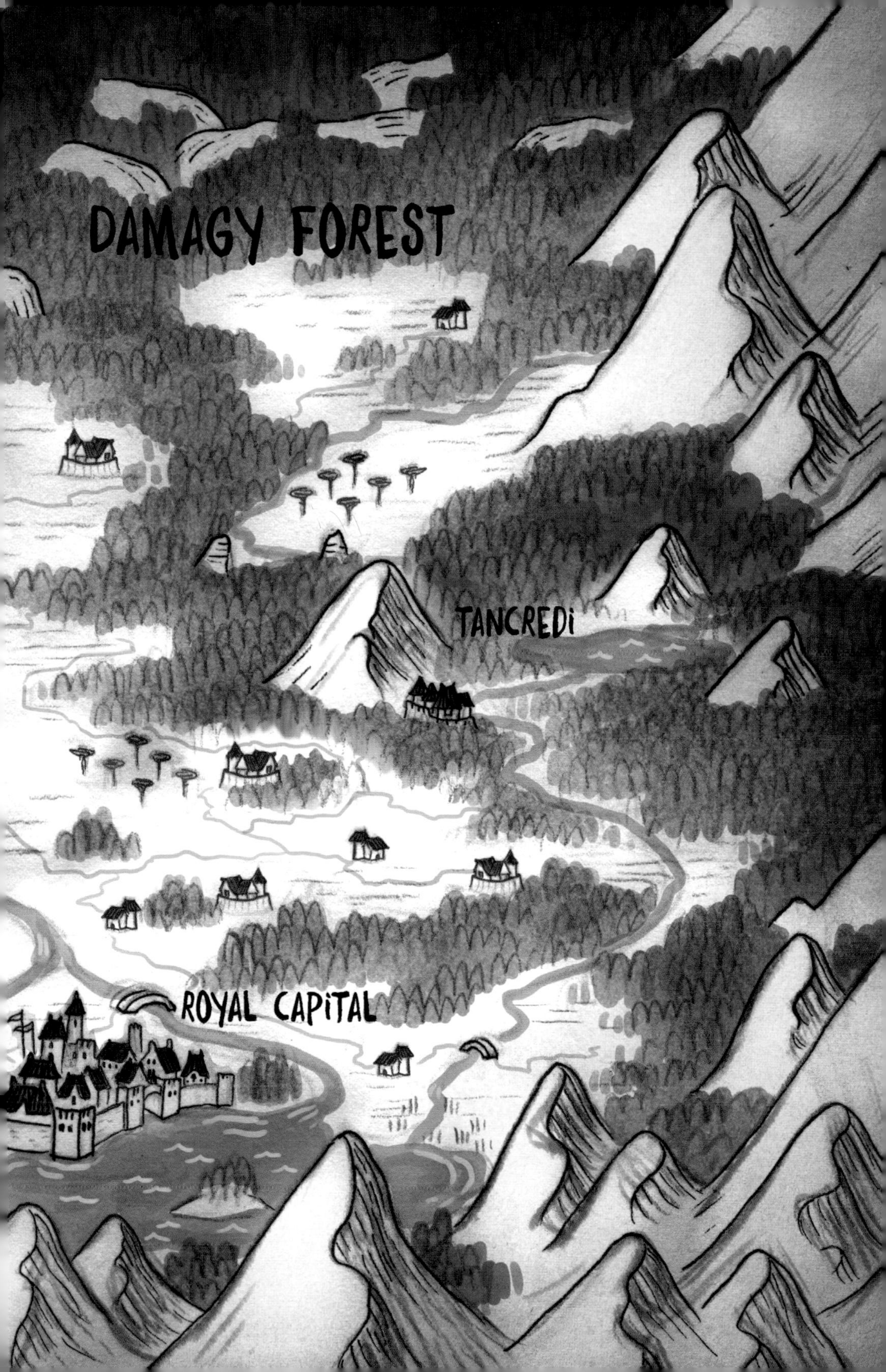
DAMAGY FOREST
TANCREDI
ROYAL CAPITAL

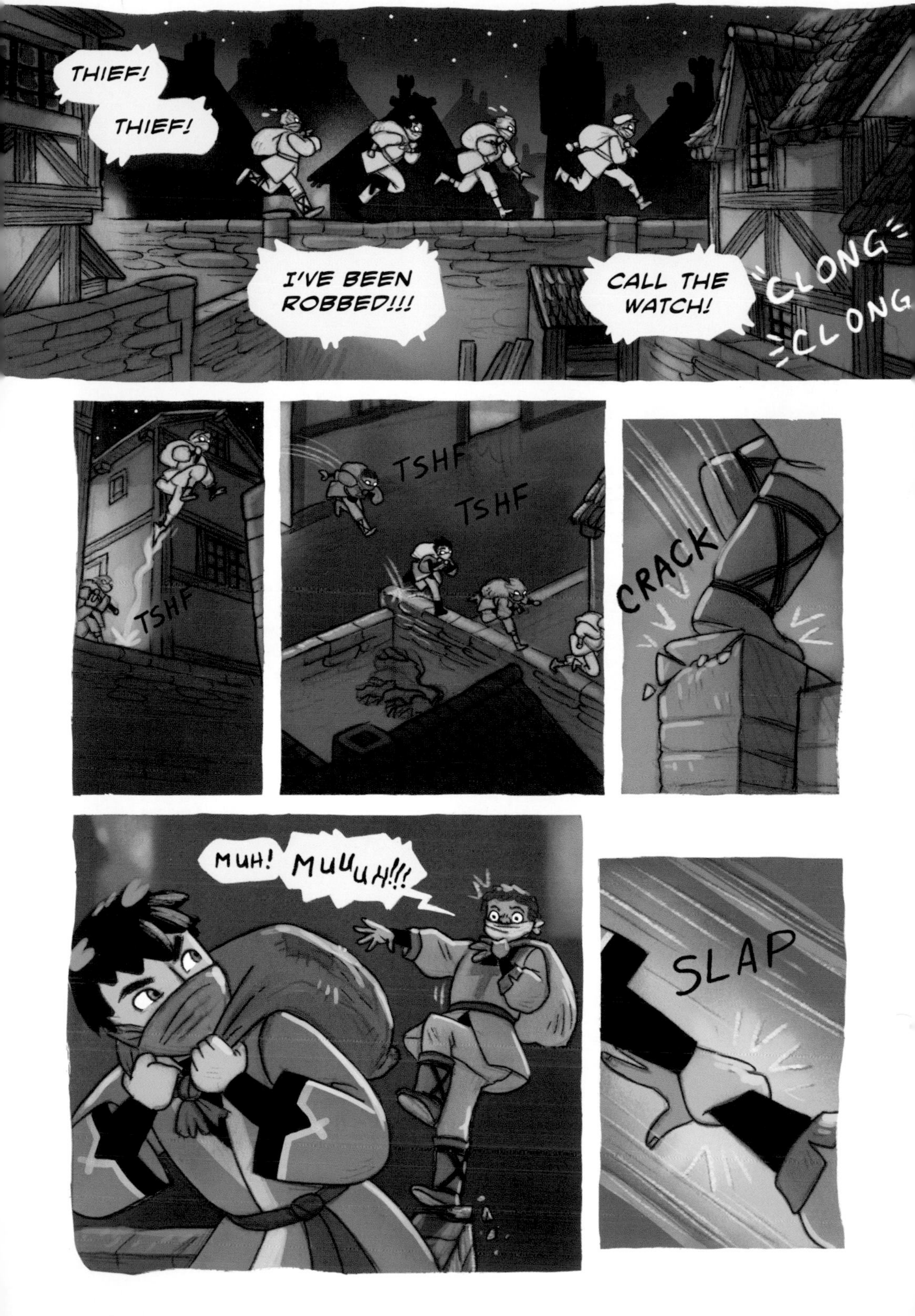
THIEF!
THIEF!
I'VE BEEN ROBBED!!!
CALL THE WATCH!
CLONG
CLONG
TSHF
TSHF
TSHF
CRACK
MUH!
MUUUH!!!
SLAP

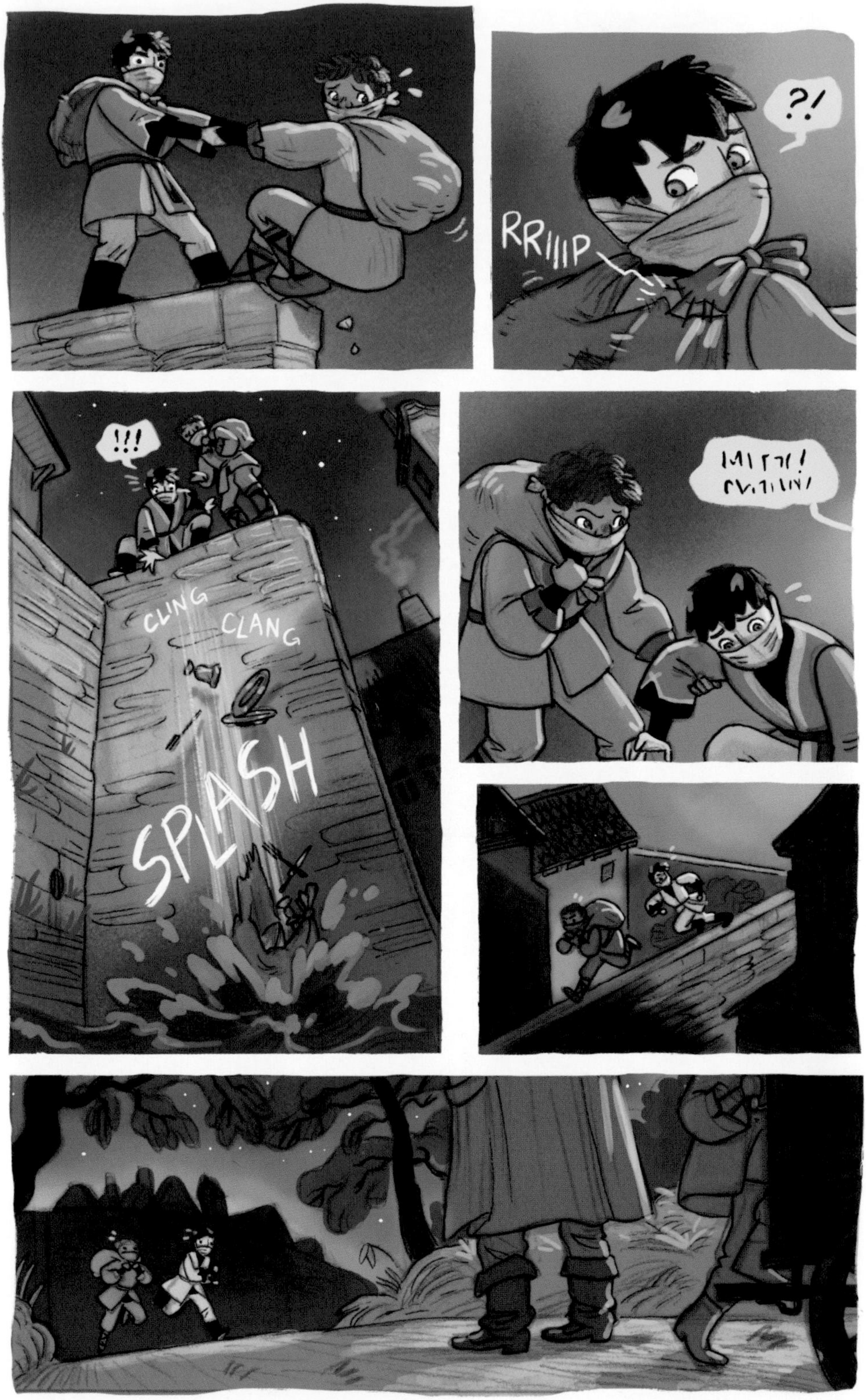
?!
RRIIIP
!!!
CLING
CLANG
SPLASH

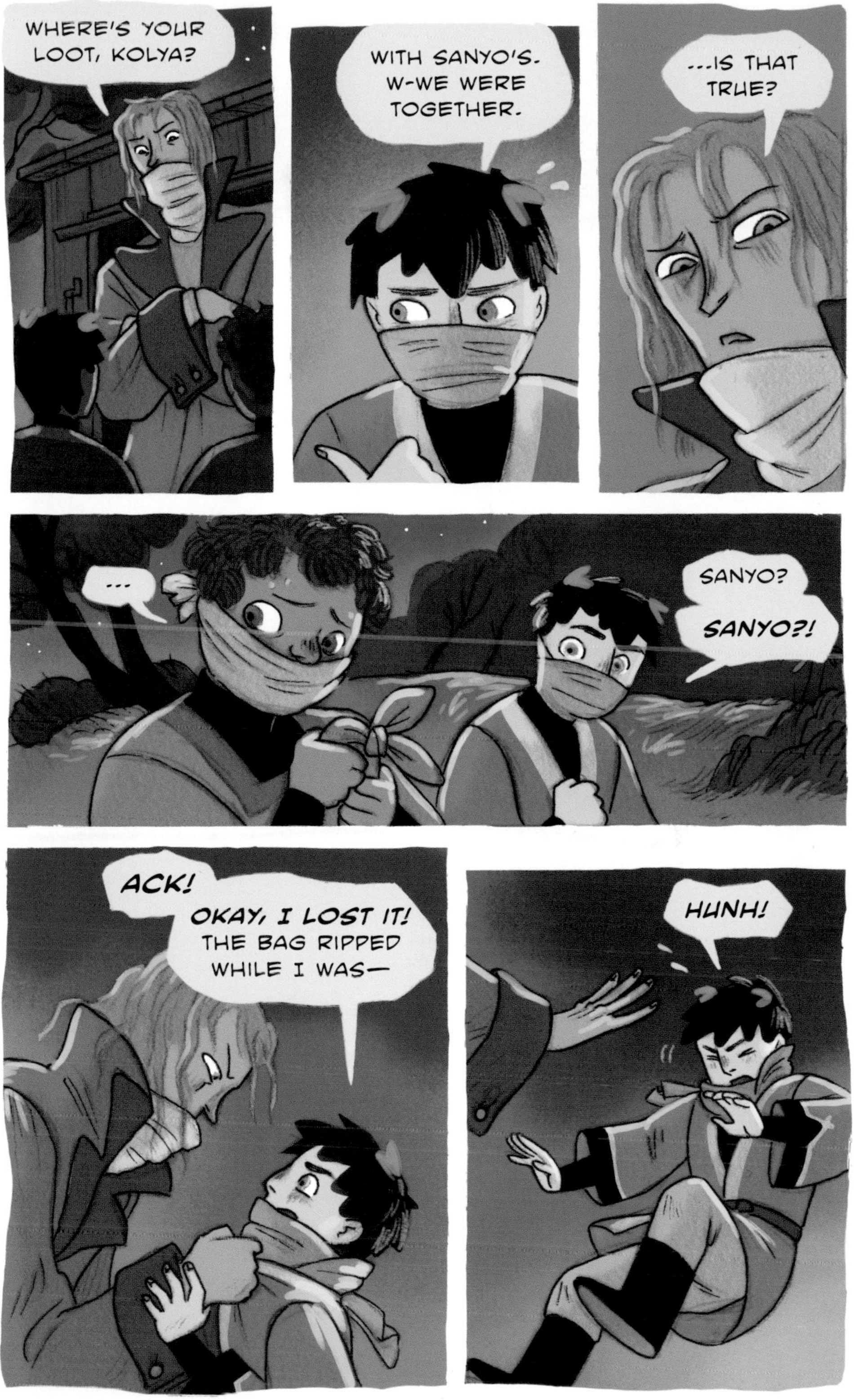
WHERE'S YOUR LOOT, KOLYA?
WITH SANYO'S. W-WE WERE TOGETHER.
...IS THAT TRUE?
...
SANYO?
SANYO?!
ACK!
OKAY, I LOST IT! THE BAG RIPPED WHILE I WAS—
HUNH!

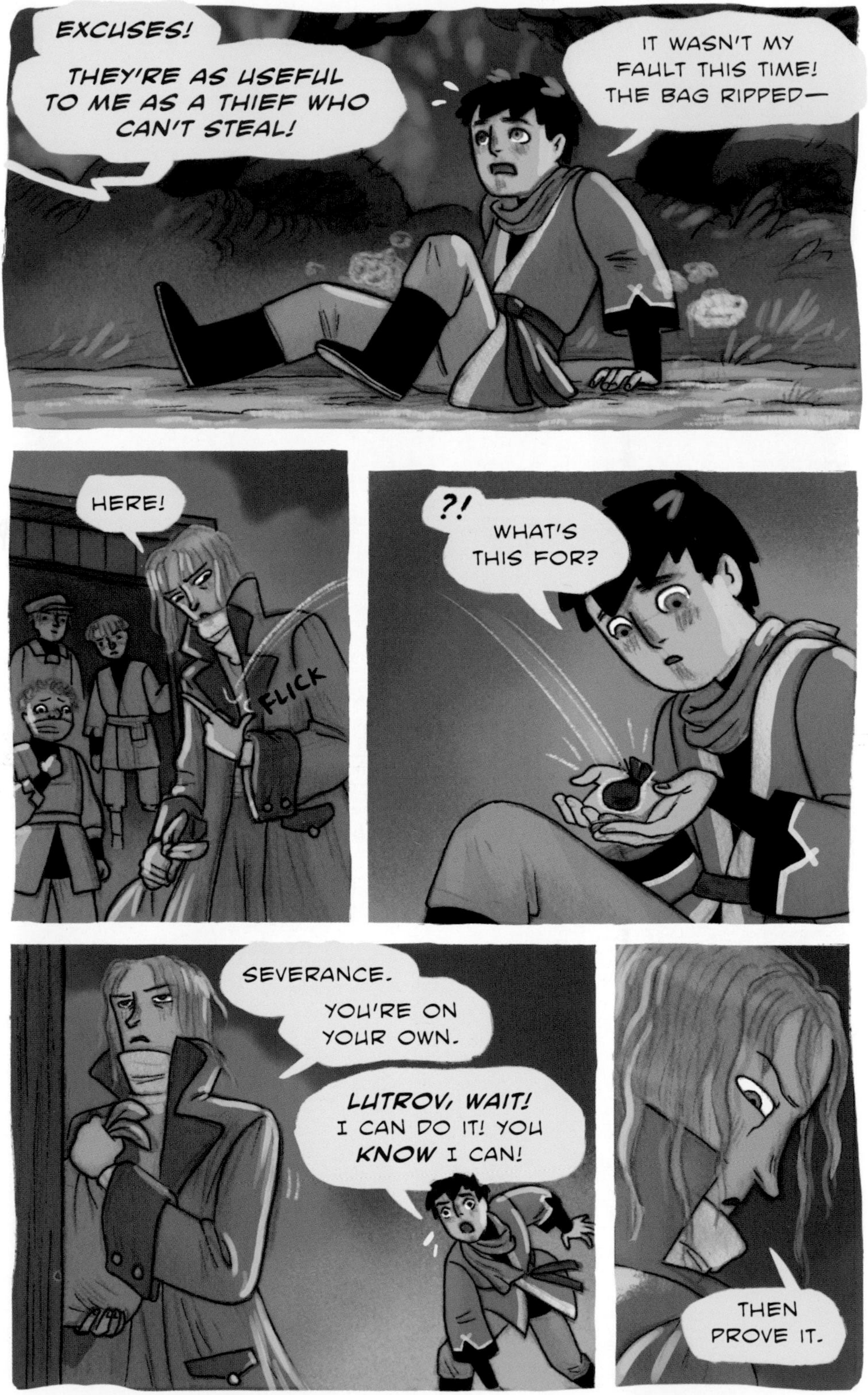
EXCUSES!
THEY'RE AS USEFUL TO ME AS A THIEF WHO CAN'T STEAL!
IT WASN'T MY FAULT THIS TIME! THE BAG RIPPED—
HERE!
FLICK
?!
WHAT'S THIS FOR?
SEVERANCE.
YOU'RE ON YOUR OWN.
LUTROV, WAIT! I CAN DO IT! YOU KNOW I CAN!
THEN PROVE IT.

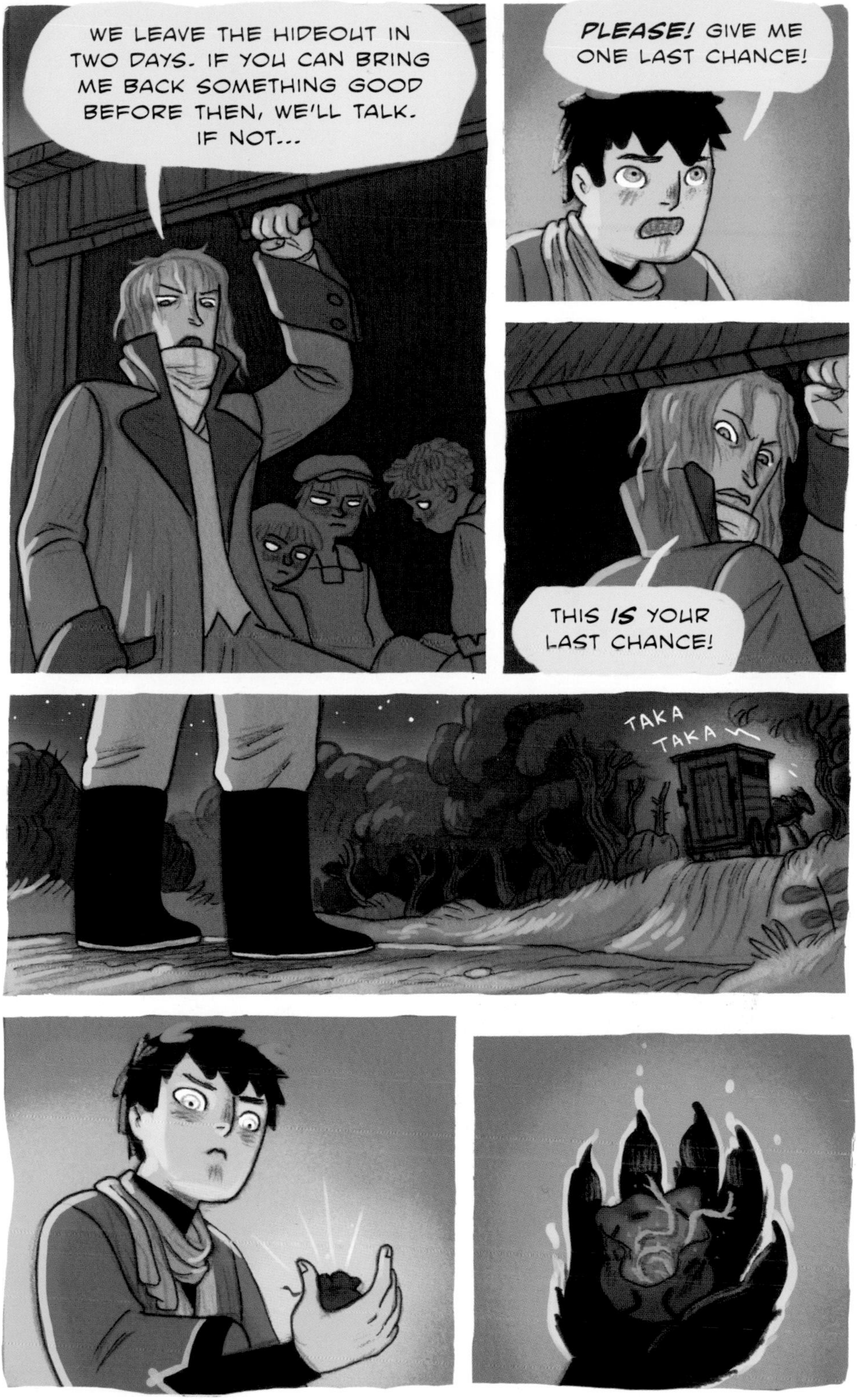
WE LEAVE THE HIDEOUT IN TWO DAYS. IF YOU CAN BRING ME BACK SOMETHING GOOD BEFORE THEN, WE'LL TALK. IF NOT...
PLEASE! GIVE ME ONE LAST CHANCE!
THIS IS YOUR LAST CHANCE!
TAKA TAKA

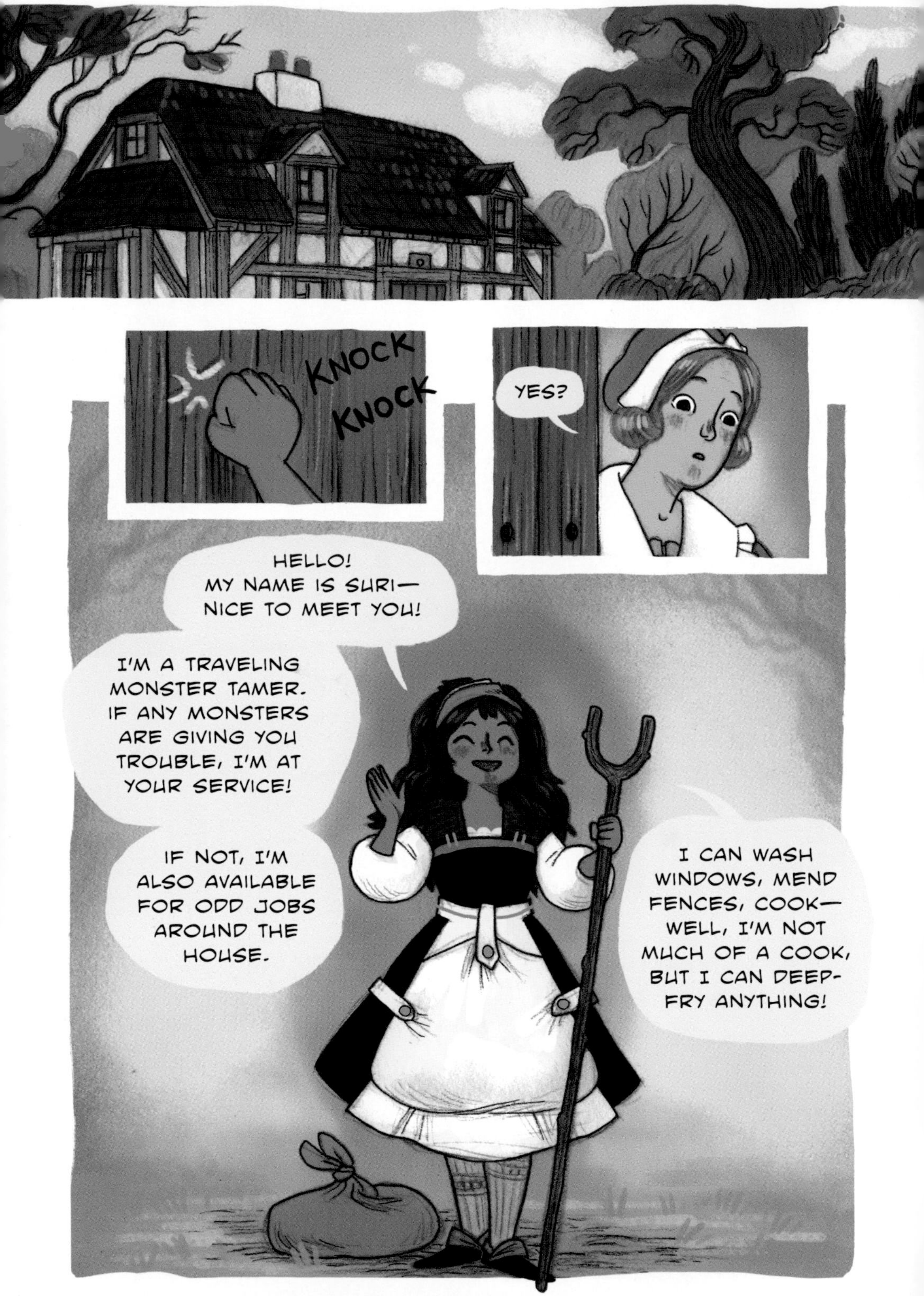
KNOCK KNOCK
YES?
HELLO! MY NAME IS SURI— NICE TO MEET YOU!
I'M A TRAVELING MONSTER TAMER. IF ANY MONSTERS ARE GIVING YOU TROUBLE, I'M AT YOUR SERVICE!
IF NOT, I'M ALSO AVAILABLE FOR ODD JOBS AROUND THE HOUSE.
I CAN WASH WINDOWS, MEND FENCES, COOK— WELL, I'M NOT MUCH OF A COOK, BUT I CAN DEEP-FRY ANYTHING!

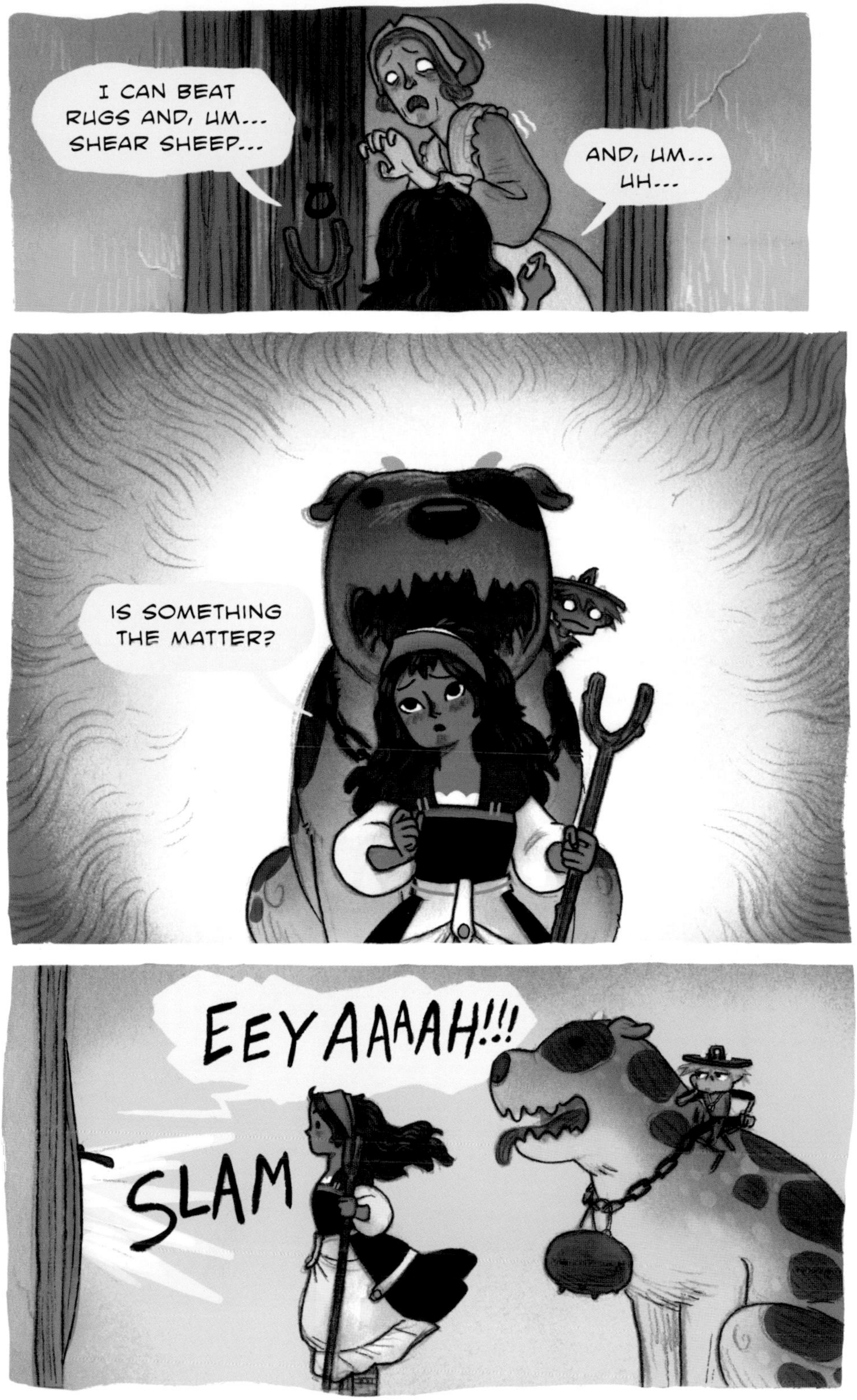
I CAN BEAT RUGS AND, UM... SHEAR SHEEP...
AND, UM... UH...
IS SOMETHING THE MATTER?
EEYAAAAH!!!
SLAM

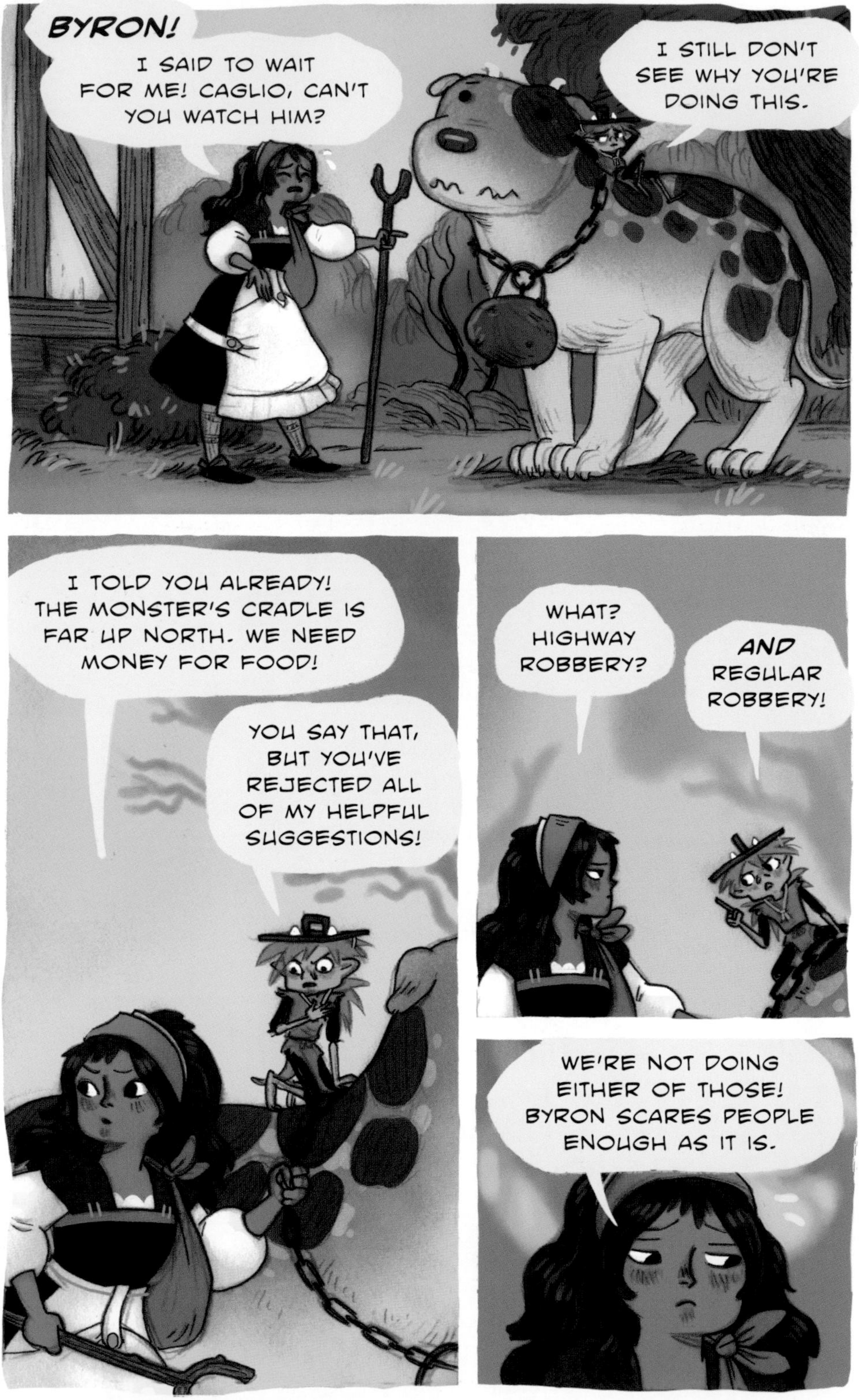
BYRON!
I SAID TO WAIT FOR ME! CAGLIO, CAN'T YOU WATCH HIM?
I STILL DON'T SEE WHY YOU'RE DOING THIS.
I TOLD YOU ALREADY! THE MONSTER'S CRADLE IS FAR UP NORTH. WE NEED MONEY FOR FOOD!
YOU SAY THAT, BUT YOU'VE REJECTED ALL OF MY HELPFUL SUGGESTIONS!
WHAT? HIGHWAY ROBBERY?
AND REGULAR ROBBERY!
WE'RE NOT DOING EITHER OF THOSE! BYRON SCARES PEOPLE ENOUGH AS IT IS.

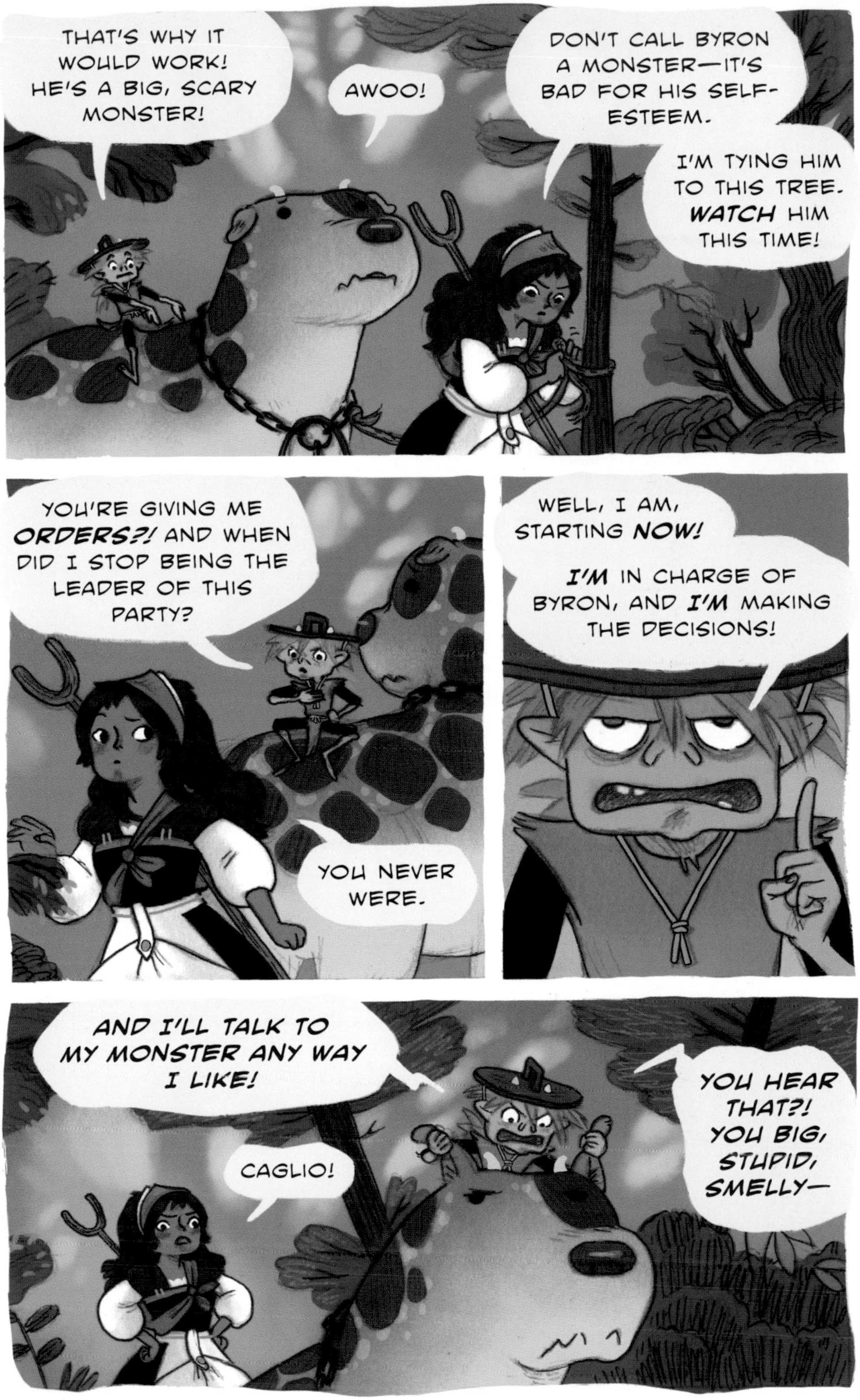
THAT'S WHY IT WOULD WORK! HE'S A BIG, SCARY MONSTER!
AWOO!
DON'T CALL BYRON A MONSTER—IT'S BAD FOR HIS SELF-ESTEEM.
I'M TYING HIM TO THIS TREE. WATCH HIM THIS TIME!
YOU'RE GIVING ME ORDERS?! AND WHEN DID I STOP BEING THE LEADER OF THIS PARTY?
YOU NEVER WERE.
WELL, I AM, STARTING NOW!
I'M IN CHARGE OF BYRON, AND I'M MAKING THE DECISIONS!
AND I'LL TALK TO MY MONSTER ANY WAY I LIKE!
CAGLIO!
YOU HEAR THAT?! YOU BIG, STUPID, SMELLY—

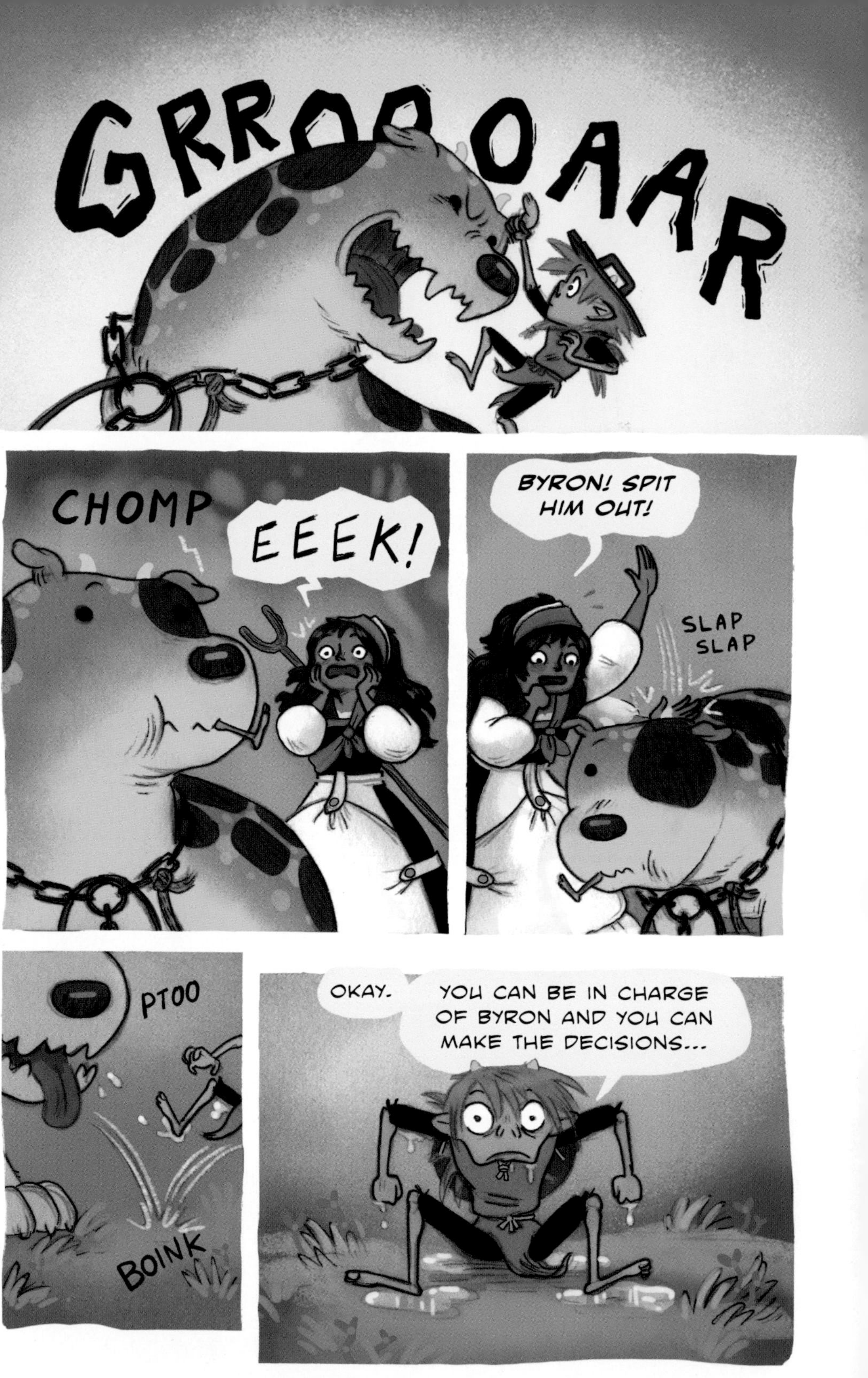
GRROOOOAAR
CHOMP
EEEK!
BYRON! SPIT HIM OUT!
SLAP SLAP
PTOO
BOINK
OKAY.
YOU CAN BE IN CHARGE OF BYRON AND YOU CAN MAKE THE DECISIONS...

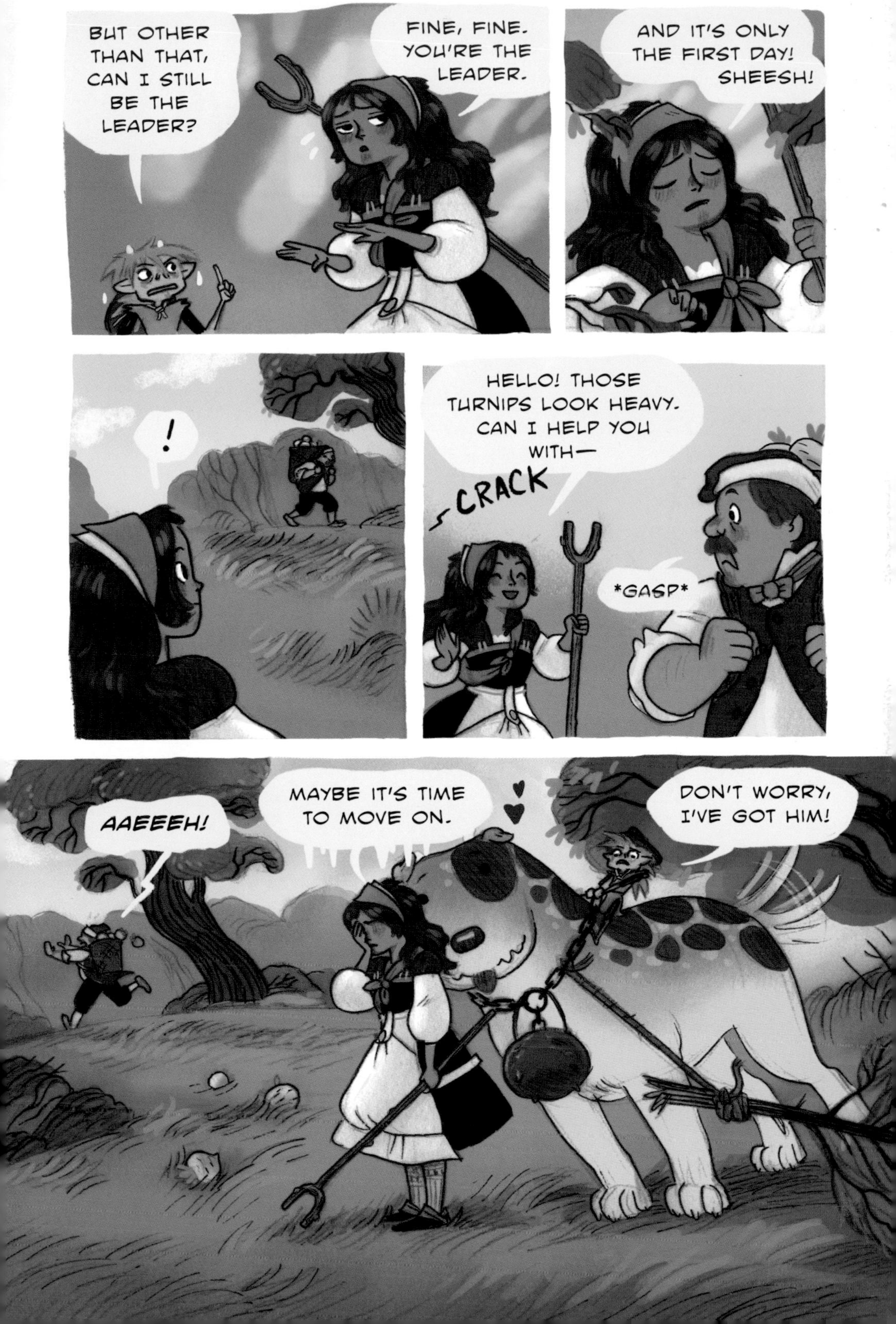
BUT OTHER THAN THAT, CAN I STILL BE THE LEADER?
FINE, FINE. YOU'RE THE LEADER.
AND IT'S ONLY THE FIRST DAY! SHEESH!
!
HELLO! THOSE TURNIPS LOOK HEAVY. CAN I HELP YOU WITH—
CRACK
GASP
AAEEEH!
MAYBE IT'S TIME TO MOVE ON.
DON'T WORRY, I'VE GOT HIM!

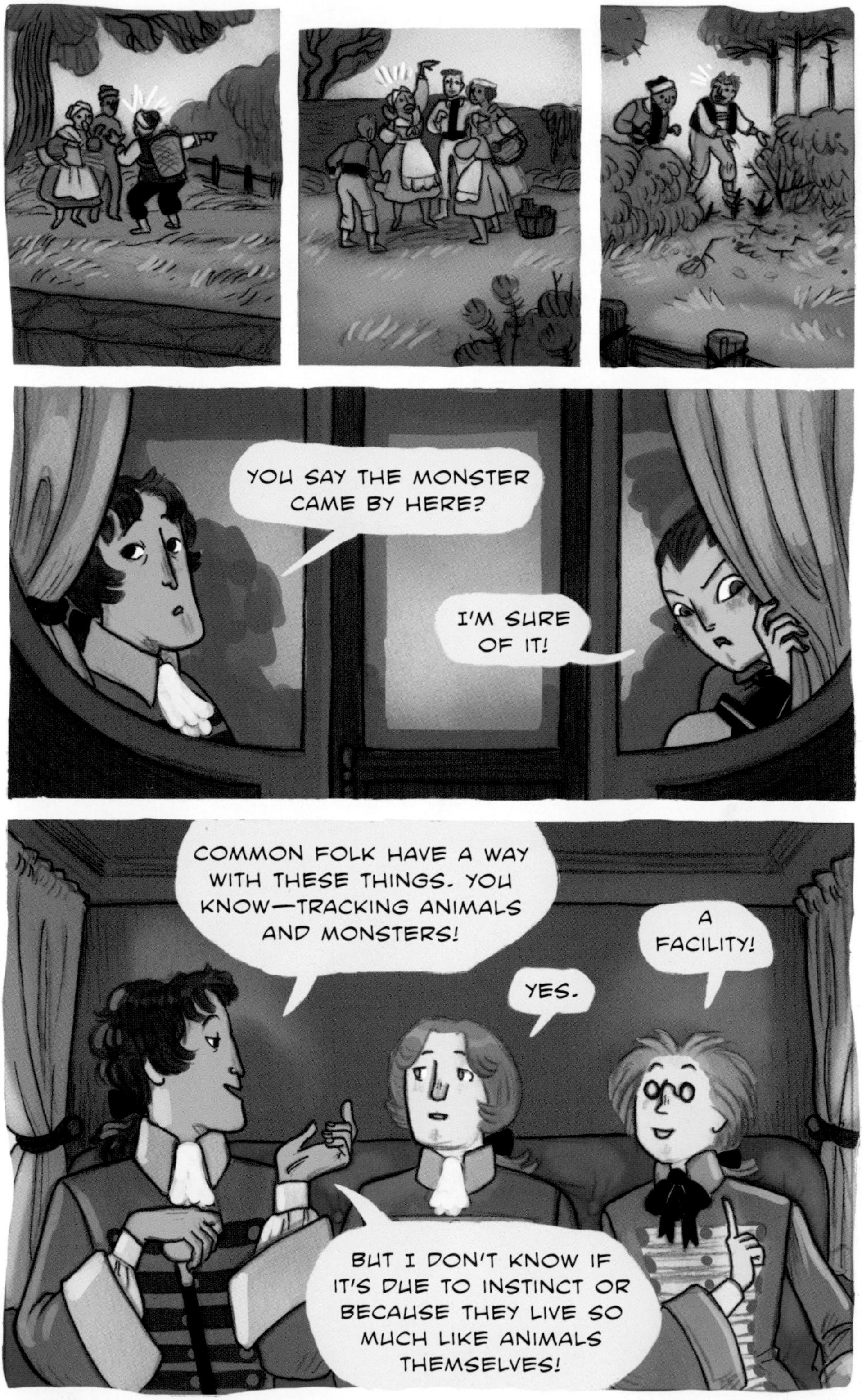
YOU SAY THE MONSTER CAME BY HERE?
I'M SURE OF IT!
COMMON FOLK HAVE A WAY WITH THESE THINGS. YOU KNOW—TRACKING ANIMALS AND MONSTERS!
YES.
A FACILITY!
BUT I DON'T KNOW IF IT'S DUE TO INSTINCT OR BECAUSE THEY LIVE SO MUCH LIKE ANIMALS THEMSELVES!

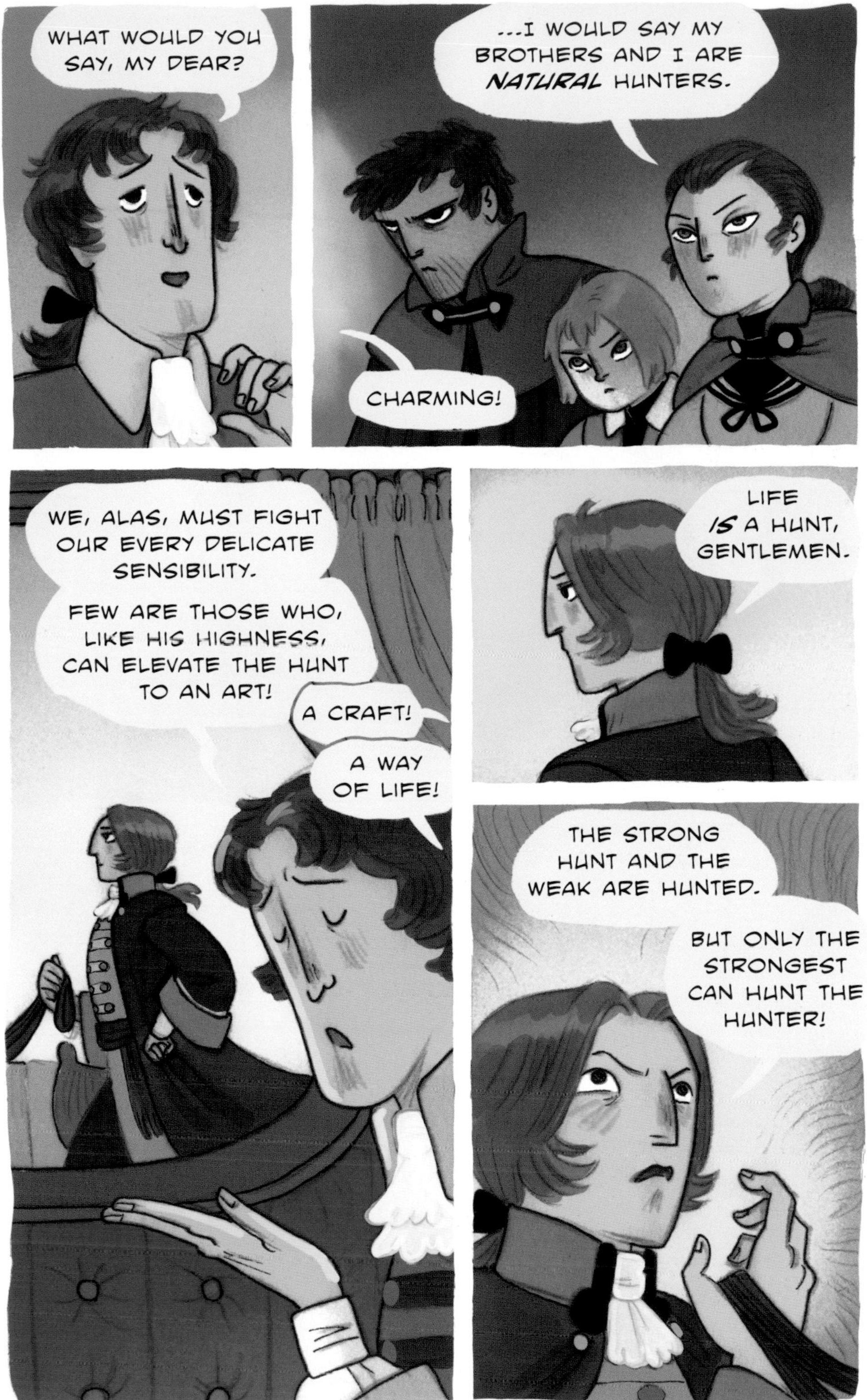
WHAT WOULD YOU SAY, MY DEAR?
...I WOULD SAY MY BROTHERS AND I ARE *NATURAL* HUNTERS.
CHARMING!
WE, ALAS, MUST FIGHT OUR EVERY DELICATE SENSIBILITY.
FEW ARE THOSE WHO, LIKE HIS HIGHNESS, CAN ELEVATE THE HUNT TO AN ART!
A CRAFT!
A WAY OF LIFE!
LIFE *IS* A HUNT, GENTLEMEN.
THE STRONG HUNT AND THE WEAK ARE HUNTED.
BUT ONLY THE STRONGEST CAN HUNT THE HUNTER!

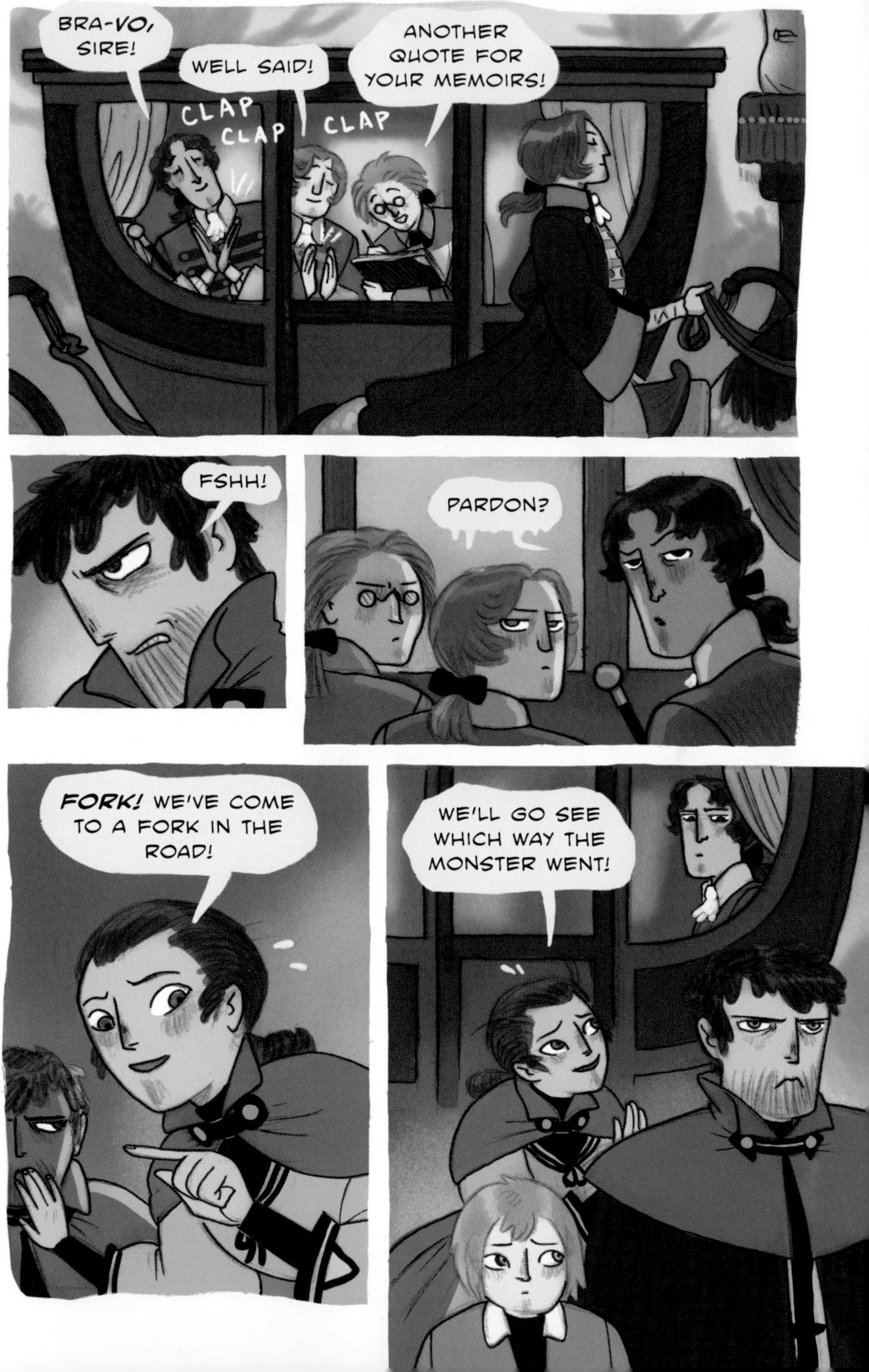
BRA-VO, SIRE!
CLAP CLAP
WELL SAID!
CLAP
ANOTHER QUOTE FOR YOUR MEMOIRS!
FSHH!
PARDON?
FORK! WE'VE COME TO A FORK IN THE ROAD!
WE'LL GO SEE WHICH WAY THE MONSTER WENT!

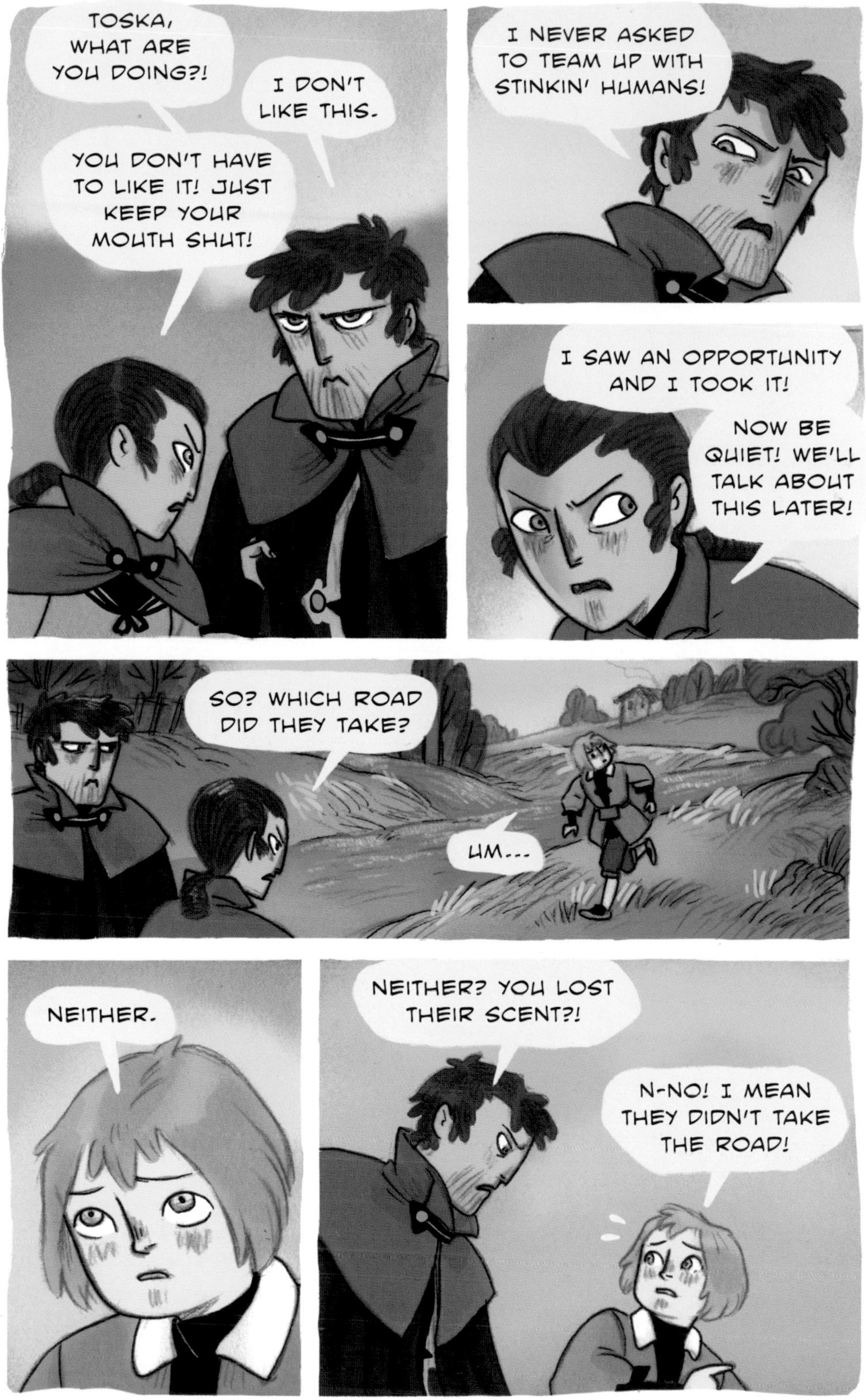
TOSKA, WHAT ARE YOU DOING?!
I DON'T LIKE THIS.
YOU DON'T HAVE TO LIKE IT! JUST KEEP YOUR MOUTH SHUT!
I NEVER ASKED TO TEAM UP WITH STINKIN' HUMANS!
I SAW AN OPPORTUNITY AND I TOOK IT!
NOW BE QUIET! WE'LL TALK ABOUT THIS LATER!
SO? WHICH ROAD DID THEY TAKE?
UM...
NEITHER.
NEITHER? YOU LOST THEIR SCENT?!
N-NO! I MEAN THEY DIDN'T TAKE THE ROAD!

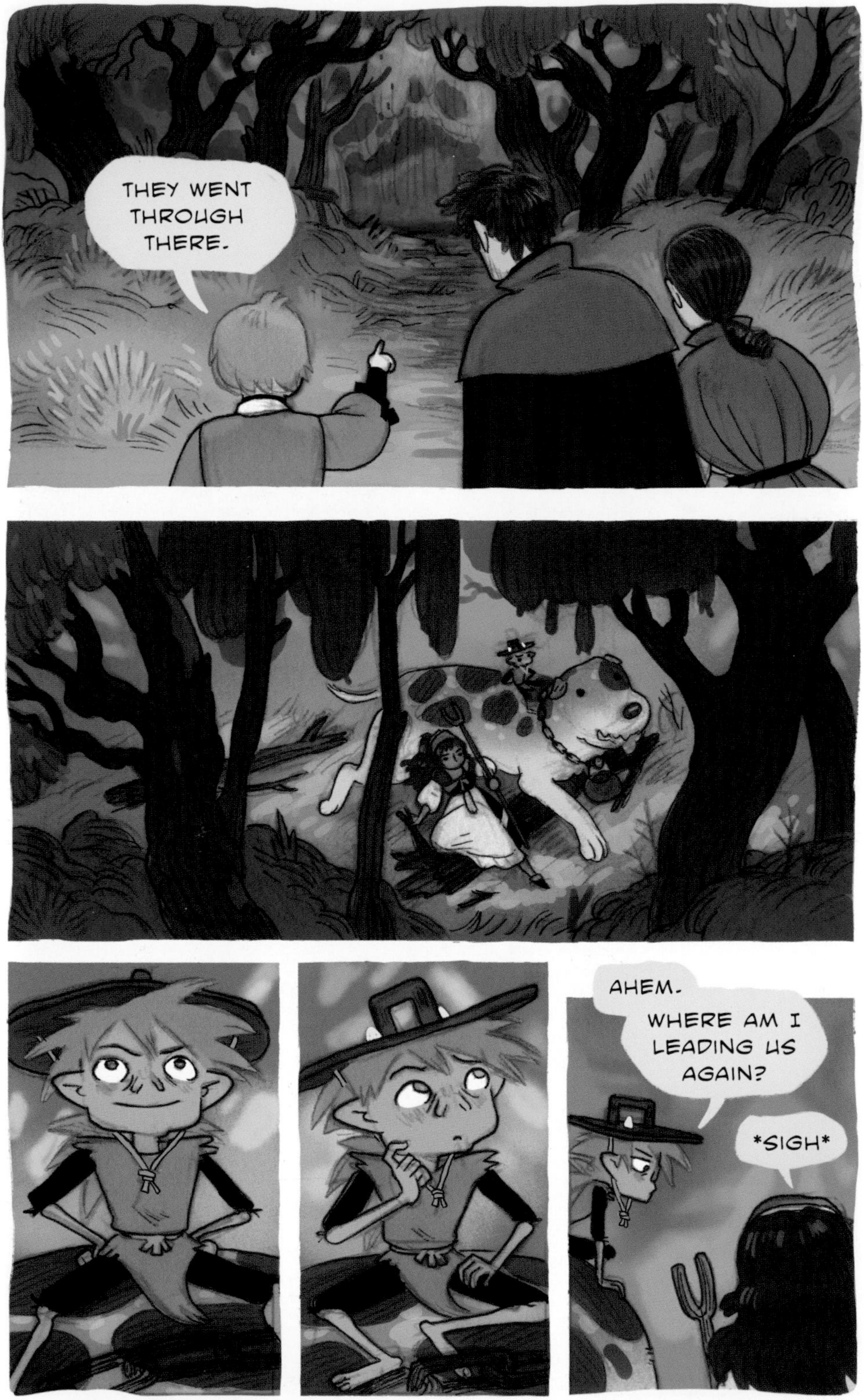
THEY WENT THROUGH THERE.
AHEM.
WHERE AM I LEADING US AGAIN?
SIGH

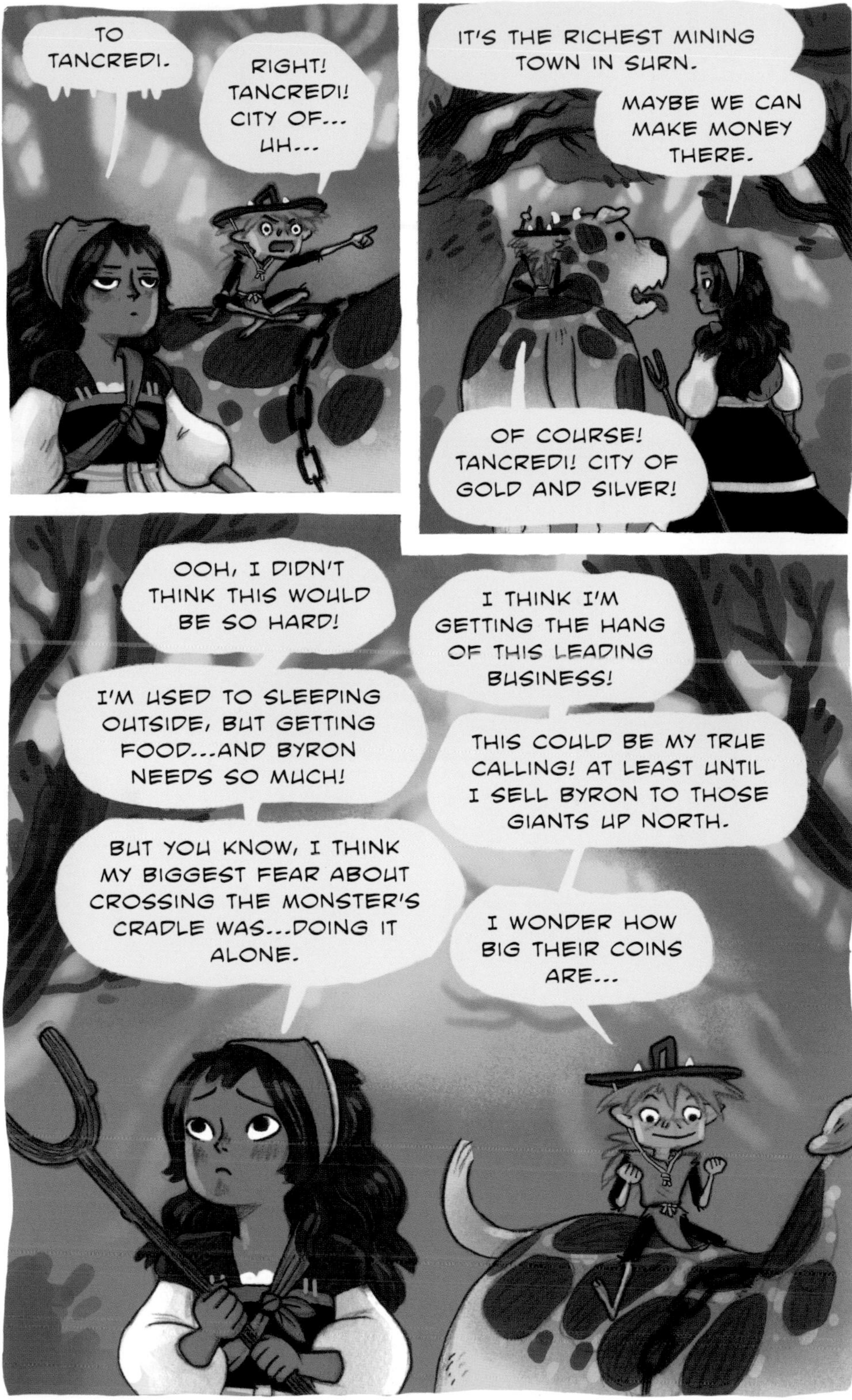
TO TANCREDI.
RIGHT! TANCREDI! CITY OF... UH...
IT'S THE RICHEST MINING TOWN IN SURN.
MAYBE WE CAN MAKE MONEY THERE.
OF COURSE! TANCREDI! CITY OF GOLD AND SILVER!
OOH, I DIDN'T THINK THIS WOULD BE SO HARD!
I'M USED TO SLEEPING OUTSIDE, BUT GETTING FOOD...AND BYRON NEEDS SO MUCH!
BUT YOU KNOW, I THINK MY BIGGEST FEAR ABOUT CROSSING THE MONSTER'S CRADLE WAS...DOING IT ALONE.
I THINK I'M GETTING THE HANG OF THIS LEADING BUSINESS!
THIS COULD BE MY TRUE CALLING! AT LEAST UNTIL I SELL BYRON TO THOSE GIANTS UP NORTH.
I WONDER HOW BIG THEIR COINS ARE...

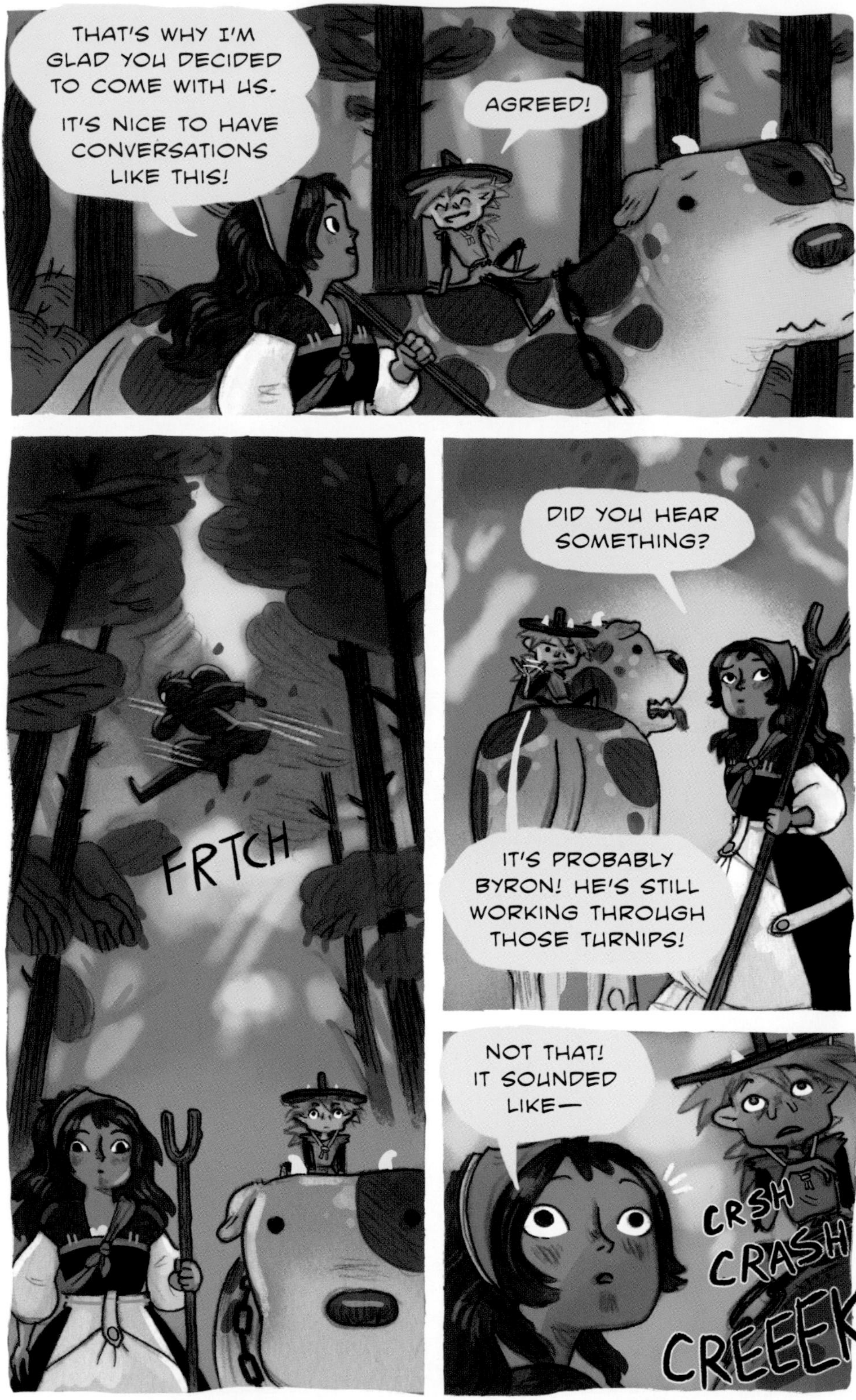
THAT'S WHY I'M GLAD YOU DECIDED TO COME WITH US.
IT'S NICE TO HAVE CONVERSATIONS LIKE THIS!
AGREED!
FRTCH
DID YOU HEAR SOMETHING?
IT'S PROBABLY BYRON! HE'S STILL WORKING THROUGH THOSE TURNIPS!
NOT THAT! IT SOUNDED LIKE—
CRSH
CRASH
CREEEK

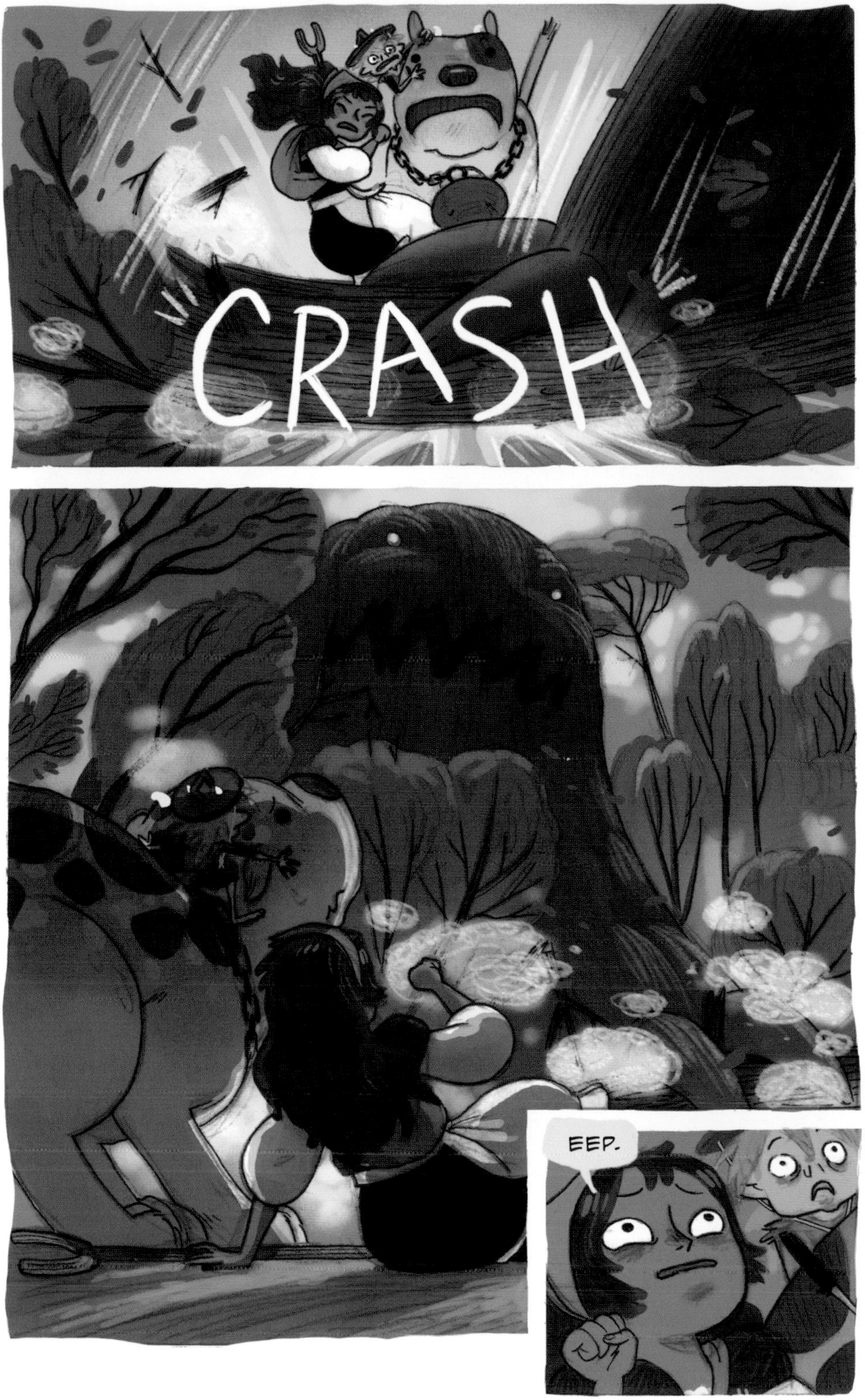
CRASH
EEP.

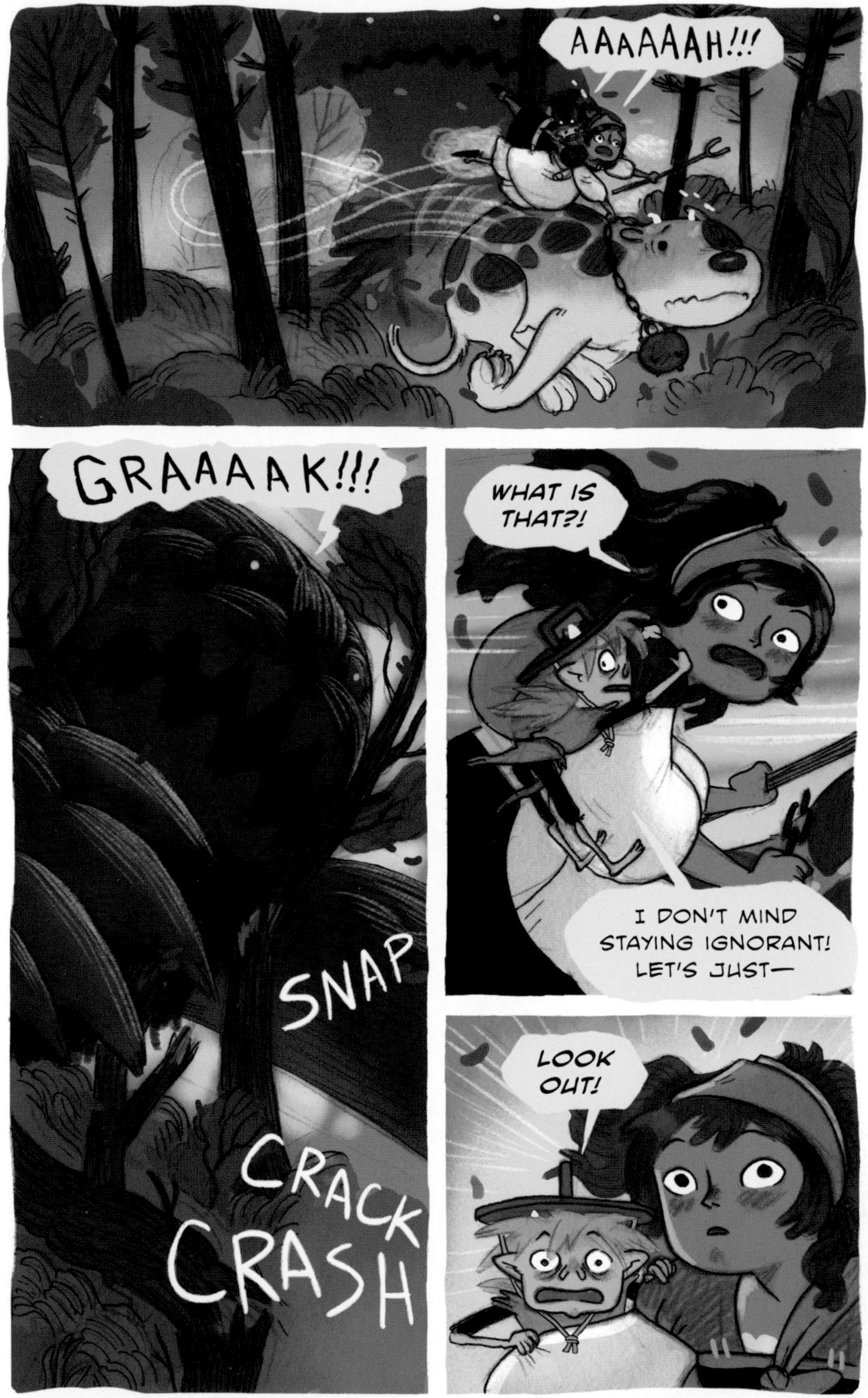
AAAAAAH!!!
GRAAAAK!!!
SNAP
CRACK
CRASH
WHAT IS THAT?!
I DON'T MIND STAYING IGNORANT! LET'S JUST—
LOOK OUT!

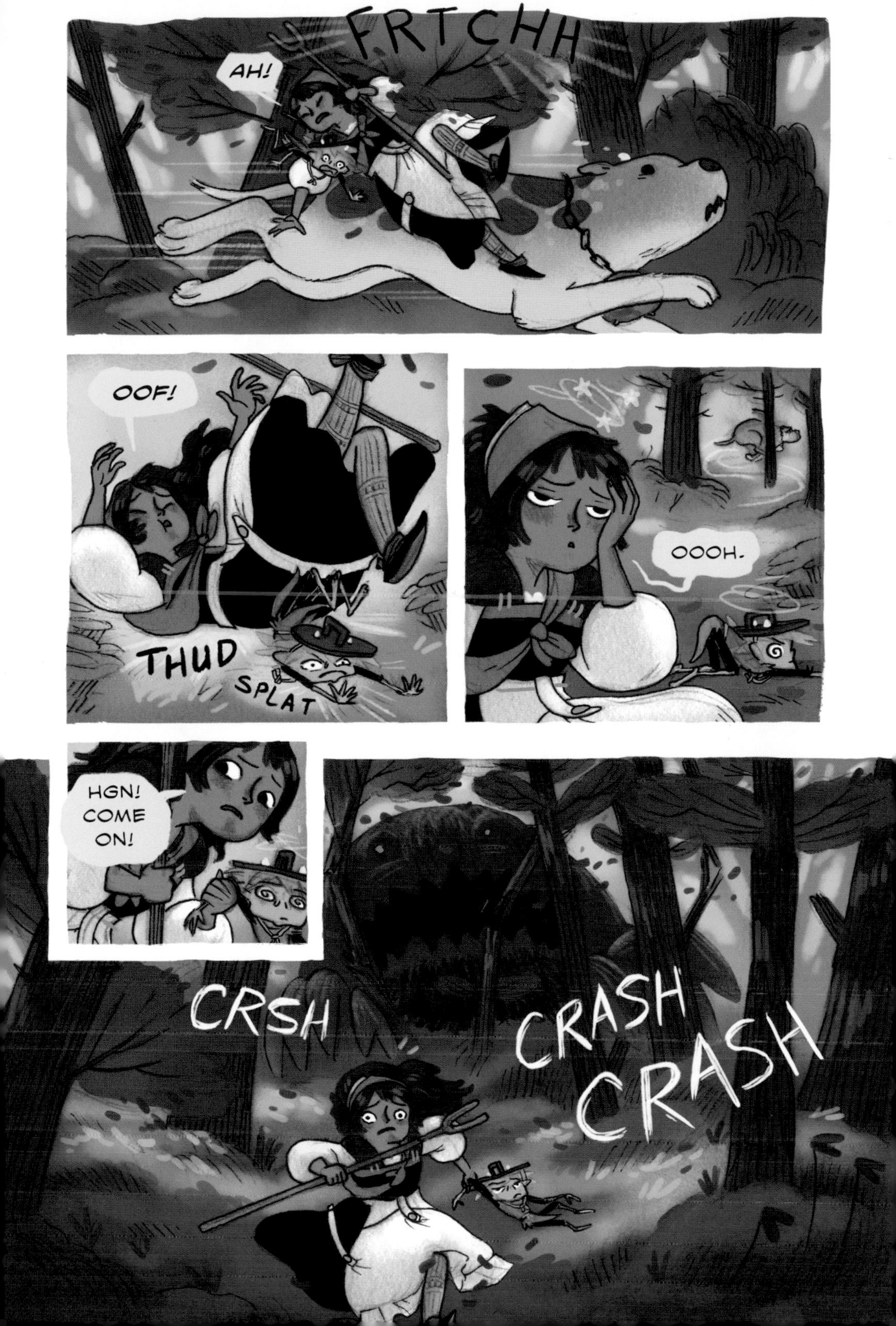
FRTCHH
AH!
OOF!
THUD
SPLAT
OOOH.
HGN! COME ON!
CRSH
CRASH
CRASH

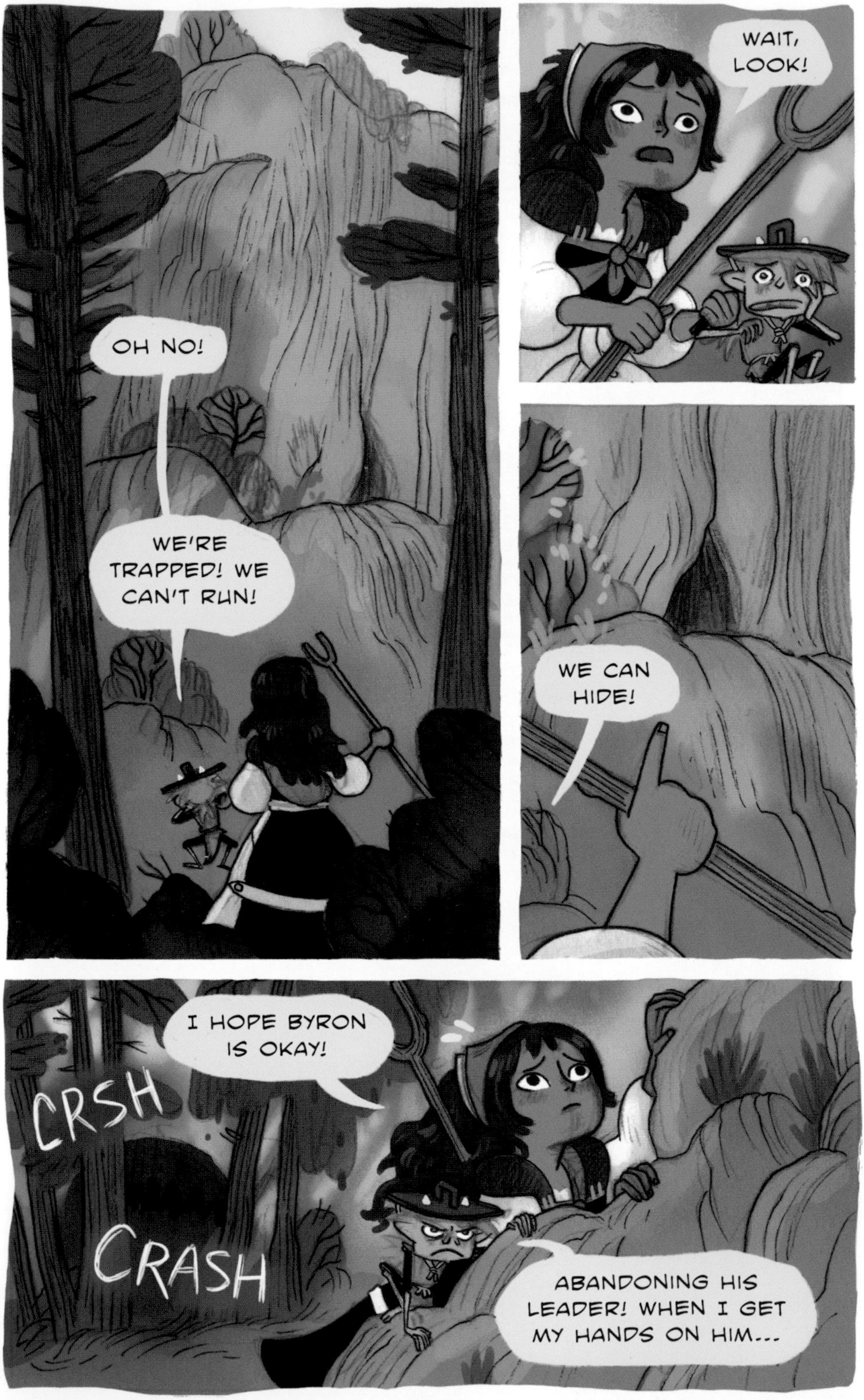
OH NO!
WE'RE TRAPPED! WE CAN'T RUN!
WAIT, LOOK!
WE CAN HIDE!
I HOPE BYRON IS OKAY!
CRSH
CRASH
ABANDONING HIS LEADER! WHEN I GET MY HANDS ON HIM...

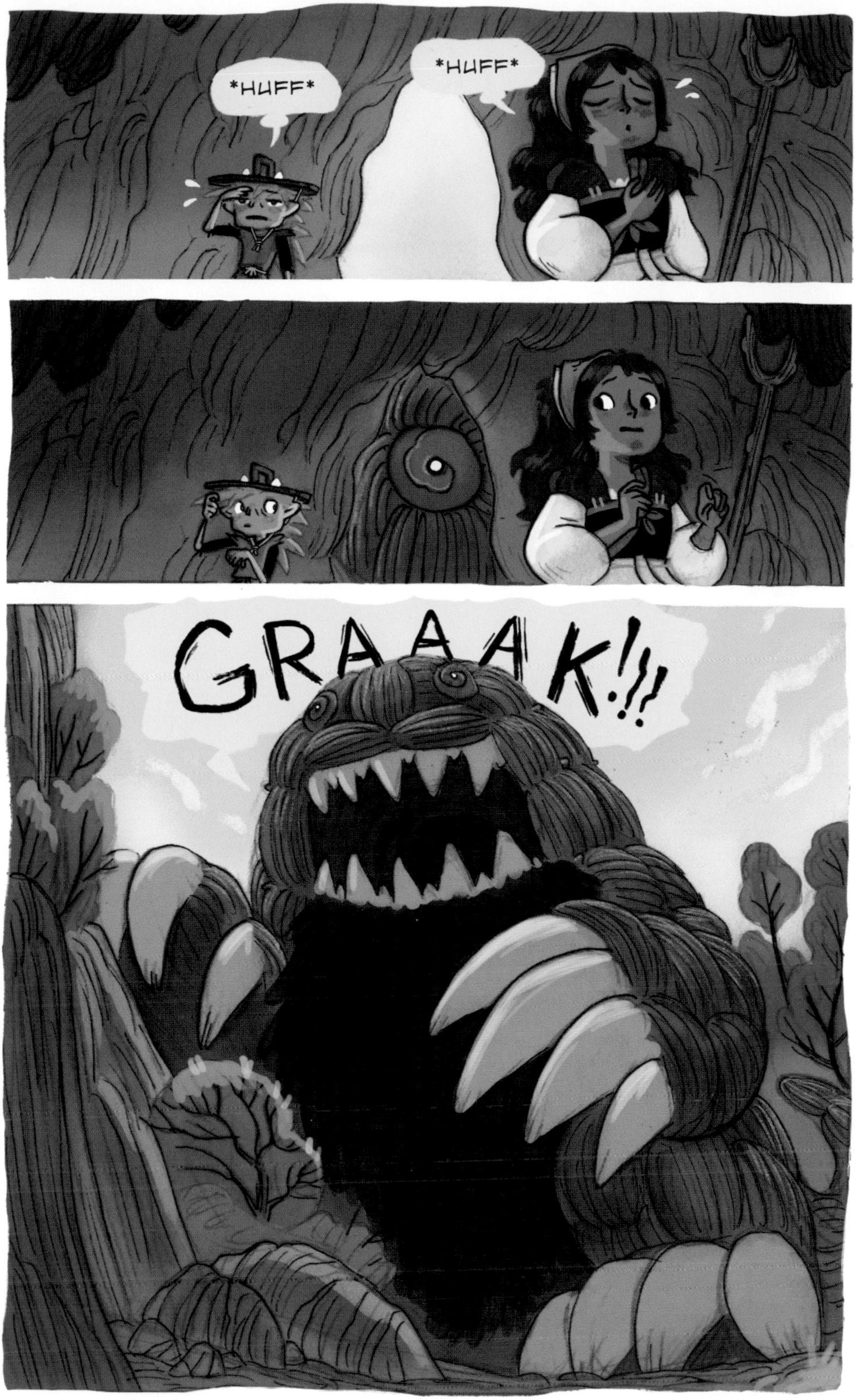
HUFF
HUFF
GRAAAK!!?

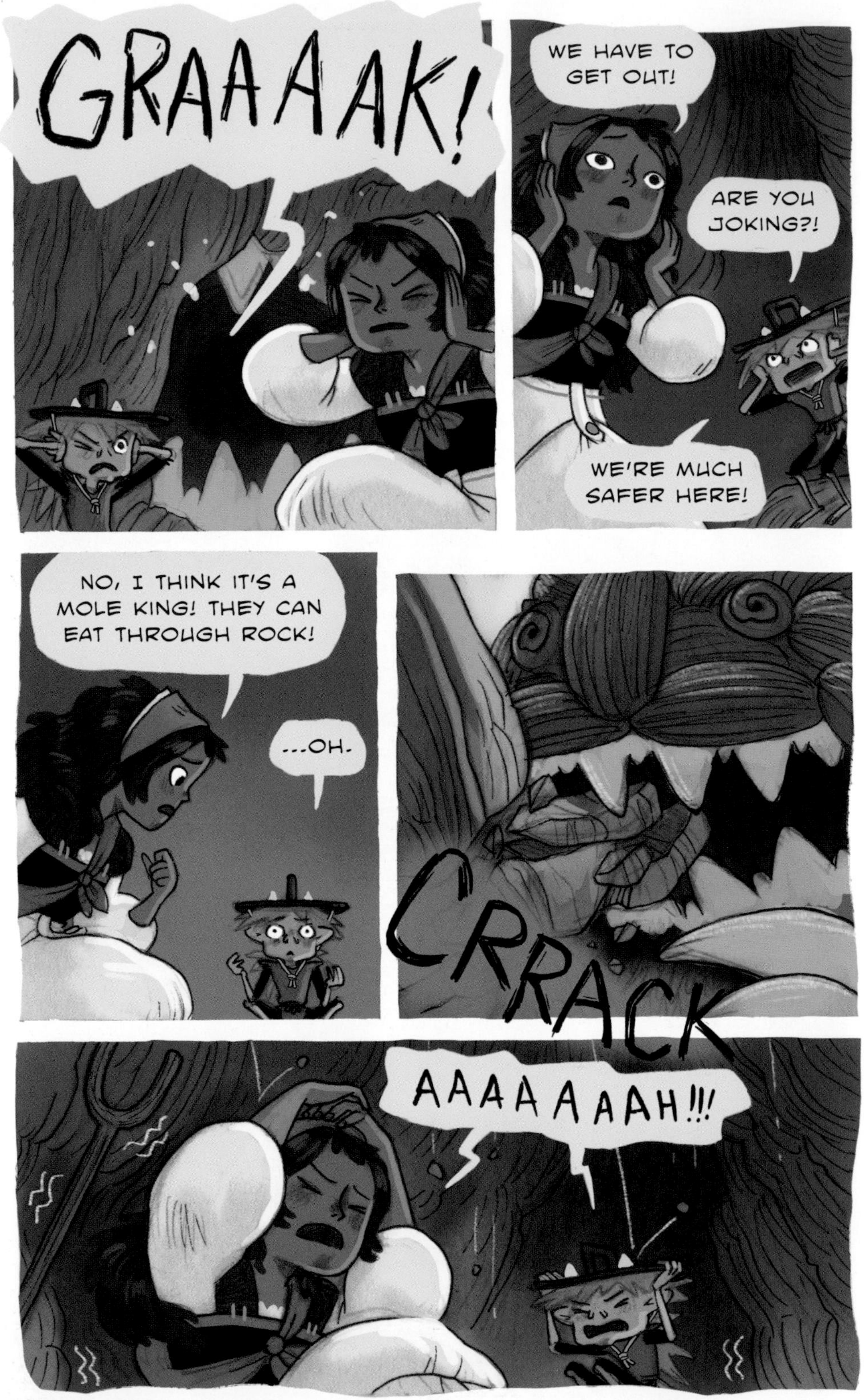
GRAAAAK!
WE HAVE TO GET OUT!
ARE YOU JOKING?!
WE'RE MUCH SAFER HERE!
NO, I THINK IT'S A MOLE KING! THEY CAN EAT THROUGH ROCK!
...OH.
CRRACK
AAAAAAAH!!!

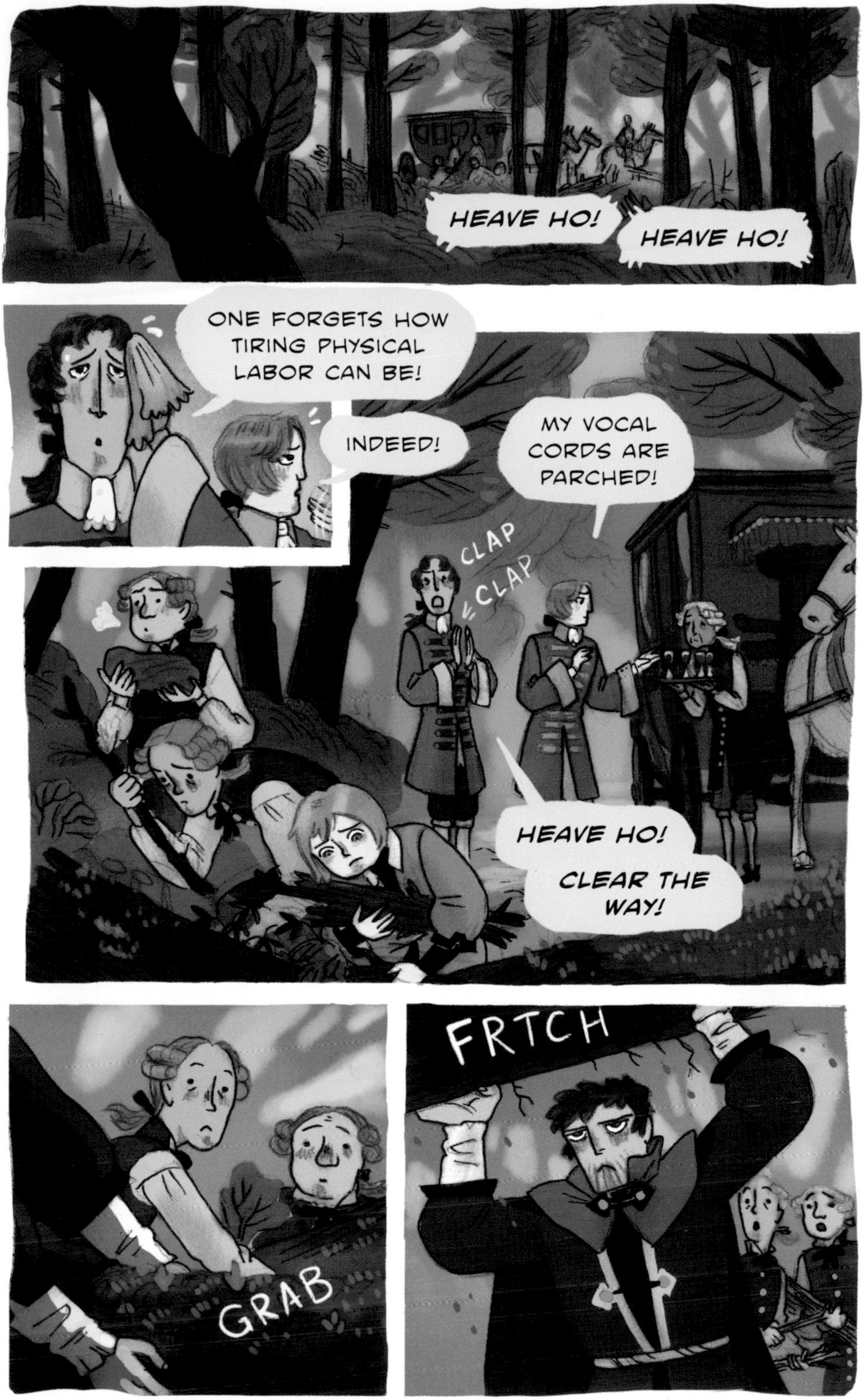
HEAVE HO!
HEAVE HO!
ONE FORGETS HOW TIRING PHYSICAL LABOR CAN BE!
INDEED!
MY VOCAL CORDS ARE PARCHED!
CLAP
CLAP
HEAVE HO!
CLEAR THE WAY!
GRAB
FRTCH

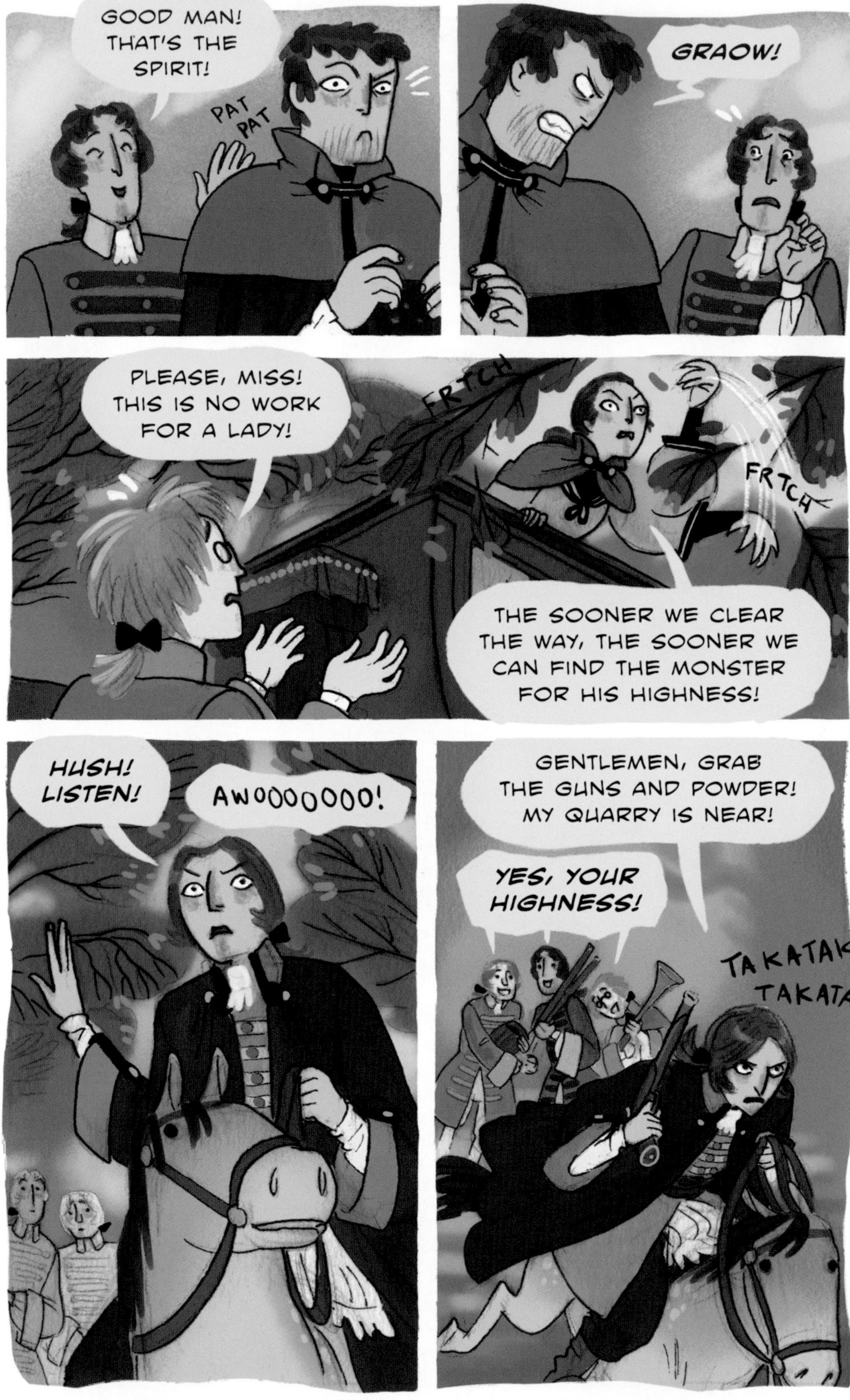
GOOD MAN! THAT'S THE SPIRIT!
PAT PAT
GRAOW!
PLEASE, MISS! THIS IS NO WORK FOR A LADY!
FRTCH
FRTCH
THE SOONER WE CLEAR THE WAY, THE SOONER WE CAN FIND THE MONSTER FOR HIS HIGHNESS!
HUSH! LISTEN!
AWOOOOOOO!
GENTLEMEN, GRAB THE GUNS AND POWDER! MY QUARRY IS NEAR!
YES, YOUR HIGHNESS!
TAKATAK
TAKATAK

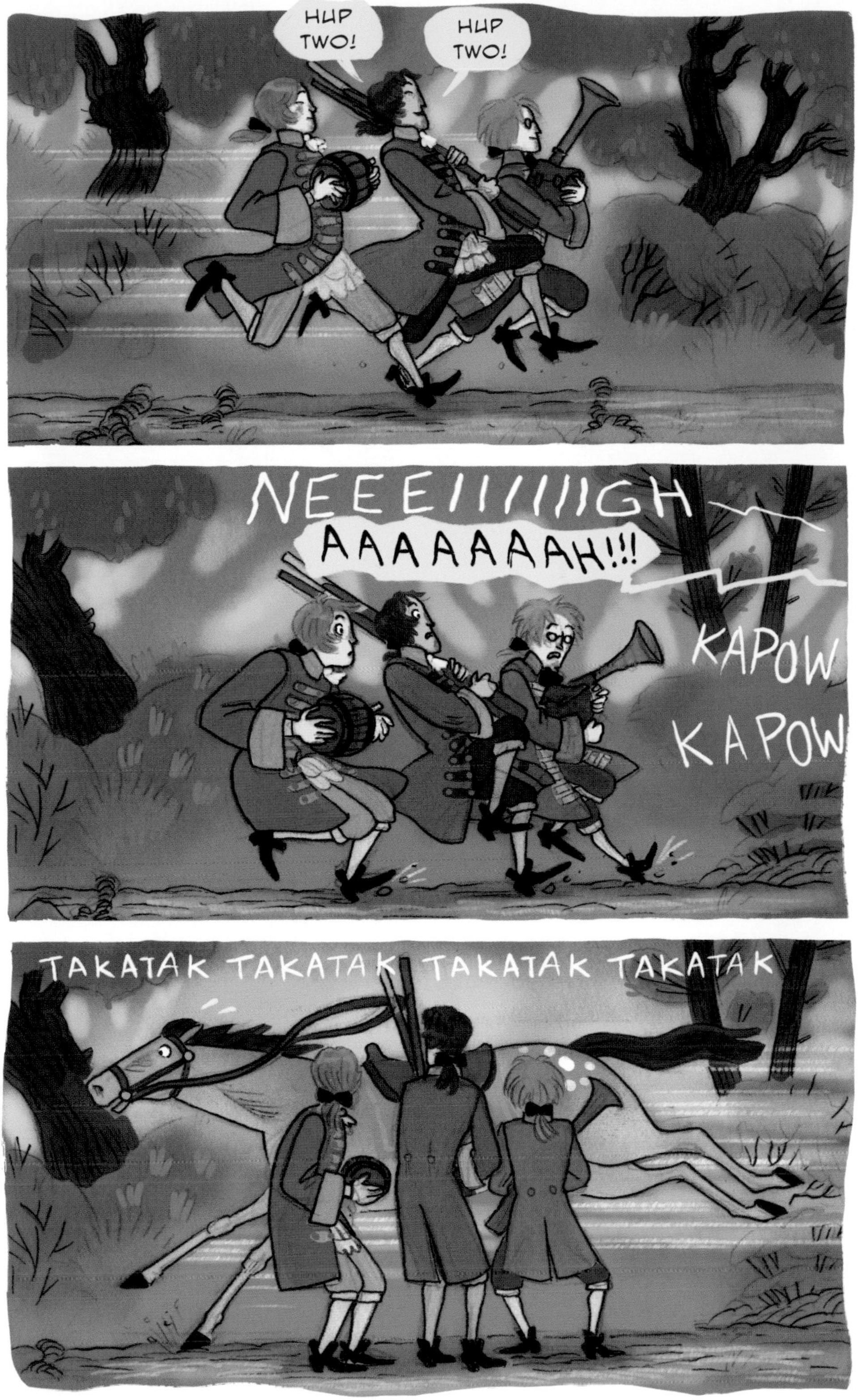
HUP TWO!
HUP TWO!
NEEEIIIIIIGH
AAAAAAAAH!!!
KAPOW
KAPOW
TAKATAK TAKATAK TAKATAK TAKATAK

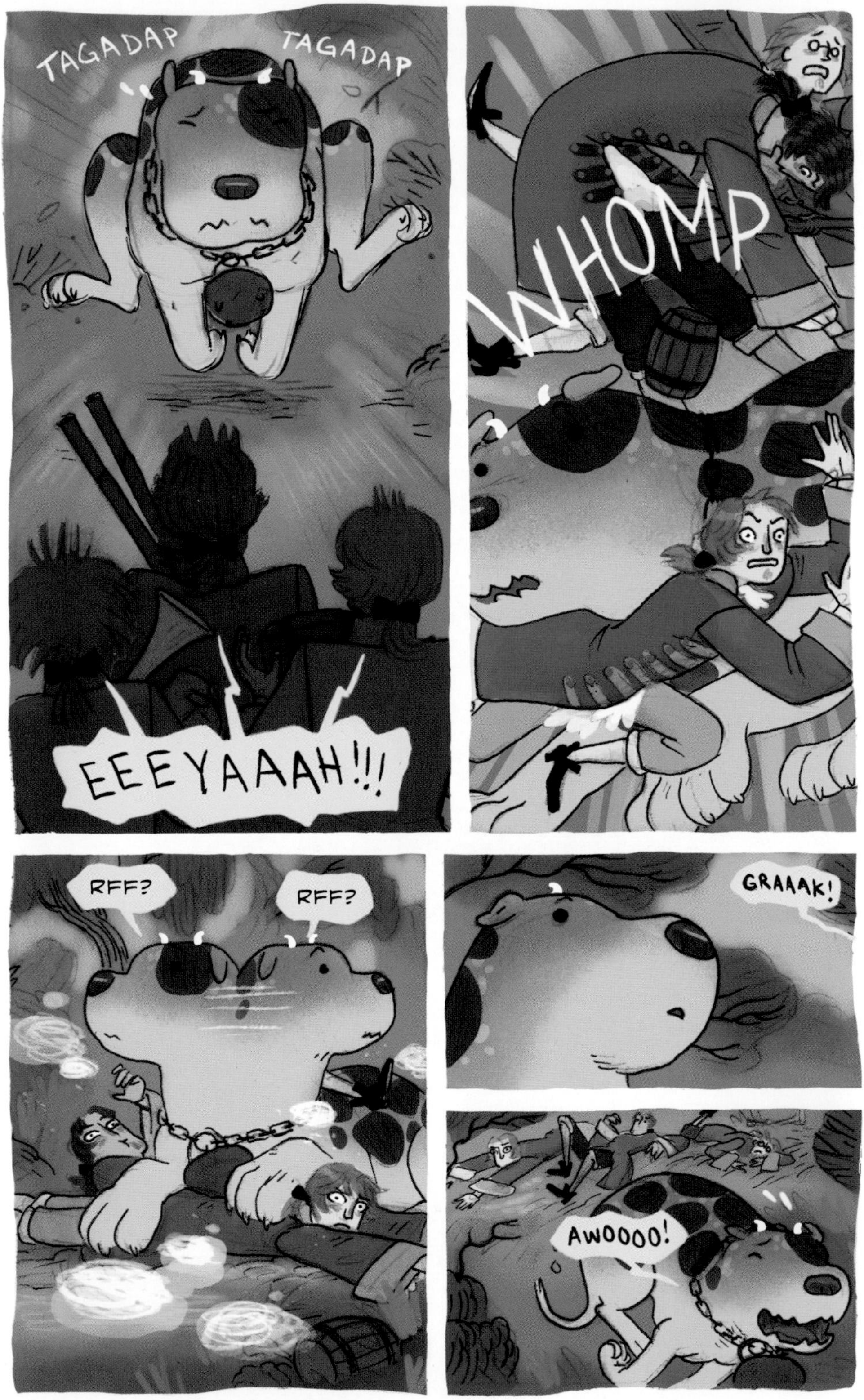
TAGADAP
TAGADAP
EEEYAAAH!!!
WHOMP
RFF?
RFF?
GRAAAK!
AWOOOO!

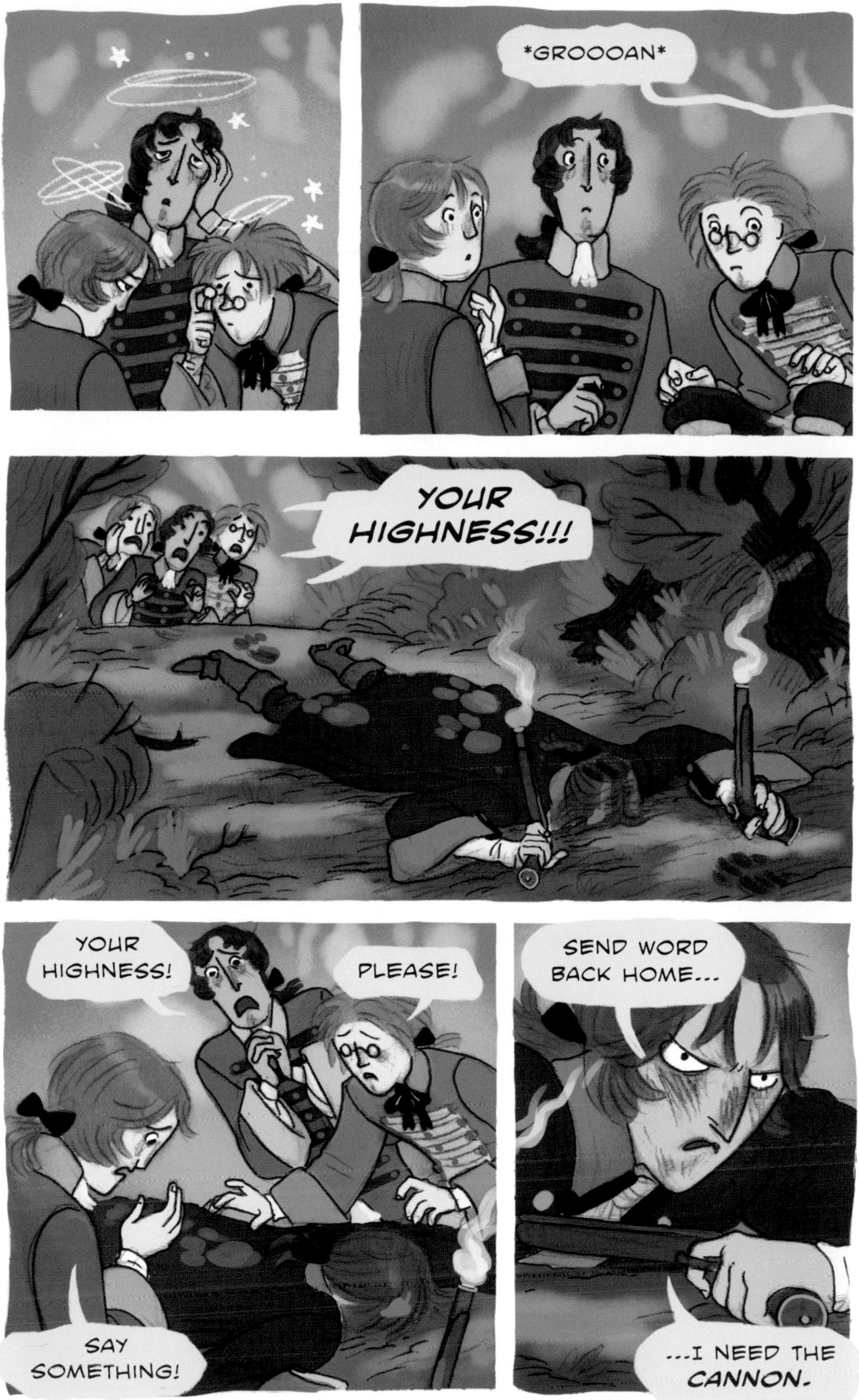
GROOOAN
YOUR HIGHNESS!!!
YOUR HIGHNESS!
PLEASE!
SAY SOMETHING!
SEND WORD BACK HOME...
...I NEED THE CANNON.

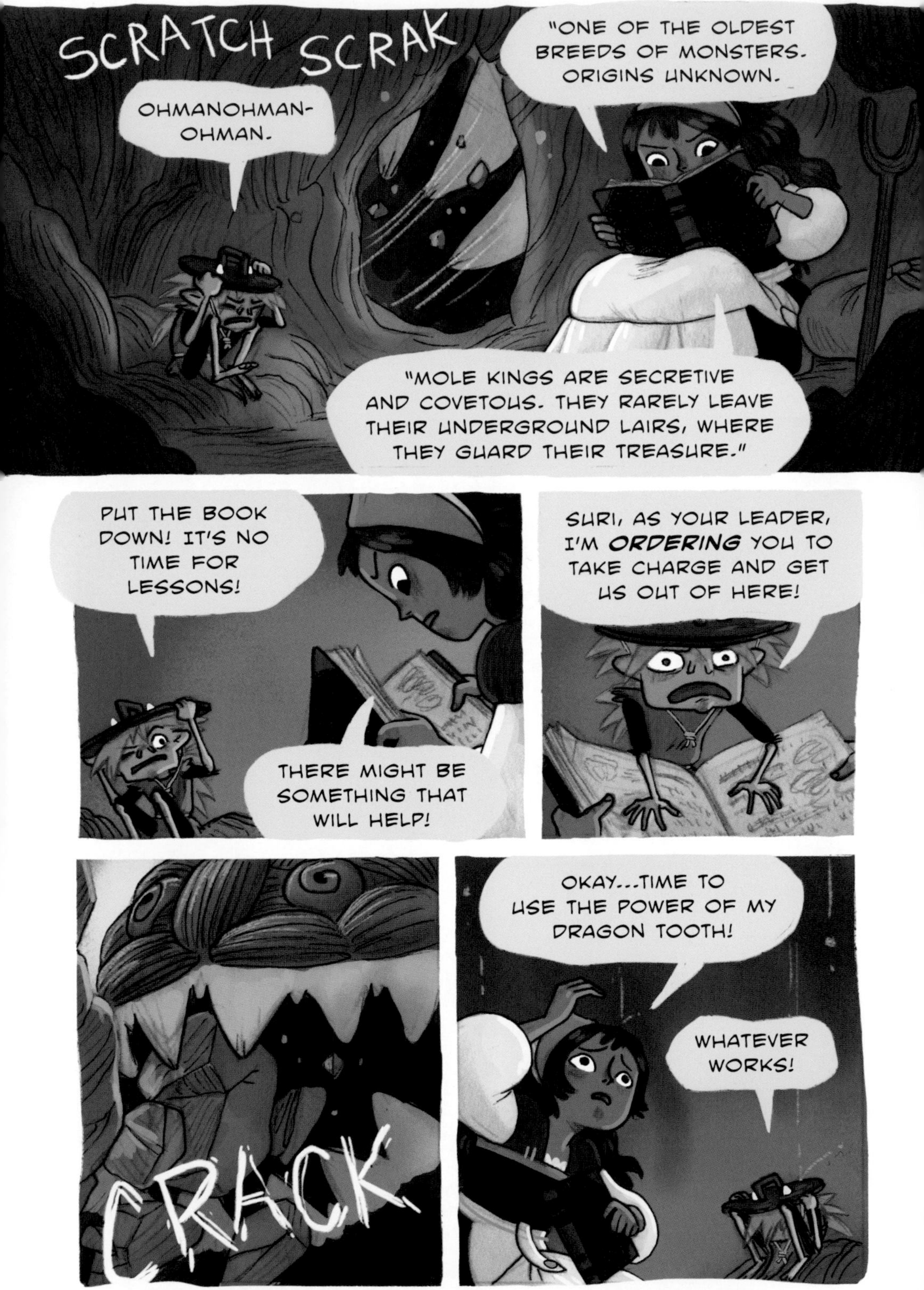
SCRATCH SCRAK
OHMANOHMAN-OHMAN.
"ONE OF THE OLDEST BREEDS OF MONSTERS. ORIGINS UNKNOWN.
"MOLE KINGS ARE SECRETIVE AND COVETOUS. THEY RARELY LEAVE THEIR UNDERGROUND LAIRS, WHERE THEY GUARD THEIR TREASURE."
PUT THE BOOK DOWN! IT'S NO TIME FOR LESSONS!
THERE MIGHT BE SOMETHING THAT WILL HELP!
SURI, AS YOUR LEADER, I'M ***ORDERING*** YOU TO TAKE CHARGE AND GET US OUT OF HERE!
CRACK
OKAY...TIME TO USE THE POWER OF MY DRAGON TOOTH!
WHATEVER WORKS!

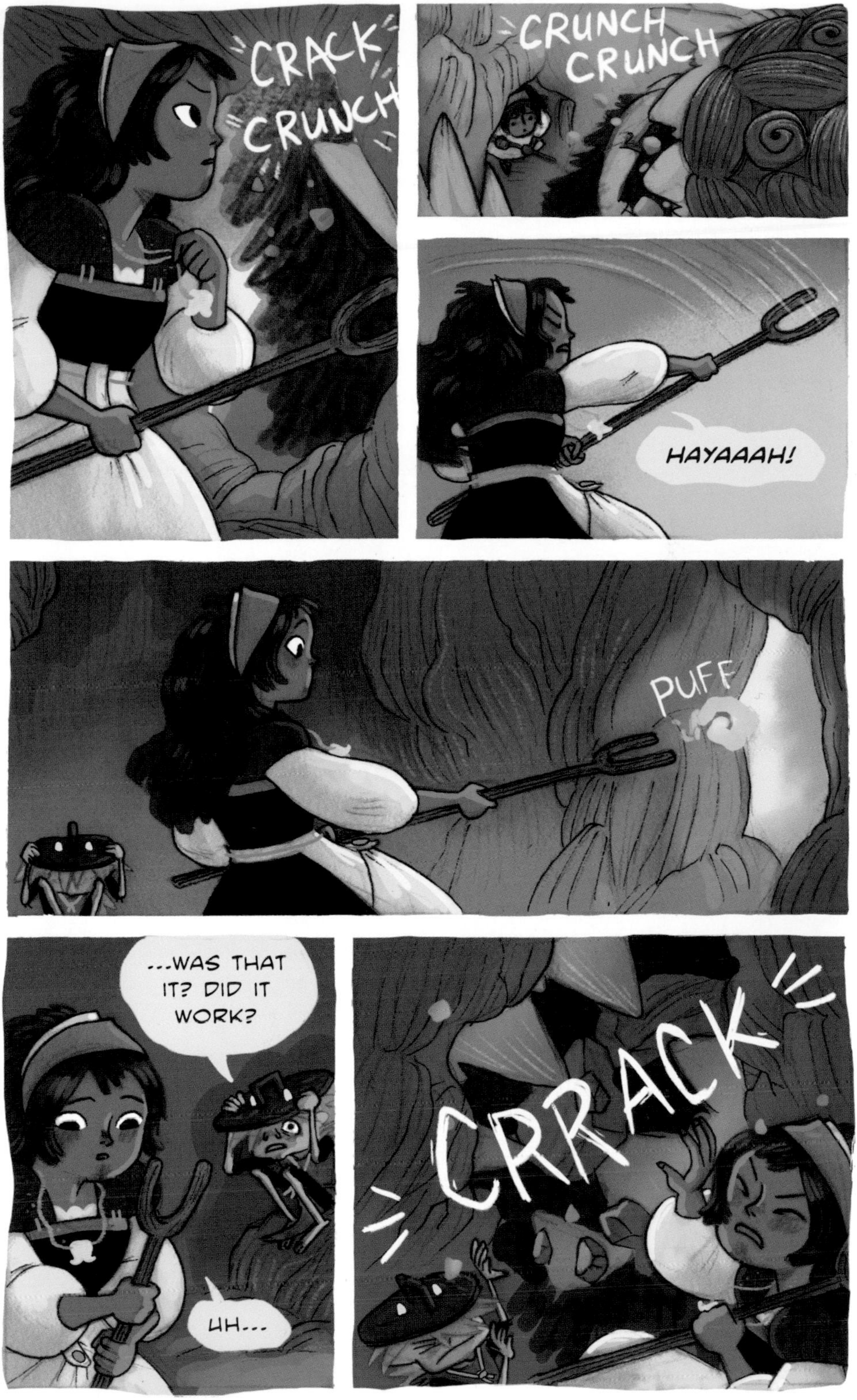
CRACK
CRUNCH
CRUNCH
CRUNCH
HAYAAAH!
PUFF
...WAS THAT IT? DID IT WORK?
UH...
CRRACK

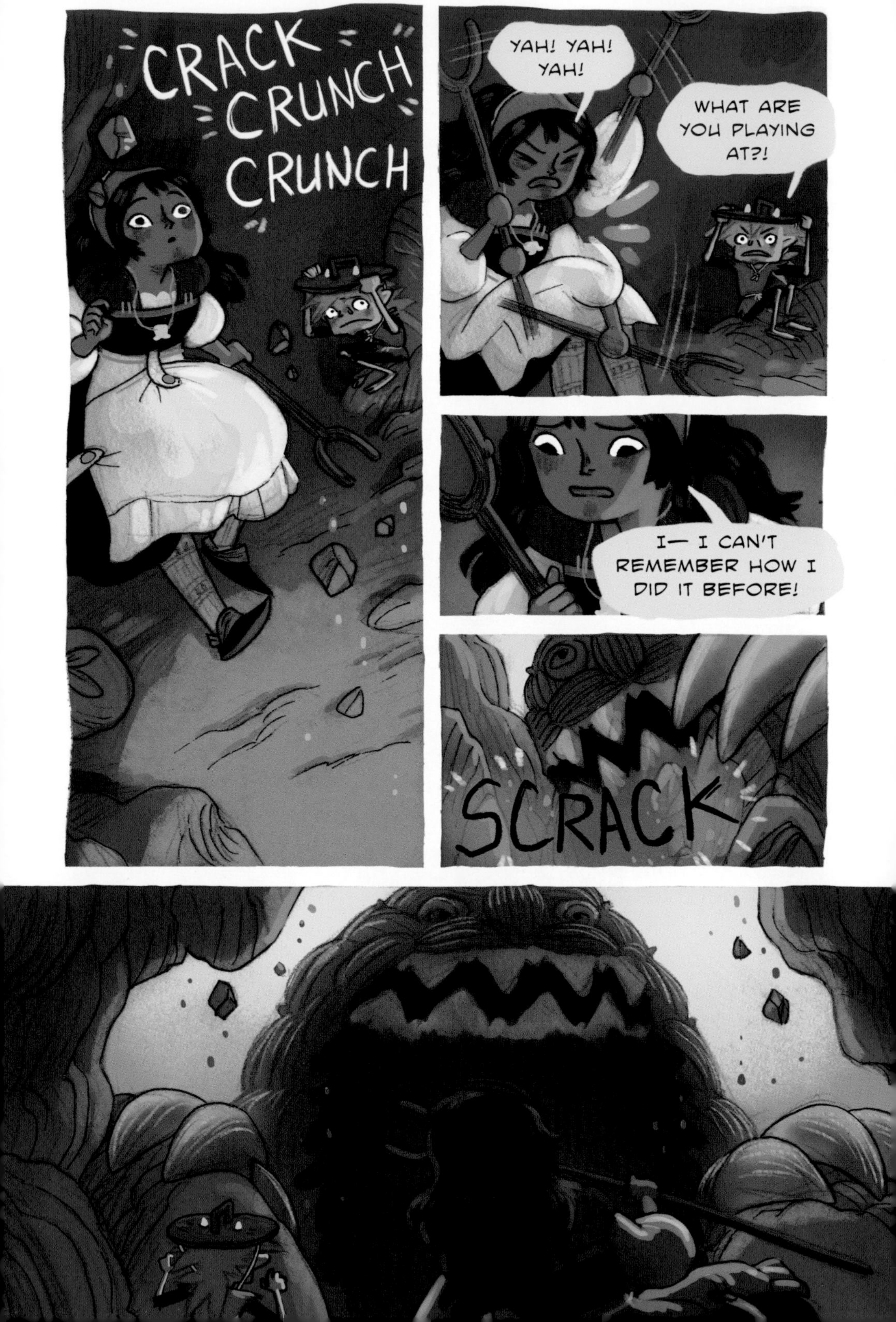
CRACK
CRUNCH
CRUNCH
YAH! YAH! YAH!
WHAT ARE YOU PLAYING AT?!
I— I CAN'T REMEMBER HOW I DID IT BEFORE!
SCRACK

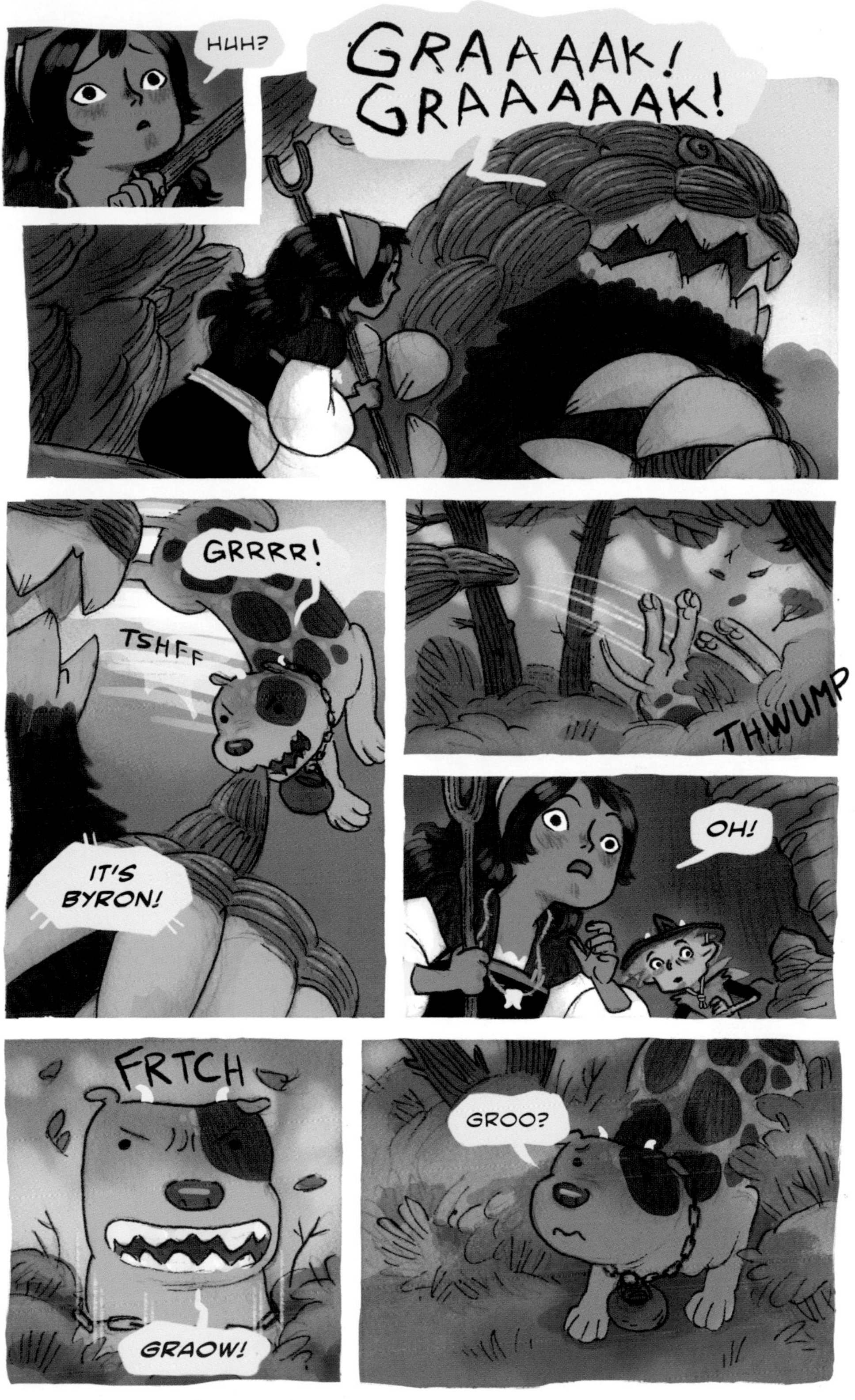
HUH?
GRAAAAK! GRAAAAAK!
GRRRR!
TSHFF
IT'S BYRON!
THWUMP
OH!
FRTCH
GRAOW!
GROO?

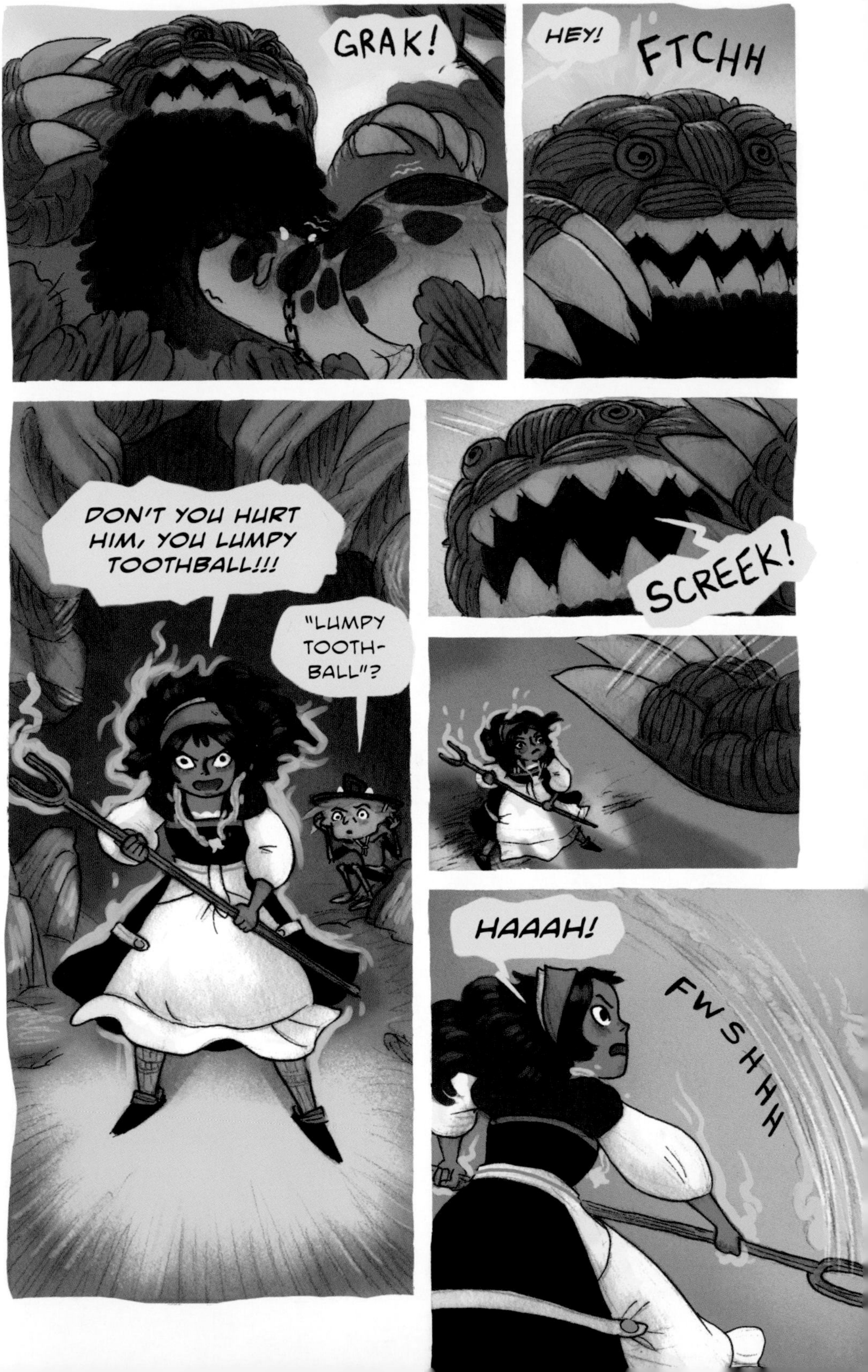
GRAK!
HEY!
FTCHH
DON'T YOU HURT HIM, YOU LUMPY TOOTHBALL!!!
"LUMPY TOOTH-BALL"?
SCREEK!
HAAAH!
FWSHHH

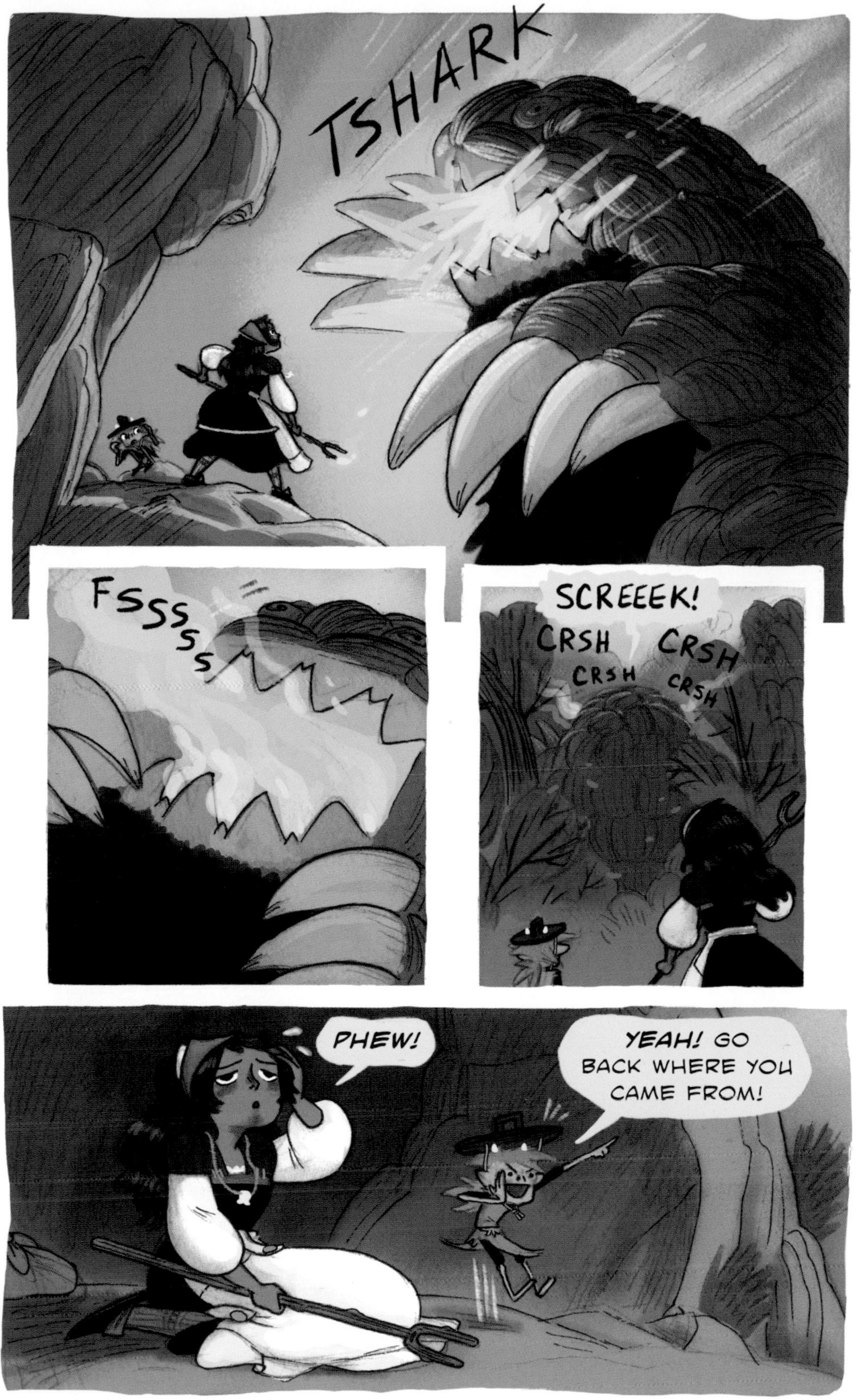
TSHARK
FSSSSSS
SCREEEK!
CRSH CRSH
CRSH CRSH
PHEW!
YEAH! GO BACK WHERE YOU CAME FROM!

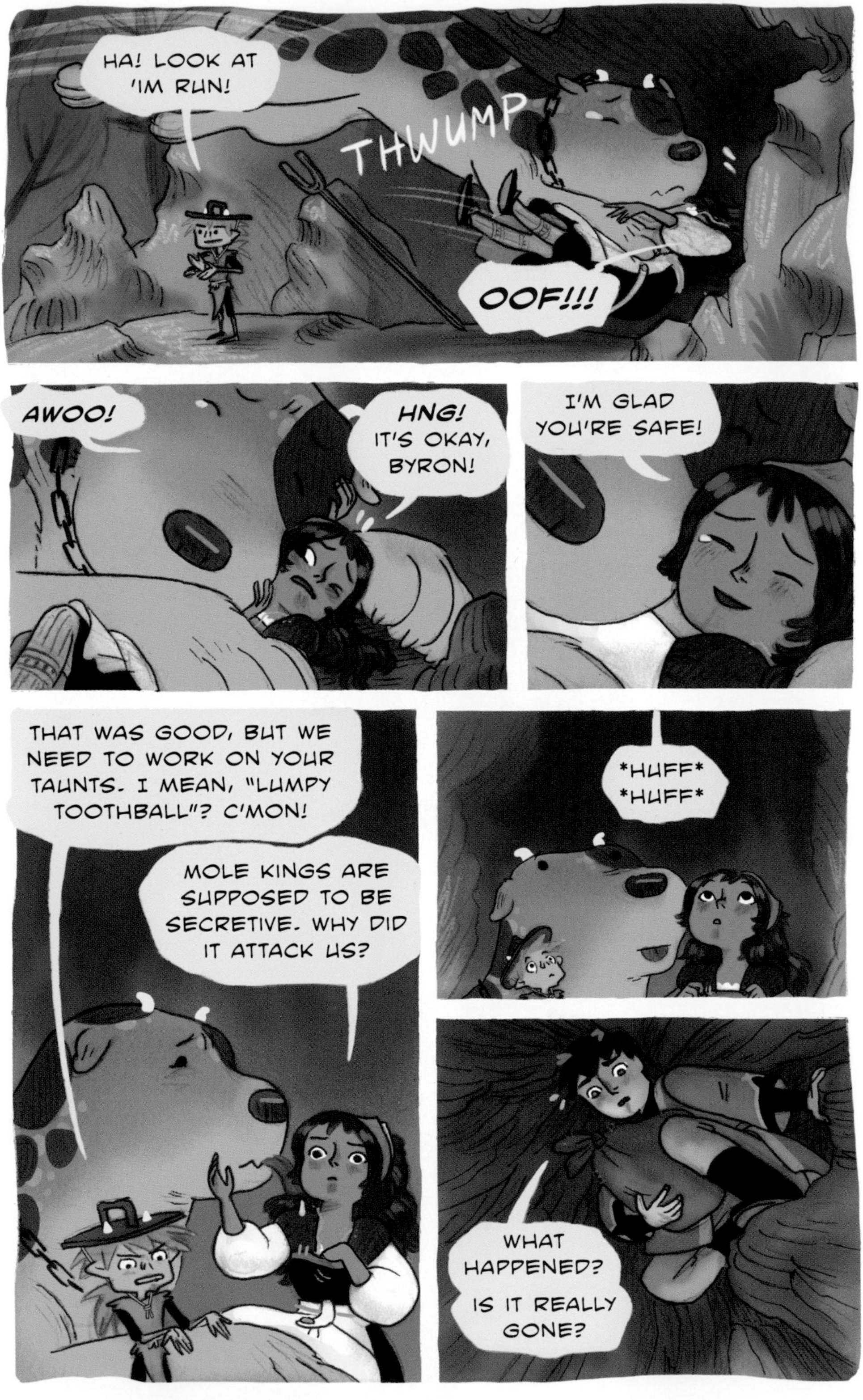
HA! LOOK AT 'IM RUN!
THWUMP
OOF!!!
AWOO!
HNG! IT'S OKAY, BYRON!
I'M GLAD YOU'RE SAFE!
THAT WAS GOOD, BUT WE NEED TO WORK ON YOUR TAUNTS. I MEAN, "LUMPY TOOTHBALL"? C'MON!
MOLE KINGS ARE SUPPOSED TO BE SECRETIVE. WHY DID IT ATTACK US?
HUFF *HUFF*
WHAT HAPPENED?
IS IT REALLY GONE?

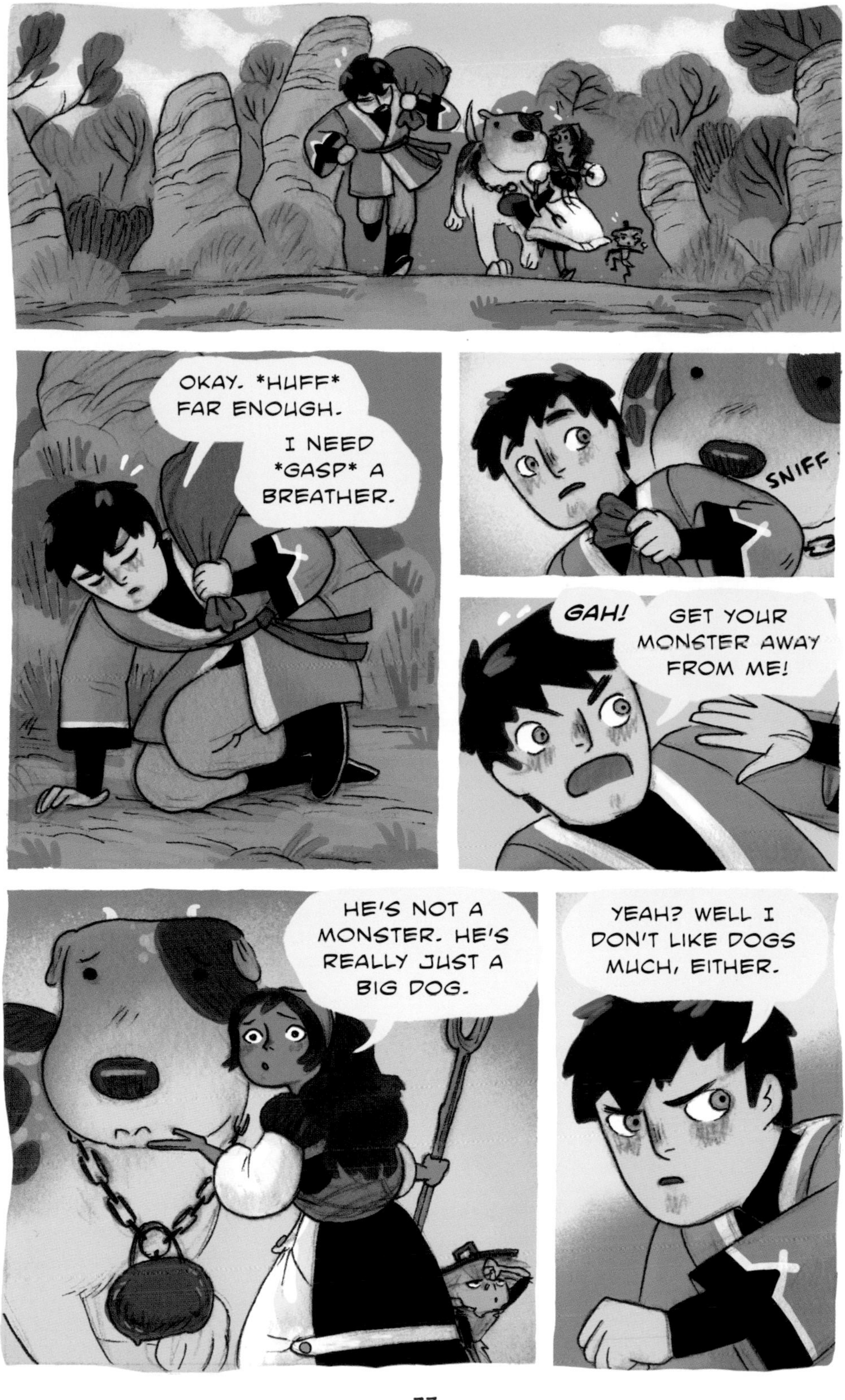

OKAY. *HUFF* FAR ENOUGH.
I NEED *GASP* A BREATHER.
SNIFF
GAH!
GET YOUR MONSTER AWAY FROM ME!
HE'S NOT A MONSTER. HE'S REALLY JUST A BIG DOG.
YEAH? WELL I DON'T LIKE DOGS MUCH, EITHER.

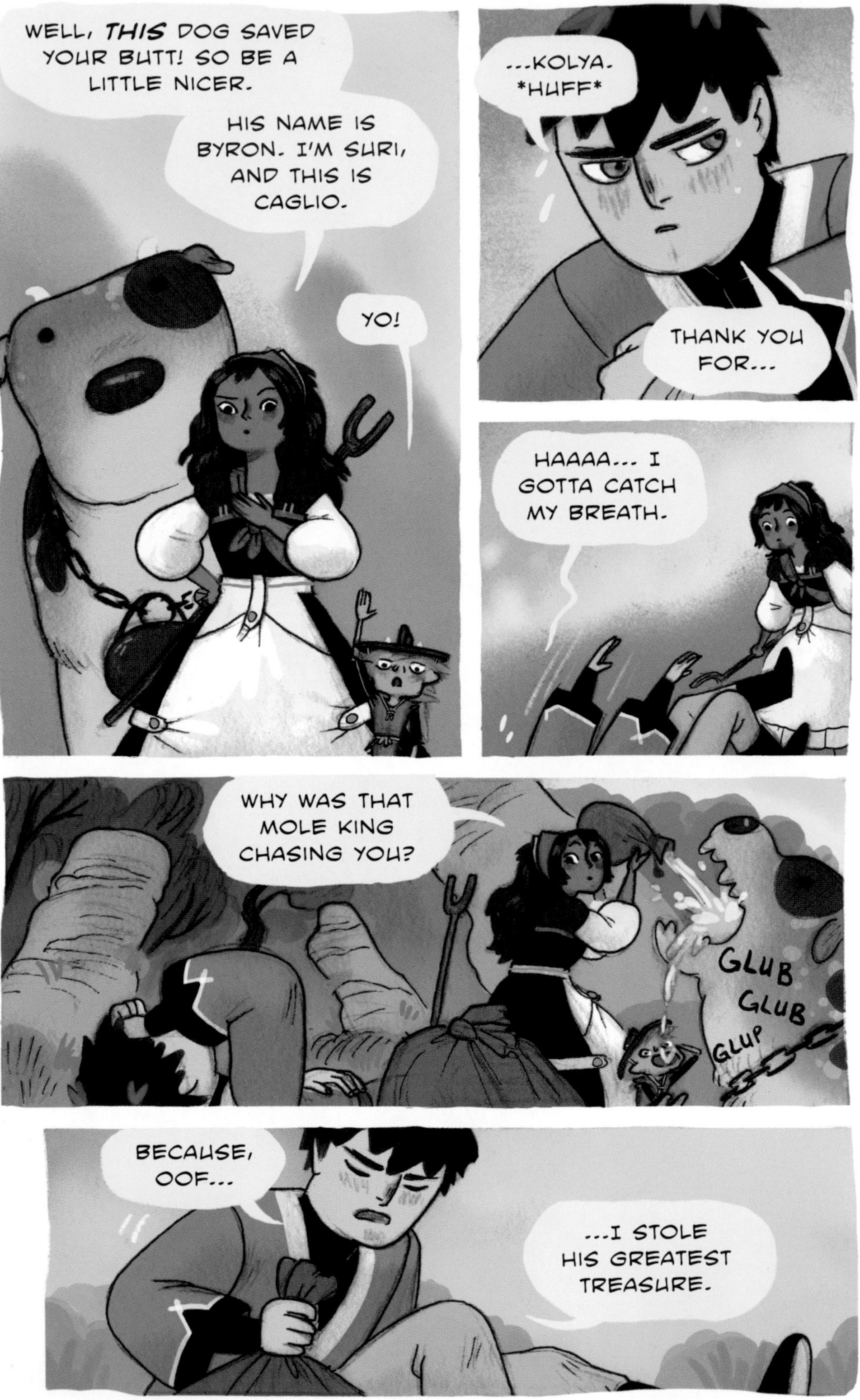

WELL, THIS DOG SAVED YOUR BUTT! SO BE A LITTLE NICER.
HIS NAME IS BYRON. I'M SURI, AND THIS IS CAGLIO.
YO!
...KOLYA. *HUFF*
THANK YOU FOR...
HAAAA... I GOTTA CATCH MY BREATH.
WHY WAS THAT MOLE KING CHASING YOU?
GLUB
GLUB
GLUP
BECAUSE, OOF...
...I STOLE HIS GREATEST TREASURE.

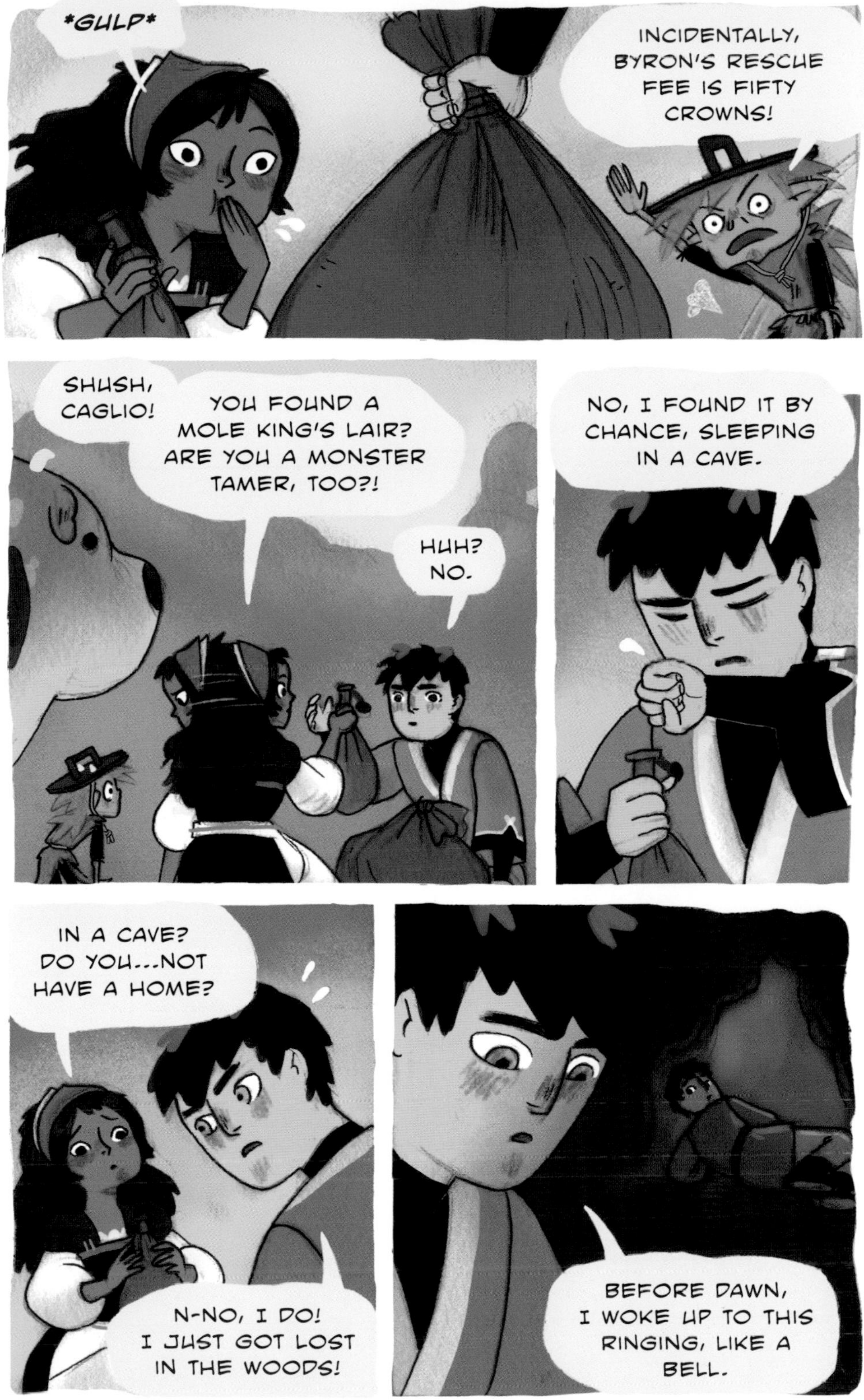
GULP
INCIDENTALLY, BYRON'S RESCUE FEE IS FIFTY CROWNS!
SHUSH, CAGLIO!
YOU FOUND A MOLE KING'S LAIR? ARE YOU A MONSTER TAMER, TOO?!
HUH? NO.
NO, I FOUND IT BY CHANCE, SLEEPING IN A CAVE.
IN A CAVE? DO YOU...NOT HAVE A HOME?
N-NO, I DO! I JUST GOT LOST IN THE WOODS!
BEFORE DAWN, I WOKE UP TO THIS RINGING, LIKE A BELL.

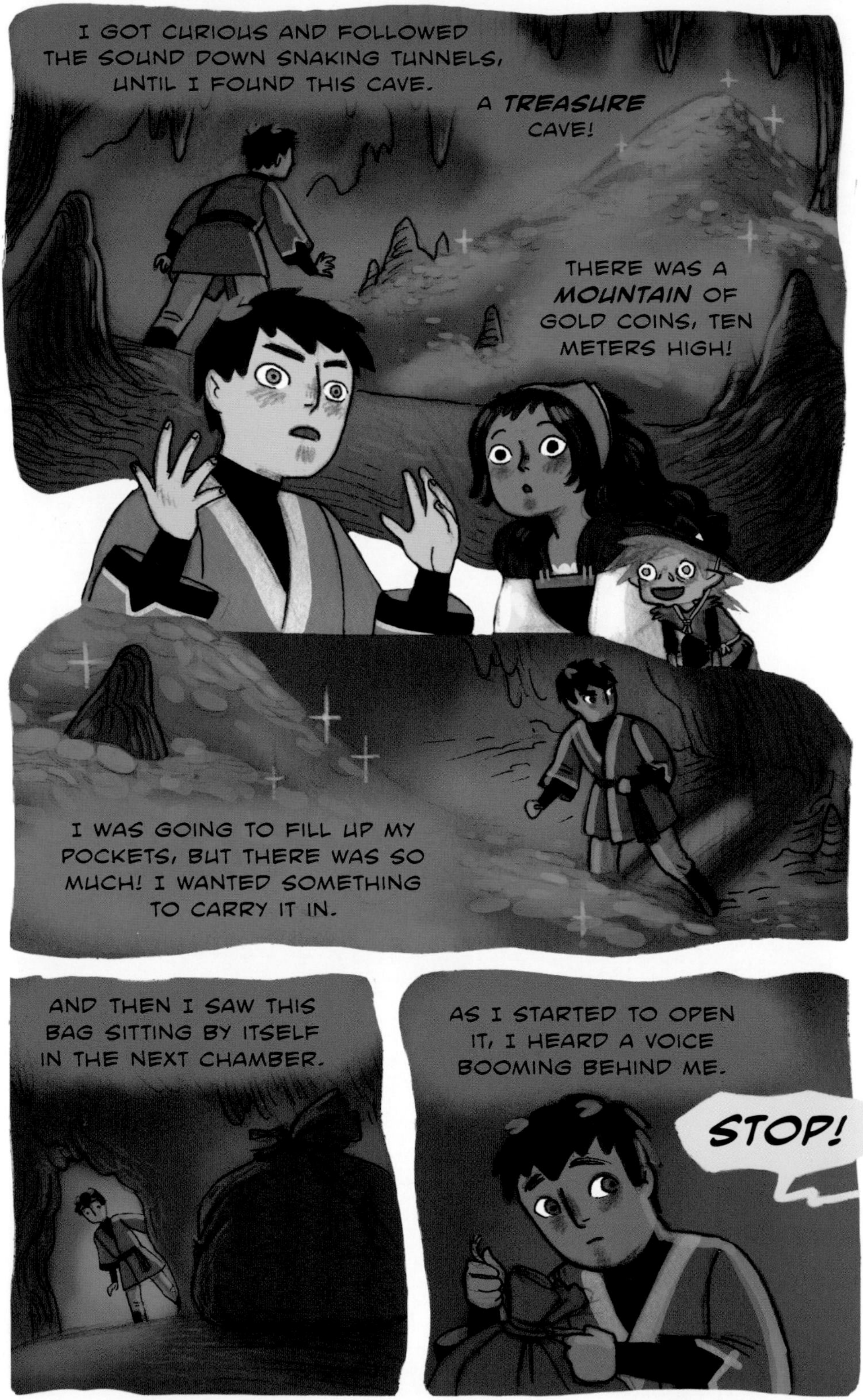
I GOT CURIOUS AND FOLLOWED THE SOUND DOWN SNAKING TUNNELS, UNTIL I FOUND THIS CAVE.
A *TREASURE* CAVE!
THERE WAS A *MOUNTAIN* OF GOLD COINS, TEN METERS HIGH!
I WAS GOING TO FILL UP MY POCKETS, BUT THERE WAS SO MUCH! I WANTED SOMETHING TO CARRY IT IN.
AND THEN I SAW THIS BAG SITTING BY ITSELF IN THE NEXT CHAMBER.
AS I STARTED TO OPEN IT, I HEARD A VOICE BOOMING BEHIND ME.
STOP!

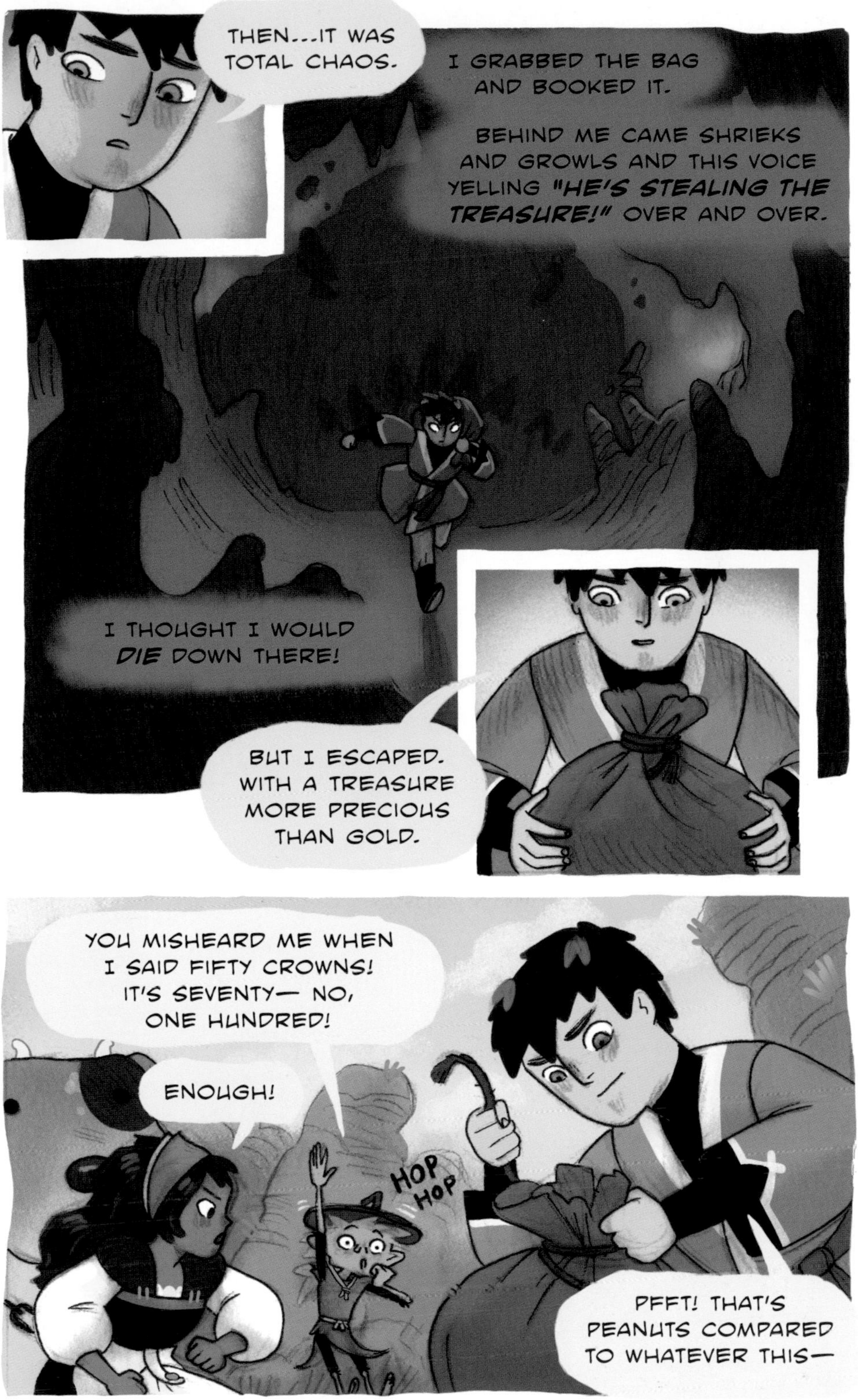
THEN...IT WAS TOTAL CHAOS.
I GRABBED THE BAG AND BOOKED IT.
BEHIND ME CAME SHRIEKS AND GROWLS AND THIS VOICE YELLING ***"HE'S STEALING THE TREASURE!"*** OVER AND OVER.
I THOUGHT I WOULD *DIE* DOWN THERE!
BUT I ESCAPED. WITH A TREASURE MORE PRECIOUS THAN GOLD.
YOU MISHEARD ME WHEN I SAID FIFTY CROWNS! IT'S SEVENTY— NO, ONE HUNDRED!
ENOUGH!
HOP HOP
PFFT! THAT'S PEANUTS COMPARED TO WHATEVER THIS—

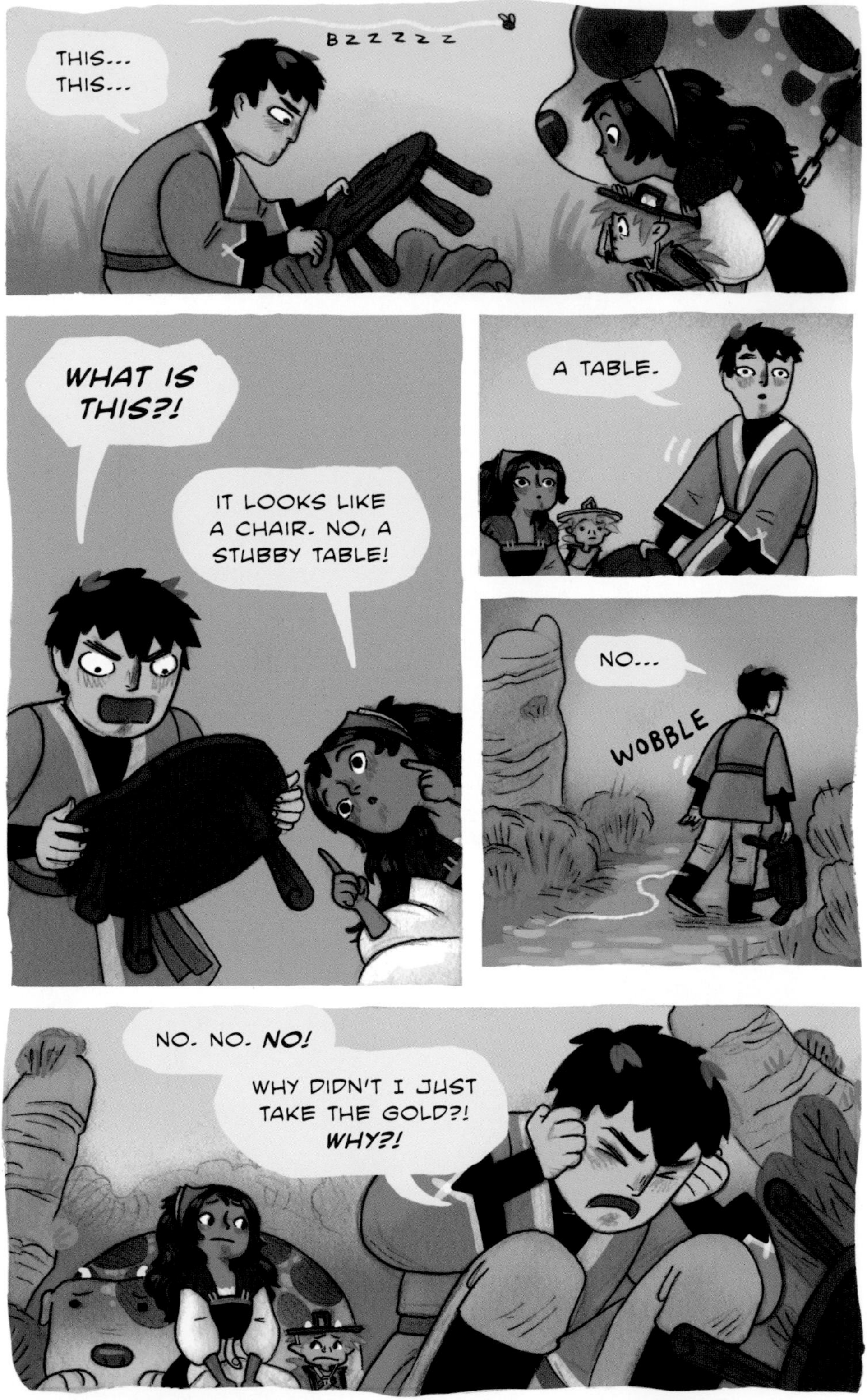
THIS...
THIS...
BZZZZZ
WHAT IS THIS?!
IT LOOKS LIKE A CHAIR. NO, A STUBBY TABLE!
A TABLE.
NO...
WOBBLE
NO. NO. NO!
WHY DIDN'T I JUST TAKE THE GOLD?! WHY?!

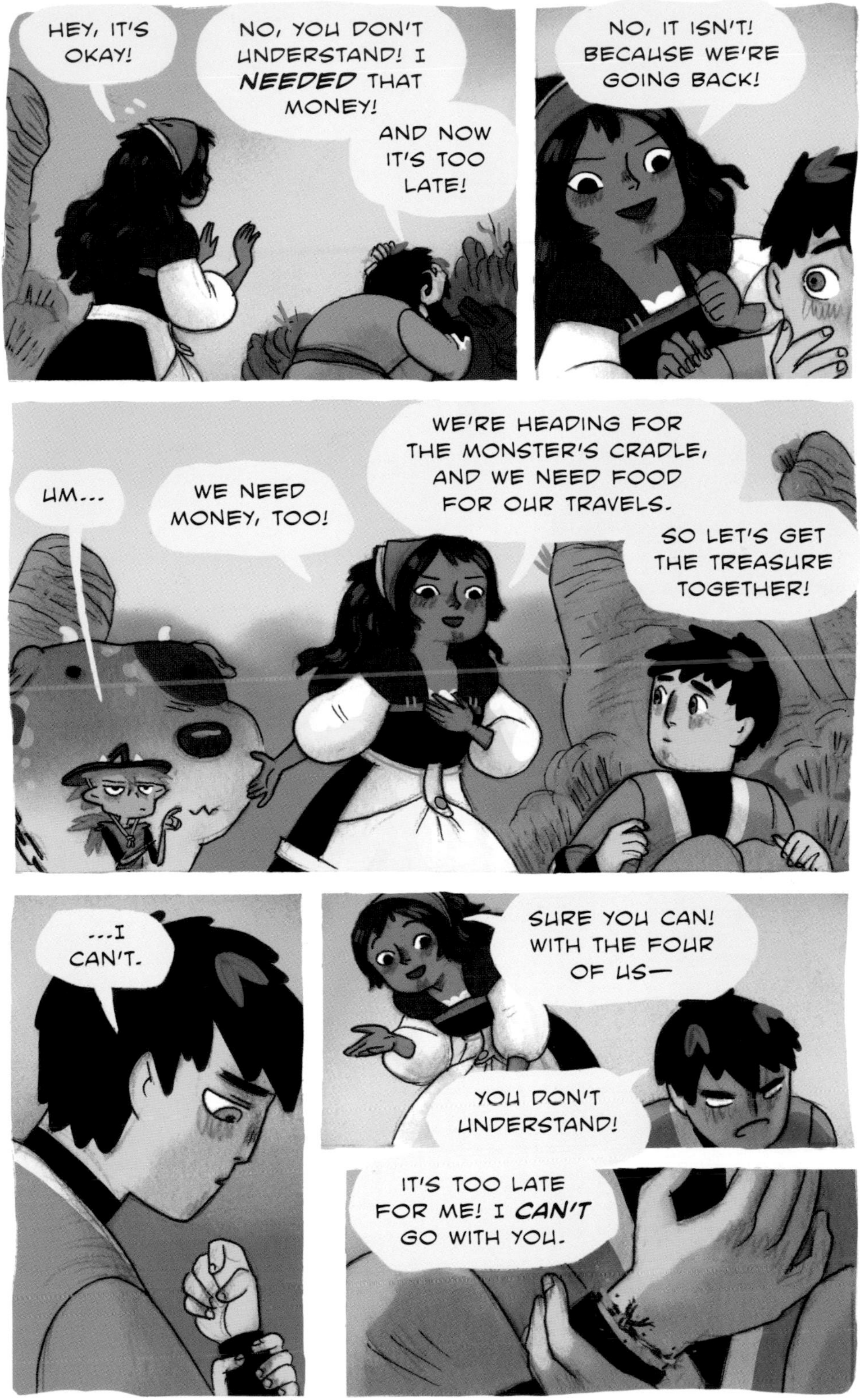
HEY, IT'S OKAY!
NO, YOU DON'T UNDERSTAND! I **NEEDED** THAT MONEY!
AND NOW IT'S TOO LATE!
NO, IT ISN'T! BECAUSE WE'RE GOING BACK!
UM...
WE NEED MONEY, TOO!
WE'RE HEADING FOR THE MONSTER'S CRADLE, AND WE NEED FOOD FOR OUR TRAVELS.
SO LET'S GET THE TREASURE TOGETHER!
...I CAN'T.
SURE YOU CAN! WITH THE FOUR OF US—
YOU DON'T UNDERSTAND!
IT'S TOO LATE FOR ME! I **CAN'T** GO WITH YOU.

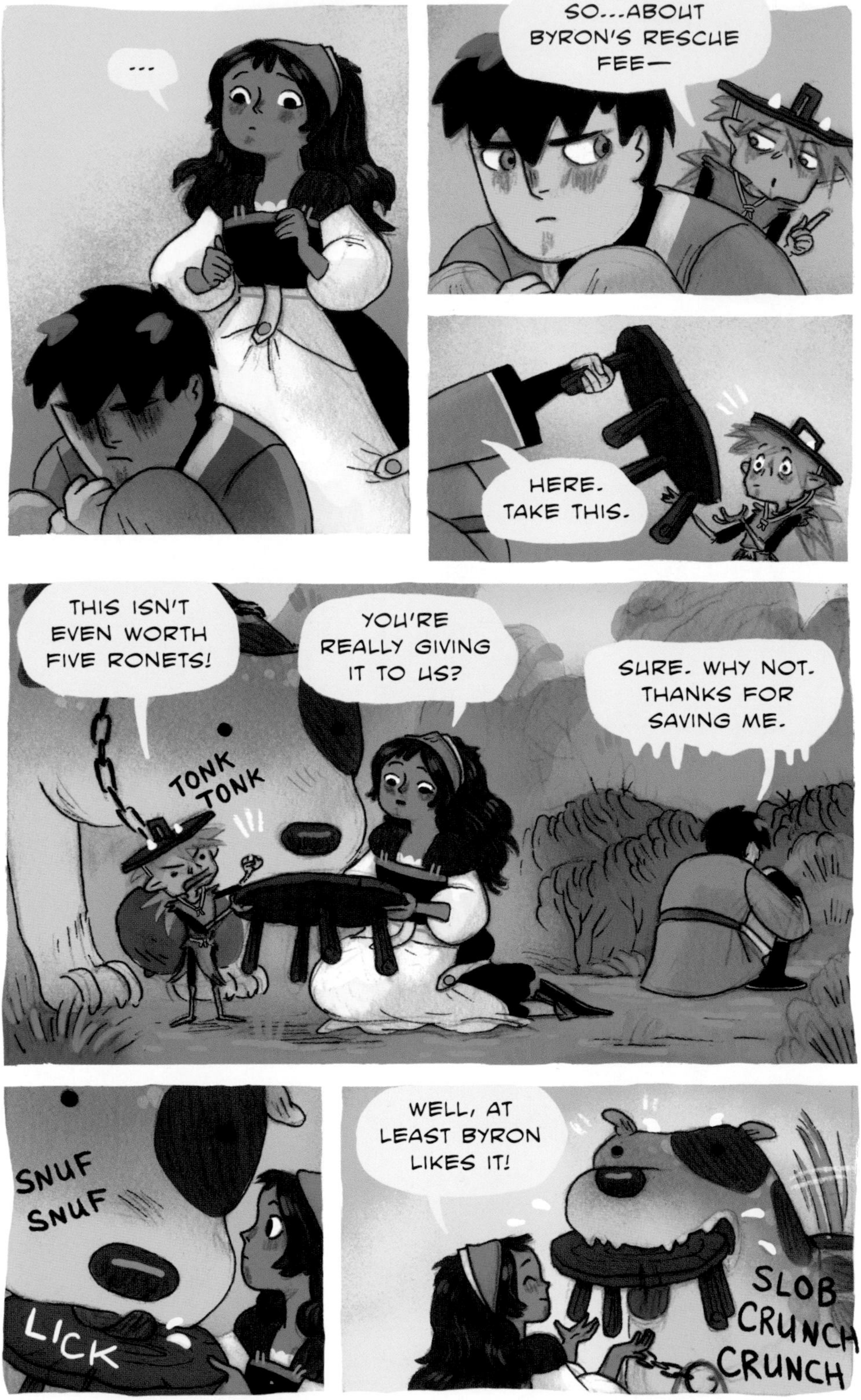
...
SO...ABOUT BYRON'S RESCUE FEE—
HERE. TAKE THIS.
THIS ISN'T EVEN WORTH FIVE RONETS!
YOU'RE REALLY GIVING IT TO US?
SURE. WHY NOT. THANKS FOR SAVING ME.
TONK TONK
SNUF SNUF
LICK
WELL, AT LEAST BYRON LIKES IT!
SLOB CRUNCH CRUNCH

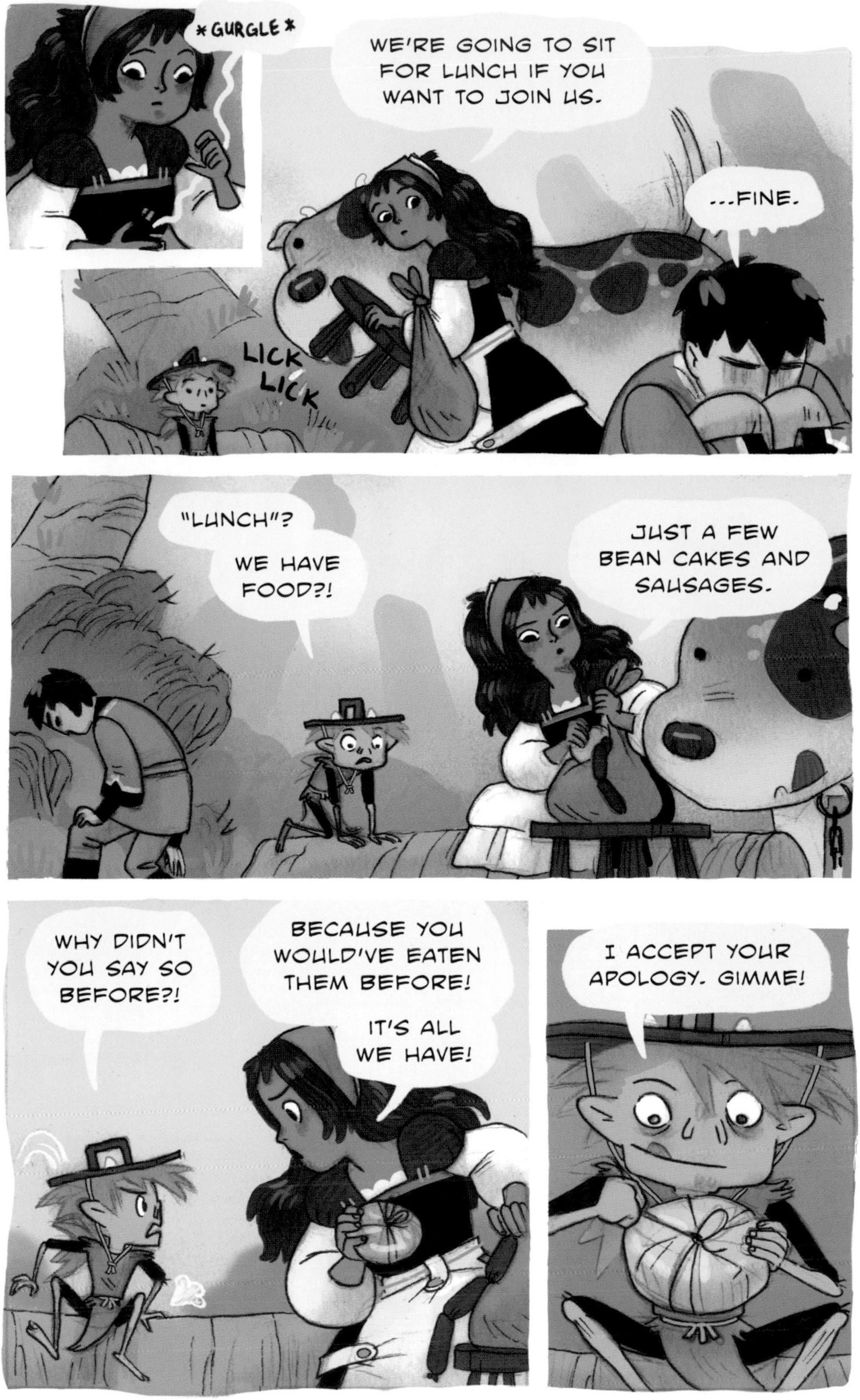
GURGLE
WE'RE GOING TO SIT FOR LUNCH IF YOU WANT TO JOIN US.
...FINE.
LICK LICK
"LUNCH"?
WE HAVE FOOD?!
JUST A FEW BEAN CAKES AND SAUSAGES.
WHY DIDN'T YOU SAY SO BEFORE?!
BECAUSE YOU WOULD'VE EATEN THEM BEFORE!
IT'S ALL WE HAVE!
I ACCEPT YOUR APOLOGY. GIMME!

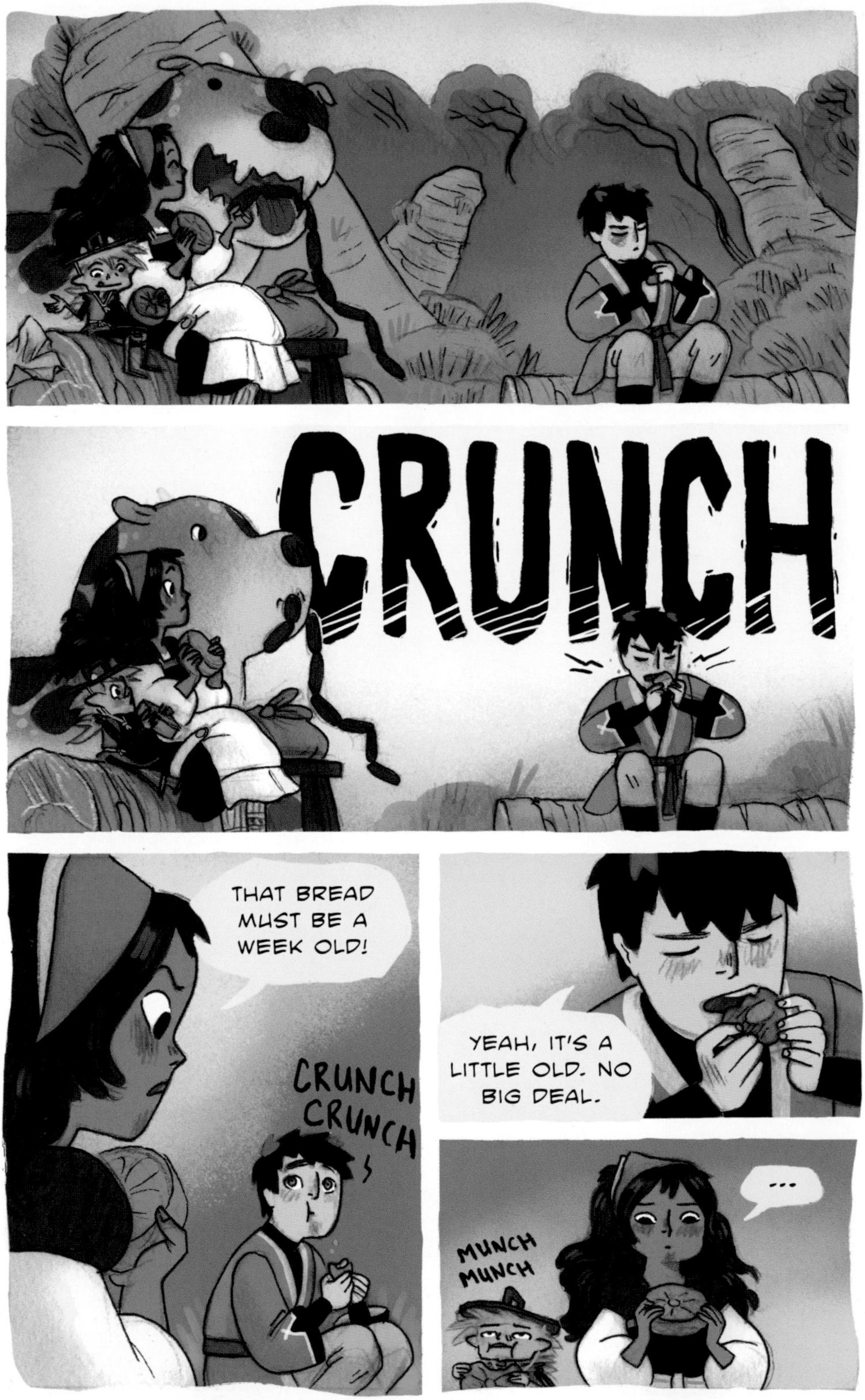
CRUNCH
THAT BREAD MUST BE A WEEK OLD!
CRUNCH CRUNCH
YEAH, IT'S A LITTLE OLD. NO BIG DEAL.
MUNCH MUNCH
...

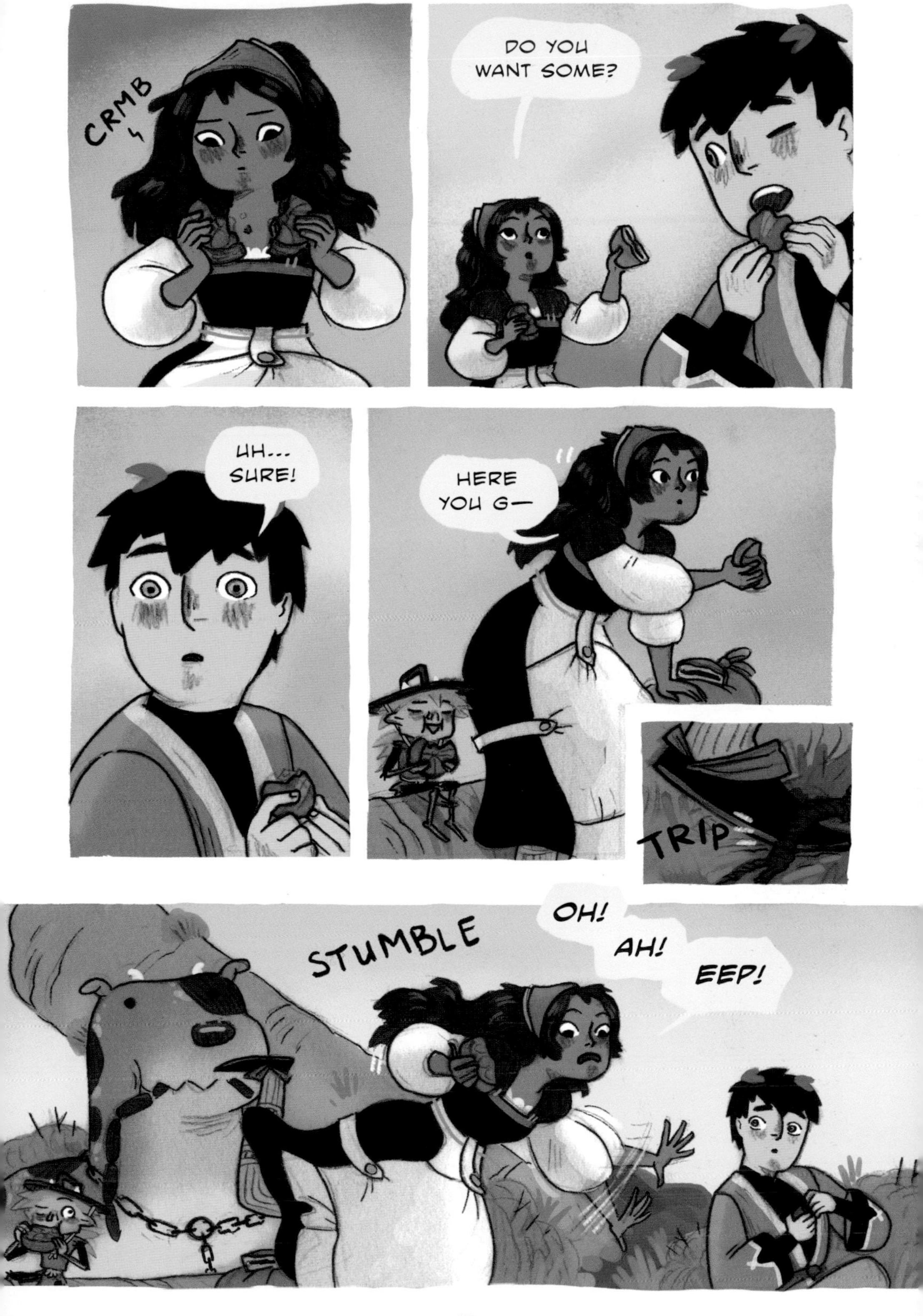
CRMB
DO YOU WANT SOME?
UH... SURE!
HERE YOU G—
TRIP
STUMBLE
OH!
AH!
EEP!

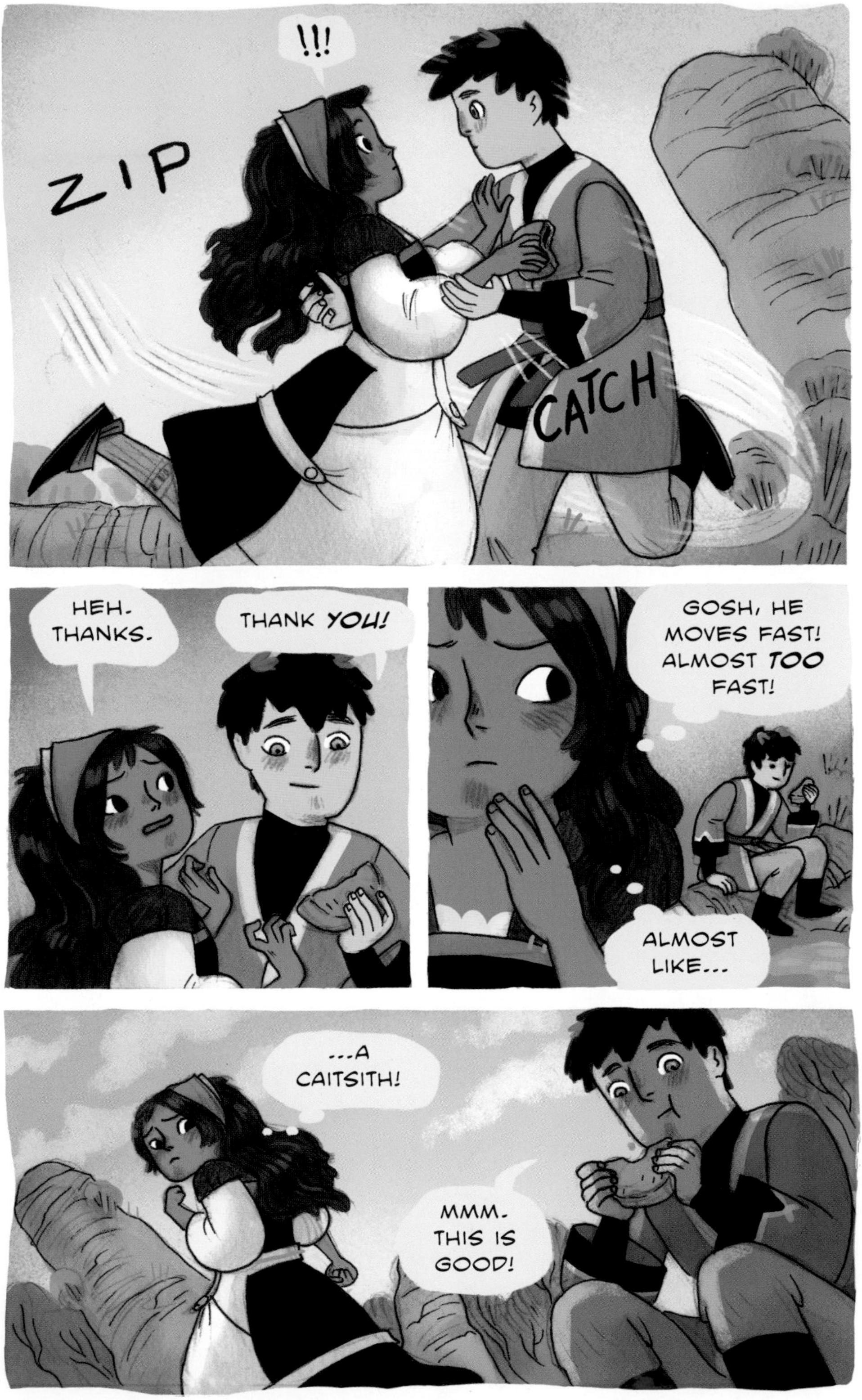
!!!
ZIP
CATCH
HEH. THANKS.
THANK YOU!
GOSH, HE MOVES FAST! ALMOST TOO FAST!
ALMOST LIKE...
...A CAITSITH!
MMM. THIS IS GOOD!

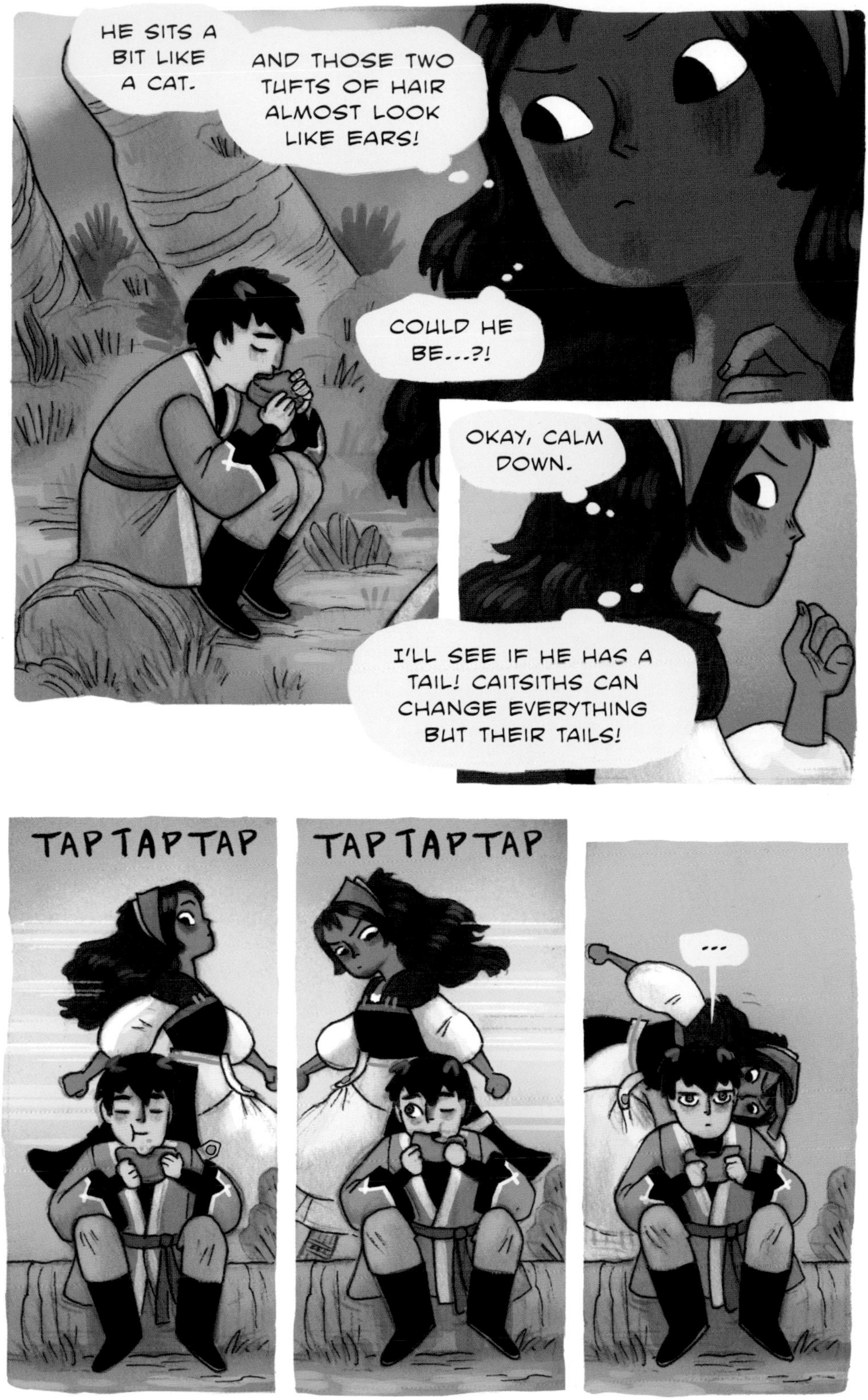
HE SITS A BIT LIKE A CAT.
AND THOSE TWO TUFTS OF HAIR ALMOST LOOK LIKE EARS!
COULD HE BE...?!
OKAY, CALM DOWN.
I'LL SEE IF HE HAS A TAIL! CAITSITHS CAN CHANGE EVERYTHING BUT THEIR TAILS!
TAP TAP TAP
TAP TAP TAP
...

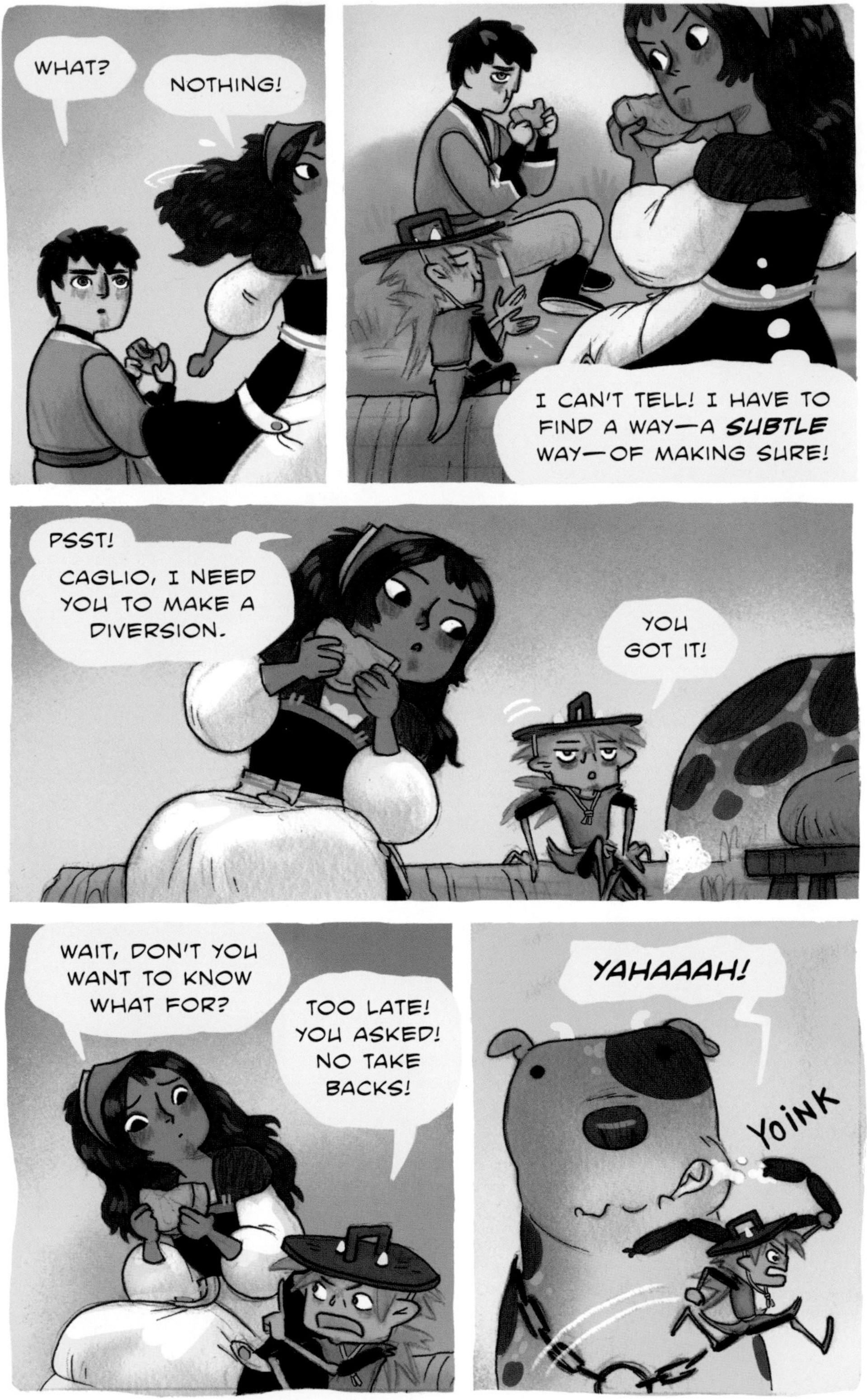
WHAT?
NOTHING!
I CAN'T TELL! I HAVE TO FIND A WAY—A SUBTLE WAY—OF MAKING SURE!
PSST!
CAGLIO, I NEED YOU TO MAKE A DIVERSION.
YOU GOT IT!
WAIT, DON'T YOU WANT TO KNOW WHAT FOR?
TOO LATE! YOU ASKED! NO TAKE BACKS!
YAHAAAH!
YOINK

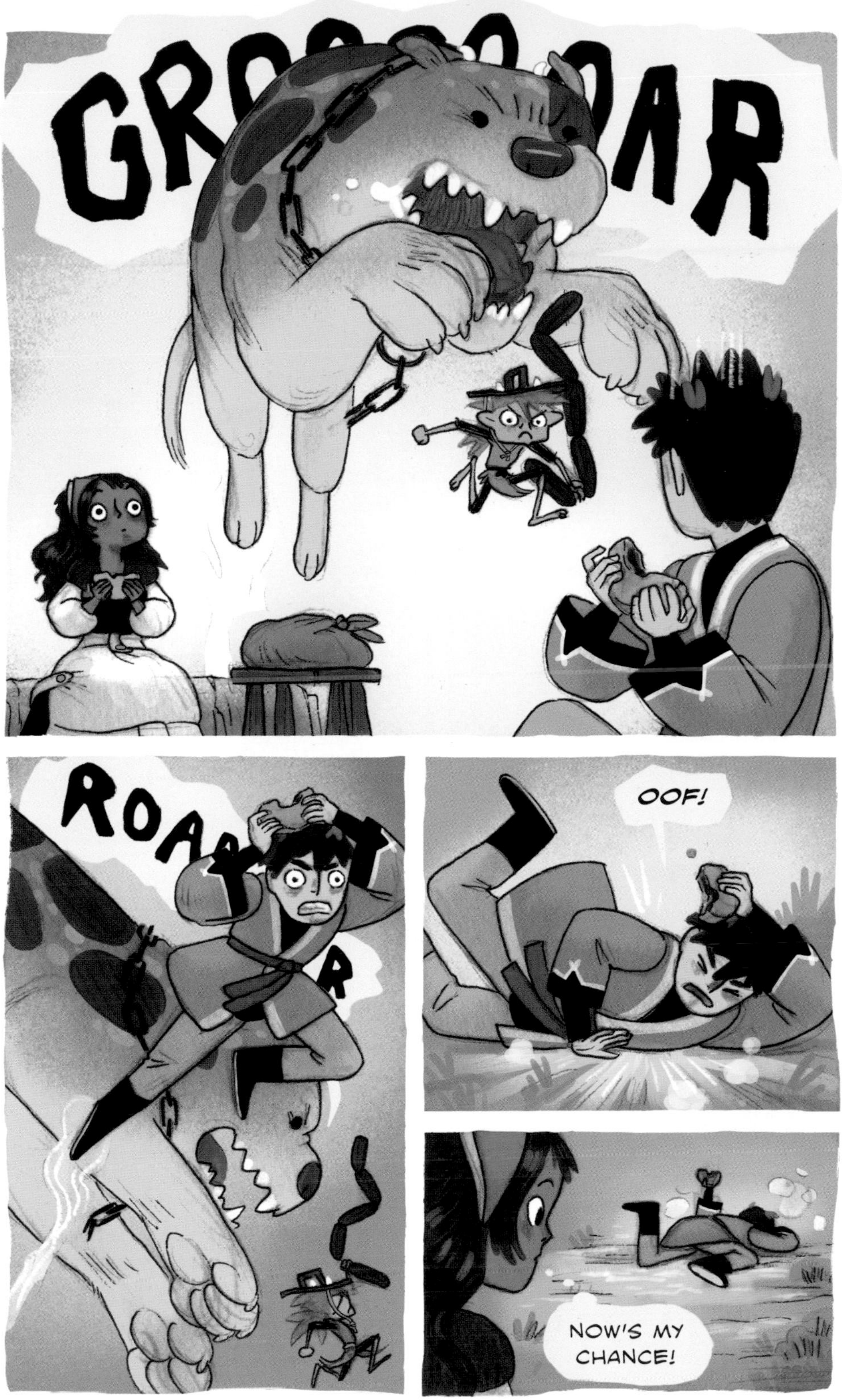
GRO OAR
ROA R
OOF!
NOW'S MY CHANCE!

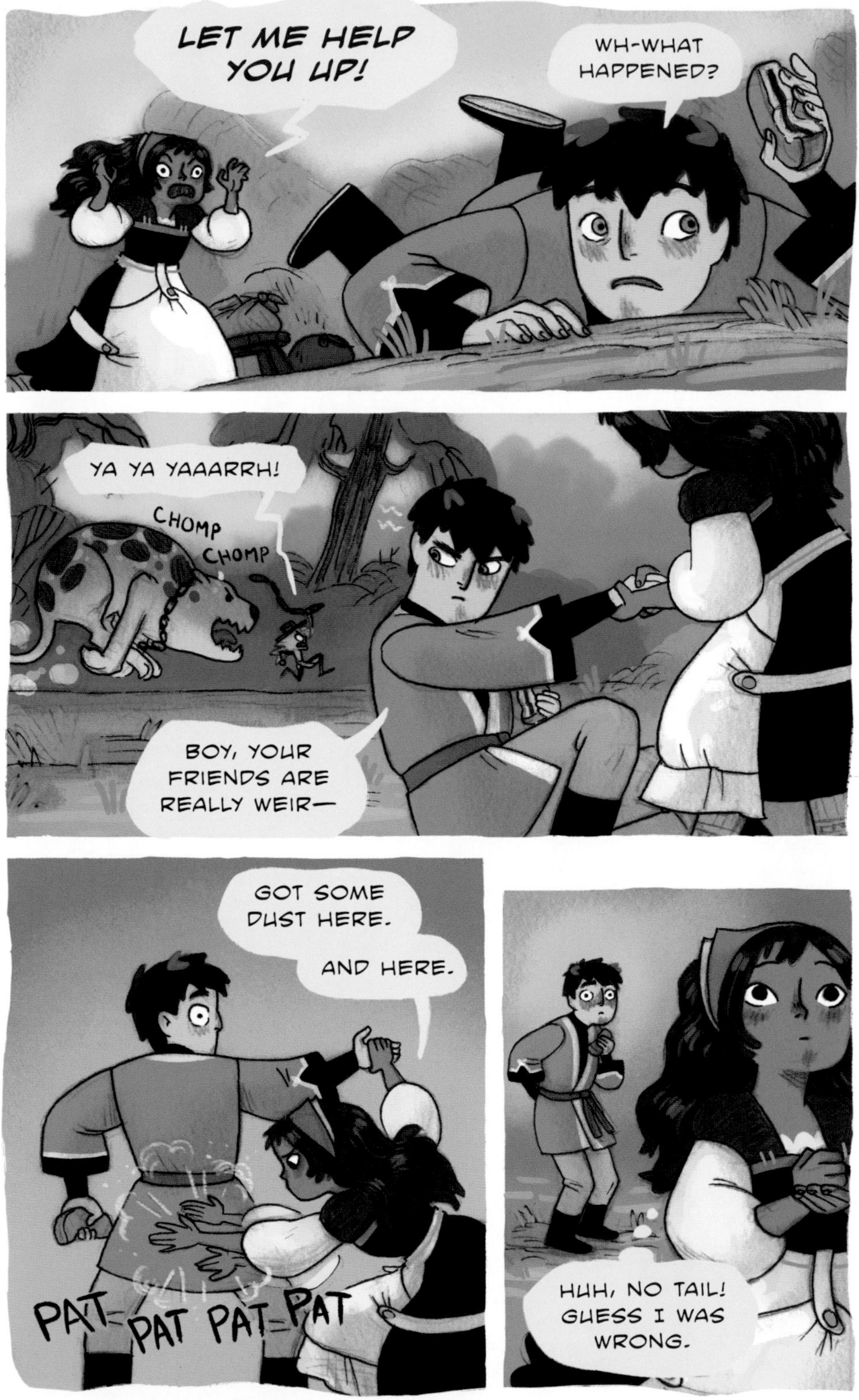

LET ME HELP YOU UP!
WH-WHAT HAPPENED?
YA YA YAAARRH!
CHOMP CHOMP
BOY, YOUR FRIENDS ARE REALLY WEIR—
GOT SOME DUST HERE.
AND HERE.
PAT PAT PAT PAT
HUH, NO TAIL! GUESS I WAS WRONG.

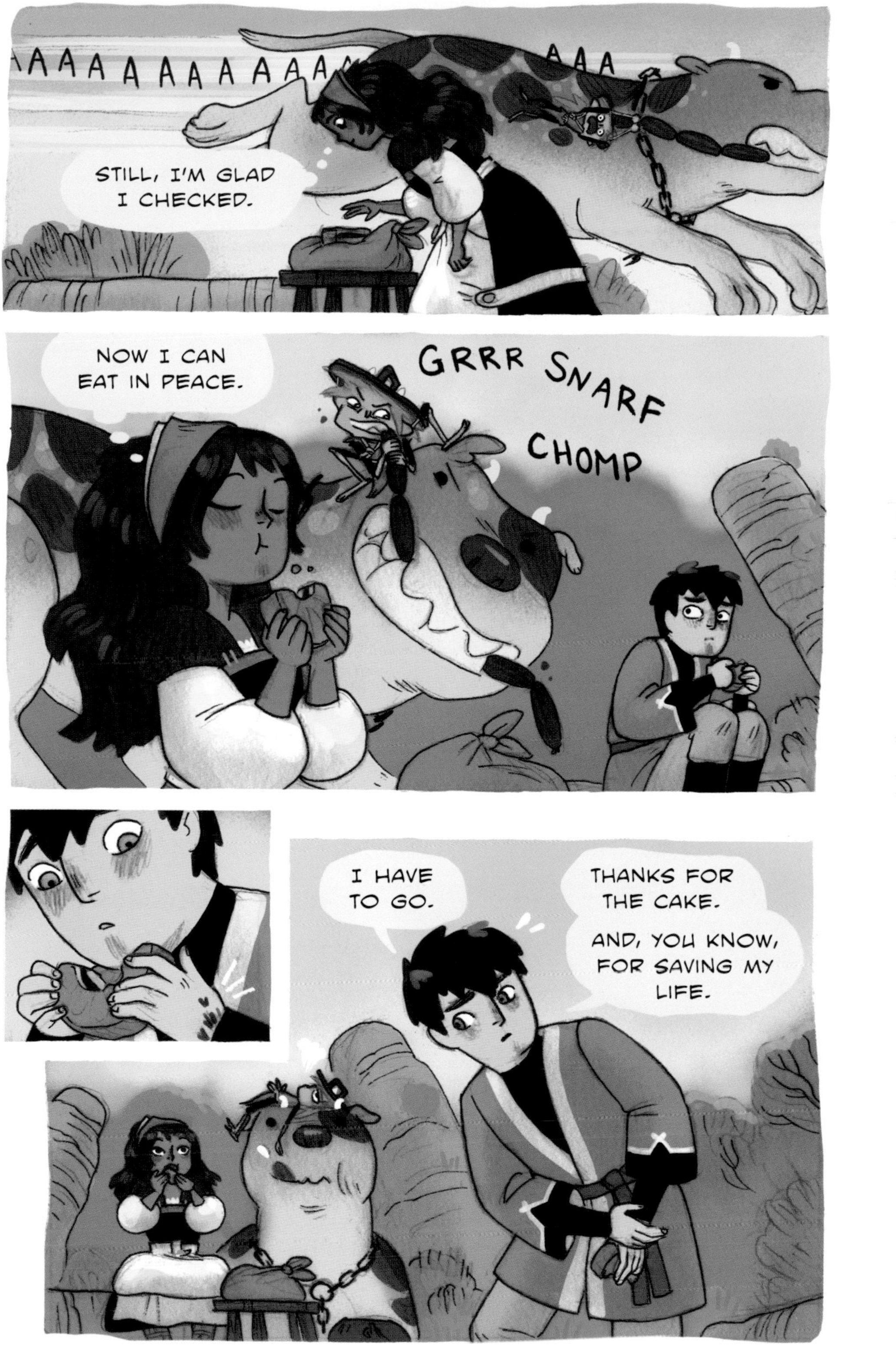
AAAAAAAAAAAAAAA
AAA
STILL, I'M GLAD I CHECKED.
NOW I CAN EAT IN PEACE.
GRRR SNARF
CHOMP
I HAVE TO GO.
THANKS FOR THE CAKE.
AND, YOU KNOW, FOR SAVING MY LIFE.

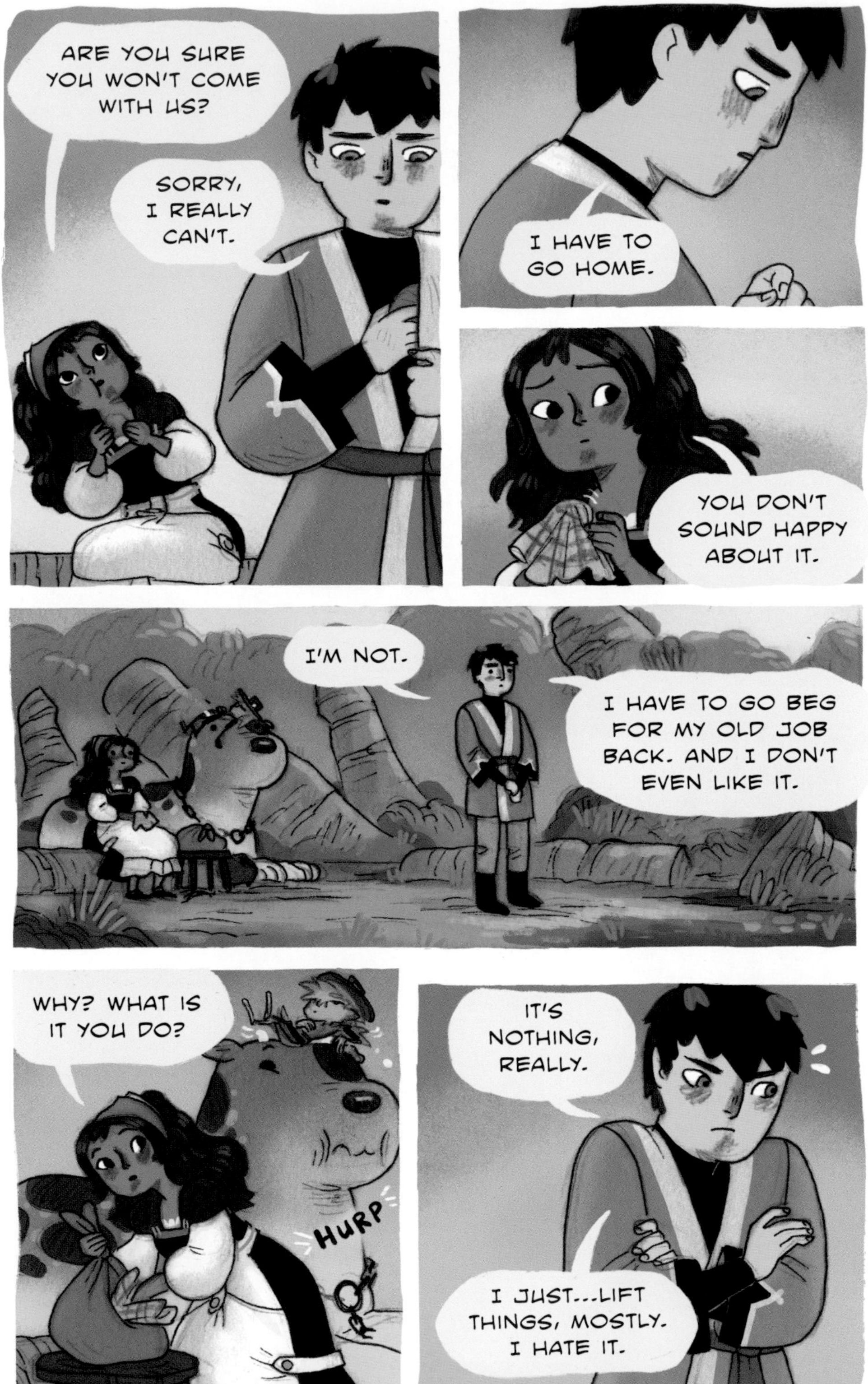
ARE YOU SURE YOU WON'T COME WITH US?
SORRY, I REALLY CAN'T.
I HAVE TO GO HOME.
YOU DON'T SOUND HAPPY ABOUT IT.
I'M NOT.
I HAVE TO GO BEG FOR MY OLD JOB BACK. AND I DON'T EVEN LIKE IT.
WHY? WHAT IS IT YOU DO?
HURP
IT'S NOTHING, REALLY.
I JUST...LIFT THINGS, MOSTLY. I HATE IT.

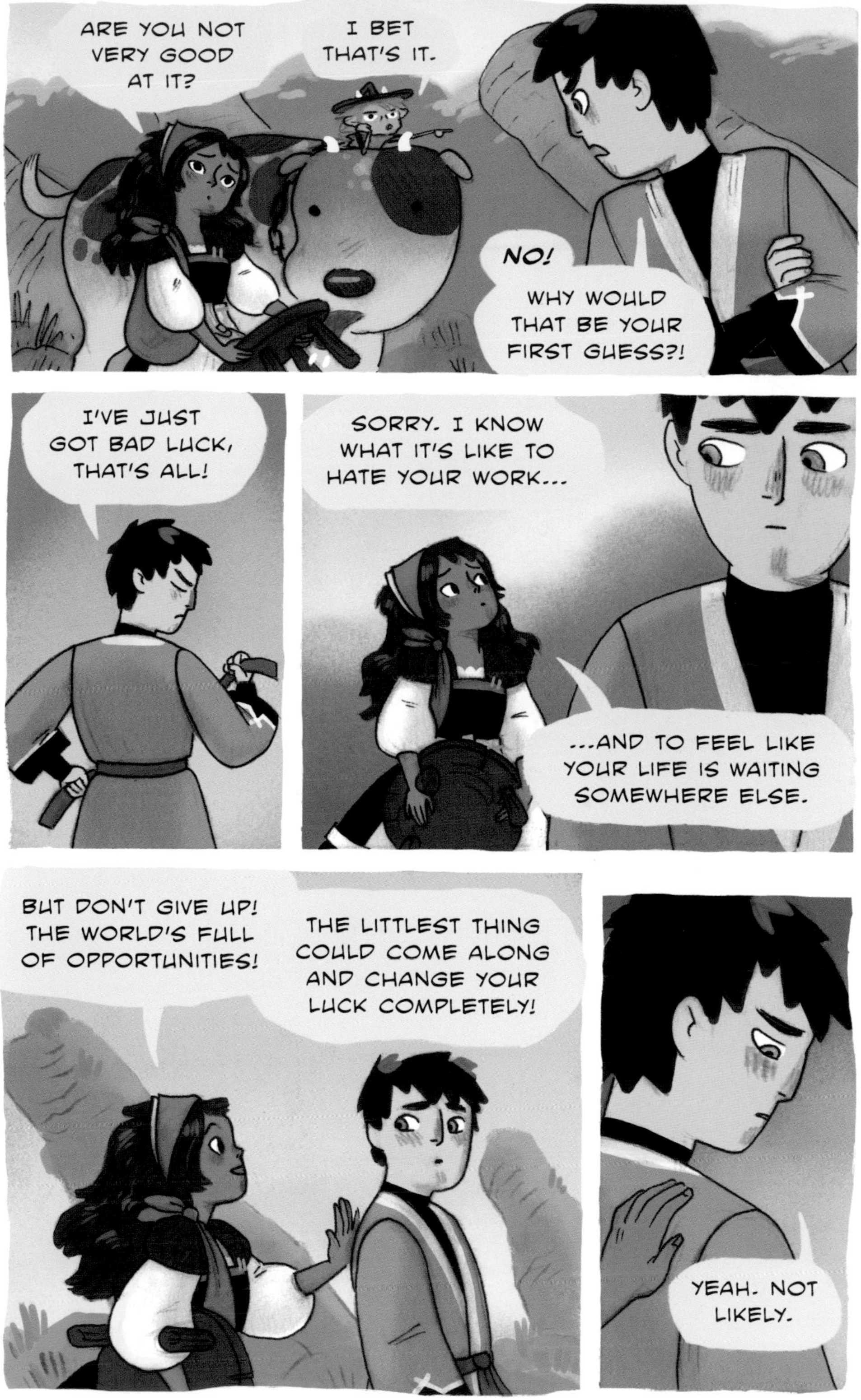
ARE YOU NOT VERY GOOD AT IT?
I BET THAT'S IT.
NO!
WHY WOULD THAT BE YOUR FIRST GUESS?!
I'VE JUST GOT BAD LUCK, THAT'S ALL!
SORRY. I KNOW WHAT IT'S LIKE TO HATE YOUR WORK...
...AND TO FEEL LIKE YOUR LIFE IS WAITING SOMEWHERE ELSE.
BUT DON'T GIVE UP! THE WORLD'S FULL OF OPPORTUNITIES!
THE LITTLEST THING COULD COME ALONG AND CHANGE YOUR LUCK COMPLETELY!
YEAH. NOT LIKELY.

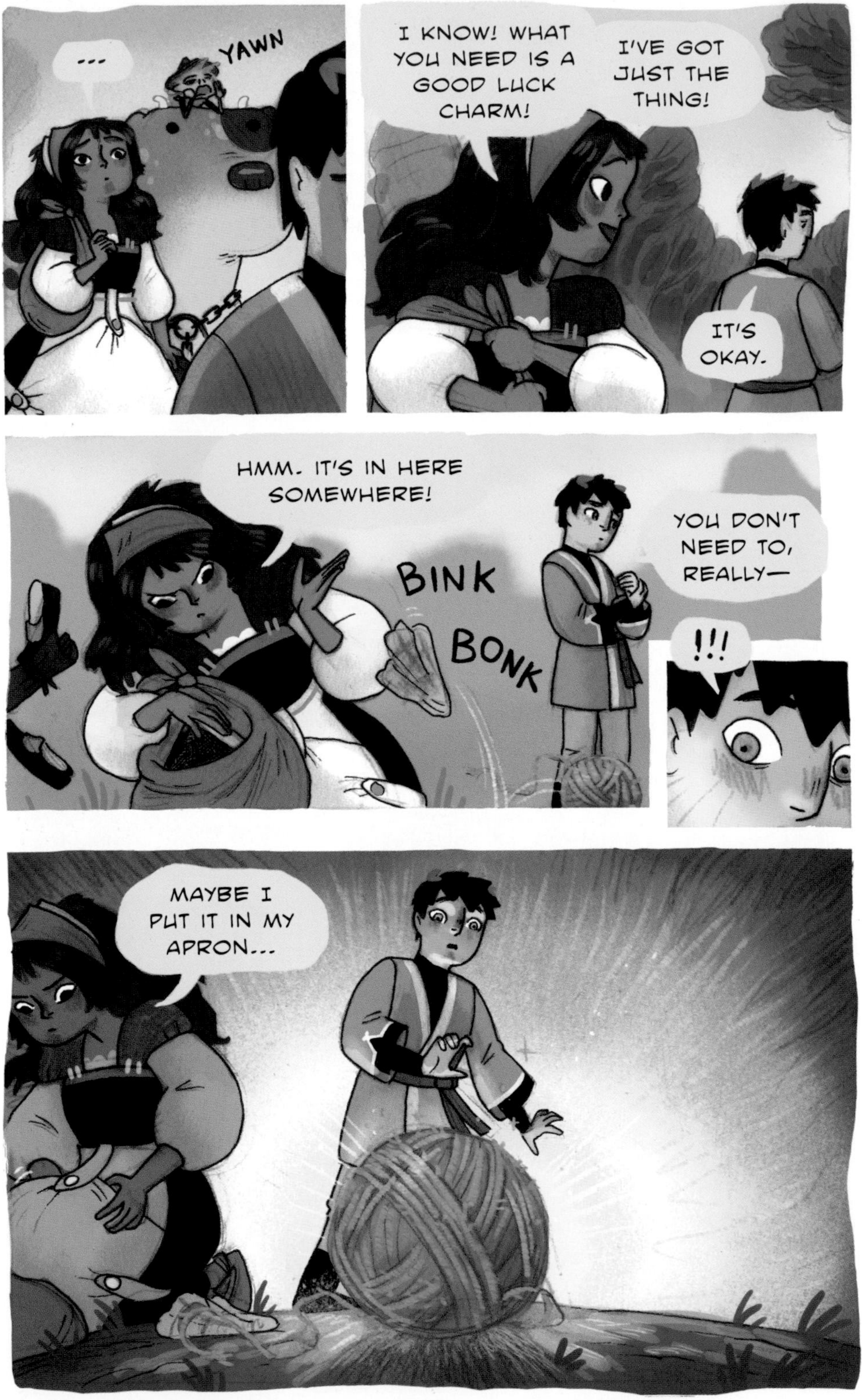

...
YAWN
I KNOW! WHAT YOU NEED IS A GOOD LUCK CHARM!
I'VE GOT JUST THE THING!
IT'S OKAY.
HMM. IT'S IN HERE SOMEWHERE!
BINK
BONK
YOU DON'T NEED TO, REALLY—
!!!
MAYBE I PUT IT IN MY APRON...

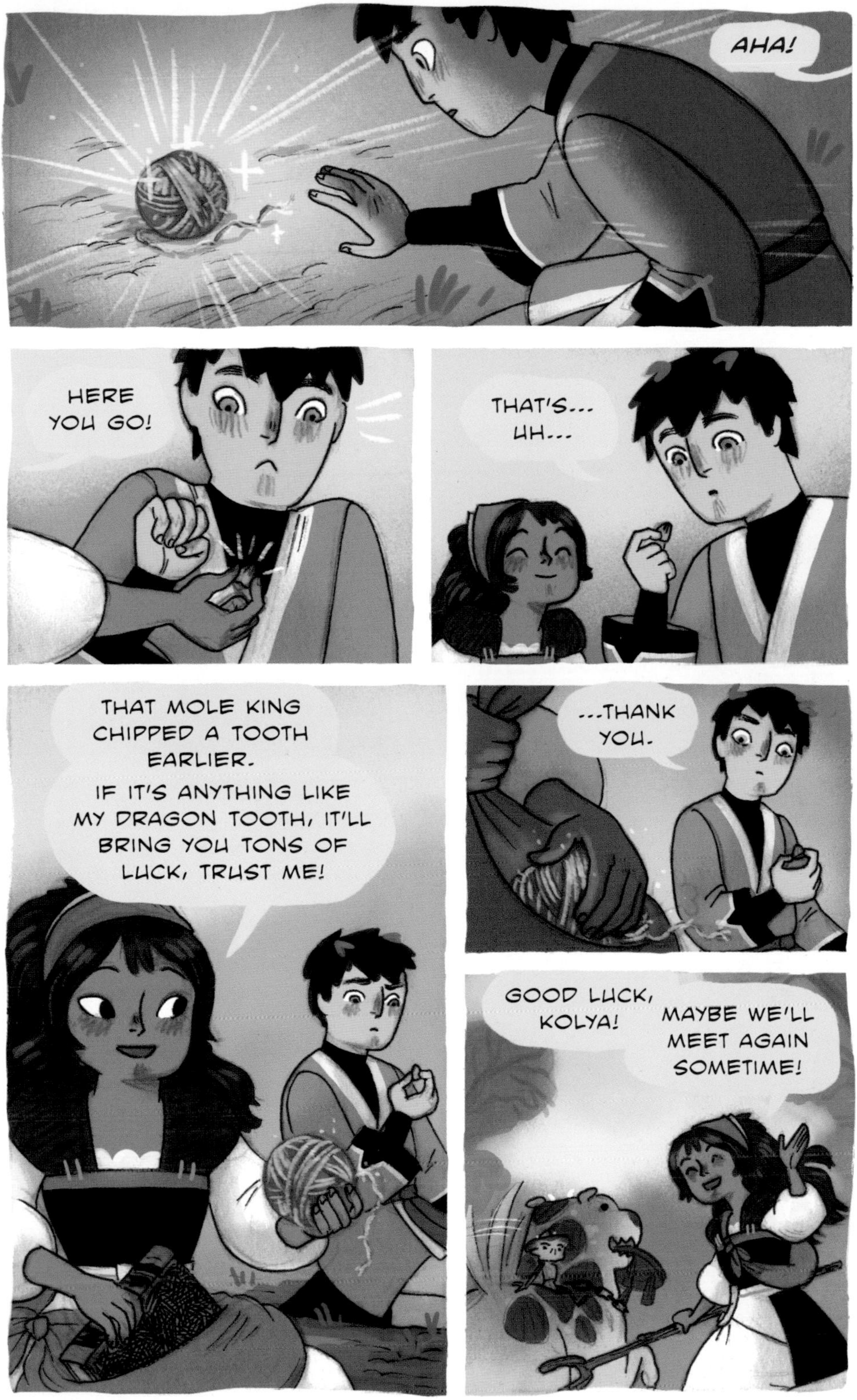
AHA!
HERE YOU GO!
THAT'S... UH...
THAT MOLE KING CHIPPED A TOOTH EARLIER.
IF IT'S ANYTHING LIKE MY DRAGON TOOTH, IT'LL BRING YOU TONS OF LUCK, TRUST ME!
...THANK YOU.
GOOD LUCK, KOLYA!
MAYBE WE'LL MEET AGAIN SOMETIME!

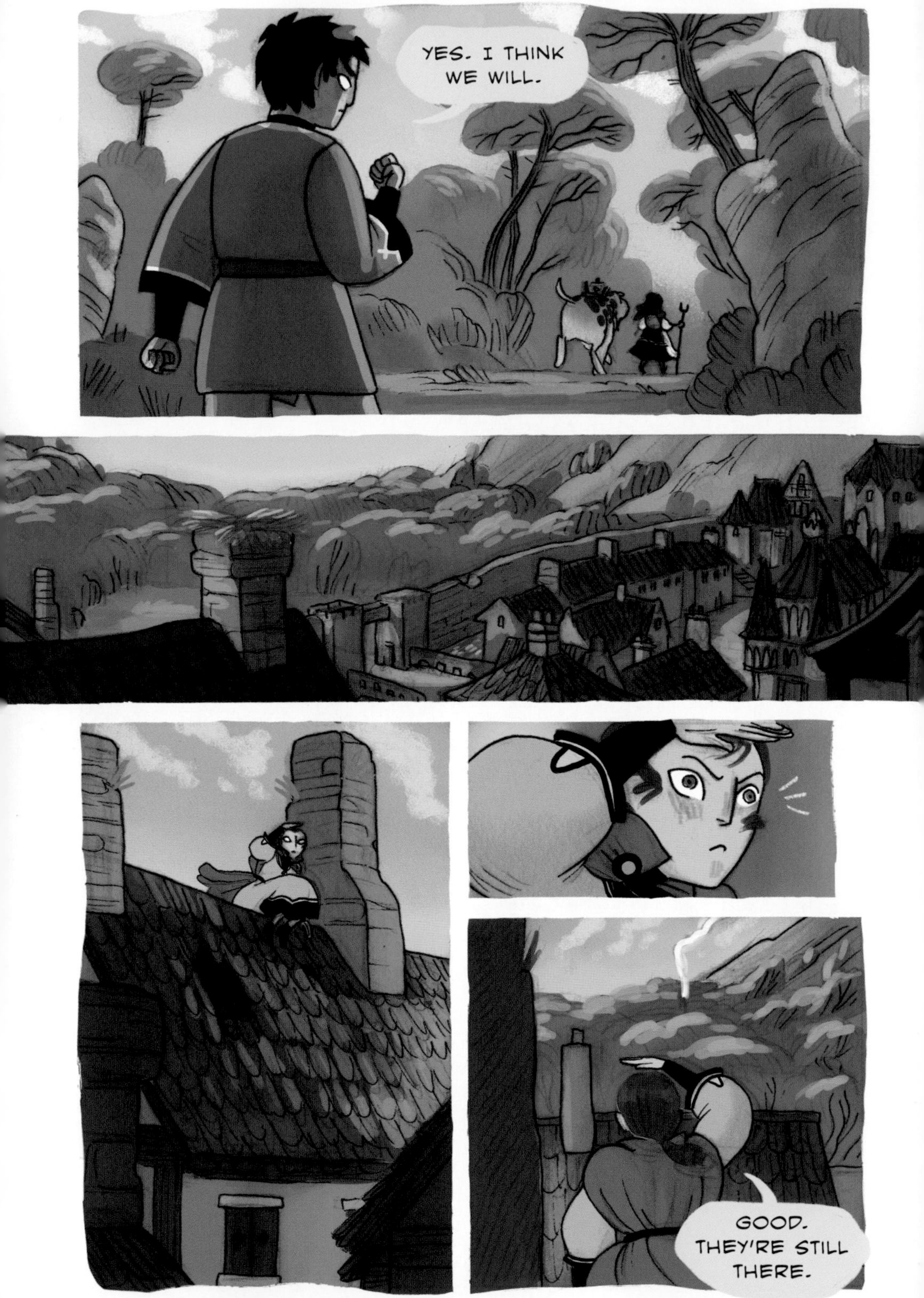
YES. I THINK WE WILL.
GOOD. THEY'RE STILL THERE.

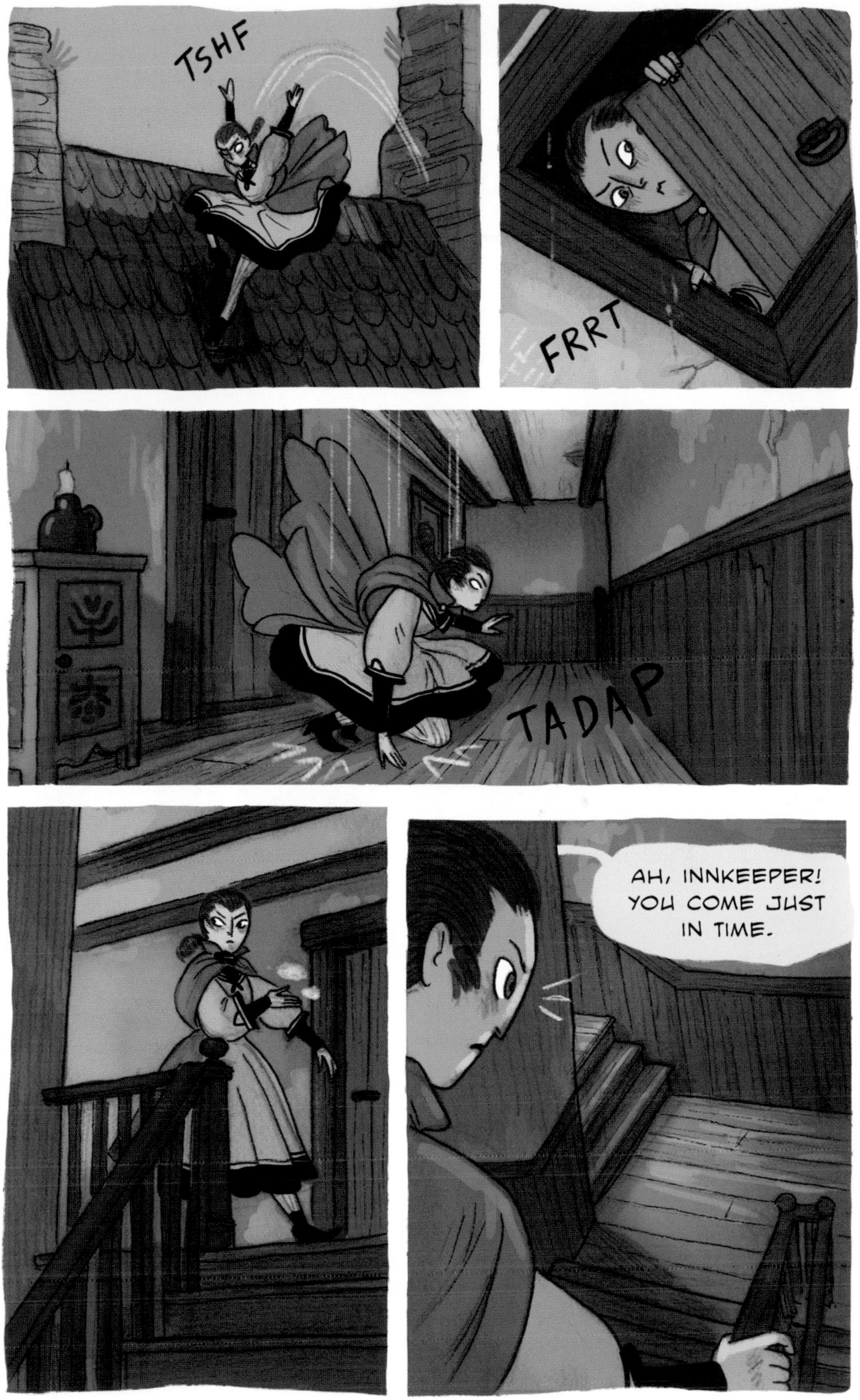
TSHF
FRRT
TADAP
AH, INNKEEPER! YOU COME JUST IN TIME.

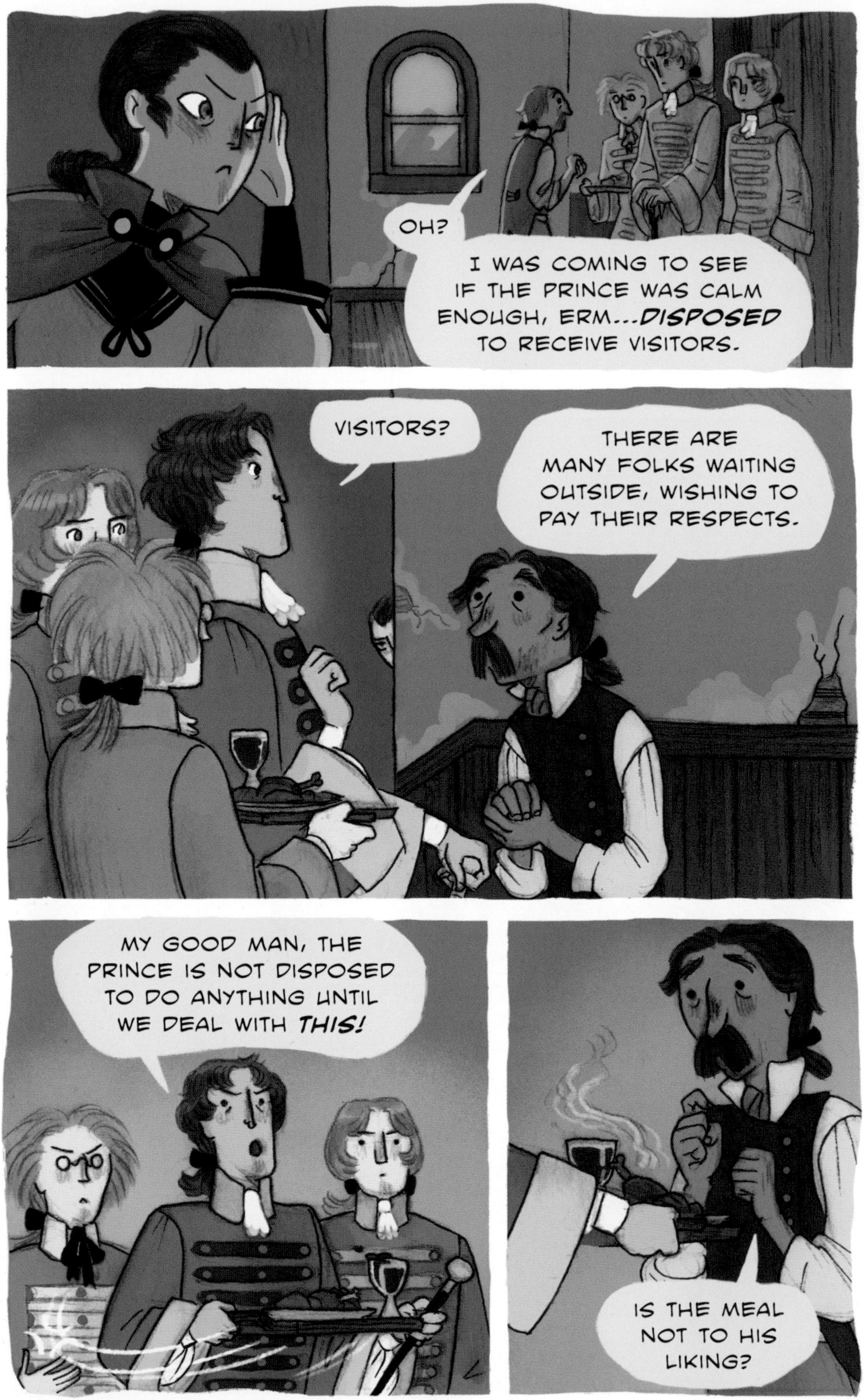
OH?
I WAS COMING TO SEE IF THE PRINCE WAS CALM ENOUGH, ERM...DISPOSED TO RECEIVE VISITORS.
VISITORS?
THERE ARE MANY FOLKS WAITING OUTSIDE, WISHING TO PAY THEIR RESPECTS.
MY GOOD MAN, THE PRINCE IS NOT DISPOSED TO DO ANYTHING UNTIL WE DEAL WITH THIS!
IS THE MEAL NOT TO HIS LIKING?

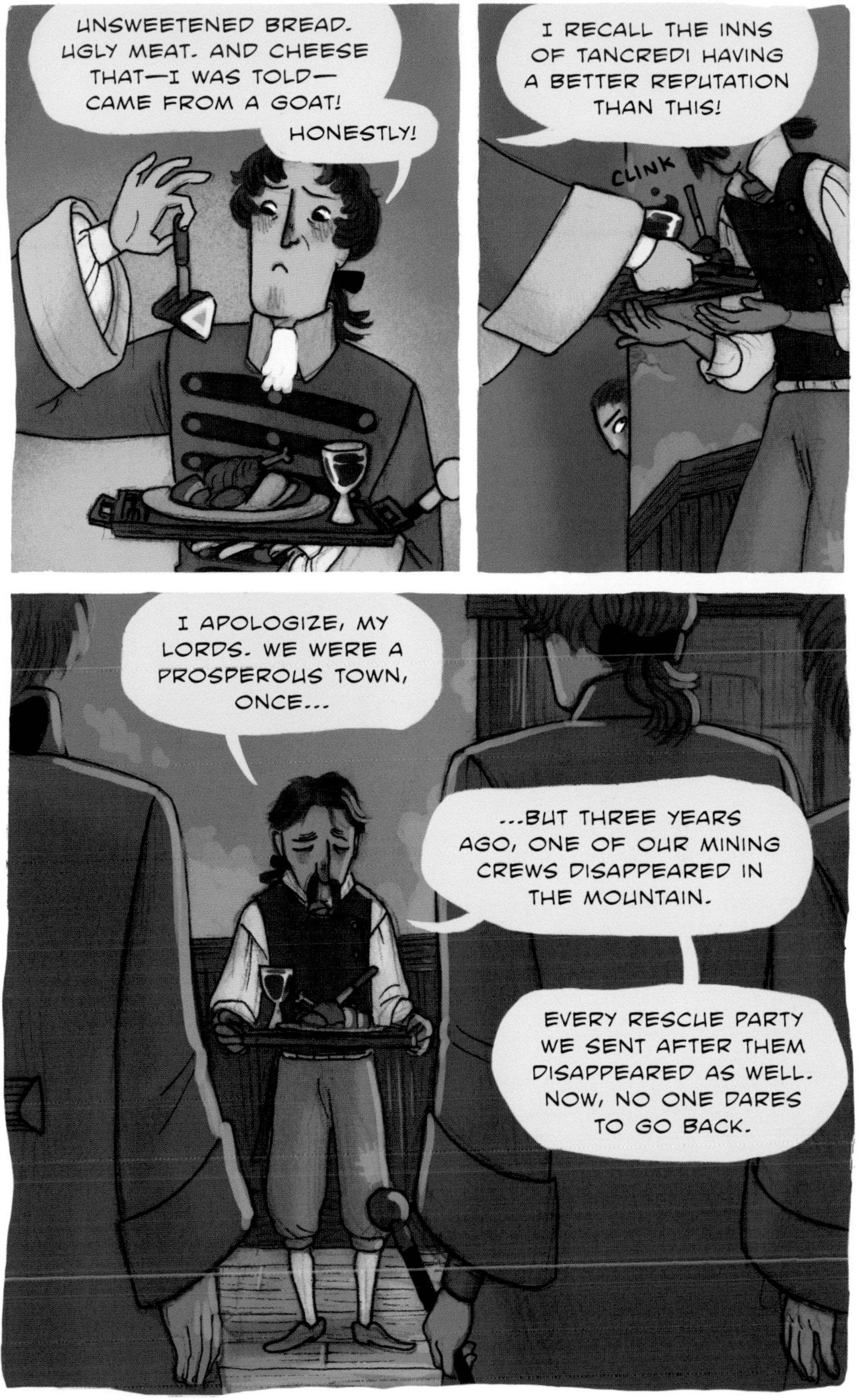

UNSWEETENED BREAD. UGLY MEAT. AND CHEESE THAT—I WAS TOLD—CAME FROM A GOAT!
HONESTLY!
I RECALL THE INNS OF TANCREDI HAVING A BETTER REPUTATION THAN THIS!
CLINK
I APOLOGIZE, MY LORDS. WE WERE A PROSPEROUS TOWN, ONCE...
...BUT THREE YEARS AGO, ONE OF OUR MINING CREWS DISAPPEARED IN THE MOUNTAIN.
EVERY RESCUE PARTY WE SENT AFTER THEM DISAPPEARED AS WELL. NOW, NO ONE DARES TO GO BACK.

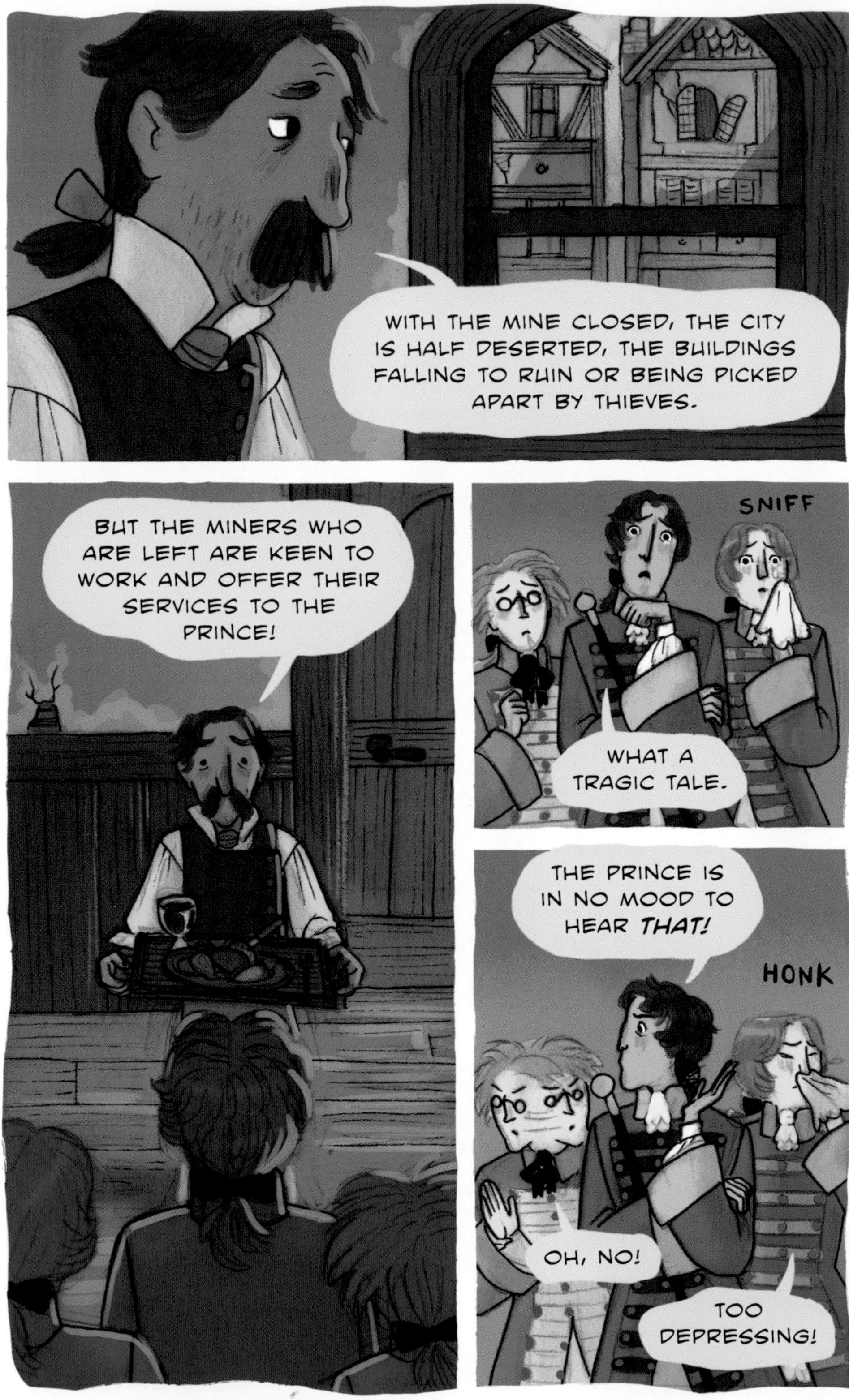
WITH THE MINE CLOSED, THE CITY IS HALF DESERTED, THE BUILDINGS FALLING TO RUIN OR BEING PICKED APART BY THIEVES.
BUT THE MINERS WHO ARE LEFT ARE KEEN TO WORK AND OFFER THEIR SERVICES TO THE PRINCE!
SNIFF
WHAT A TRAGIC TALE.
THE PRINCE IS IN NO MOOD TO HEAR *THAT!*
HONK
OH, NO!
TOO DEPRESSING!

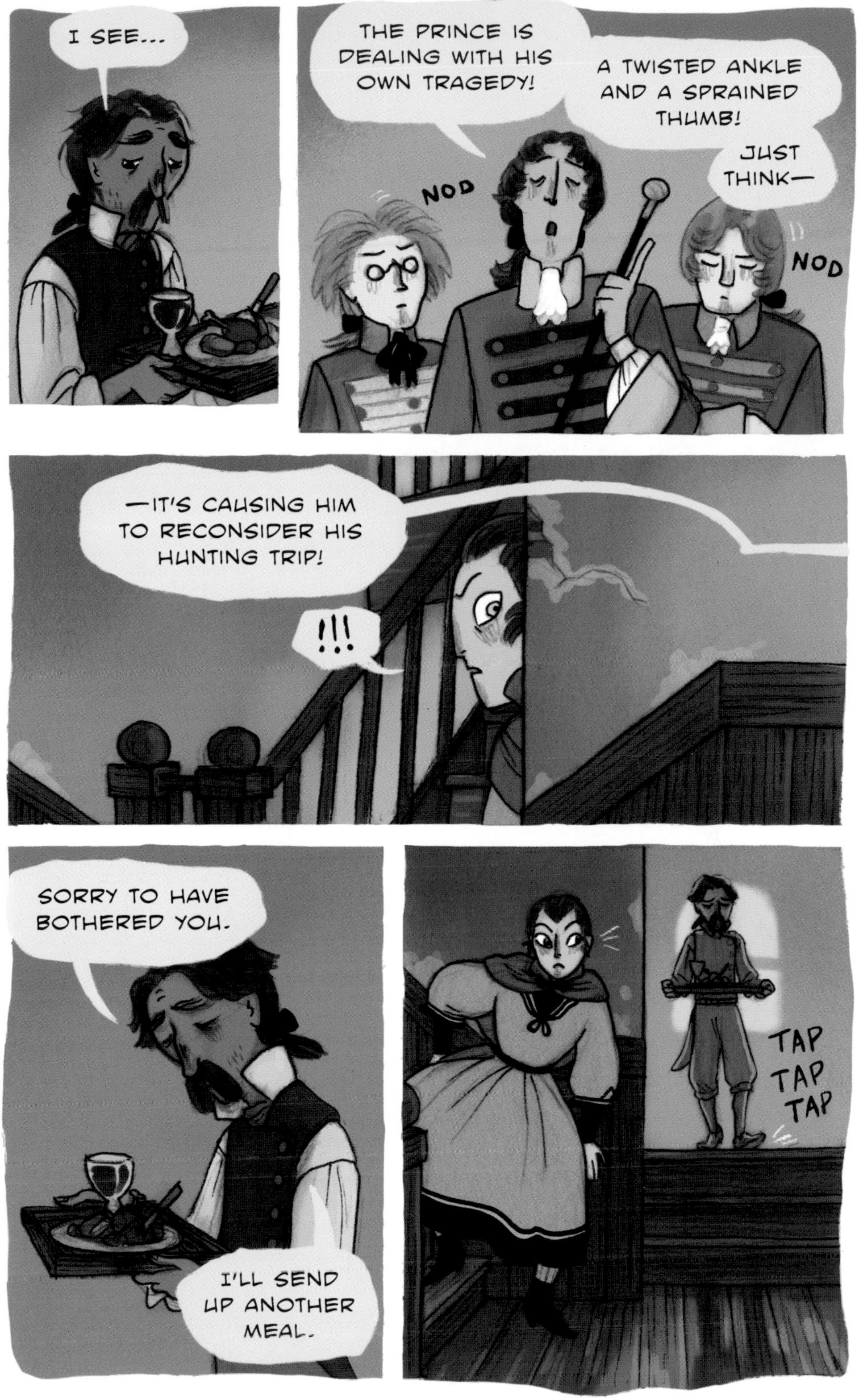
I SEE...
THE PRINCE IS DEALING WITH HIS OWN TRAGEDY!
A TWISTED ANKLE AND A SPRAINED THUMB!
JUST THINK—
NOD
NOD
—IT'S CAUSING HIM TO RECONSIDER HIS HUNTING TRIP!
!!!
SORRY TO HAVE BOTHERED YOU.
I'LL SEND UP ANOTHER MEAL.
TAP
TAP
TAP

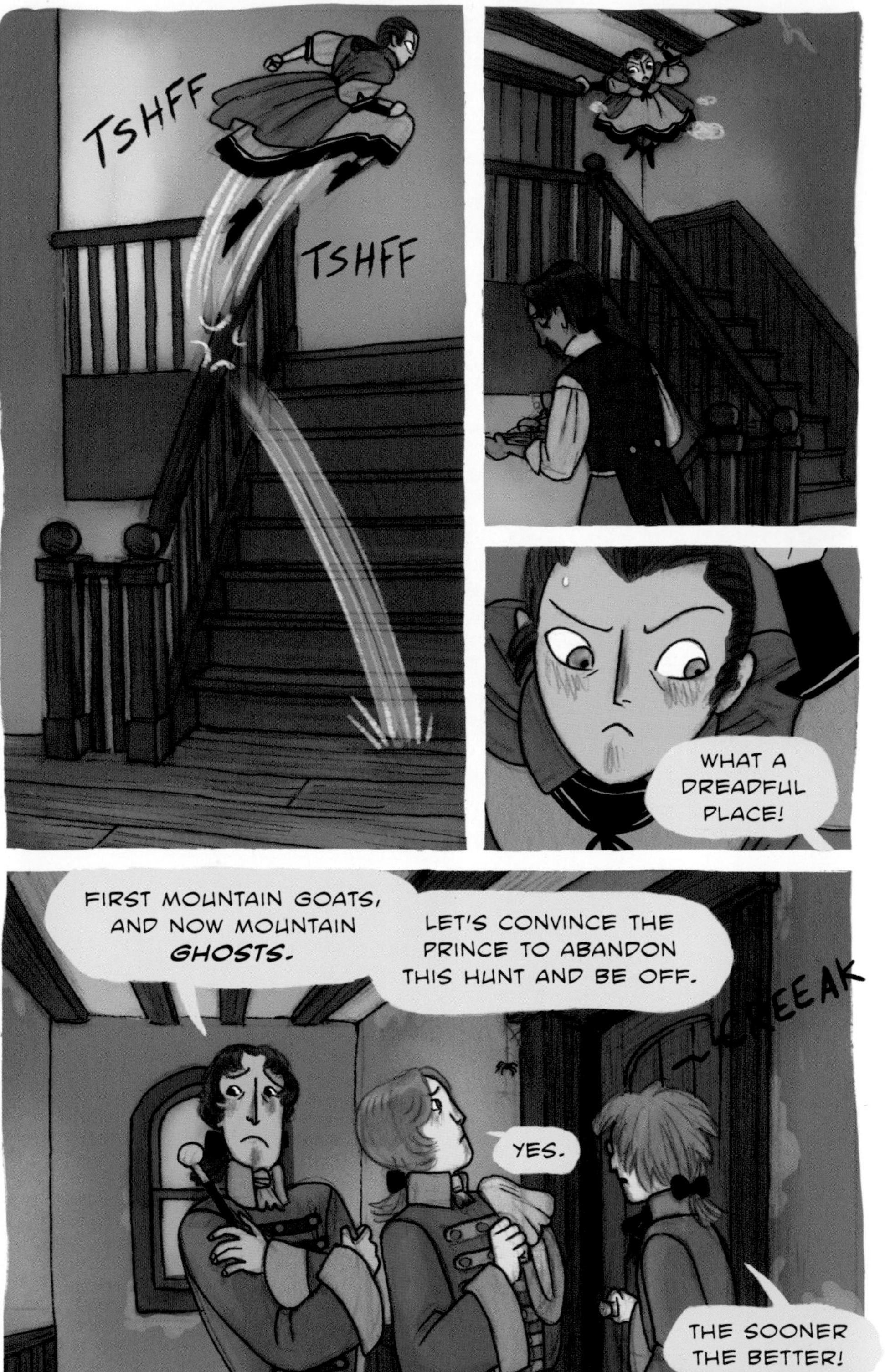
TSHFF
TSHFF
WHAT A DREADFUL PLACE!
FIRST MOUNTAIN GOATS, AND NOW MOUNTAIN GHOSTS.
LET'S CONVINCE THE PRINCE TO ABANDON THIS HUNT AND BE OFF.
CREEEAK
YES.
THE SOONER THE BETTER!

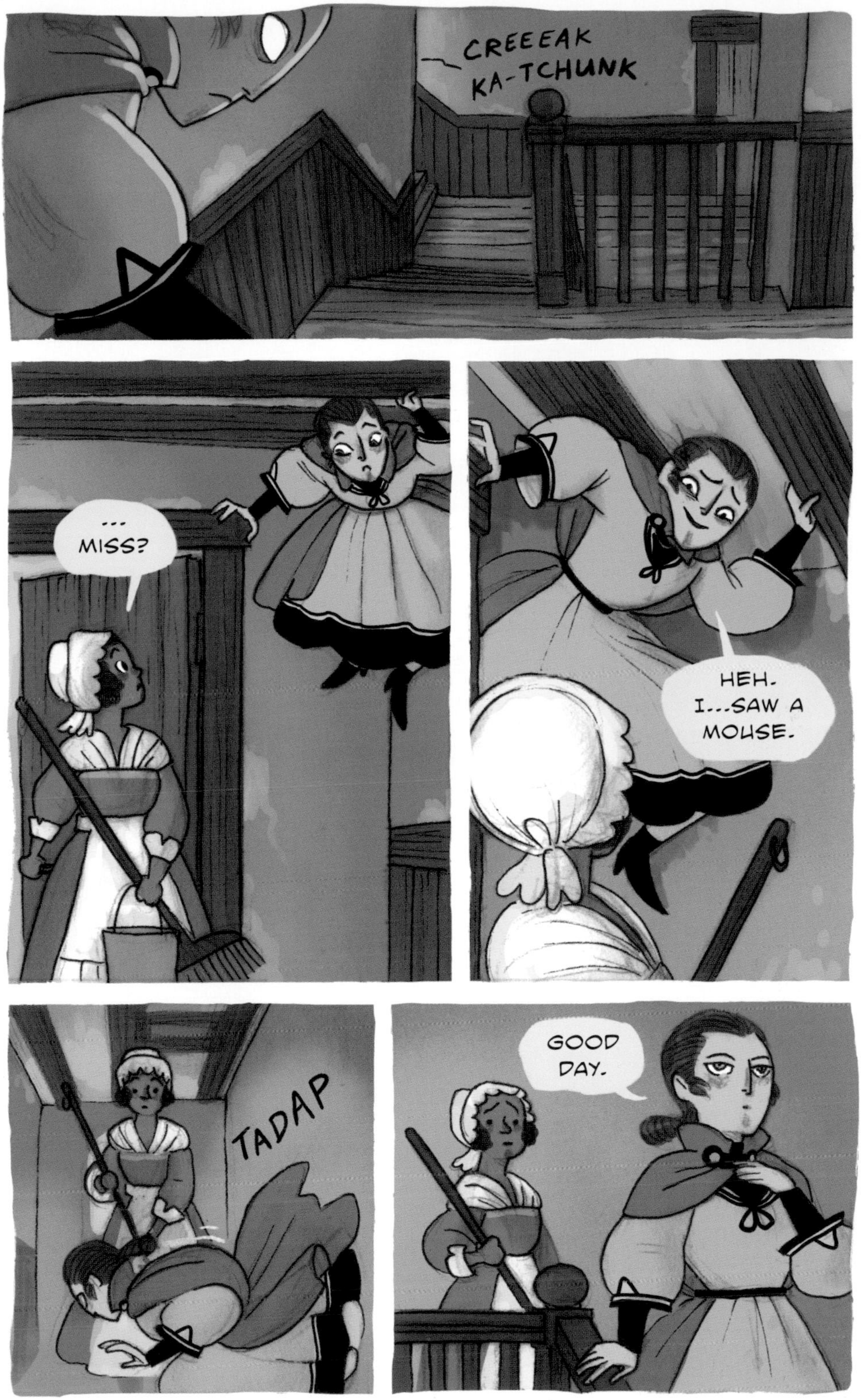
CREEEAK
KA-TCHUNK
... MISS?
HEH. I...SAW A MOUSE.
TADAP
GOOD DAY.

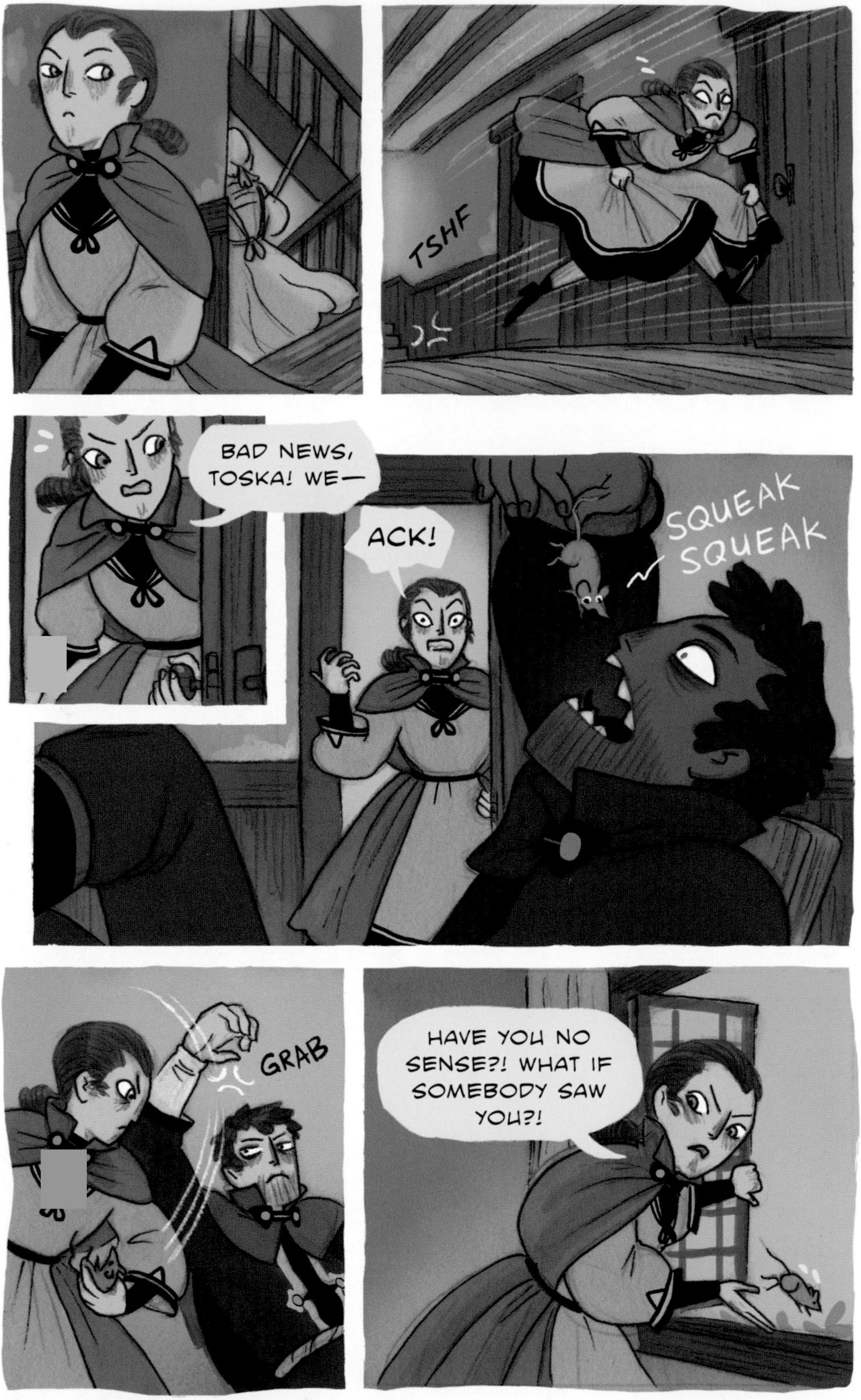
TSHF
BAD NEWS, TOSKA! WE—
ACK!
SQUEAK SQUEAK
GRAB
HAVE YOU NO SENSE?! WHAT IF SOMEBODY SAW YOU?!

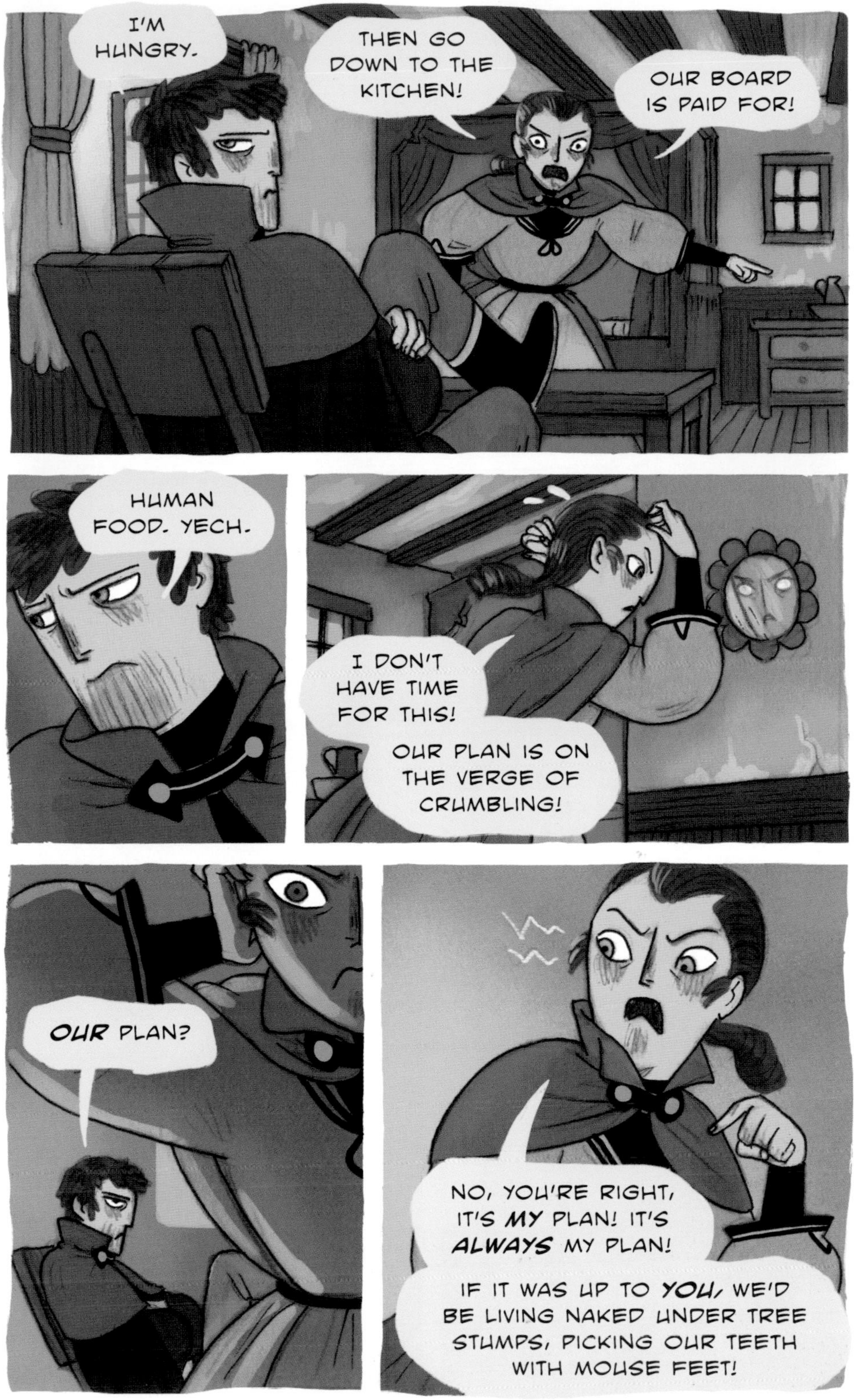
I'M HUNGRY.
THEN GO DOWN TO THE KITCHEN!
OUR BOARD IS PAID FOR!
HUMAN FOOD. YECH.
I DON'T HAVE TIME FOR THIS!
OUR PLAN IS ON THE VERGE OF CRUMBLING!
OUR PLAN?
NO, YOU'RE RIGHT, IT'S MY PLAN! IT'S ALWAYS MY PLAN!
IF IT WAS UP TO YOU, WE'D BE LIVING NAKED UNDER TREE STUMPS, PICKING OUR TEETH WITH MOUSE FEET!

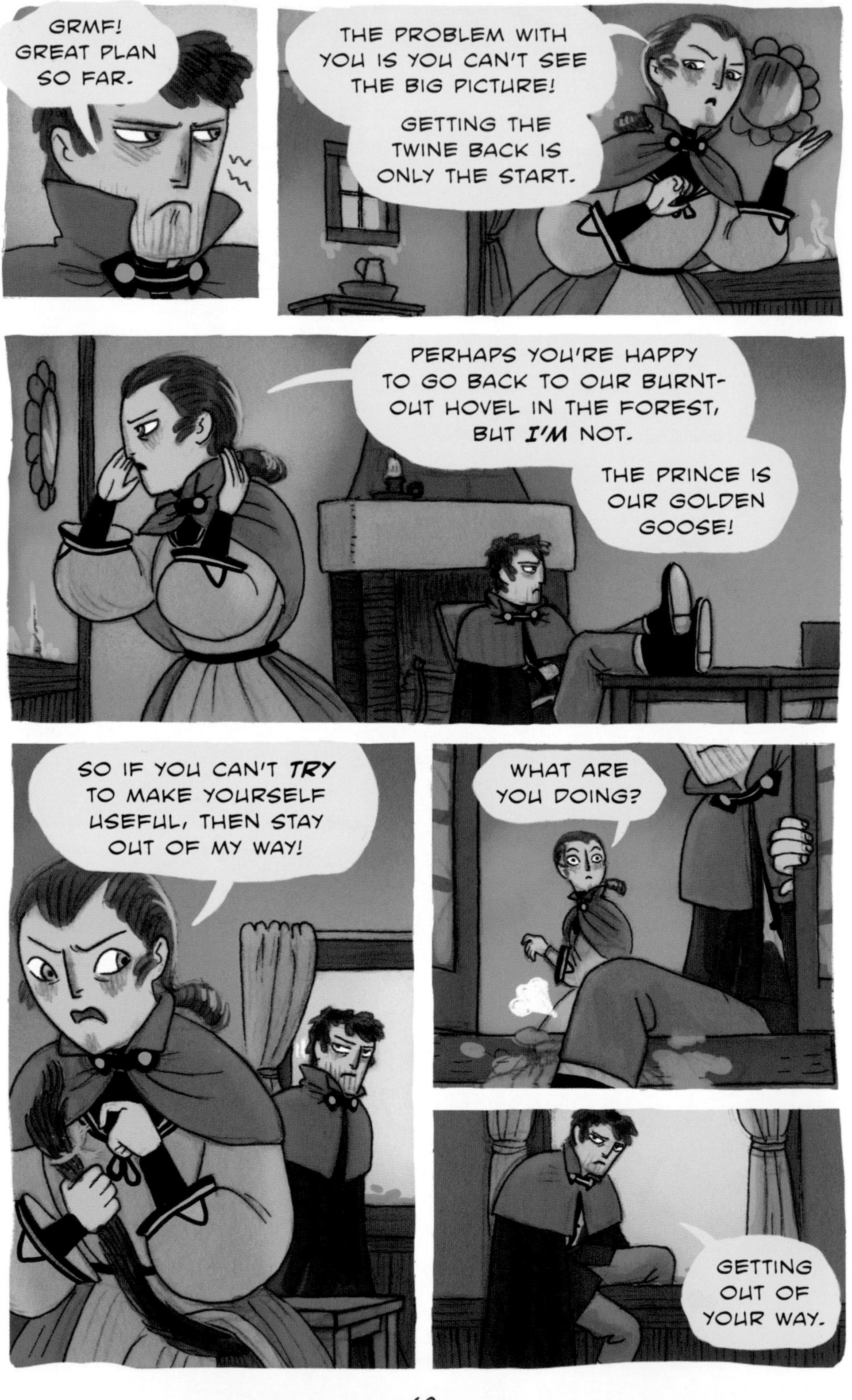
GRMF! GREAT PLAN SO FAR.
THE PROBLEM WITH YOU IS YOU CAN'T SEE THE BIG PICTURE!
GETTING THE TWINE BACK IS ONLY THE START.
PERHAPS YOU'RE HAPPY TO GO BACK TO OUR BURNT-OUT HOVEL IN THE FOREST, BUT *I'M* NOT.
THE PRINCE IS OUR GOLDEN GOOSE!
SO IF YOU CAN'T *TRY* TO MAKE YOURSELF USEFUL, THEN STAY OUT OF MY WAY!
WHAT ARE YOU DOING?
GETTING OUT OF YOUR WAY.

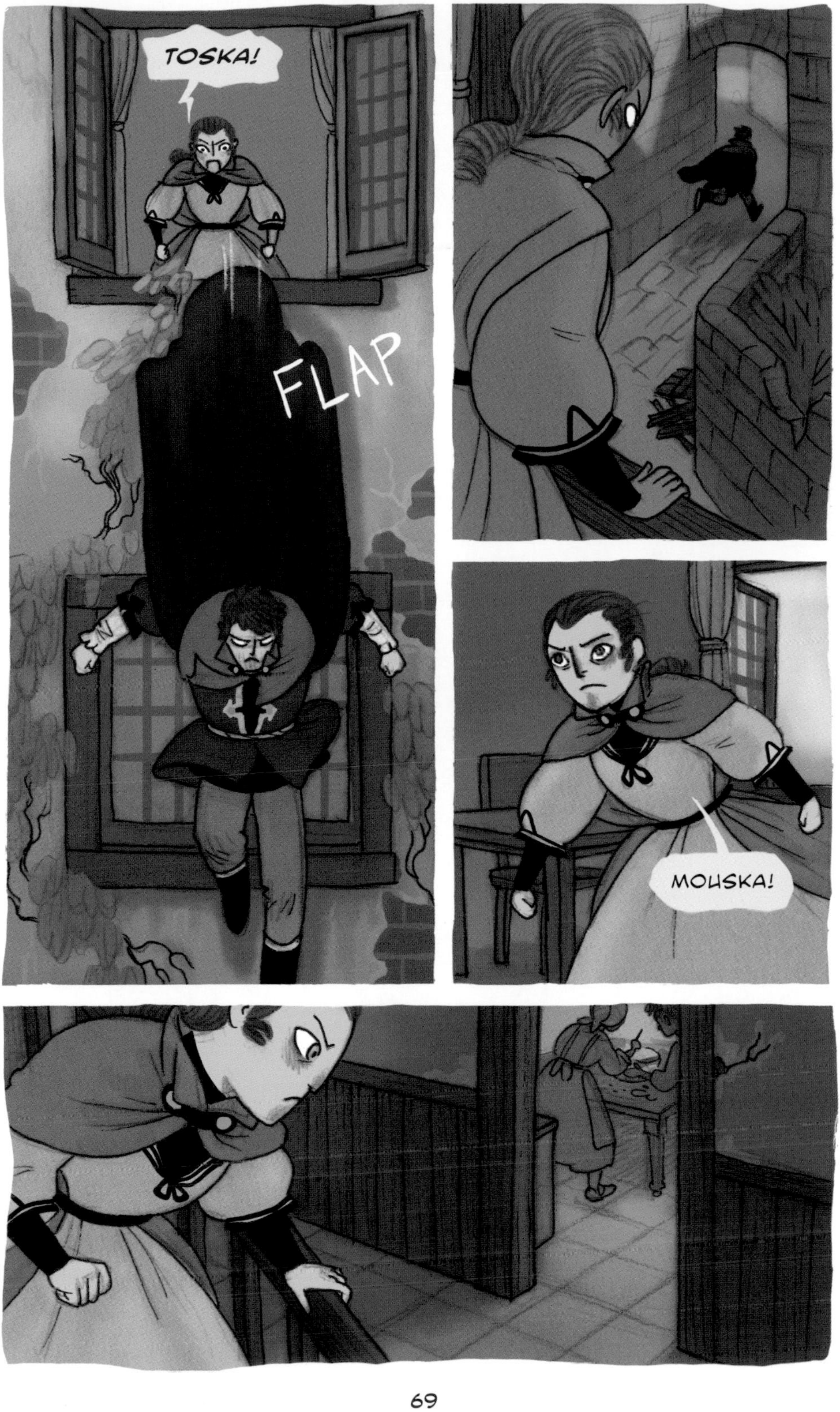
TOSKA!
FLAP
MOUSKA!

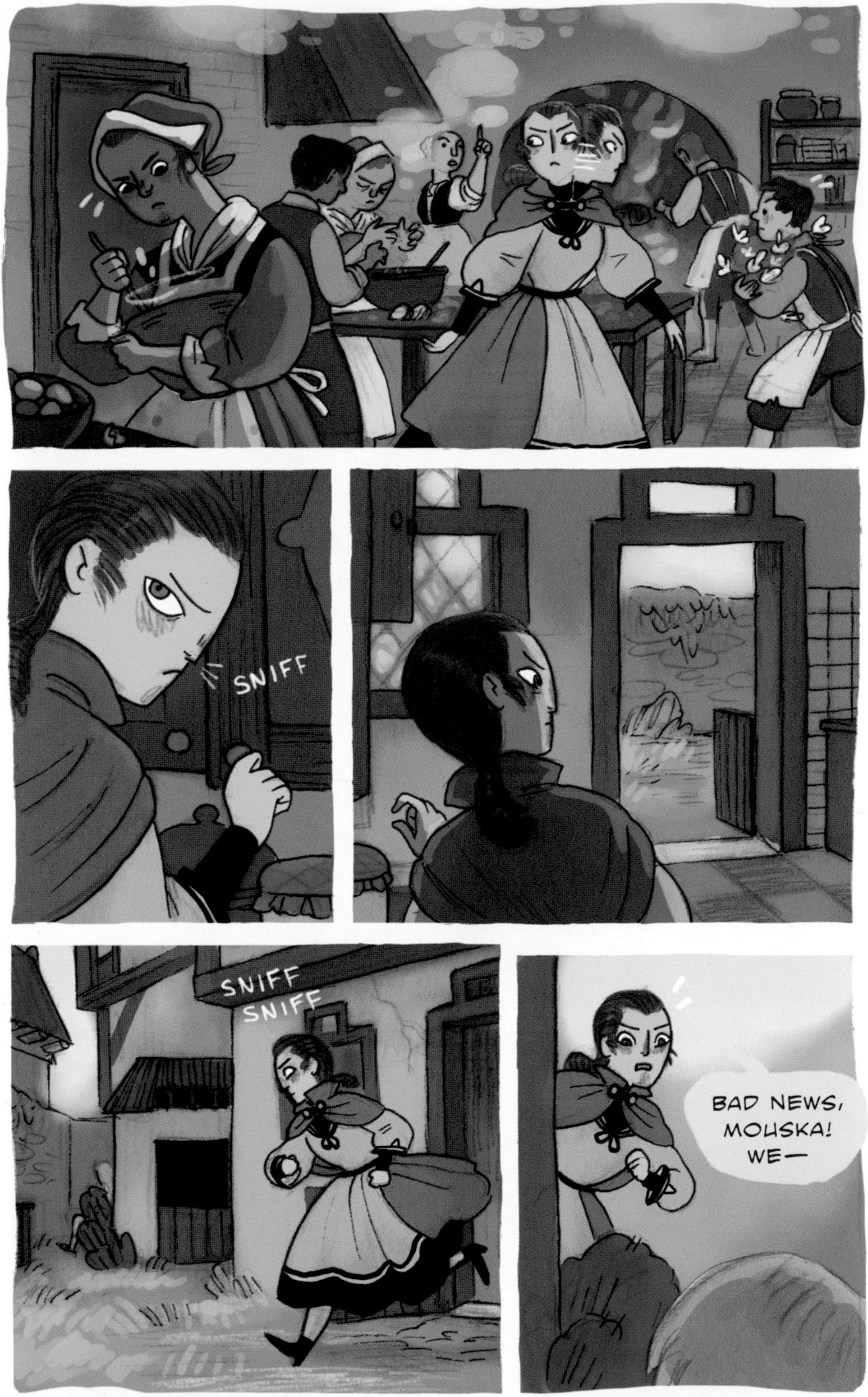
SNIFF
SNIFF
SNIFF
BAD NEWS, MOUSKA! WE—

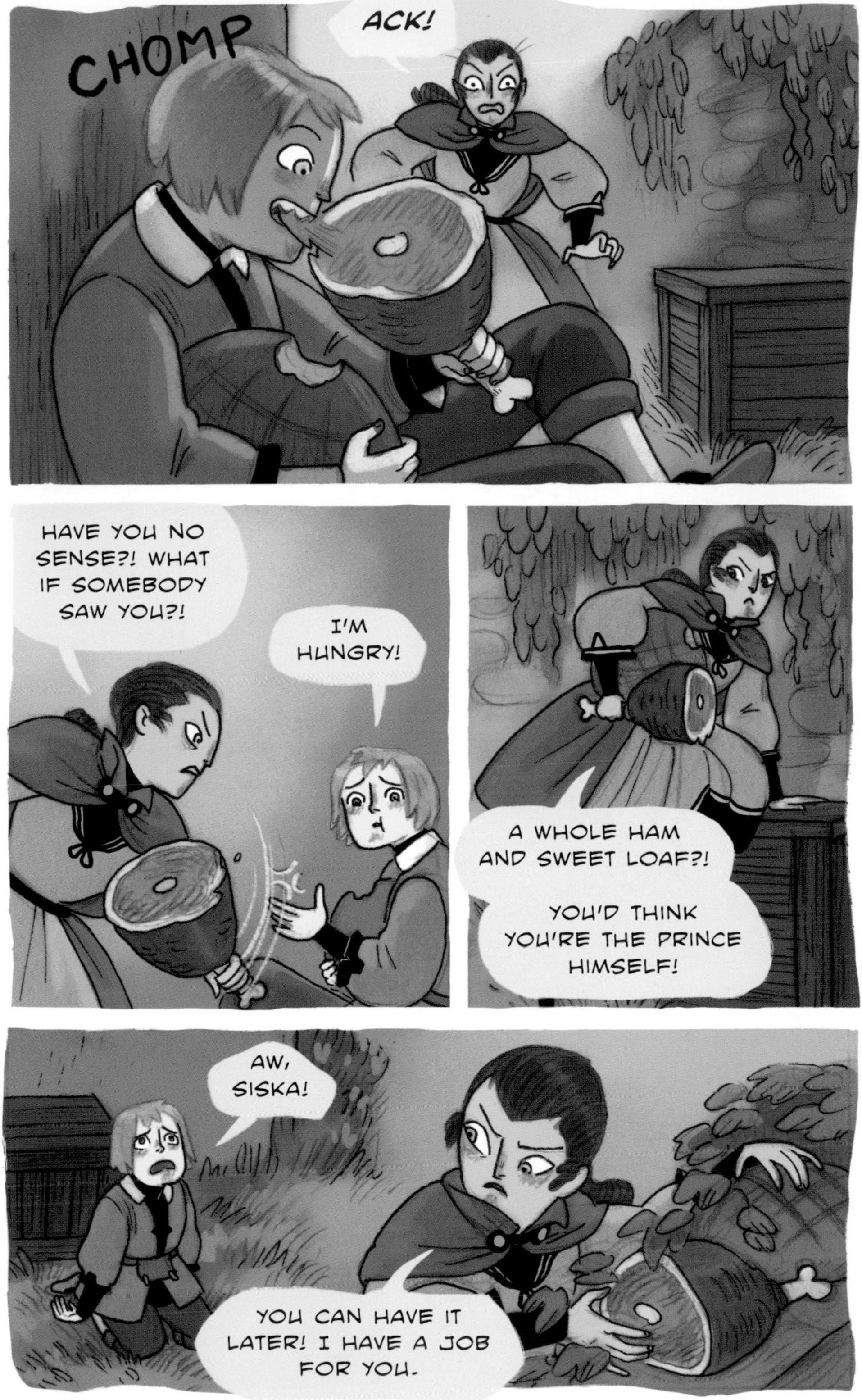
CHOMP
ACK!
HAVE YOU NO SENSE?! WHAT IF SOMEBODY SAW YOU?!
I'M HUNGRY!
A WHOLE HAM AND SWEET LOAF?!
YOU'D THINK YOU'RE THE PRINCE HIMSELF!
AW, SISKA!
YOU CAN HAVE IT LATER! I HAVE A JOB FOR YOU.

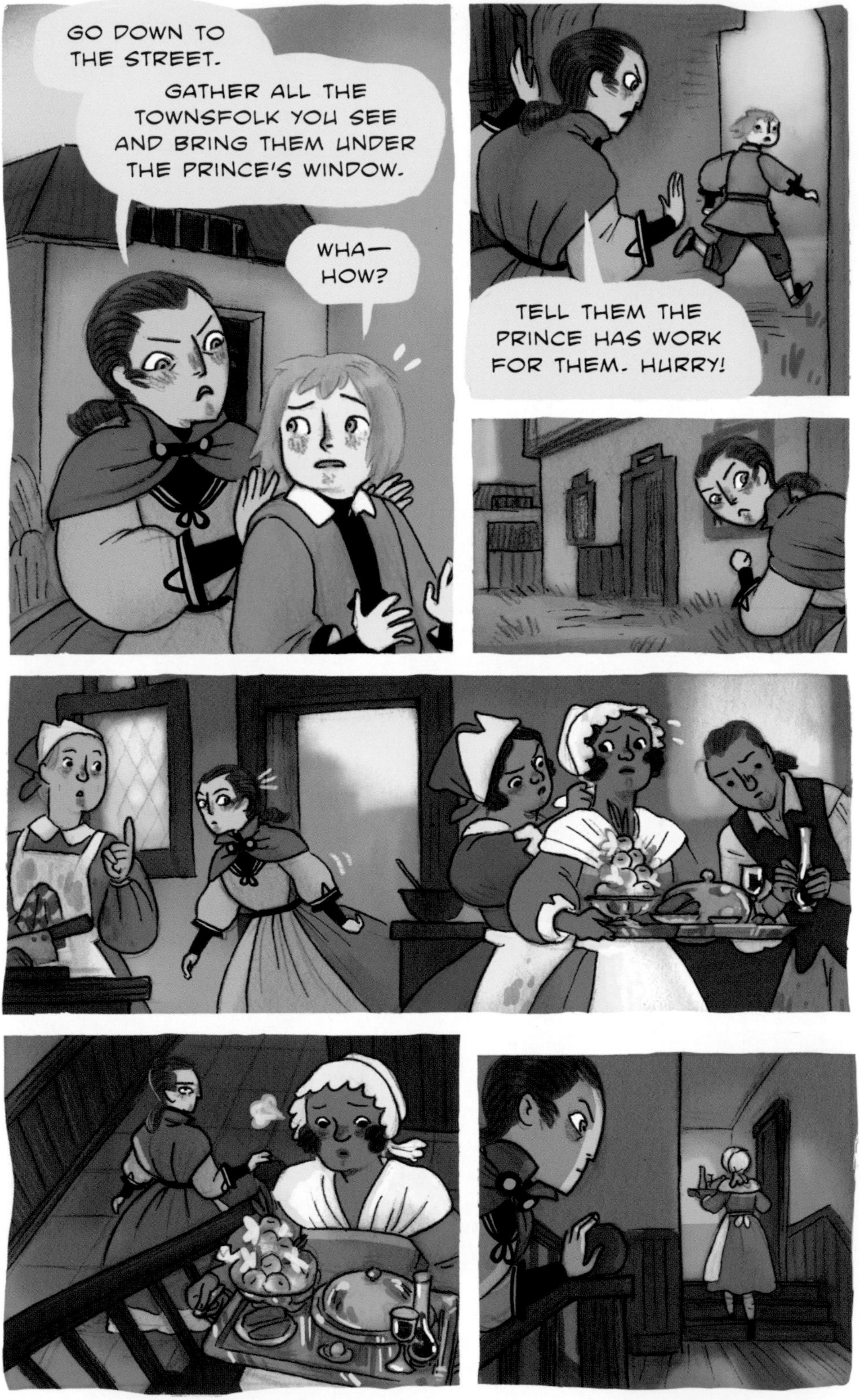
GO DOWN TO THE STREET.
GATHER ALL THE TOWNSFOLK YOU SEE AND BRING THEM UNDER THE PRINCE'S WINDOW.
WHA— HOW?
TELL THEM THE PRINCE HAS WORK FOR THEM. HURRY!

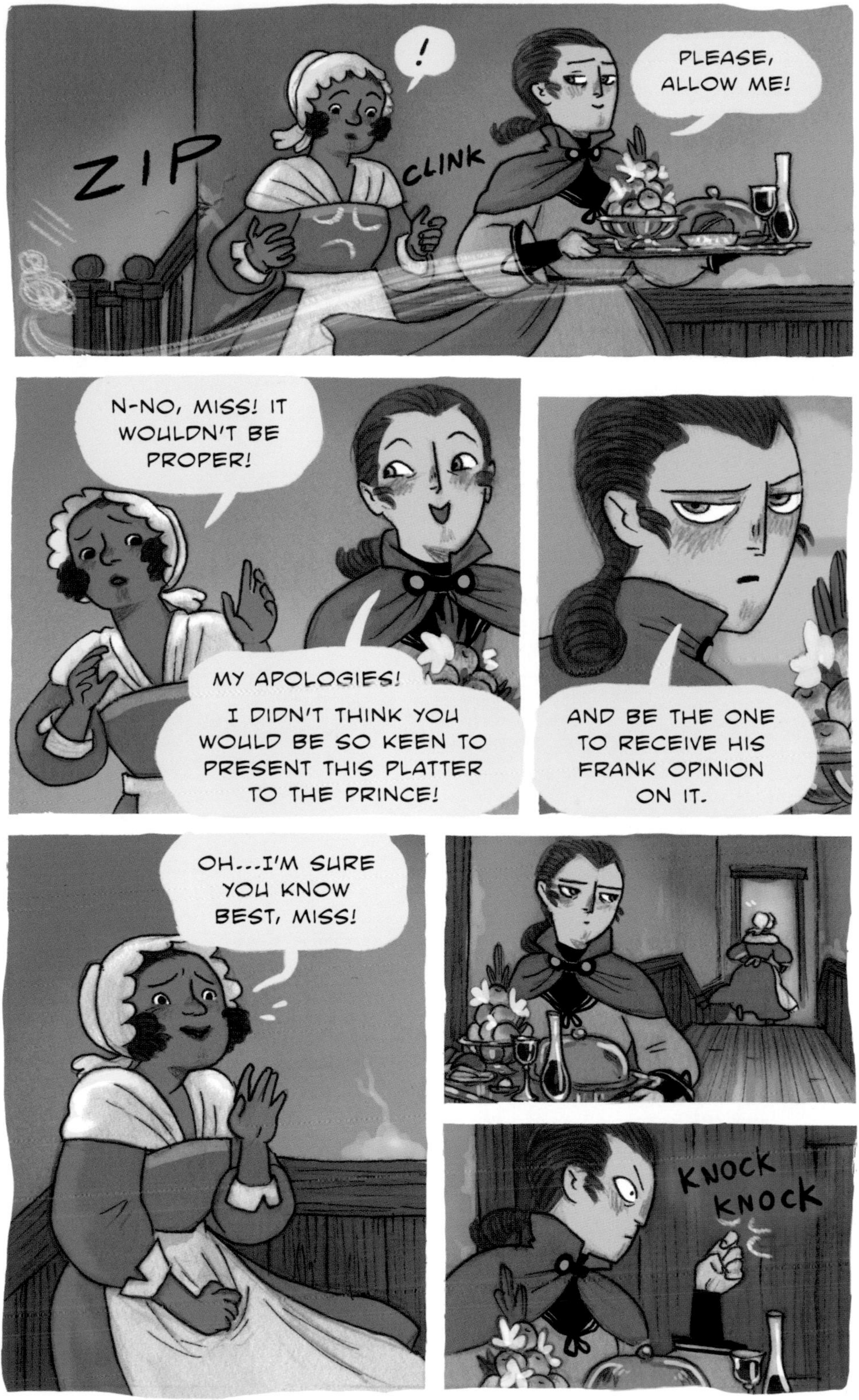
!
PLEASE, ALLOW ME!
ZIP
CLINK
N-NO, MISS! IT WOULDN'T BE PROPER!
MY APOLOGIES!
I DIDN'T THINK YOU WOULD BE SO KEEN TO PRESENT THIS PLATTER TO THE PRINCE!
AND BE THE ONE TO RECEIVE HIS FRANK OPINION ON IT.
OH...I'M SURE YOU KNOW BEST, MISS!
KNOCK KNOCK

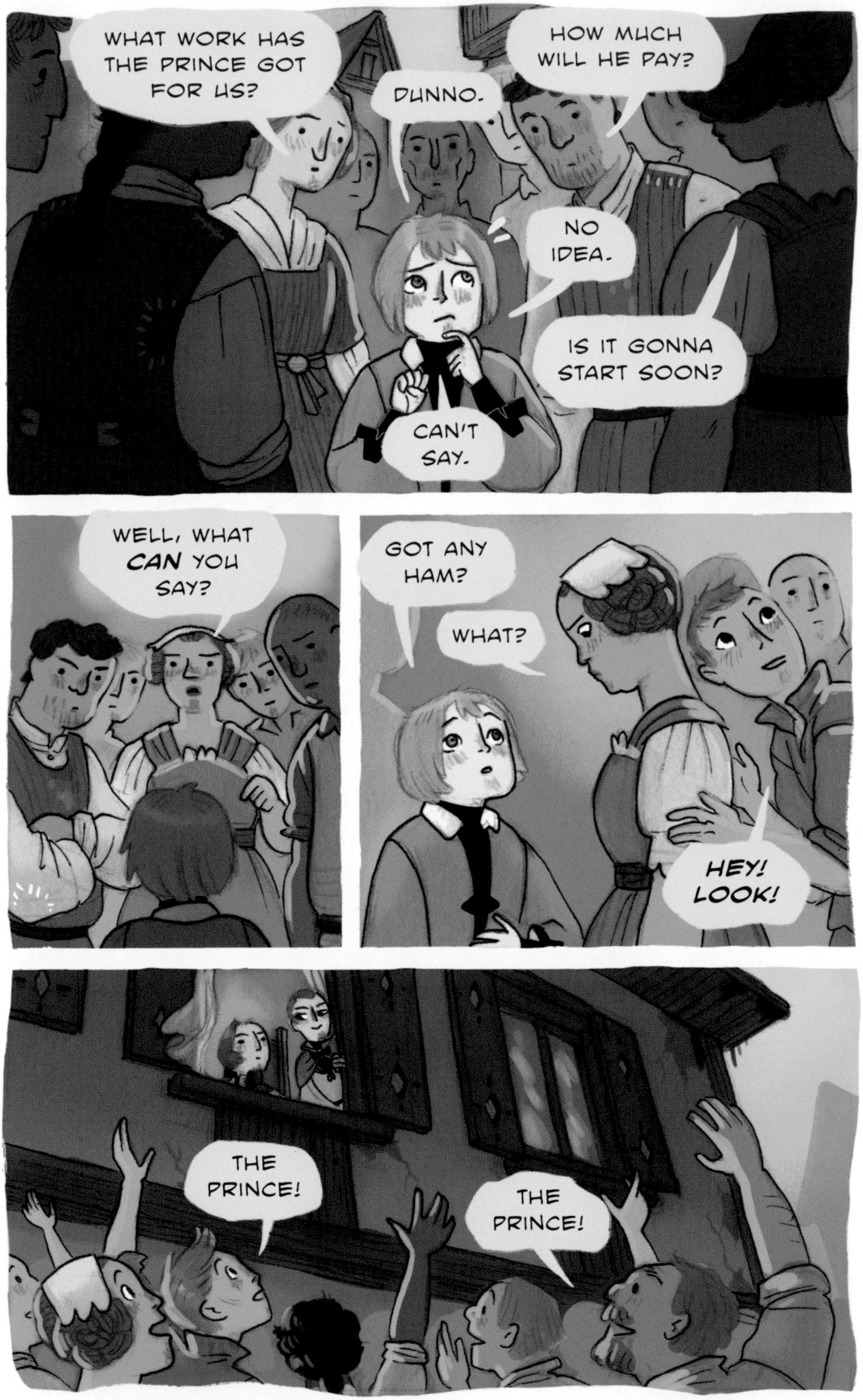
WHAT WORK HAS THE PRINCE GOT FOR US?
DUNNO.
HOW MUCH WILL HE PAY?
NO IDEA.
IS IT GONNA START SOON?
CAN'T SAY.
WELL, WHAT **CAN** YOU SAY?
GOT ANY HAM?
WHAT?
HEY! LOOK!
THE PRINCE!
THE PRINCE!

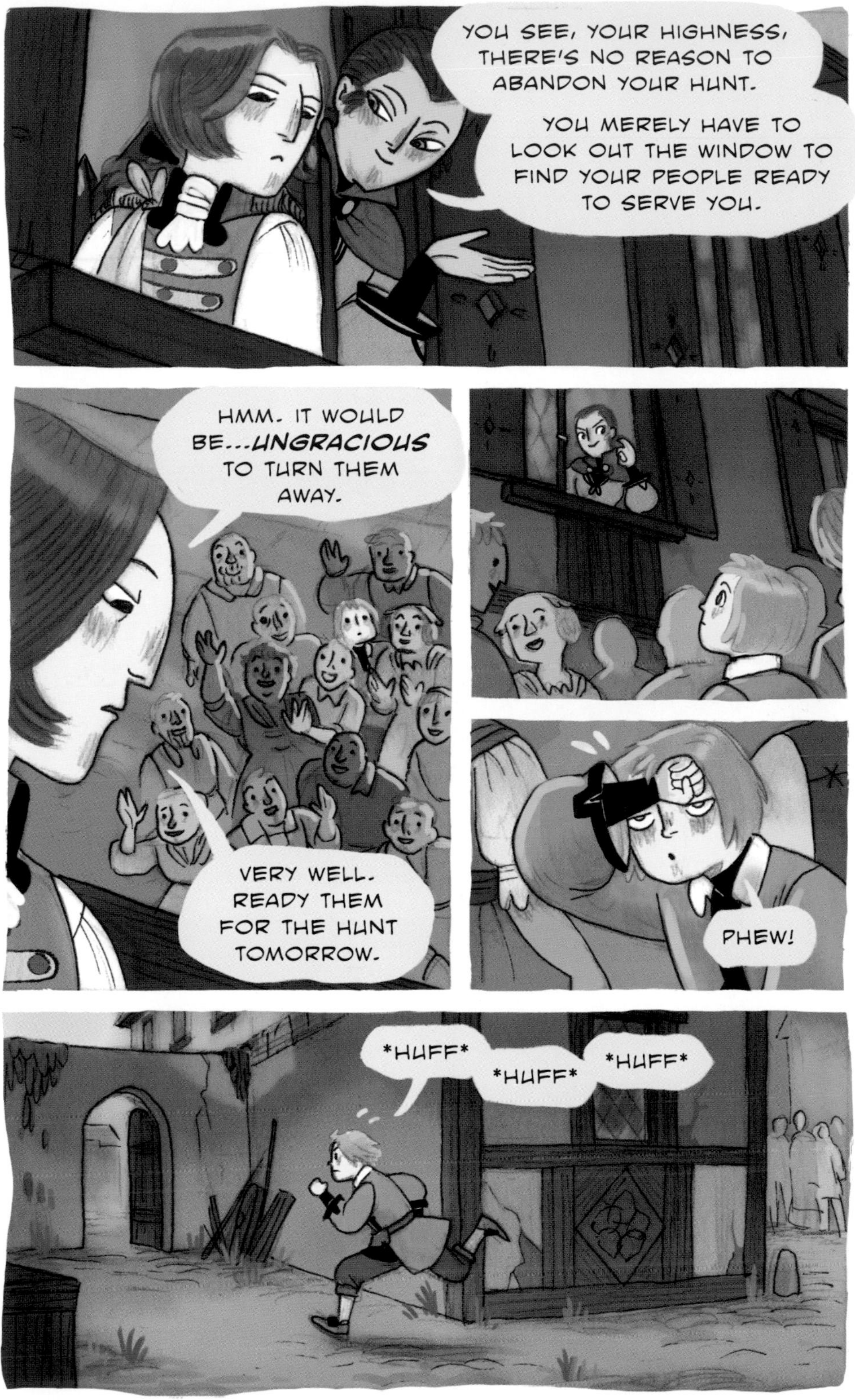
YOU SEE, YOUR HIGHNESS, THERE'S NO REASON TO ABANDON YOUR HUNT.
YOU MERELY HAVE TO LOOK OUT THE WINDOW TO FIND YOUR PEOPLE READY TO SERVE YOU.
HMM. IT WOULD BE...*UNGRACIOUS* TO TURN THEM AWAY.
VERY WELL. READY THEM FOR THE HUNT TOMORROW.
PHEW!
HUFF
HUFF
HUFF

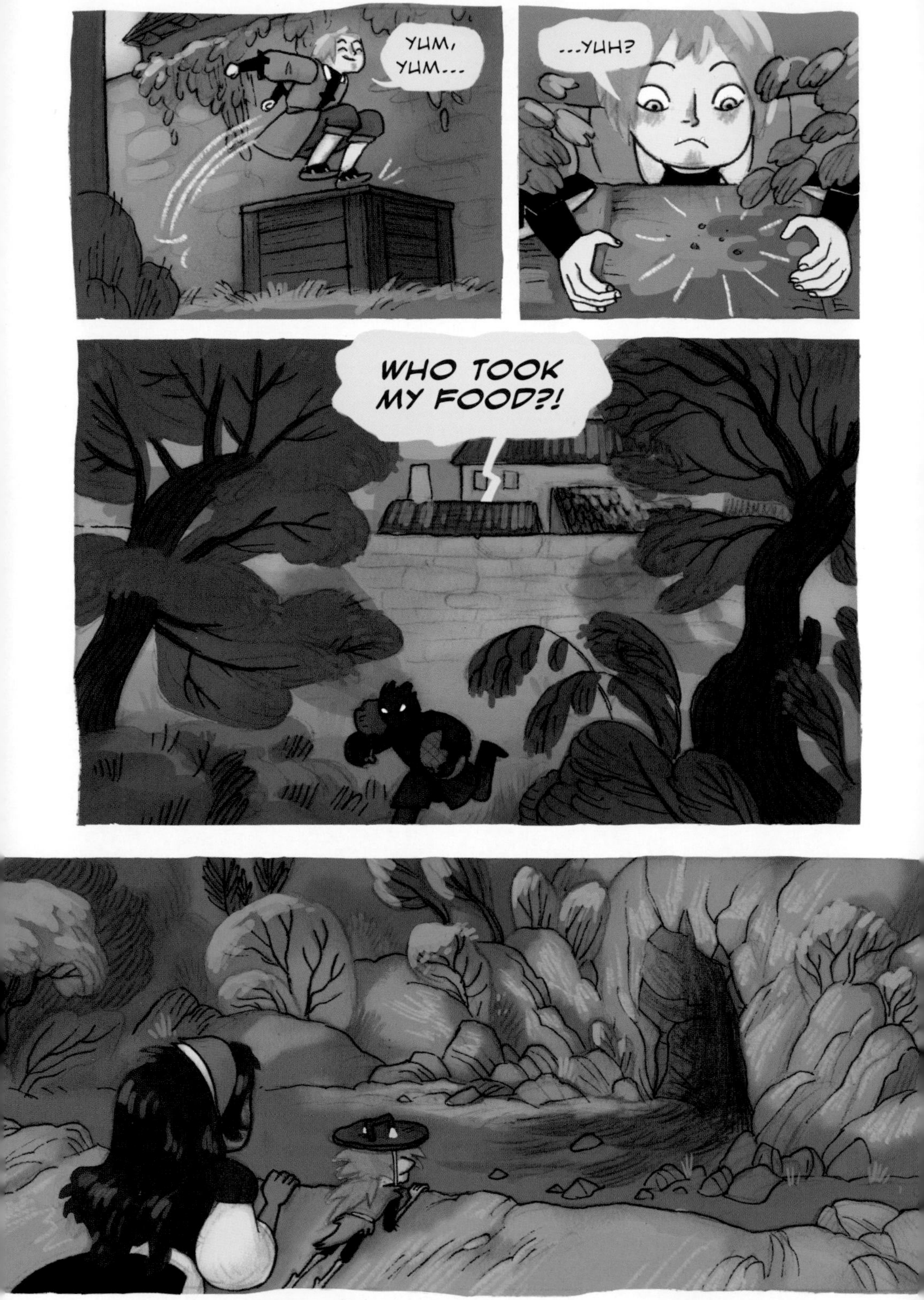
YUM, YUM...
...YUH?
WHO TOOK MY FOOD?!

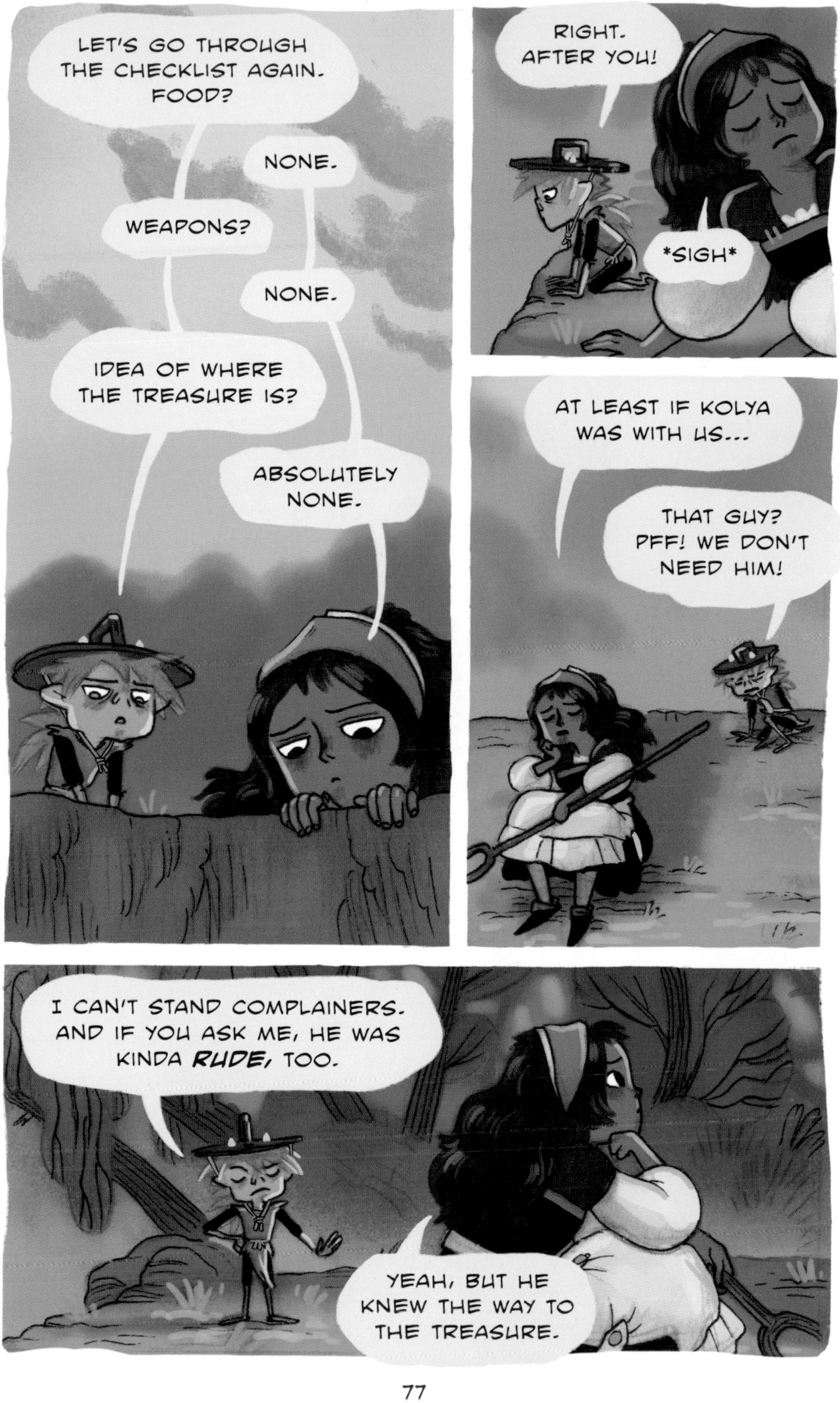
LET'S GO THROUGH THE CHECKLIST AGAIN. FOOD?
NONE.
WEAPONS?
NONE.
IDEA OF WHERE THE TREASURE IS?
ABSOLUTELY NONE.
RIGHT. AFTER YOU!
SIGH
AT LEAST IF KOLYA WAS WITH US...
THAT GUY? PFF! WE DON'T NEED HIM!
I CAN'T STAND COMPLAINERS. AND IF YOU ASK ME, HE WAS KINDA ***RUDE***, TOO.
YEAH, BUT HE KNEW THE WAY TO THE TREASURE.

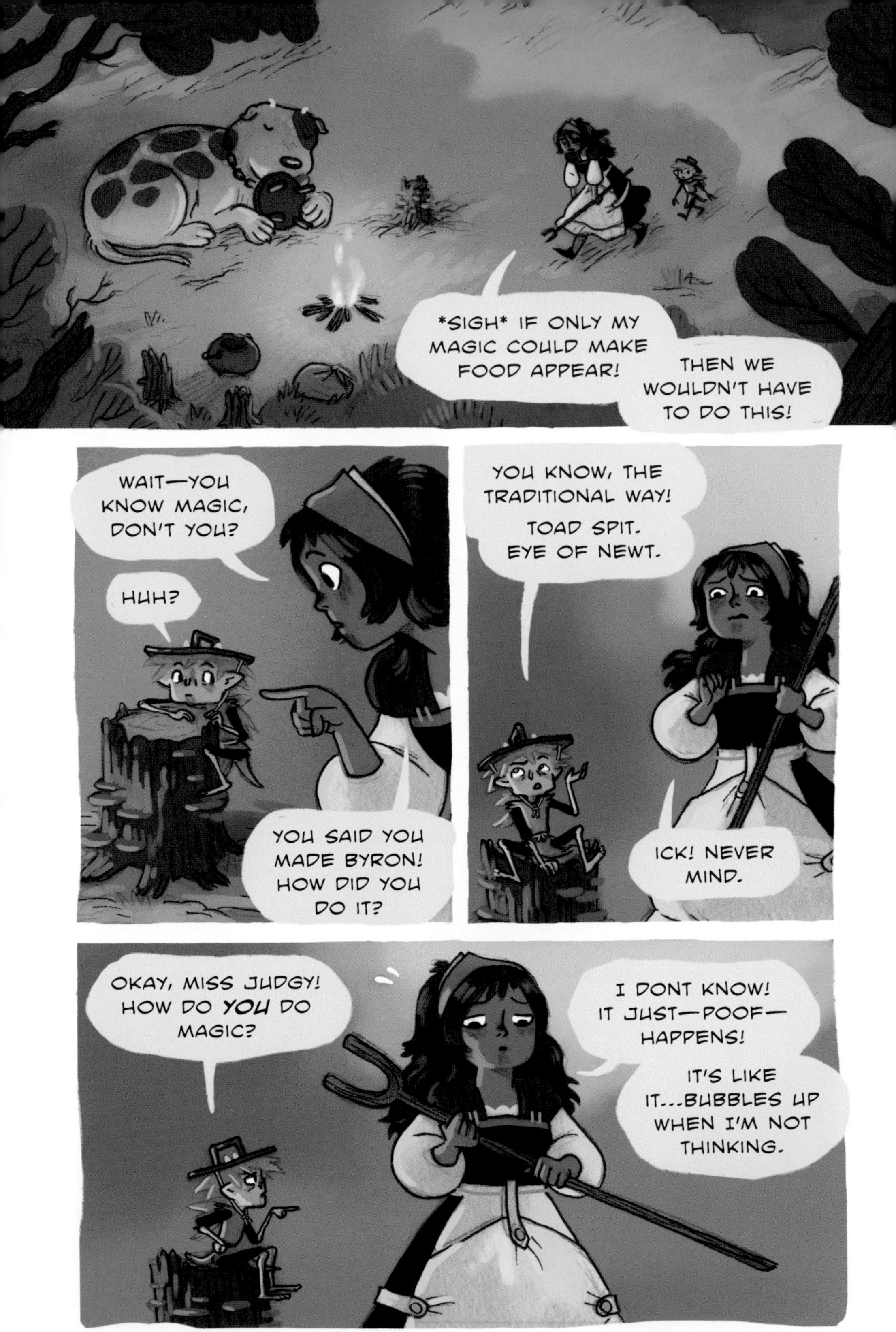
SIGH IF ONLY MY MAGIC COULD MAKE FOOD APPEAR!
THEN WE WOULDN'T HAVE TO DO THIS!
WAIT—YOU KNOW MAGIC, DON'T YOU?
HUH?
YOU SAID YOU MADE BYRON! HOW DID YOU DO IT?
YOU KNOW, THE TRADITIONAL WAY!
TOAD SPIT. EYE OF NEWT.
ICK! NEVER MIND.
OKAY, MISS JUDGY! HOW DO YOU DO MAGIC?
I DONT KNOW! IT JUST—POOF—HAPPENS!
IT'S LIKE IT...BUBBLES UP WHEN I'M NOT THINKING.

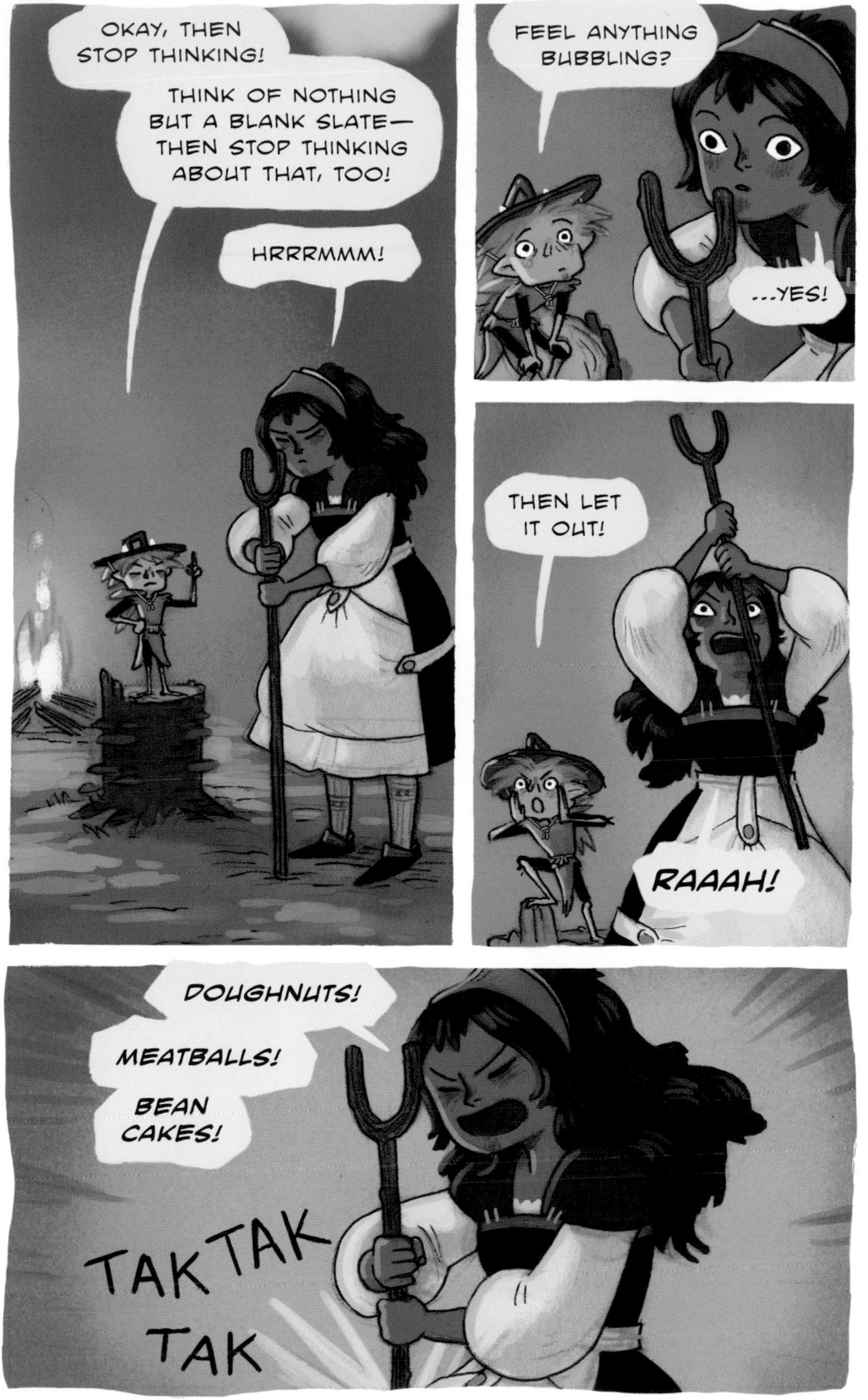
OKAY, THEN STOP THINKING!
THINK OF NOTHING BUT A BLANK SLATE— THEN STOP THINKING ABOUT THAT, TOO!
HRRRMMM!
FEEL ANYTHING BUBBLING?
...YES!
THEN LET IT OUT!
RAAAH!
DOUGHNUTS!
MEATBALLS!
BEAN CAKES!
TAK TAK
TAK

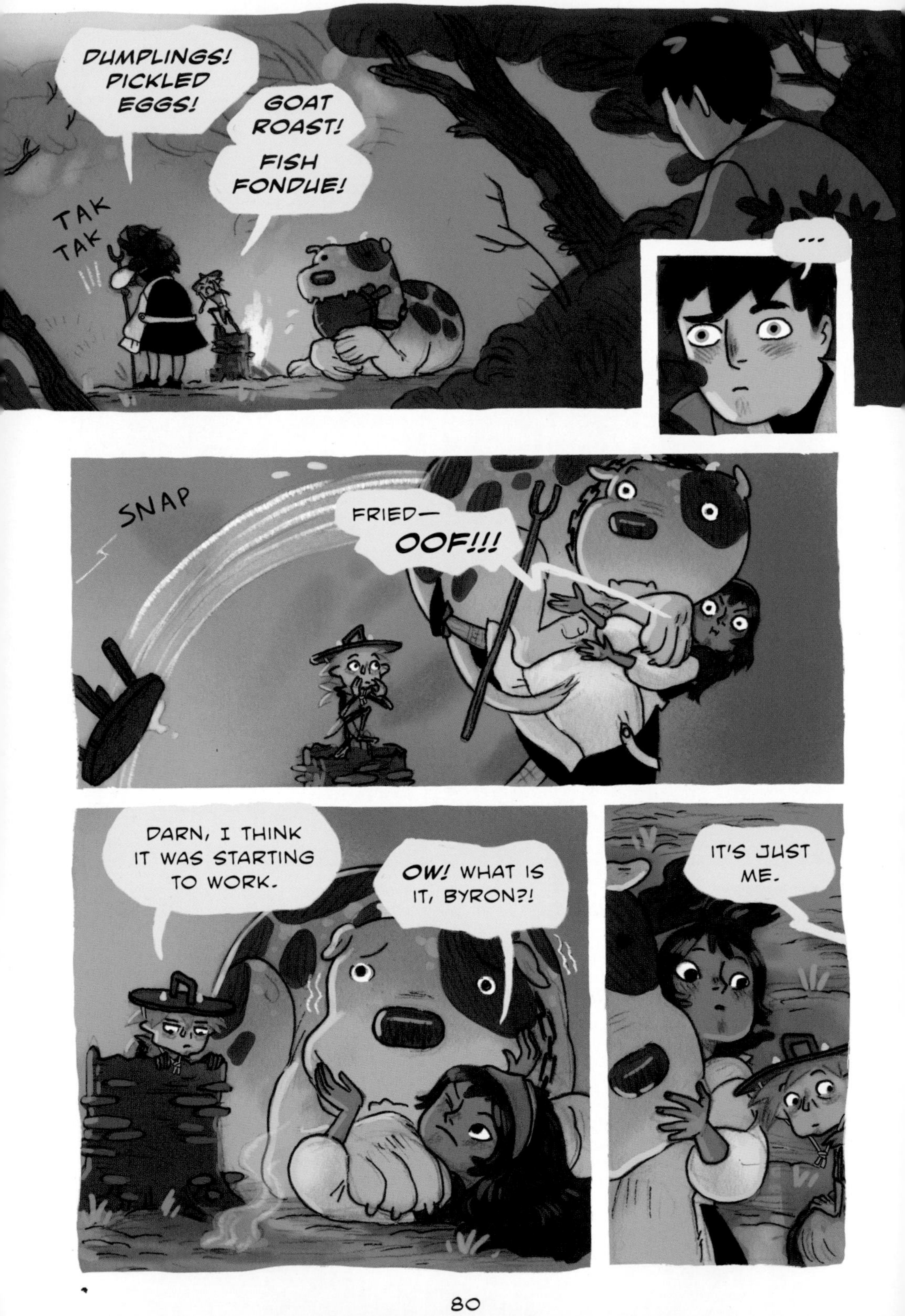
DUMPLINGS! PICKLED EGGS!
GOAT ROAST!
FISH FONDUE!
TAK TAK
...
SNAP
FRIED—
OOF!!!
DARN, I THINK IT WAS STARTING TO WORK.
OW! WHAT IS IT, BYRON?!
IT'S JUST ME.

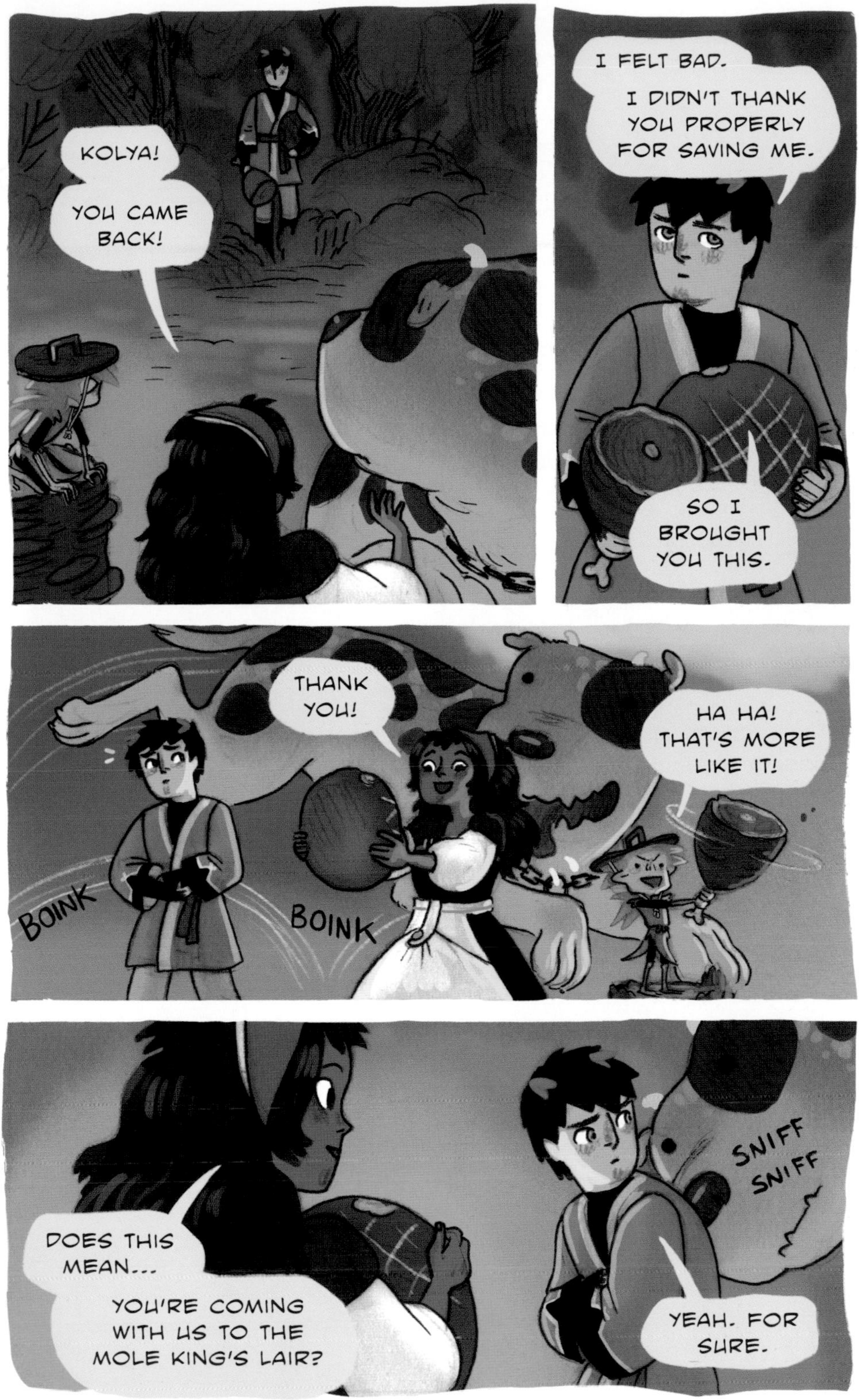
KOLYA!
YOU CAME BACK!
I FELT BAD.
I DIDN'T THANK YOU PROPERLY FOR SAVING ME.
SO I BROUGHT YOU THIS.
THANK YOU!
HA HA! THAT'S MORE LIKE IT!
BOINK
BOINK
DOES THIS MEAN...
YOU'RE COMING WITH US TO THE MOLE KING'S LAIR?
SNIFF SNIFF
YEAH. FOR SURE.

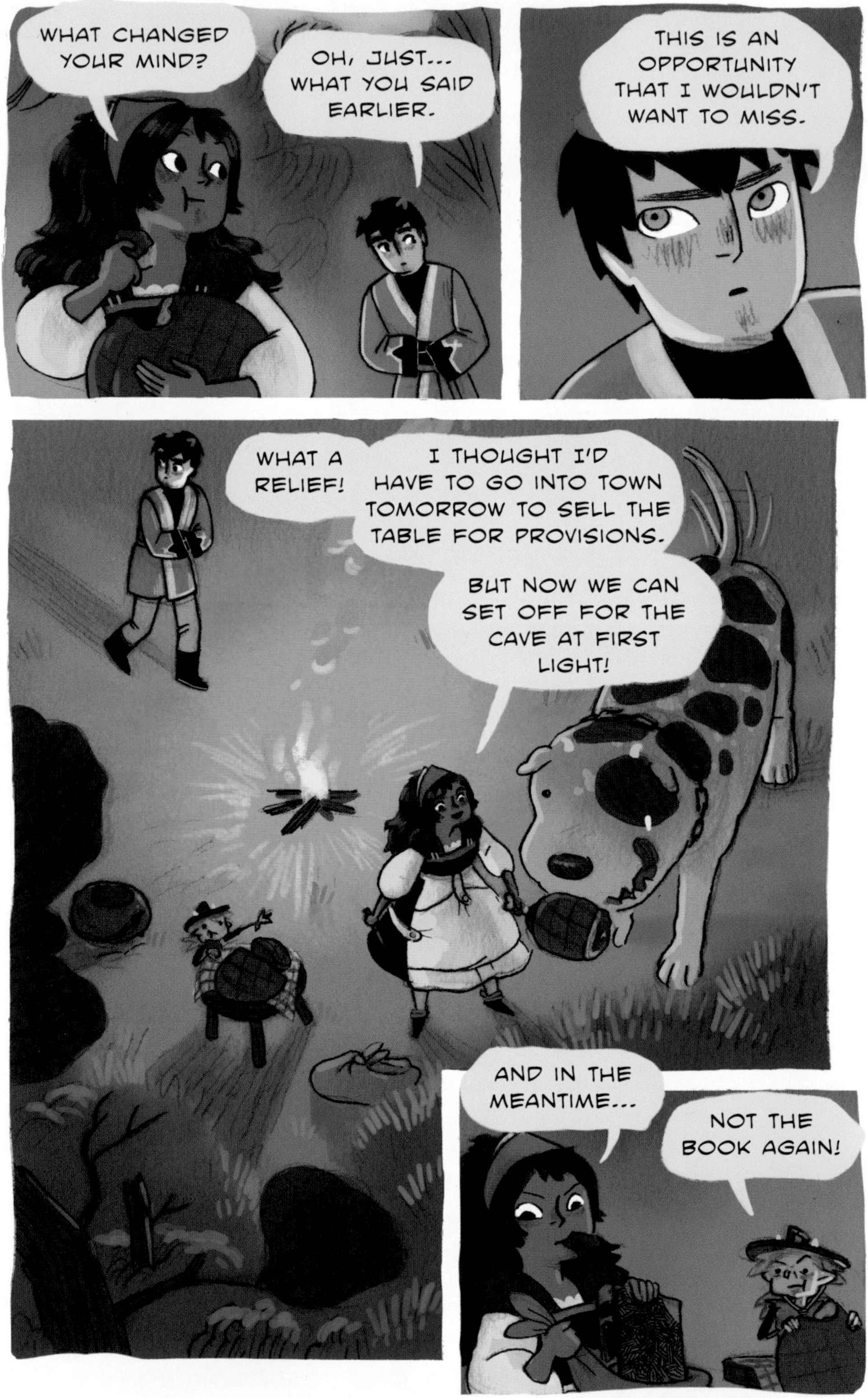
WHAT CHANGED YOUR MIND?
OH, JUST... WHAT YOU SAID EARLIER.
THIS IS AN OPPORTUNITY THAT I WOULDN'T WANT TO MISS.
WHAT A RELIEF!
I THOUGHT I'D HAVE TO GO INTO TOWN TOMORROW TO SELL THE TABLE FOR PROVISIONS.
BUT NOW WE CAN SET OFF FOR THE CAVE AT FIRST LIGHT!
AND IN THE MEANTIME...
NOT THE BOOK AGAIN!

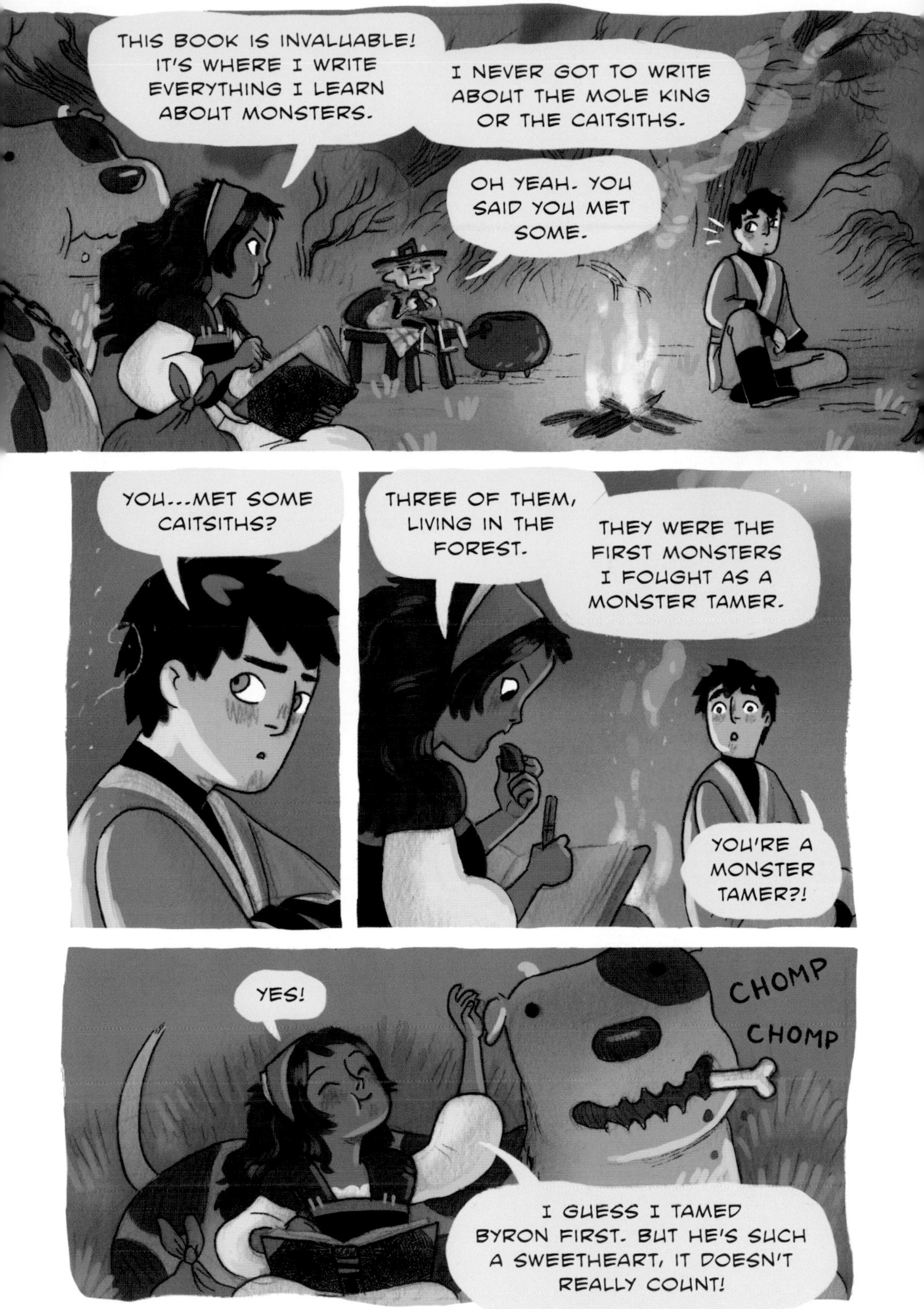
THIS BOOK IS INVALUABLE! IT'S WHERE I WRITE EVERYTHING I LEARN ABOUT MONSTERS.
I NEVER GOT TO WRITE ABOUT THE MOLE KING OR THE CAITSITHS.
OH YEAH. YOU SAID YOU MET SOME.
YOU...MET SOME CAITSITHS?
THREE OF THEM, LIVING IN THE FOREST.
THEY WERE THE FIRST MONSTERS I FOUGHT AS A MONSTER TAMER.
YOU'RE A MONSTER TAMER?!
YES!
CHOMP
CHOMP
I GUESS I TAMED BYRON FIRST. BUT HE'S SUCH A SWEETHEART, IT DOESN'T REALLY COUNT!

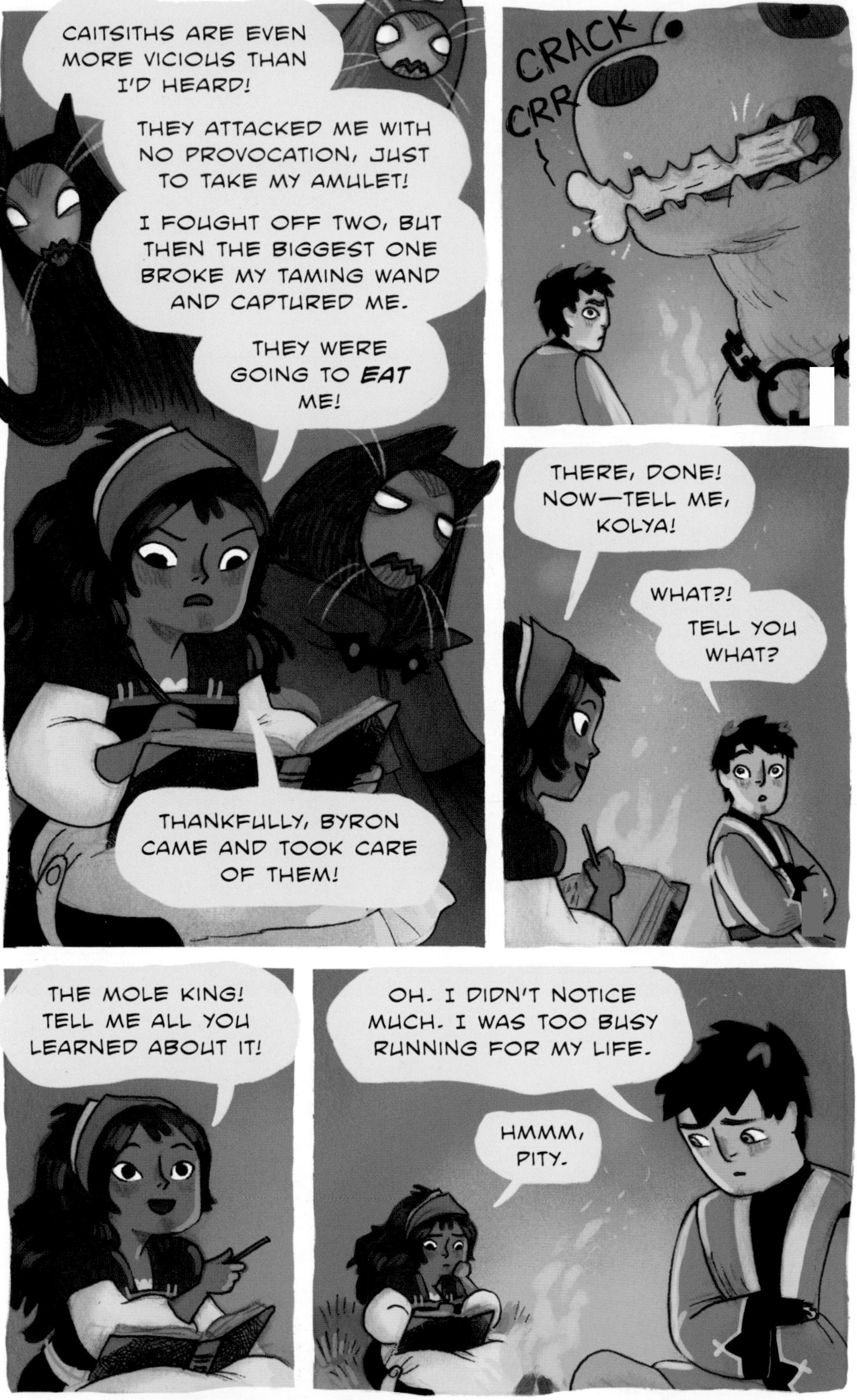
CAITSITHS ARE EVEN MORE VICIOUS THAN I'D HEARD!
THEY ATTACKED ME WITH NO PROVOCATION, JUST TO TAKE MY AMULET!
I FOUGHT OFF TWO, BUT THEN THE BIGGEST ONE BROKE MY TAMING WAND AND CAPTURED ME.
THEY WERE GOING TO EAT ME!
THANKFULLY, BYRON CAME AND TOOK CARE OF THEM!
CRACK
CRR
THERE, DONE! NOW—TELL ME, KOLYA!
WHAT?!
TELL YOU WHAT?
THE MOLE KING! TELL ME ALL YOU LEARNED ABOUT IT!
OH. I DIDN'T NOTICE MUCH. I WAS TOO BUSY RUNNING FOR MY LIFE.
HMMM, PITY.

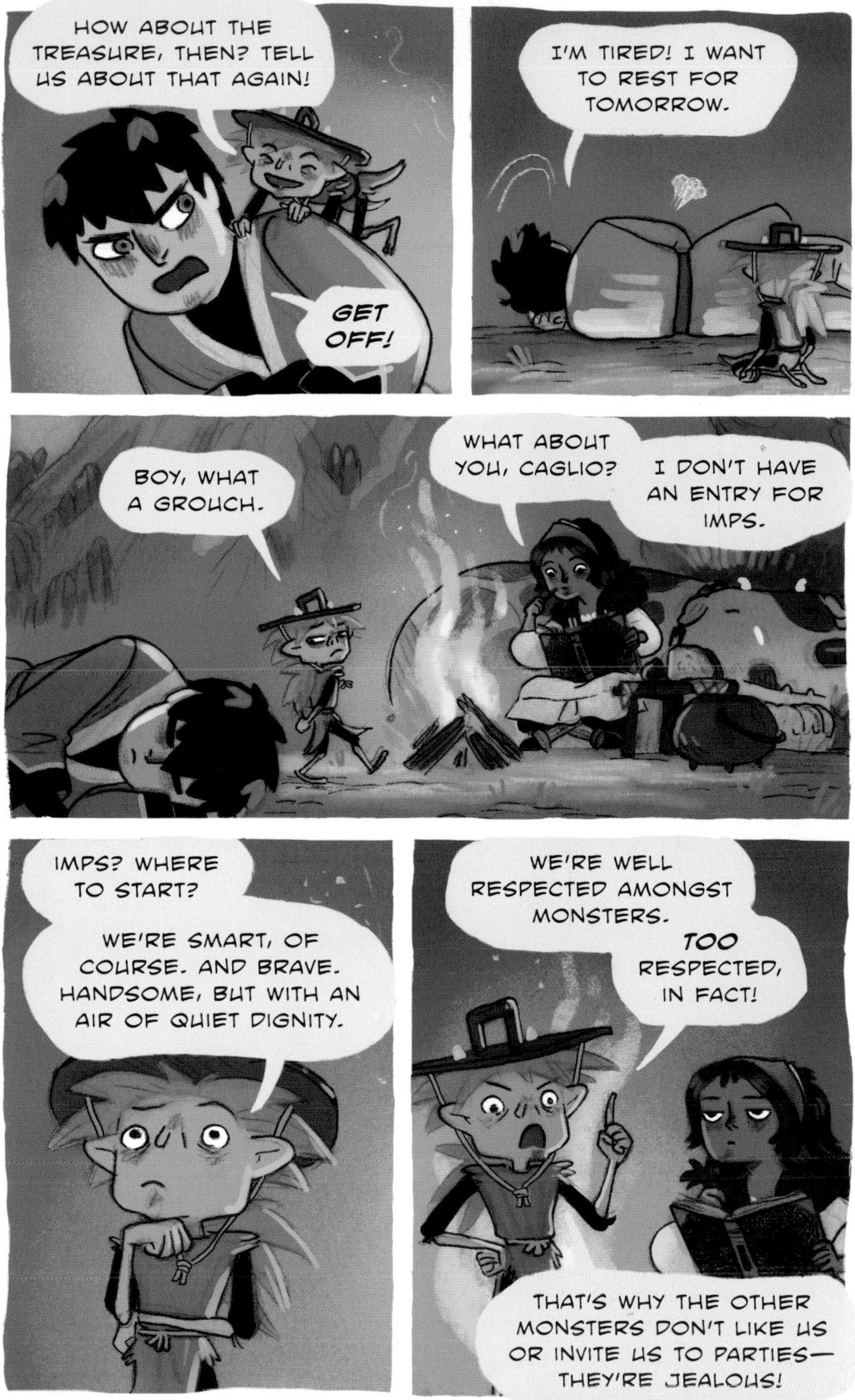
HOW ABOUT THE TREASURE, THEN? TELL US ABOUT THAT AGAIN!
GET OFF!
I'M TIRED! I WANT TO REST FOR TOMORROW.
BOY, WHAT A GROUCH.
WHAT ABOUT YOU, CAGLIO?
I DON'T HAVE AN ENTRY FOR IMPS.
IMPS? WHERE TO START?
WE'RE SMART, OF COURSE. AND BRAVE. HANDSOME, BUT WITH AN AIR OF QUIET DIGNITY.
WE'RE WELL RESPECTED AMONGST MONSTERS.
TOO RESPECTED, IN FACT!
THAT'S WHY THE OTHER MONSTERS DON'T LIKE US OR INVITE US TO PARTIES—THEY'RE JEALOUS!

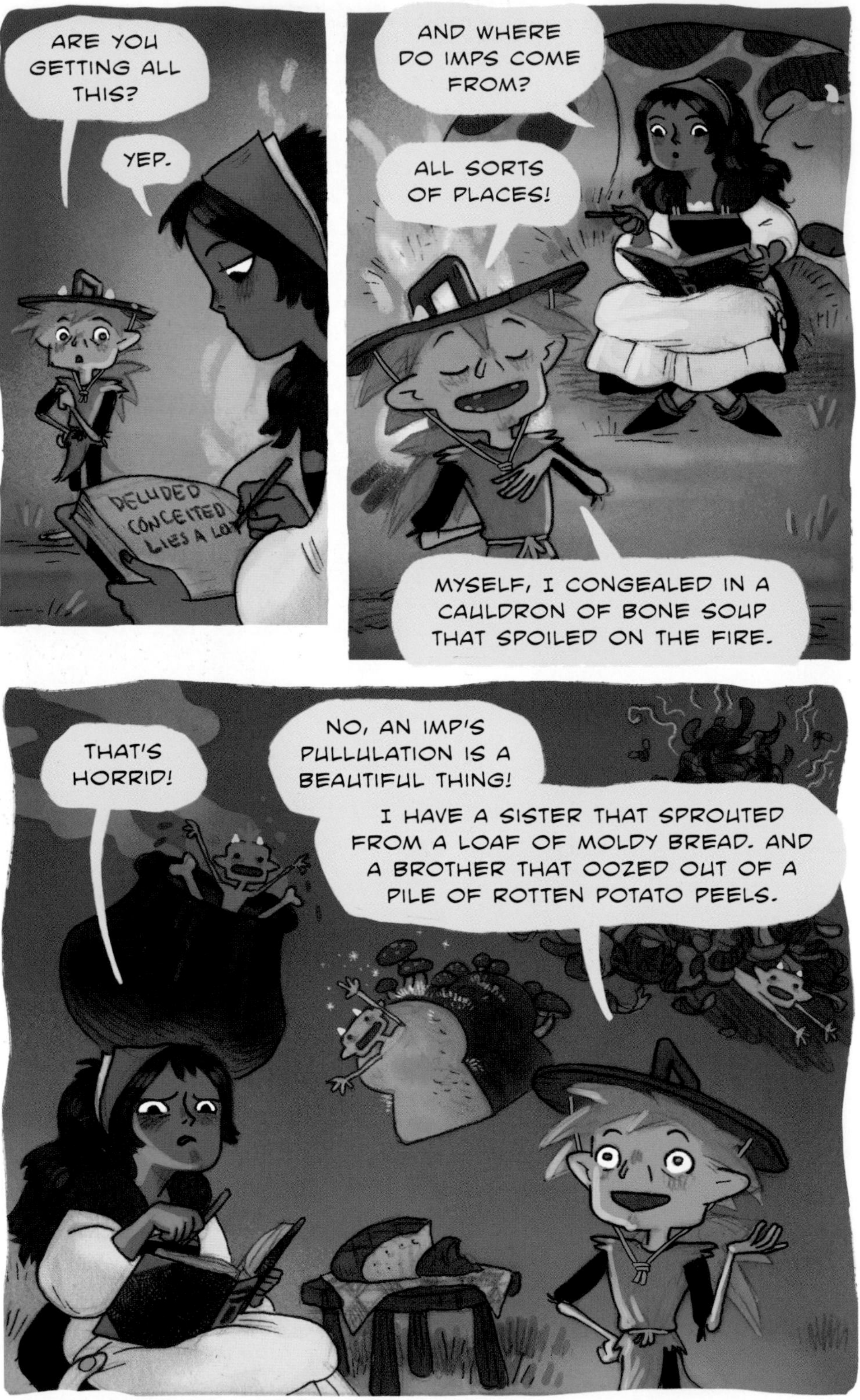
ARE YOU GETTING ALL THIS?
YEP.
DELUDED
CONCEITED
LIES A LOT
AND WHERE DO IMPS COME FROM?
ALL SORTS OF PLACES!
MYSELF, I CONGEALED IN A CAULDRON OF BONE SOUP THAT SPOILED ON THE FIRE.
THAT'S HORRID!
NO, AN IMP'S PULLULATION IS A BEAUTIFUL THING!
I HAVE A SISTER THAT SPROUTED FROM A LOAF OF MOLDY BREAD. AND A BROTHER THAT OOZED OUT OF A PILE OF ROTTEN POTATO PEELS.

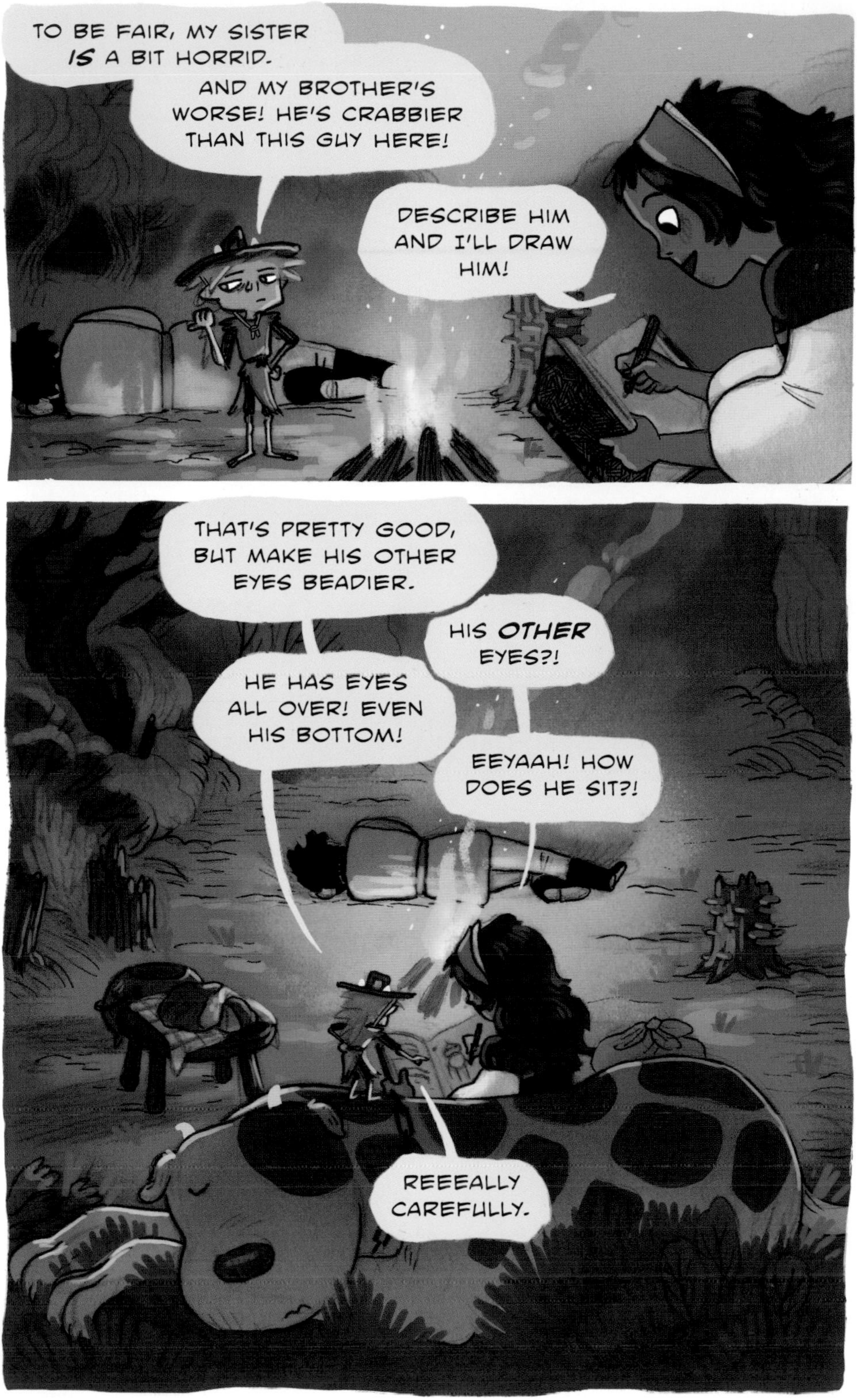

TO BE FAIR, MY SISTER *IS* A BIT HORRID.
AND MY BROTHER'S WORSE! HE'S CRABBIER THAN THIS GUY HERE!
DESCRIBE HIM AND I'LL DRAW HIM!
THAT'S PRETTY GOOD, BUT MAKE HIS OTHER EYES BEADIER.
HIS ***OTHER*** EYES?!
HE HAS EYES ALL OVER! EVEN HIS BOTTOM!
EEYAAH! HOW DOES HE SIT?!
REEEALLY CAREFULLY.

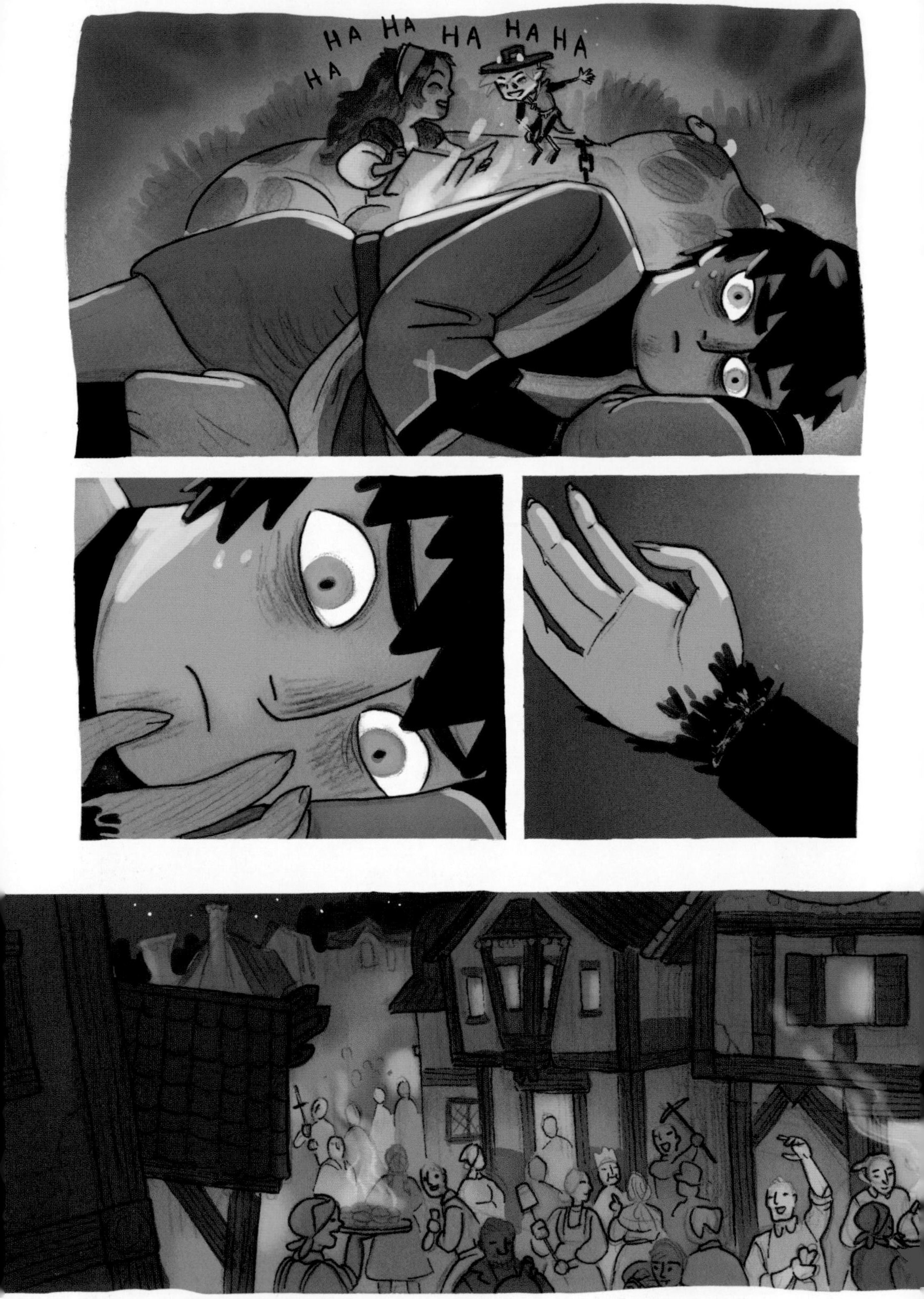
HA HA HA HA HA HA HA

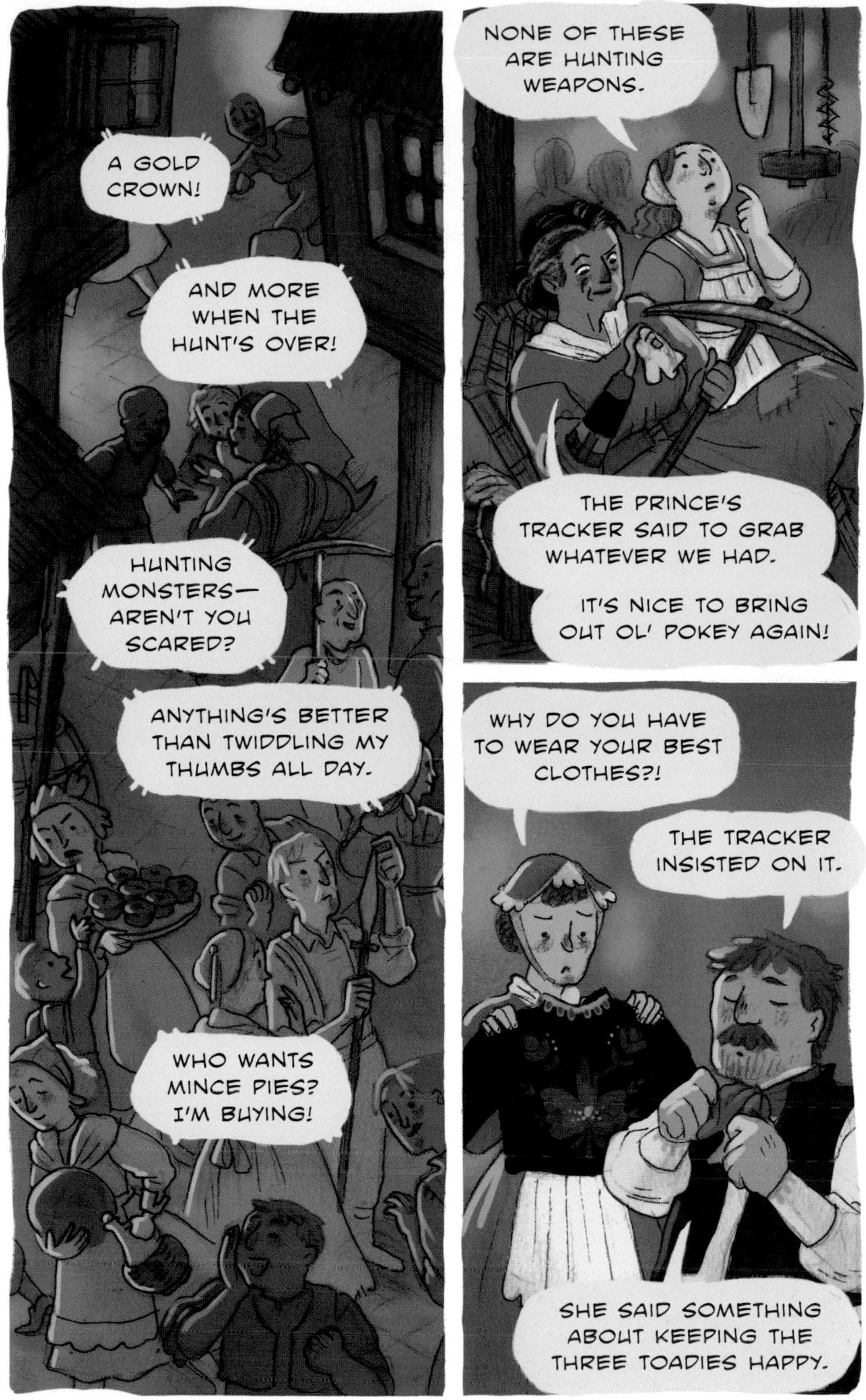
A GOLD CROWN!
AND MORE WHEN THE HUNT'S OVER!
HUNTING MONSTERS—AREN'T YOU SCARED?
ANYTHING'S BETTER THAN TWIDDLING MY THUMBS ALL DAY.
WHO WANTS MINCE PIES? I'M BUYING!
NONE OF THESE ARE HUNTING WEAPONS.
THE PRINCE'S TRACKER SAID TO GRAB WHATEVER WE HAD.
IT'S NICE TO BRING OUT OL' POKEY AGAIN!
WHY DO YOU HAVE TO WEAR YOUR BEST CLOTHES?!
THE TRACKER INSISTED ON IT.
SHE SAID SOMETHING ABOUT KEEPING THE THREE TOADIES HAPPY.

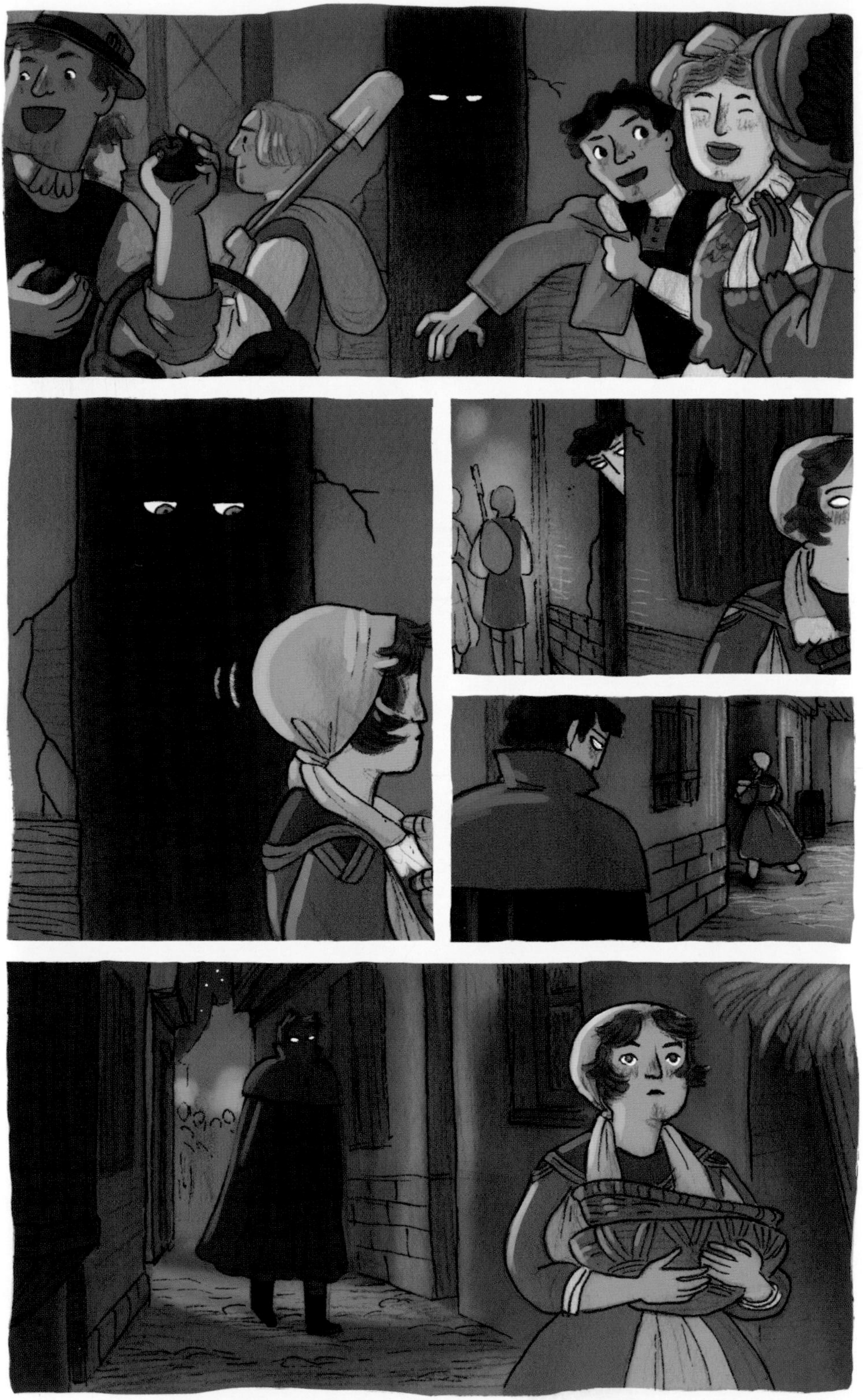

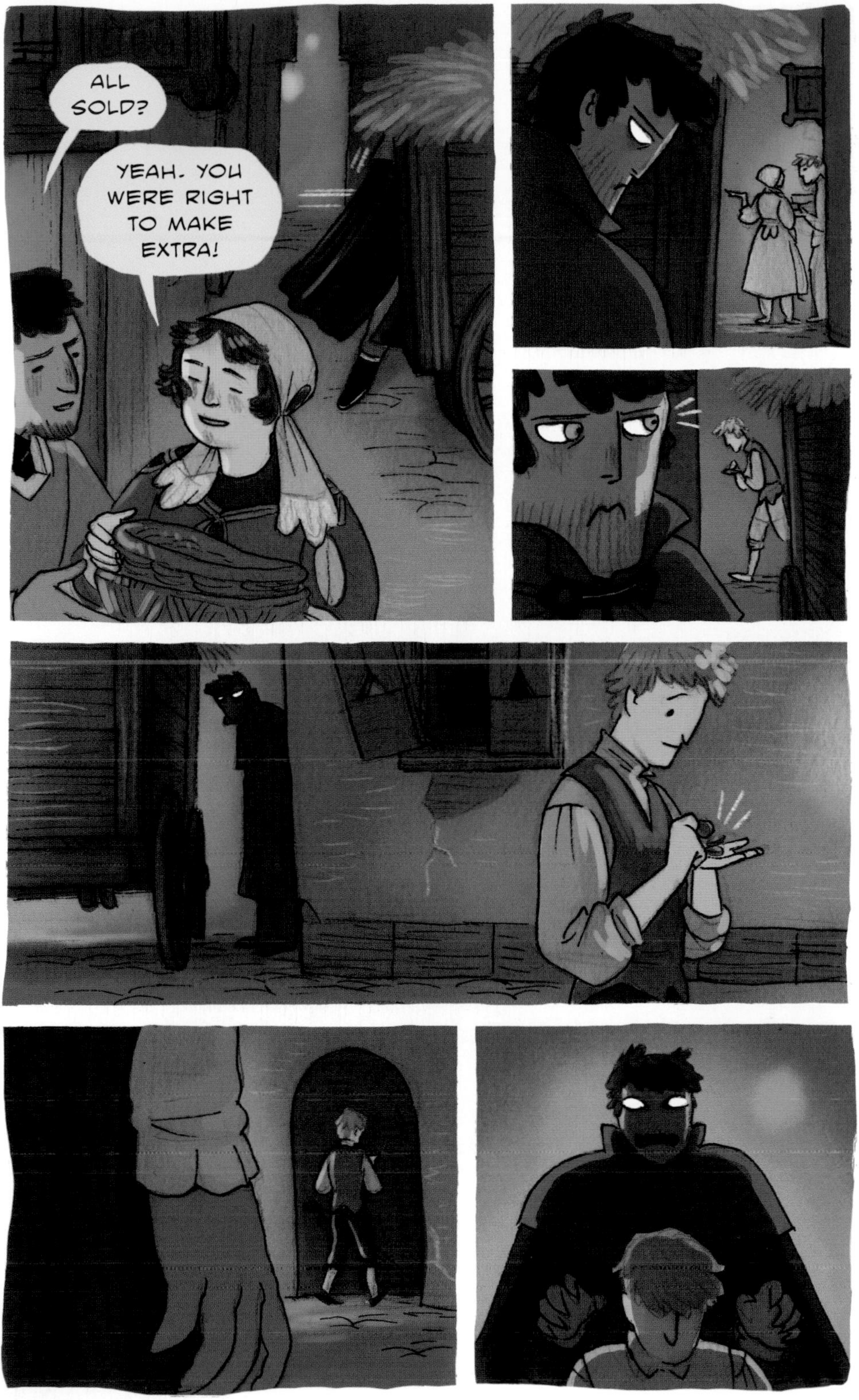
ALL SOLD?
YEAH. YOU WERE RIGHT TO MAKE EXTRA!

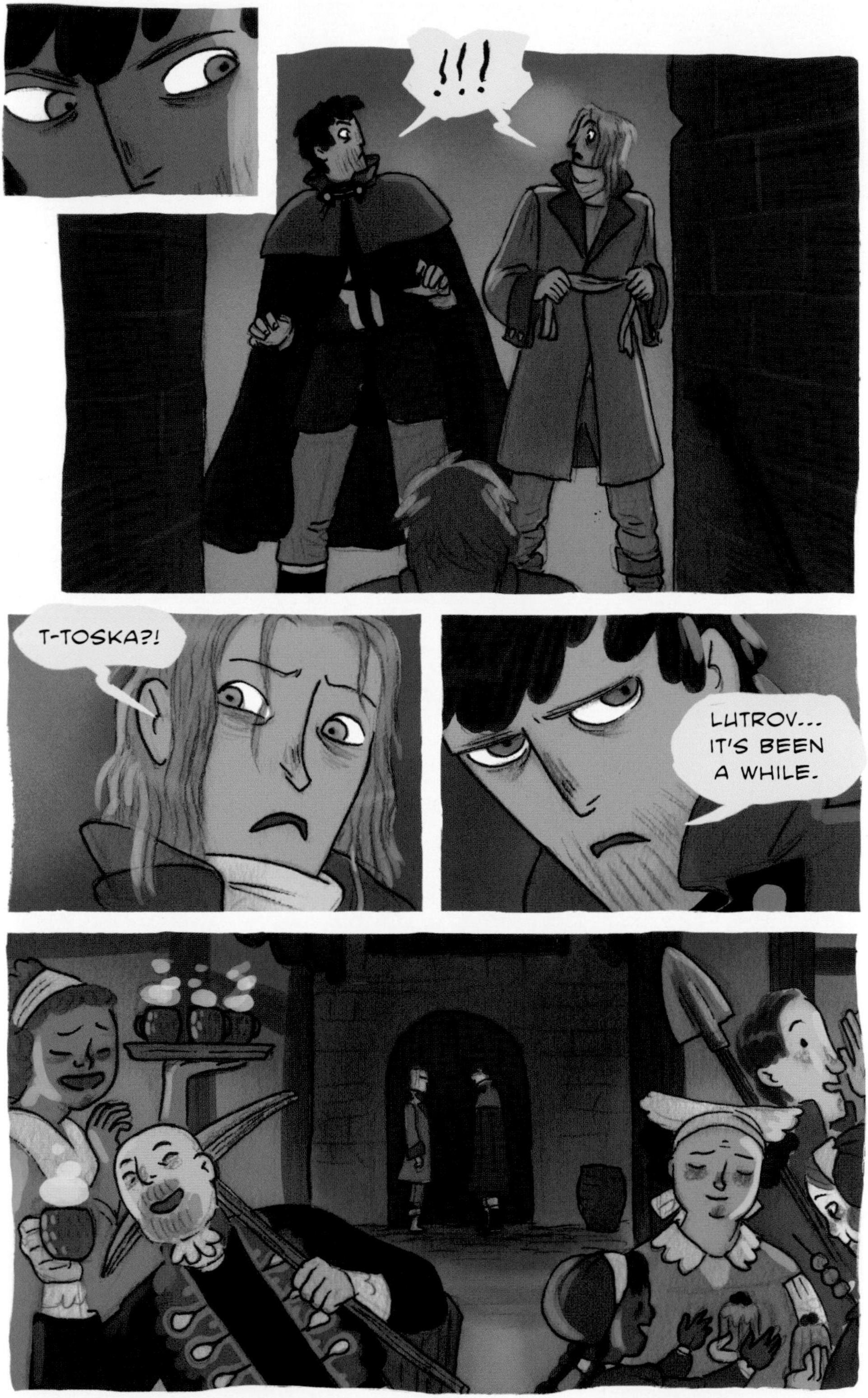
!!!
T-TOSKA?!
LUTROV...
IT'S BEEN
A WHILE.

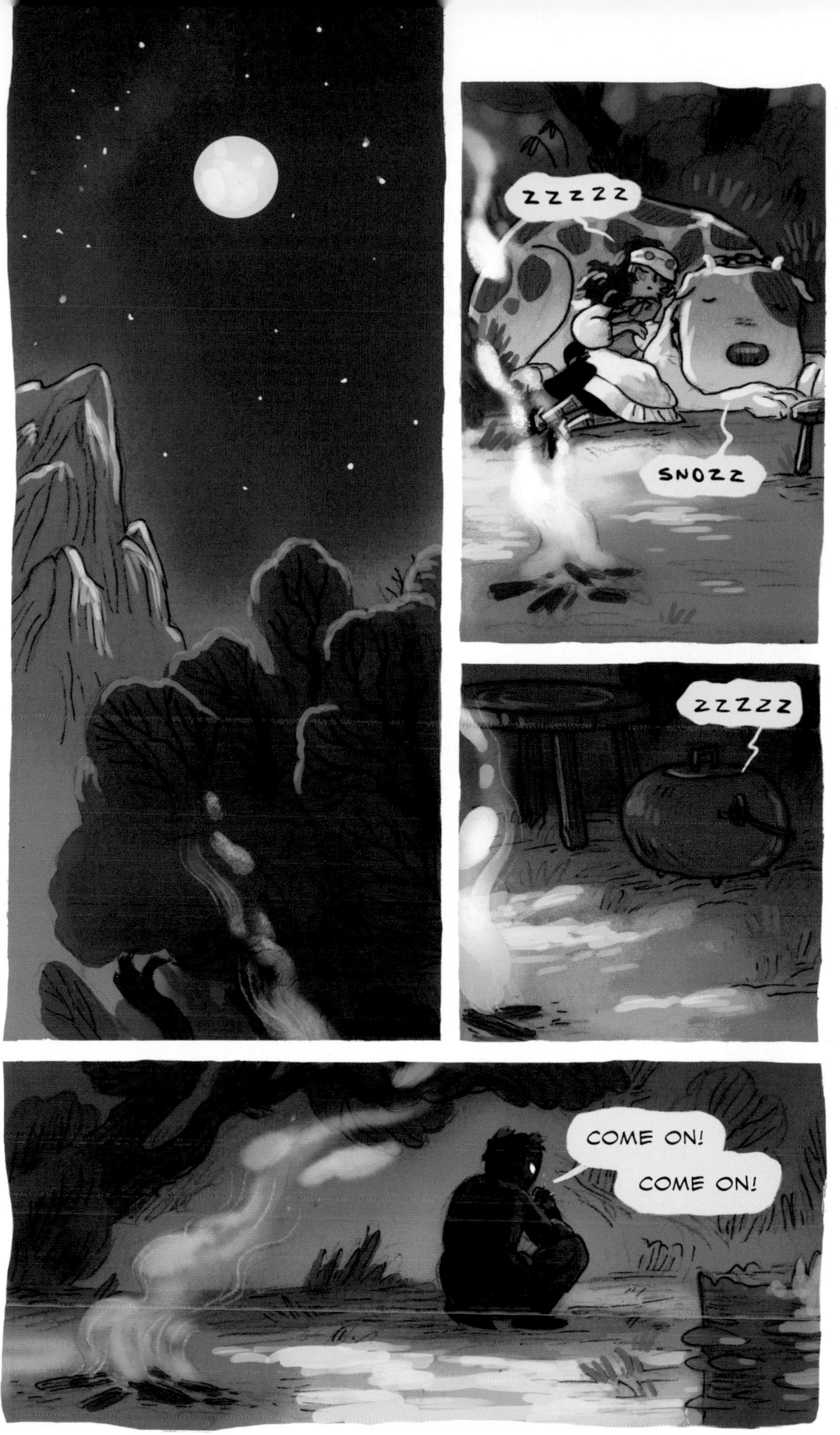
ZZZZZ
SNOZZ
ZZZZZ
COME ON!
COME ON!

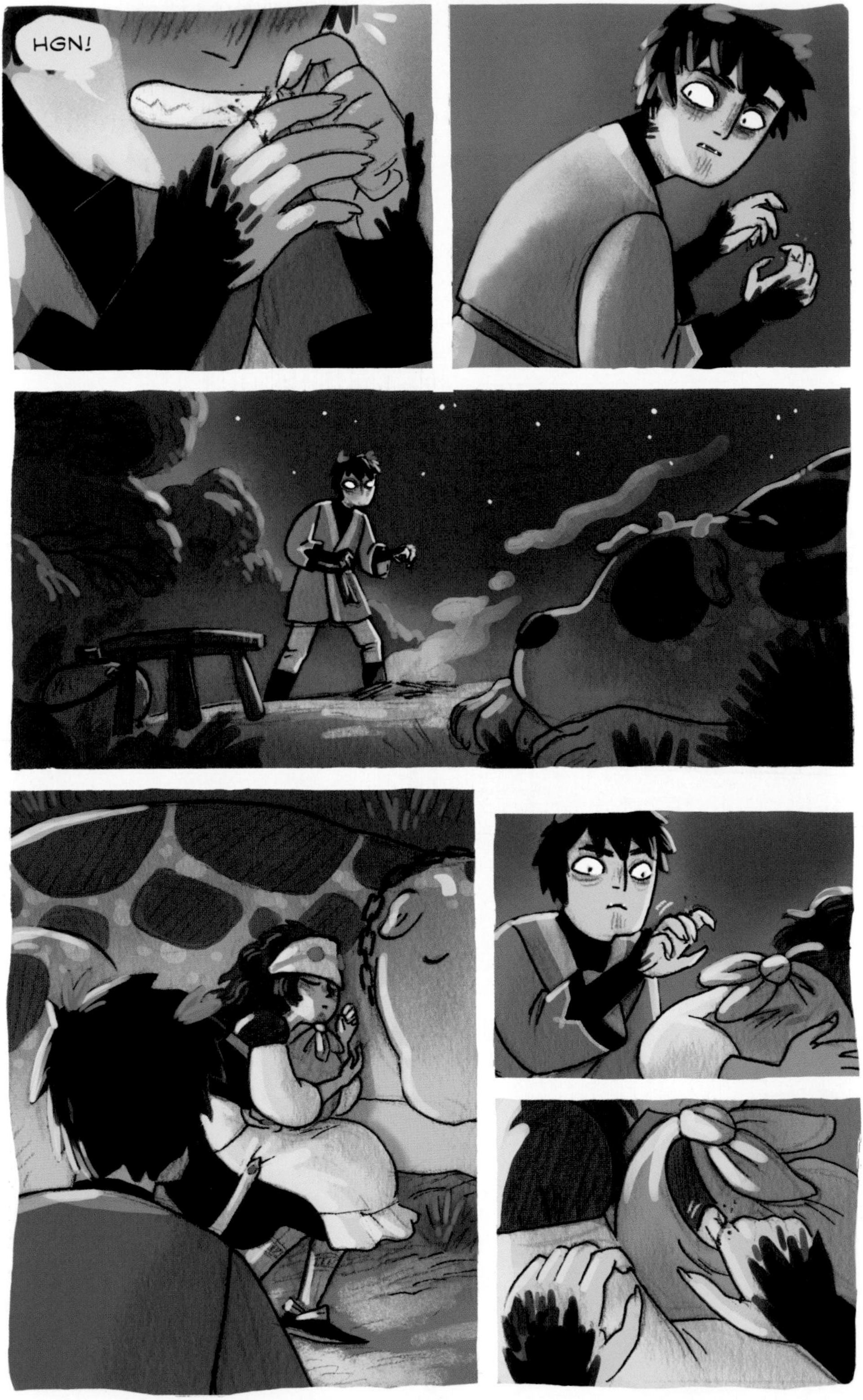
HGN!

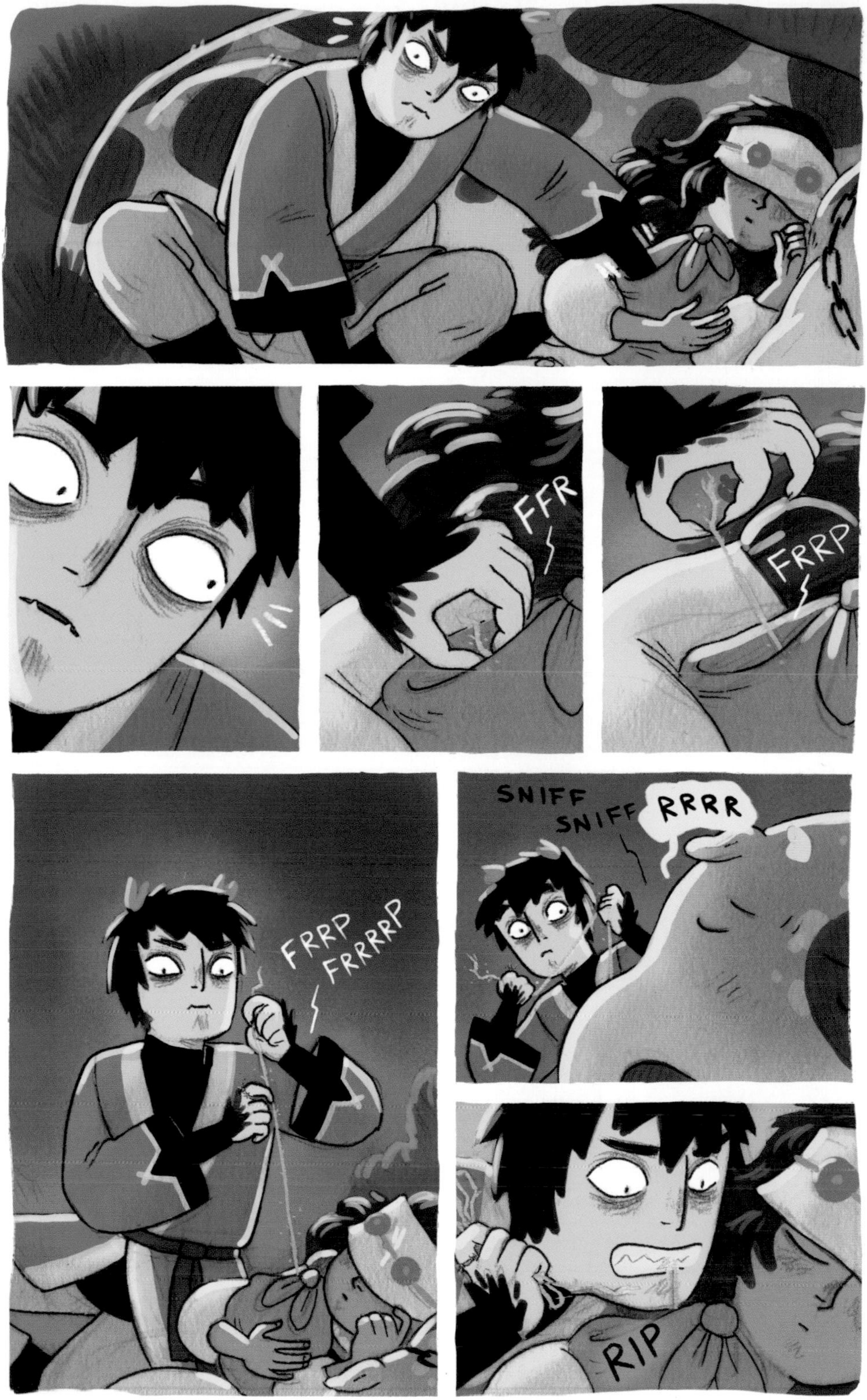
FFR
FRRP
FRRP
FRRRP
SNIFF
SNIFF
RRRR
RIP

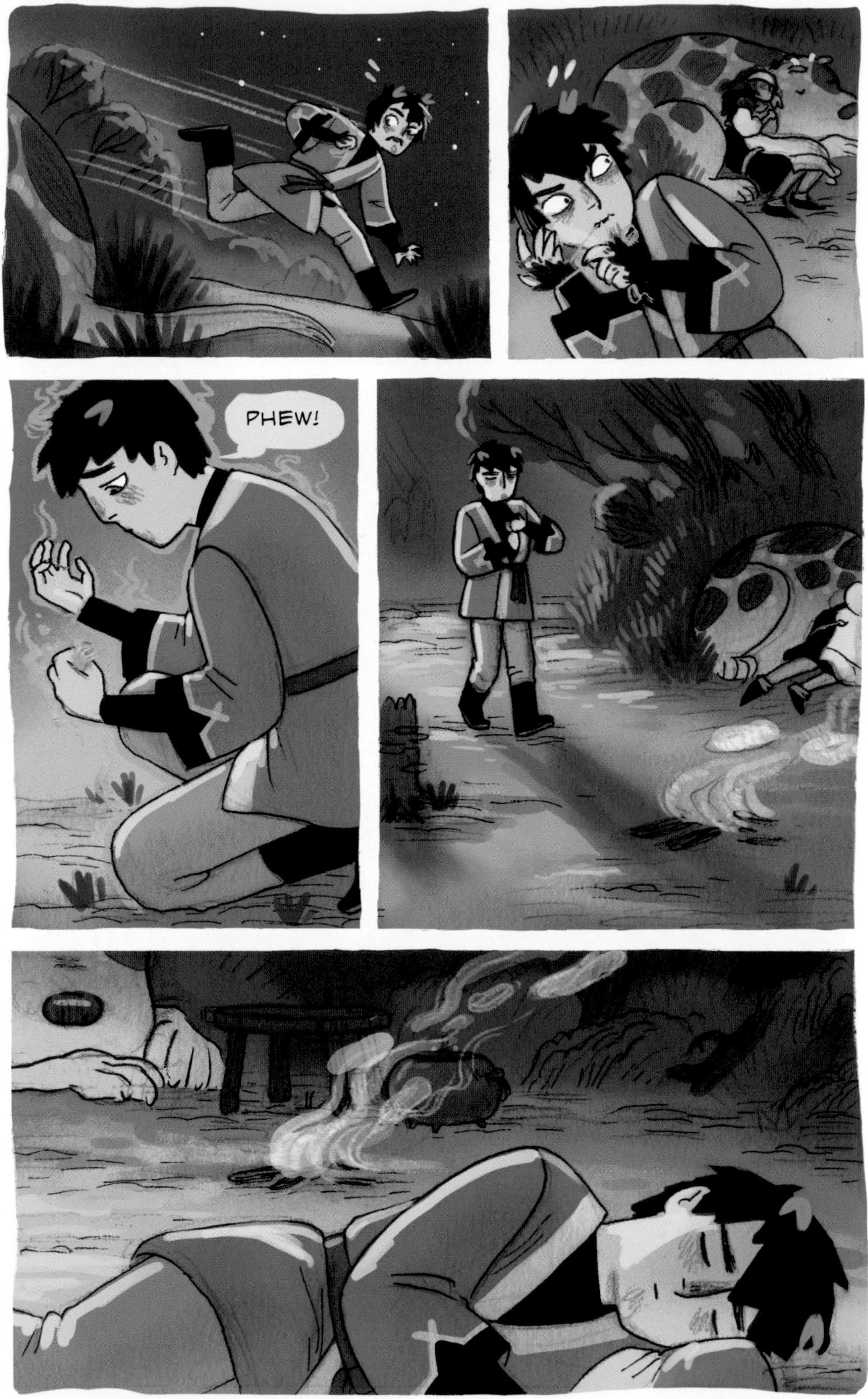
PHEW!

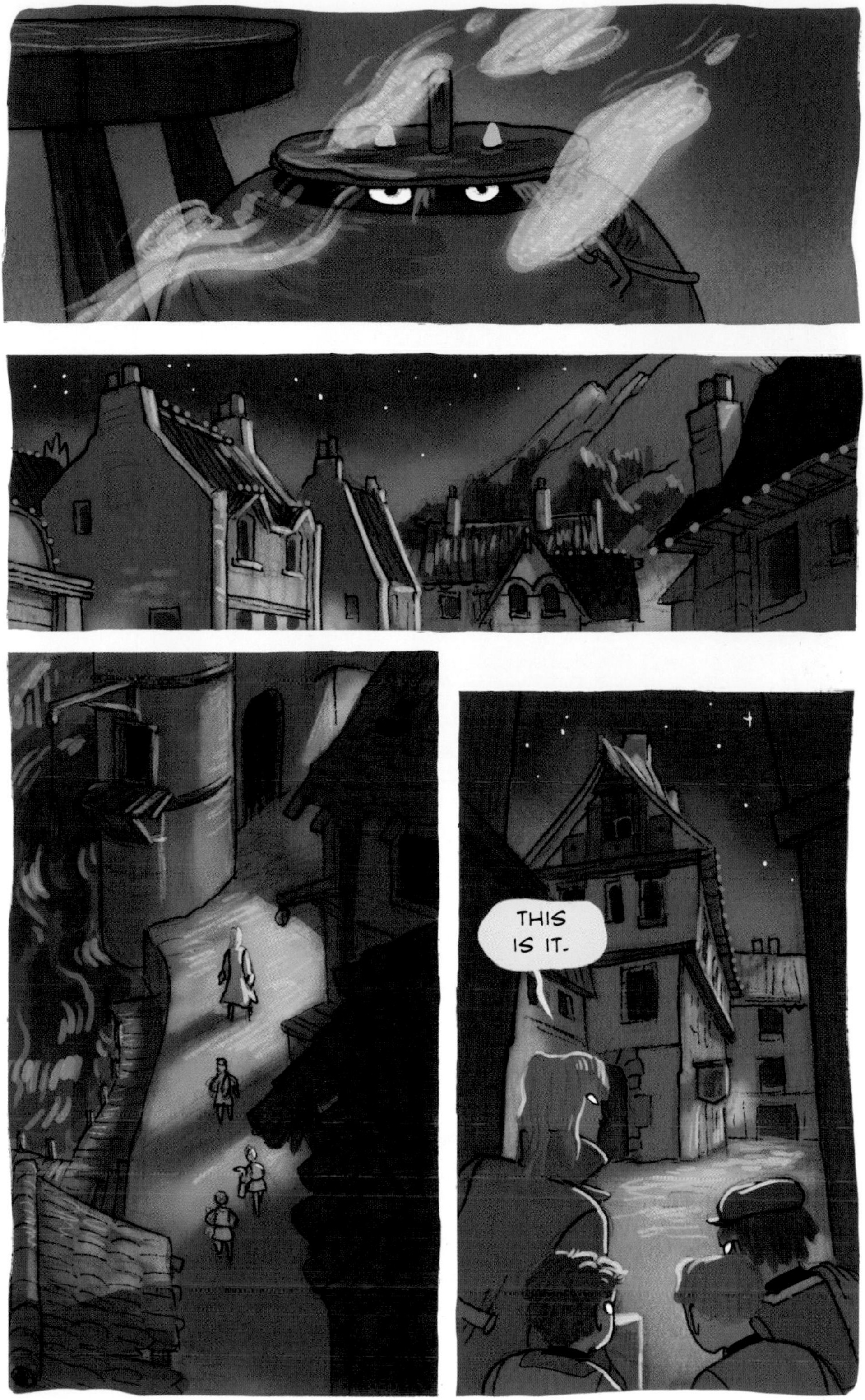
THIS IS IT.

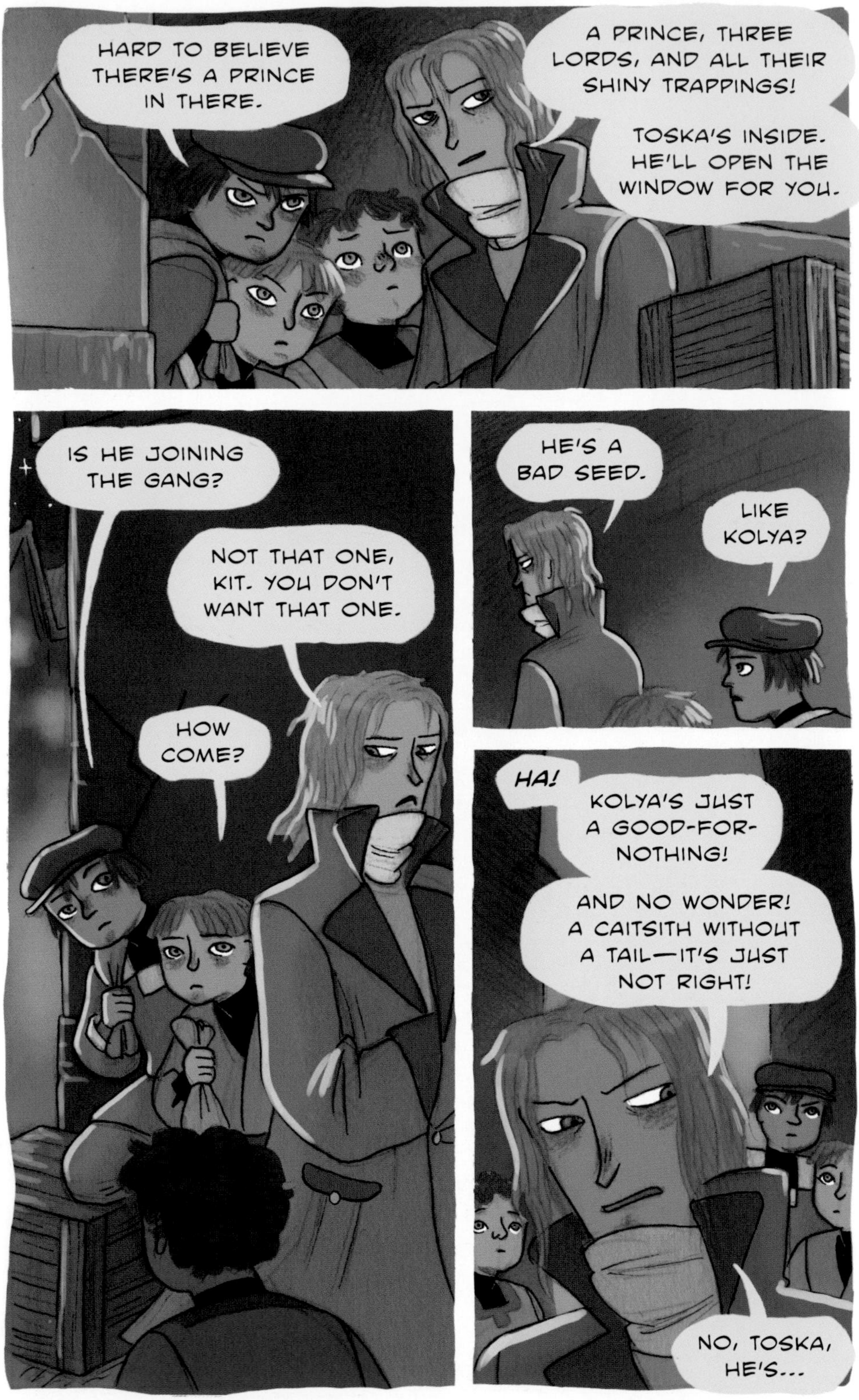
HARD TO BELIEVE THERE'S A PRINCE IN THERE.
A PRINCE, THREE LORDS, AND ALL THEIR SHINY TRAPPINGS!
TOSKA'S INSIDE. HE'LL OPEN THE WINDOW FOR YOU.
IS HE JOINING THE GANG?
NOT THAT ONE, KIT. YOU DON'T WANT THAT ONE.
HOW COME?
HE'S A BAD SEED.
LIKE KOLYA?
HA!
KOLYA'S JUST A GOOD-FOR-NOTHING!
AND NO WONDER! A CAITSITH WITHOUT A TAIL—IT'S JUST NOT RIGHT!
NO, TOSKA, HE'S...

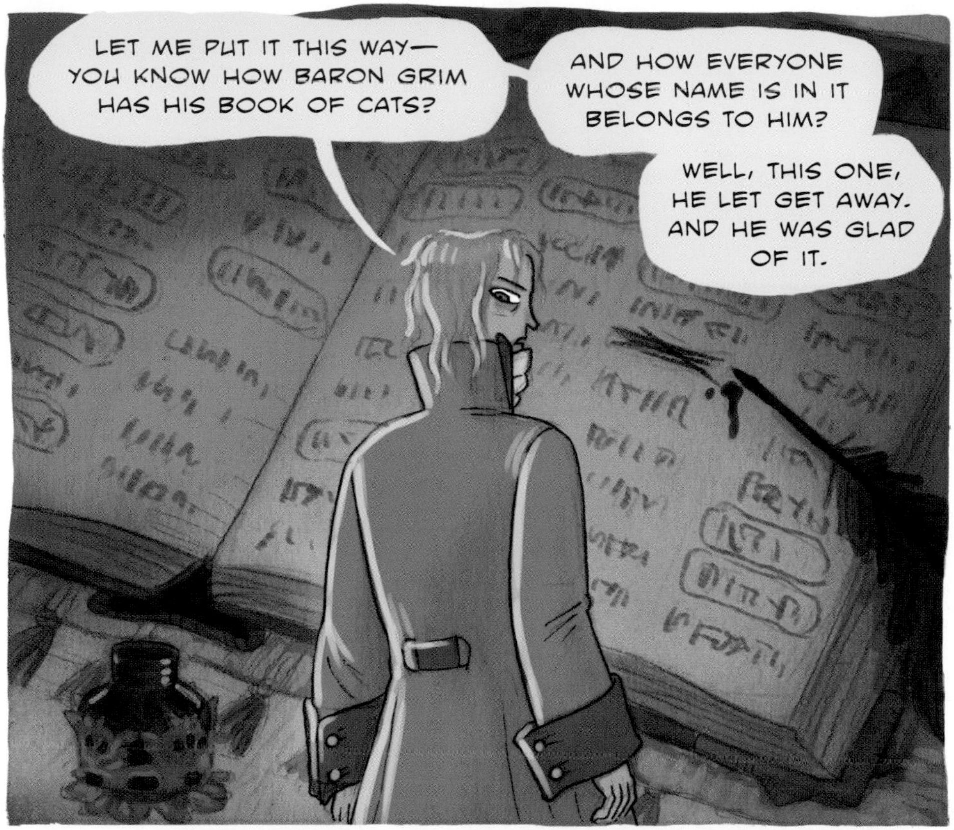
LET ME PUT IT THIS WAY— YOU KNOW HOW BARON GRIM HAS HIS BOOK OF CATS?
AND HOW EVERYONE WHOSE NAME IS IN IT BELONGS TO HIM?
WELL, THIS ONE, HE LET GET AWAY. AND HE WAS GLAD OF IT.

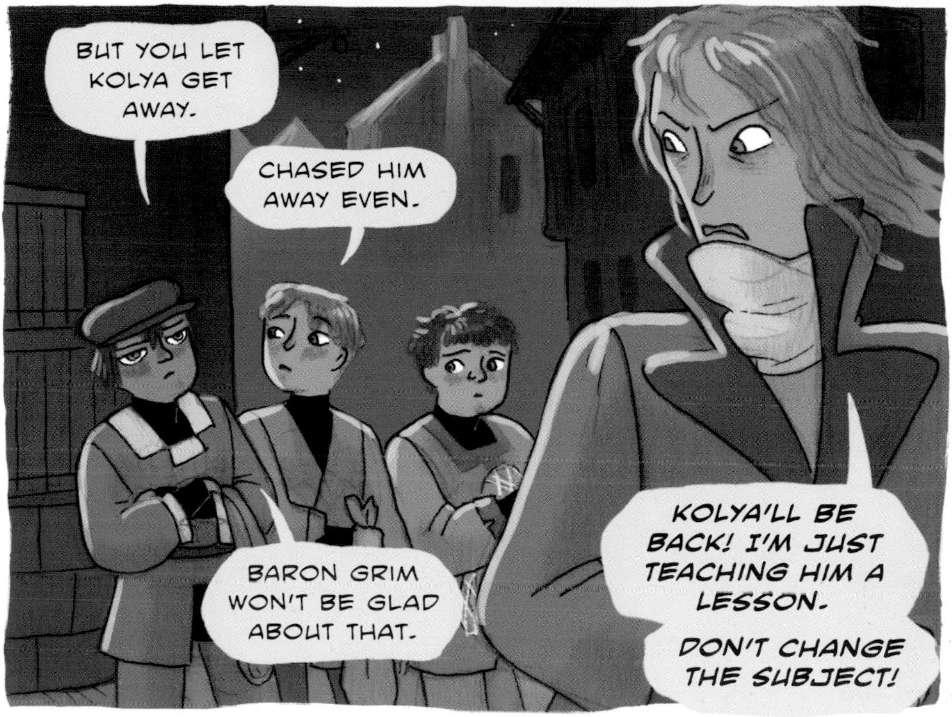
BUT YOU LET KOLYA GET AWAY.
CHASED HIM AWAY EVEN.
BARON GRIM WON'T BE GLAD ABOUT THAT.
KOLYA'LL BE BACK! I'M JUST TEACHING HIM A LESSON.
DON'T CHANGE THE SUBJECT!

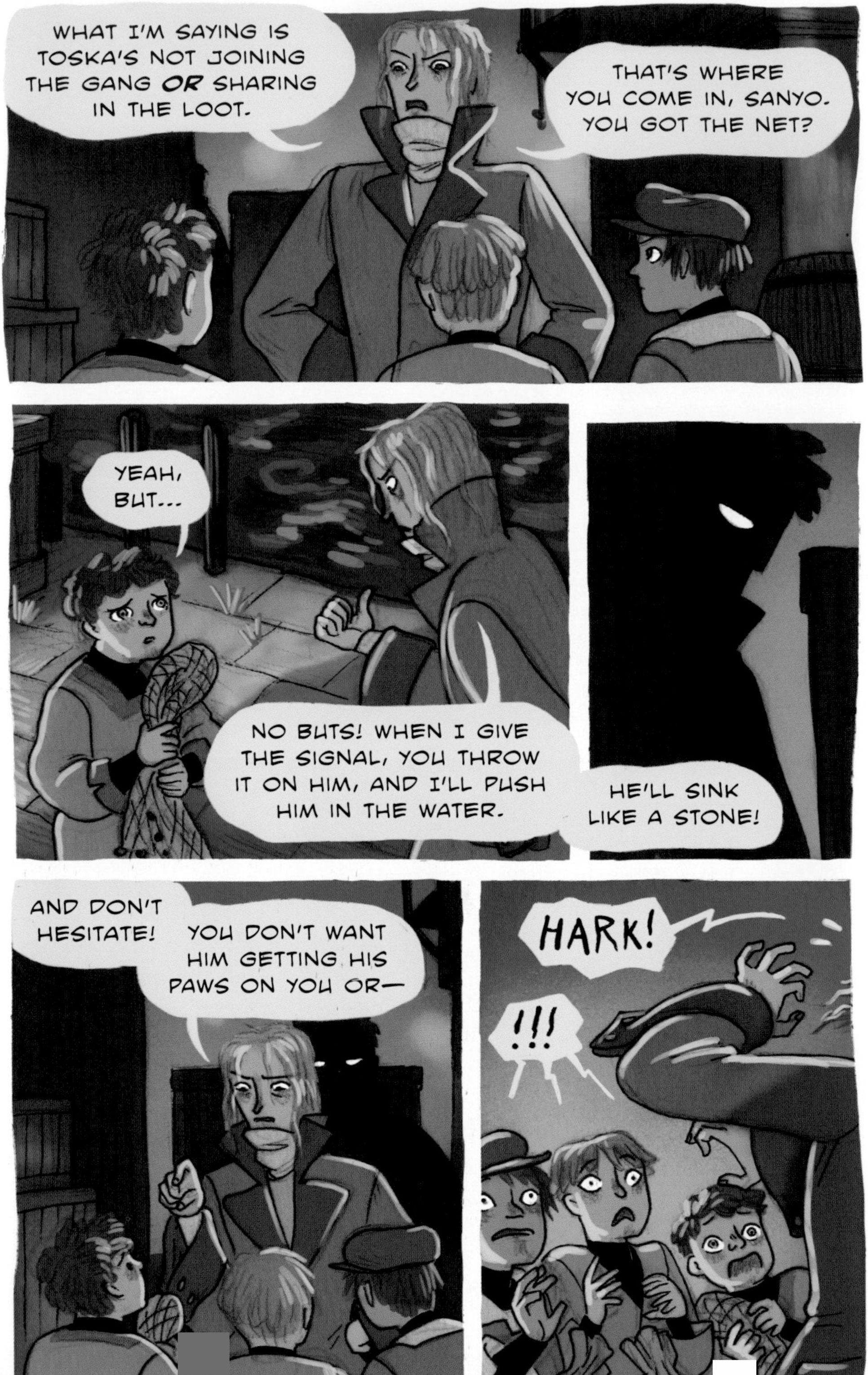
WHAT I'M SAYING IS TOSKA'S NOT JOINING THE GANG *OR* SHARING IN THE LOOT.
THAT'S WHERE YOU COME IN, SANYO. YOU GOT THE NET?
YEAH, BUT...
NO BUTS! WHEN I GIVE THE SIGNAL, YOU THROW IT ON HIM, AND I'LL PUSH HIM IN THE WATER.
HE'LL SINK LIKE A STONE!
AND DON'T HESITATE!
YOU DON'T WANT HIM GETTING HIS PAWS ON YOU OR—
HARK!
!!!

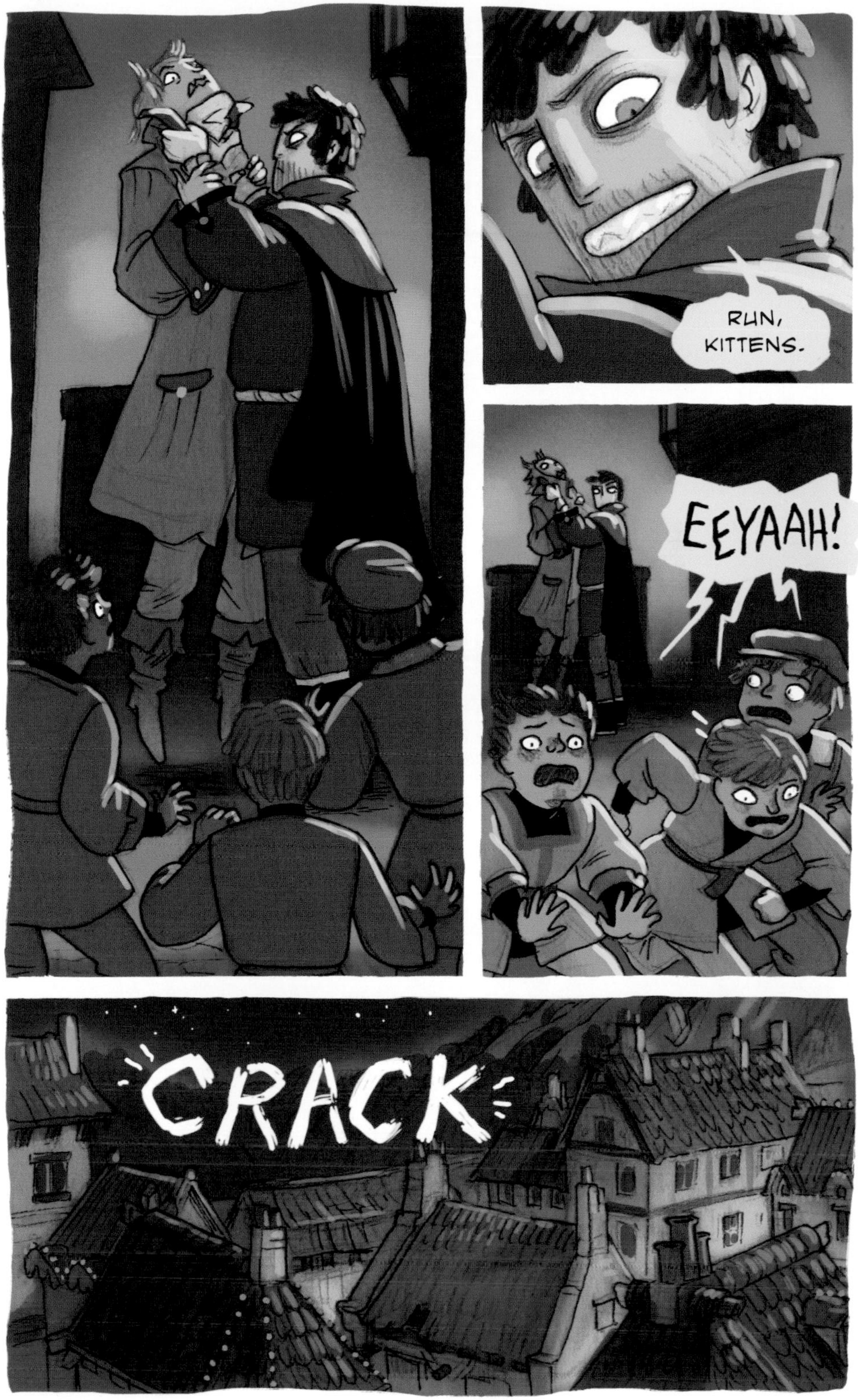
RUN, KITTENS.
EEYAAH!
CRACK

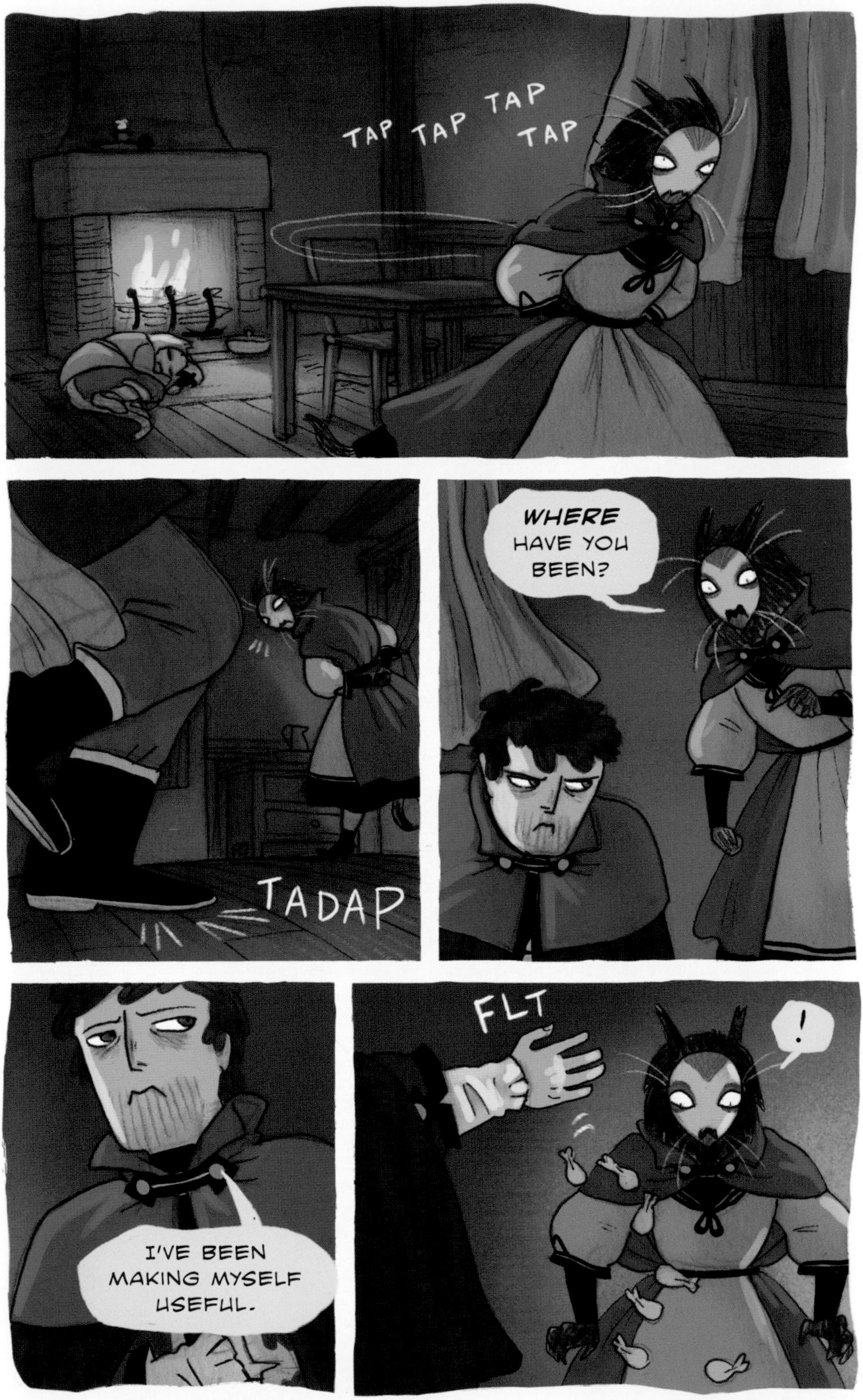
TAP TAP TAP
TAP
TADAP
WHERE HAVE YOU BEEN?
I'VE BEEN MAKING MYSELF USEFUL.
FLT
!

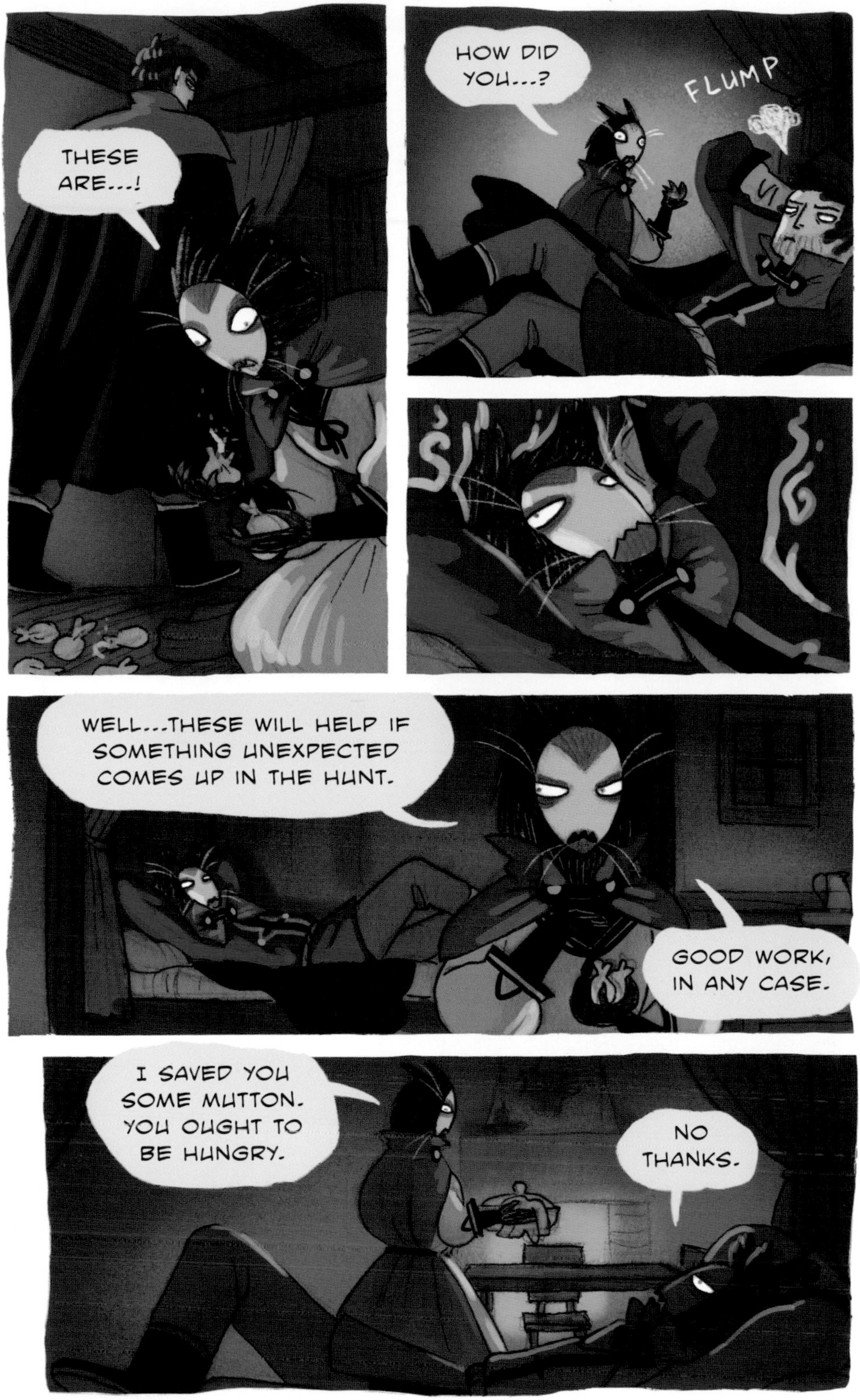
THESE ARE...!
HOW DID YOU...?
FLUMP
WELL...THESE WILL HELP IF SOMETHING UNEXPECTED COMES UP IN THE HUNT.
GOOD WORK, IN ANY CASE.
I SAVED YOU SOME MUTTON. YOU OUGHT TO BE HUNGRY.
NO THANKS.

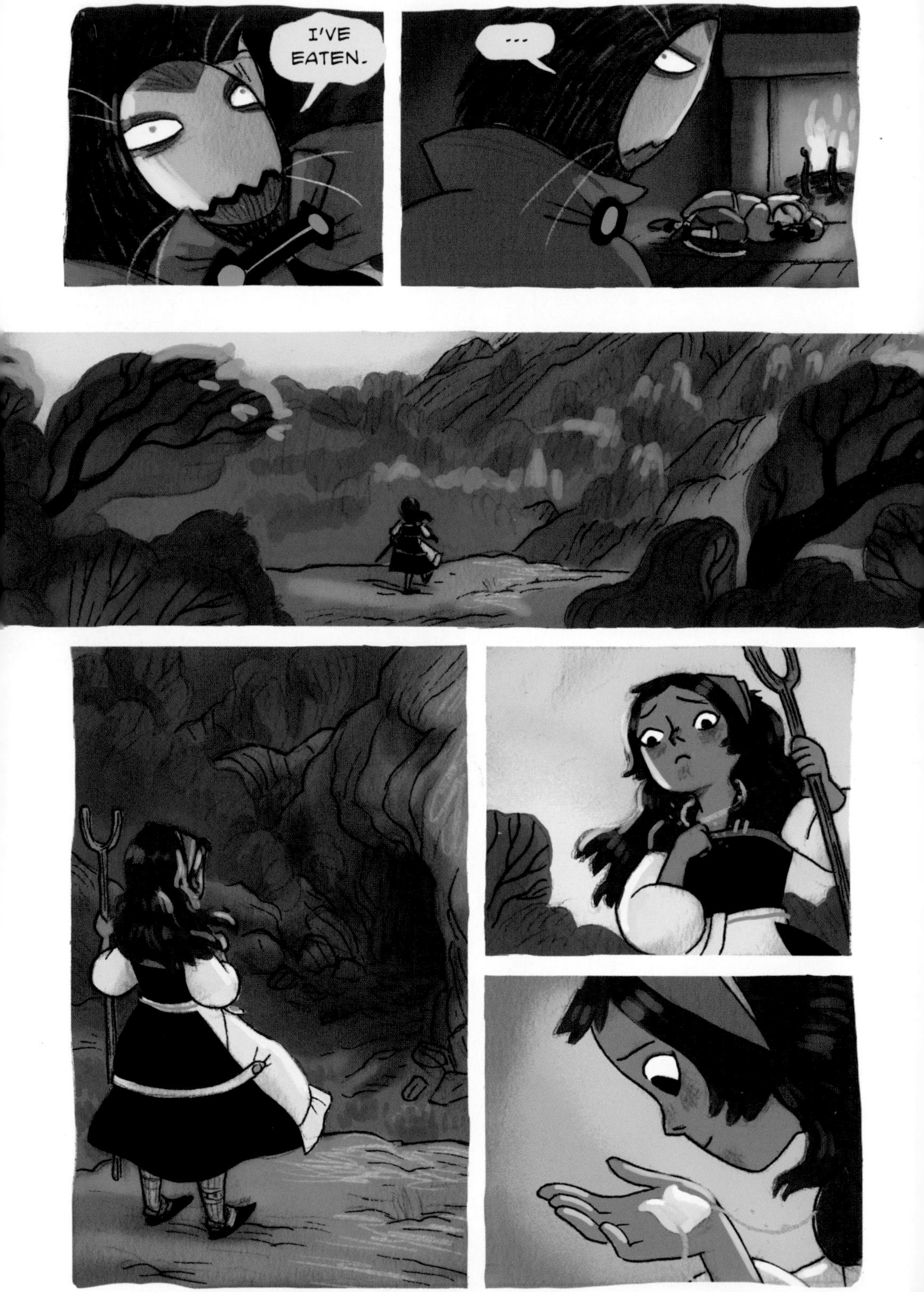
I'VE EATEN.
...

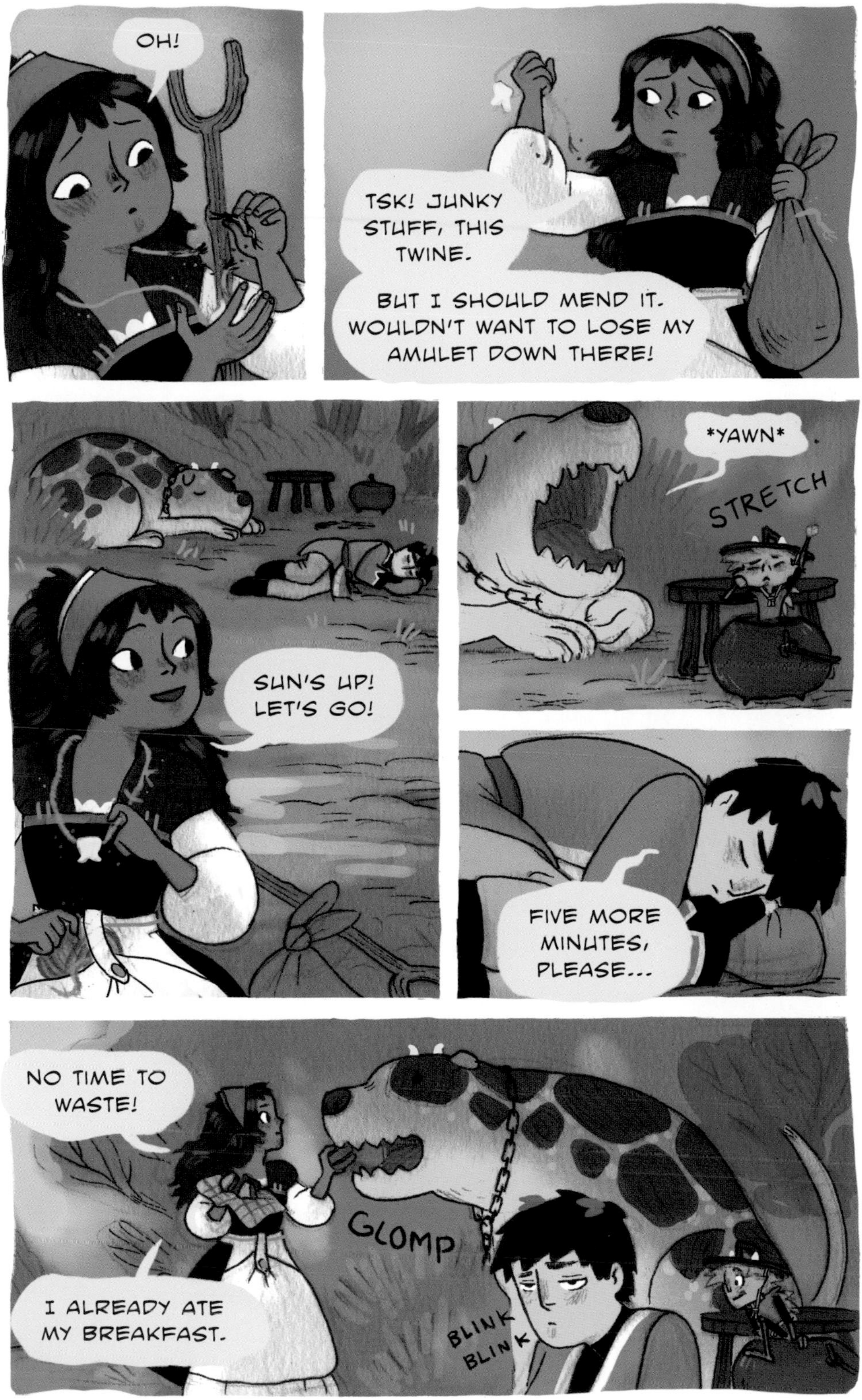
OH!
TSK! JUNKY STUFF, THIS TWINE.
BUT I SHOULD MEND IT. WOULDN'T WANT TO LOSE MY AMULET DOWN THERE!
SUN'S UP! LET'S GO!
YAWN
STRETCH
FIVE MORE MINUTES, PLEASE...
NO TIME TO WASTE!
GLOMP
I ALREADY ATE MY BREAKFAST.
BLINK BLINK

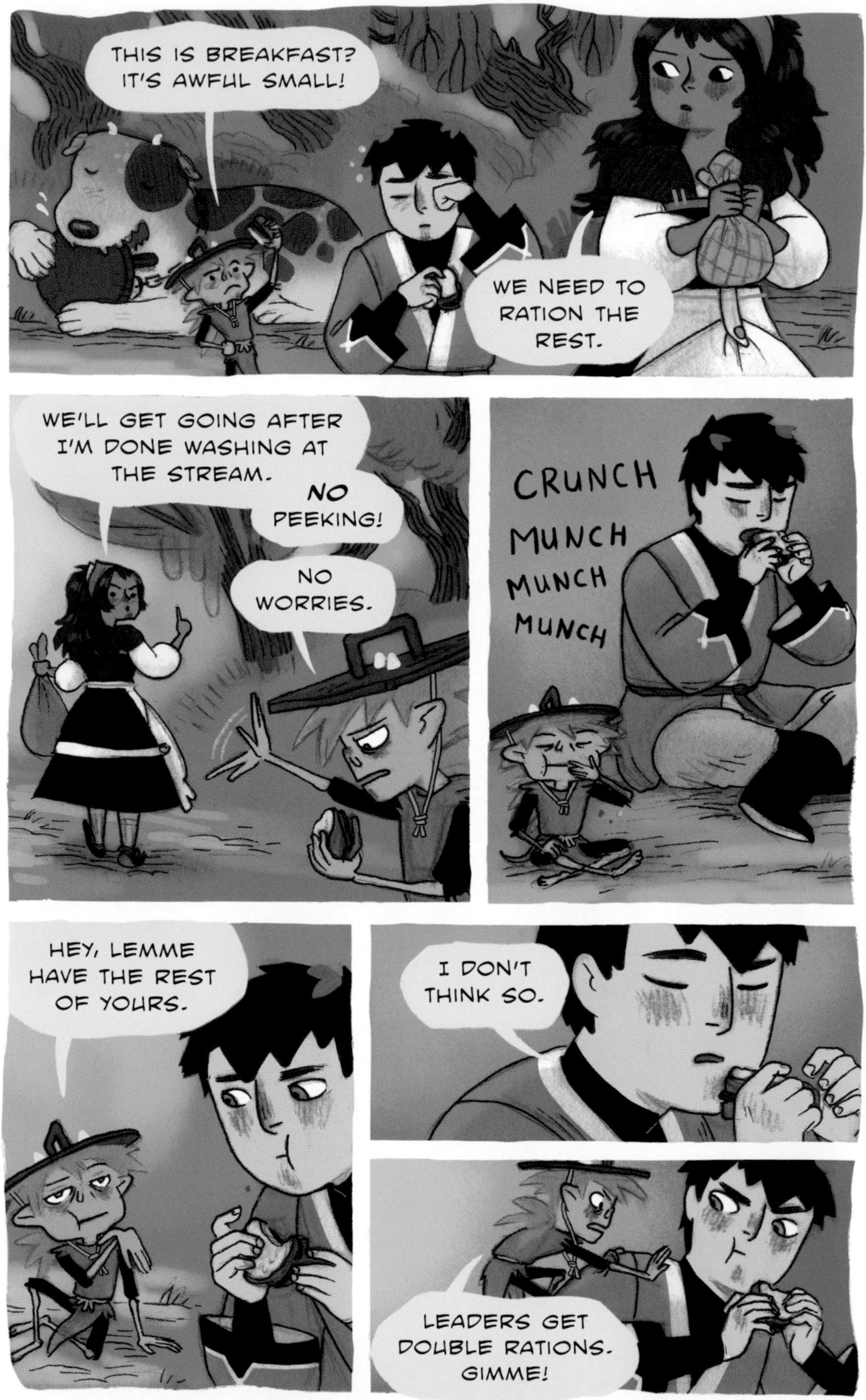
THIS IS BREAKFAST? IT'S AWFUL SMALL!
WE NEED TO RATION THE REST.
WE'LL GET GOING AFTER I'M DONE WASHING AT THE STREAM.
NO PEEKING!
NO WORRIES.
CRUNCH
MUNCH
MUNCH
MUNCH
HEY, LEMME HAVE THE REST OF YOURS.
I DON'T THINK SO.
LEADERS GET DOUBLE RATIONS. GIMME!

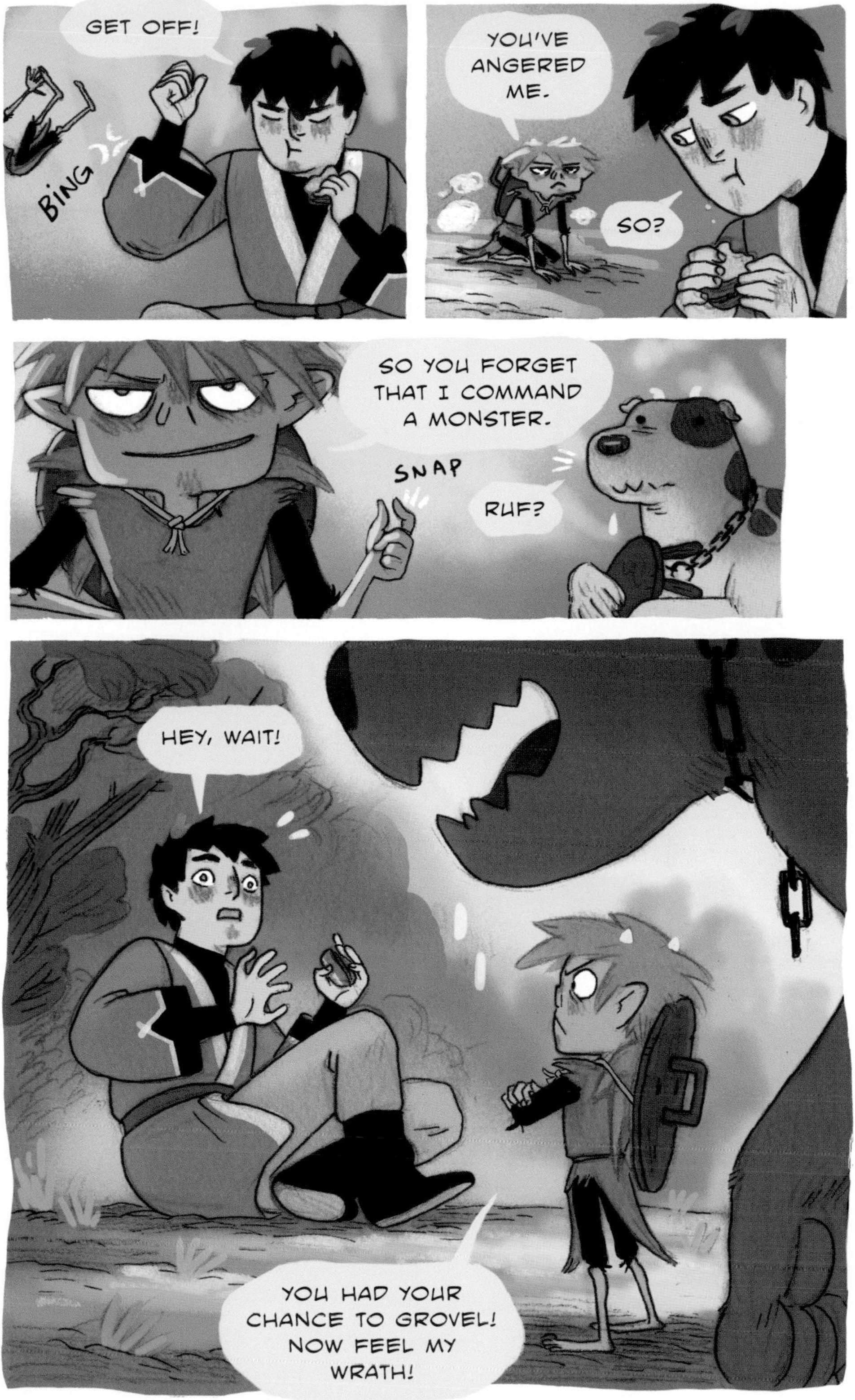
GET OFF!
BING
YOU'VE ANGERED ME.
SO?
SO YOU FORGET THAT I COMMAND A MONSTER.
SNAP
RUF?
HEY, WAIT!
YOU HAD YOUR CHANCE TO GROVEL! NOW FEEL MY WRATH!

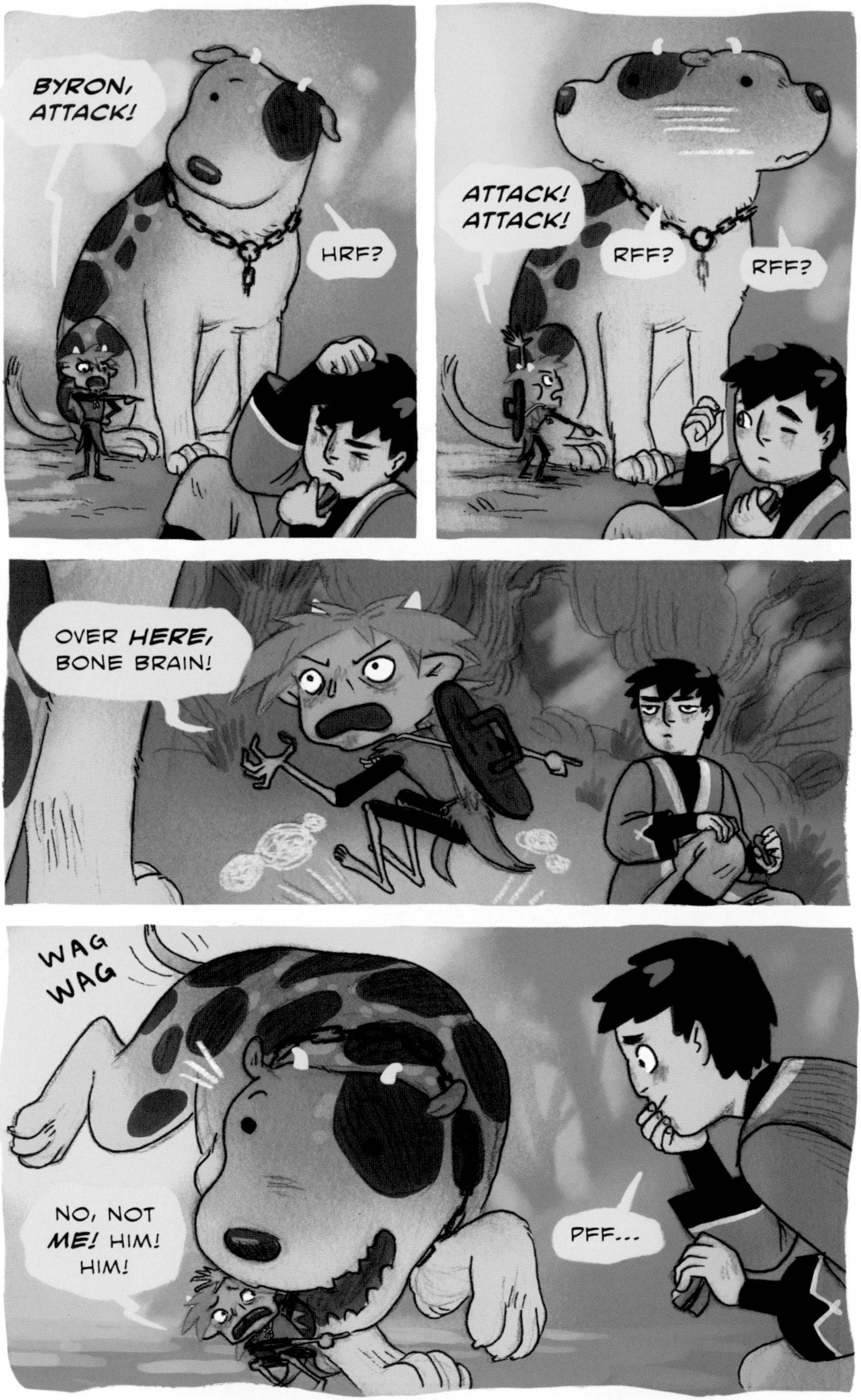
BYRON, ATTACK!
HRF?
ATTACK! ATTACK!
RFF?
RFF?
OVER HERE, BONE BRAIN!
WAG WAG
NO, NOT ME! HIM! HIM!
PFF...

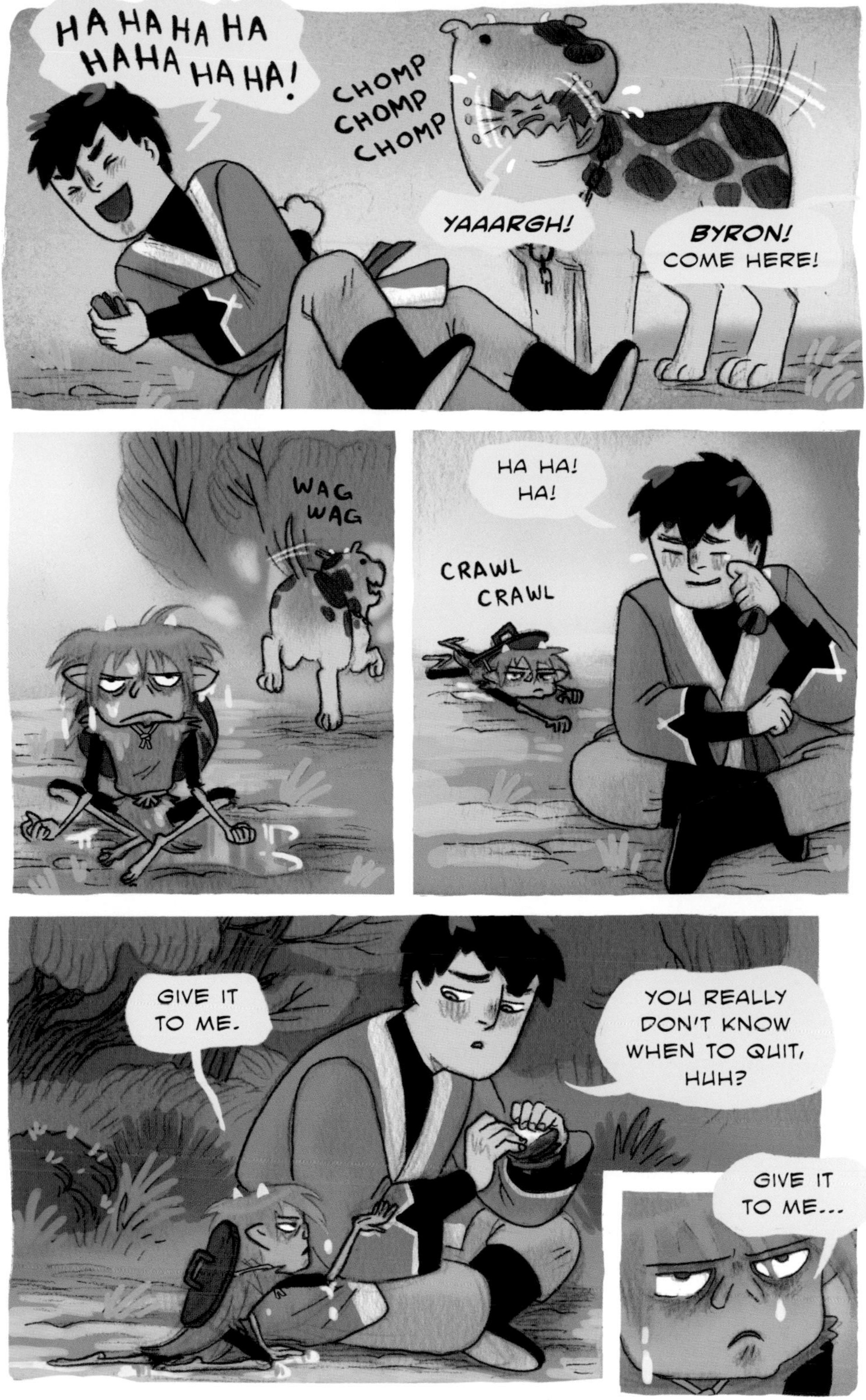
HA HA HA HA HA
HAHA HA HA!
CHOMP
CHOMP
CHOMP
YAAARGH!
BYRON!
COME HERE!
WAG
WAG
HA HA!
HA!
CRAWL
CRAWL
GIVE IT
TO ME.
YOU REALLY
DON'T KNOW
WHEN TO QUIT,
HUH?
GIVE IT
TO ME...

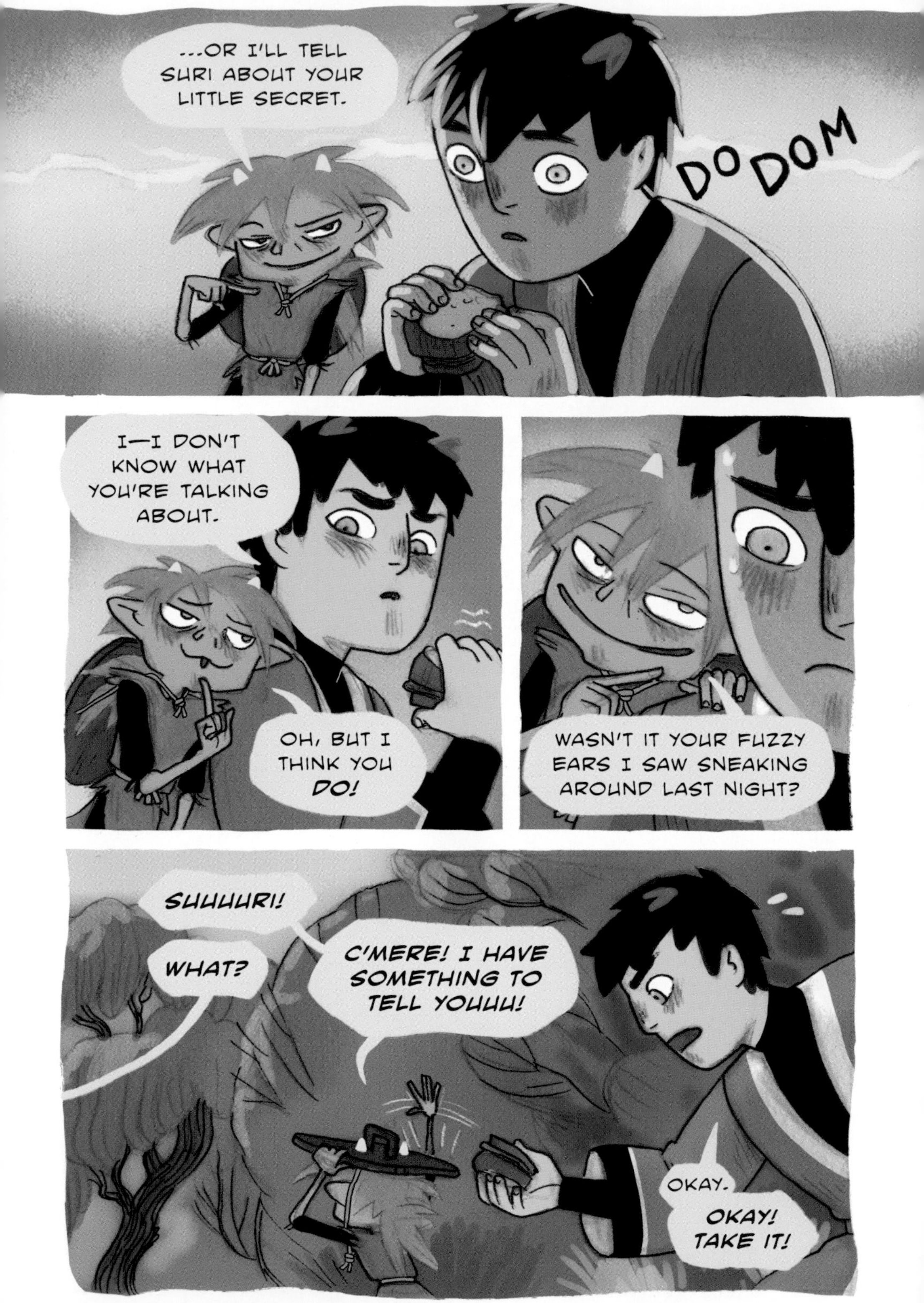
...OR I'LL TELL SURI ABOUT YOUR LITTLE SECRET.
DO DOM
I—I DON'T KNOW WHAT YOU'RE TALKING ABOUT.
OH, BUT I THINK YOU *DO!*
WASN'T IT YOUR FUZZY EARS I SAW SNEAKING AROUND LAST NIGHT?
SUUUURI!
WHAT?
C'MERE! I HAVE SOMETHING TO TELL YOUUU!
OKAY.
OKAY! TAKE IT!

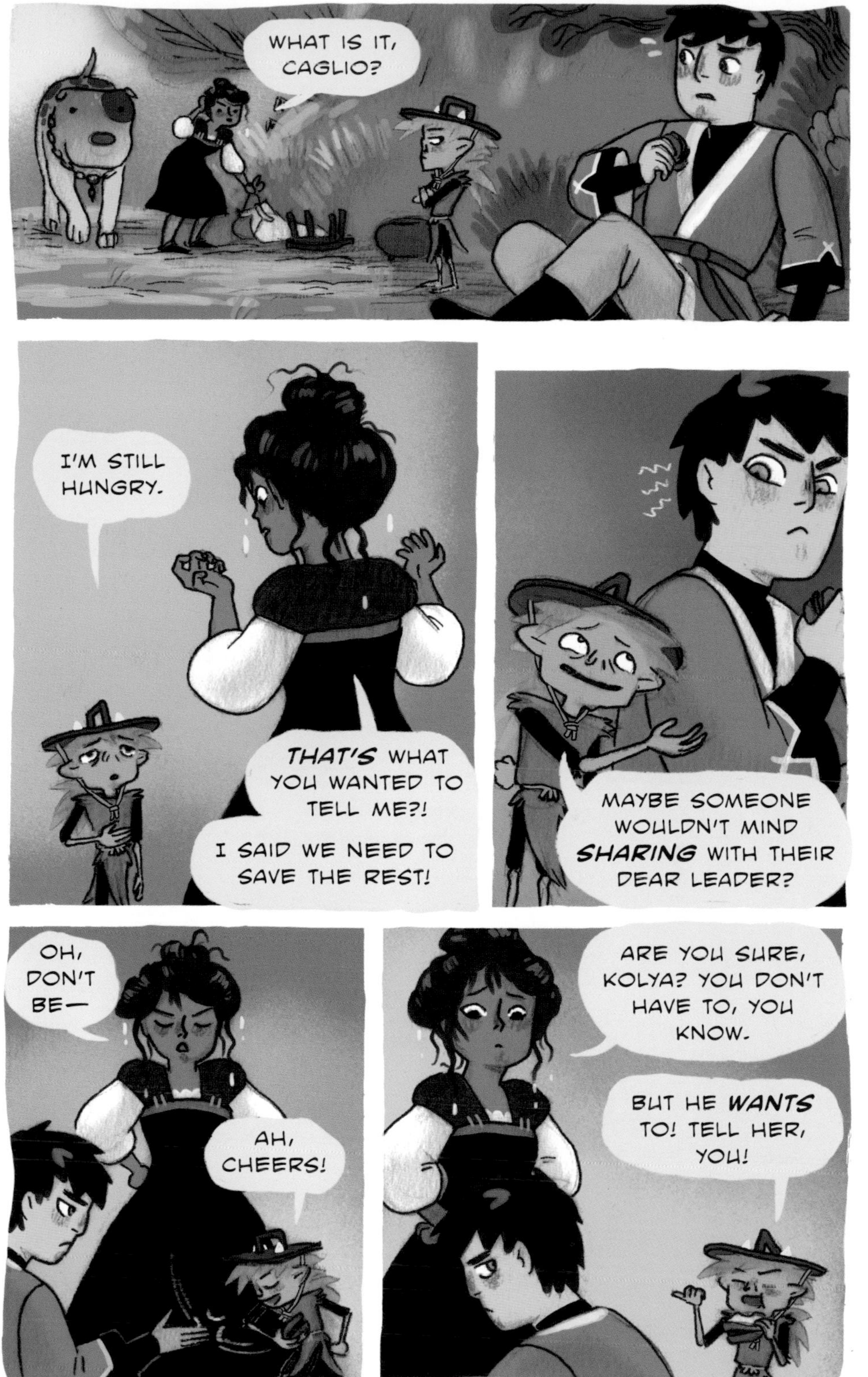
WHAT IS IT, CAGLIO?
I'M STILL HUNGRY.
THAT'S WHAT YOU WANTED TO TELL ME?!
I SAID WE NEED TO SAVE THE REST!
MAYBE SOMEONE WOULDN'T MIND SHARING WITH THEIR DEAR LEADER?
OH, DON'T BE—
AH, CHEERS!
ARE YOU SURE, KOLYA? YOU DON'T HAVE TO, YOU KNOW.
BUT HE WANTS TO! TELL HER, YOU!

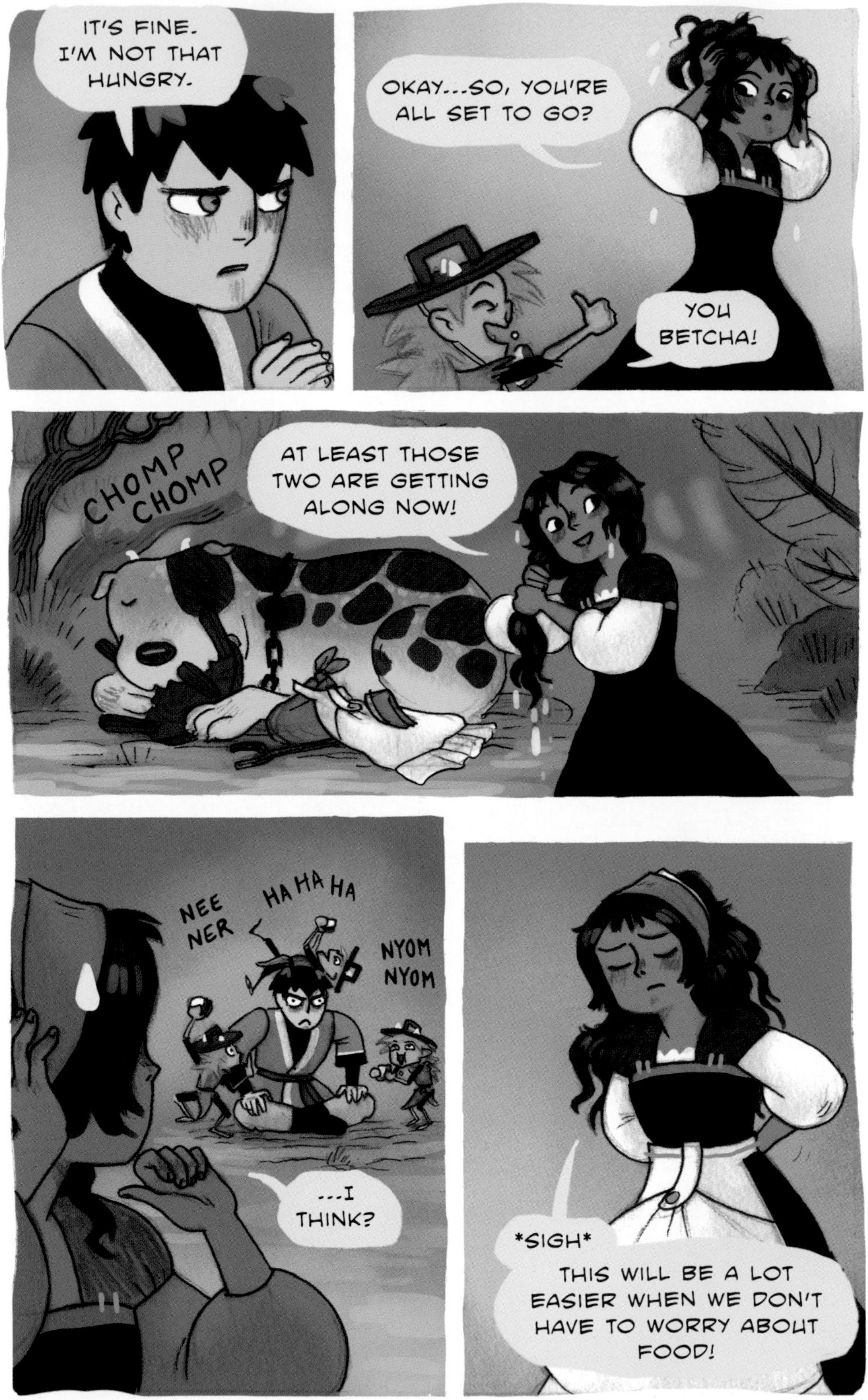
IT'S FINE. I'M NOT THAT HUNGRY.
OKAY...SO, YOU'RE ALL SET TO GO?
YOU BETCHA!
CHOMP CHOMP
AT LEAST THOSE TWO ARE GETTING ALONG NOW!
NEE NER
HA HA HA HA
NYOM NYOM
...I THINK?
SIGH
THIS WILL BE A LOT EASIER WHEN WE DON'T HAVE TO WORRY ABOUT FOOD!

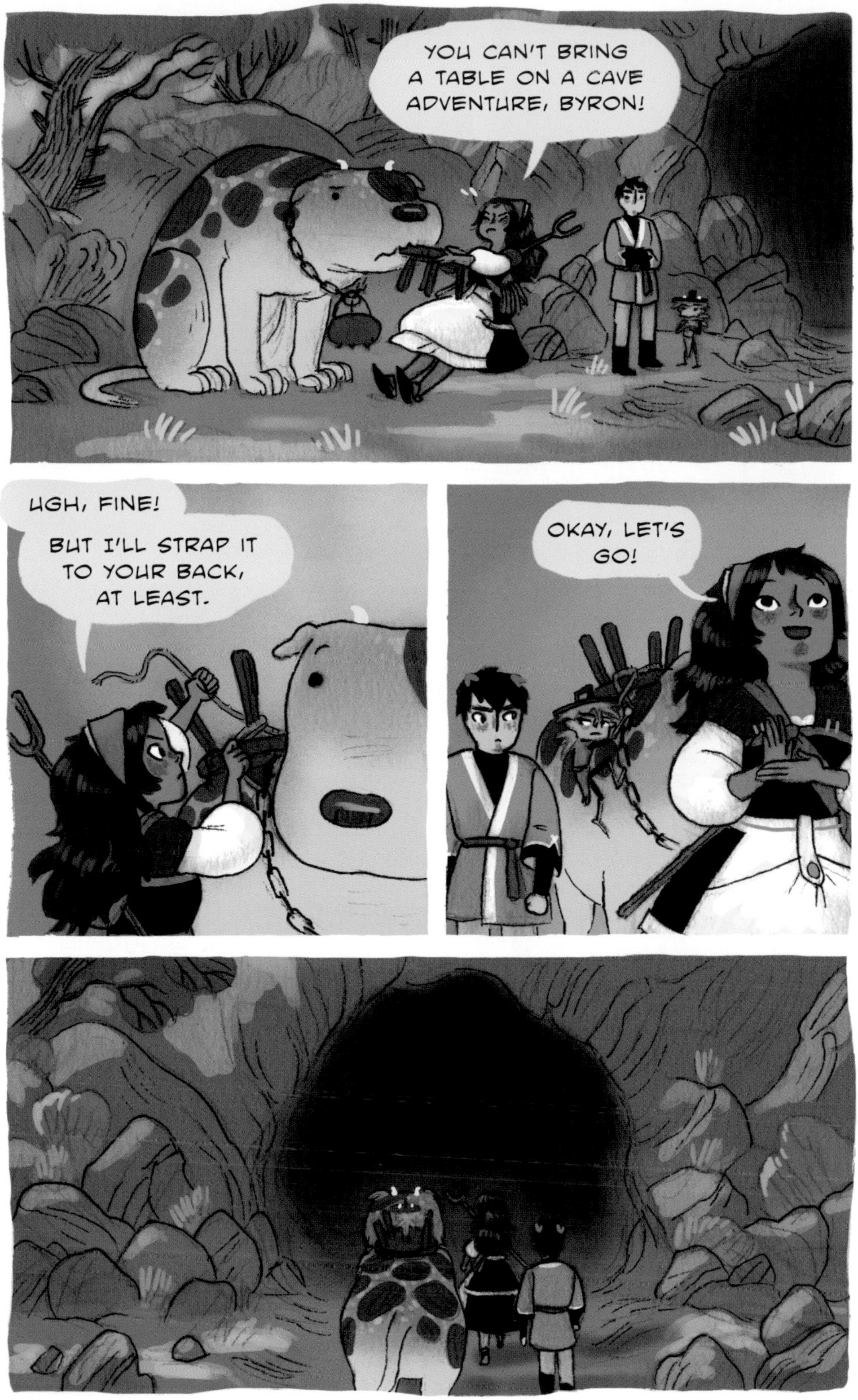
YOU CAN'T BRING A TABLE ON A CAVE ADVENTURE, BYRON!
UGH, FINE!
BUT I'LL STRAP IT TO YOUR BACK, AT LEAST.
OKAY, LET'S GO!

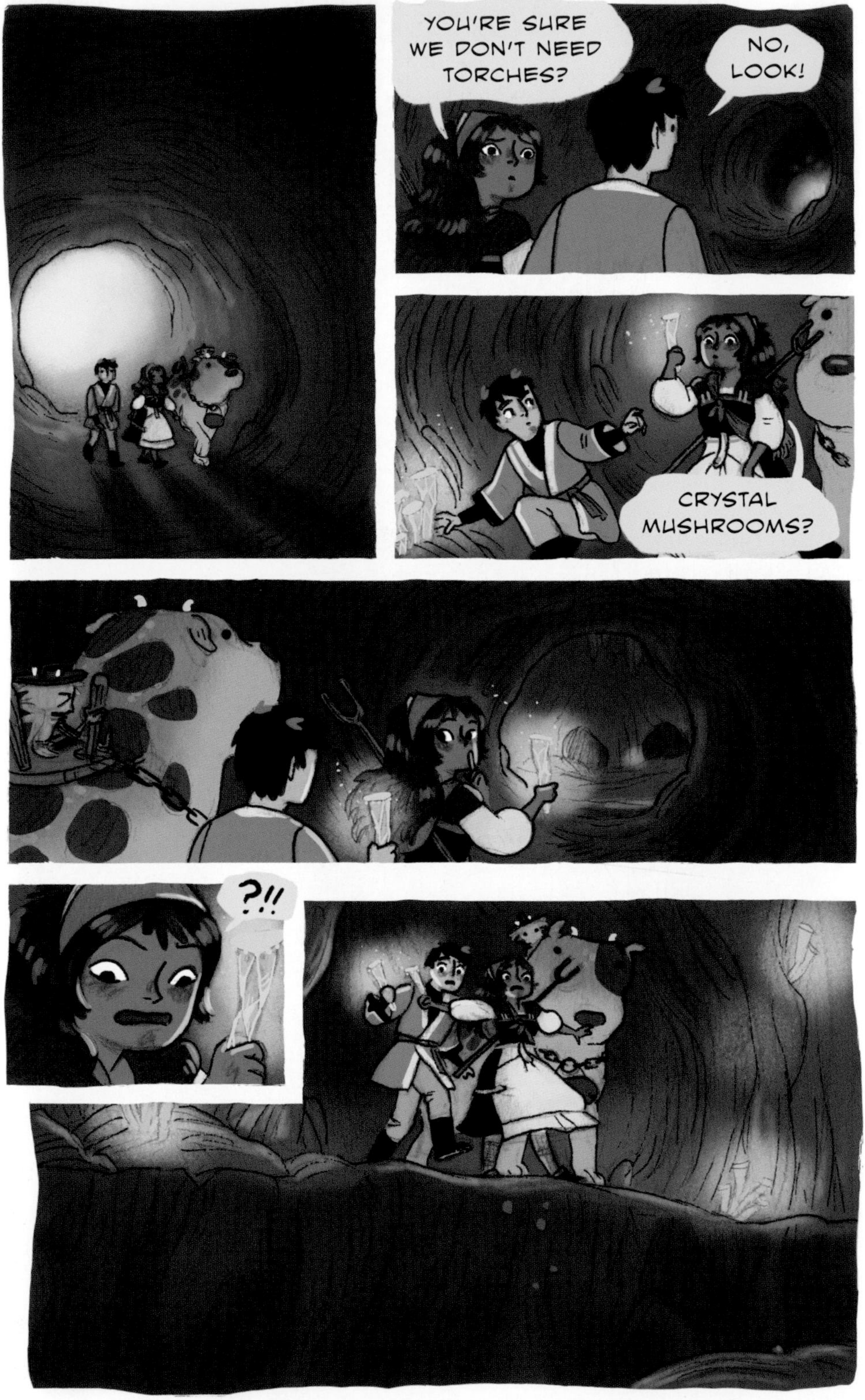
YOU'RE SURE WE DON'T NEED TORCHES?
NO, LOOK!
CRYSTAL MUSHROOMS?
?!!

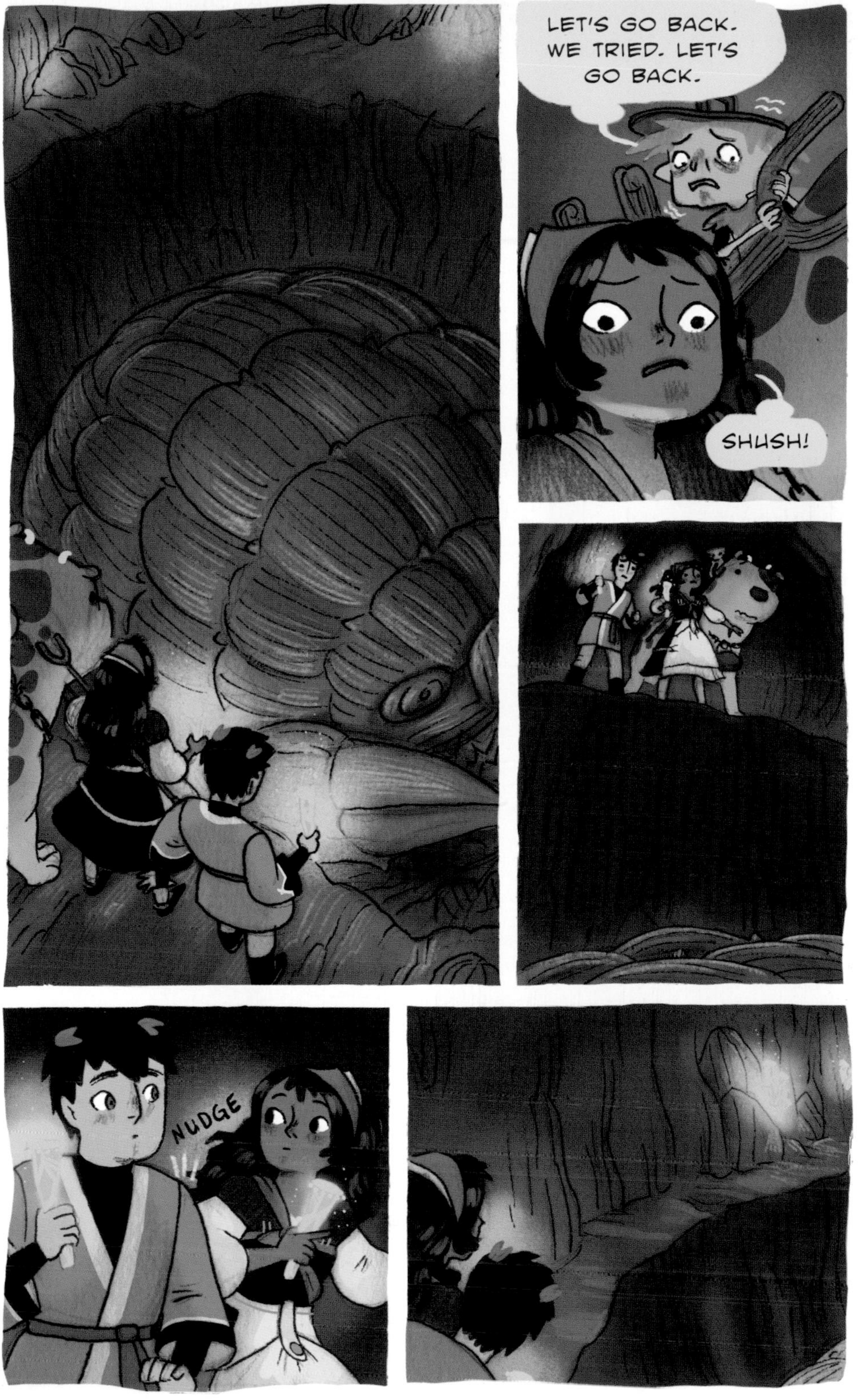
LET'S GO BACK. WE TRIED. LET'S GO BACK.
SHUSH!
NUDGE

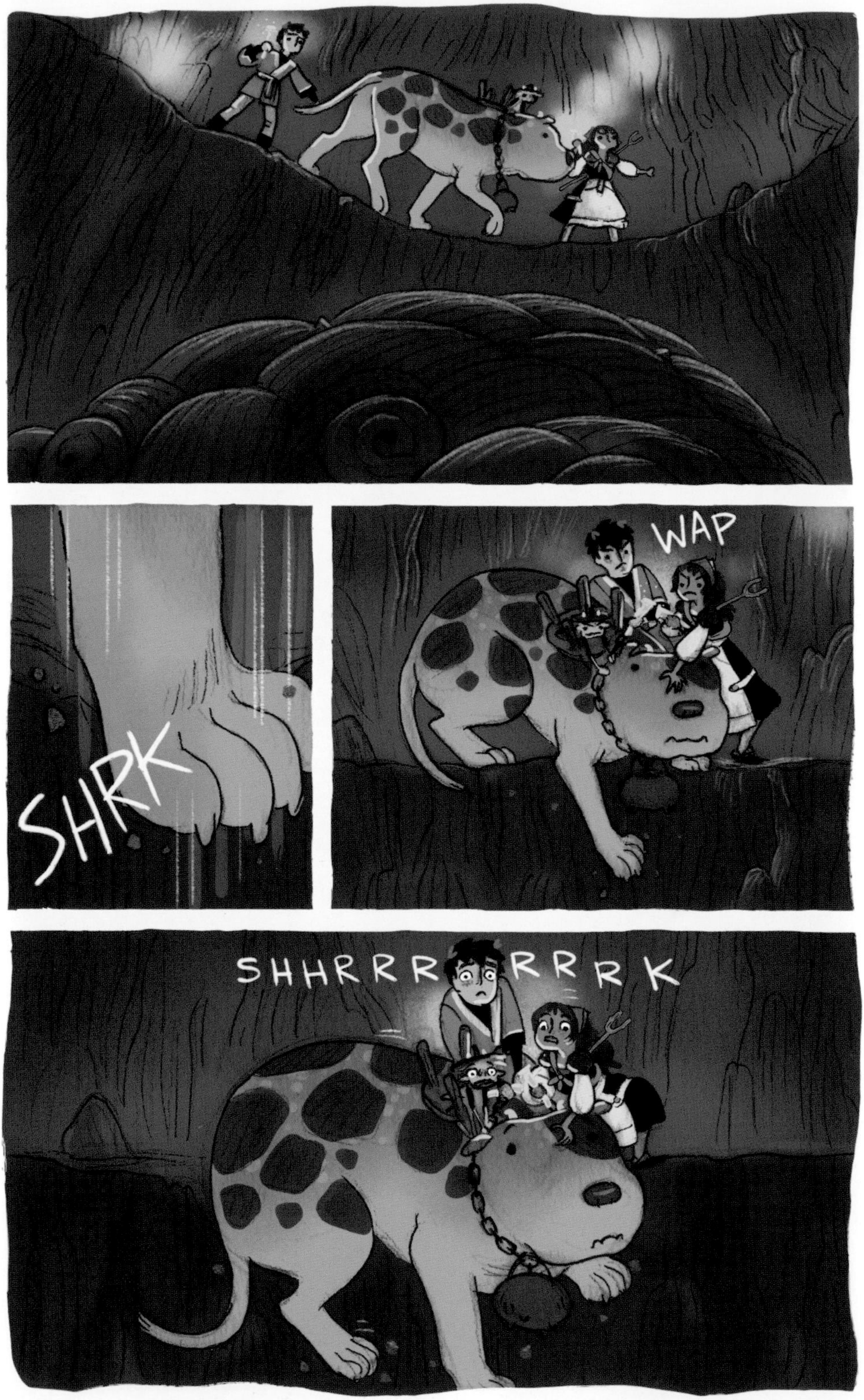
SHRK
WAP
SHHRRRRRRK

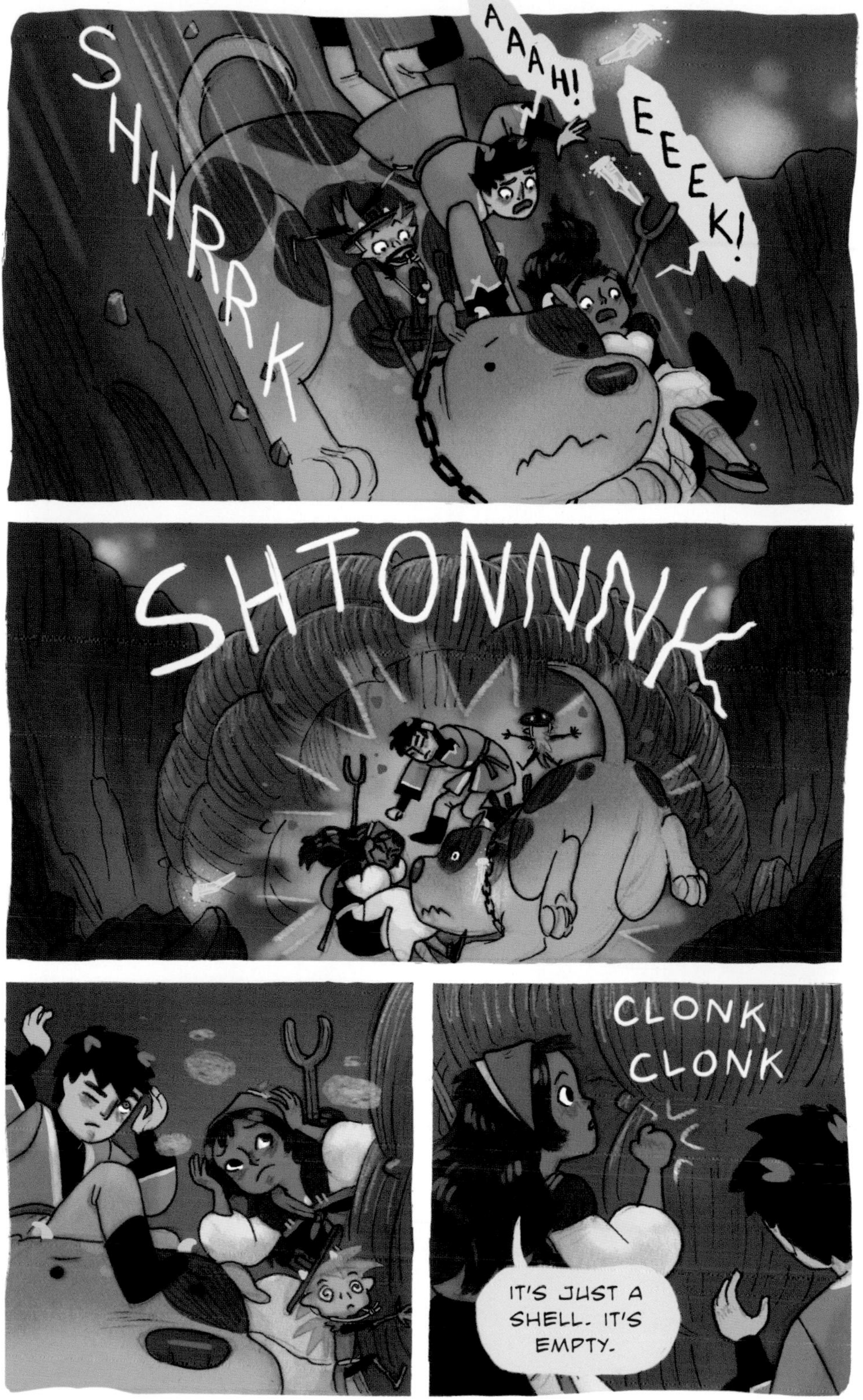
SHHRRK
AAAH!
EEEK!
SHTONNNK
CLONK CLONK
IT'S JUST A SHELL. IT'S EMPTY.

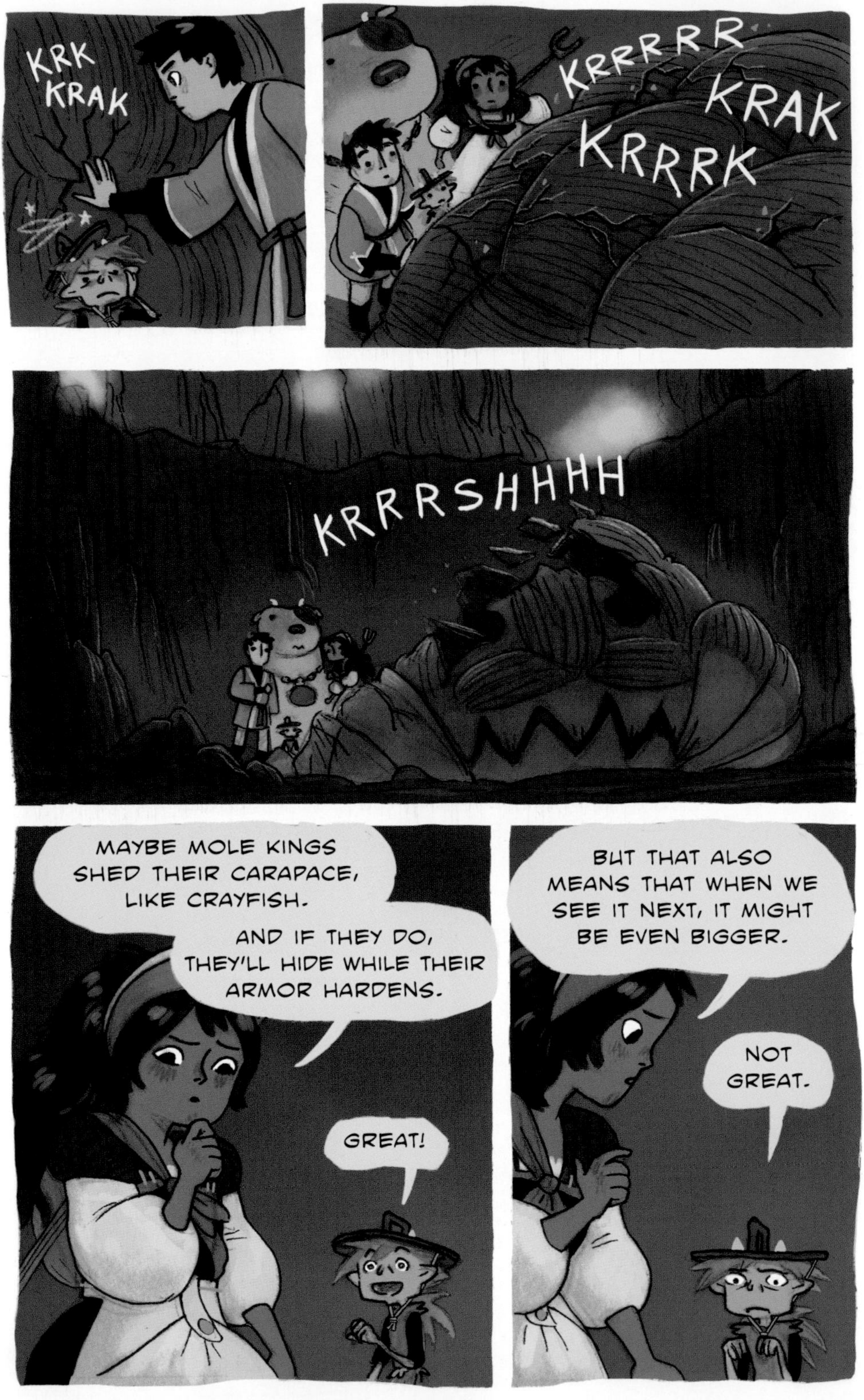
KRK
KRAK
KRRRRR
KRAK
KRRRK
KRRRSHHHH
MAYBE MOLE KINGS SHED THEIR CARAPACE, LIKE CRAYFISH.
AND IF THEY DO, THEY'LL HIDE WHILE THEIR ARMOR HARDENS.
GREAT!
BUT THAT ALSO MEANS THAT WHEN WE SEE IT NEXT, IT MIGHT BE EVEN BIGGER.
NOT GREAT.

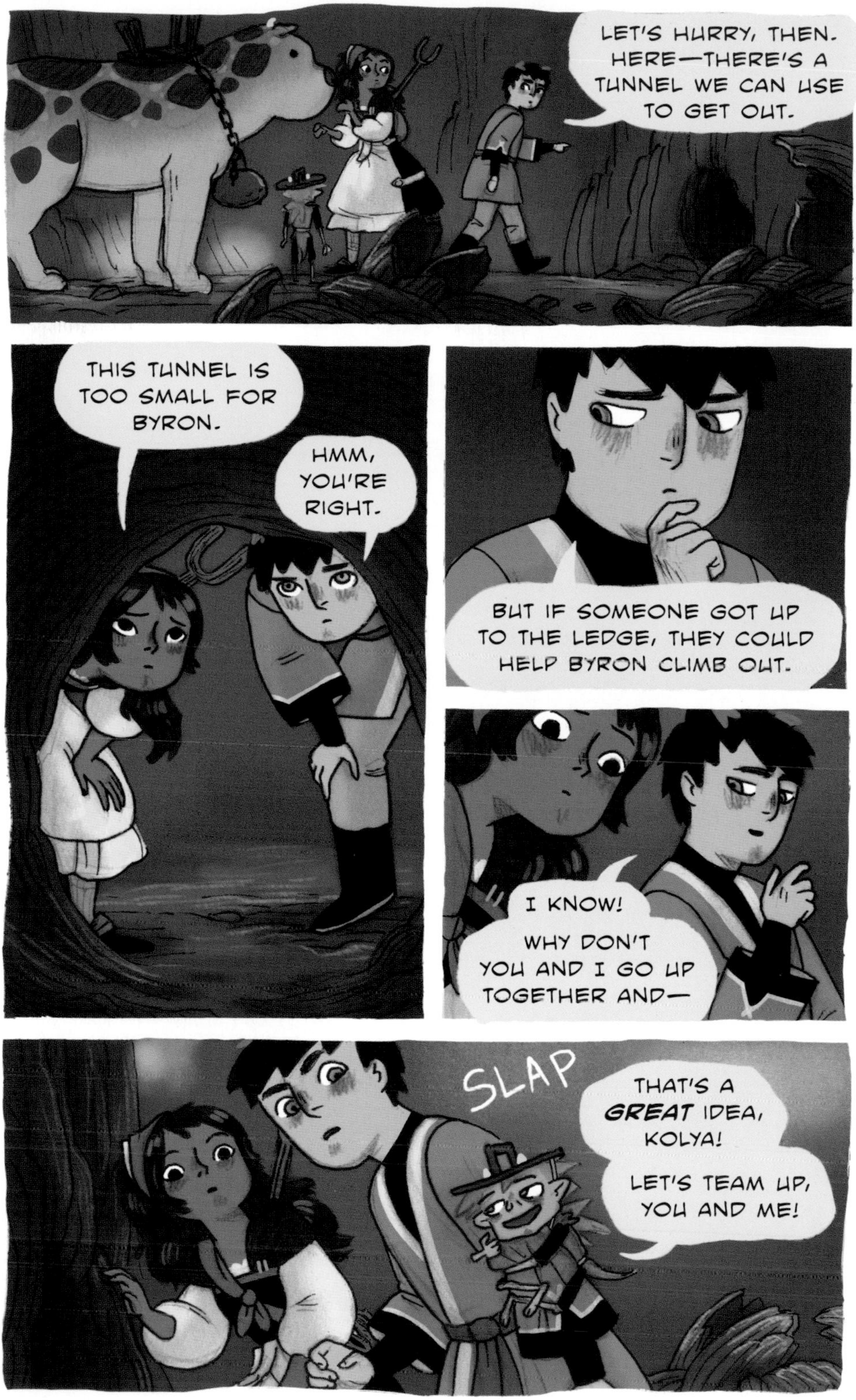
LET'S HURRY, THEN. HERE—THERE'S A TUNNEL WE CAN USE TO GET OUT.
THIS TUNNEL IS TOO SMALL FOR BYRON.
HMM, YOU'RE RIGHT.
BUT IF SOMEONE GOT UP TO THE LEDGE, THEY COULD HELP BYRON CLIMB OUT.
I KNOW!
WHY DON'T YOU AND I GO UP TOGETHER AND—
SLAP
THAT'S A ***GREAT*** IDEA, KOLYA!
LET'S TEAM UP, YOU AND ME!

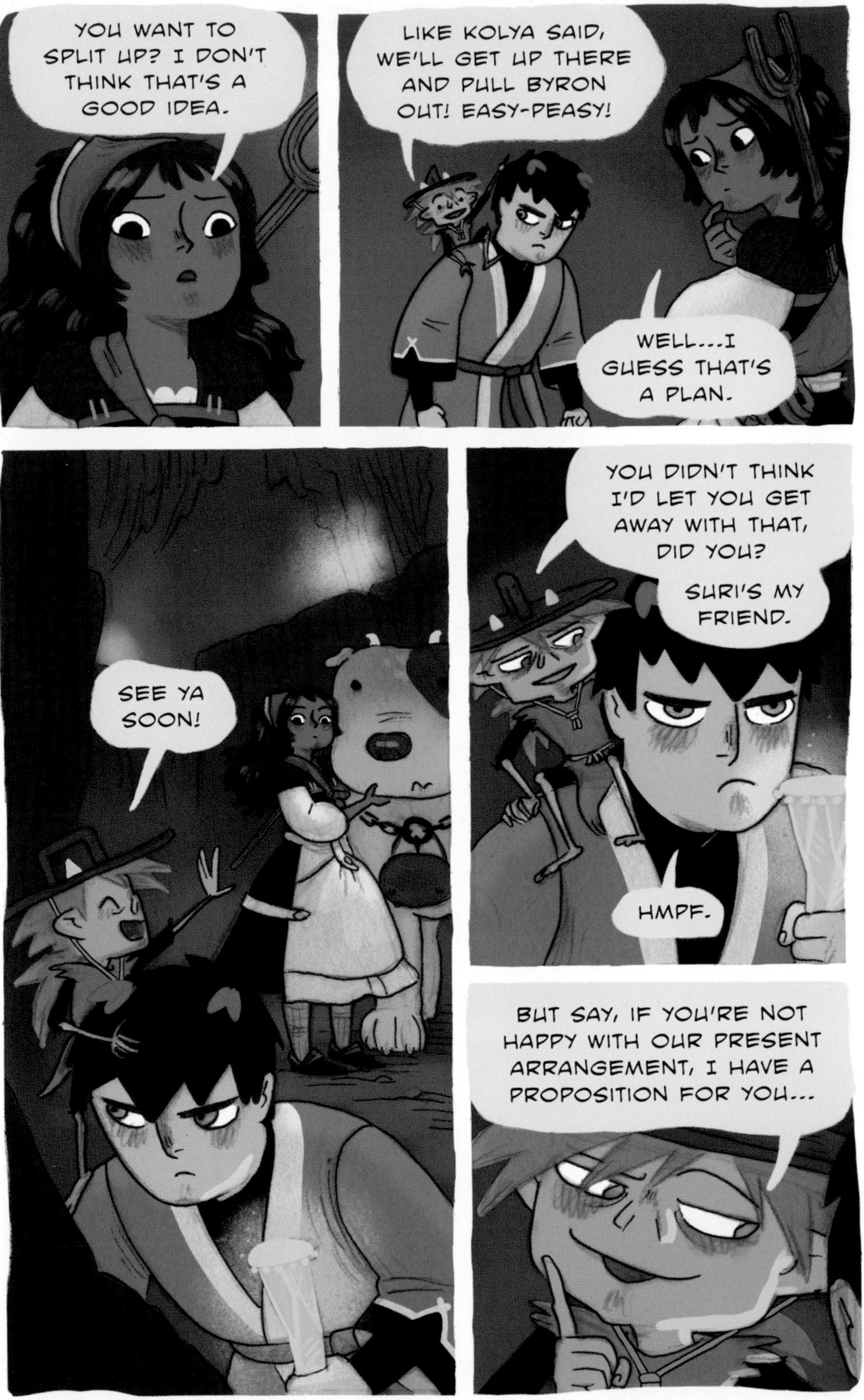
YOU WANT TO SPLIT UP? I DON'T THINK THAT'S A GOOD IDEA.
LIKE KOLYA SAID, WE'LL GET UP THERE AND PULL BYRON OUT! EASY-PEASY!
WELL...I GUESS THAT'S A PLAN.
SEE YA SOON!
YOU DIDN'T THINK I'D LET YOU GET AWAY WITH THAT, DID YOU?
SURI'S MY FRIEND.
HMPF.
BUT SAY, IF YOU'RE NOT HAPPY WITH OUR PRESENT ARRANGEMENT, I HAVE A PROPOSITION FOR YOU...

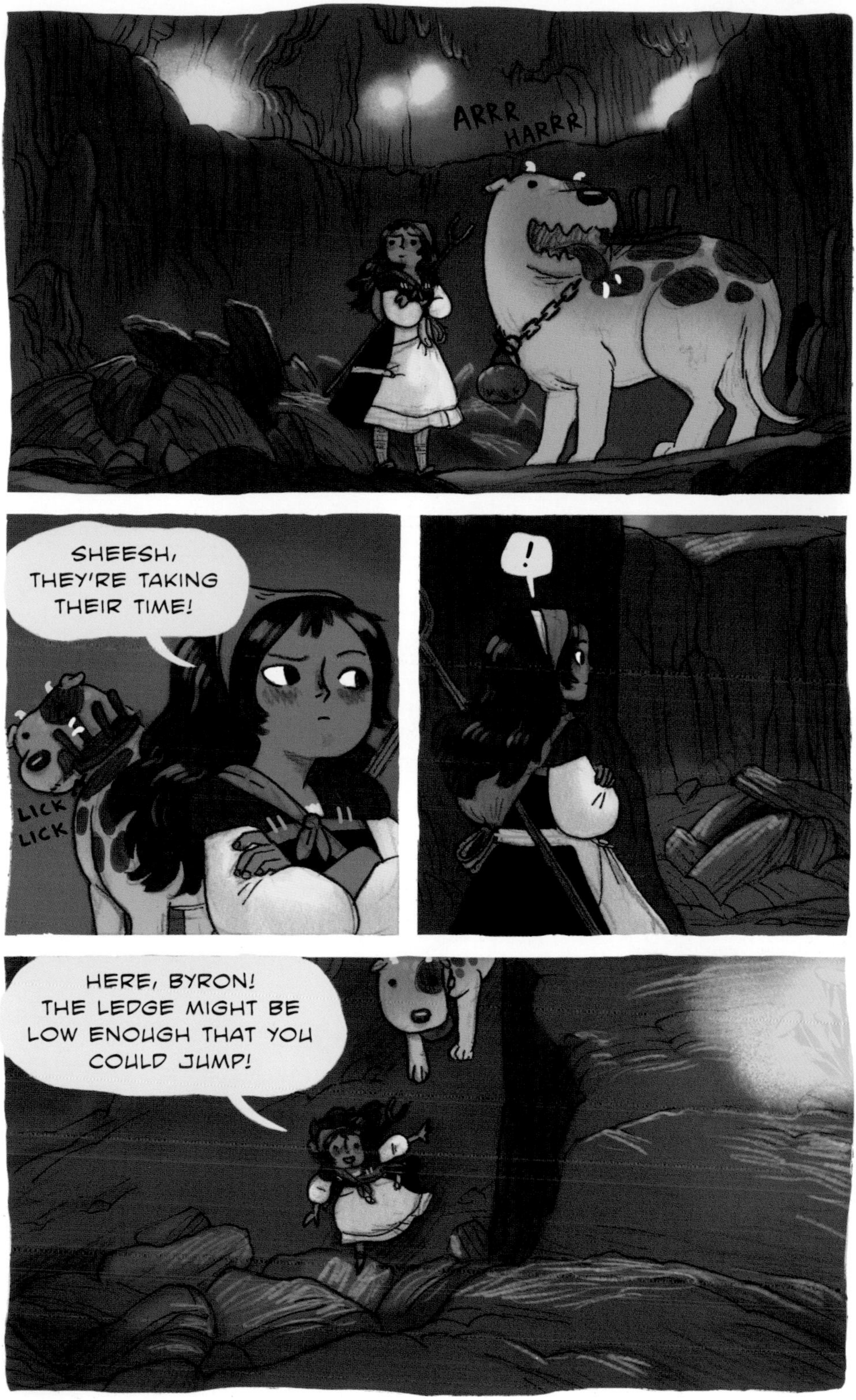
ARRR
HARRR
SHEESH, THEY'RE TAKING THEIR TIME!
LICK
LICK
!
HERE, BYRON! THE LEDGE MIGHT BE LOW ENOUGH THAT YOU COULD JUMP!

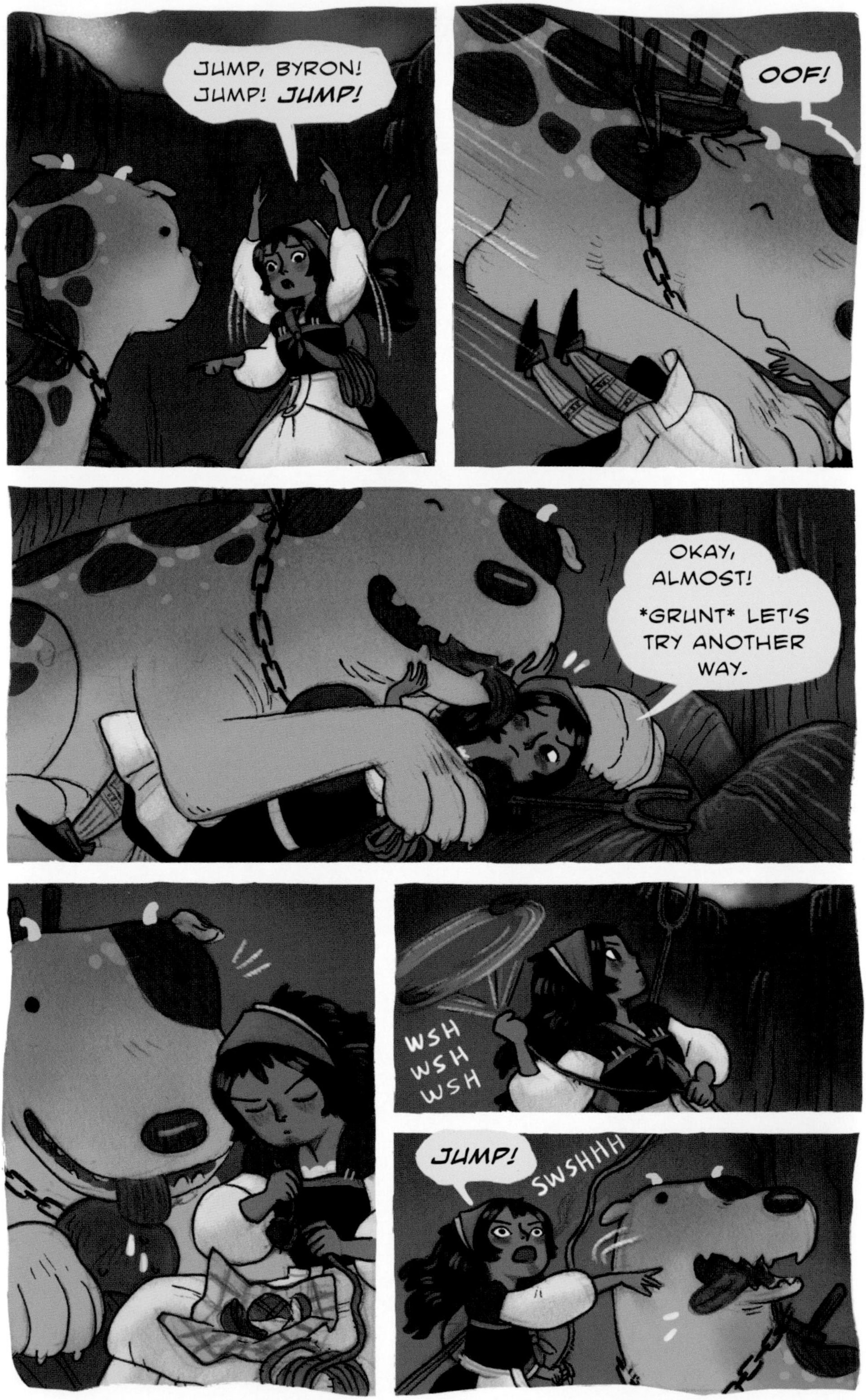
JUMP, BYRON! JUMP! JUMP!
OOF!
OKAY, ALMOST!
GRUNT LET'S TRY ANOTHER WAY.
WSH WSH WSH
JUMP!
SWSHHH

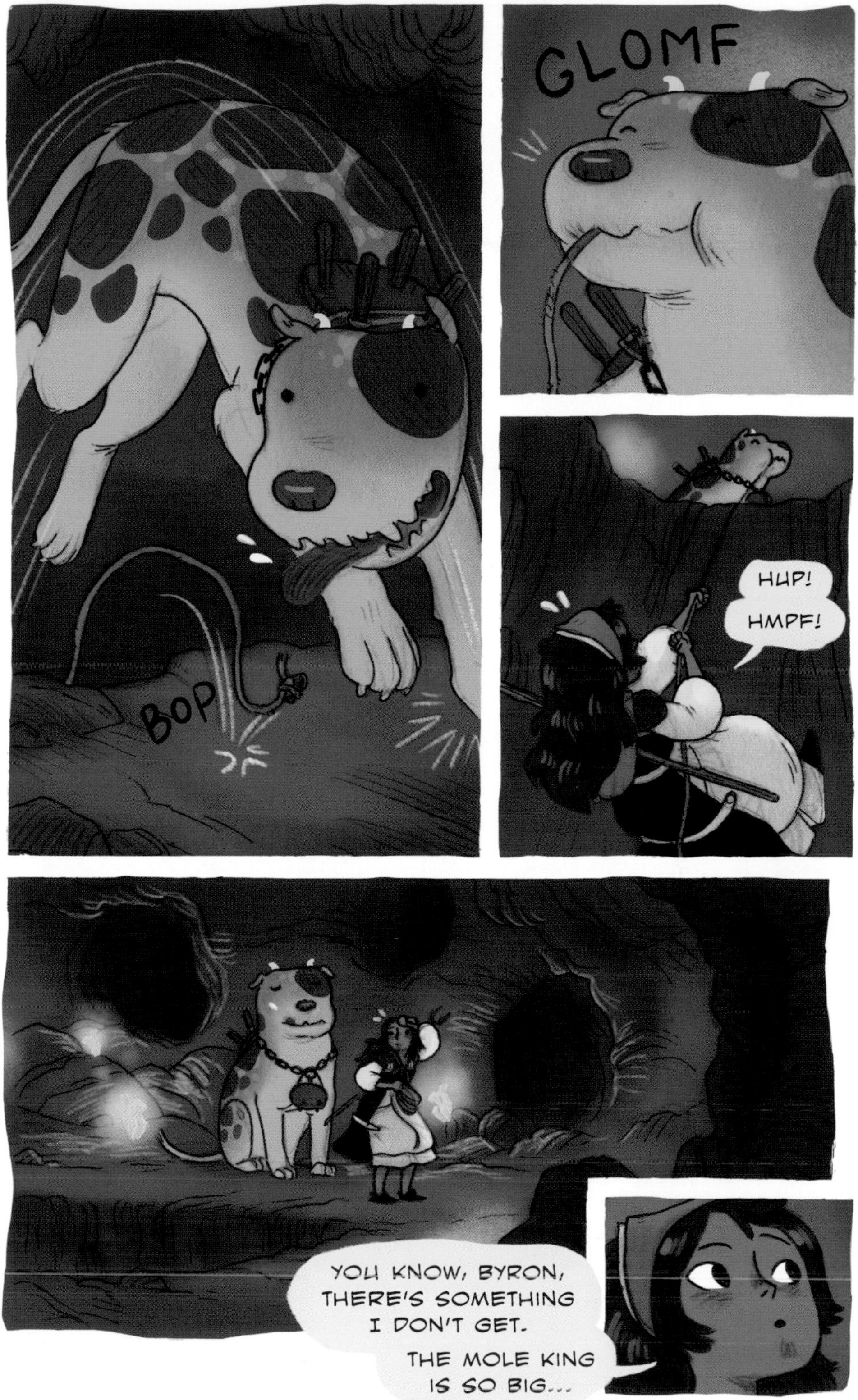
GLOMF
BOP
HUP!
HMPF!
YOU KNOW, BYRON, THERE'S SOMETHING I DON'T GET.
THE MOLE KING IS SO BIG...

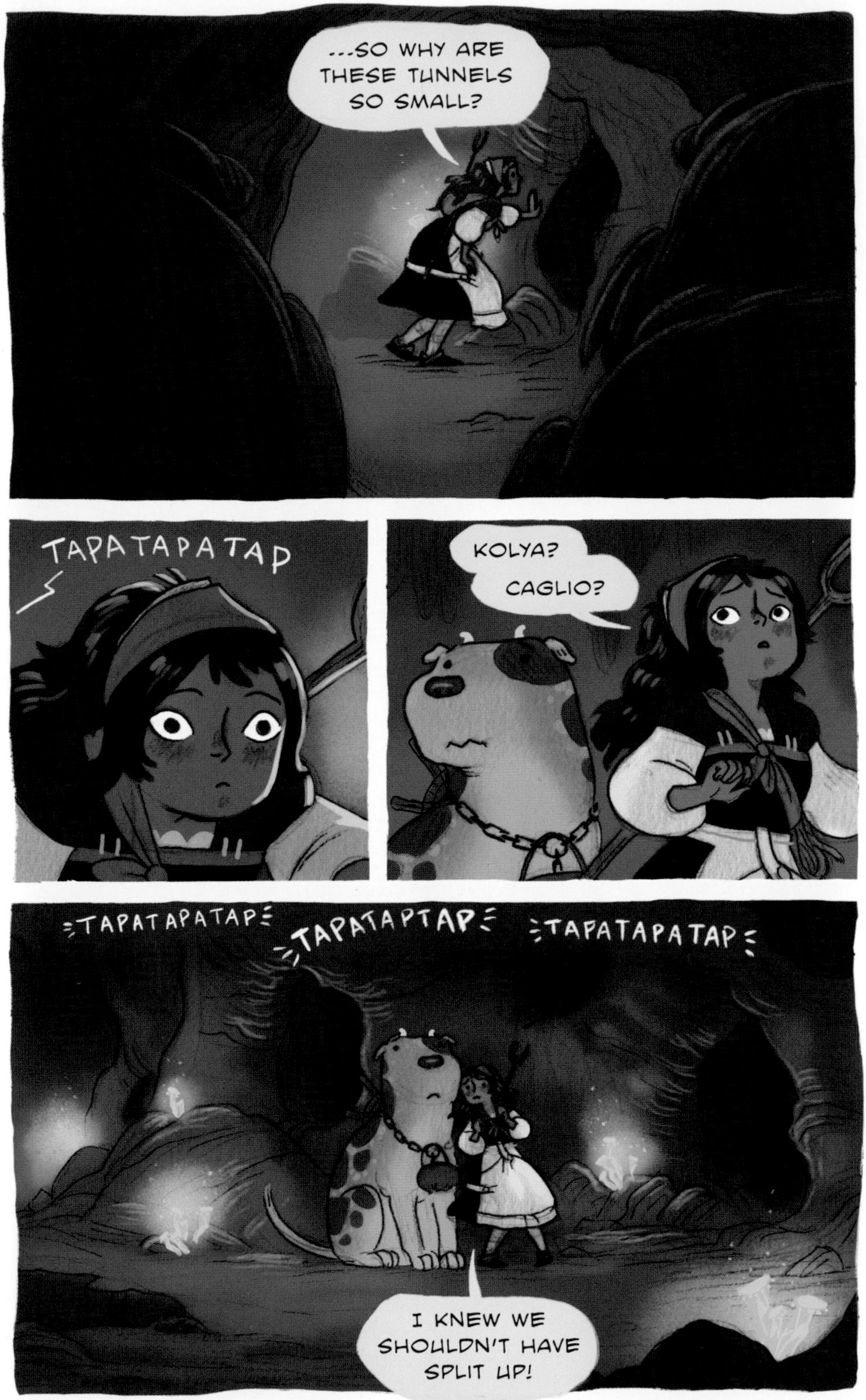
...SO WHY ARE THESE TUNNELS SO SMALL?
TAPATAPATAP
KOLYA?
CAGLIO?
TAPATAPATAP
TAPATAPTAP
TAPATAPATAP
I KNEW WE SHOULDN'T HAVE SPLIT UP!

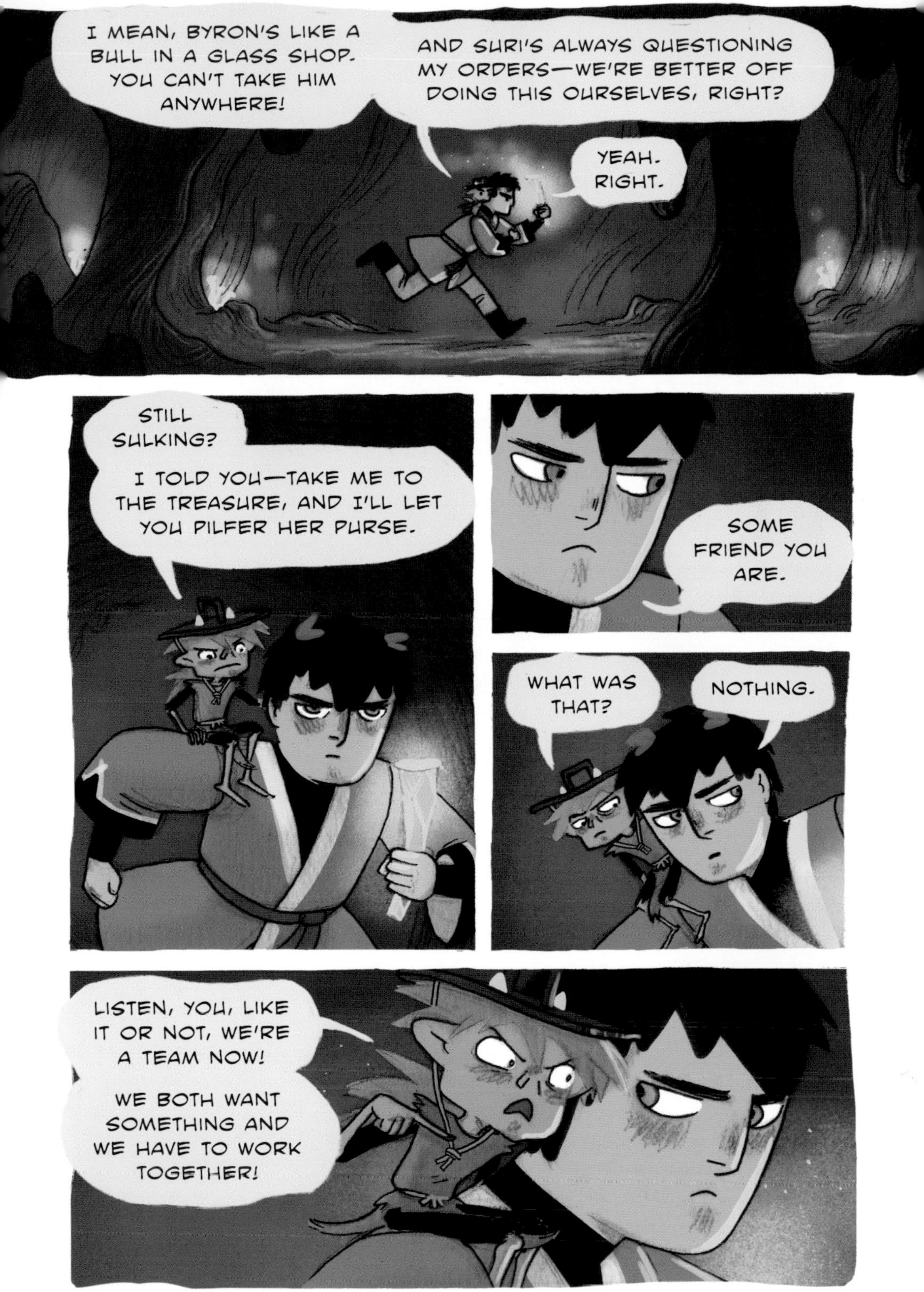
I MEAN, BYRON'S LIKE A BULL IN A GLASS SHOP. YOU CAN'T TAKE HIM ANYWHERE!
AND SURI'S ALWAYS QUESTIONING MY ORDERS—WE'RE BETTER OFF DOING THIS OURSELVES, RIGHT?
YEAH. RIGHT.
STILL SULKING?
I TOLD YOU—TAKE ME TO THE TREASURE, AND I'LL LET YOU PILFER HER PURSE.
SOME FRIEND YOU ARE.
WHAT WAS THAT?
NOTHING.
LISTEN, YOU, LIKE IT OR NOT, WE'RE A TEAM NOW!
WE BOTH WANT SOMETHING AND WE HAVE TO WORK TOGETHER!

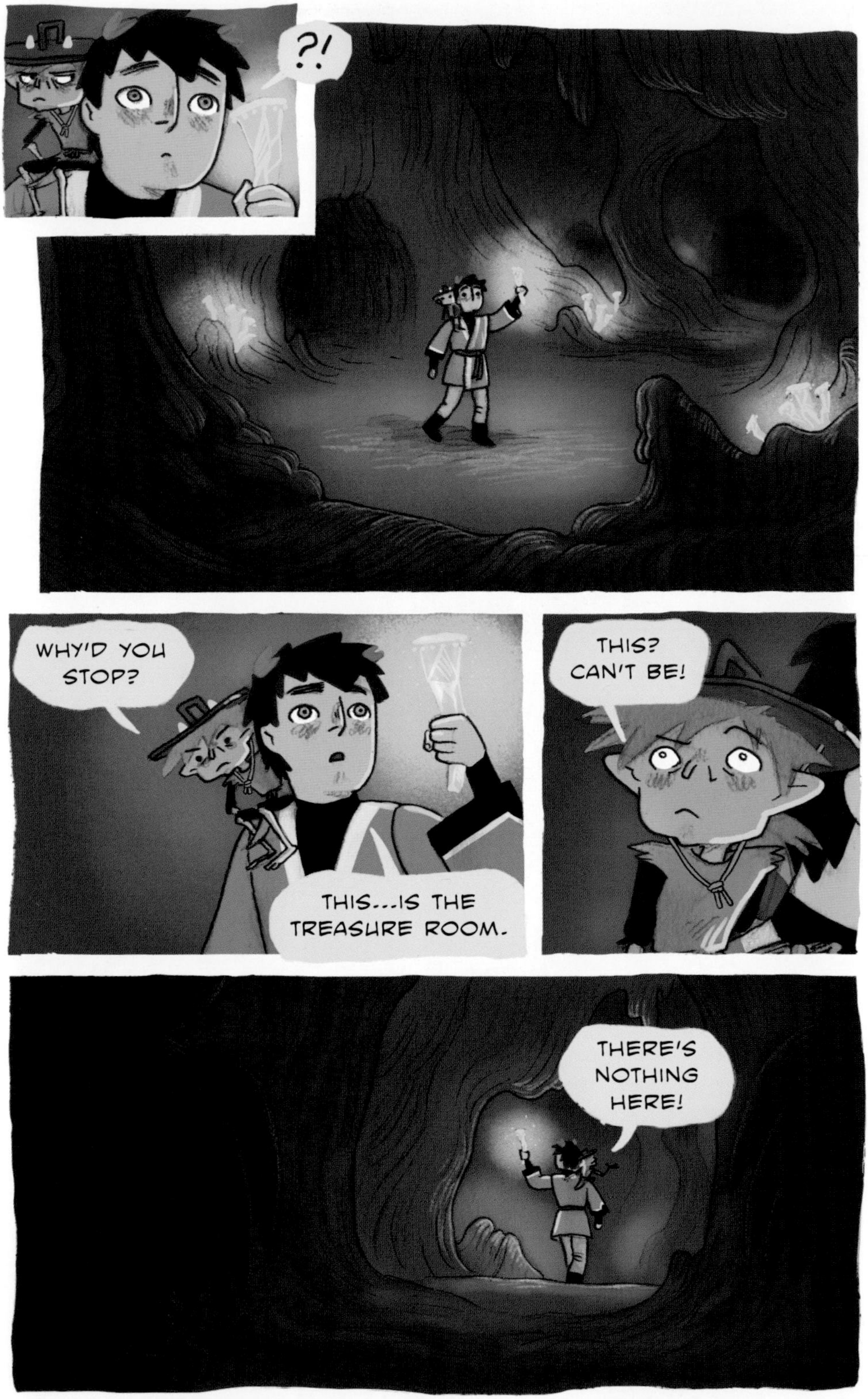
?!
WHY'D YOU STOP?
THIS...IS THE TREASURE ROOM.
THIS? CAN'T BE!
THERE'S NOTHING HERE!

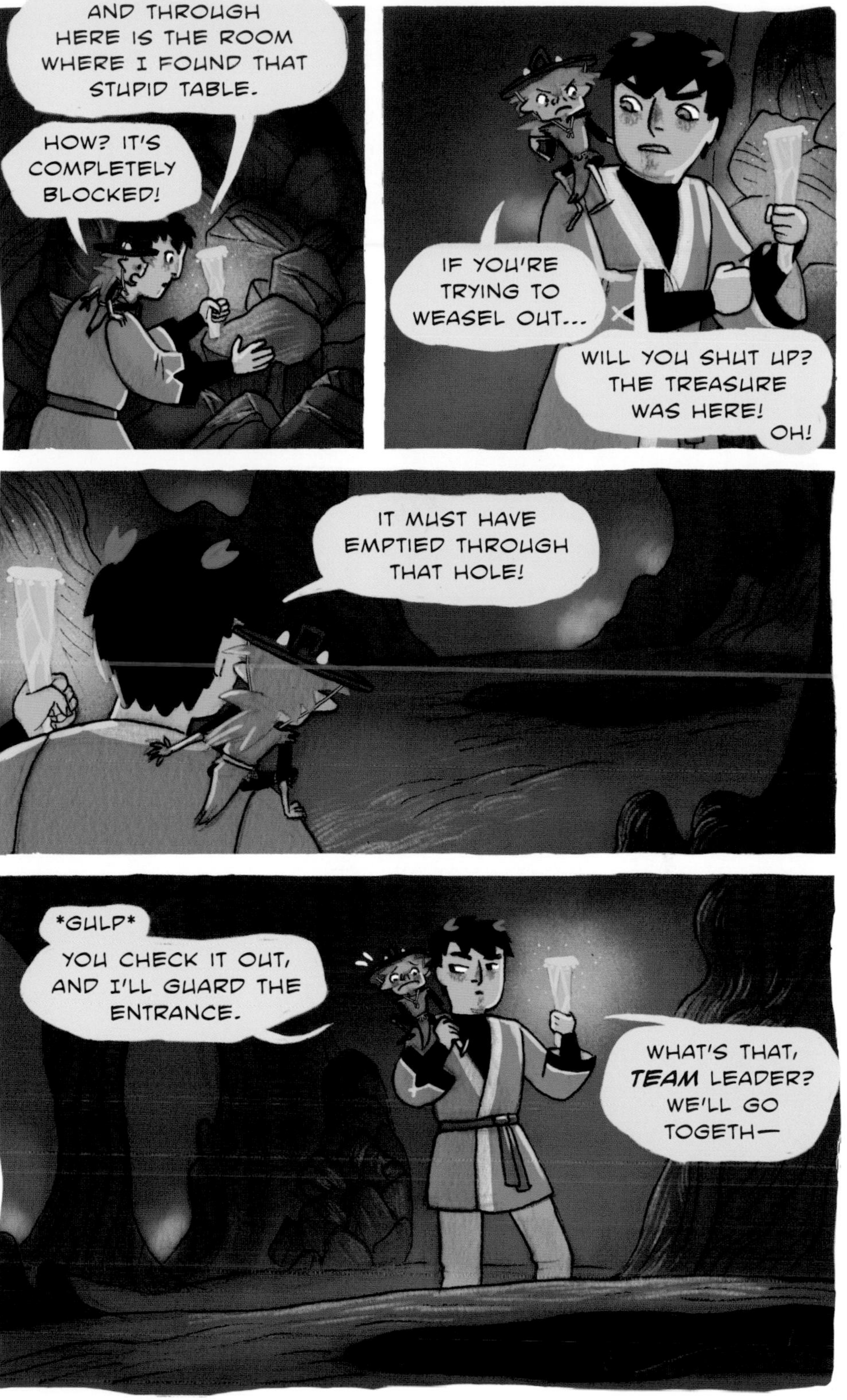
AND THROUGH HERE IS THE ROOM WHERE I FOUND THAT STUPID TABLE.
HOW? IT'S COMPLETELY BLOCKED!
IF YOU'RE TRYING TO WEASEL OUT...
WILL YOU SHUT UP? THE TREASURE WAS HERE!
OH!
IT MUST HAVE EMPTIED THROUGH THAT HOLE!
GULP
YOU CHECK IT OUT, AND I'LL GUARD THE ENTRANCE.
WHAT'S THAT, TEAM LEADER? WE'LL GO TOGETH—

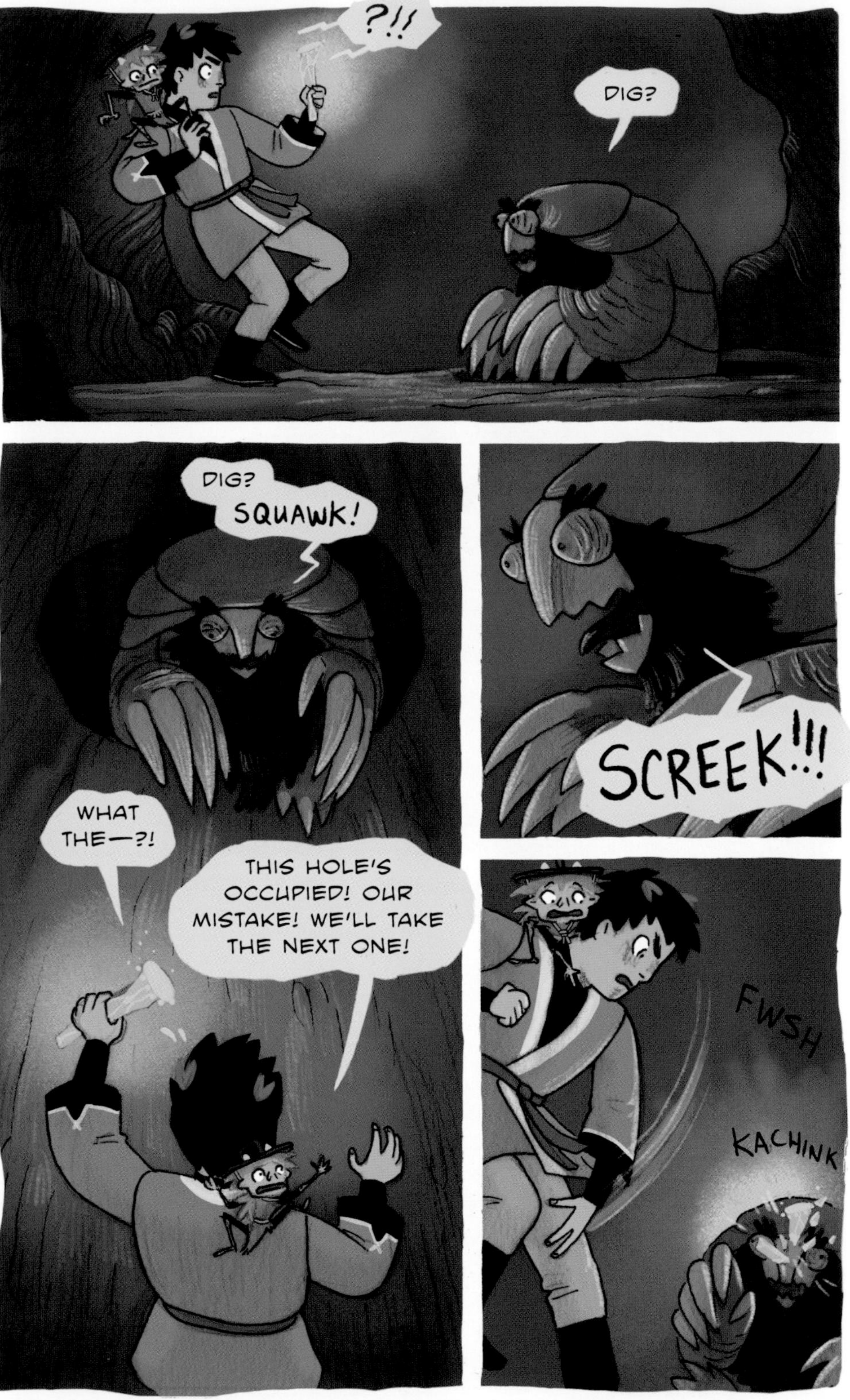
?!!
DIG?
DIG? SQUAWK!
SCREEK!!!
WHAT THE—?!
THIS HOLE'S OCCUPIED! OUR MISTAKE! WE'LL TAKE THE NEXT ONE!
FWSH
KACHINK

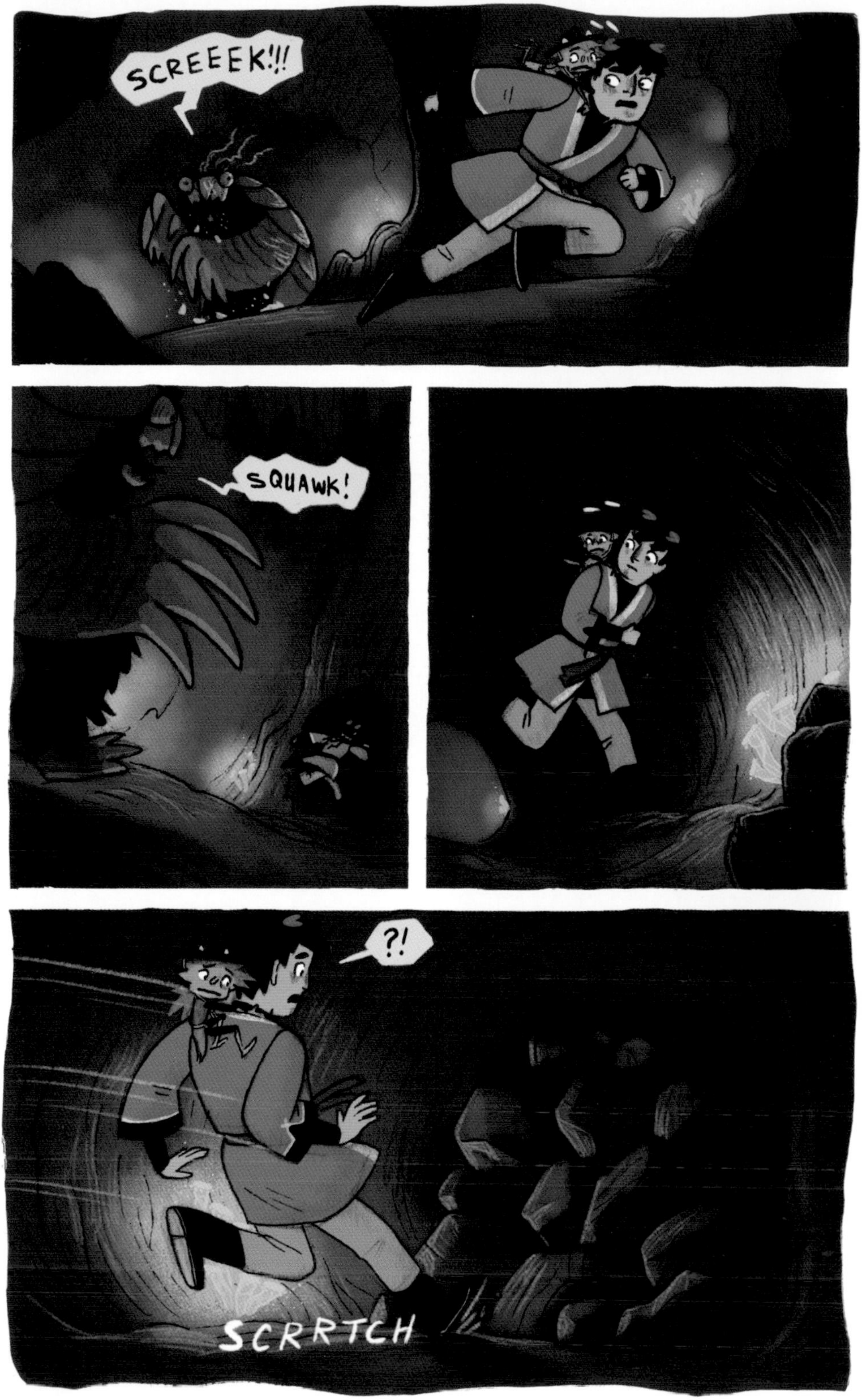
SCREEEK!!!
SQUAWK!
?!
SCRRTCH

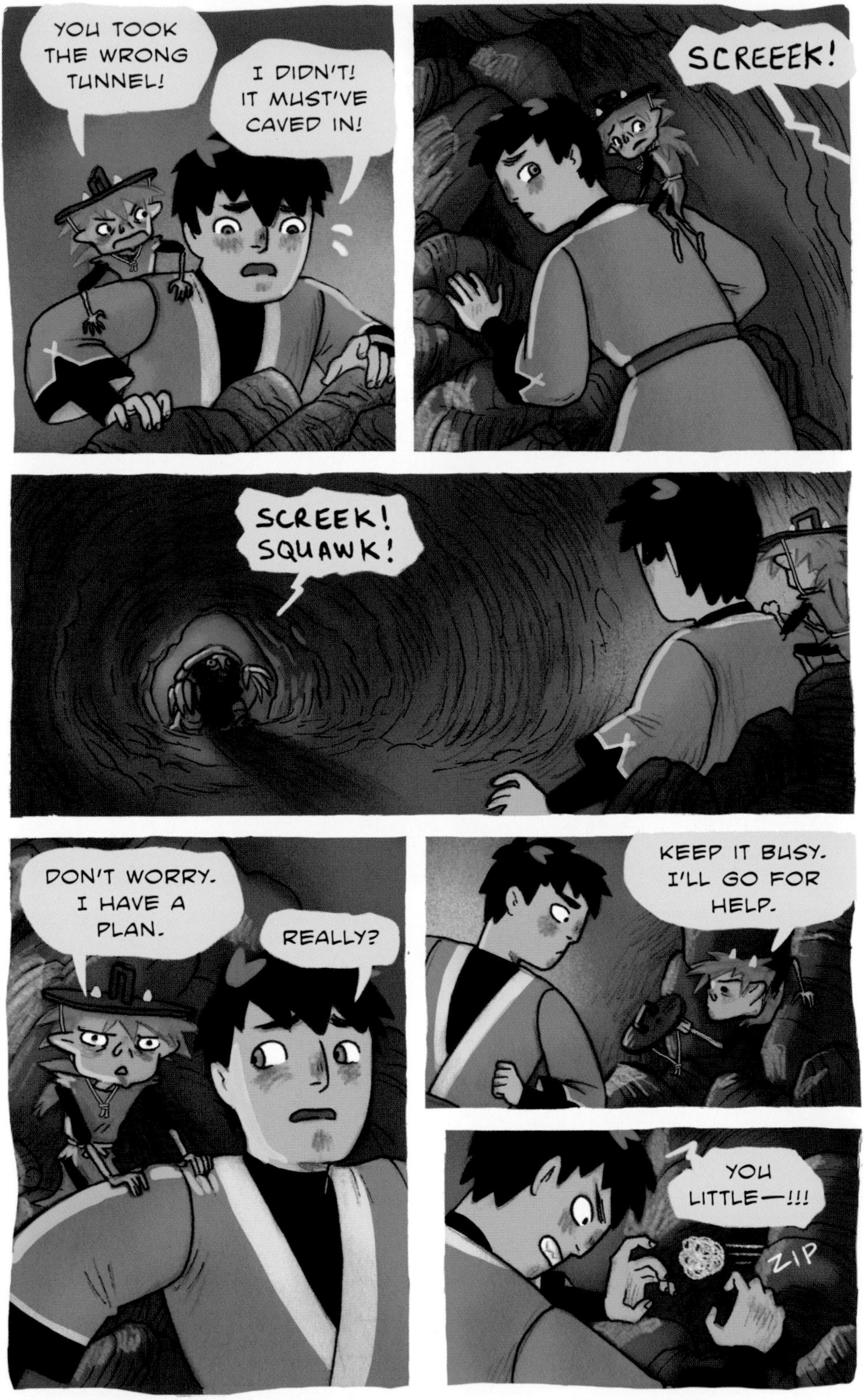
YOU TOOK THE WRONG TUNNEL!
I DIDN'T! IT MUST'VE CAVED IN!
SCREEEK!
SCREEK! SQUAWK!
DON'T WORRY. I HAVE A PLAN.
REALLY?
KEEP IT BUSY. I'LL GO FOR HELP.
YOU LITTLE—!!!
ZIP

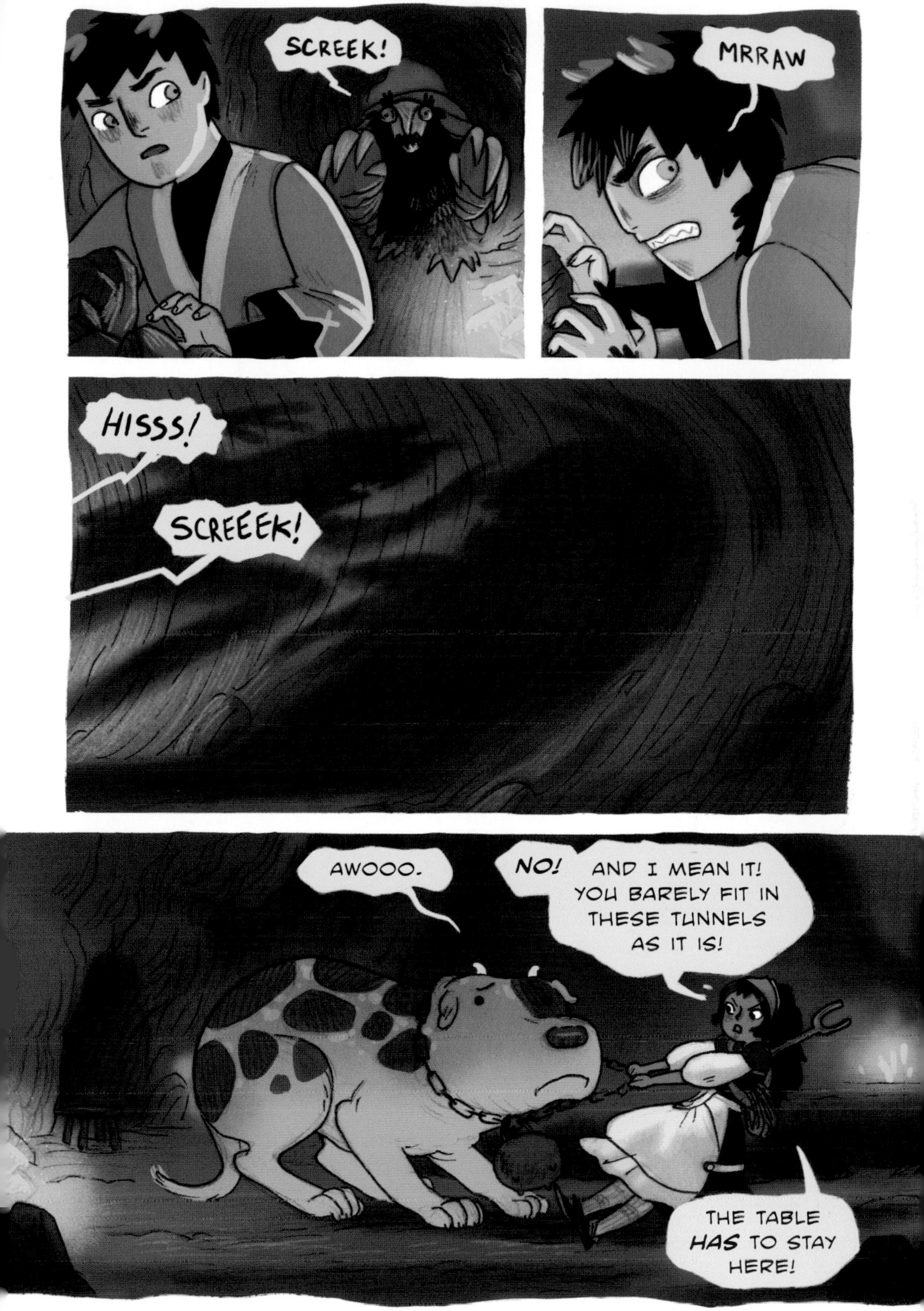
SCREEK!
MRRAW
HISSS!
SCREEEK!
AWOOO.
NO! AND I MEAN IT! YOU BARELY FIT IN THESE TUNNELS AS IT IS!
THE TABLE HAS TO STAY HERE!

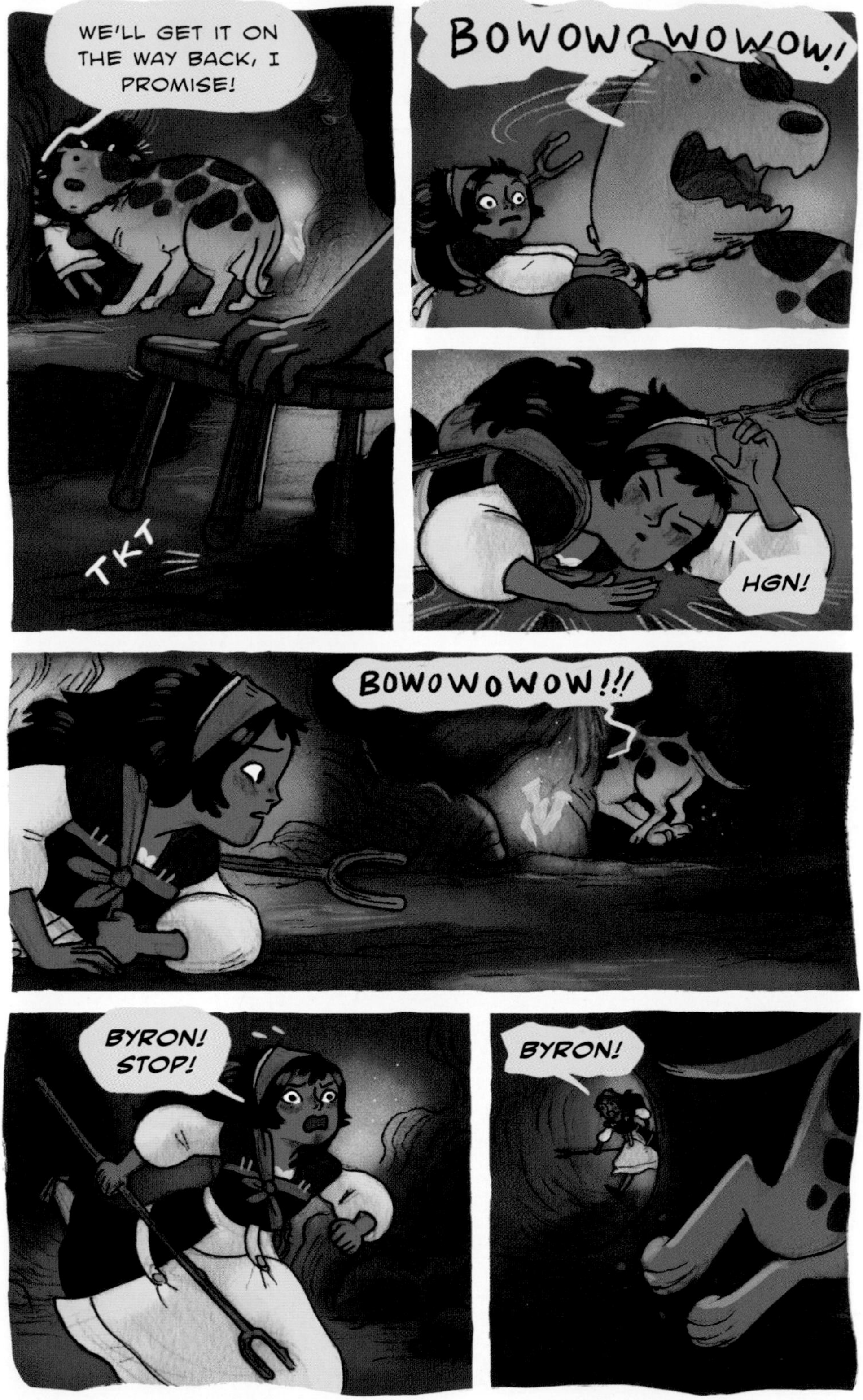
WE'LL GET IT ON THE WAY BACK, I PROMISE!
TKT
BOWOWOWOWOWOW!
HGN!
BOWOWOWOW!!!
BYRON! STOP!
BYRON!

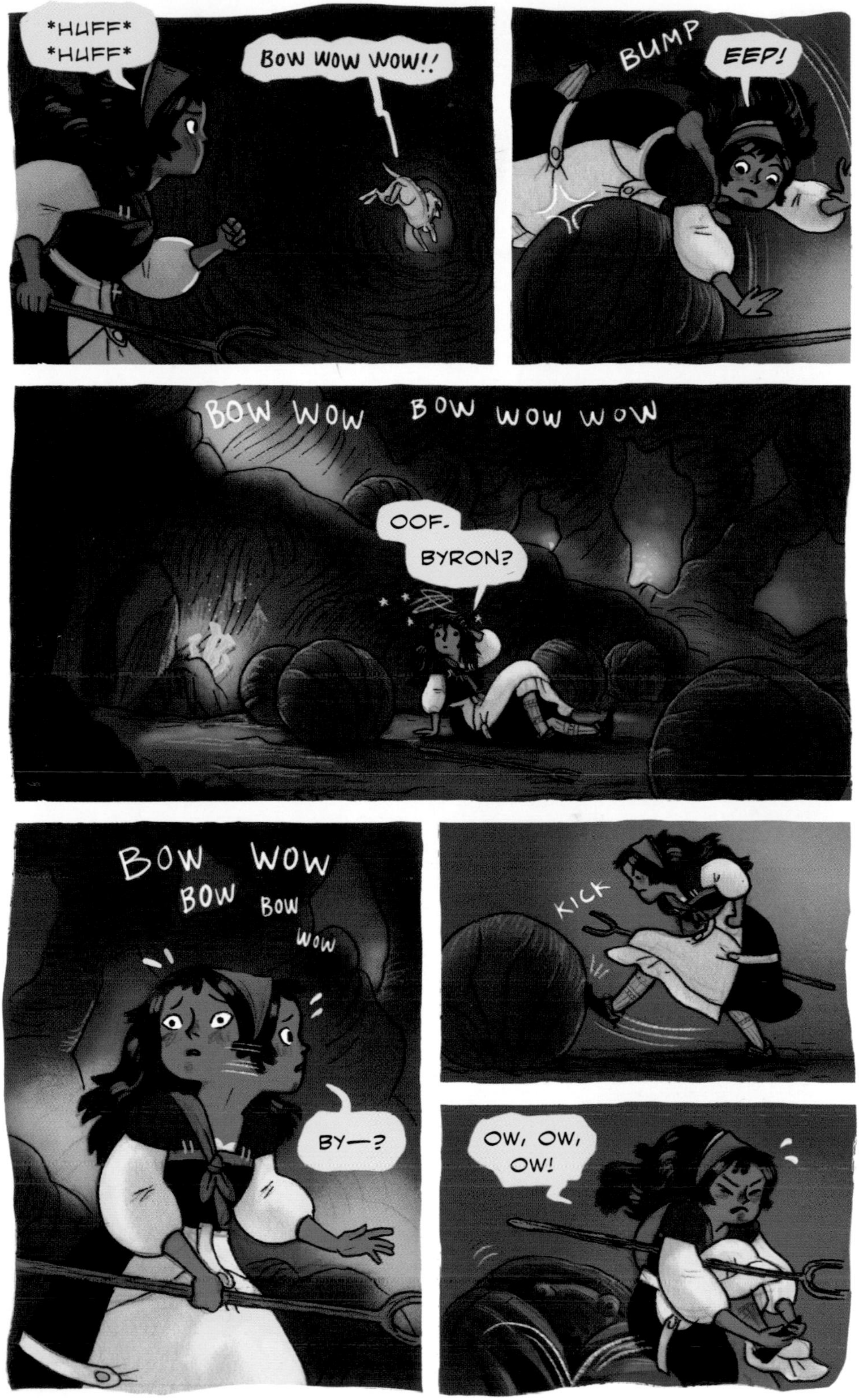
HUFF
HUFF
BOW WOW WOW!!
BUMP
EEP!
BOW WOW BOW WOW WOW WOW
OOF-
BYRON?
BOW WOW
BOW BOW
WOW
BY—?
KICK
OW, OW,
OW!

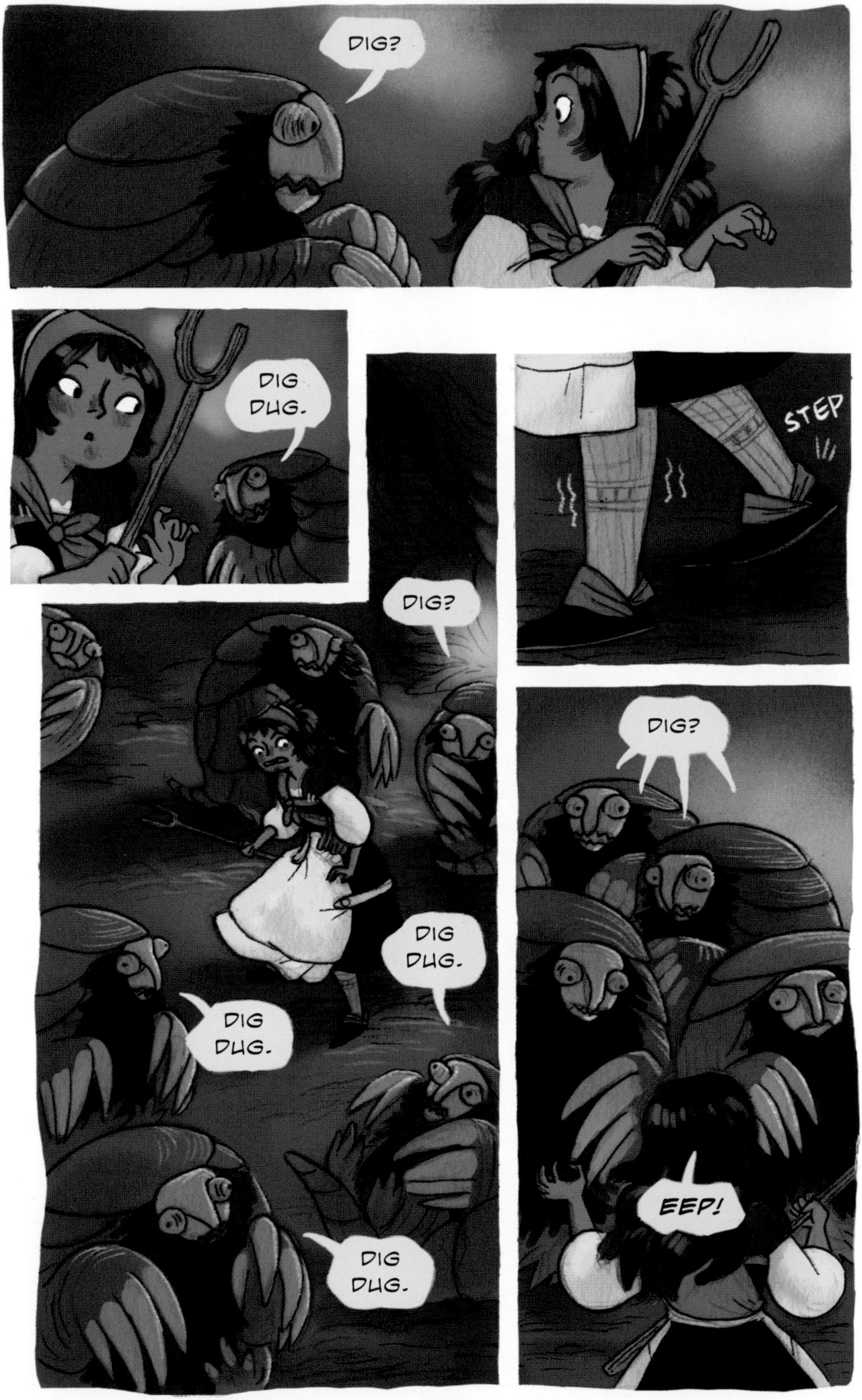
DIG?
DIG DUG.
STEP
DIG?
DIG DUG.
DIG DUG.
DIG DUG.
DIG?
EEP!

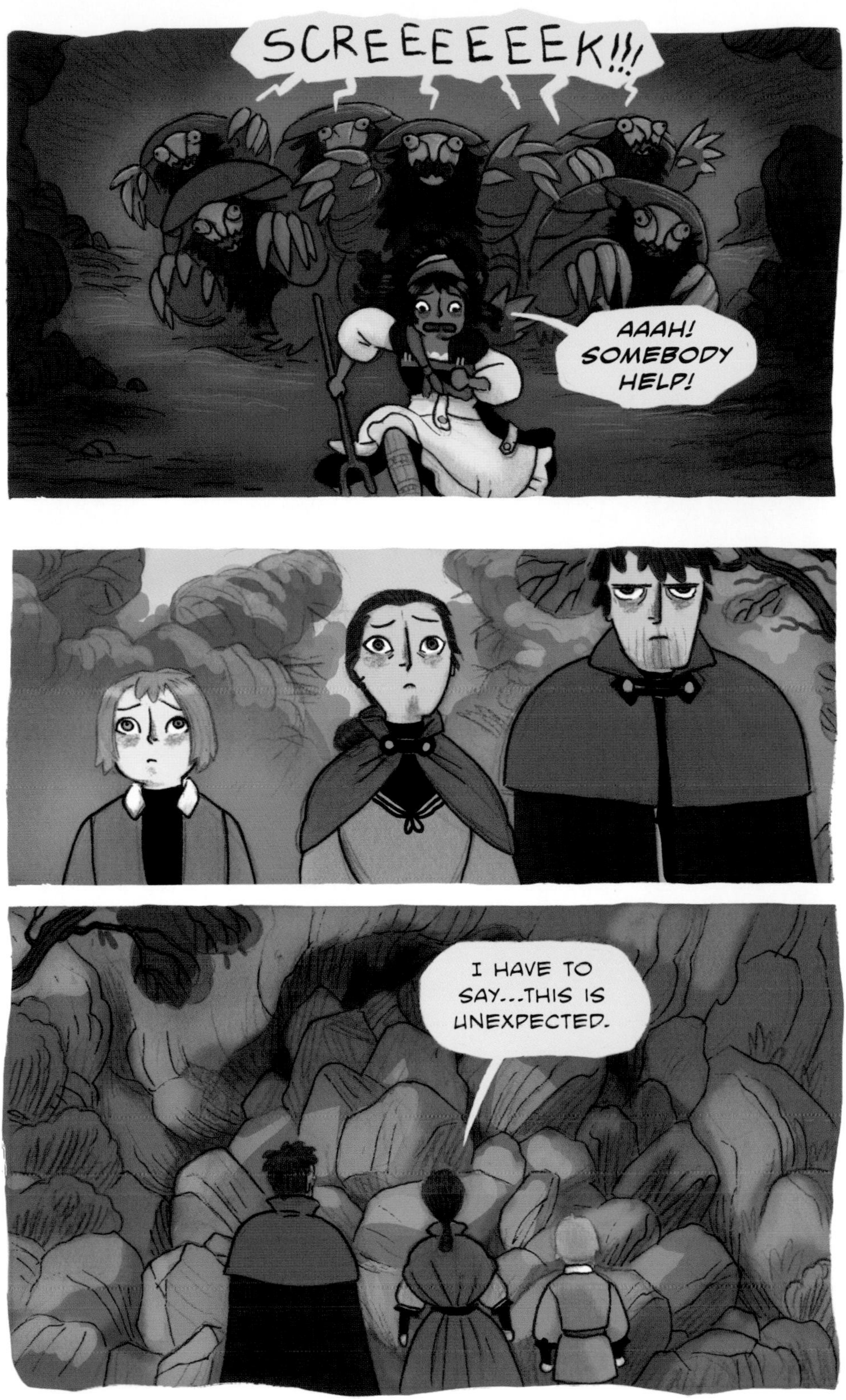
SCREEEEEEEK!!!
AAAH! SOMEBODY HELP!
I HAVE TO SAY...THIS IS UNEXPECTED.

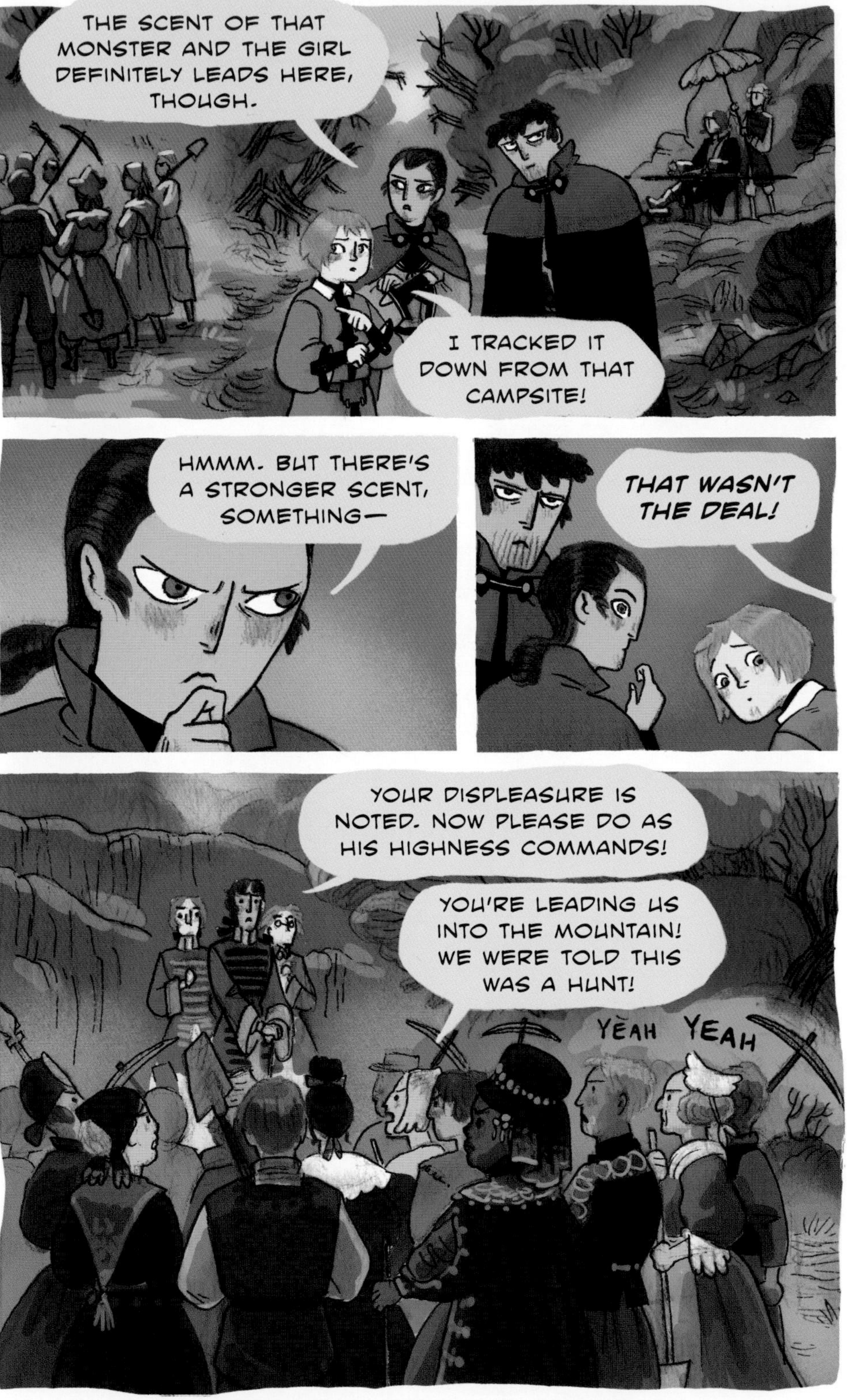
THE SCENT OF THAT MONSTER AND THE GIRL DEFINITELY LEADS HERE, THOUGH.
I TRACKED IT DOWN FROM THAT CAMPSITE!
HMMM. BUT THERE'S A STRONGER SCENT, SOMETHING—
THAT WASN'T THE DEAL!
YOUR DISPLEASURE IS NOTED. NOW PLEASE DO AS HIS HIGHNESS COMMANDS!
YOU'RE LEADING US INTO THE MOUNTAIN! WE WERE TOLD THIS WAS A HUNT!
YEAH
YEAH

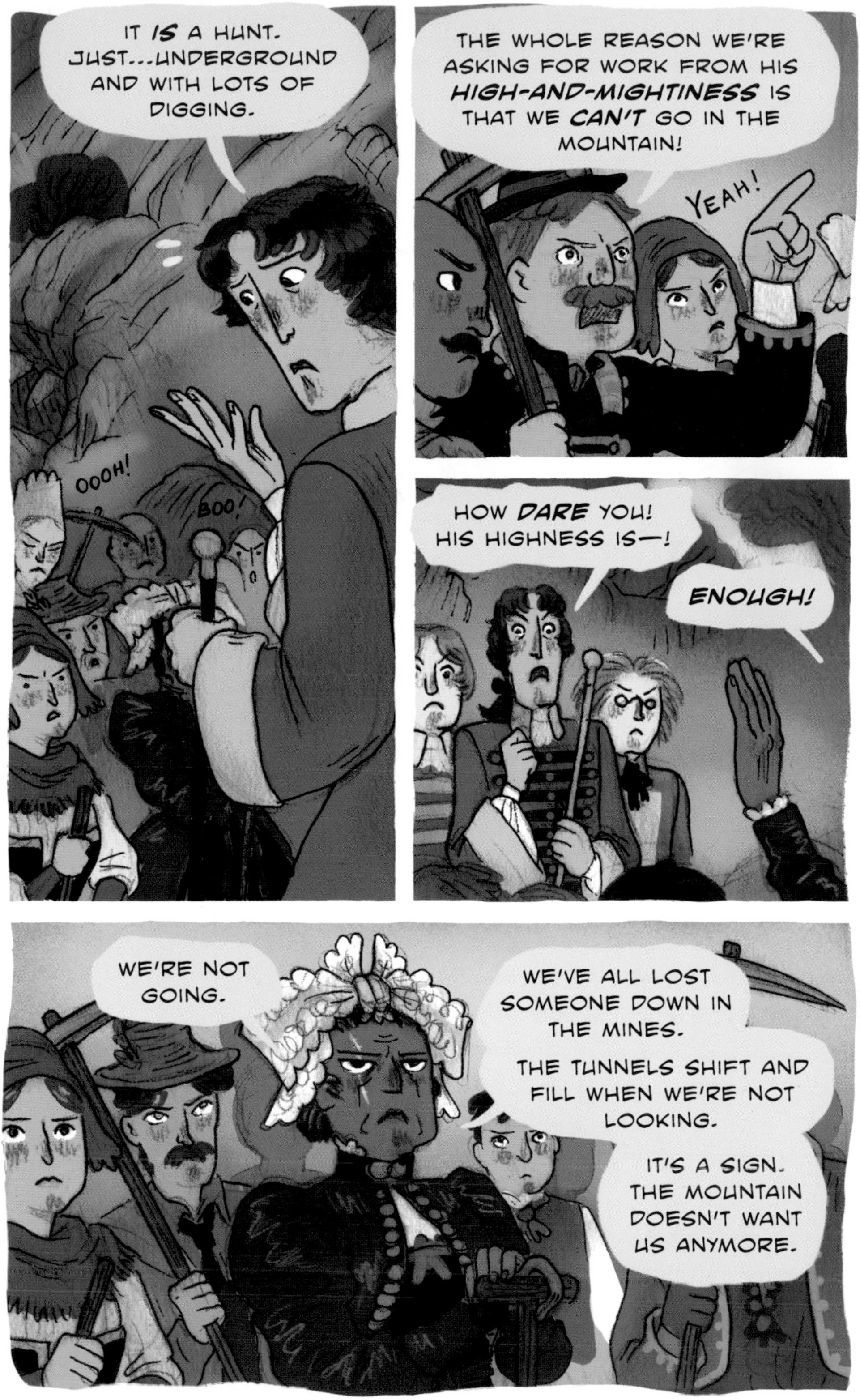
IT *IS* A HUNT. JUST...UNDERGROUND AND WITH LOTS OF DIGGING.
OOOH!
BOO!
THE WHOLE REASON WE'RE ASKING FOR WORK FROM HIS *HIGH-AND-MIGHTINESS* IS THAT WE *CAN'T* GO IN THE MOUNTAIN!
YEAH!
HOW *DARE* YOU! HIS HIGHNESS IS—!
ENOUGH!
WE'RE NOT GOING.
WE'VE ALL LOST SOMEONE DOWN IN THE MINES.
THE TUNNELS SHIFT AND FILL WHEN WE'RE NOT LOOKING.
IT'S A SIGN. THE MOUNTAIN DOESN'T WANT US ANYMORE.

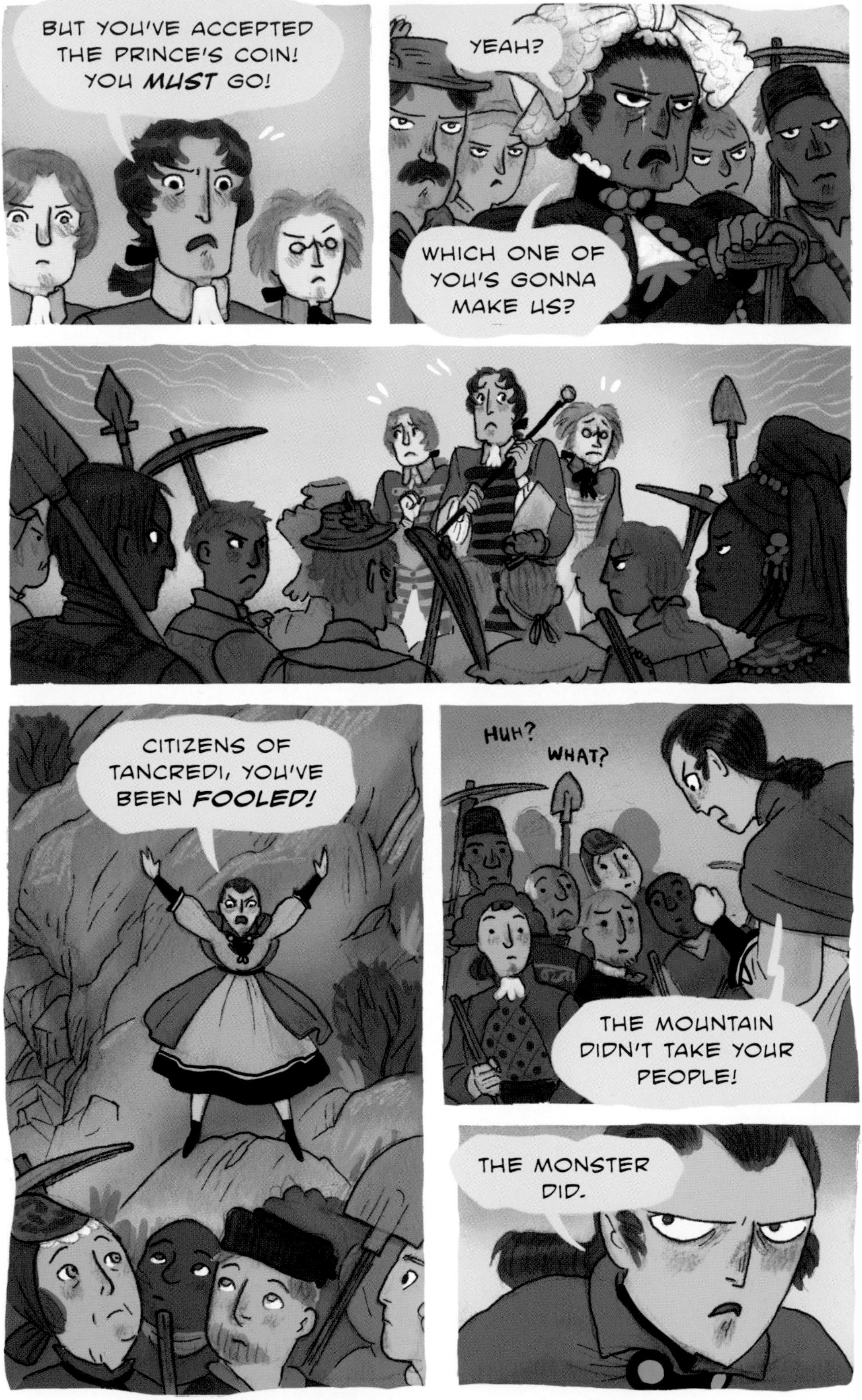
BUT YOU'VE ACCEPTED THE PRINCE'S COIN! YOU *MUST* GO!
YEAH?
WHICH ONE OF YOU'S GONNA MAKE US?
CITIZENS OF TANCREDI, YOU'VE BEEN *FOOLED*!
HUH?
WHAT?
THE MOUNTAIN DIDN'T TAKE YOUR PEOPLE!
THE MONSTER DID.

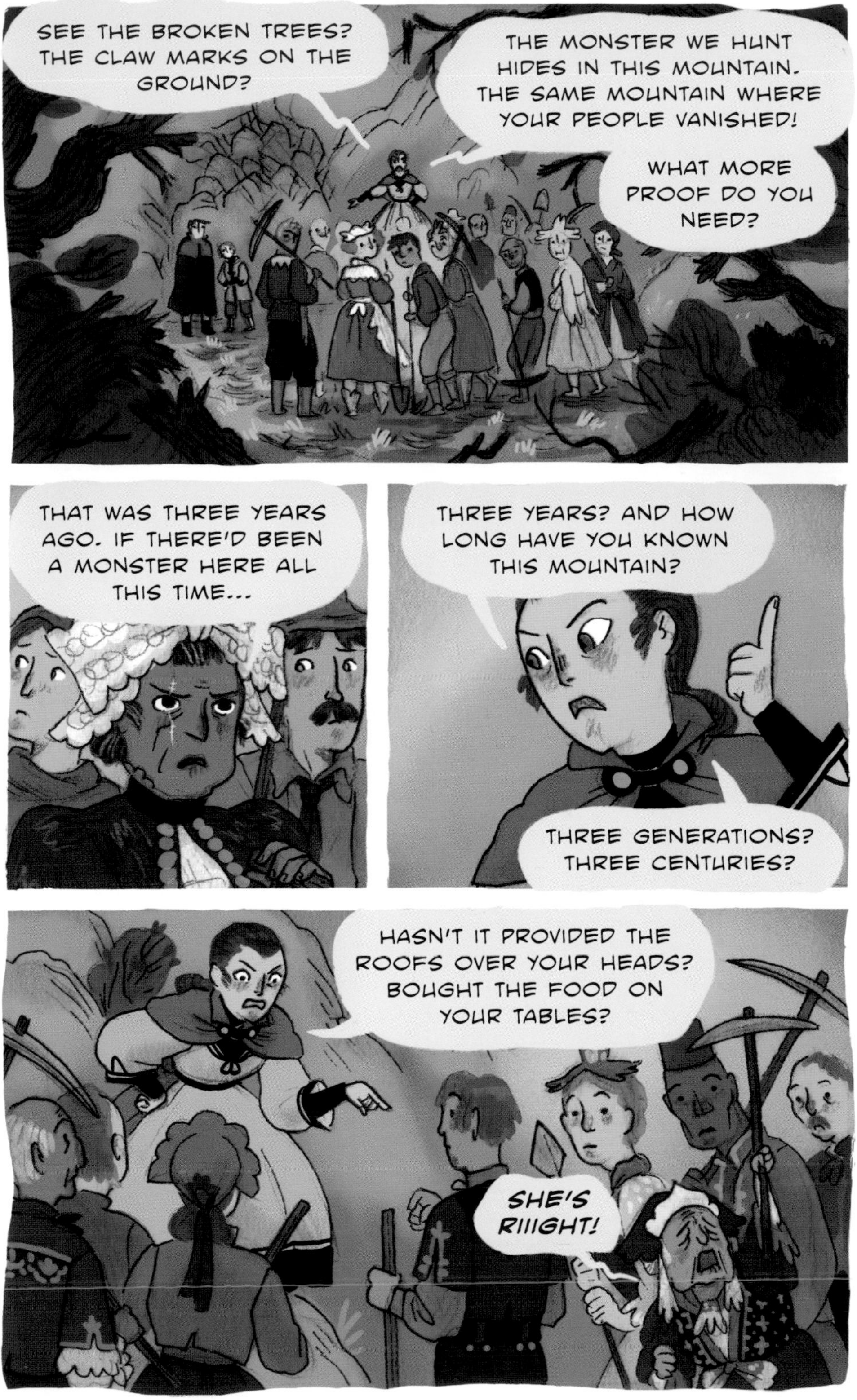
SEE THE BROKEN TREES? THE CLAW MARKS ON THE GROUND?
THE MONSTER WE HUNT HIDES IN THIS MOUNTAIN. THE SAME MOUNTAIN WHERE YOUR PEOPLE VANISHED!
WHAT MORE PROOF DO YOU NEED?
THAT WAS THREE YEARS AGO. IF THERE'D BEEN A MONSTER HERE ALL THIS TIME...
THREE YEARS? AND HOW LONG HAVE YOU KNOWN THIS MOUNTAIN?
THREE GENERATIONS? THREE CENTURIES?
HASN'T IT PROVIDED THE ROOFS OVER YOUR HEADS? BOUGHT THE FOOD ON YOUR TABLES?
SHE'S RIIIGHT!

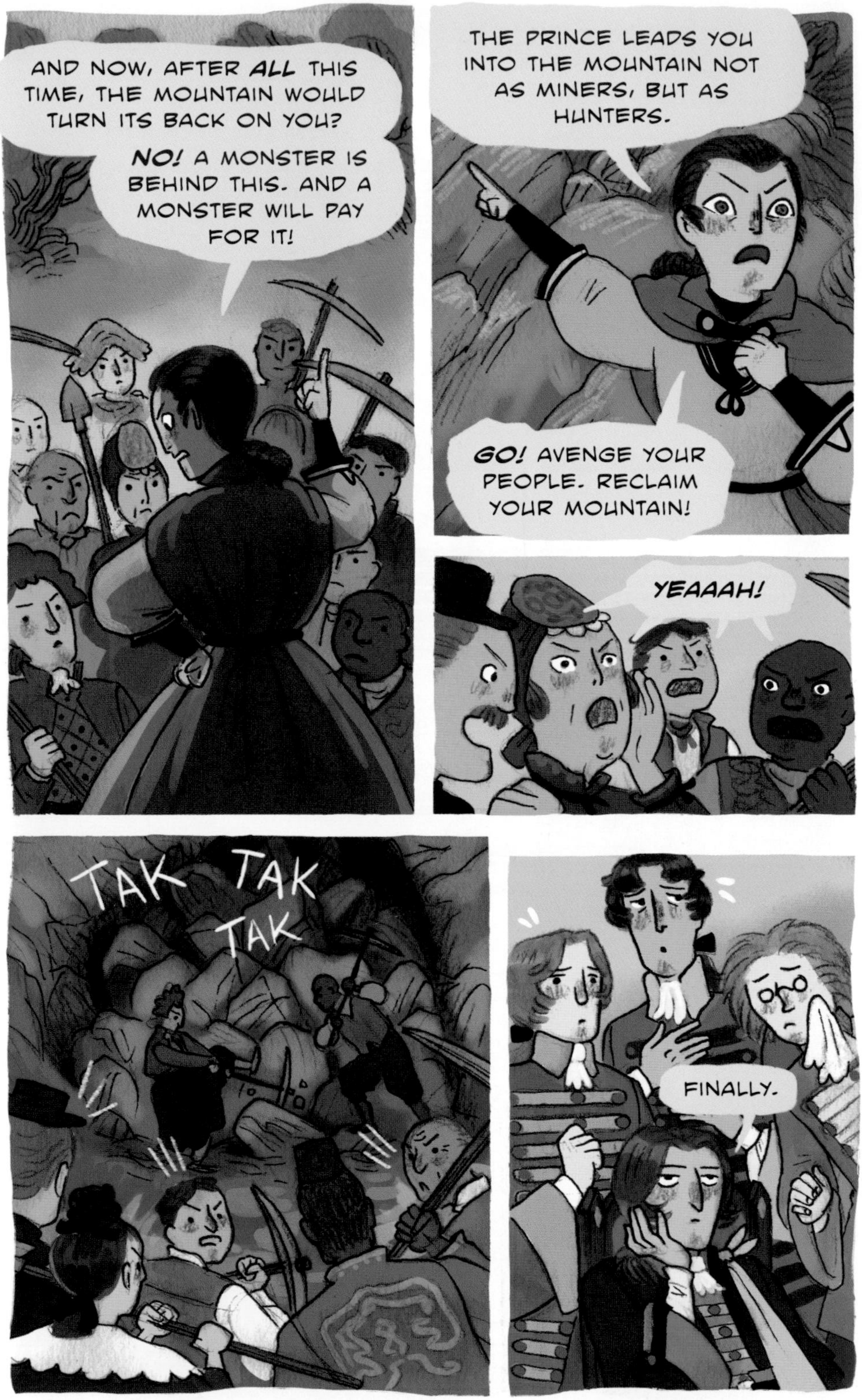

AND NOW, AFTER ALL THIS TIME, THE MOUNTAIN WOULD TURN ITS BACK ON YOU?
NO! A MONSTER IS BEHIND THIS. AND A MONSTER WILL PAY FOR IT!
THE PRINCE LEADS YOU INTO THE MOUNTAIN NOT AS MINERS, BUT AS HUNTERS.
GO! AVENGE YOUR PEOPLE. RECLAIM YOUR MOUNTAIN!
YEAAAH!
TAK TAK TAK
FINALLY.

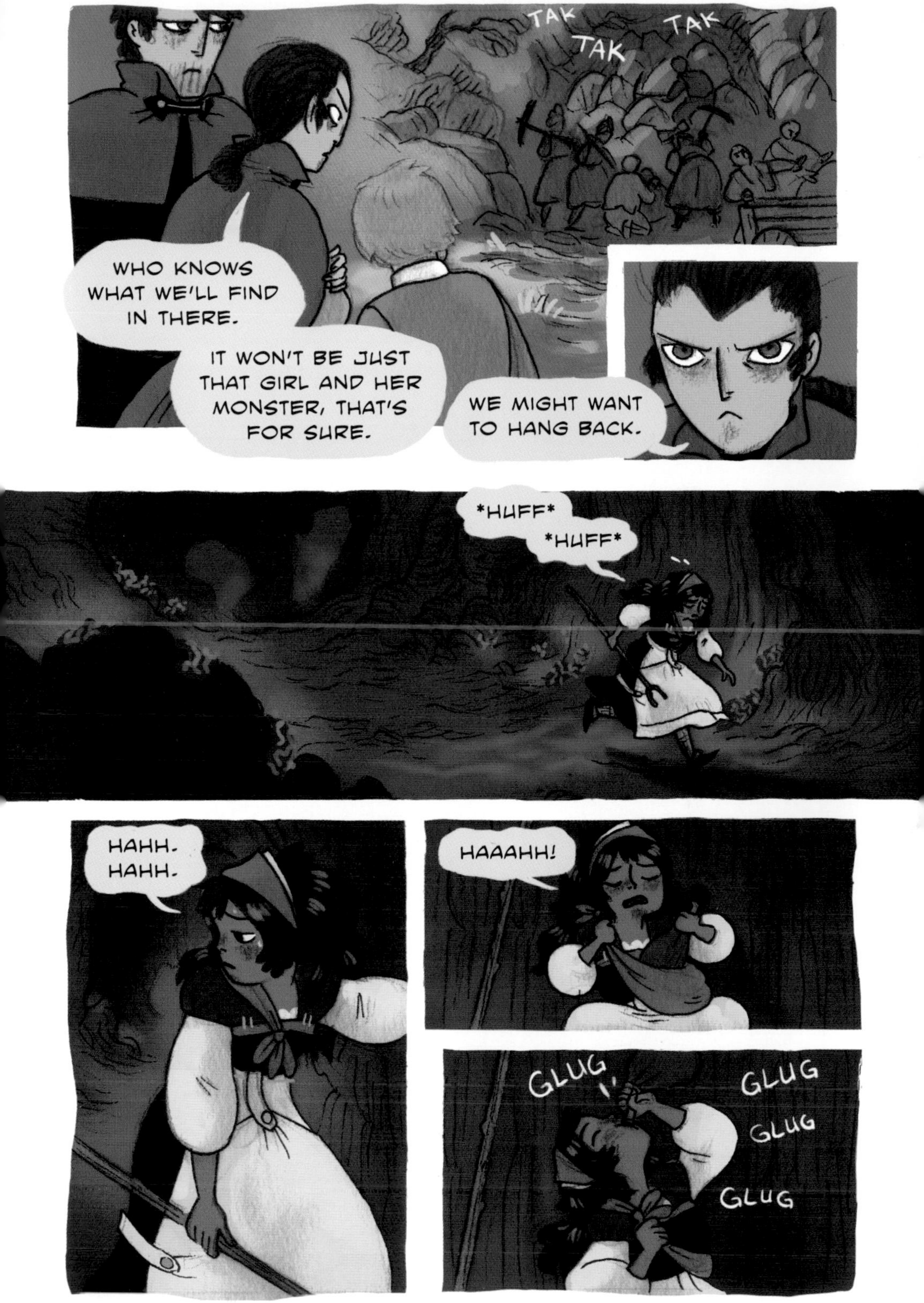
TAK
TAK
TAK
WHO KNOWS WHAT WE'LL FIND IN THERE.
IT WON'T BE JUST THAT GIRL AND HER MONSTER, THAT'S FOR SURE.
WE MIGHT WANT TO HANG BACK.
HUFF
HUFF
HAHH. HAHH.
HAAAHH!
GLUG
GLUG
GLUG
GLUG

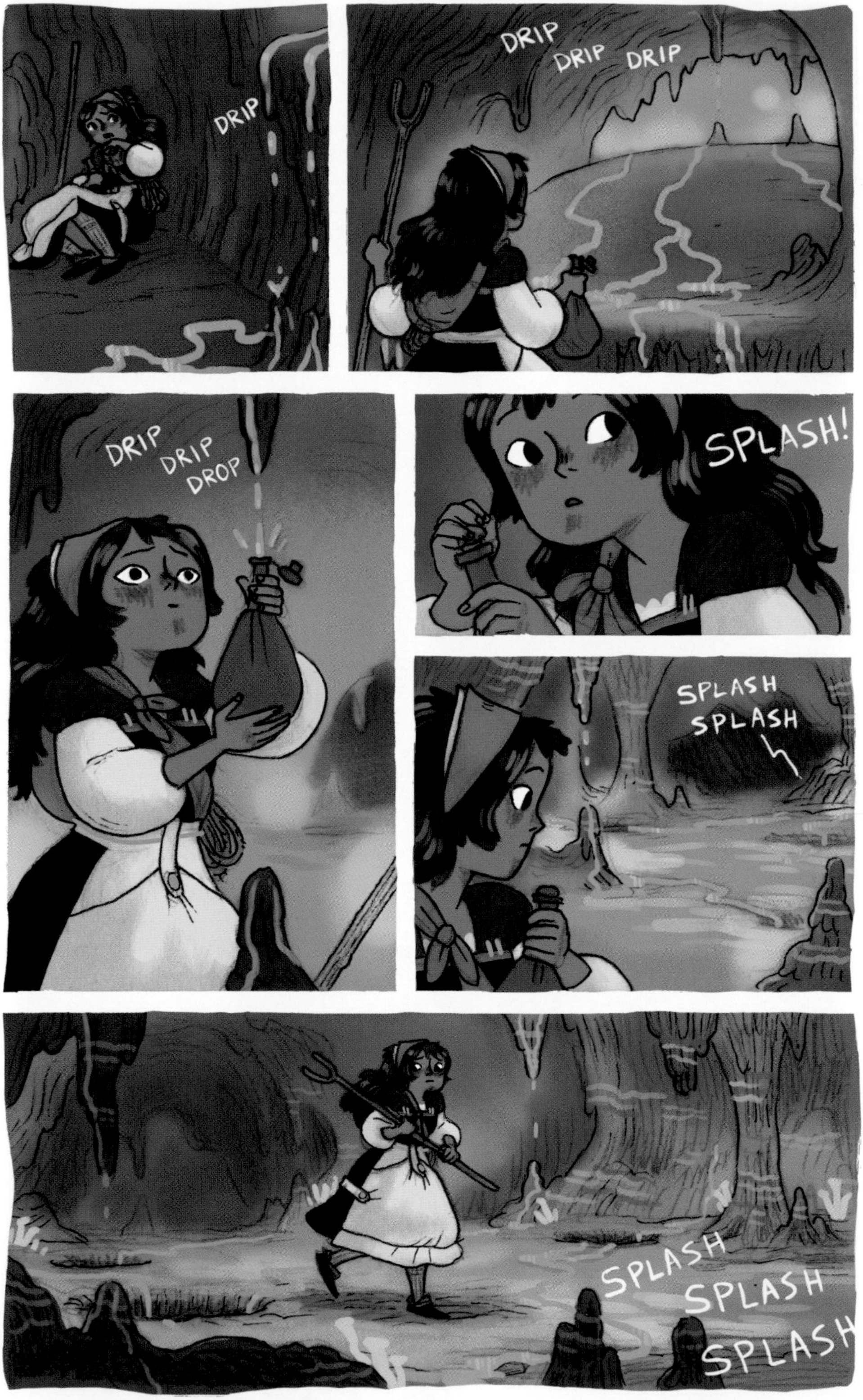
DRIP
DRIP
DRIP
DRIP
DRIP
DRIP
DRIP
DROP
SPLASH!
SPLASH
SPLASH
SPLASH
SPLASH
SPLASH

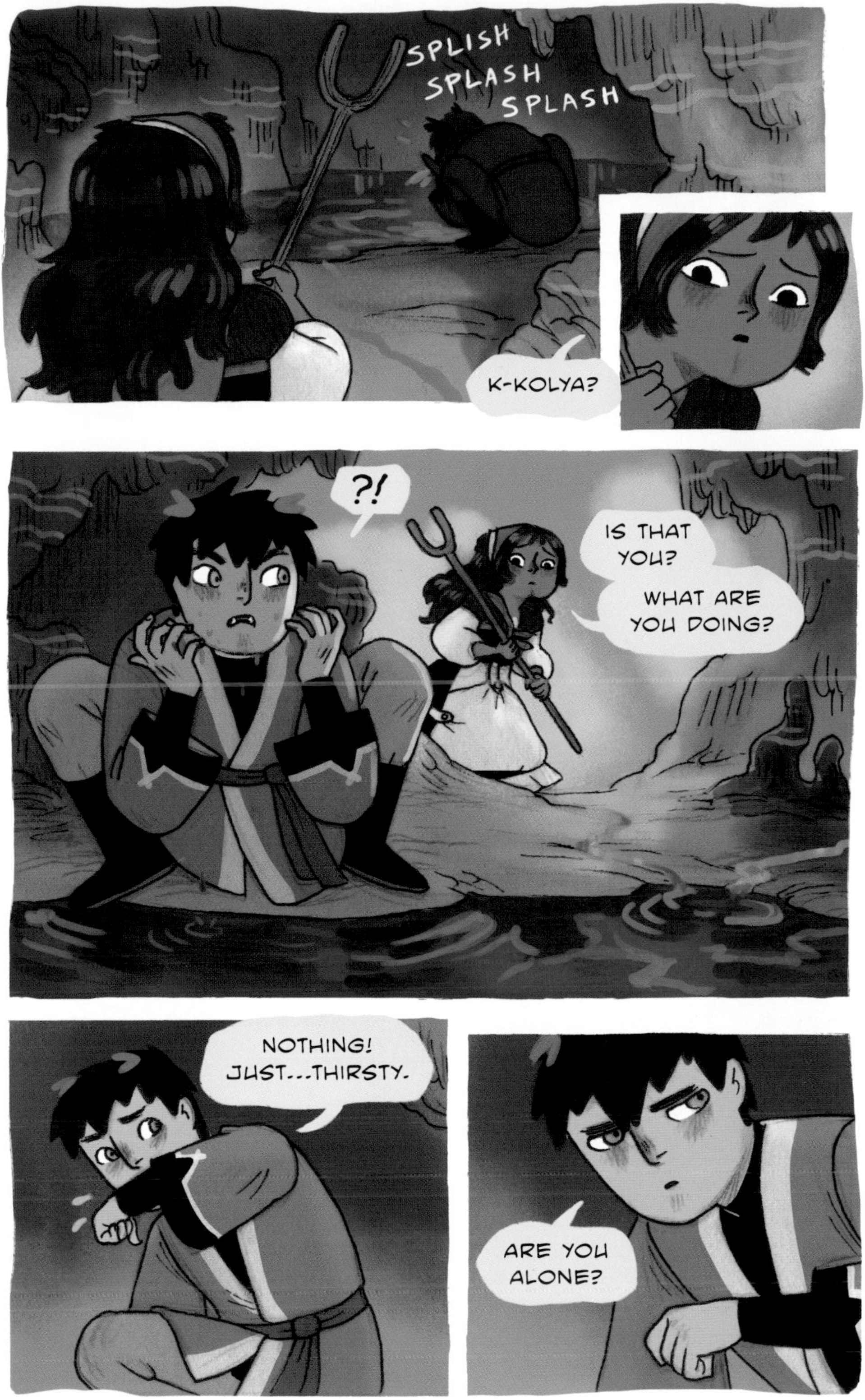

SPLISH
SPLASH
SPLASH
K-KOLYA?
?!
IS THAT YOU?
WHAT ARE YOU DOING?
NOTHING! JUST...THIRSTY.
ARE YOU ALONE?

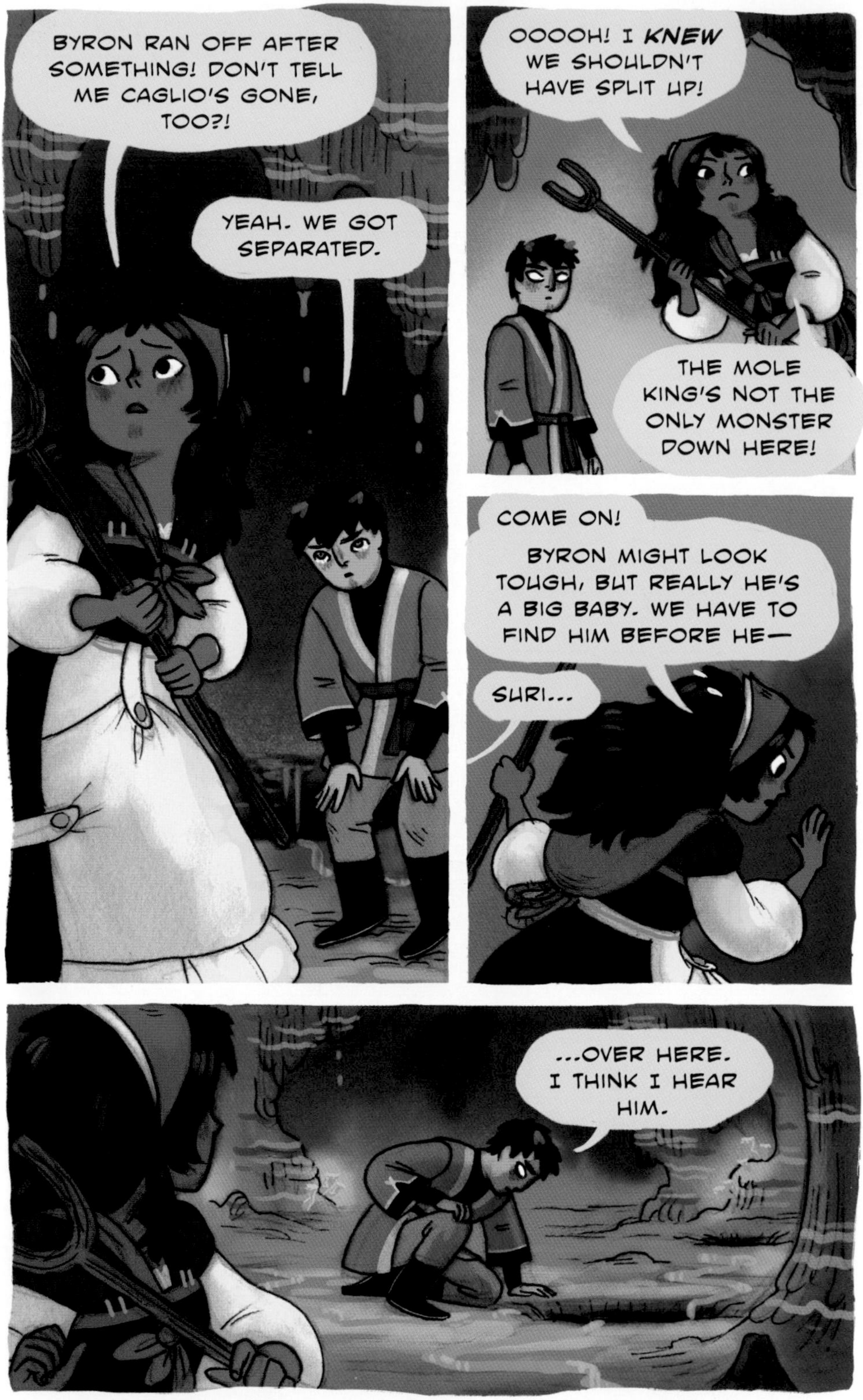
BYRON RAN OFF AFTER SOMETHING! DON'T TELL ME CAGLIO'S GONE, TOO?!
YEAH. WE GOT SEPARATED.
OOOOH! I *KNEW* WE SHOULDN'T HAVE SPLIT UP!
THE MOLE KING'S NOT THE ONLY MONSTER DOWN HERE!
COME ON!
BYRON MIGHT LOOK TOUGH, BUT REALLY HE'S A BIG BABY. WE HAVE TO FIND HIM BEFORE HE—
SURI...
...OVER HERE. I THINK I HEAR HIM.

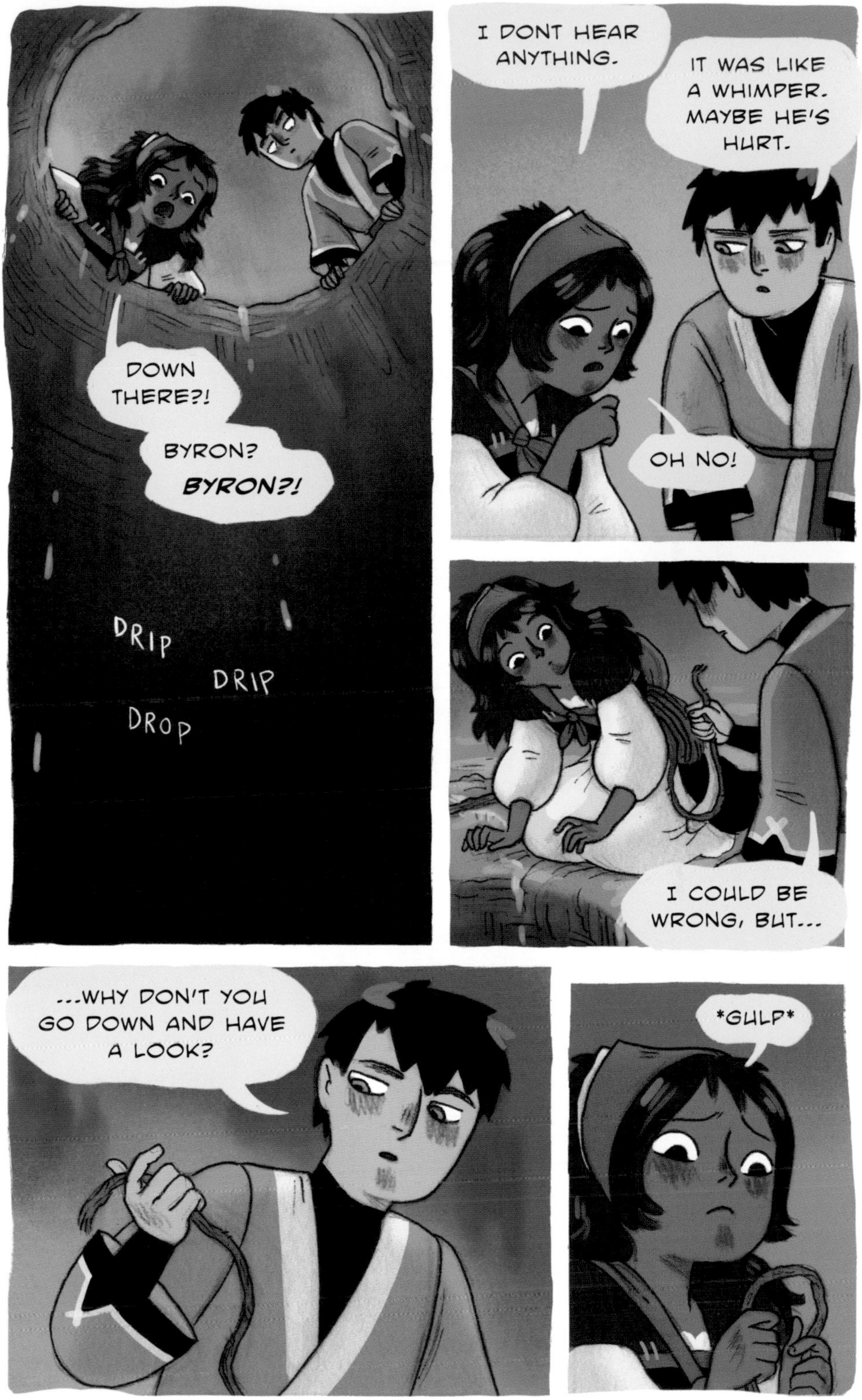
DOWN THERE?!
BYRON? BYRON?!
DRIP DRIP DROP
I DONT HEAR ANYTHING.
IT WAS LIKE A WHIMPER. MAYBE HE'S HURT.
OH NO!
I COULD BE WRONG, BUT...
...WHY DON'T YOU GO DOWN AND HAVE A LOOK?
GULP

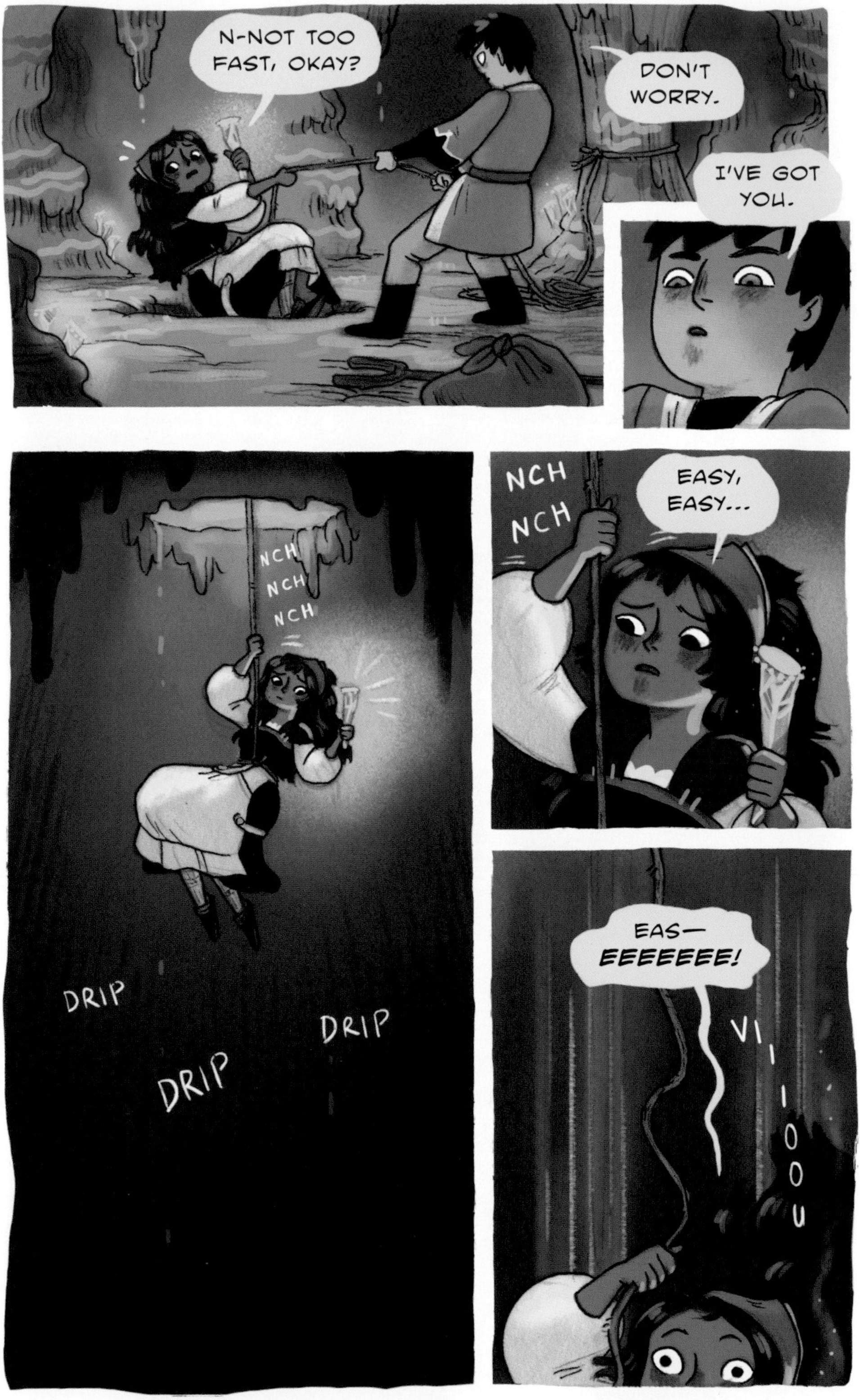
N-NOT TOO FAST, OKAY?
DON'T WORRY.
I'VE GOT YOU.
NCH
NCH
NCH
DRIP
DRIP
DRIP
NCH
NCH
EASY, EASY...
EAS—
EEEEEEE!
VIIIOOU

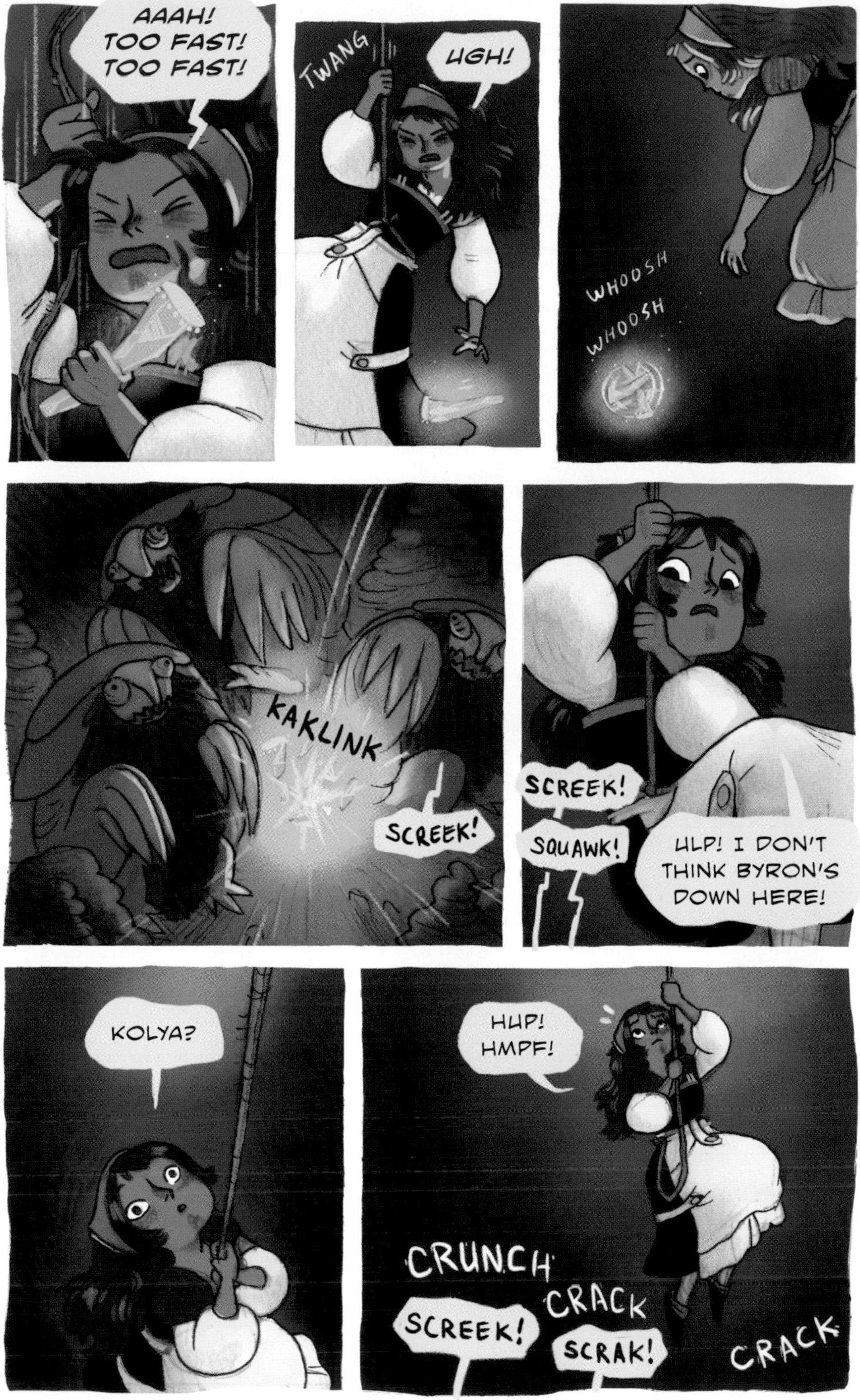
AAAH! TOO FAST! TOO FAST!
TWANG
UGH!
WHOOSH
WHOOSH
KAKLINK
SCREEK!
SCREEK!
SQUAWK!
ULP! I DON'T THINK BYRON'S DOWN HERE!
KOLYA?
HUP! HMPF!
CRUNCH
CRACK
SCREEK!
SCRAK!
CRACK

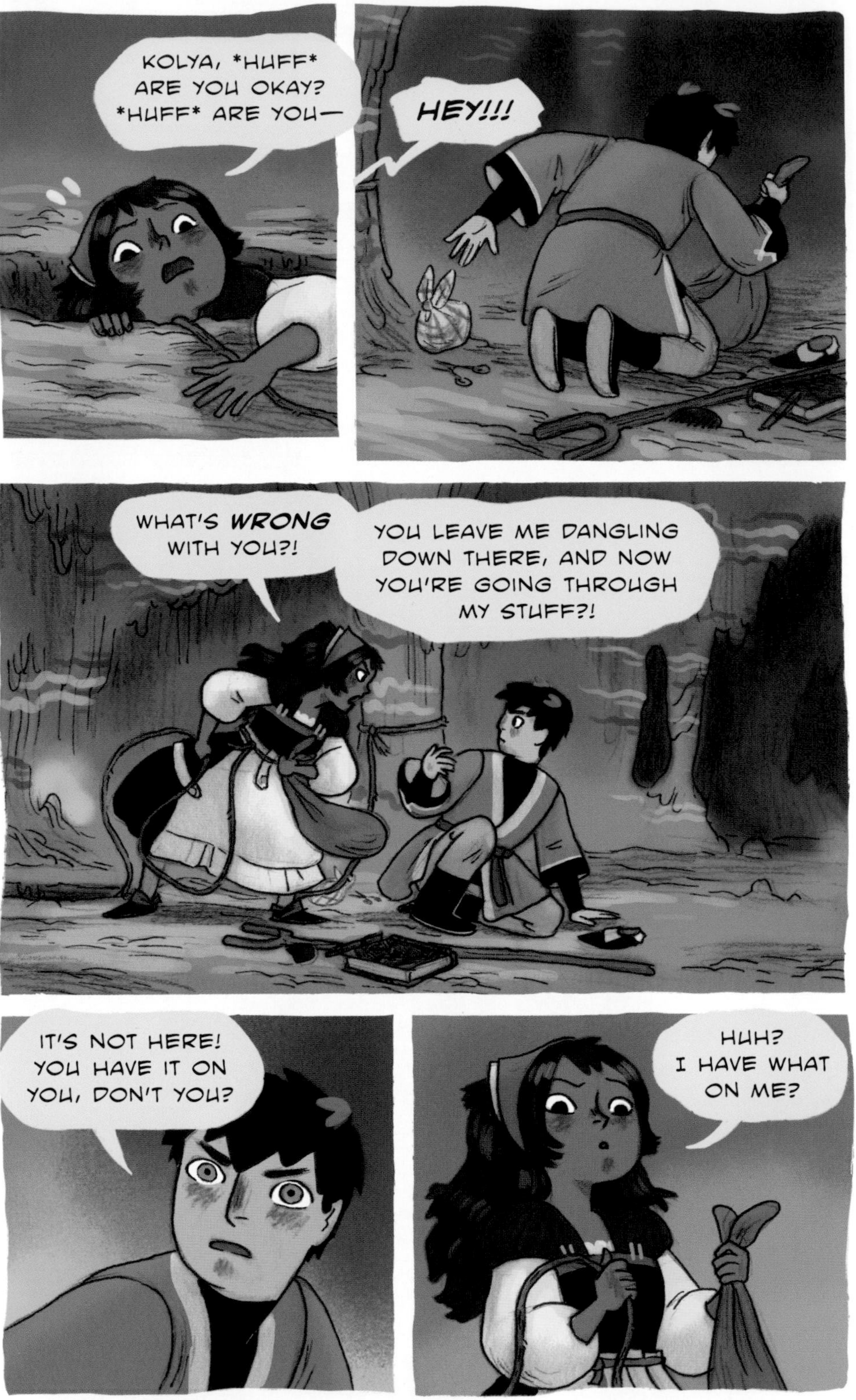
KOLYA, *HUFF* ARE YOU OKAY? *HUFF* ARE YOU—
HEY!!!
WHAT'S WRONG WITH YOU?!
YOU LEAVE ME DANGLING DOWN THERE, AND NOW YOU'RE GOING THROUGH MY STUFF?!
IT'S NOT HERE! YOU HAVE IT ON YOU, DON'T YOU?
HUH? I HAVE WHAT ON ME?

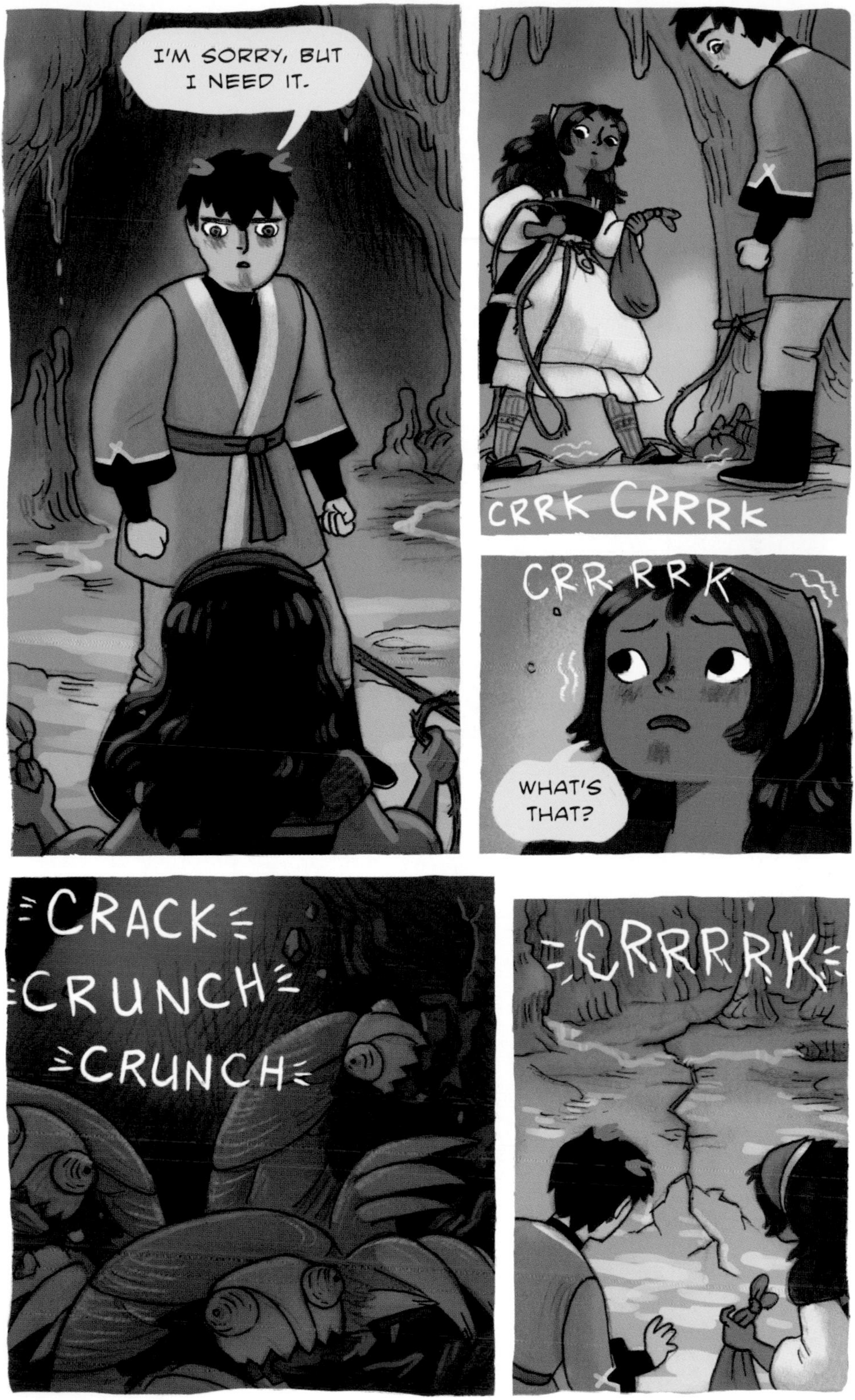
I'M SORRY, BUT I NEED IT.
CRRK CRRRK
CRRRRK
WHAT'S THAT?
CRACK
CRUNCH
CRUNCH
CRRRRK

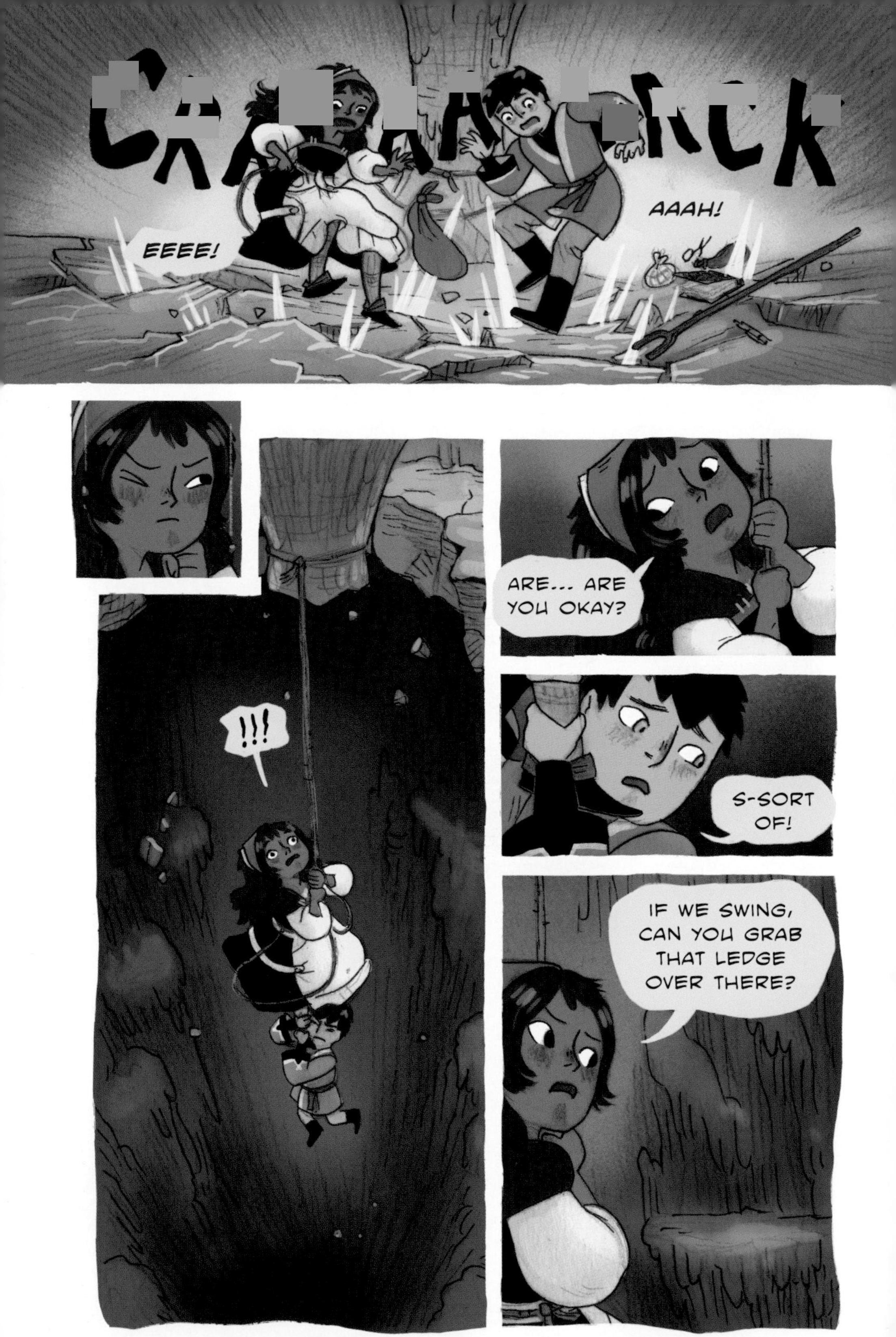
EEEE!
AAAH!
!!!
ARE... ARE YOU OKAY?
S-SORT OF!
IF WE SWING, CAN YOU GRAB THAT LEDGE OVER THERE?

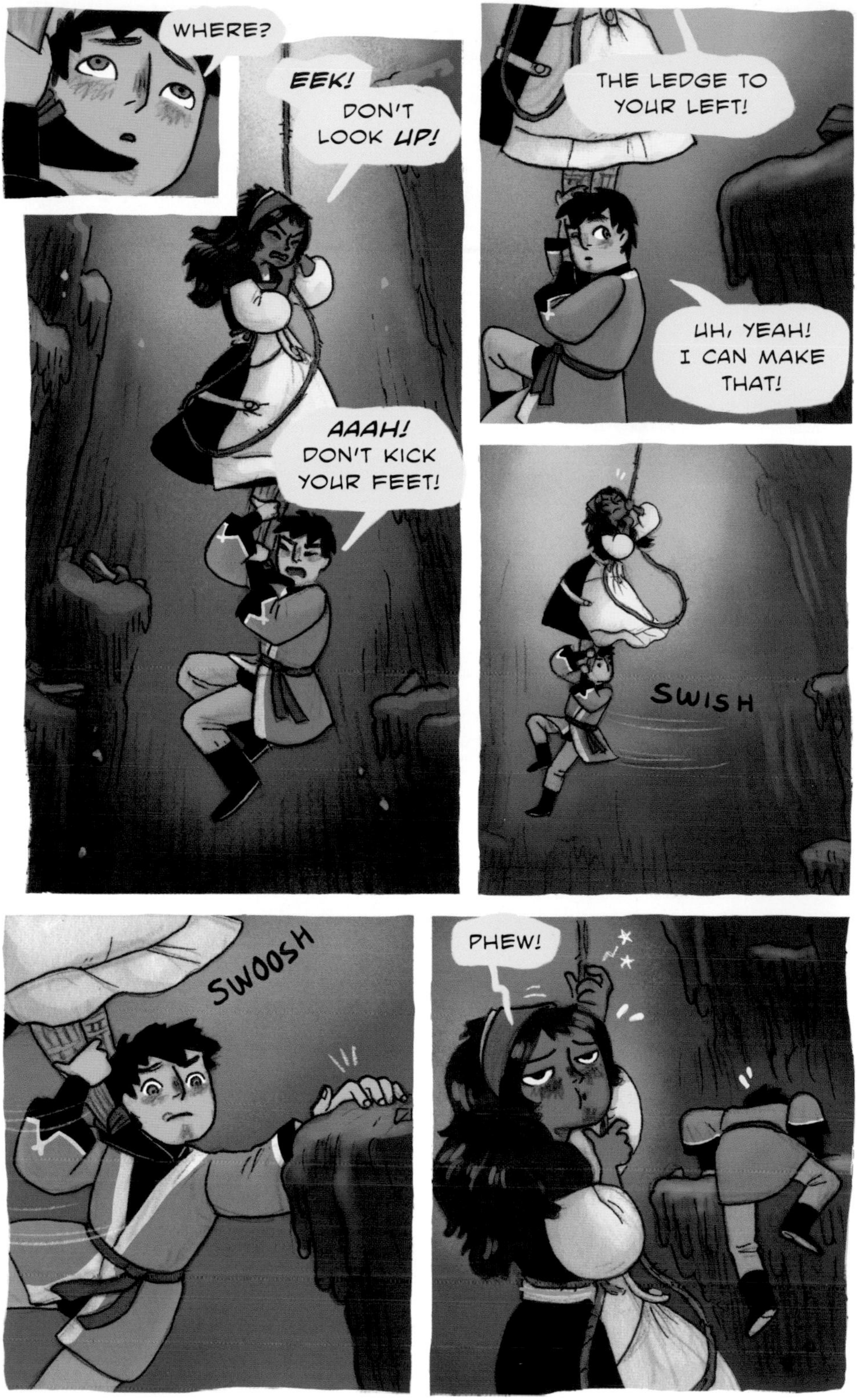
WHERE?
EEK! DON'T LOOK UP!
AAAH! DON'T KICK YOUR FEET!
THE LEDGE TO YOUR LEFT!
UH, YEAH! I CAN MAKE THAT!
SWISH
SWOOSH
PHEW!

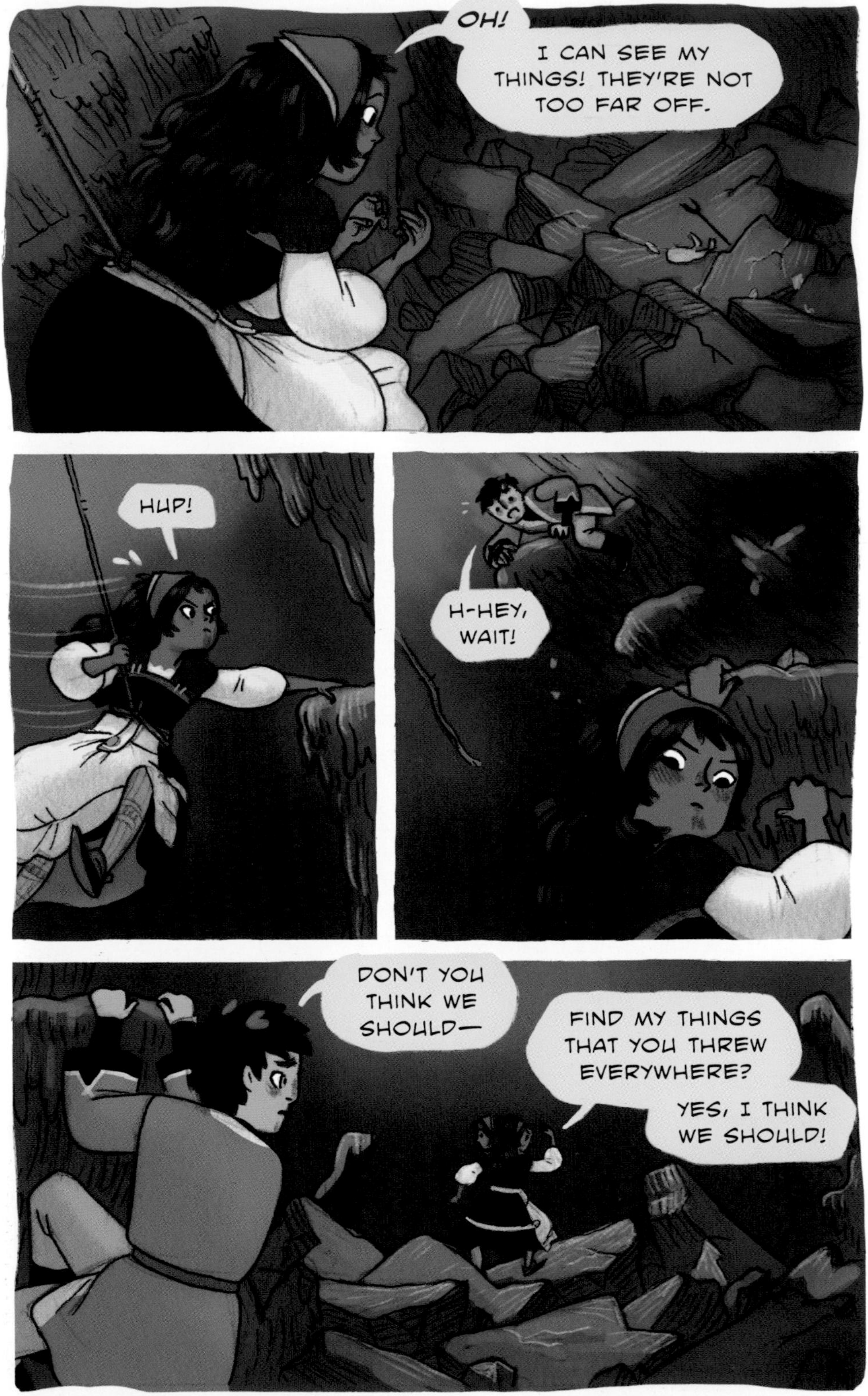
OH!
I CAN SEE MY THINGS! THEY'RE NOT TOO FAR OFF.
HUP!
H-HEY, WAIT!
DON'T YOU THINK WE SHOULD—
FIND MY THINGS THAT YOU THREW EVERYWHERE?
YES, I THINK WE SHOULD!

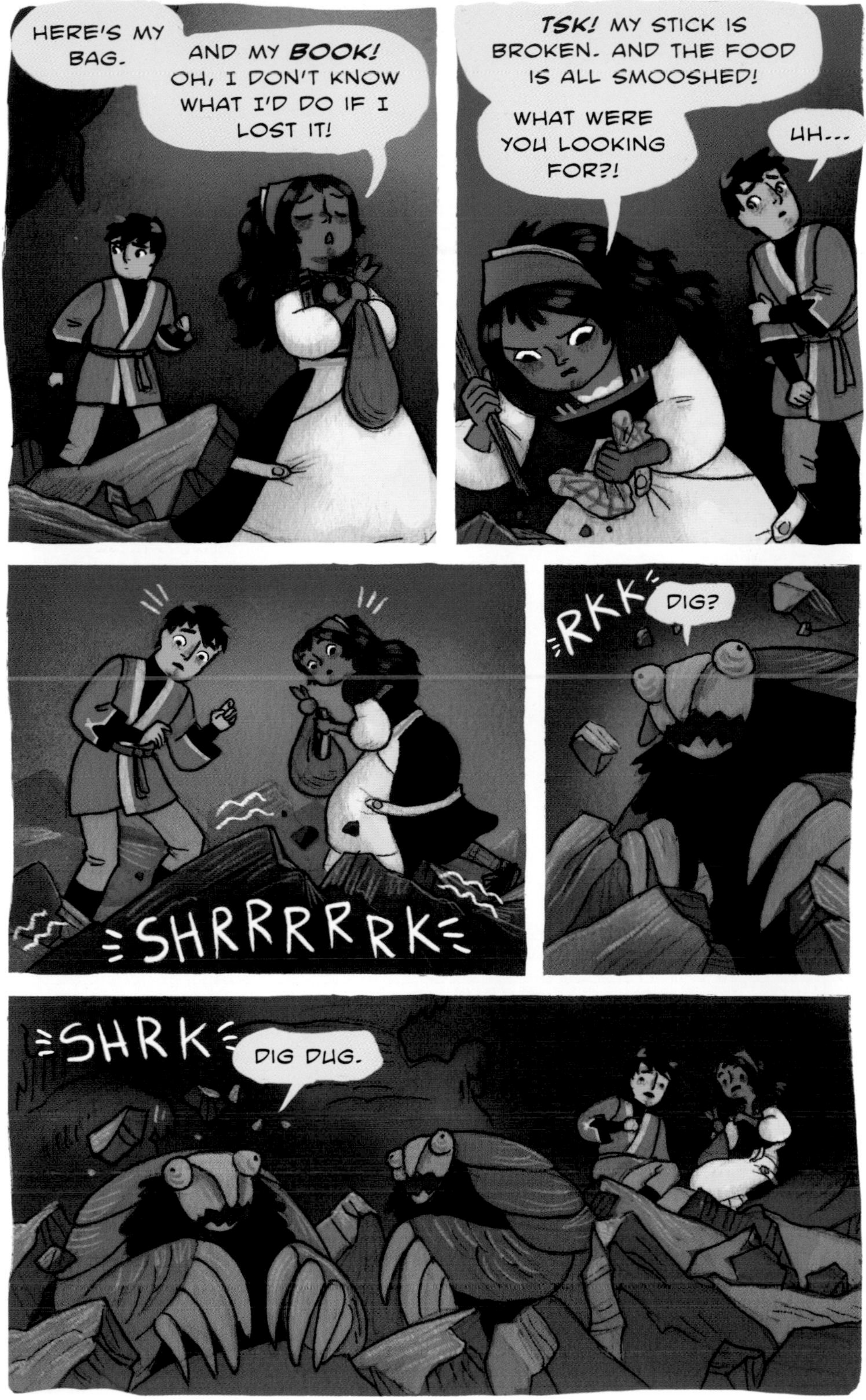
HERE'S MY BAG.
AND MY **BOOK!** OH, I DON'T KNOW WHAT I'D DO IF I LOST IT!
TSK! MY STICK IS BROKEN. AND THE FOOD IS ALL SMOOSHED!
WHAT WERE YOU LOOKING FOR?!
UH...
SHRRRRRK
RKK
DIG?
SHRK
DIG DUG.

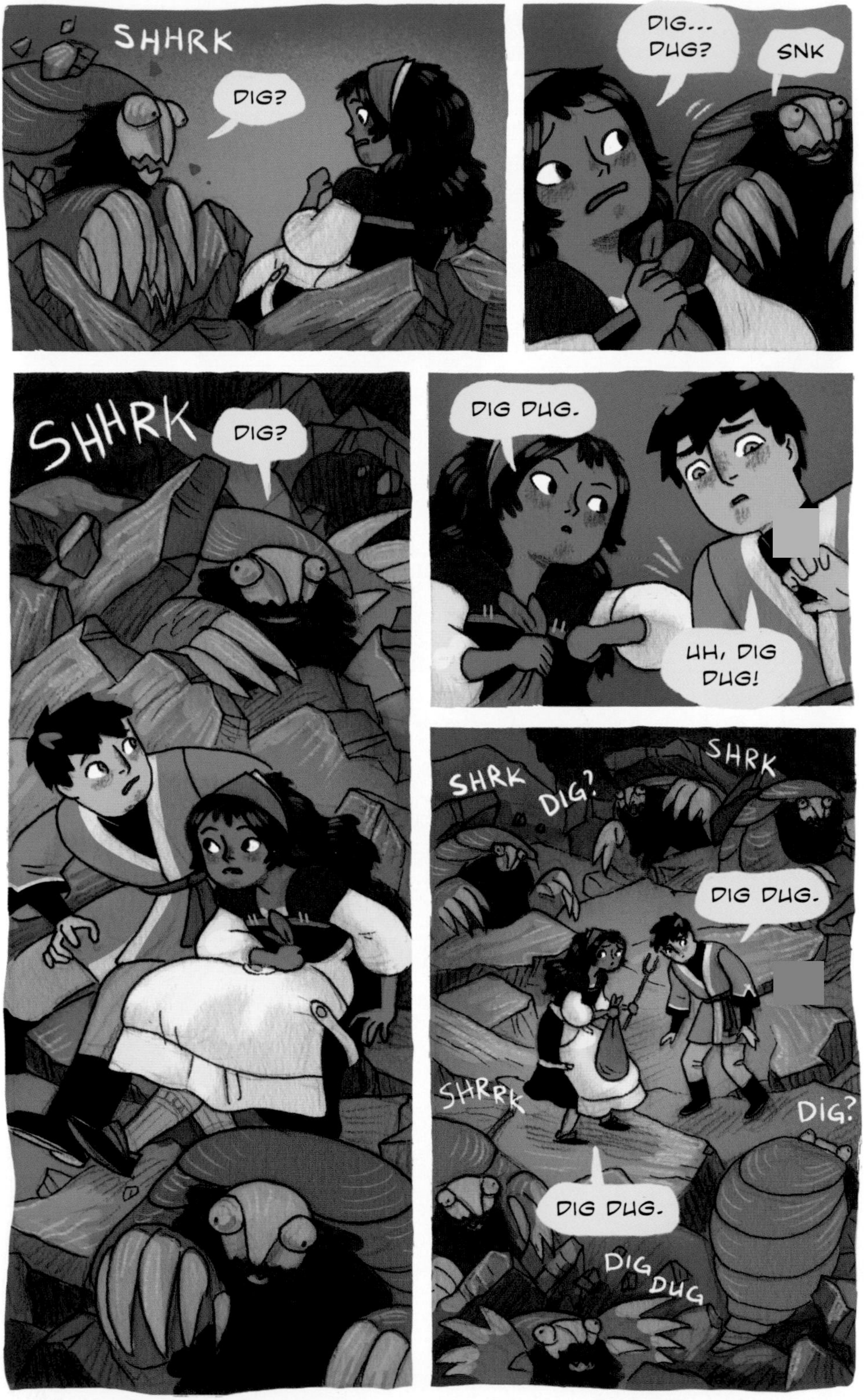
SHHRK
DIG?
DIG... DUG?
SNK
SHHRK
DIG?
DIG DUG.
UH, DIG DUG!
SHRK
DIG?
SHRK
DIG DUG.
SHRRK
DIG?
DIG DUG.
DIG DUG

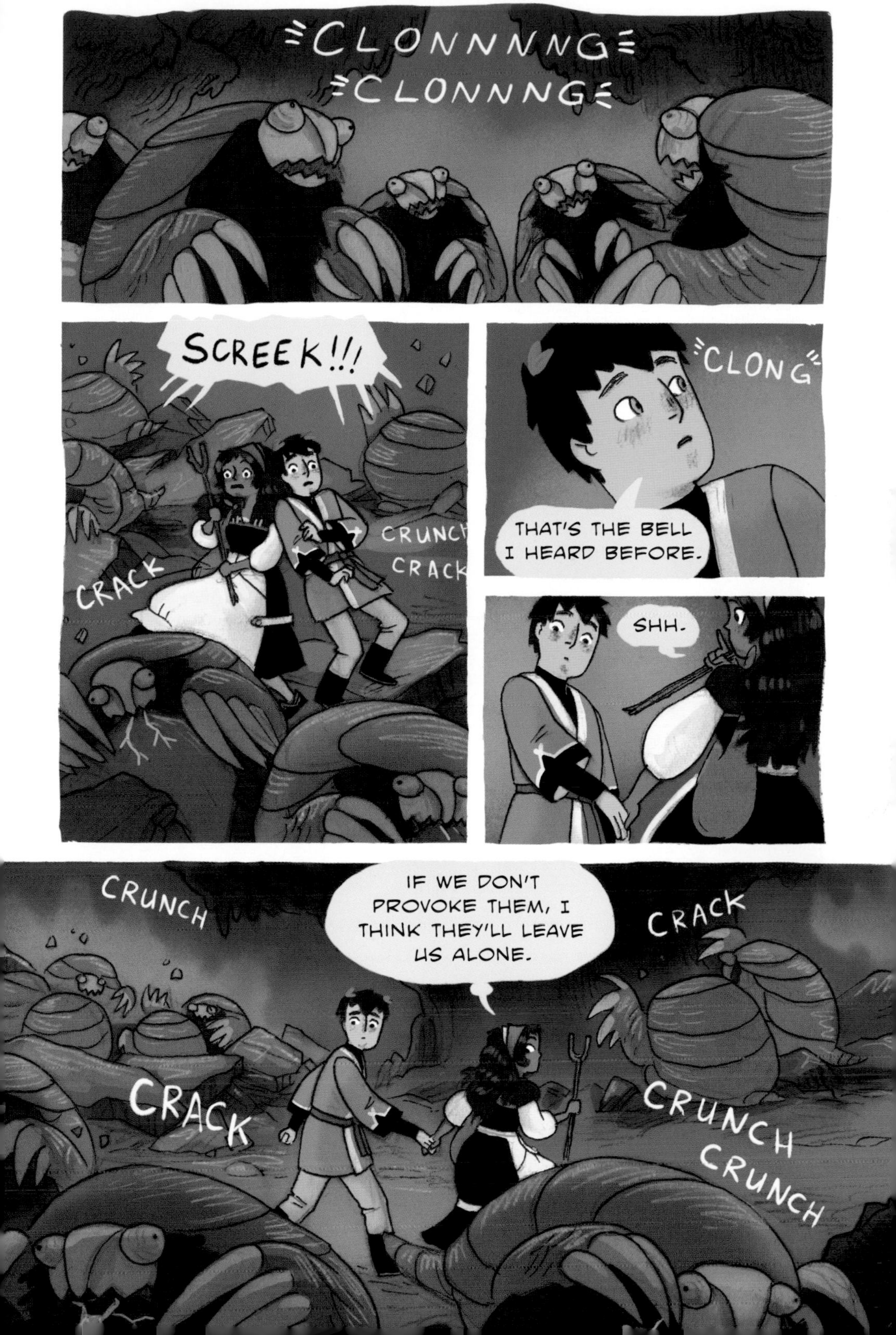
CLONNNNG
CLONNNG
SCREEK!!!
CRUNCH
CRACK
CRACK
CLONG
THAT'S THE BELL I HEARD BEFORE.
SHH.
CRUNCH
IF WE DON'T PROVOKE THEM, I THINK THEY'LL LEAVE US ALONE.
CRACK
CRACK
CRUNCH
CRUNCH

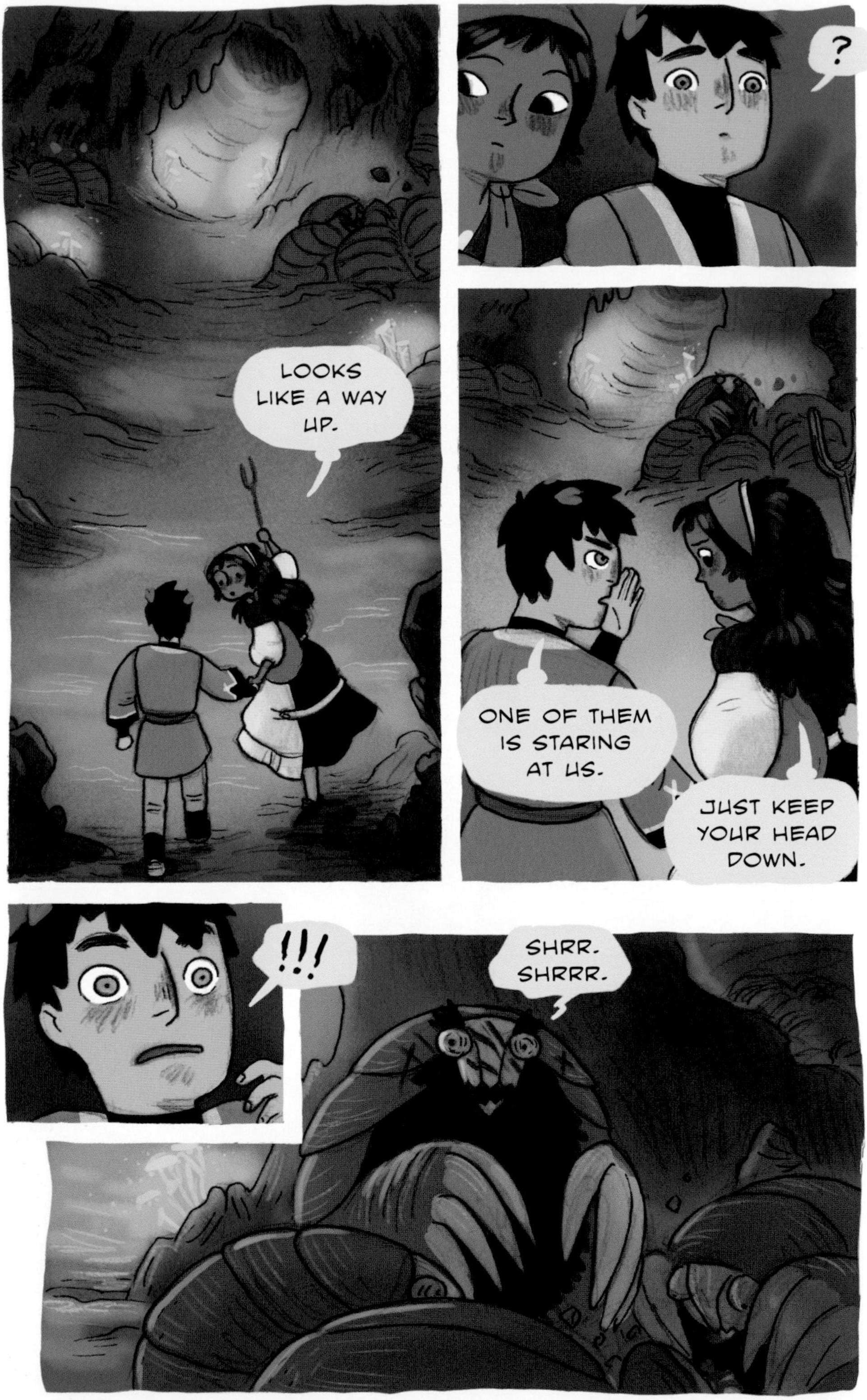
LOOKS LIKE A WAY UP.
?
ONE OF THEM IS STARING AT US.
JUST KEEP YOUR HEAD DOWN.
!!!
SHRR. SHRRR.

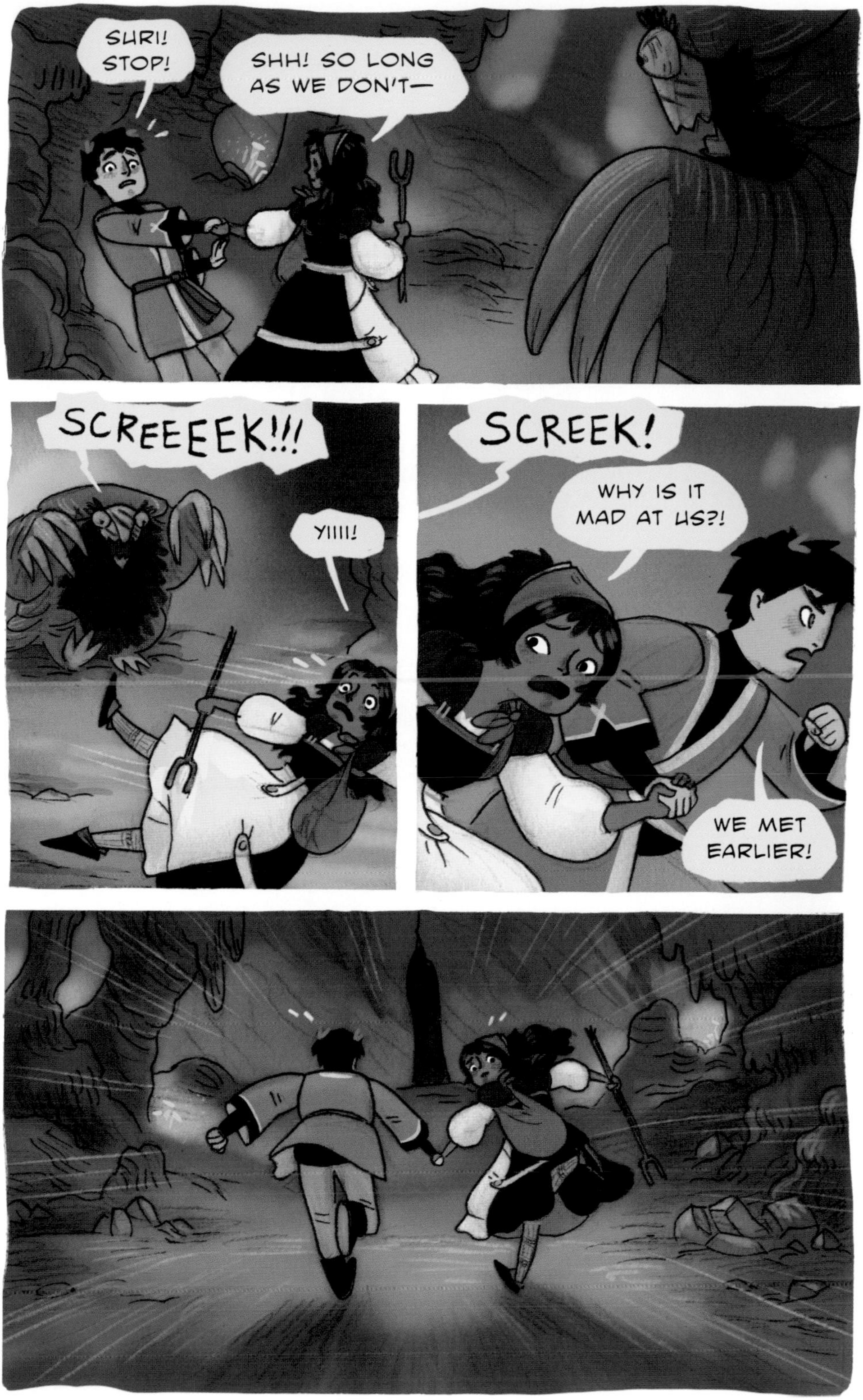
SURI! STOP!
SHH! SO LONG AS WE DON'T—
SCREEEEK!!!
YIIII!
SCREEK!
WHY IS IT MAD AT US?!
WE MET EARLIER!

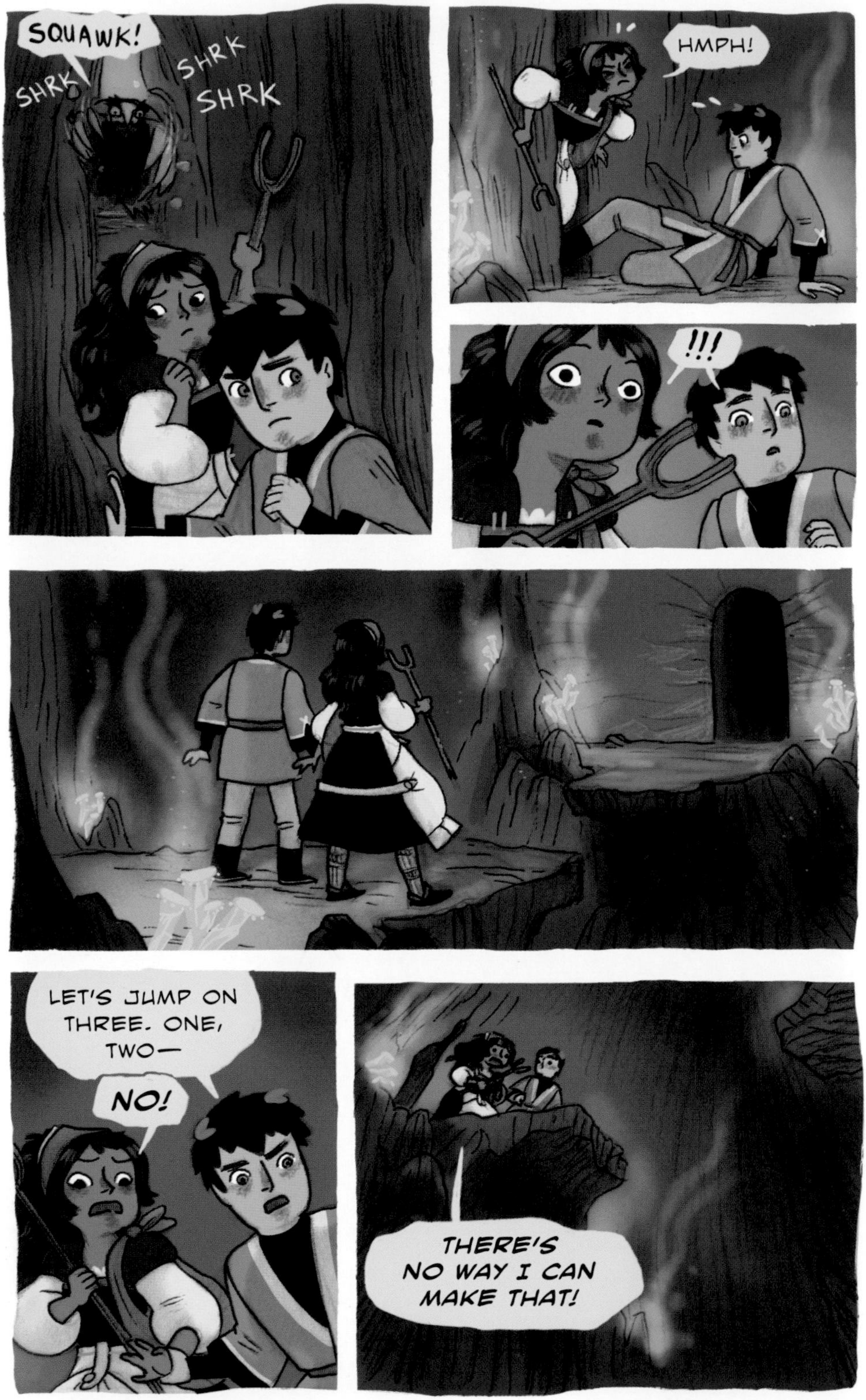

SQUAWK!
SHRK
SHRK
SHRK
HMPH!
!!!
LET'S JUMP ON THREE. ONE, TWO—
NO!
THERE'S NO WAY I CAN MAKE THAT!

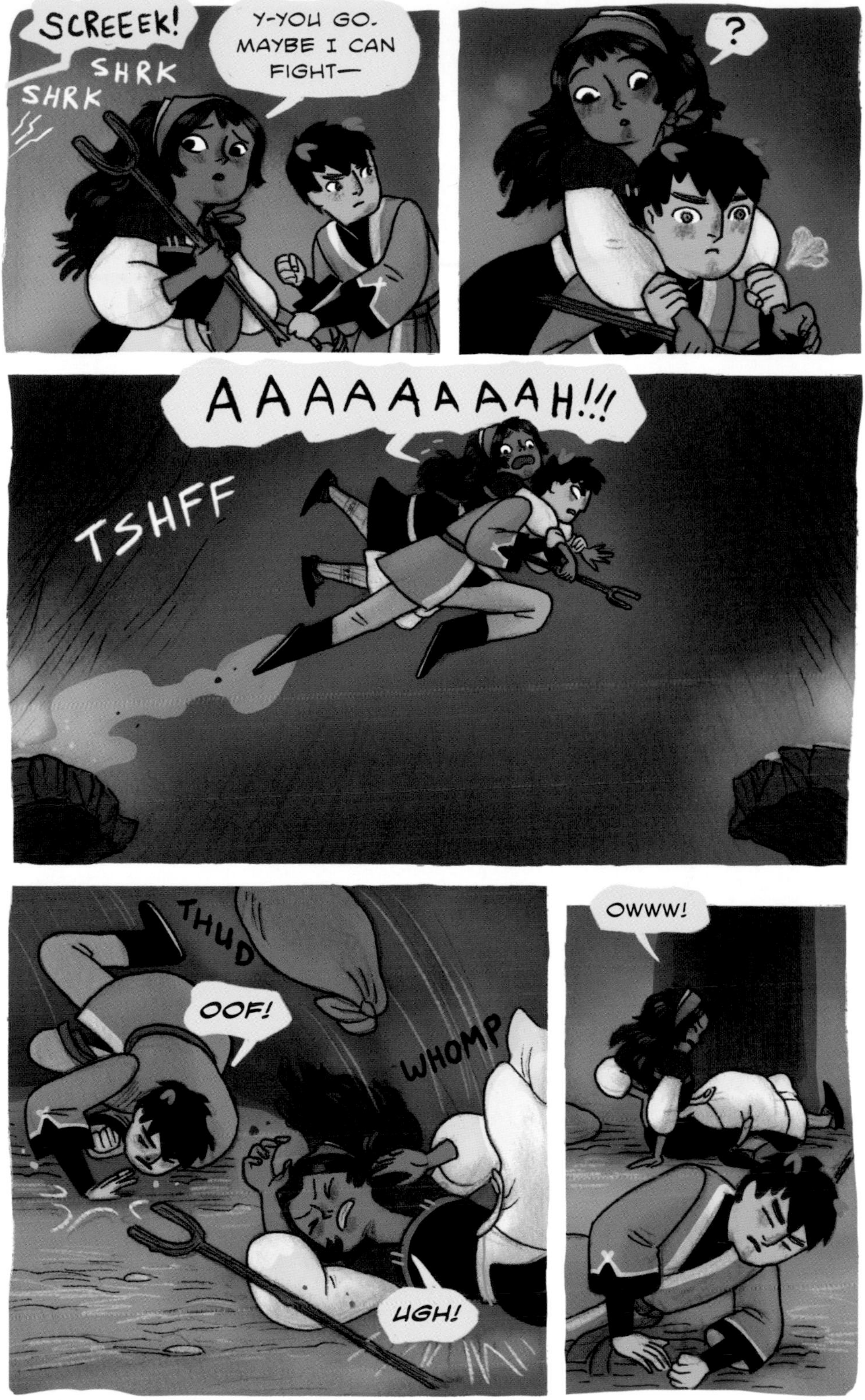
SCREEEK!
SHRK
SHRK
Y-YOU GO. MAYBE I CAN FIGHT—
?
AAAAAAAAH!!!
TSHFF
THUD
OOF!
WHOMP
UGH!
OWWW!

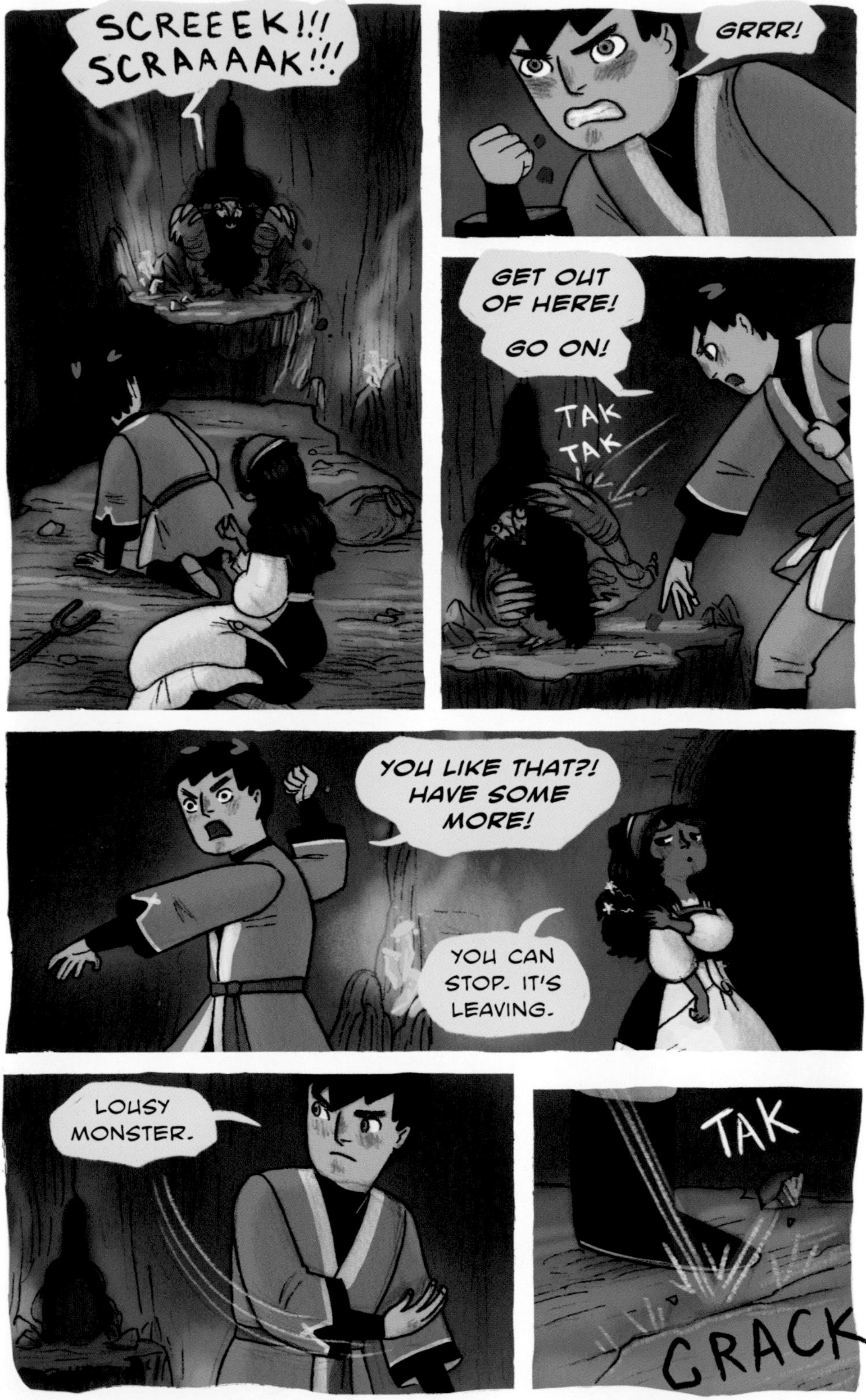
SCREEEK!!! SCRAAAAK!!!
GRRR!
GET OUT OF HERE!
GO ON!
TAK TAK
YOU LIKE THAT?! HAVE SOME MORE!
YOU CAN STOP. IT'S LEAVING.
LOUSY MONSTER.
TAK
CRACK

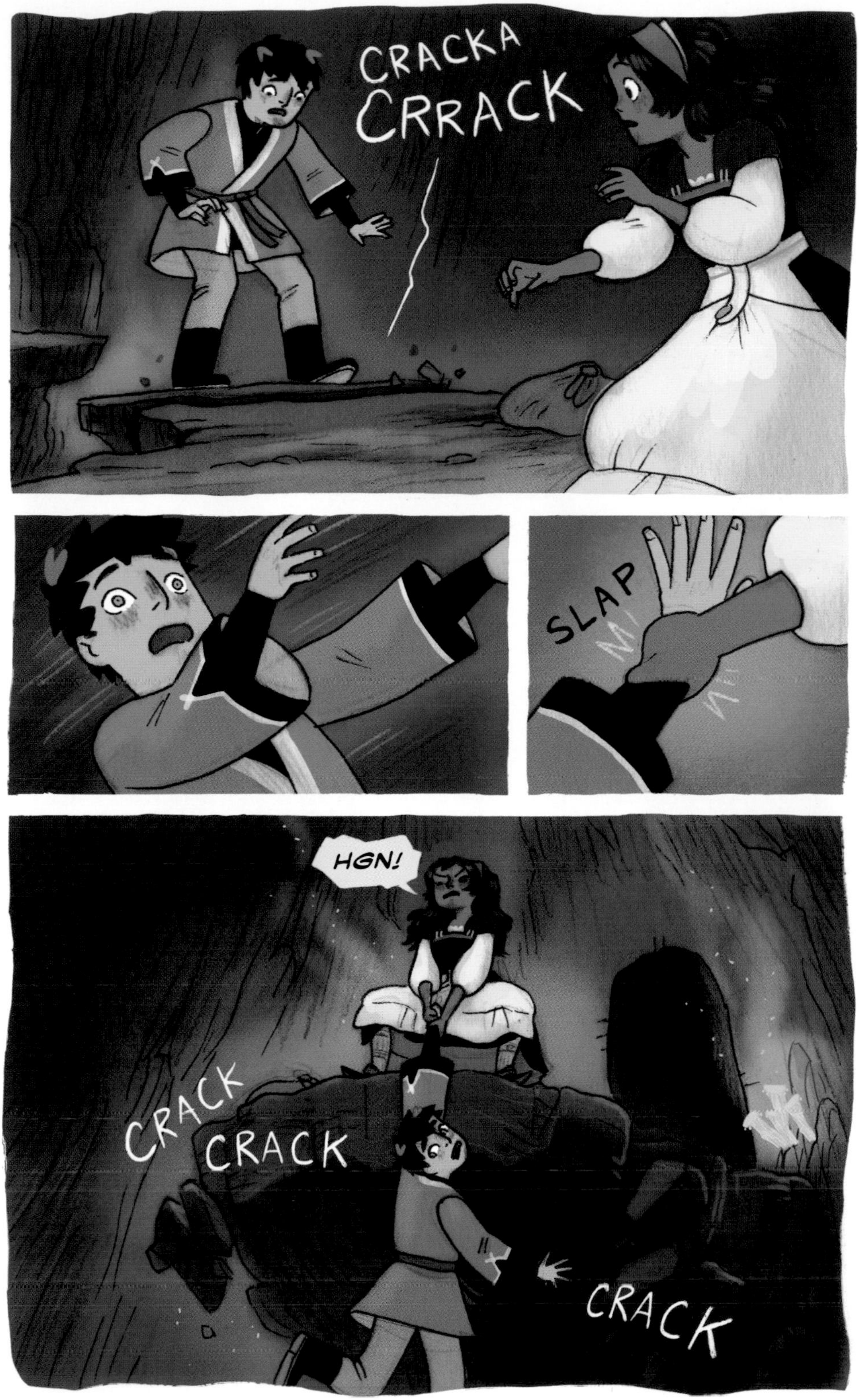
CRACKA
CRRACK
SLAP
HGN!
CRACK
CRACK
CRACK

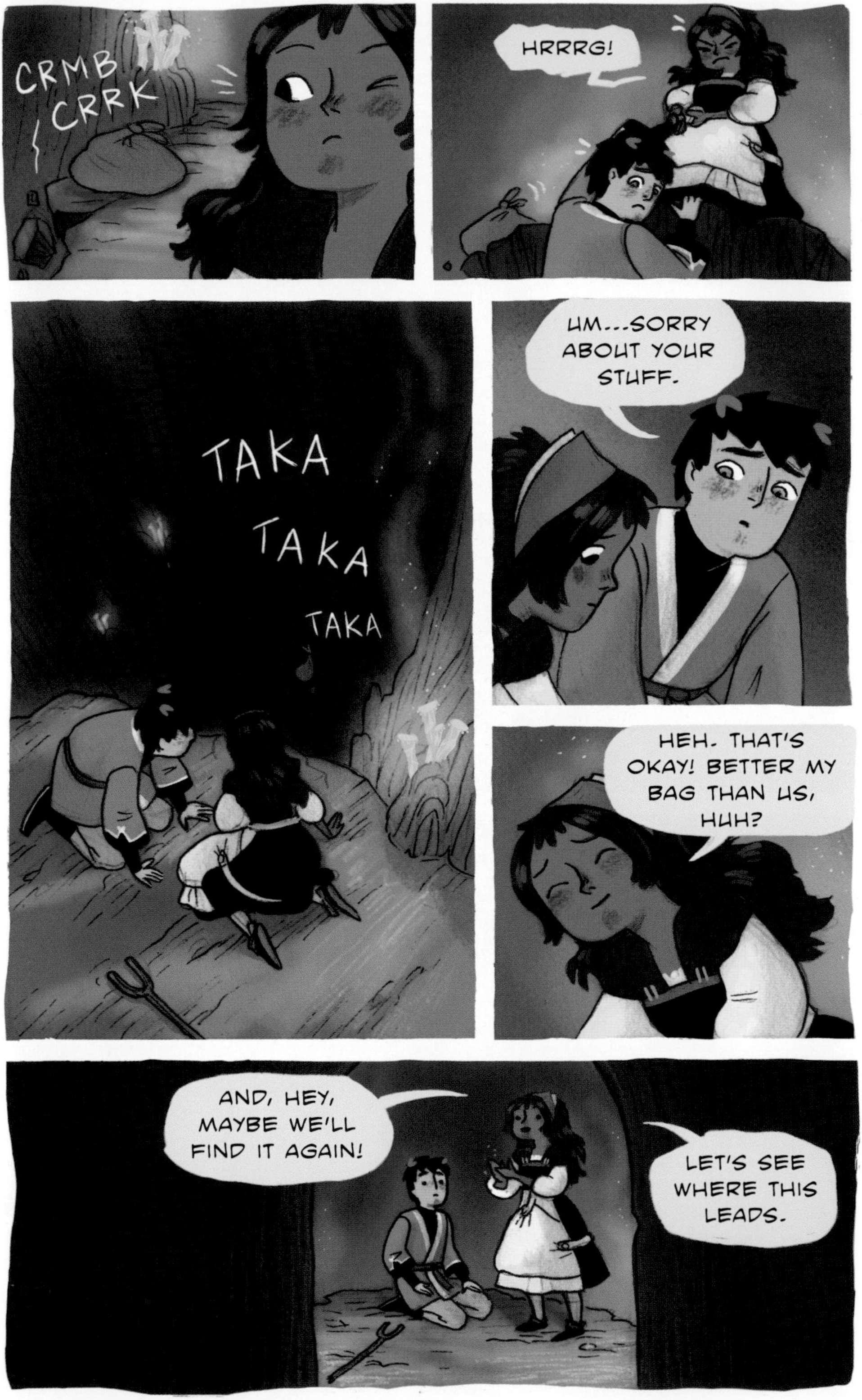
CRMB CRRK
HRRRG!
TAKA TAKA TAKA
UM...SORRY ABOUT YOUR STUFF.
HEH. THAT'S OKAY! BETTER MY BAG THAN US, HUH?
AND, HEY, MAYBE WE'LL FIND IT AGAIN!
LET'S SEE WHERE THIS LEADS.

THIS LOOKS
LIKE AN OLD
MINE SHAFT.

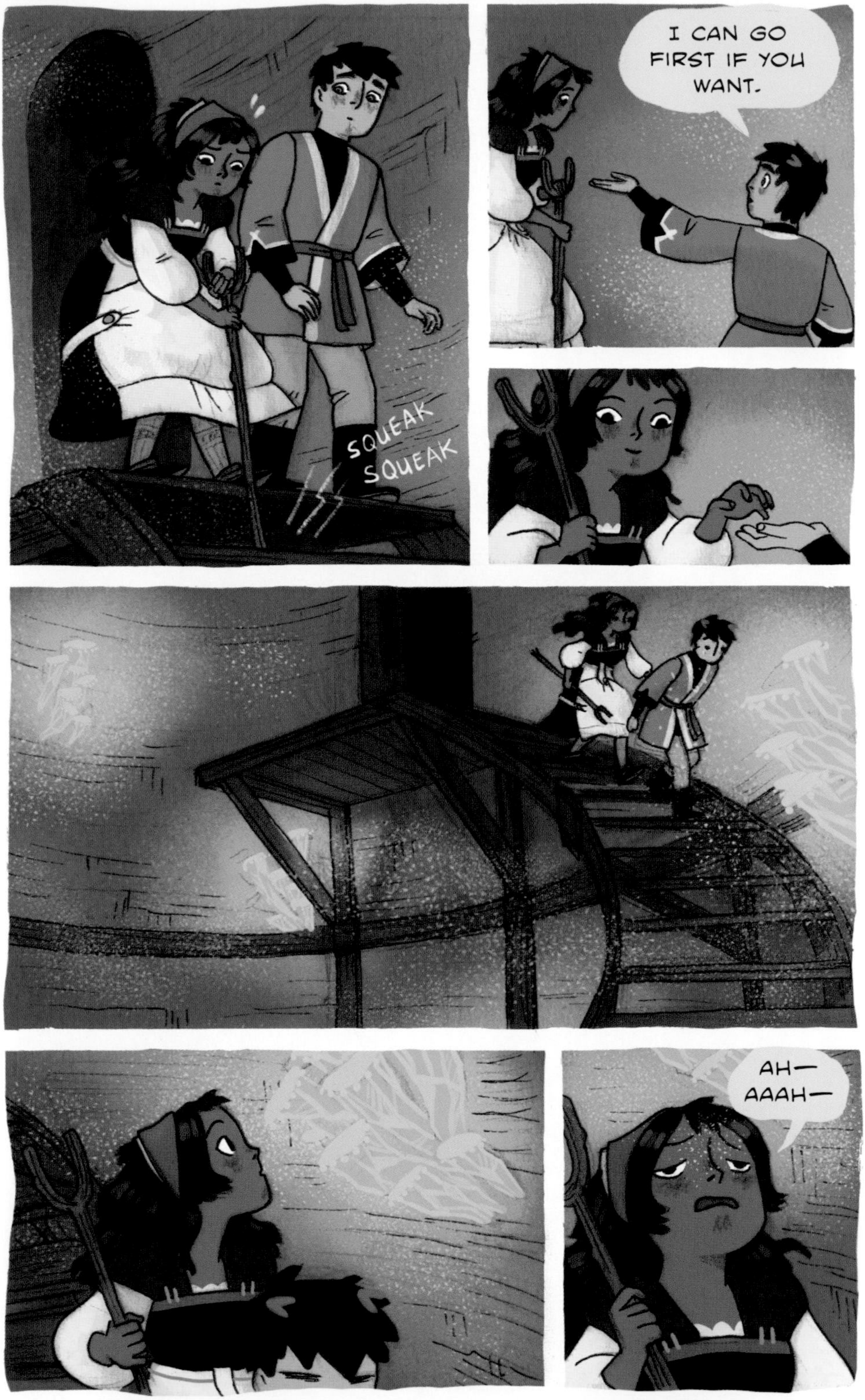
SQUEAK
SQUEAK
I CAN GO FIRST IF YOU WANT.
AH—
AAAH—

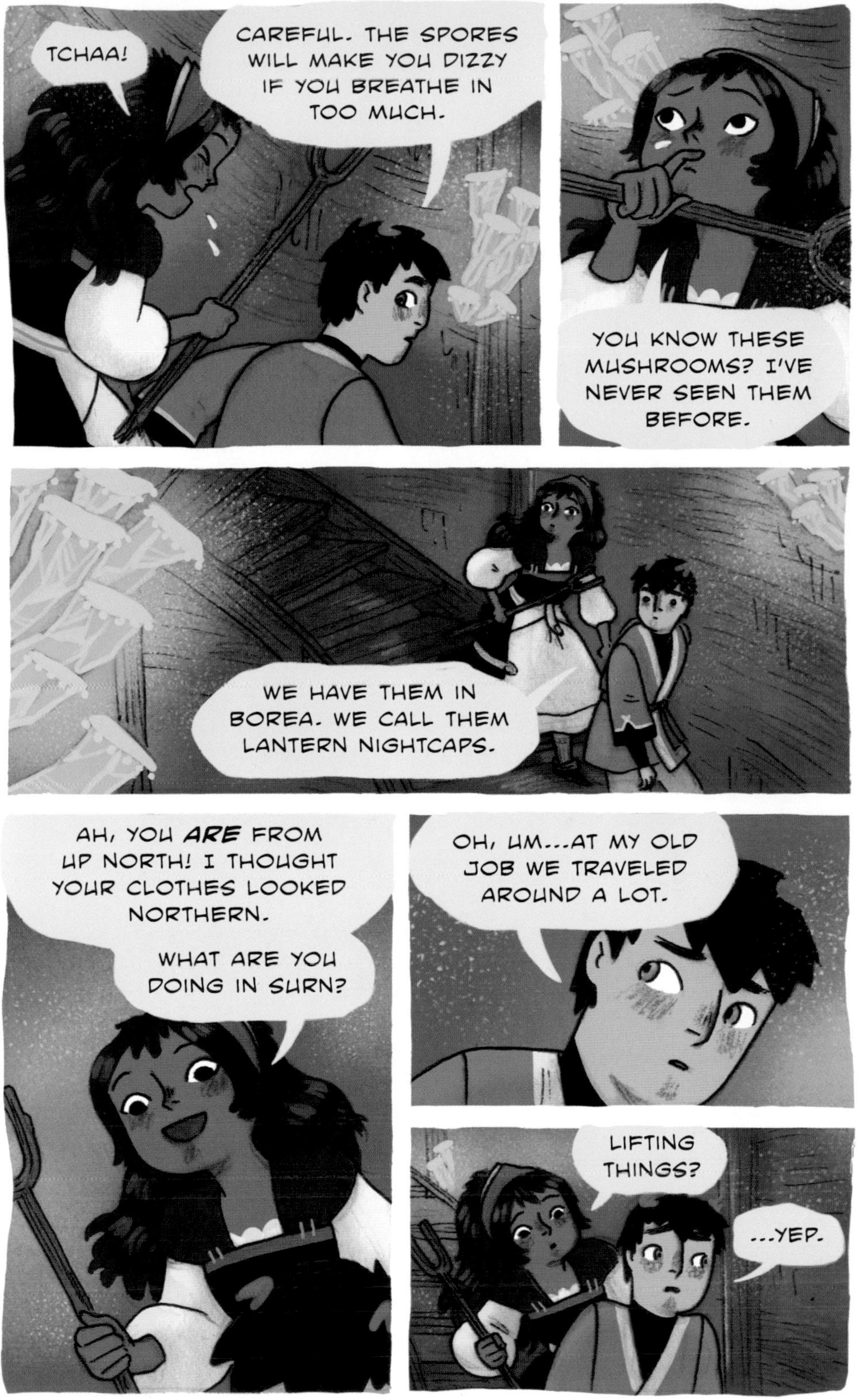
TCHAA!
CAREFUL. THE SPORES WILL MAKE YOU DIZZY IF YOU BREATHE IN TOO MUCH.
YOU KNOW THESE MUSHROOMS? I'VE NEVER SEEN THEM BEFORE.
WE HAVE THEM IN BOREA. WE CALL THEM LANTERN NIGHTCAPS.
AH, YOU **ARE** FROM UP NORTH! I THOUGHT YOUR CLOTHES LOOKED NORTHERN.
WHAT ARE YOU DOING IN SURN?
OH, UM...AT MY OLD JOB WE TRAVELED AROUND A LOT.
LIFTING THINGS?
...YEP.

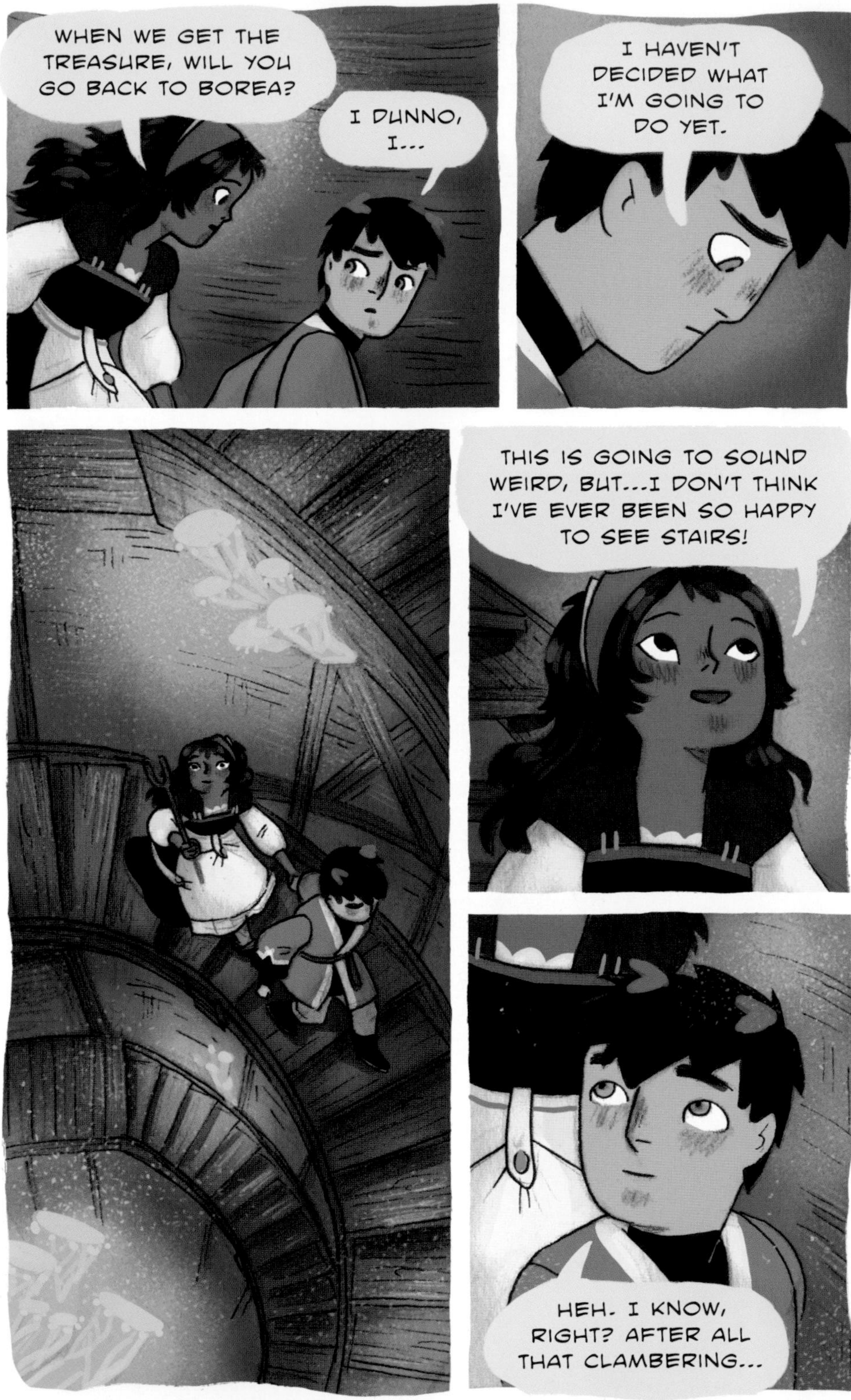
WHEN WE GET THE TREASURE, WILL YOU GO BACK TO BOREA?
I DUNNO, I...
I HAVEN'T DECIDED WHAT I'M GOING TO DO YET.
THIS IS GOING TO SOUND WEIRD, BUT...I DON'T THINK I'VE EVER BEEN SO HAPPY TO SEE STAIRS!
HEH. I KNOW, RIGHT? AFTER ALL THAT CLAMBERING...

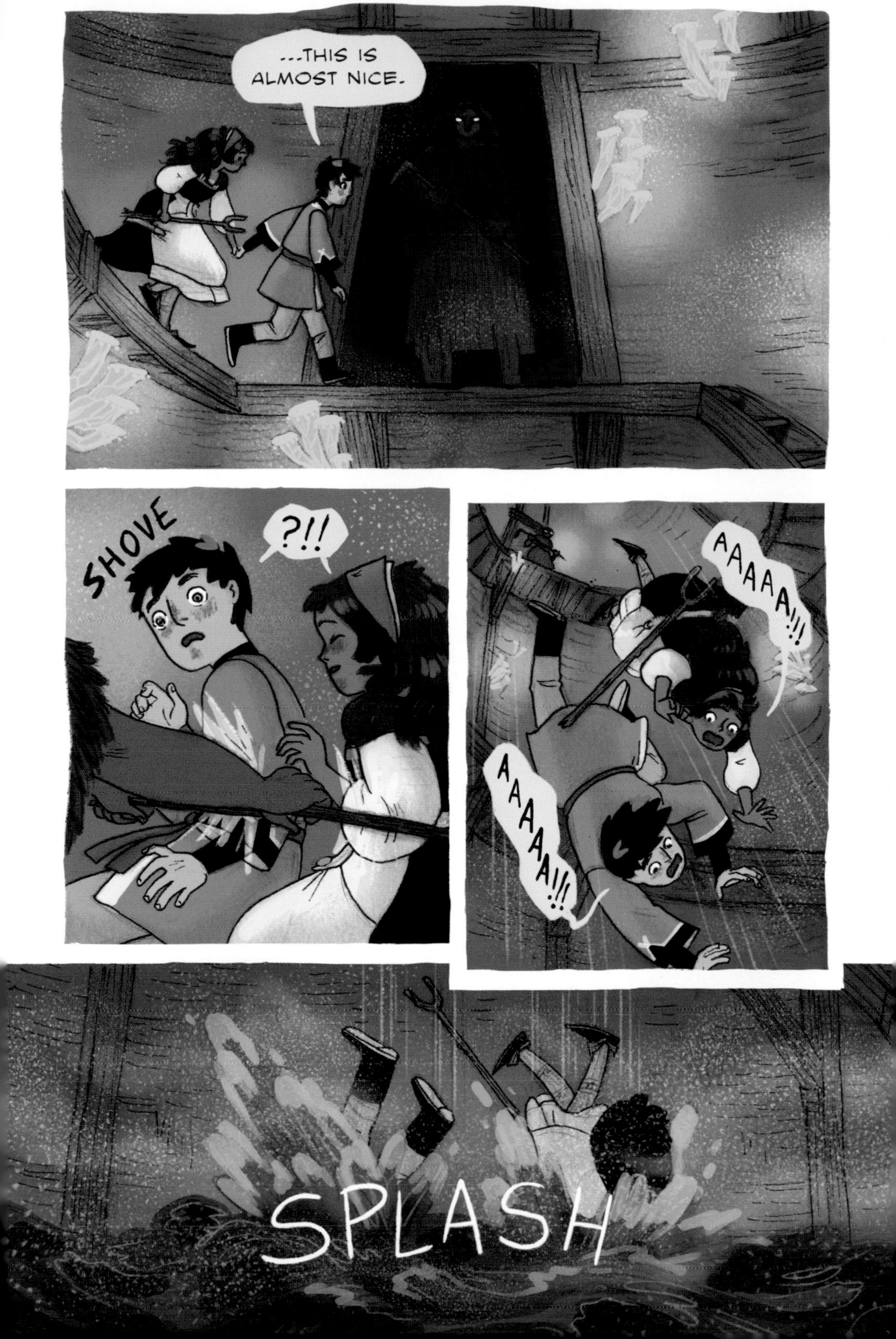
...THIS IS ALMOST NICE.
SHOVE
?!!
AAAAA!!!
AAAAA!!!
SPLASH

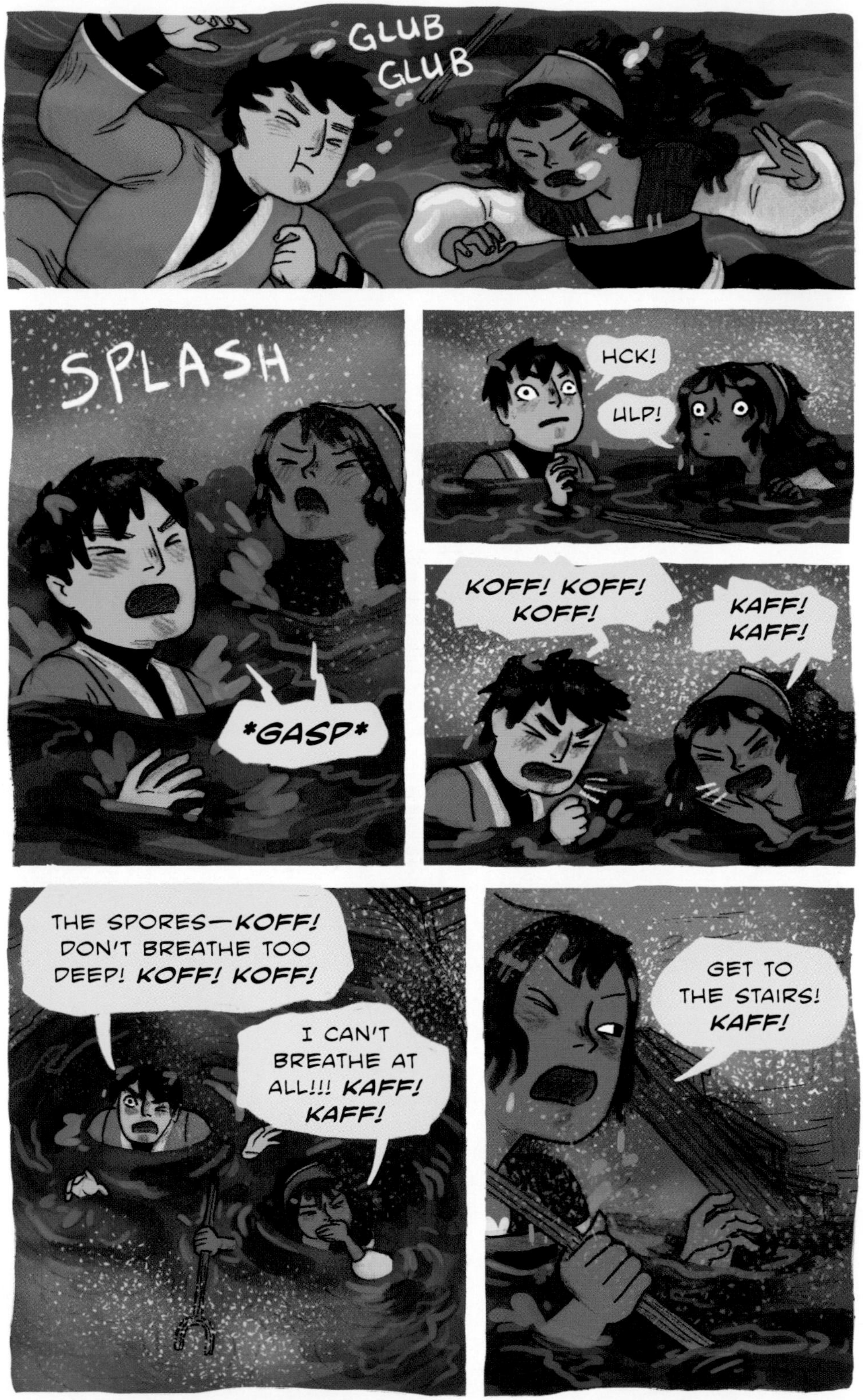
GLUB
GLUB
SPLASH
GASP
HCK!
ULP!
KOFF! KOFF! KOFF!
KAFF! KAFF!
THE SPORES—KOFF! DON'T BREATHE TOO DEEP! KOFF! KOFF!
I CAN'T BREATHE AT ALL!!! KAFF! KAFF!
GET TO THE STAIRS! KAFF!

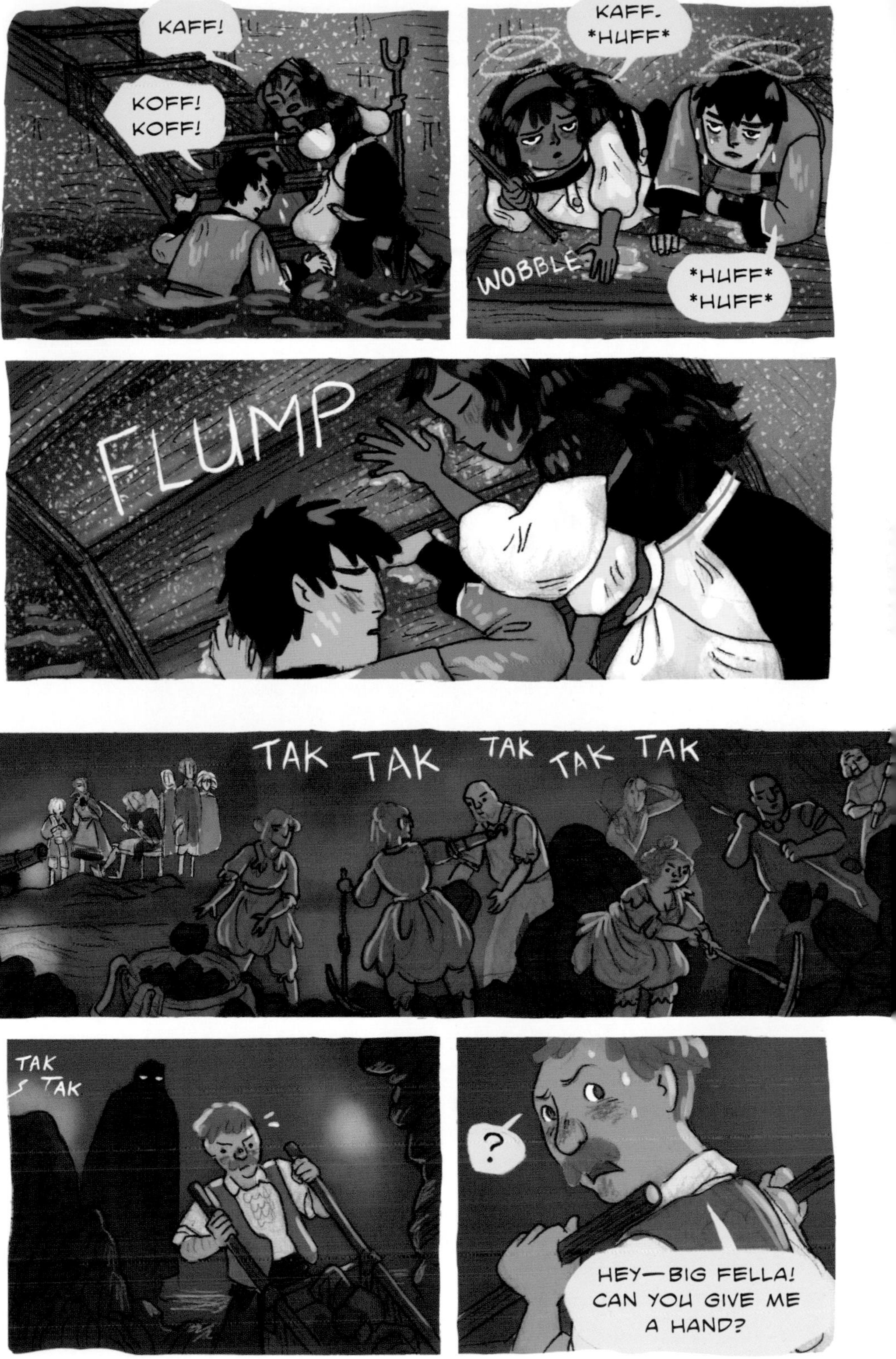
KAFF!
KOFF! KOFF!
KAFF- *HUFF*
WOBBLE
HUFF *HUFF*
FLUMP
TAK TAK TAK TAK TAK
TAK TAK
?
HEY—BIG FELLA! CAN YOU GIVE ME A HAND?

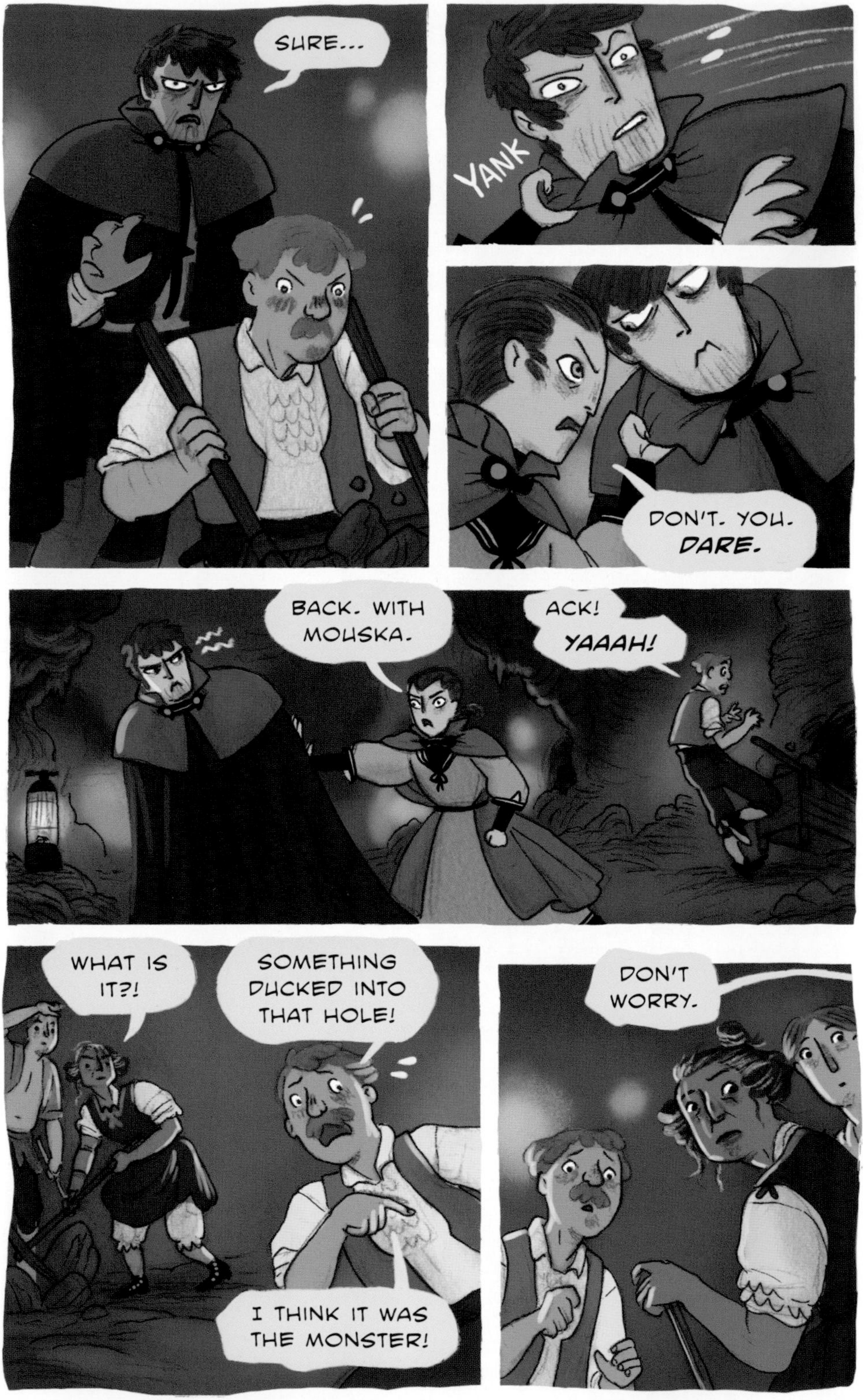
SURE...
YANK
DON'T. YOU. DARE.
BACK. WITH MOUSKA.
ACK! YAAAH!
WHAT IS IT?!
SOMETHING DUCKED INTO THAT HOLE!
I THINK IT WAS THE MONSTER!
DON'T WORRY.

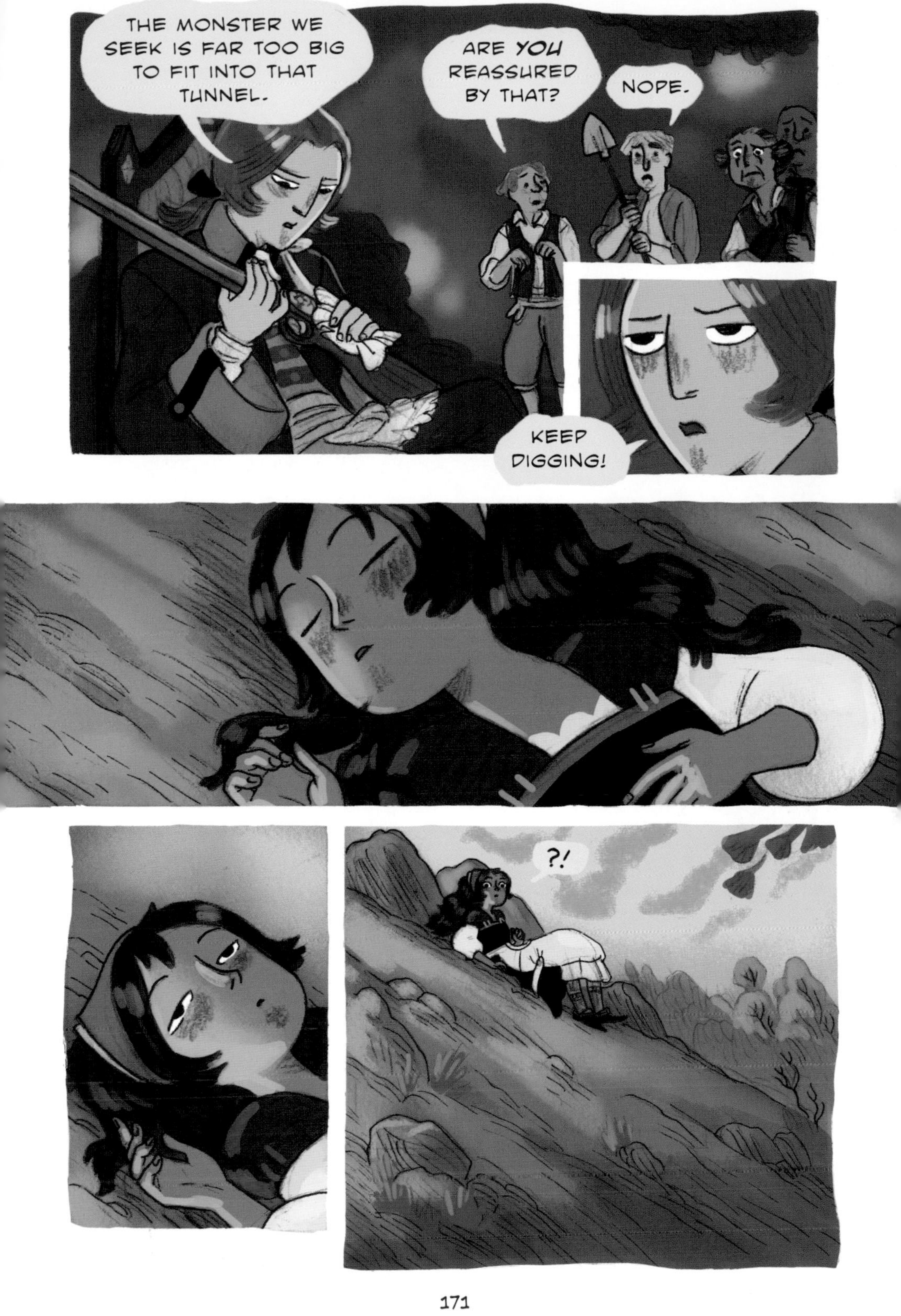
THE MONSTER WE SEEK IS FAR TOO BIG TO FIT INTO THAT TUNNEL.
ARE YOU REASSURED BY THAT?
NOPE.
KEEP DIGGING!
?!

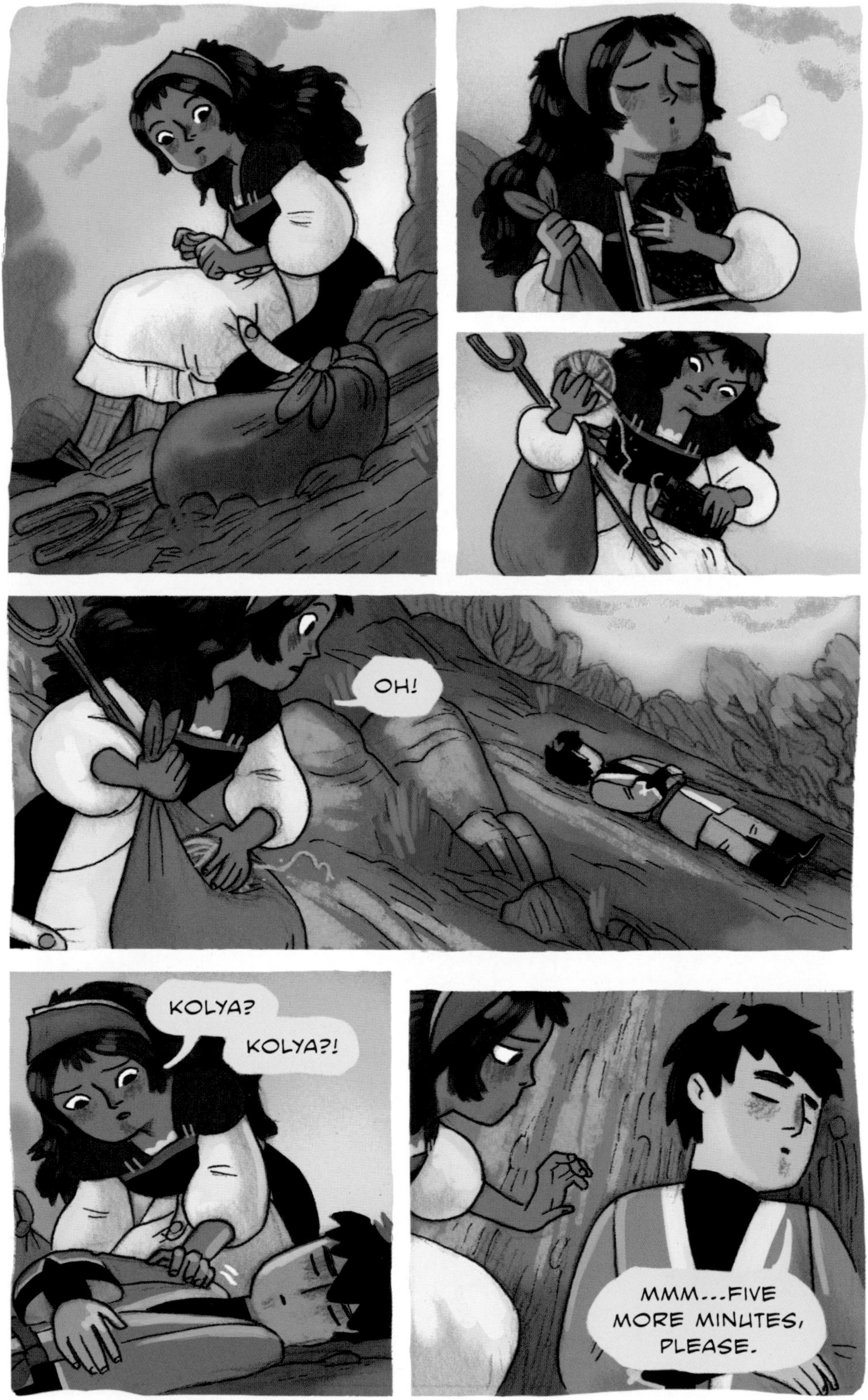
OH!
KOLYA?
KOLYA?!
MMM...FIVE MORE MINUTES, PLEASE.

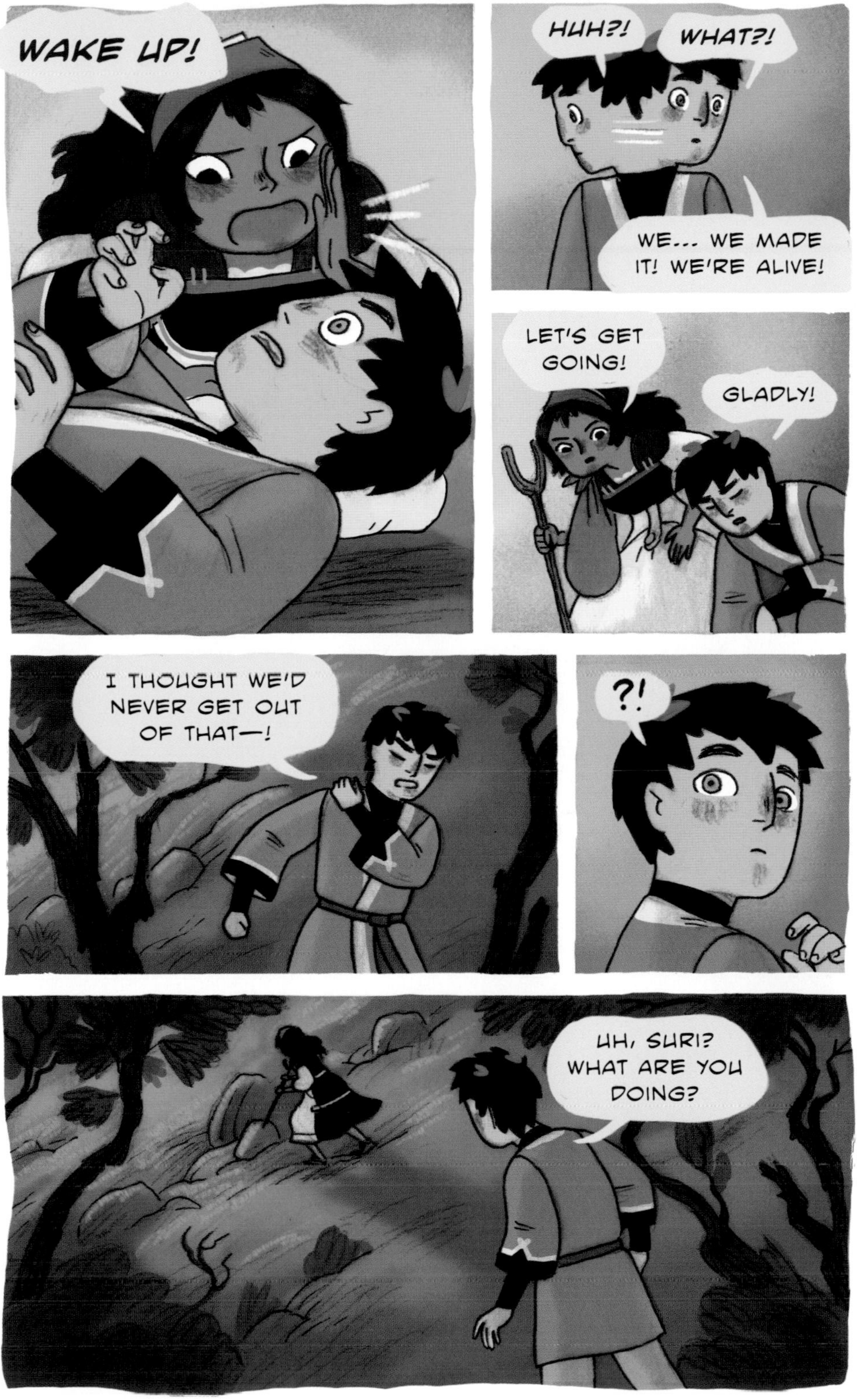
WAKE UP!
HUH?!
WHAT?!
WE... WE MADE IT! WE'RE ALIVE!
LET'S GET GOING!
GLADLY!
I THOUGHT WE'D NEVER GET OUT OF THAT—!
?!
UH, SURI? WHAT ARE YOU DOING?

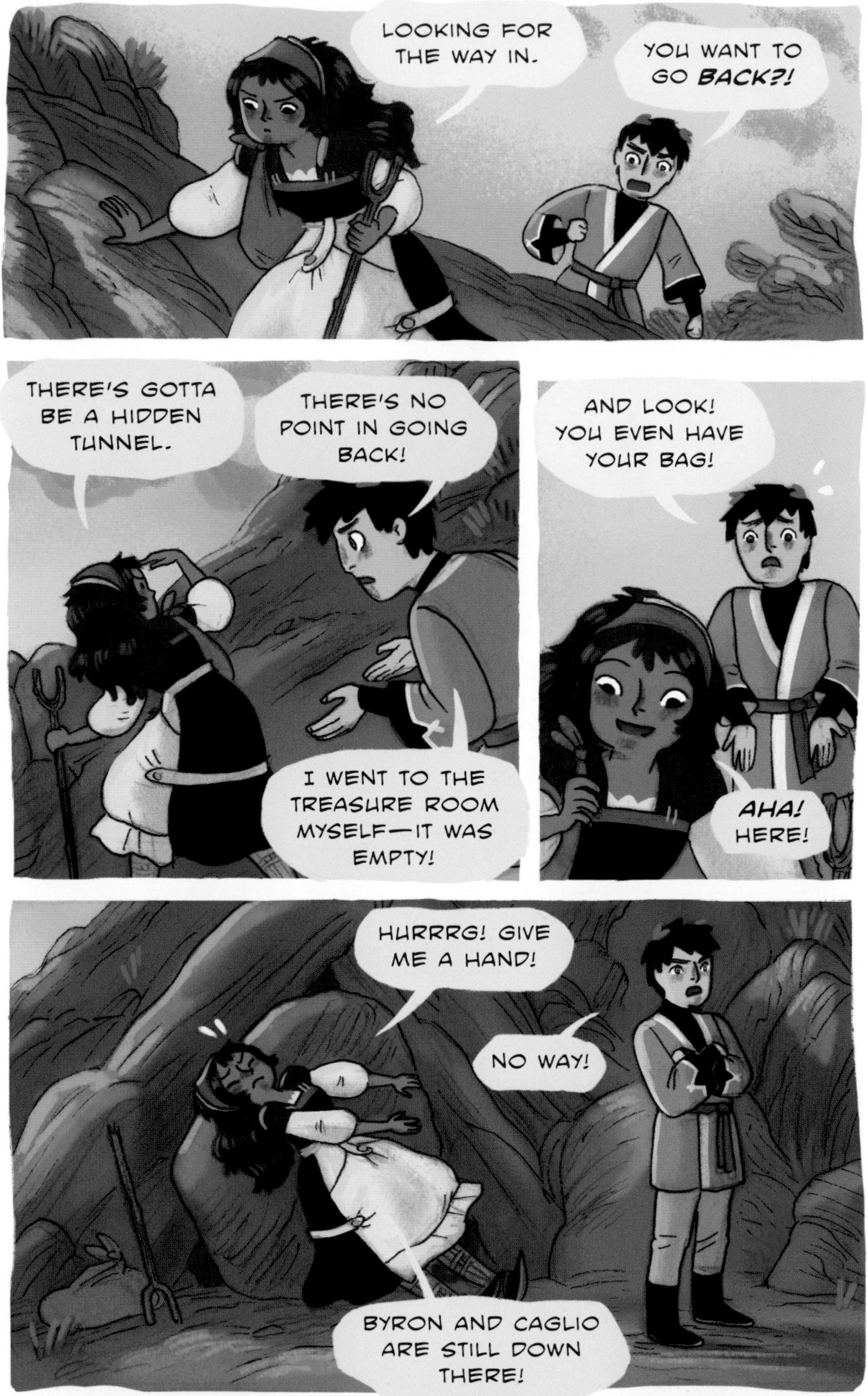
LOOKING FOR THE WAY IN.
YOU WANT TO GO *BACK?!*
THERE'S GOTTA BE A HIDDEN TUNNEL.
THERE'S NO POINT IN GOING BACK!
I WENT TO THE TREASURE ROOM MYSELF—IT WAS EMPTY!
AND LOOK! YOU EVEN HAVE YOUR BAG!
AHA! HERE!
HURRRG! GIVE ME A HAND!
NO WAY!
BYRON AND CAGLIO ARE STILL DOWN THERE!

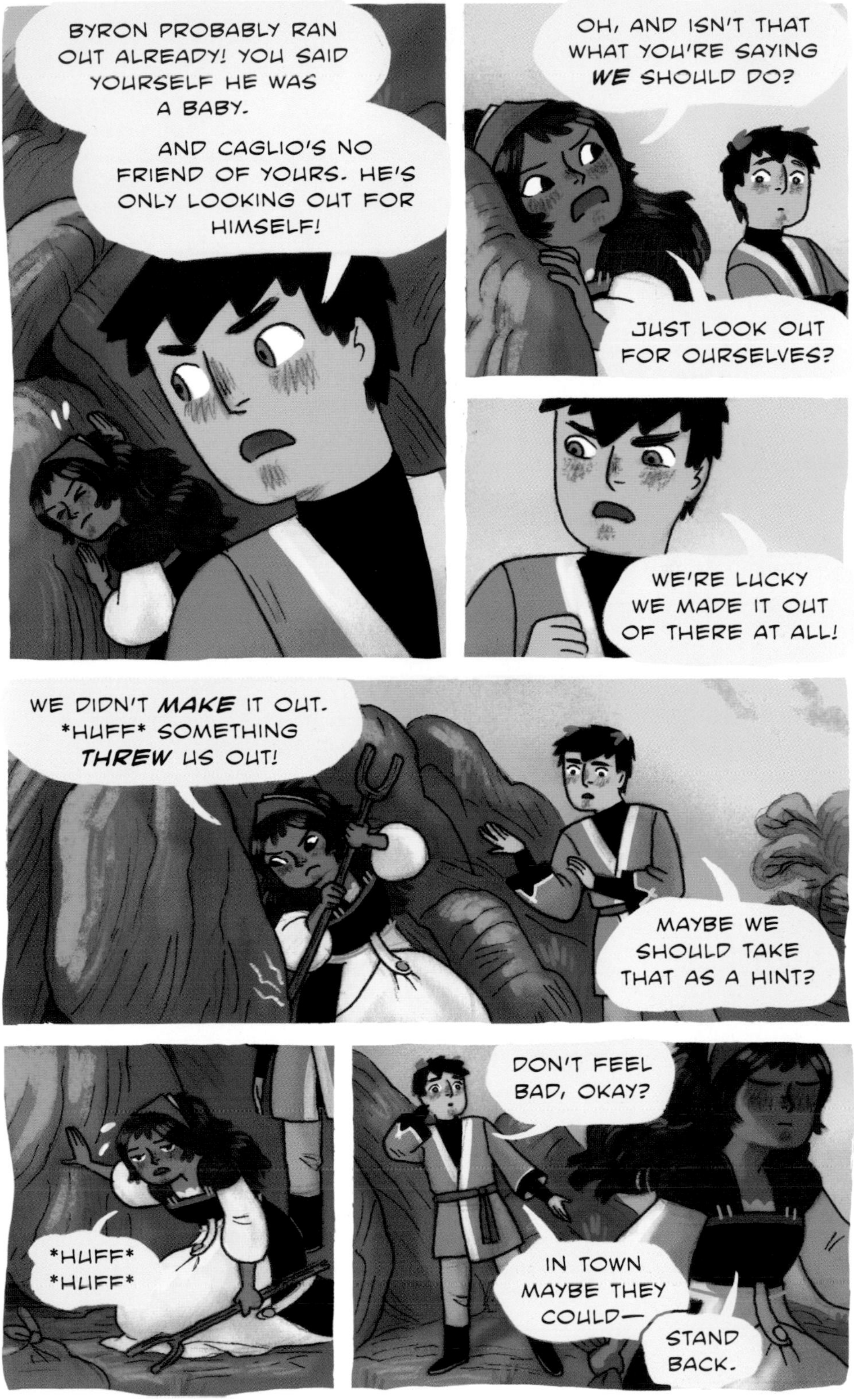
BYRON PROBABLY RAN OUT ALREADY! YOU SAID YOURSELF HE WAS A BABY.
AND CAGLIO'S NO FRIEND OF YOURS. HE'S ONLY LOOKING OUT FOR HIMSELF!
OH, AND ISN'T THAT WHAT YOU'RE SAYING *WE* SHOULD DO?
JUST LOOK OUT FOR OURSELVES?
WE'RE LUCKY WE MADE IT OUT OF THERE AT ALL!
WE DIDN'T *MAKE* IT OUT. *HUFF* SOMETHING *THREW* US OUT!
MAYBE WE SHOULD TAKE THAT AS A HINT?
HUFF *HUFF*
DON'T FEEL BAD, OKAY?
IN TOWN MAYBE THEY COULD—
STAND BACK.

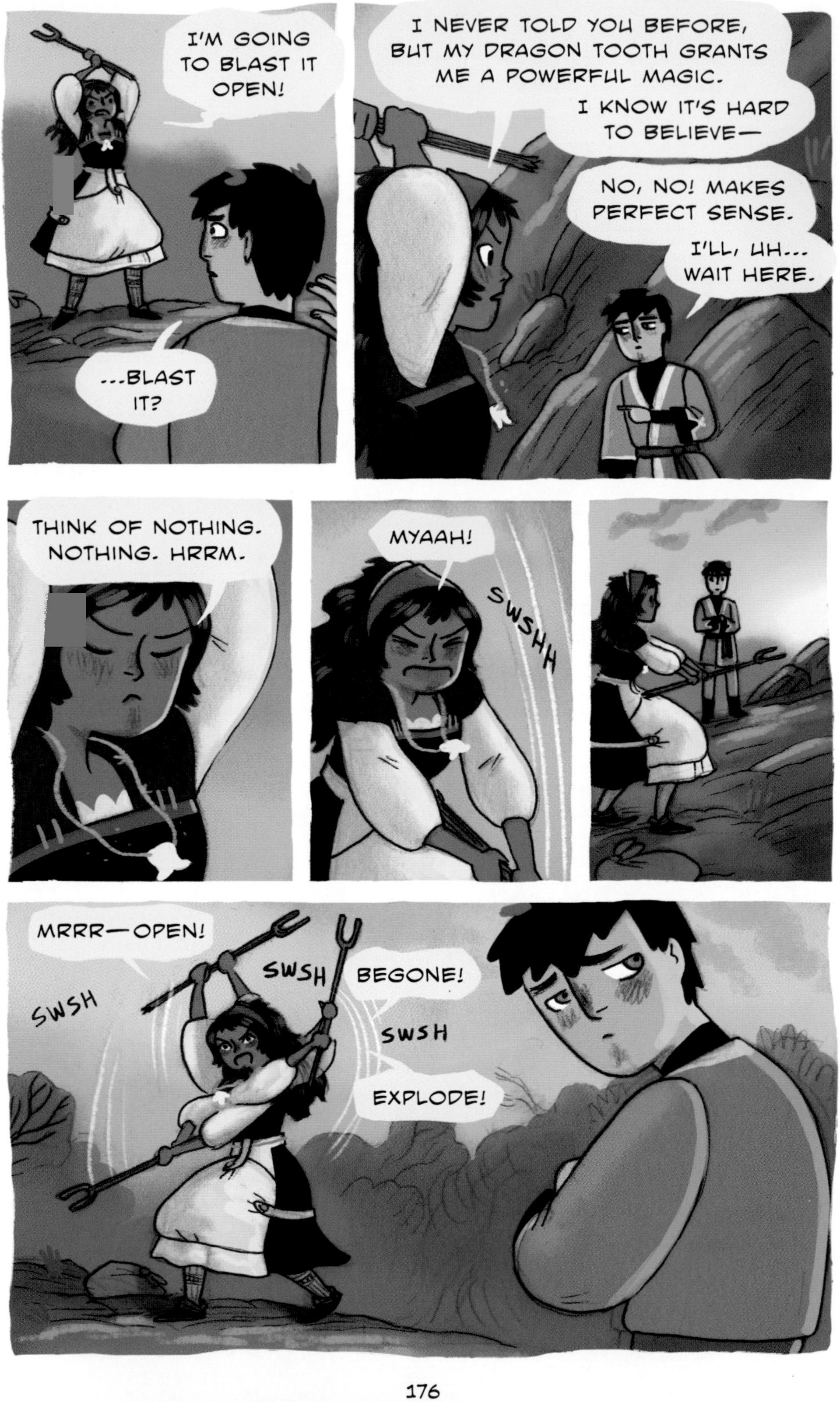
I'M GOING TO BLAST IT OPEN!
...BLAST IT?
I NEVER TOLD YOU BEFORE, BUT MY DRAGON TOOTH GRANTS ME A POWERFUL MAGIC.
I KNOW IT'S HARD TO BELIEVE—
NO, NO! MAKES PERFECT SENSE.
I'LL, UH... WAIT HERE.
THINK OF NOTHING. NOTHING. HRRM.
MYAAH!
SWSHH
MRRR—OPEN!
SWSH
SWSH
BEGONE!
SWSH
EXPLODE!

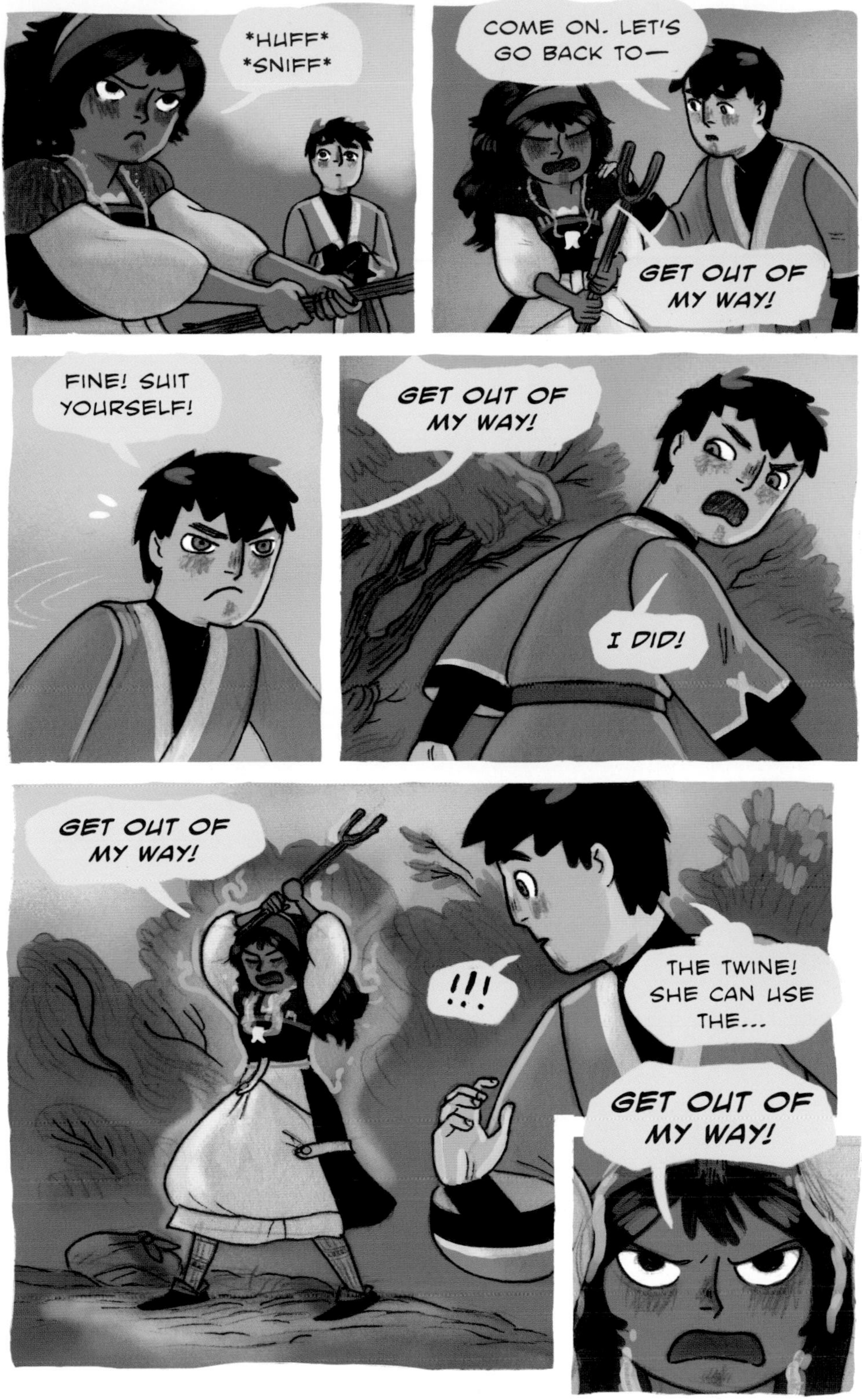
HUFF
SNIFF
COME ON. LET'S GO BACK TO—
GET OUT OF MY WAY!
FINE! SUIT YOURSELF!
GET OUT OF MY WAY!
I DID!
GET OUT OF MY WAY!
!!!
THE TWINE! SHE CAN USE THE...
GET OUT OF MY WAY!

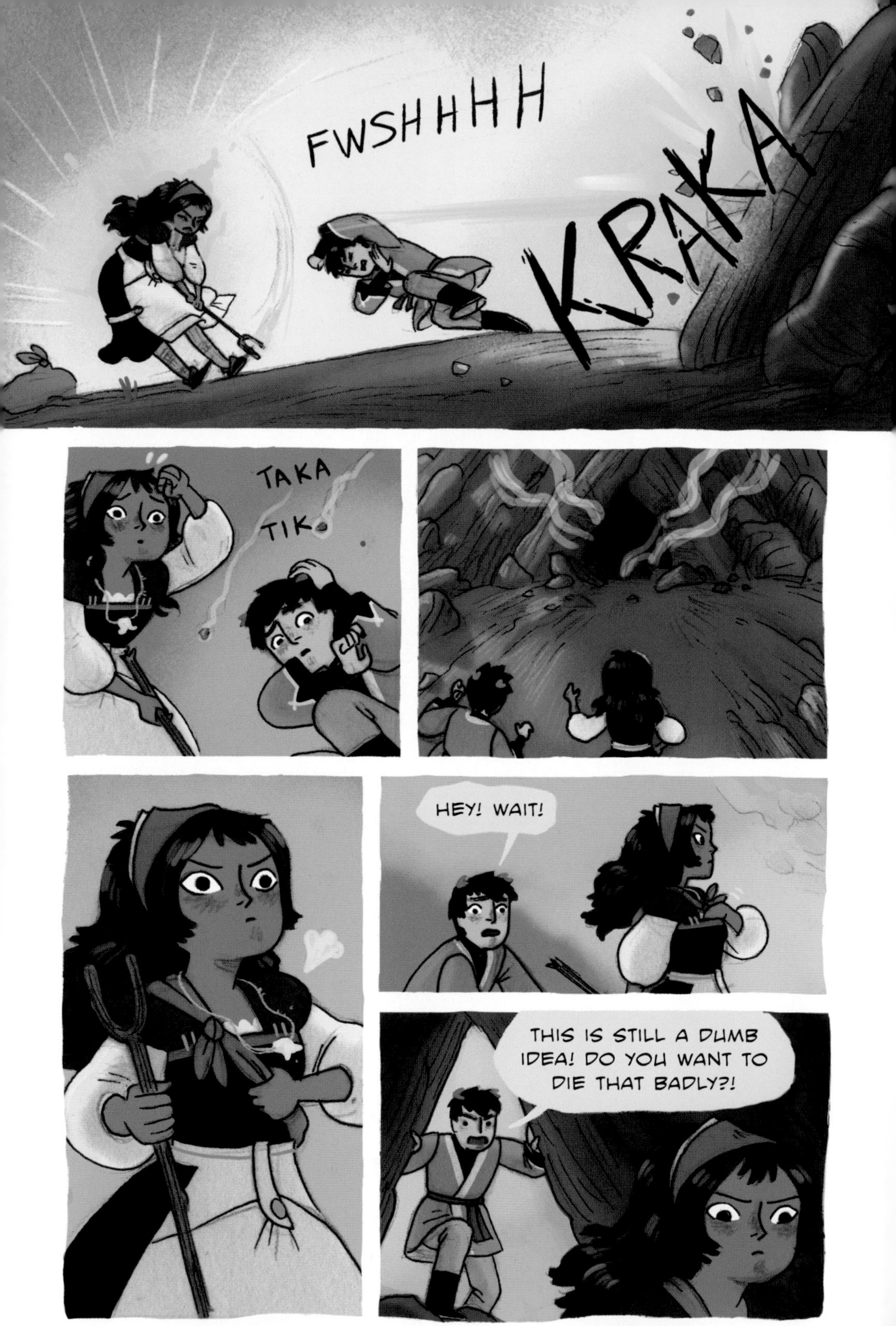
FWSHHHHH
KRAKA
TAKA
TIK
HEY! WAIT!
THIS IS STILL A DUMB IDEA! DO YOU WANT TO DIE THAT BADLY?!

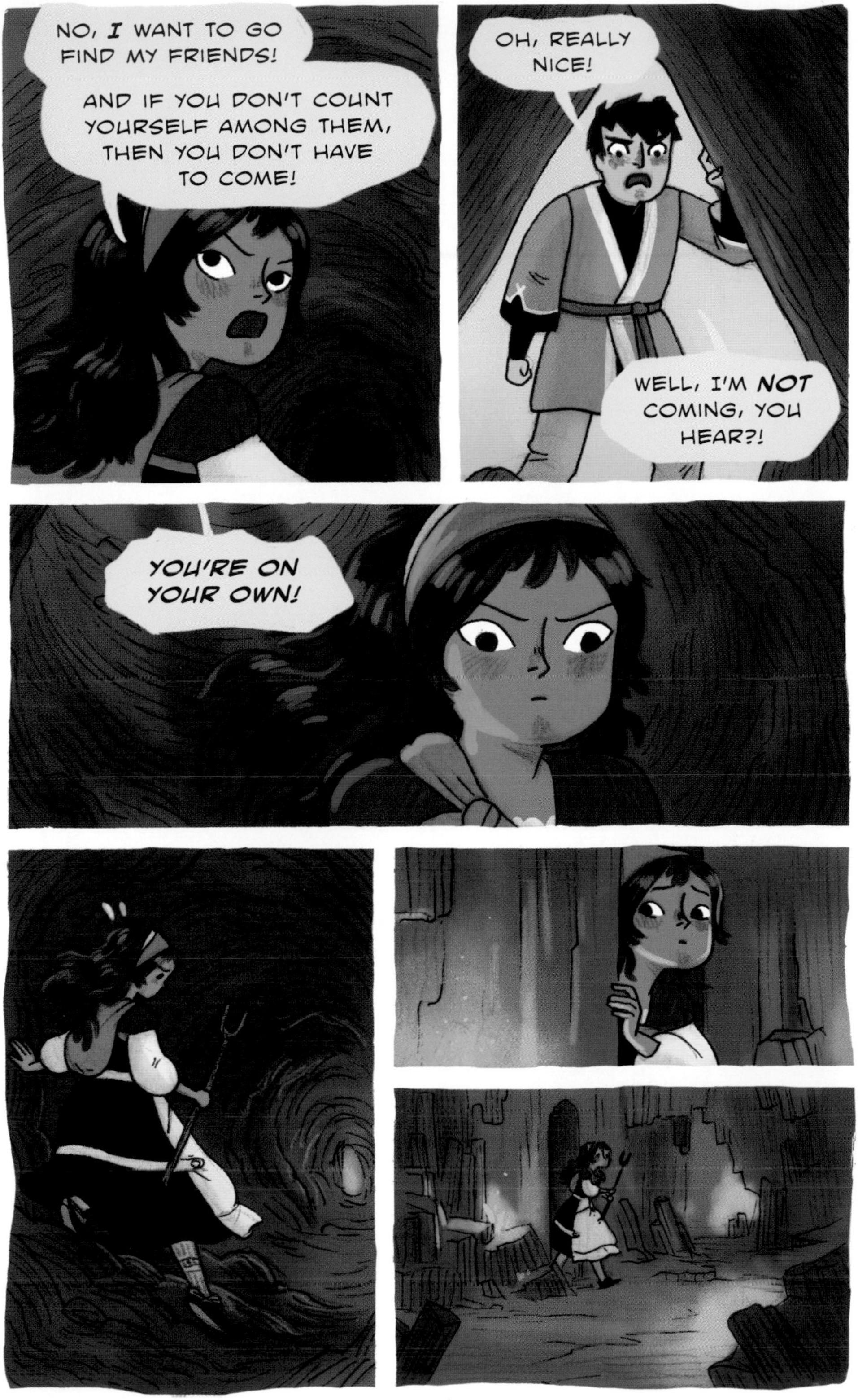
NO, *I* WANT TO GO FIND MY FRIENDS!
AND IF YOU DON'T COUNT YOURSELF AMONG THEM, THEN YOU DON'T HAVE TO COME!
OH, REALLY NICE!
WELL, I'M **NOT** COMING, YOU HEAR?!
YOU'RE ON YOUR OWN!

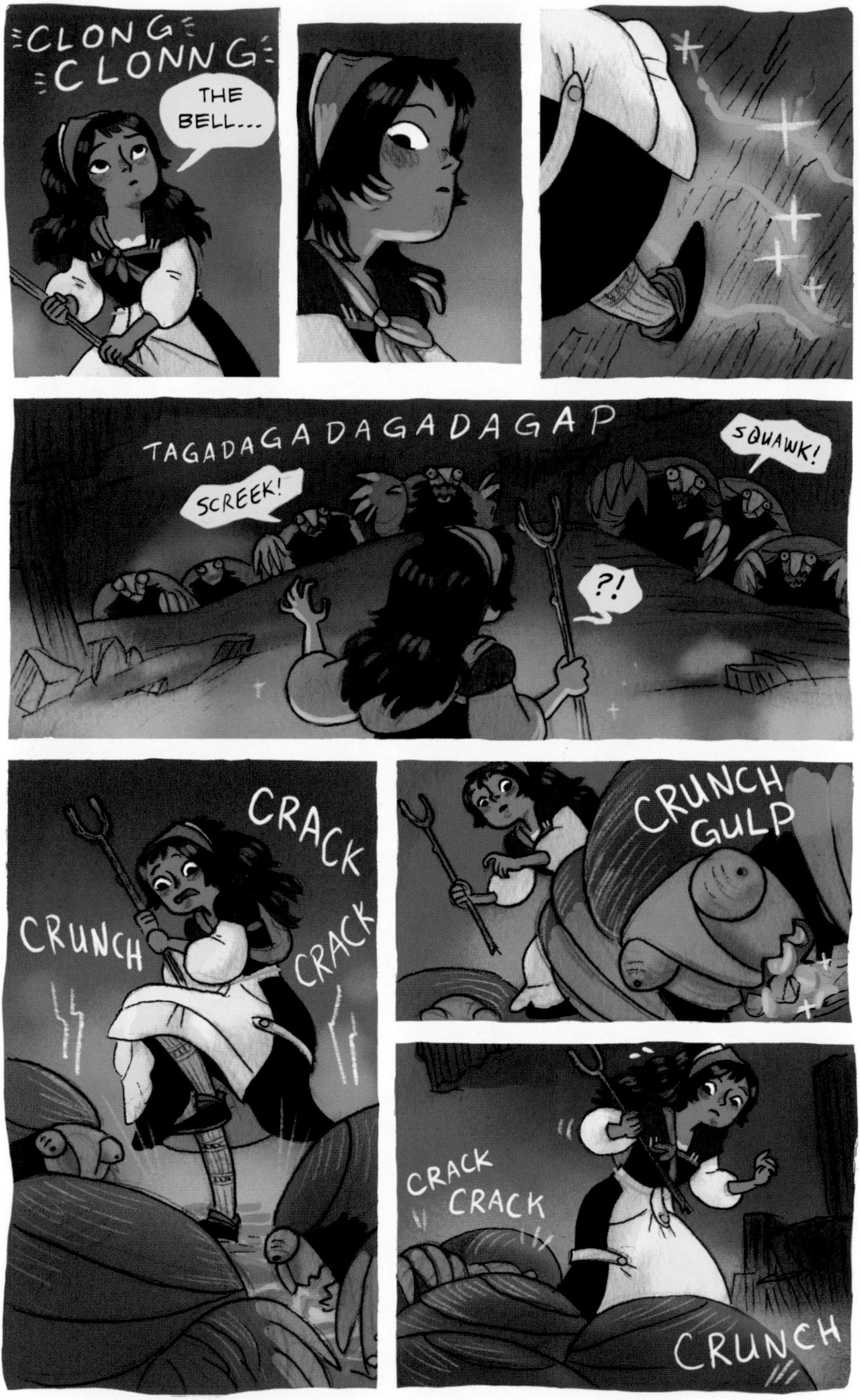
CLONG
CLONNG
THE BELL...
TAGADAGADAGADAGAP
SCREEK!
SQUAWK!
?!
CRACK
CRUNCH
CRACK
CRUNCH
GULP
CRACK
CRACK
CRUNCH

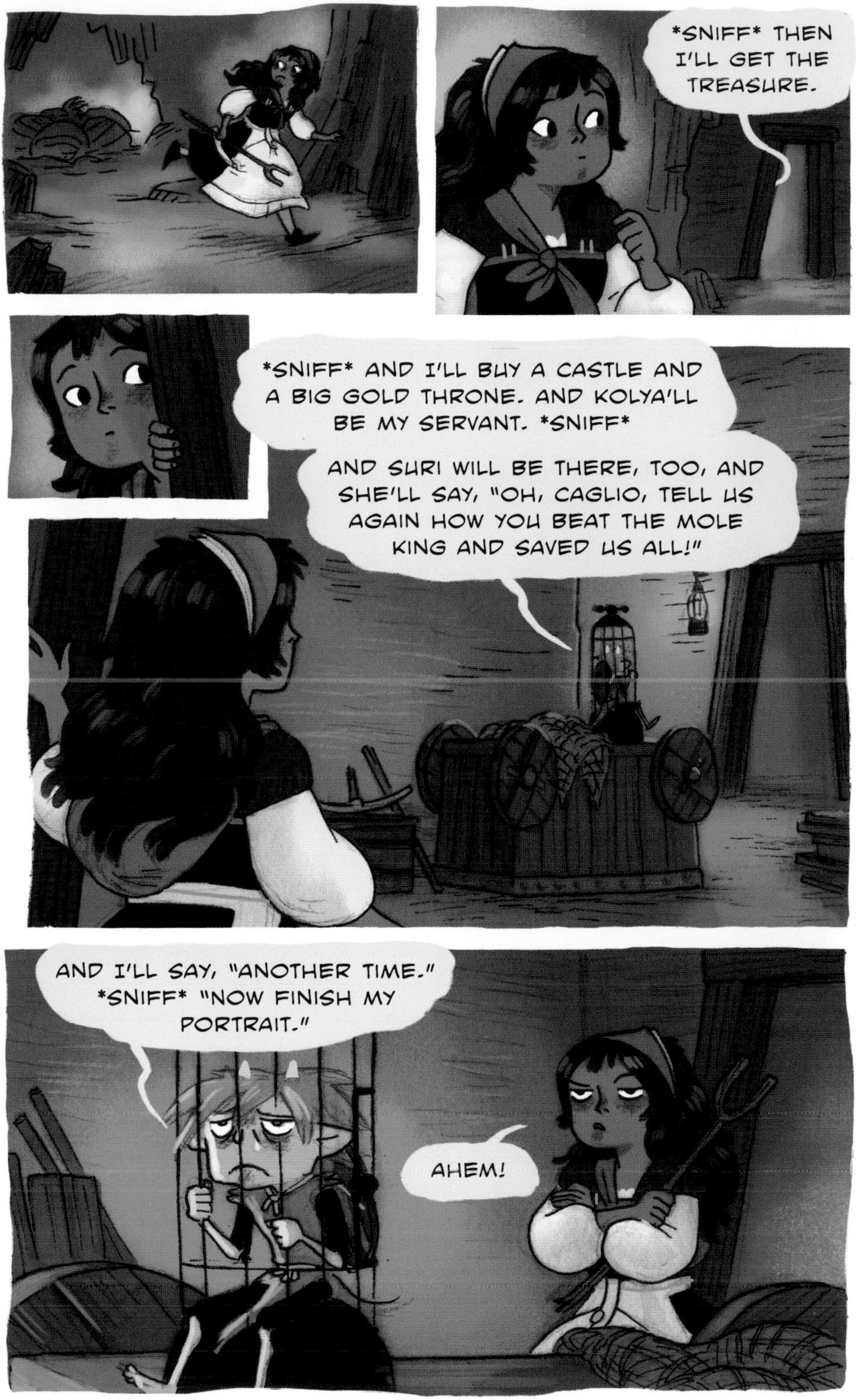
SNIFF THEN I'LL GET THE TREASURE.
SNIFF AND I'LL BUY A CASTLE AND A BIG GOLD THRONE. AND KOLYA'LL BE MY SERVANT. *SNIFF*
AND SURI WILL BE THERE, TOO, AND SHE'LL SAY, "OH, CAGLIO, TELL US AGAIN HOW YOU BEAT THE MOLE KING AND SAVED US ALL!"
AND I'LL SAY, "ANOTHER TIME." *SNIFF* "NOW FINISH MY PORTRAIT."
AHEM!

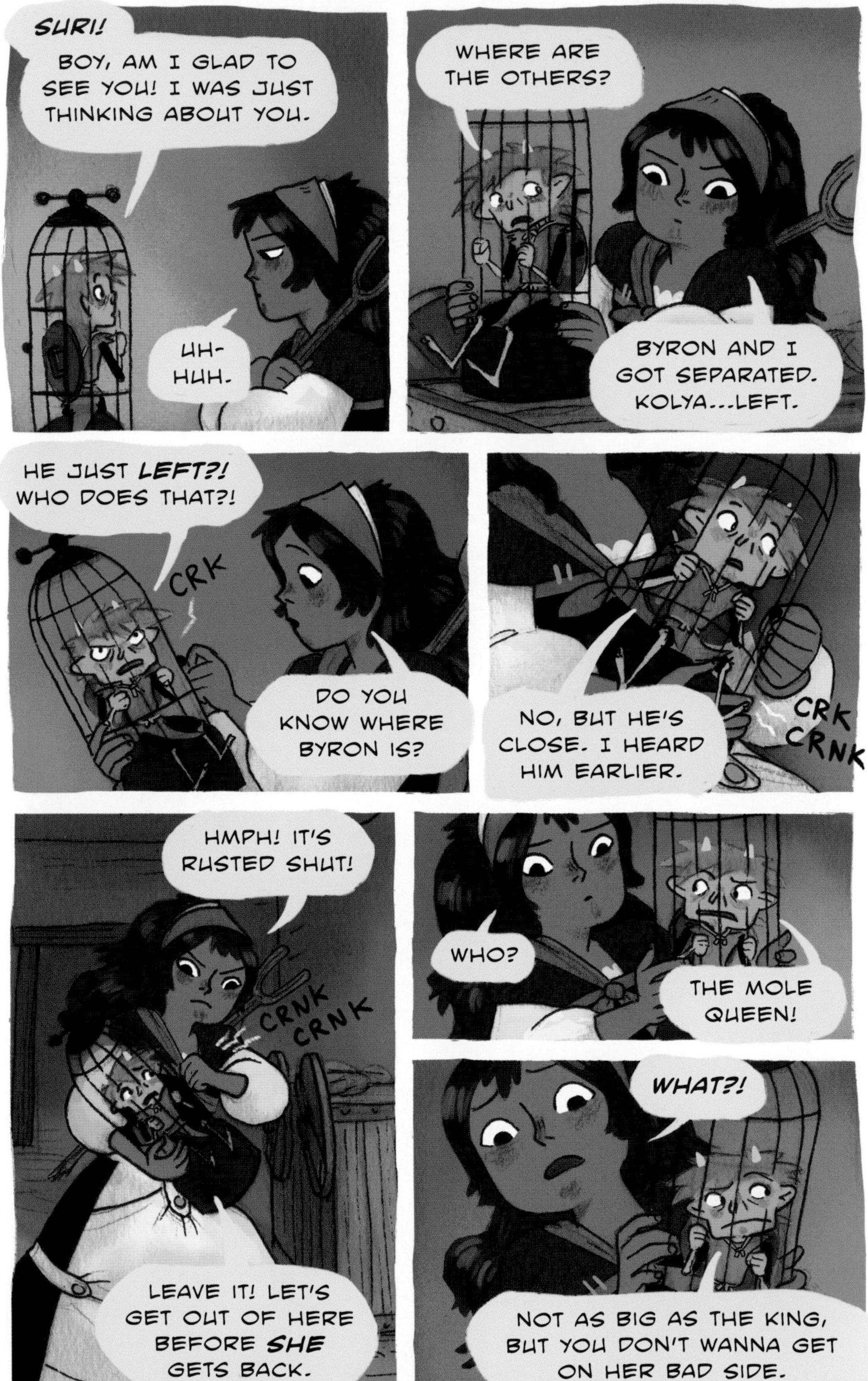
SURI!
BOY, AM I GLAD TO SEE YOU! I WAS JUST THINKING ABOUT YOU.
UH-HUH.
WHERE ARE THE OTHERS?
BYRON AND I GOT SEPARATED. KOLYA...LEFT.
HE JUST LEFT?! WHO DOES THAT?!
CRK
DO YOU KNOW WHERE BYRON IS?
NO, BUT HE'S CLOSE. I HEARD HIM EARLIER.
CRK CRNK
HMPH! IT'S RUSTED SHUT!
CRNK CRNK
LEAVE IT! LET'S GET OUT OF HERE BEFORE SHE GETS BACK.
WHO?
THE MOLE QUEEN!
WHAT?!
NOT AS BIG AS THE KING, BUT YOU DON'T WANNA GET ON HER BAD SIDE.

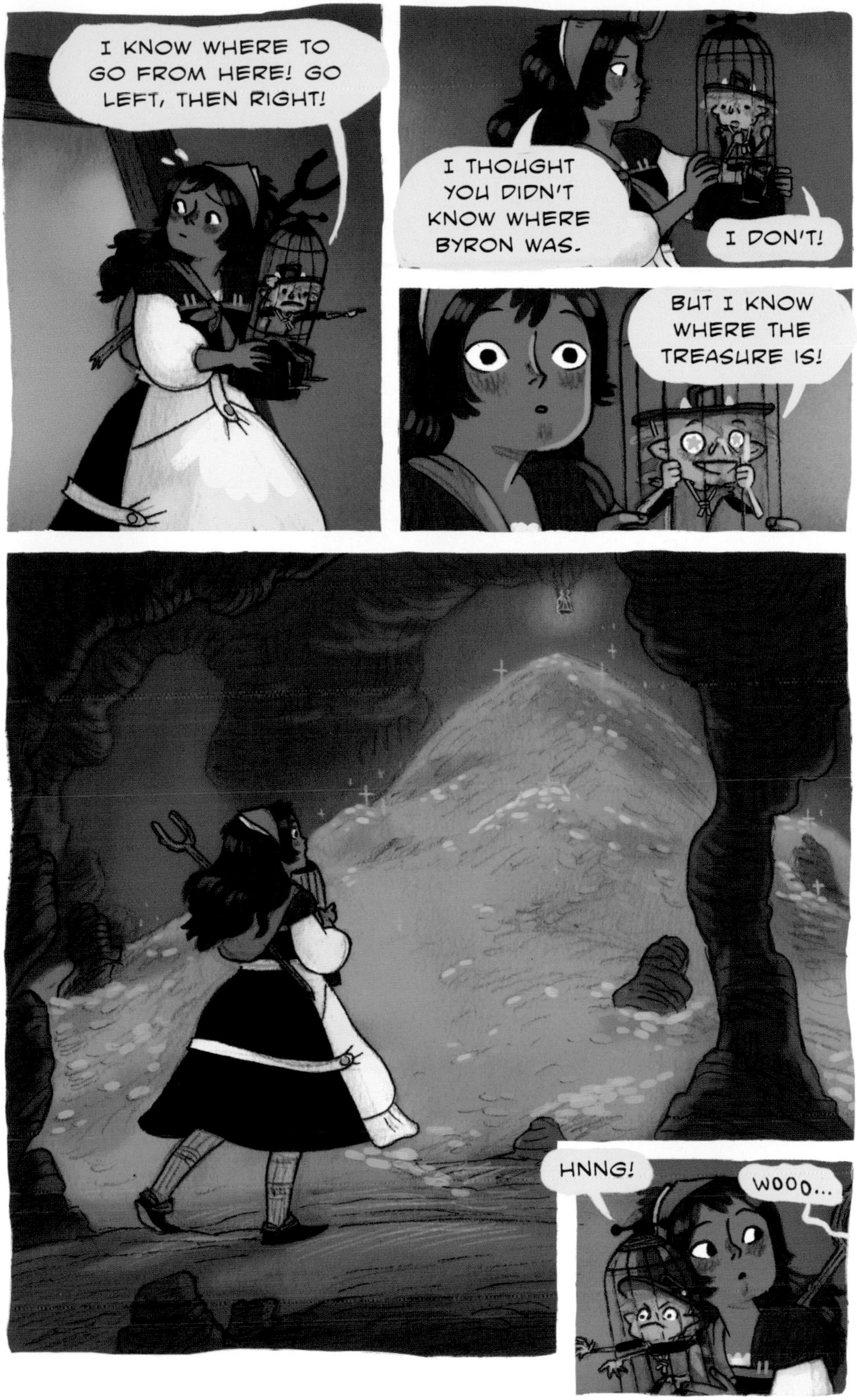
I KNOW WHERE TO GO FROM HERE! GO LEFT, THEN RIGHT!
I THOUGHT YOU DIDN'T KNOW WHERE BYRON WAS.
I DON'T!
BUT I KNOW WHERE THE TREASURE IS!
HNNG!
WOOO...

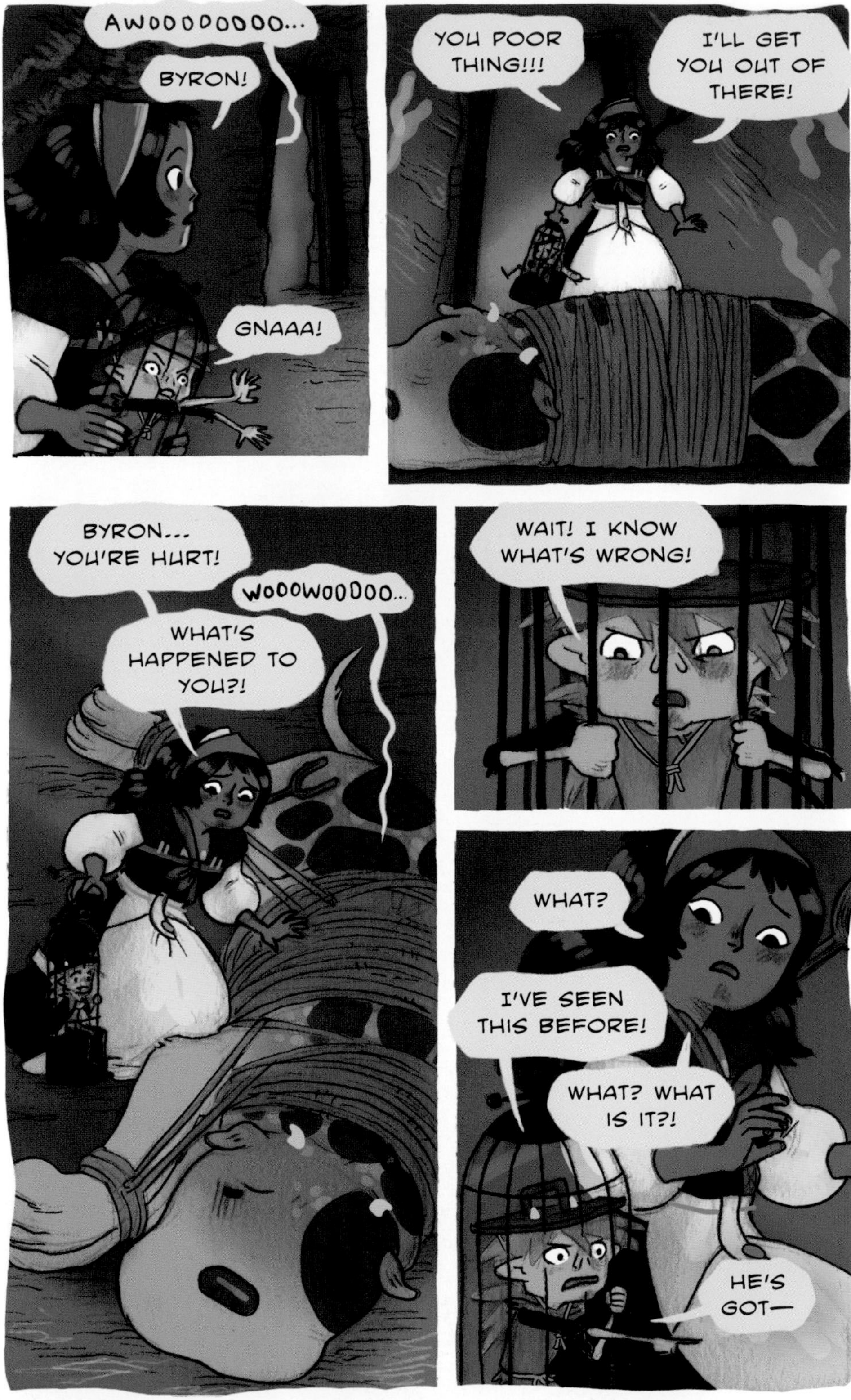
AWOOOOOOOO...
BYRON!
GNAAA!
YOU POOR THING!!!
I'LL GET YOU OUT OF THERE!
BYRON... YOU'RE HURT!
WOOOWOODOO...
WHAT'S HAPPENED TO YOU?!
WAIT! I KNOW WHAT'S WRONG!
WHAT?
I'VE SEEN THIS BEFORE!
WHAT? WHAT IS IT?!
HE'S GOT—

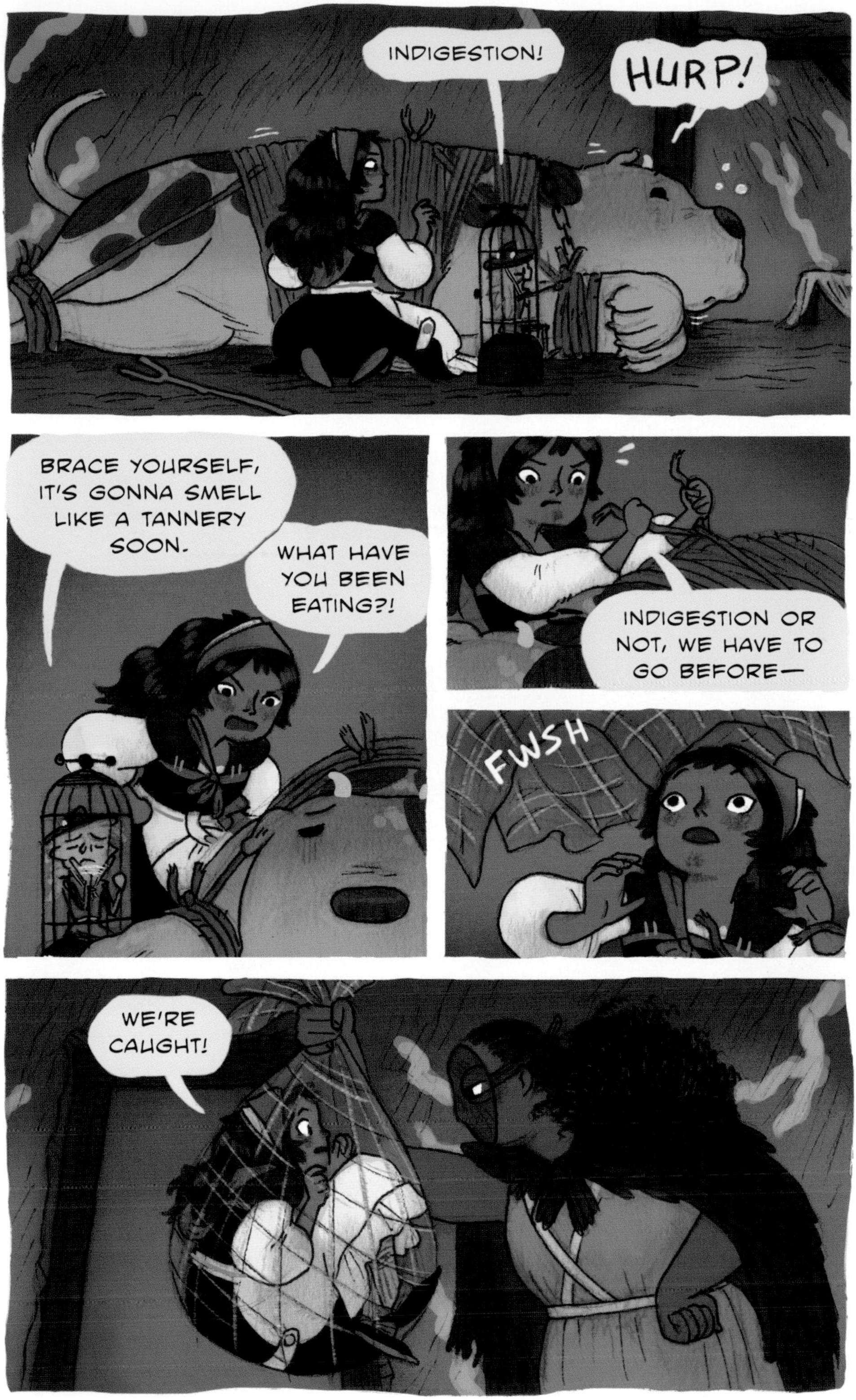
INDIGESTION!
HURP!
BRACE YOURSELF, IT'S GONNA SMELL LIKE A TANNERY SOON.
WHAT HAVE YOU BEEN EATING?!
INDIGESTION OR NOT, WE HAVE TO GO BEFORE—
FWSH
WE'RE CAUGHT!

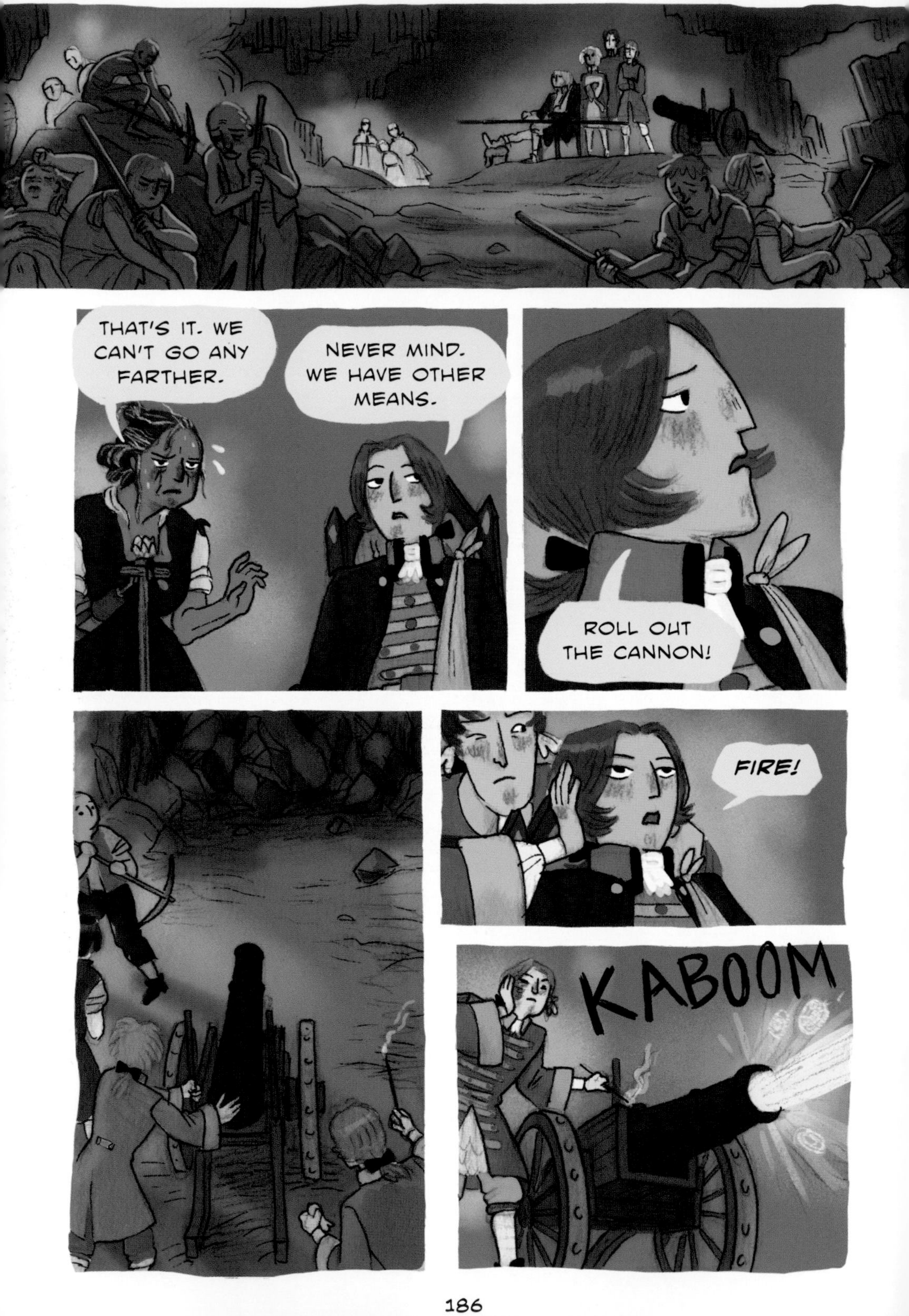
THAT'S IT. WE CAN'T GO ANY FARTHER.
NEVER MIND. WE HAVE OTHER MEANS.
ROLL OUT THE CANNON!
FIRE!
KABOOM

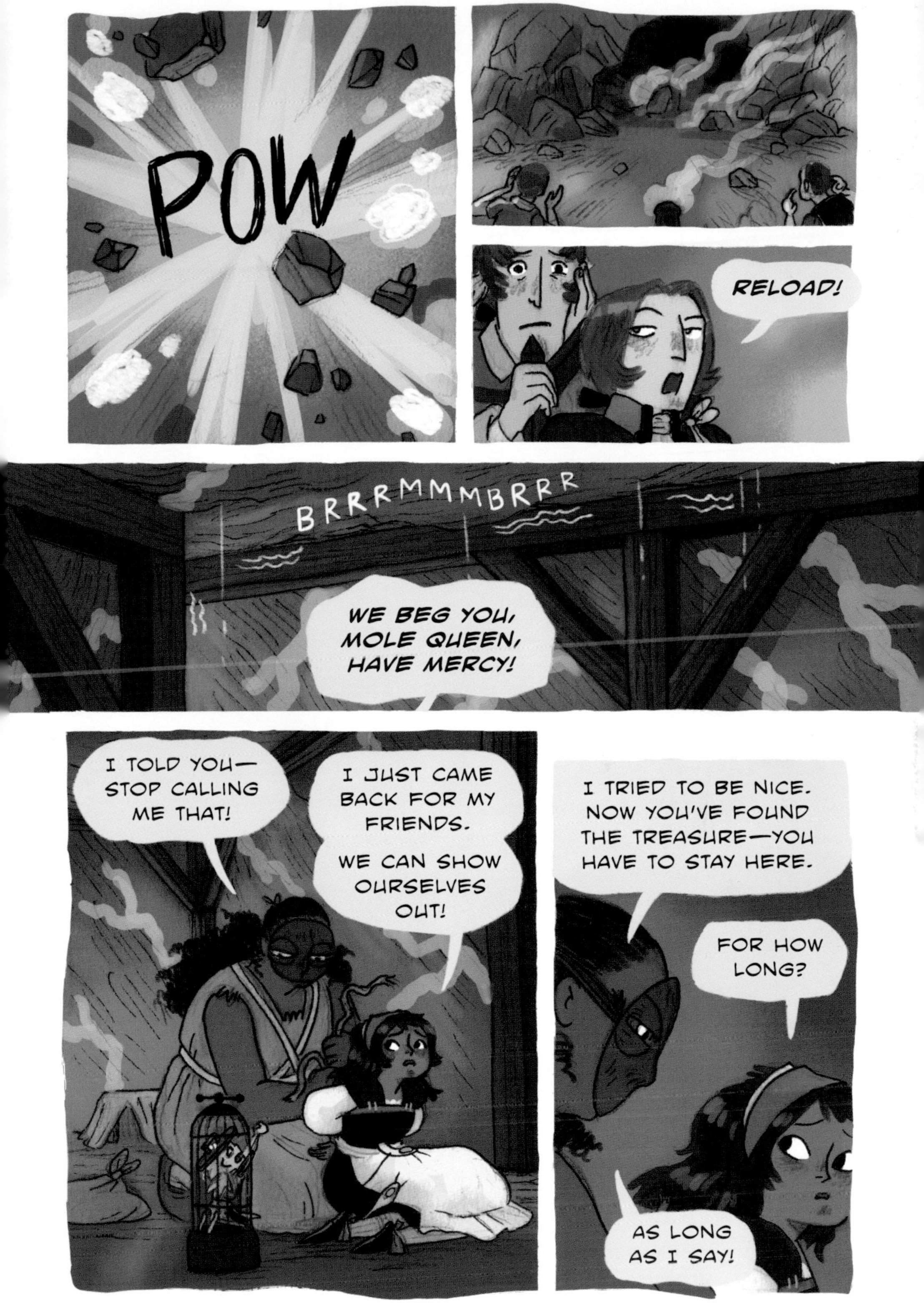
POW
RELOAD!
BRRRMMMMBRRR
WE BEG YOU, MOLE QUEEN, HAVE MERCY!
I TOLD YOU— STOP CALLING ME THAT!
I JUST CAME BACK FOR MY FRIENDS.
WE CAN SHOW OURSELVES OUT!
I TRIED TO BE NICE. NOW YOU'VE FOUND THE TREASURE—YOU HAVE TO STAY HERE.
FOR HOW LONG?
AS LONG AS I SAY!

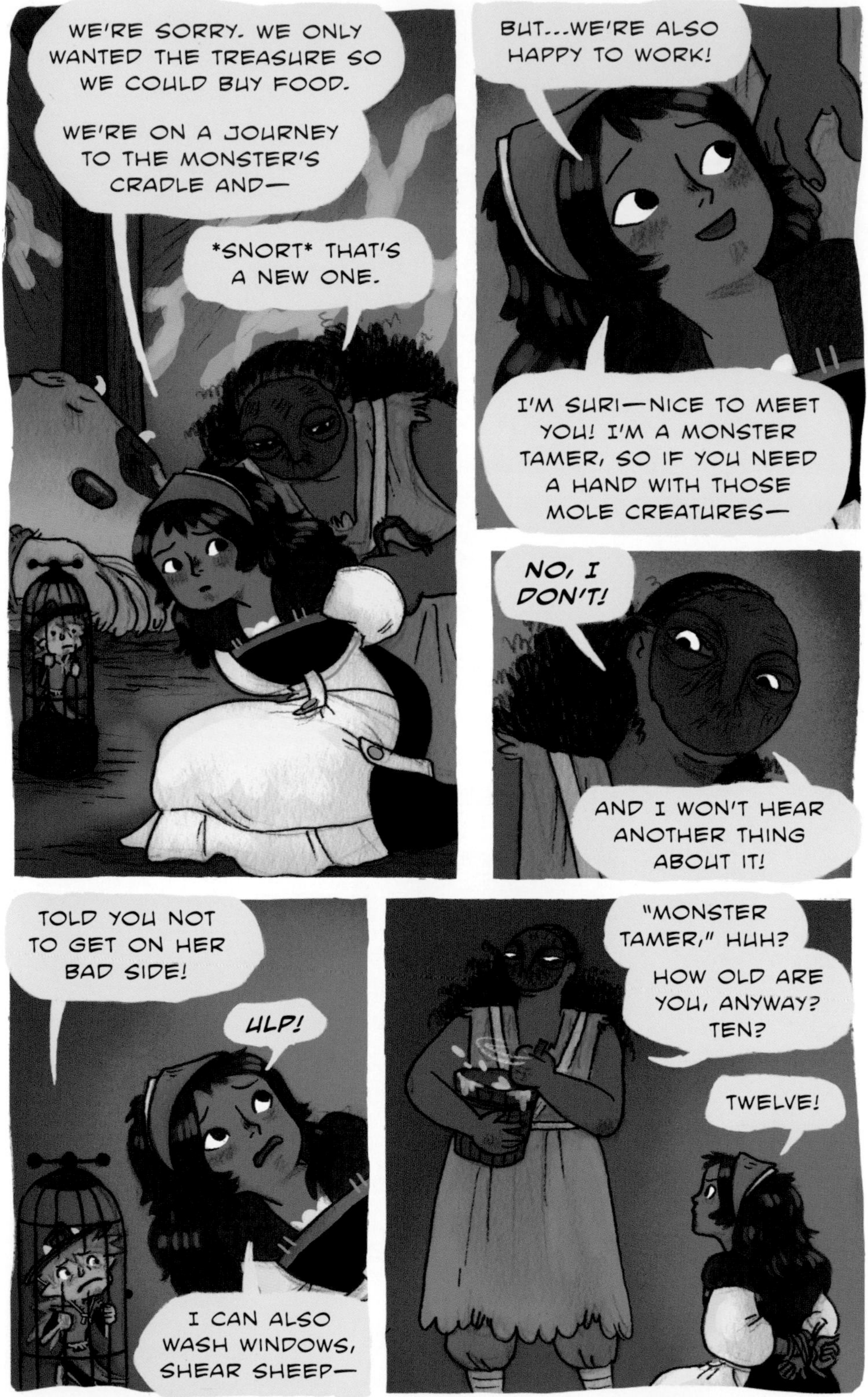
WE'RE SORRY. WE ONLY WANTED THE TREASURE SO WE COULD BUY FOOD.
WE'RE ON A JOURNEY TO THE MONSTER'S CRADLE AND—
SNORT THAT'S A NEW ONE.
BUT...WE'RE ALSO HAPPY TO WORK!
I'M SURI—NICE TO MEET YOU! I'M A MONSTER TAMER, SO IF YOU NEED A HAND WITH THOSE MOLE CREATURES—
NO, I DON'T!
AND I WON'T HEAR ANOTHER THING ABOUT IT!
TOLD YOU NOT TO GET ON HER BAD SIDE!
ULP!
I CAN ALSO WASH WINDOWS, SHEAR SHEEP—
"MONSTER TAMER," HUH?
HOW OLD ARE YOU, ANYWAY? TEN?
TWELVE!

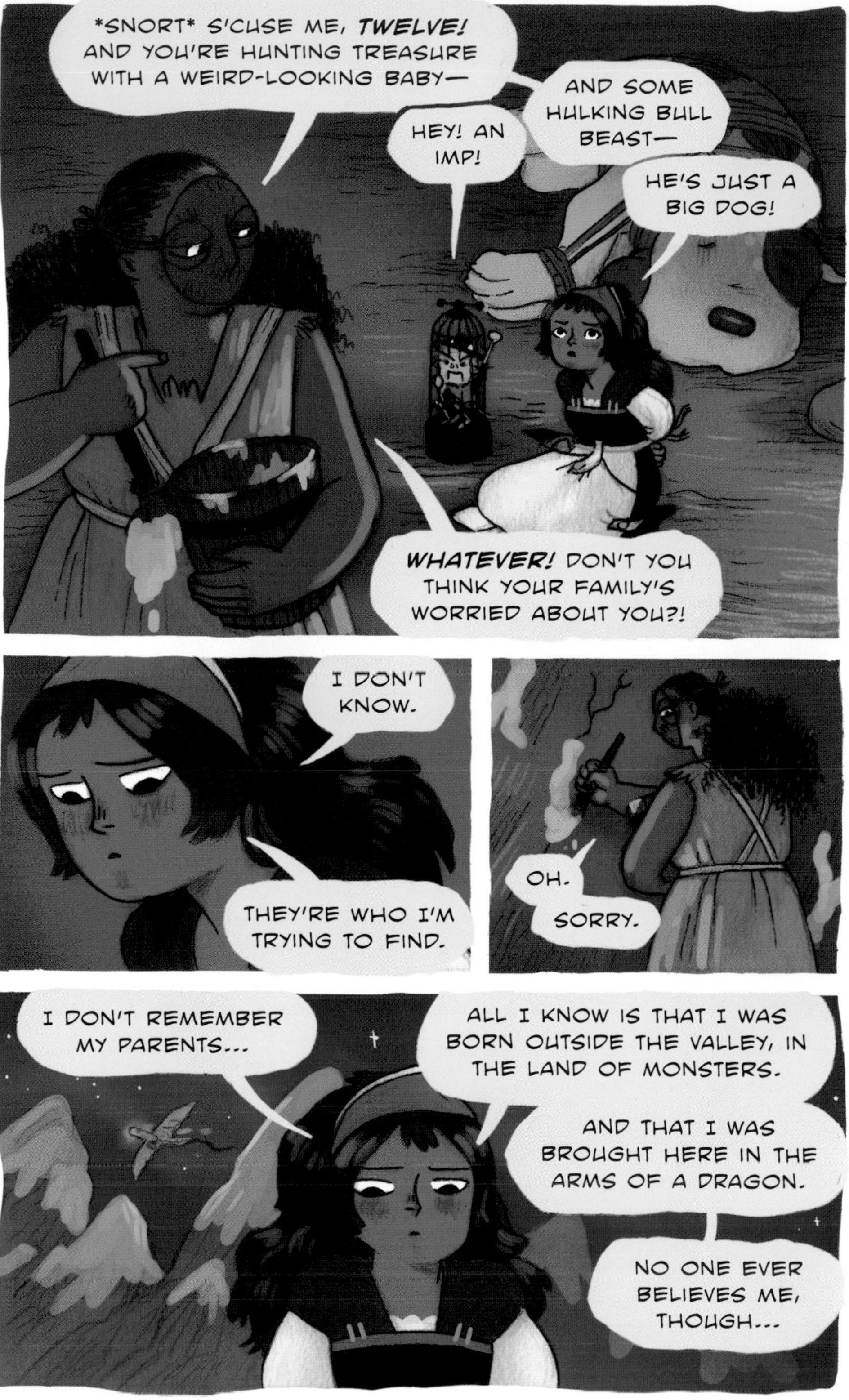
SNORT S'CUSE ME, TWELVE! AND YOU'RE HUNTING TREASURE WITH A WEIRD-LOOKING BABY—
AND SOME HULKING BULL BEAST—
HEY! AN IMP!
HE'S JUST A BIG DOG!
WHATEVER! DON'T YOU THINK YOUR FAMILY'S WORRIED ABOUT YOU?!
I DON'T KNOW.
THEY'RE WHO I'M TRYING TO FIND.
OH.
SORRY.
I DON'T REMEMBER MY PARENTS...
ALL I KNOW IS THAT I WAS BORN OUTSIDE THE VALLEY, IN THE LAND OF MONSTERS.
AND THAT I WAS BROUGHT HERE IN THE ARMS OF A DRAGON.
NO ONE EVER BELIEVES ME, THOUGH...

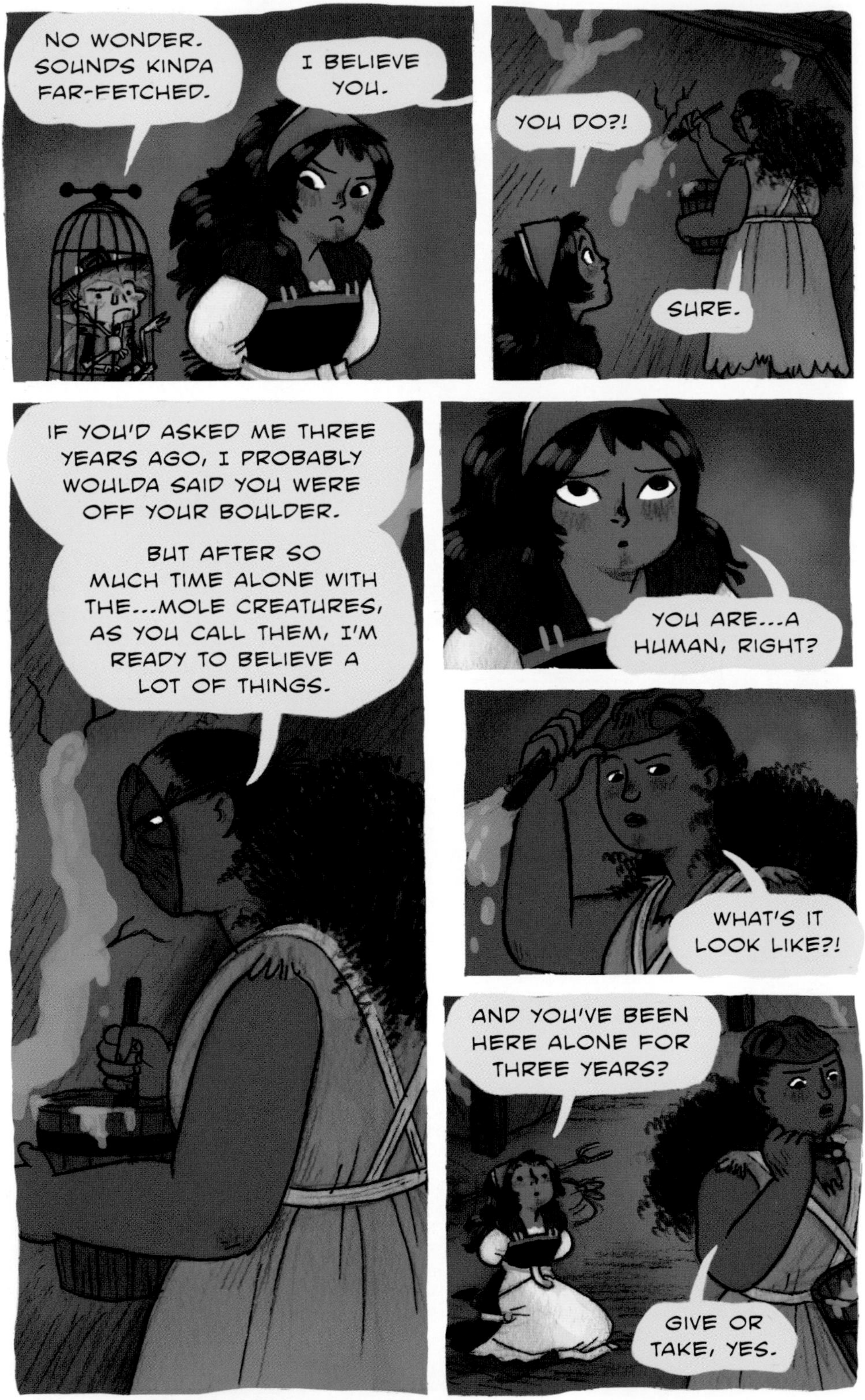
NO WONDER. SOUNDS KINDA FAR-FETCHED.
I BELIEVE YOU.
YOU DO?!
SURE.
IF YOU'D ASKED ME THREE YEARS AGO, I PROBABLY WOULDA SAID YOU WERE OFF YOUR BOULDER.
BUT AFTER SO MUCH TIME ALONE WITH THE...MOLE CREATURES, AS YOU CALL THEM, I'M READY TO BELIEVE A LOT OF THINGS.
YOU ARE...A HUMAN, RIGHT?
WHAT'S IT LOOK LIKE?!
AND YOU'VE BEEN HERE ALONE FOR THREE YEARS?
GIVE OR TAKE, YES.

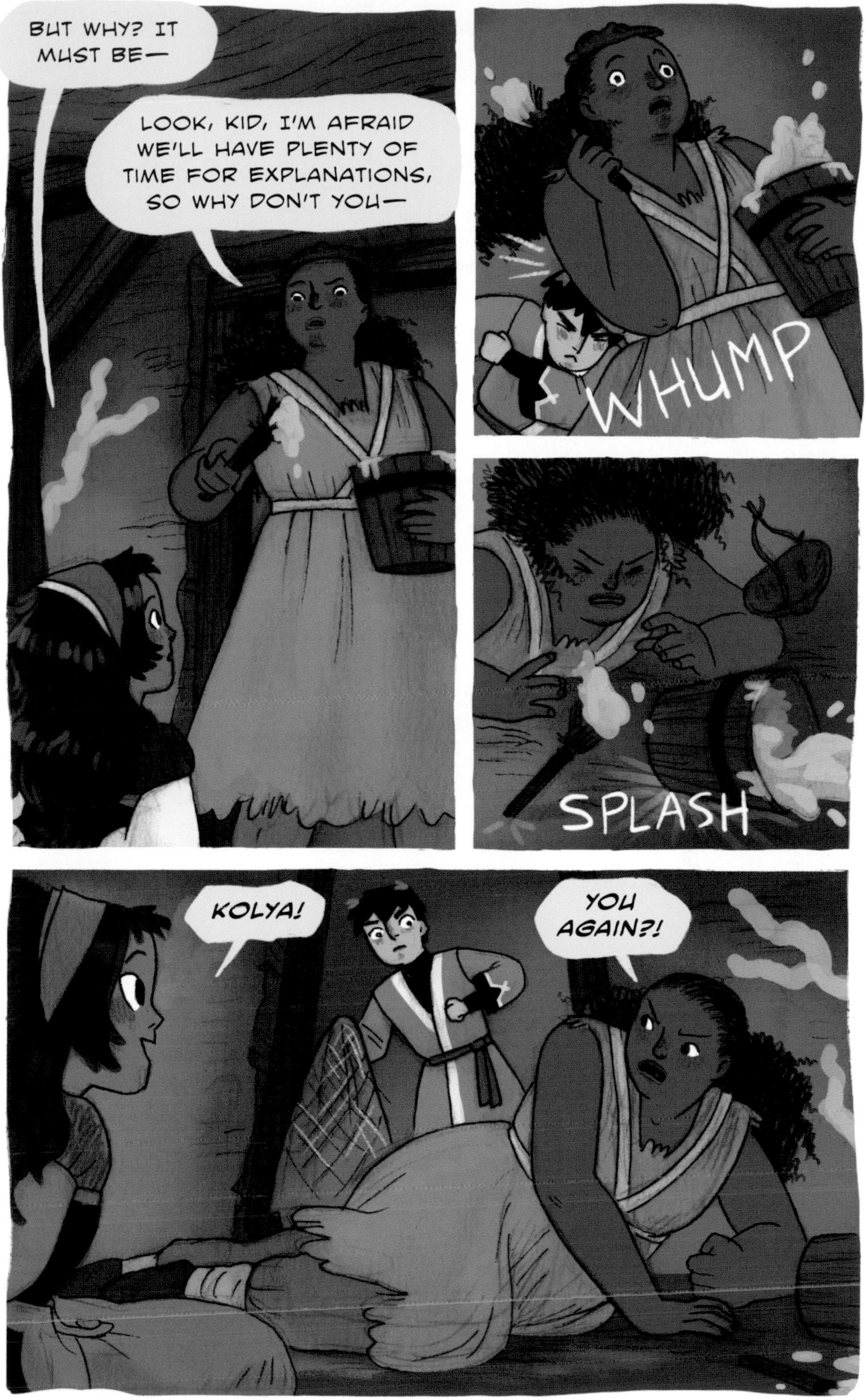
BUT WHY? IT MUST BE—
LOOK, KID, I'M AFRAID WE'LL HAVE PLENTY OF TIME FOR EXPLANATIONS, SO WHY DON'T YOU—
WHUMP
SPLASH
KOLYA!
YOU AGAIN?!

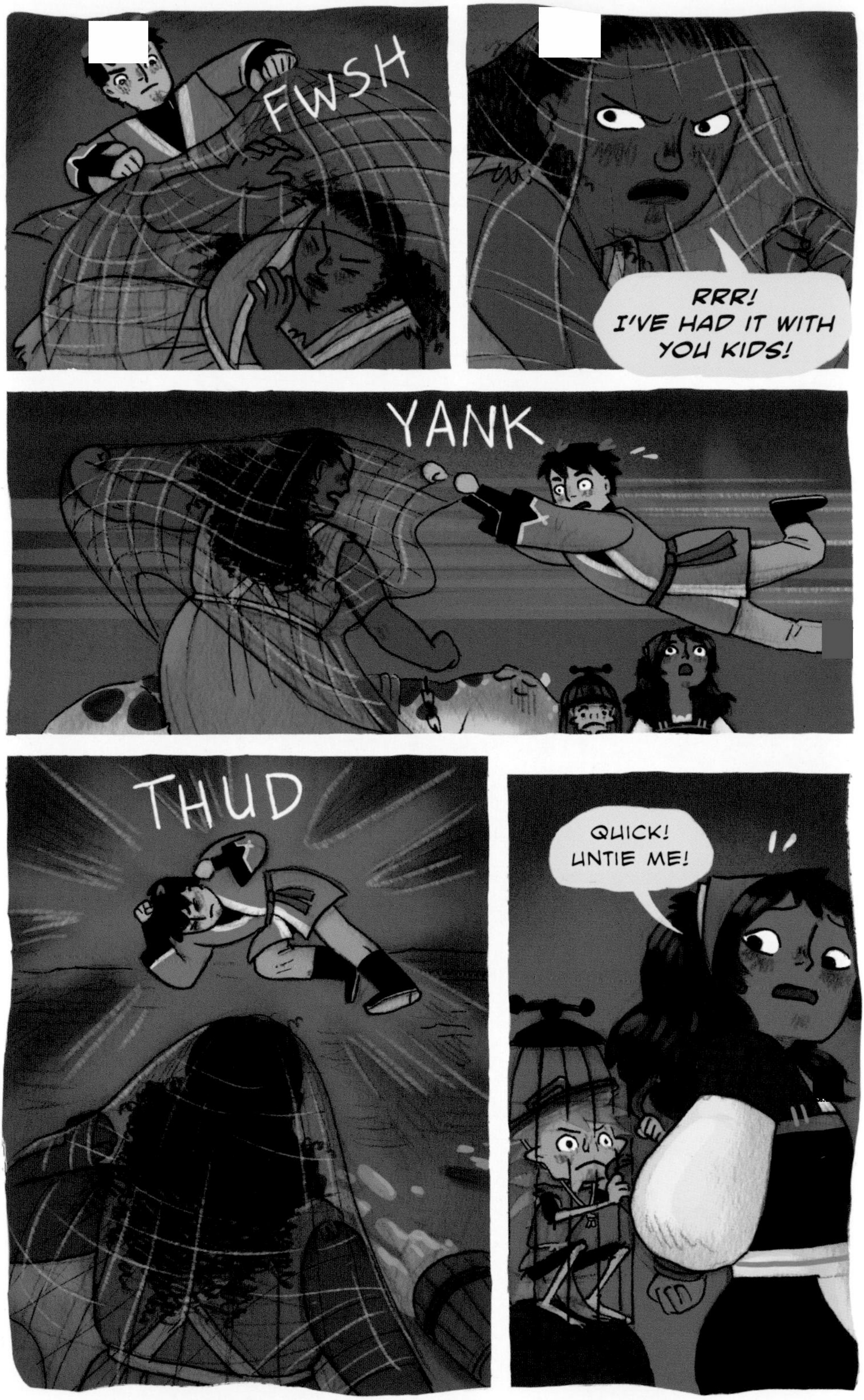
FWSH
RRR! I'VE HAD IT WITH YOU KIDS!
YANK
THUD
QUICK! UNTIE ME!

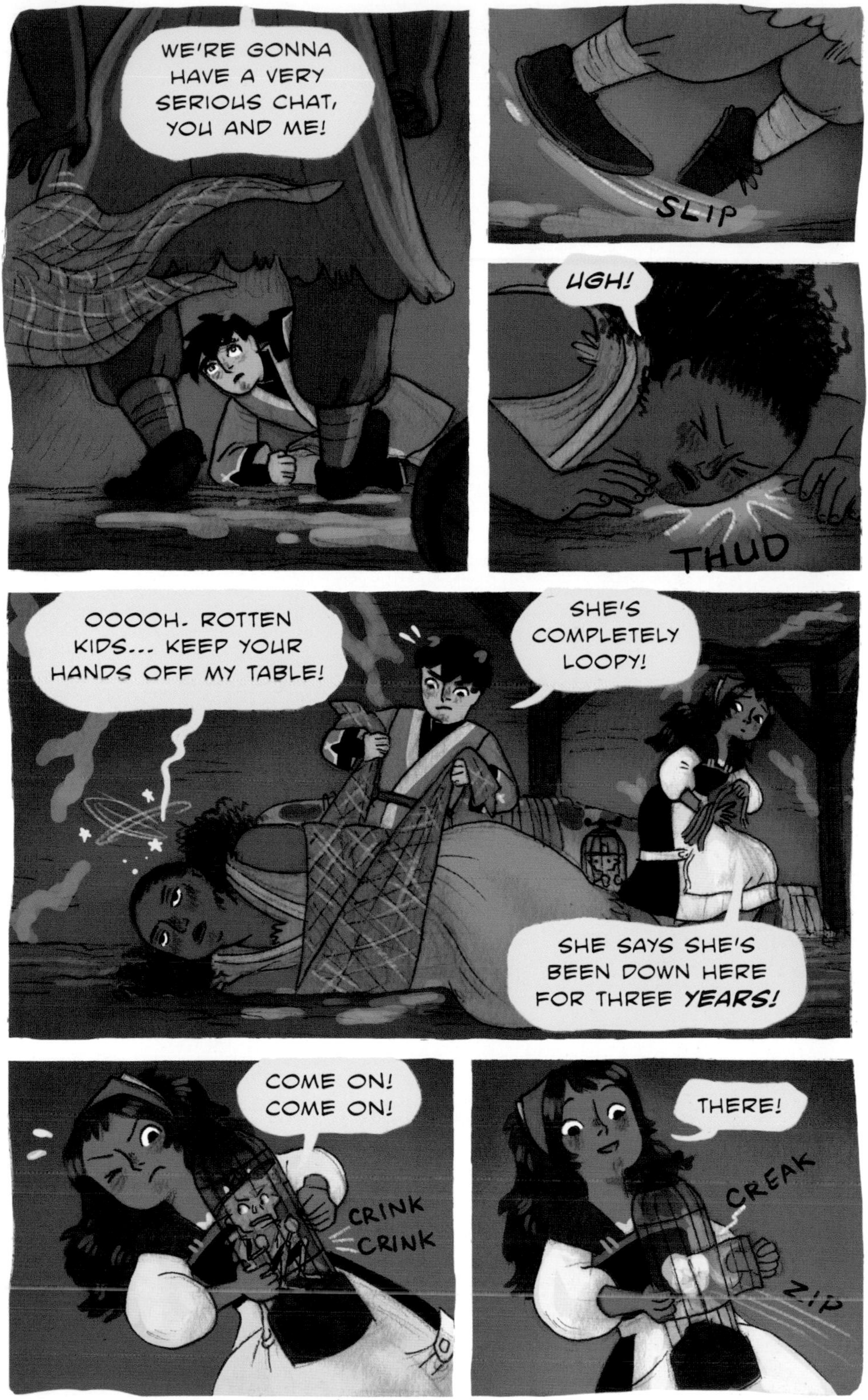
WE'RE GONNA HAVE A VERY SERIOUS CHAT, YOU AND ME!
SLIP
UGH!
THUD
OOOOH. ROTTEN KIDS... KEEP YOUR HANDS OFF MY TABLE!
SHE'S COMPLETELY LOOPY!
SHE SAYS SHE'S BEEN DOWN HERE FOR THREE *YEARS!*
COME ON! COME ON!
CRINK
CRINK
THERE!
CREAK
ZIP

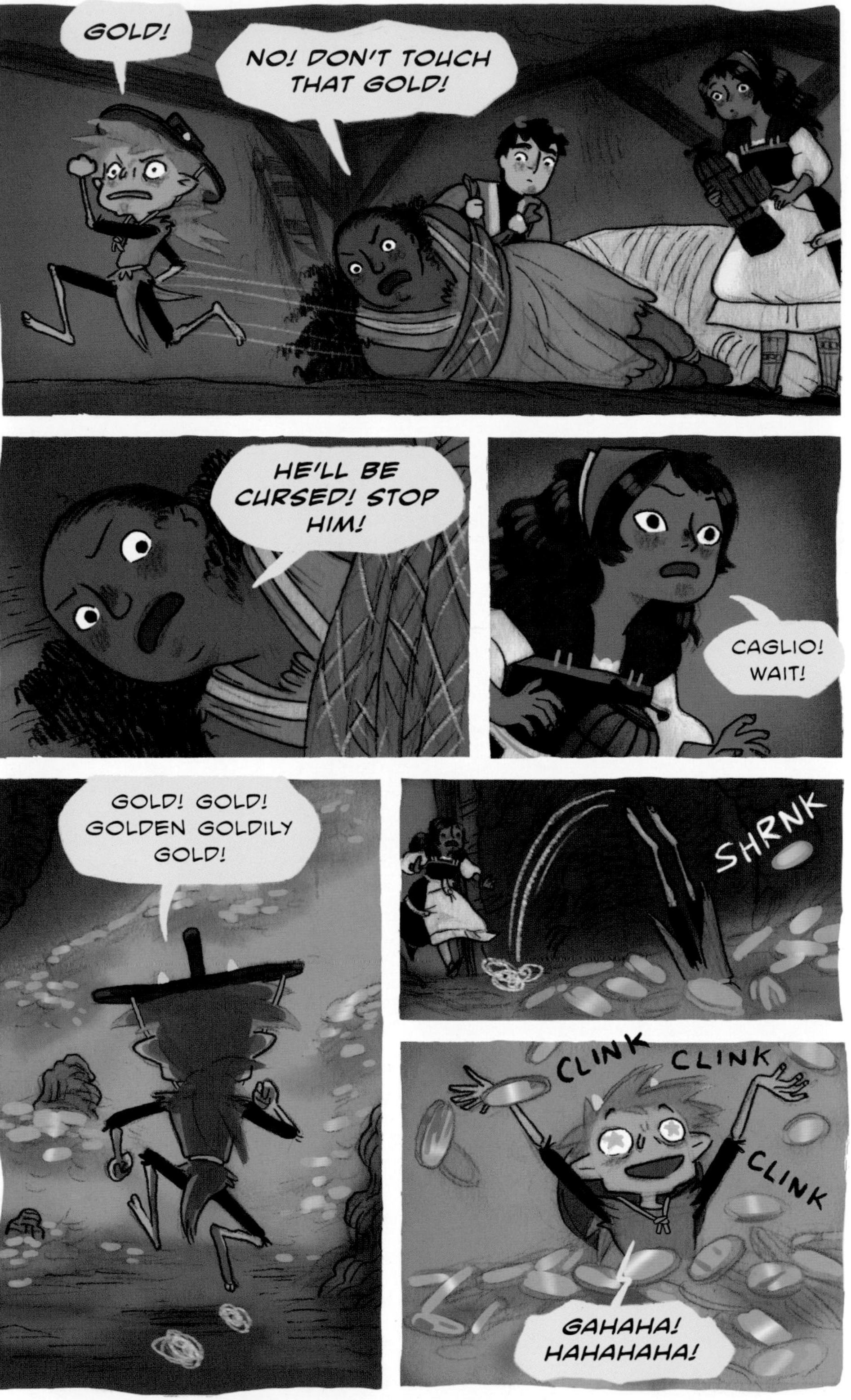
GOLD!
NO! DON'T TOUCH THAT GOLD!
HE'LL BE CURSED! STOP HIM!
CAGLIO! WAIT!
GOLD! GOLD! GOLDEN GOLDILY GOLD!
SHRNK
CLINK
CLINK
CLINK
GAHAHA! HAHAHAHA!

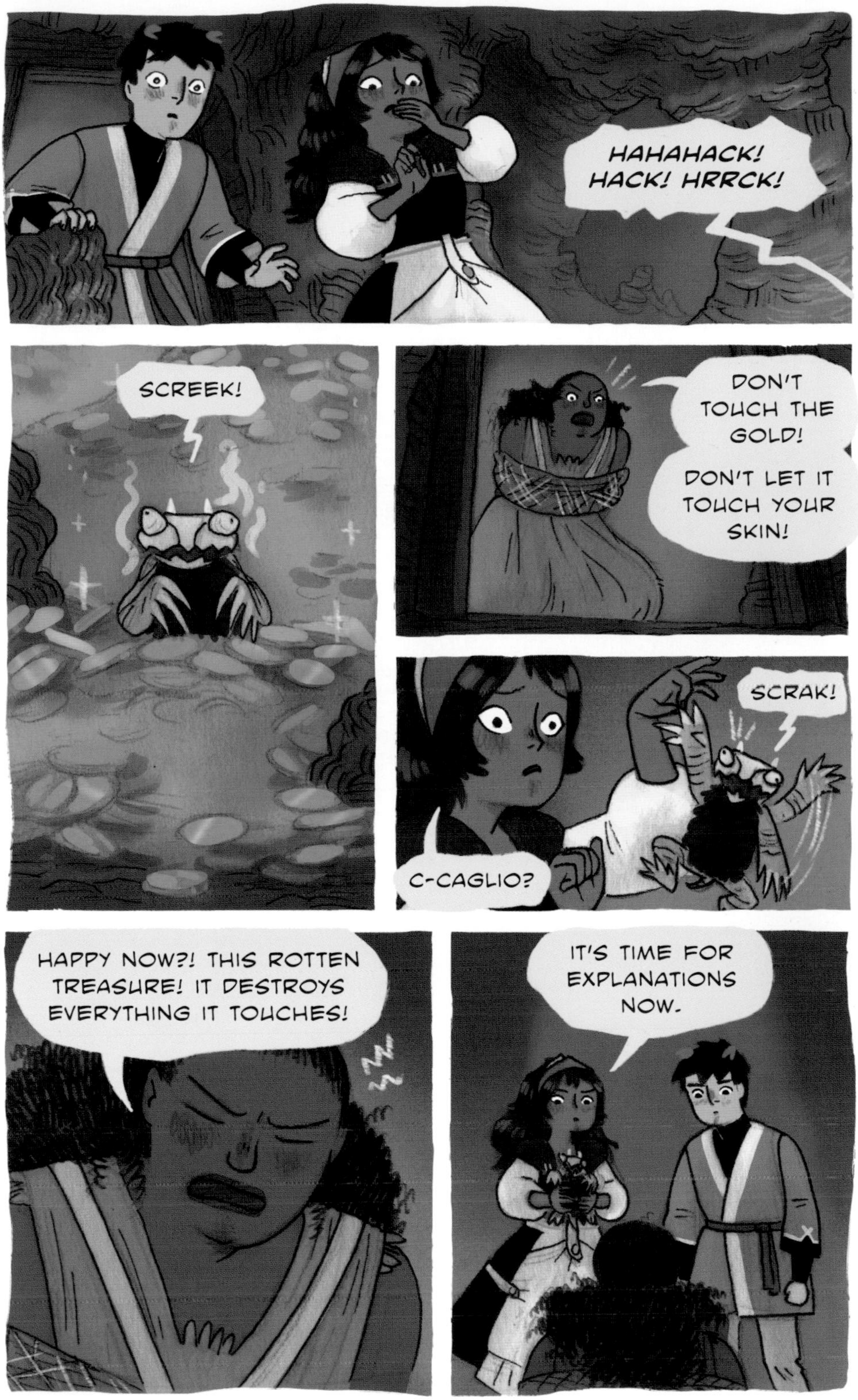
HAHAHACK! HACK! HRRCK!
SCREEK!
DON'T TOUCH THE GOLD!
DON'T LET IT TOUCH YOUR SKIN!
SCRAK!
C-CAGLIO?
HAPPY NOW?! THIS ROTTEN TREASURE! IT DESTROYS EVERYTHING IT TOUCHES!
IT'S TIME FOR EXPLANATIONS NOW.

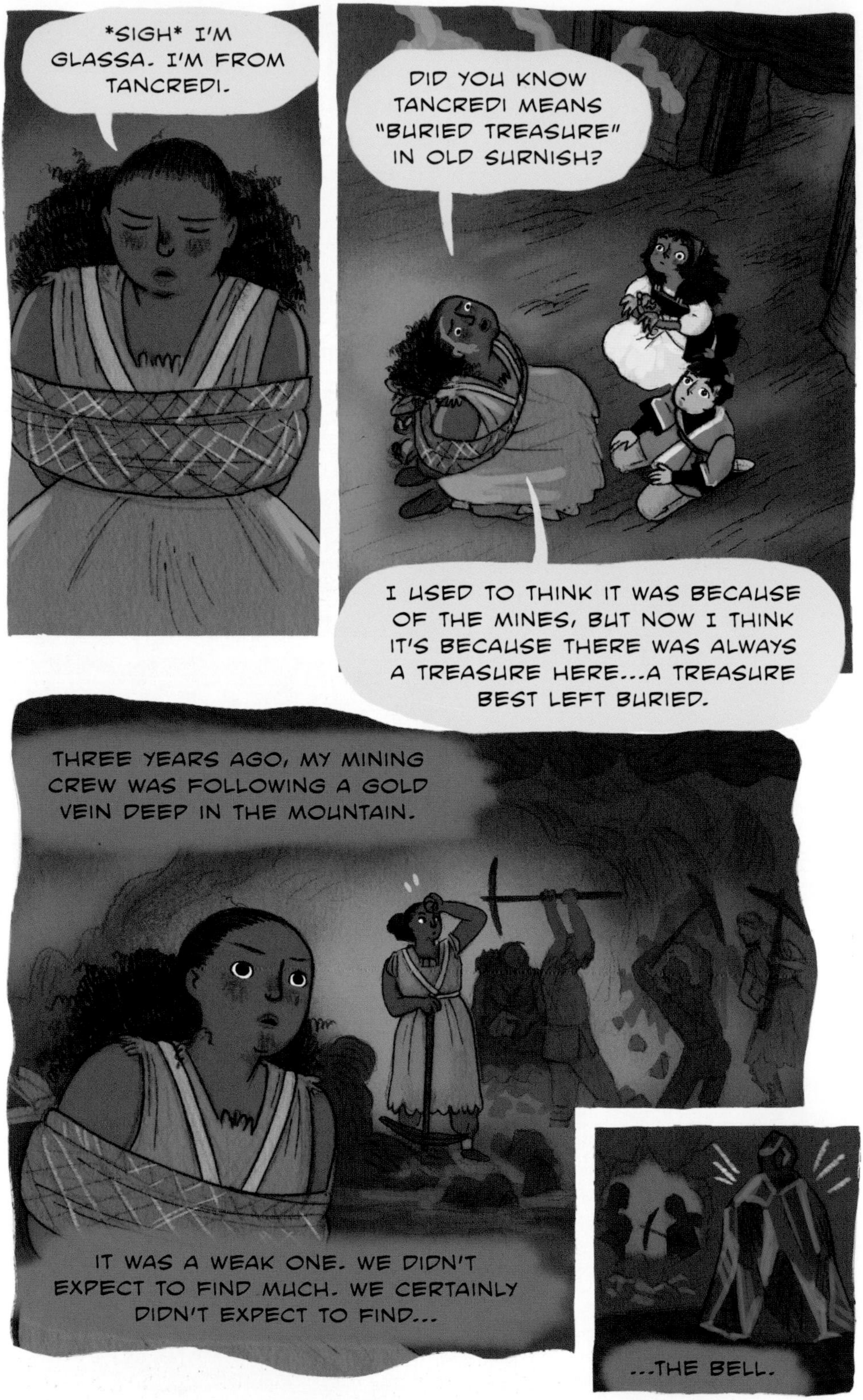
SIGH I'M GLASSA. I'M FROM TANCREDI.
DID YOU KNOW TANCREDI MEANS "BURIED TREASURE" IN OLD SURNISH?
I USED TO THINK IT WAS BECAUSE OF THE MINES, BUT NOW I THINK IT'S BECAUSE THERE WAS ALWAYS A TREASURE HERE...A TREASURE BEST LEFT BURIED.
THREE YEARS AGO, MY MINING CREW WAS FOLLOWING A GOLD VEIN DEEP IN THE MOUNTAIN.
IT WAS A WEAK ONE. WE DIDN'T EXPECT TO FIND MUCH. WE CERTAINLY DIDN'T EXPECT TO FIND...
...THE BELL.

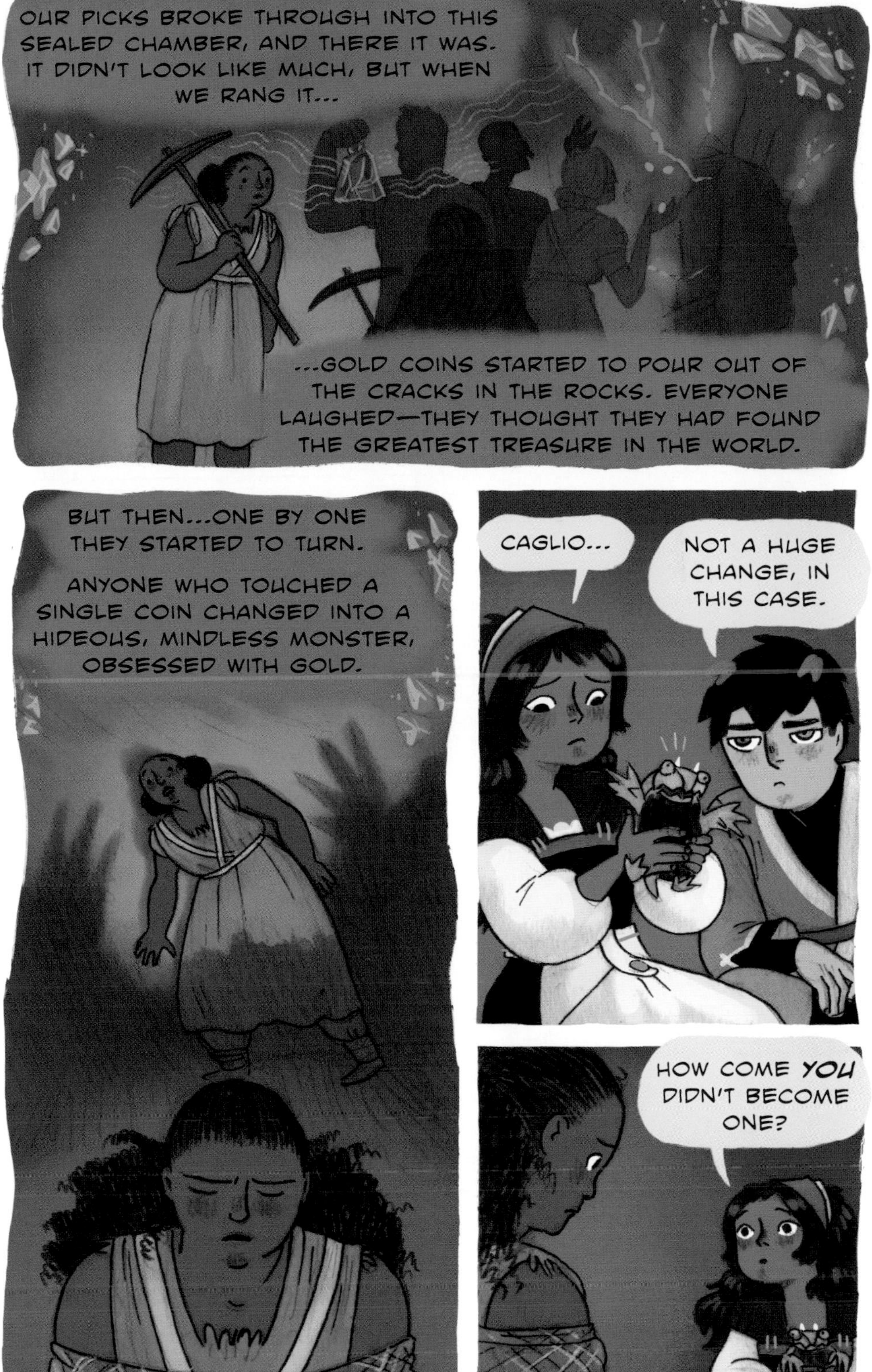
OUR PICKS BROKE THROUGH INTO THIS SEALED CHAMBER, AND THERE IT WAS. IT DIDN'T LOOK LIKE MUCH, BUT WHEN WE RANG IT...
...GOLD COINS STARTED TO POUR OUT OF THE CRACKS IN THE ROCKS. EVERYONE LAUGHED—THEY THOUGHT THEY HAD FOUND THE GREATEST TREASURE IN THE WORLD.
BUT THEN...ONE BY ONE THEY STARTED TO TURN.
ANYONE WHO TOUCHED A SINGLE COIN CHANGED INTO A HIDEOUS, MINDLESS MONSTER, OBSESSED WITH GOLD.
CAGLIO...
NOT A HUGE CHANGE, IN THIS CASE.
HOW COME *YOU* DIDN'T BECOME ONE?

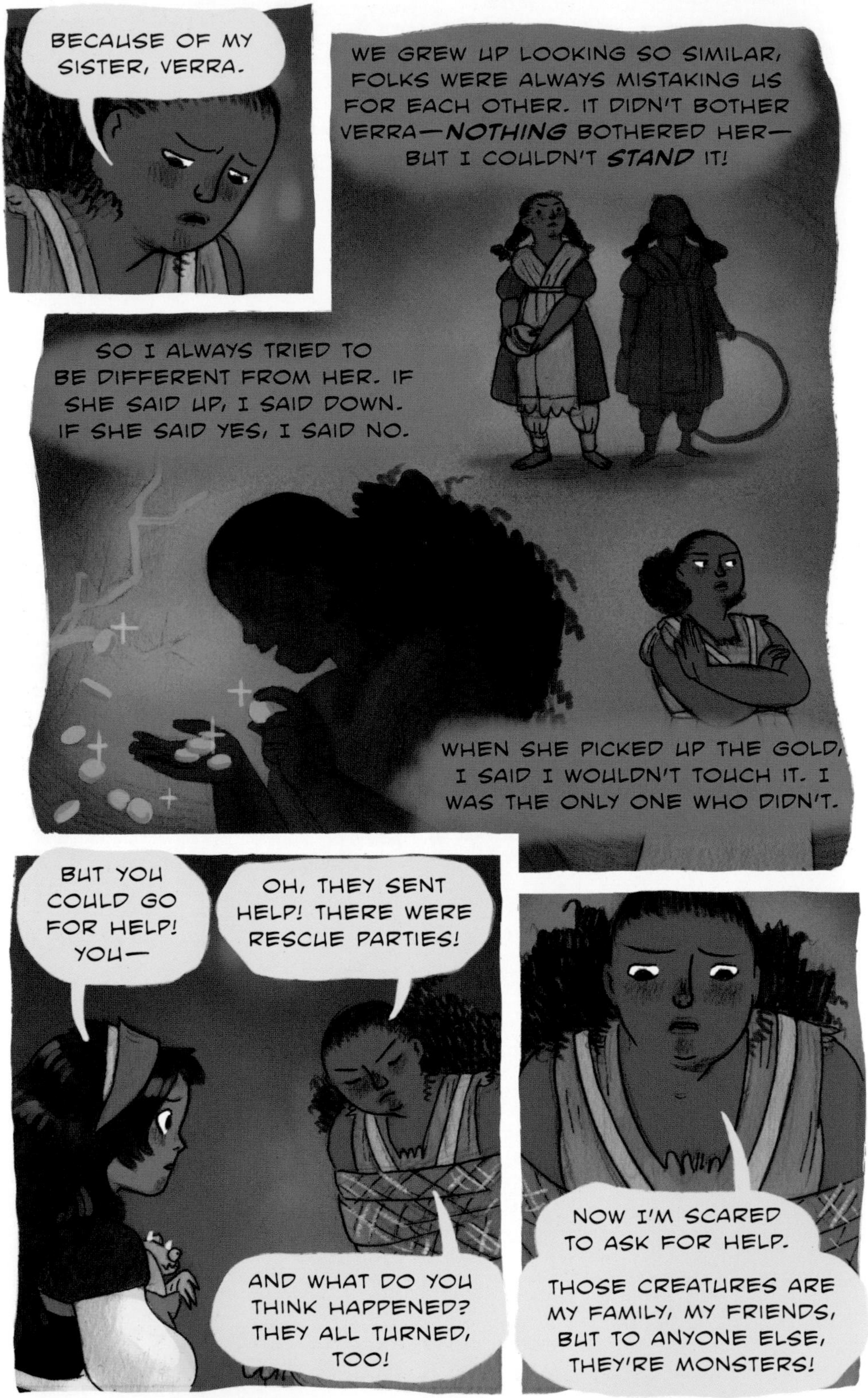
BECAUSE OF MY SISTER, VERRA.
WE GREW UP LOOKING SO SIMILAR, FOLKS WERE ALWAYS MISTAKING US FOR EACH OTHER. IT DIDN'T BOTHER VERRA—*NOTHING* BOTHERED HER—BUT I COULDN'T *STAND* IT!
SO I ALWAYS TRIED TO BE DIFFERENT FROM HER. IF SHE SAID UP, I SAID DOWN. IF SHE SAID YES, I SAID NO.
WHEN SHE PICKED UP THE GOLD, I SAID I WOULDN'T TOUCH IT. I WAS THE ONLY ONE WHO DIDN'T.
BUT YOU COULD GO FOR HELP! YOU—
OH, THEY SENT HELP! THERE WERE RESCUE PARTIES!
AND WHAT DO YOU THINK HAPPENED? THEY ALL TURNED, TOO!
NOW I'M SCARED TO ASK FOR HELP.
THOSE CREATURES ARE MY FAMILY, MY FRIENDS, BUT TO ANYONE ELSE, THEY'RE MONSTERS!

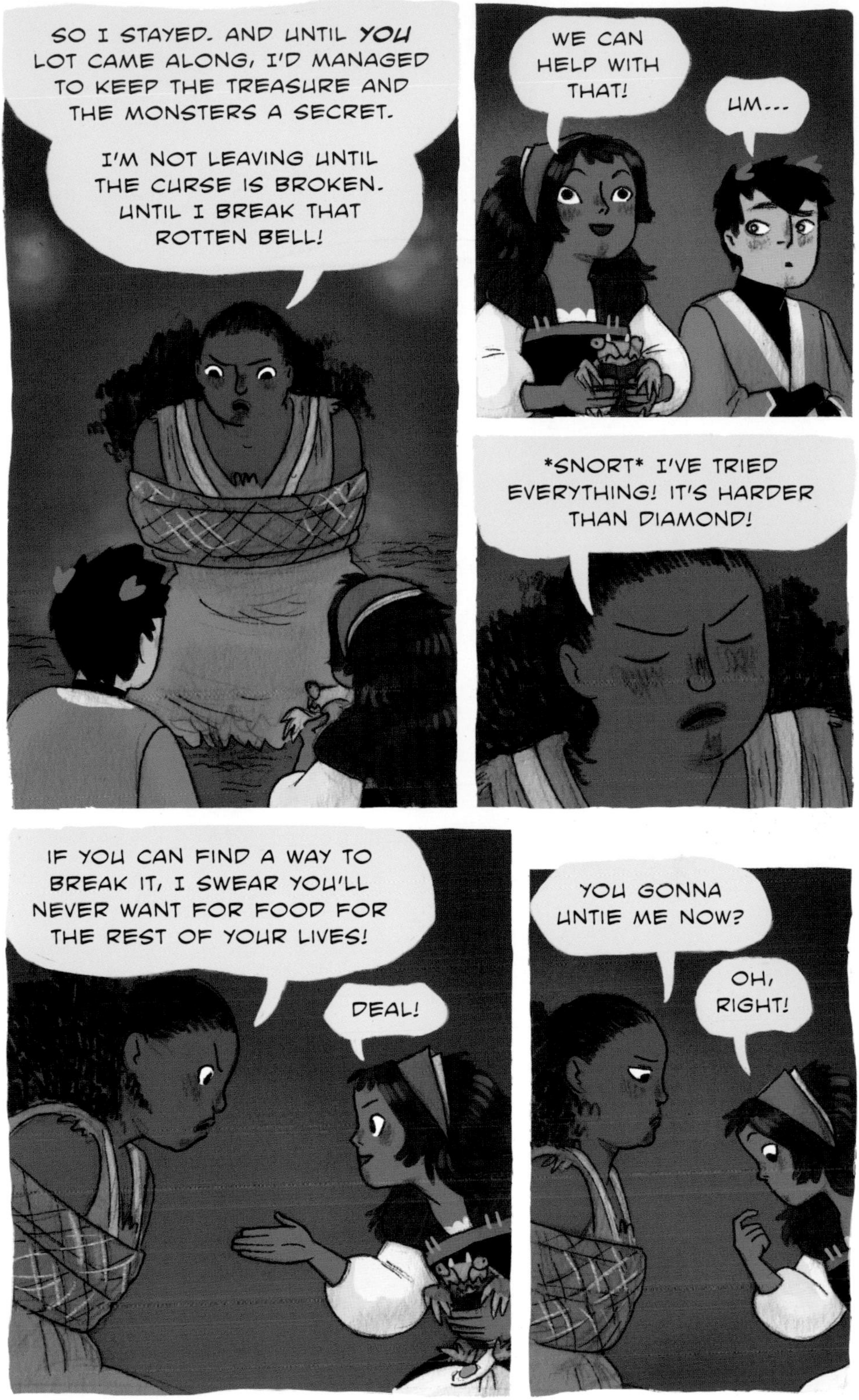
SO I STAYED. AND UNTIL YOU LOT CAME ALONG, I'D MANAGED TO KEEP THE TREASURE AND THE MONSTERS A SECRET.
I'M NOT LEAVING UNTIL THE CURSE IS BROKEN. UNTIL I BREAK THAT ROTTEN BELL!
WE CAN HELP WITH THAT!
UM...
SNORT I'VE TRIED EVERYTHING! IT'S HARDER THAN DIAMOND!
IF YOU CAN FIND A WAY TO BREAK IT, I SWEAR YOU'LL NEVER WANT FOR FOOD FOR THE REST OF YOUR LIVES!
DEAL!
YOU GONNA UNTIE ME NOW?
OH, RIGHT!

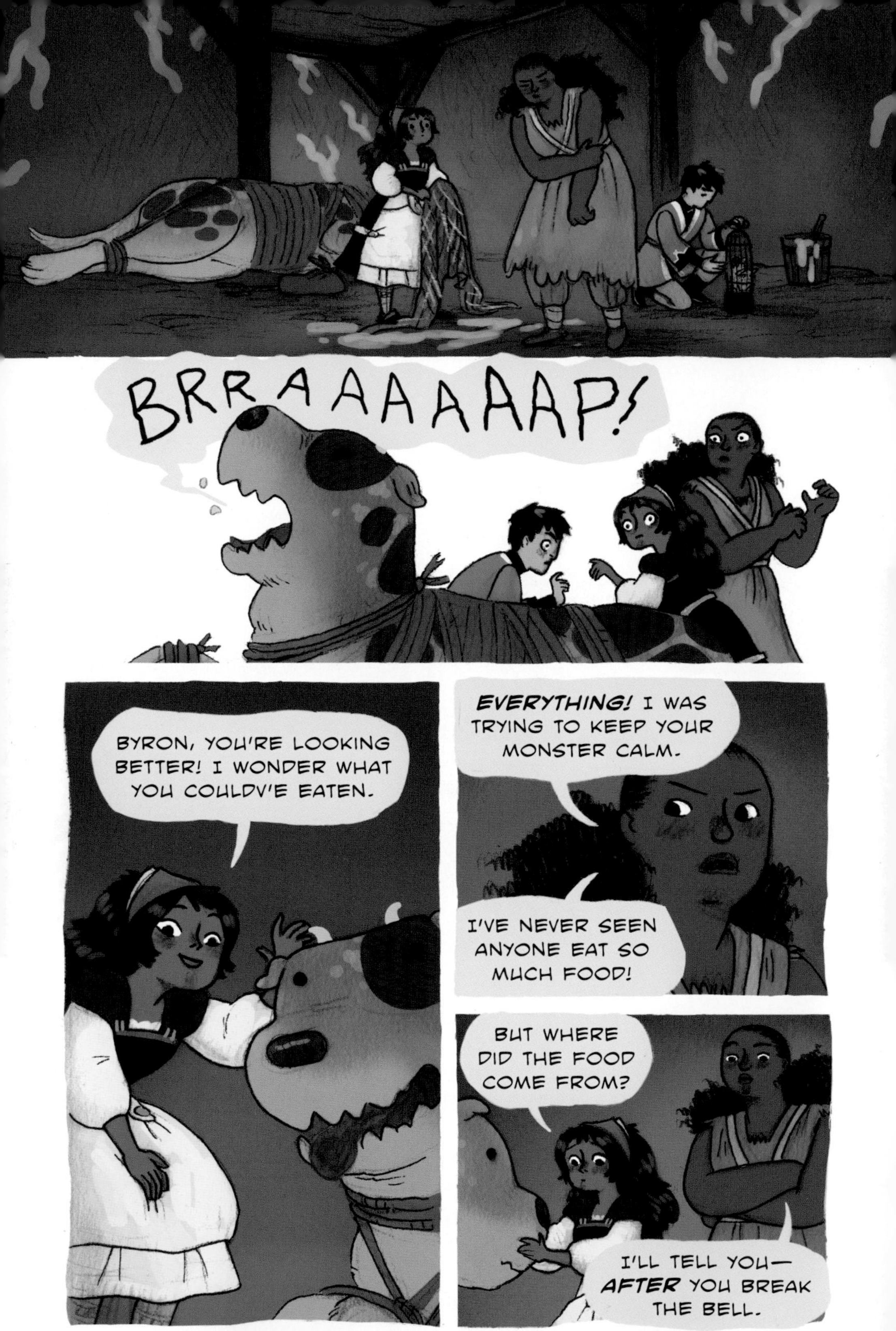
BRRAAAAAAP!
BYRON, YOU'RE LOOKING BETTER! I WONDER WHAT YOU COULDV'E EATEN.
EVERYTHING! I WAS TRYING TO KEEP YOUR MONSTER CALM.
I'VE NEVER SEEN ANYONE EAT SO MUCH FOOD!
BUT WHERE DID THE FOOD COME FROM?
I'LL TELL YOU—AFTER YOU BREAK THE BELL.

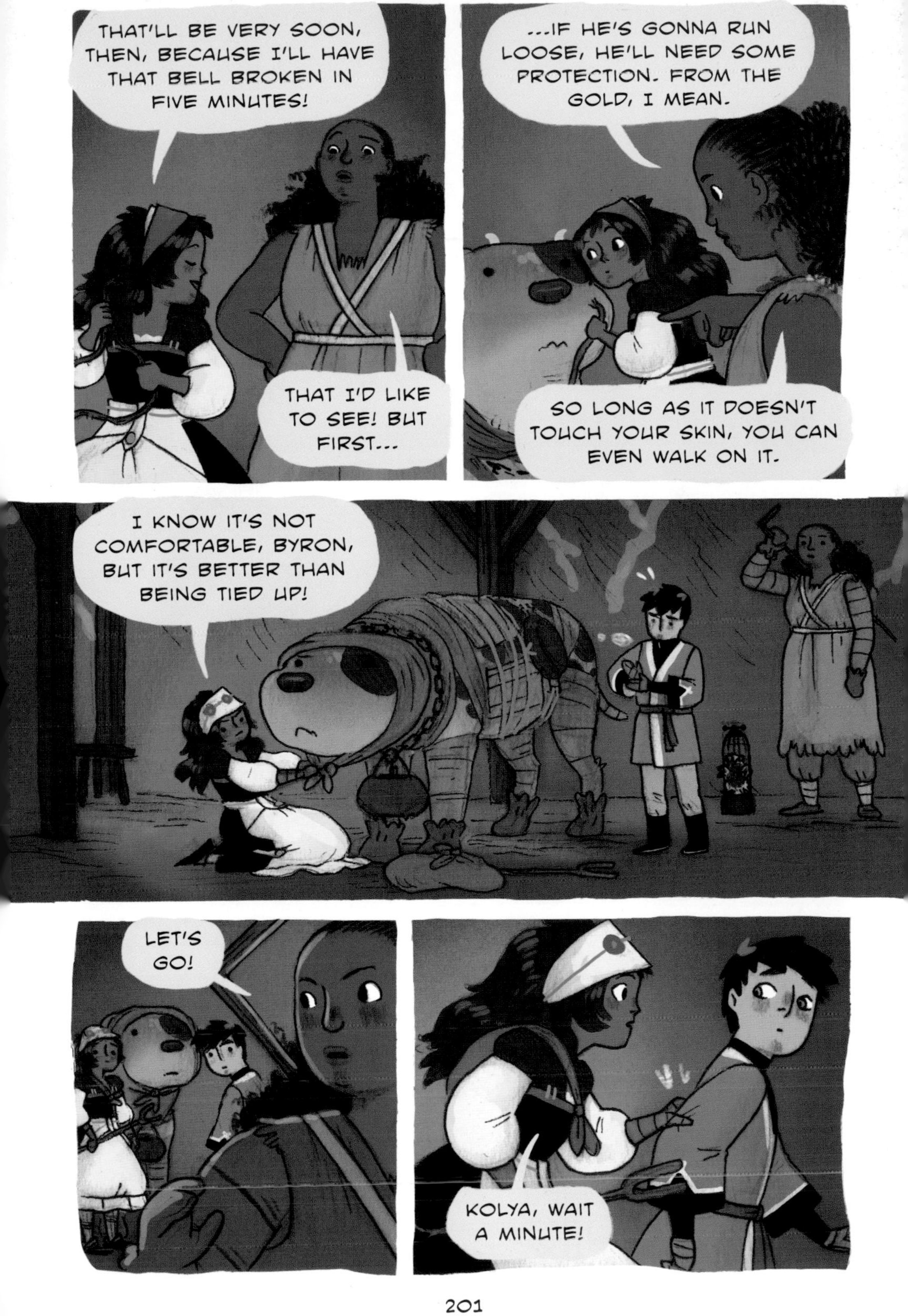
THAT'LL BE VERY SOON, THEN, BECAUSE I'LL HAVE THAT BELL BROKEN IN FIVE MINUTES!
THAT I'D LIKE TO SEE! BUT FIRST...
...IF HE'S GONNA RUN LOOSE, HE'LL NEED SOME PROTECTION. FROM THE GOLD, I MEAN.
SO LONG AS IT DOESN'T TOUCH YOUR SKIN, YOU CAN EVEN WALK ON IT.
I KNOW IT'S NOT COMFORTABLE, BYRON, BUT IT'S BETTER THAN BEING TIED UP!
LET'S GO!
KOLYA, WAIT A MINUTE!

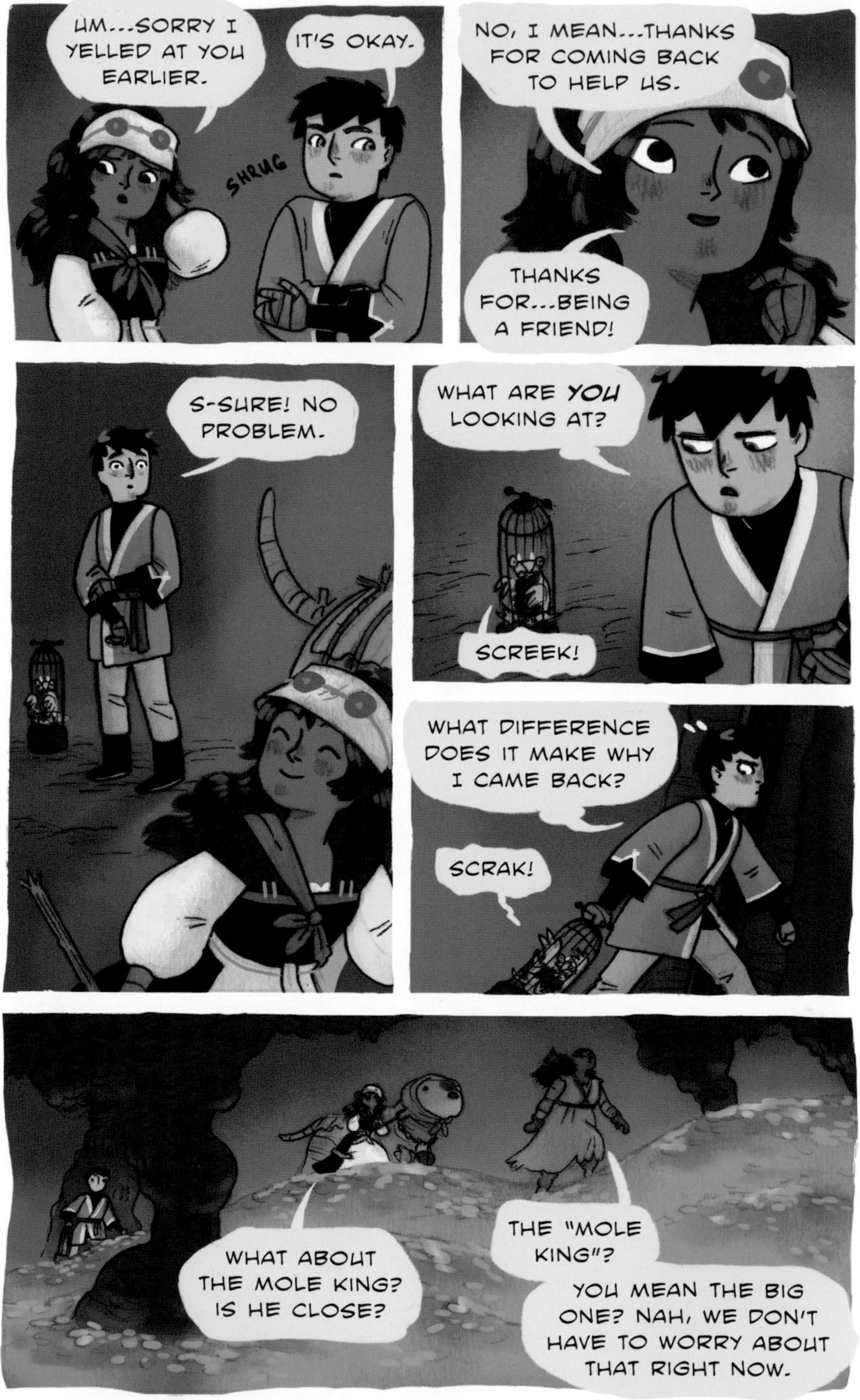
UM...SORRY I YELLED AT YOU EARLIER.
IT'S OKAY.
SHRUG
NO, I MEAN...THANKS FOR COMING BACK TO HELP US.
THANKS FOR...BEING A FRIEND!
S-SURE! NO PROBLEM.
WHAT ARE YOU LOOKING AT?
SCREEK!
WHAT DIFFERENCE DOES IT MAKE WHY I CAME BACK?
SCRAK!
WHAT ABOUT THE MOLE KING? IS HE CLOSE?
THE "MOLE KING"?
YOU MEAN THE BIG ONE? NAH, WE DON'T HAVE TO WORRY ABOUT THAT RIGHT NOW.

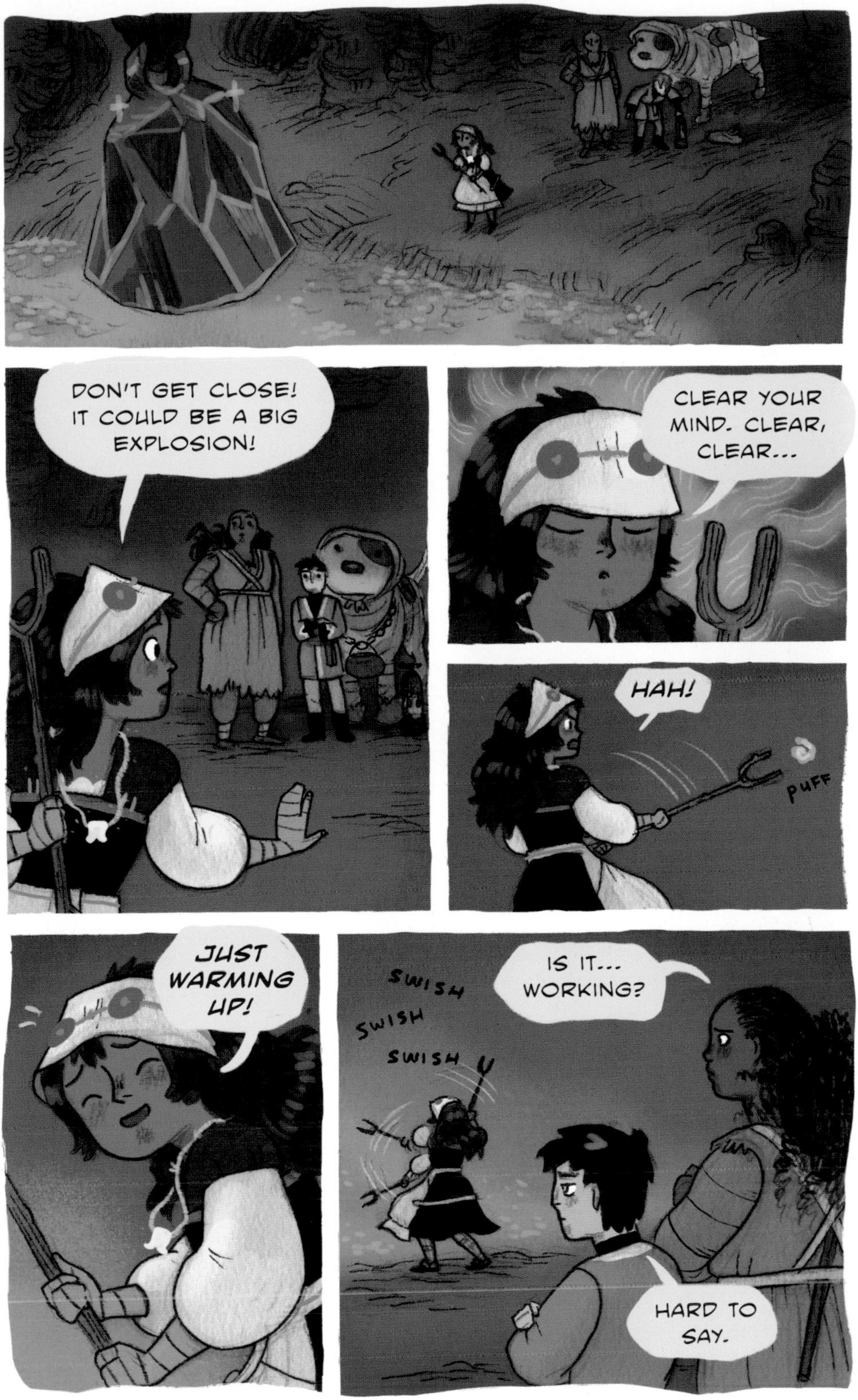
DON'T GET CLOSE! IT COULD BE A BIG EXPLOSION!
CLEAR YOUR MIND. CLEAR, CLEAR...
HAH!
PUFF
JUST WARMING UP!
SWISH
SWISH
SWISH
IS IT... WORKING?
HARD TO SAY.

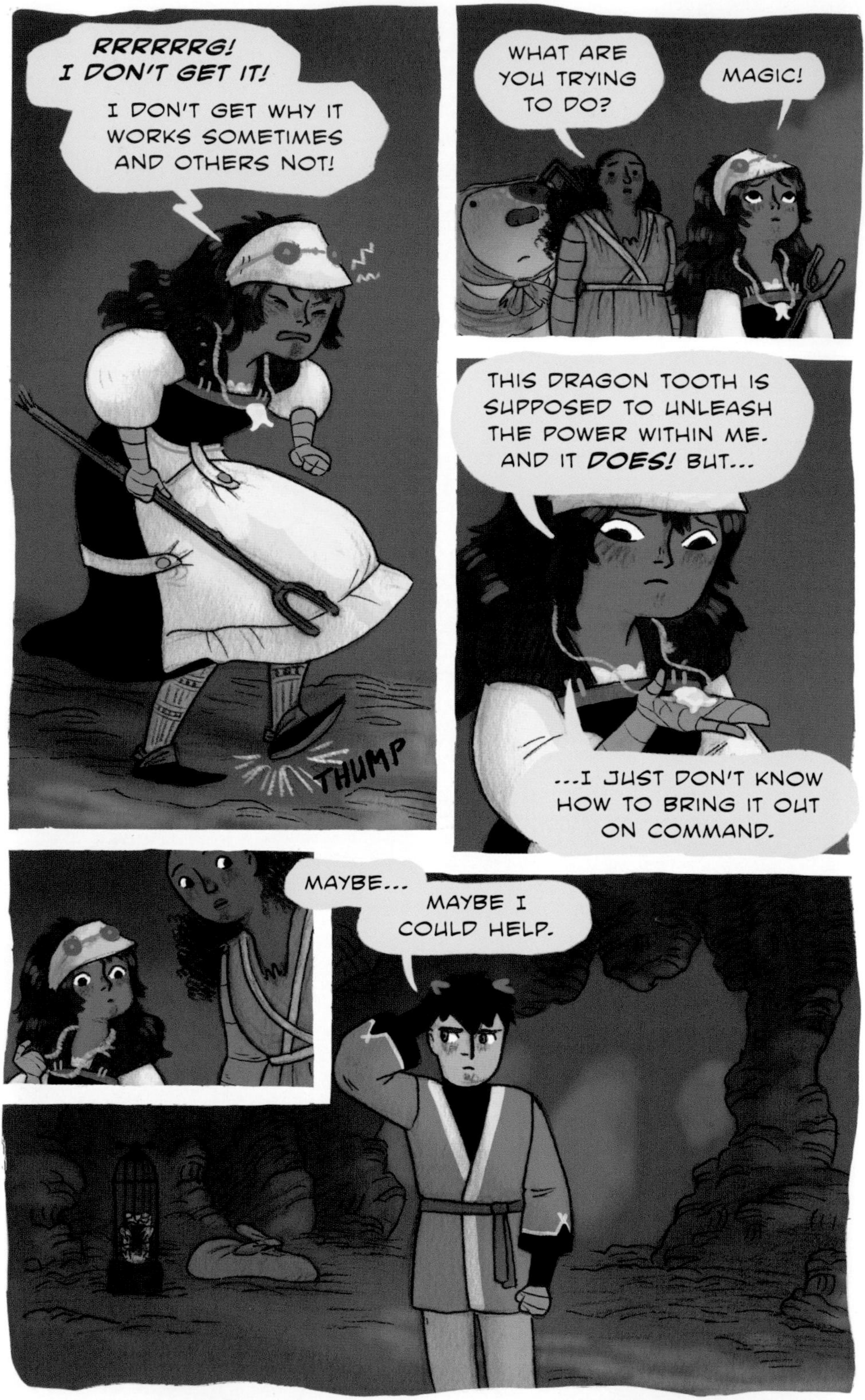
RRRRRRG! I DON'T GET IT!
I DON'T GET WHY IT WORKS SOMETIMES AND OTHERS NOT!
THUMP
WHAT ARE YOU TRYING TO DO?
MAGIC!
THIS DRAGON TOOTH IS SUPPOSED TO UNLEASH THE POWER WITHIN ME. AND IT DOES! BUT...
...I JUST DON'T KNOW HOW TO BRING IT OUT ON COMMAND.
MAYBE...
MAYBE I COULD HELP.

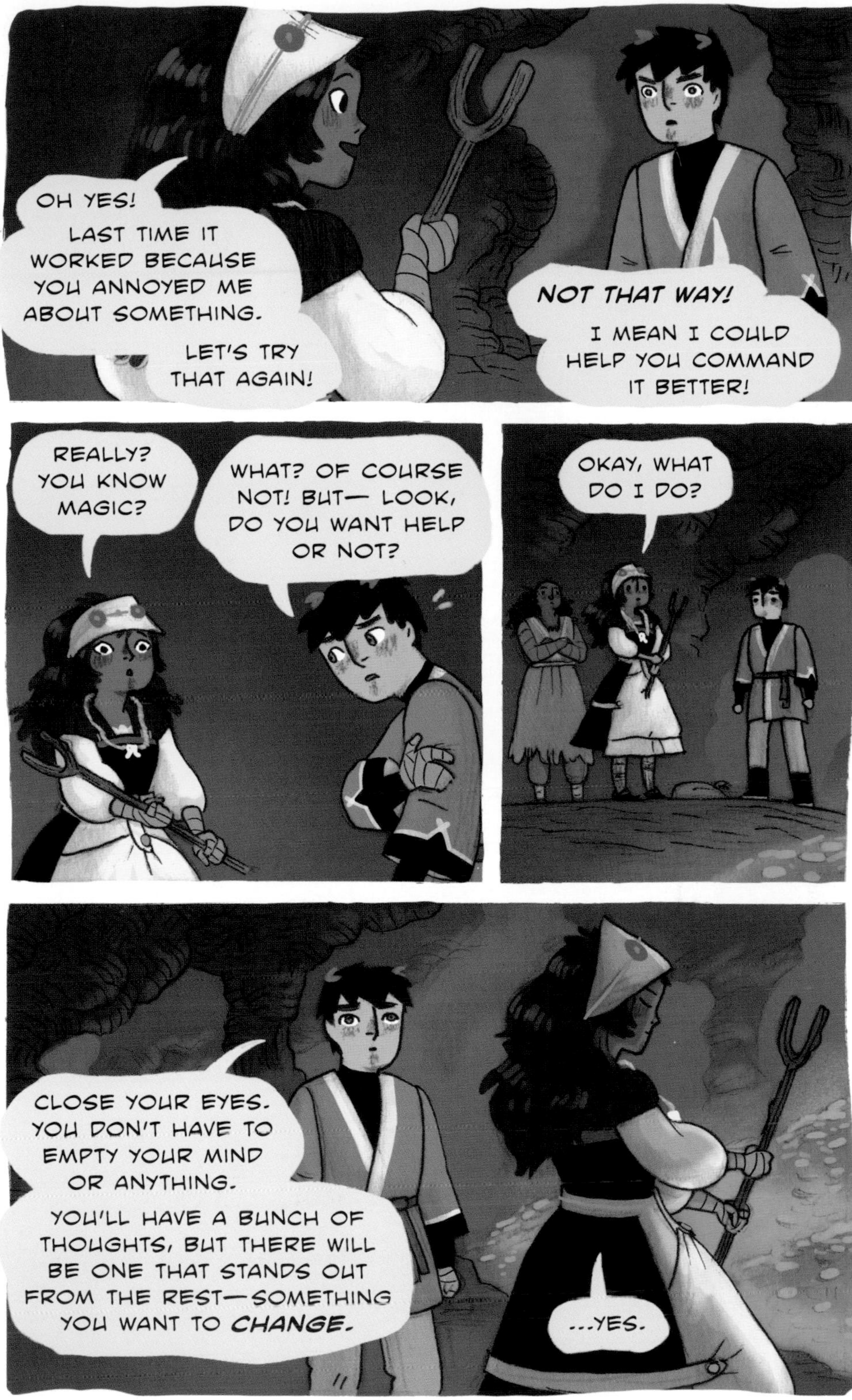
OH YES!
LAST TIME IT WORKED BECAUSE YOU ANNOYED ME ABOUT SOMETHING.
LET'S TRY THAT AGAIN!
NOT THAT WAY!
I MEAN I COULD HELP YOU COMMAND IT BETTER!
REALLY? YOU KNOW MAGIC?
WHAT? OF COURSE NOT! BUT— LOOK, DO YOU WANT HELP OR NOT?
OKAY, WHAT DO I DO?
CLOSE YOUR EYES. YOU DON'T HAVE TO EMPTY YOUR MIND OR ANYTHING.
YOU'LL HAVE A BUNCH OF THOUGHTS, BUT THERE WILL BE ONE THAT STANDS OUT FROM THE REST—SOMETHING YOU WANT TO CHANGE.
...YES.

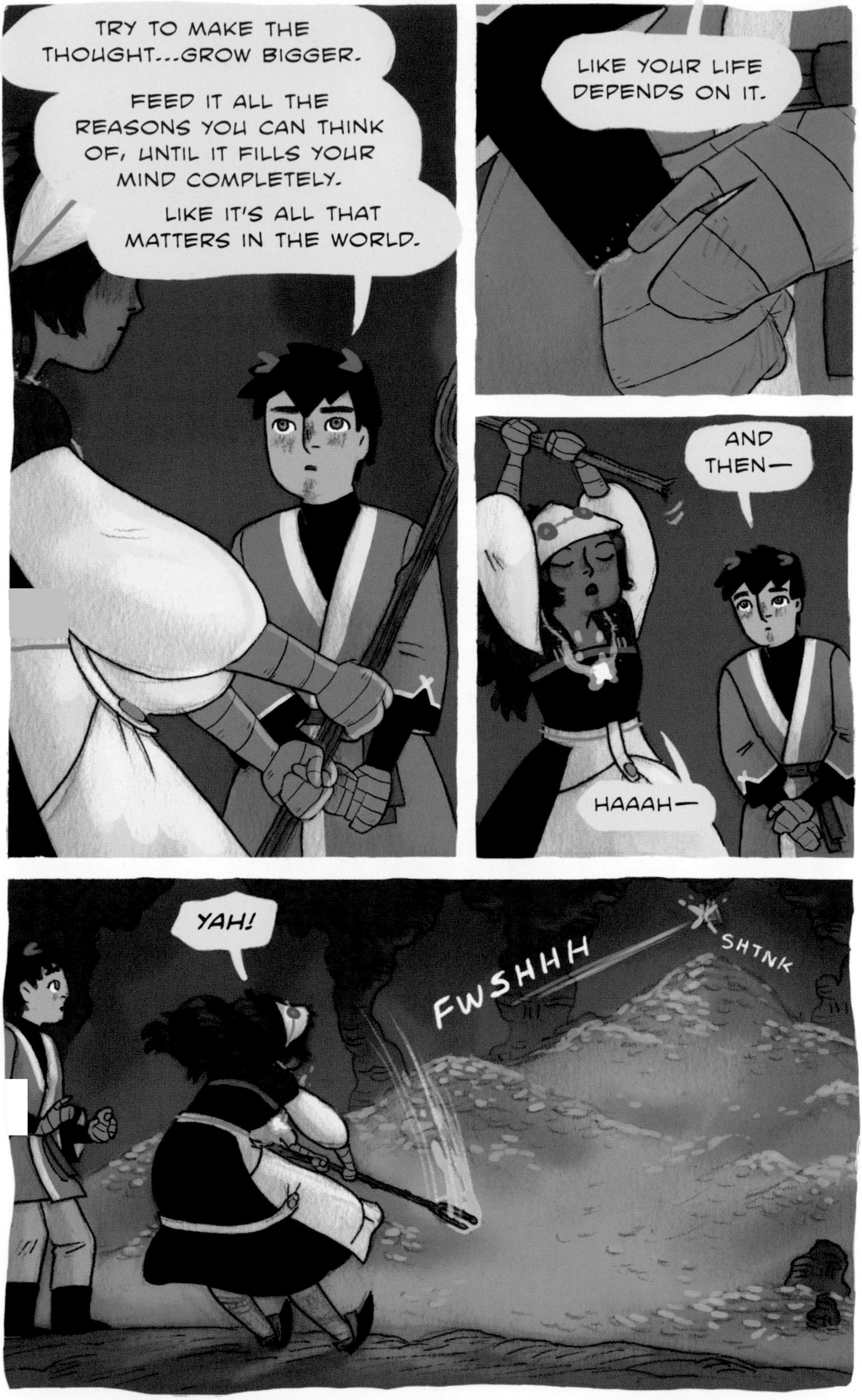
TRY TO MAKE THE THOUGHT...GROW BIGGER.
FEED IT ALL THE REASONS YOU CAN THINK OF, UNTIL IT FILLS YOUR MIND COMPLETELY.
LIKE IT'S ALL THAT MATTERS IN THE WORLD.
LIKE YOUR LIFE DEPENDS ON IT.
AND THEN—
HAAAH—
YAH!
FWSHHH
SHTNK

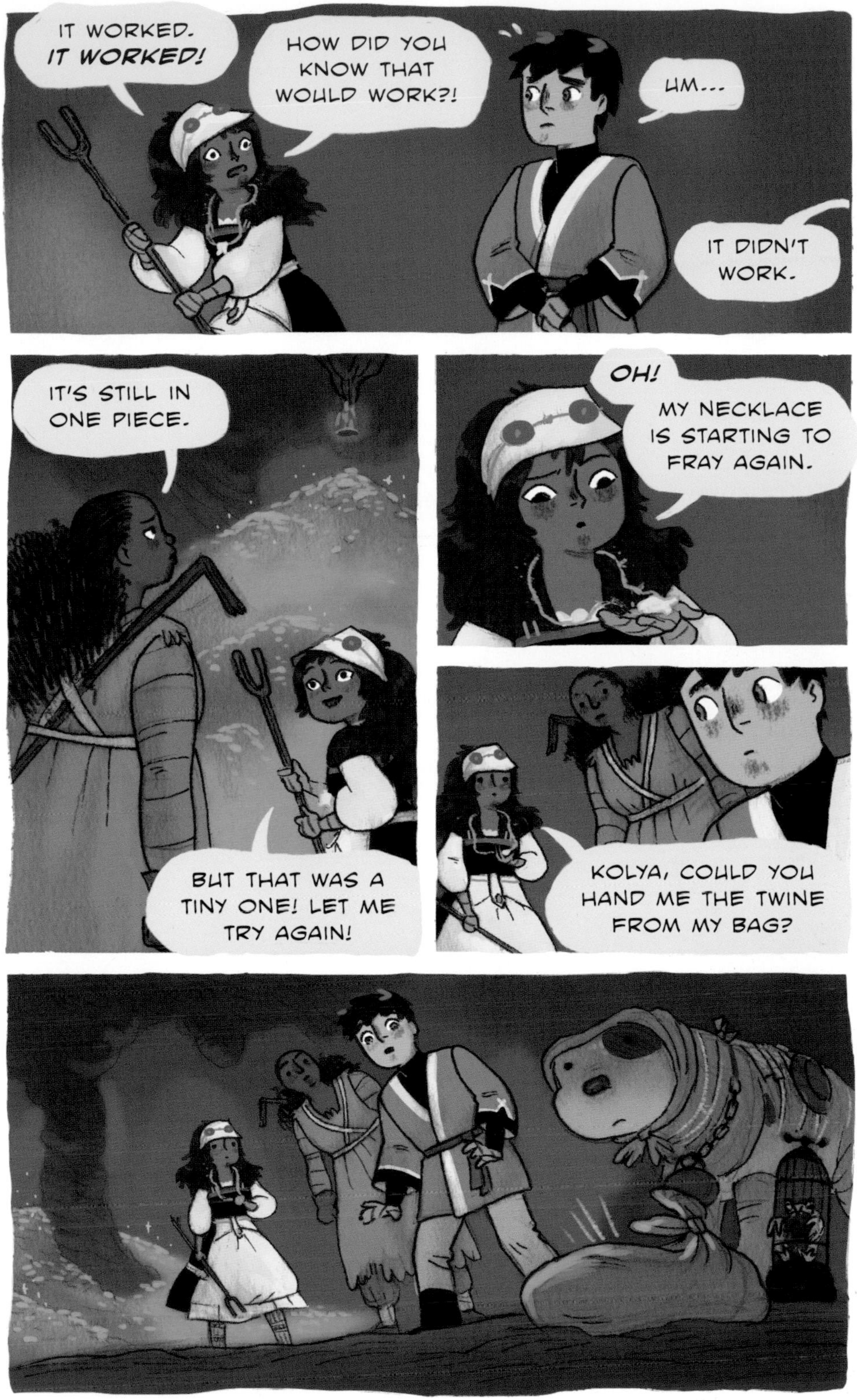
IT WORKED. *IT WORKED!*
HOW DID YOU KNOW THAT WOULD WORK?!
UM...
IT DIDN'T WORK.
IT'S STILL IN ONE PIECE.
BUT THAT WAS A TINY ONE! LET ME TRY AGAIN!
OH!
MY NECKLACE IS STARTING TO FRAY AGAIN.
KOLYA, COULD YOU HAND ME THE TWINE FROM MY BAG?

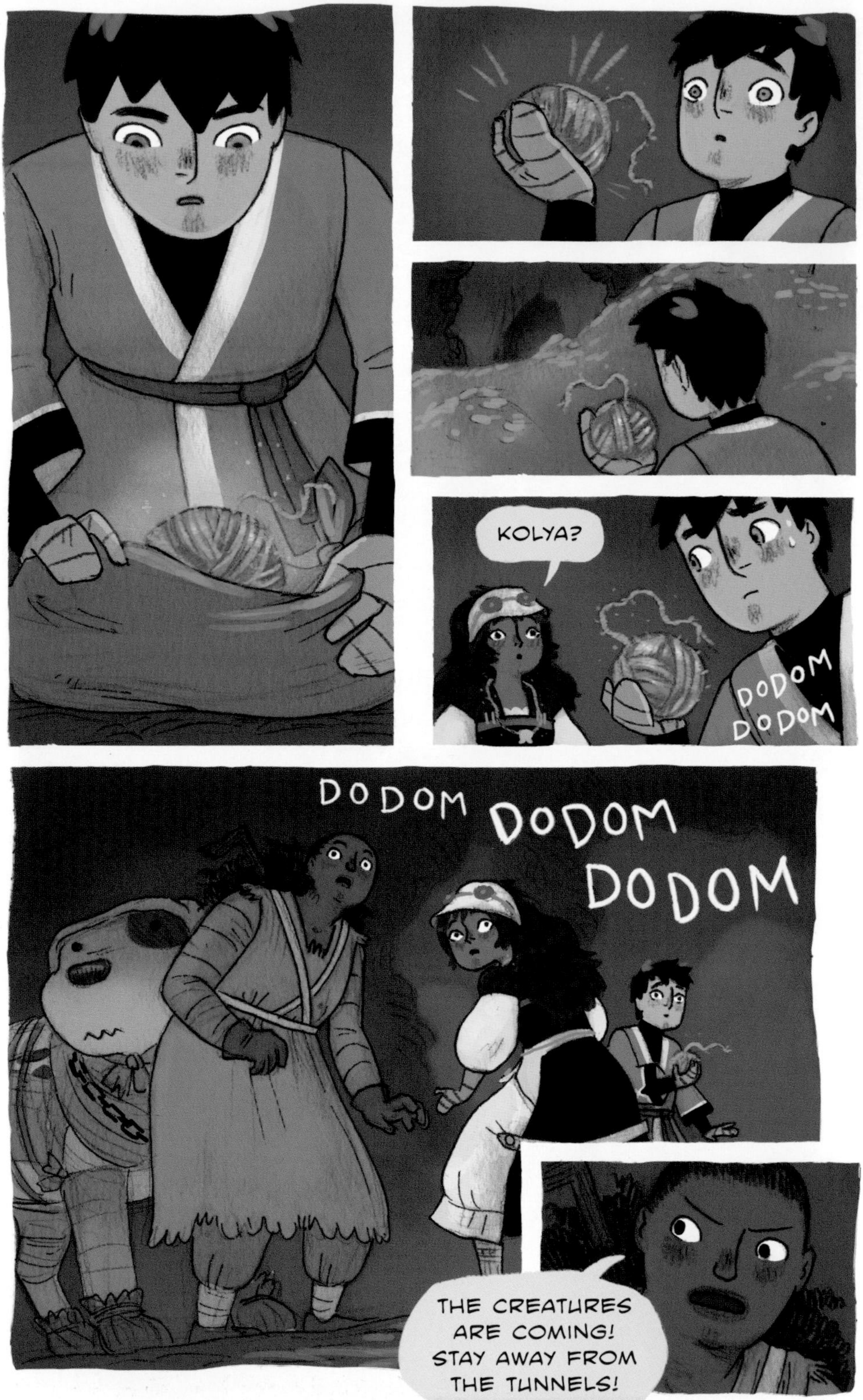
KOLYA?
DODOM DODOM
DODOM DODOM DODOM
THE CREATURES ARE COMING! STAY AWAY FROM THE TUNNELS!

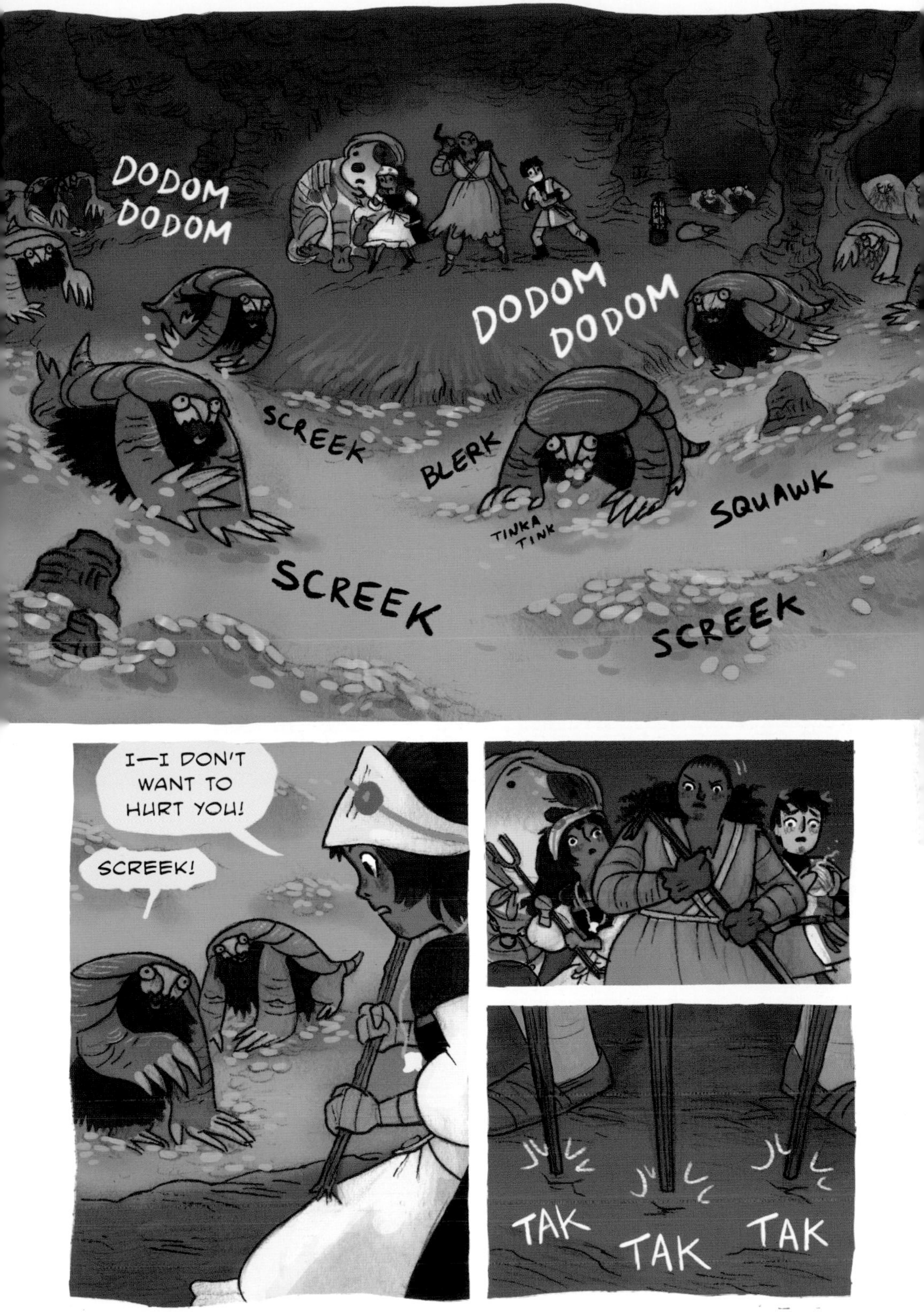
DODOM
DODOM
DODOM
DODOM
SCREEK
BLERK
SQUAWK
TINKA TINK
SCREEK
SCREEK
I—I DON'T WANT TO HURT YOU!
SCREEK!
TAK
TAK
TAK

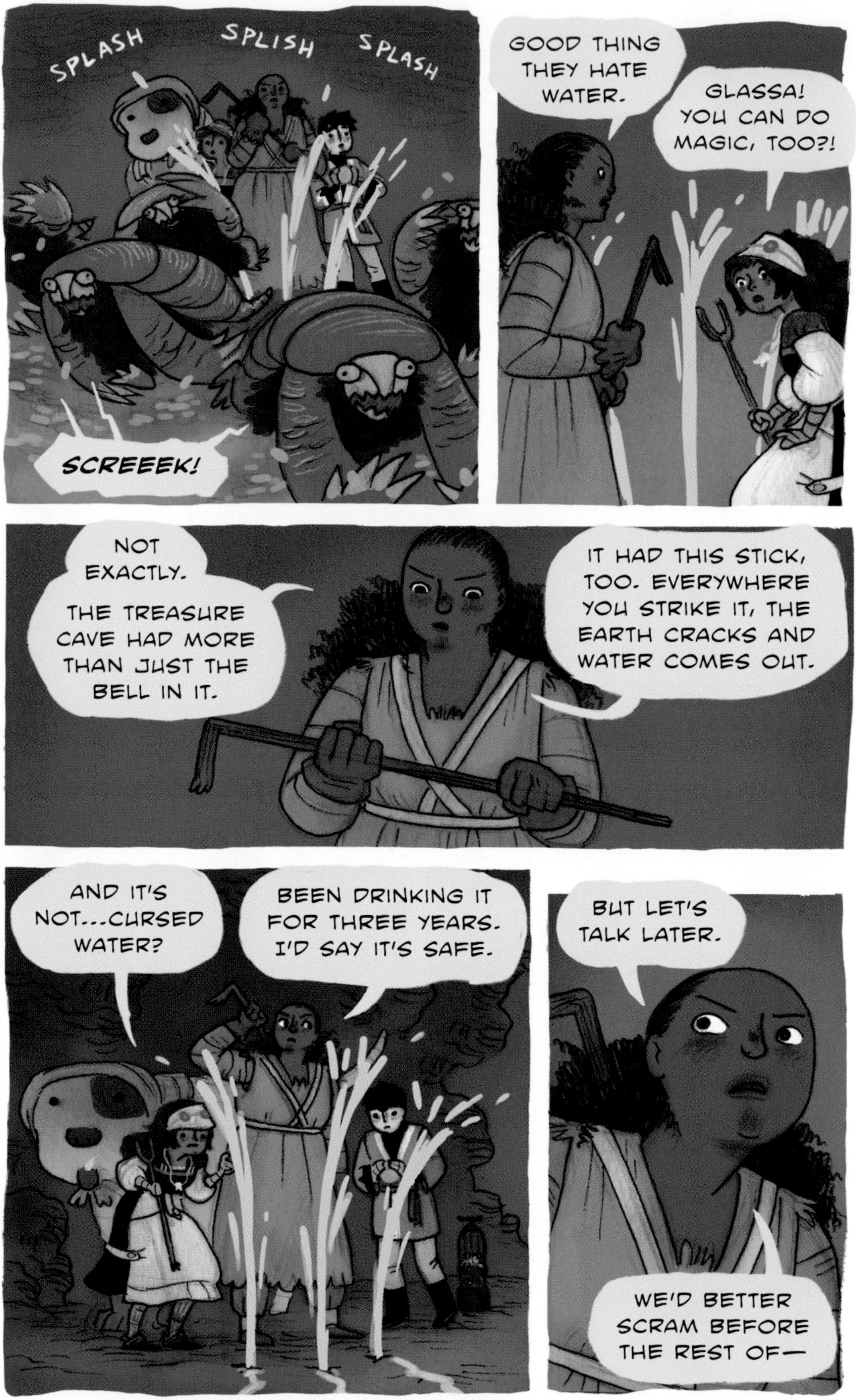
SPLASH
SPLISH
SPLASH
SCREEEK!
GOOD THING THEY HATE WATER.
GLASSA! YOU CAN DO MAGIC, TOO?!
NOT EXACTLY.
THE TREASURE CAVE HAD MORE THAN JUST THE BELL IN IT.
IT HAD THIS STICK, TOO. EVERYWHERE YOU STRIKE IT, THE EARTH CRACKS AND WATER COMES OUT.
AND IT'S NOT...CURSED WATER?
BEEN DRINKING IT FOR THREE YEARS. I'D SAY IT'S SAFE.
BUT LET'S TALK LATER.
WE'D BETTER SCRAM BEFORE THE REST OF—

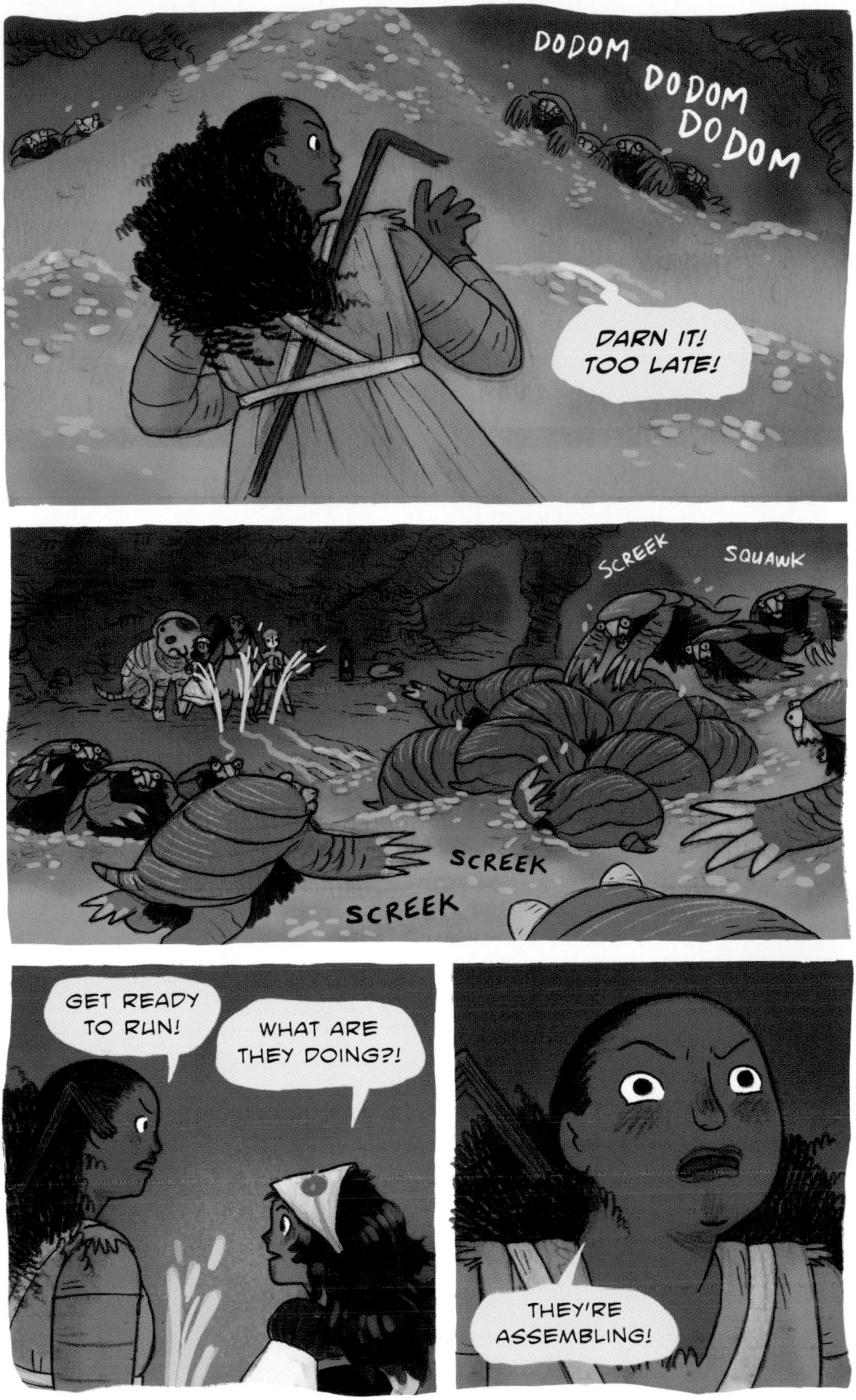
DODOM
DODOM
DODOM
DARN IT! TOO LATE!
SCREEK
SQUAWK
SCREEK
SCREEK
GET READY TO RUN!
WHAT ARE THEY DOING?!
THEY'RE ASSEMBLING!

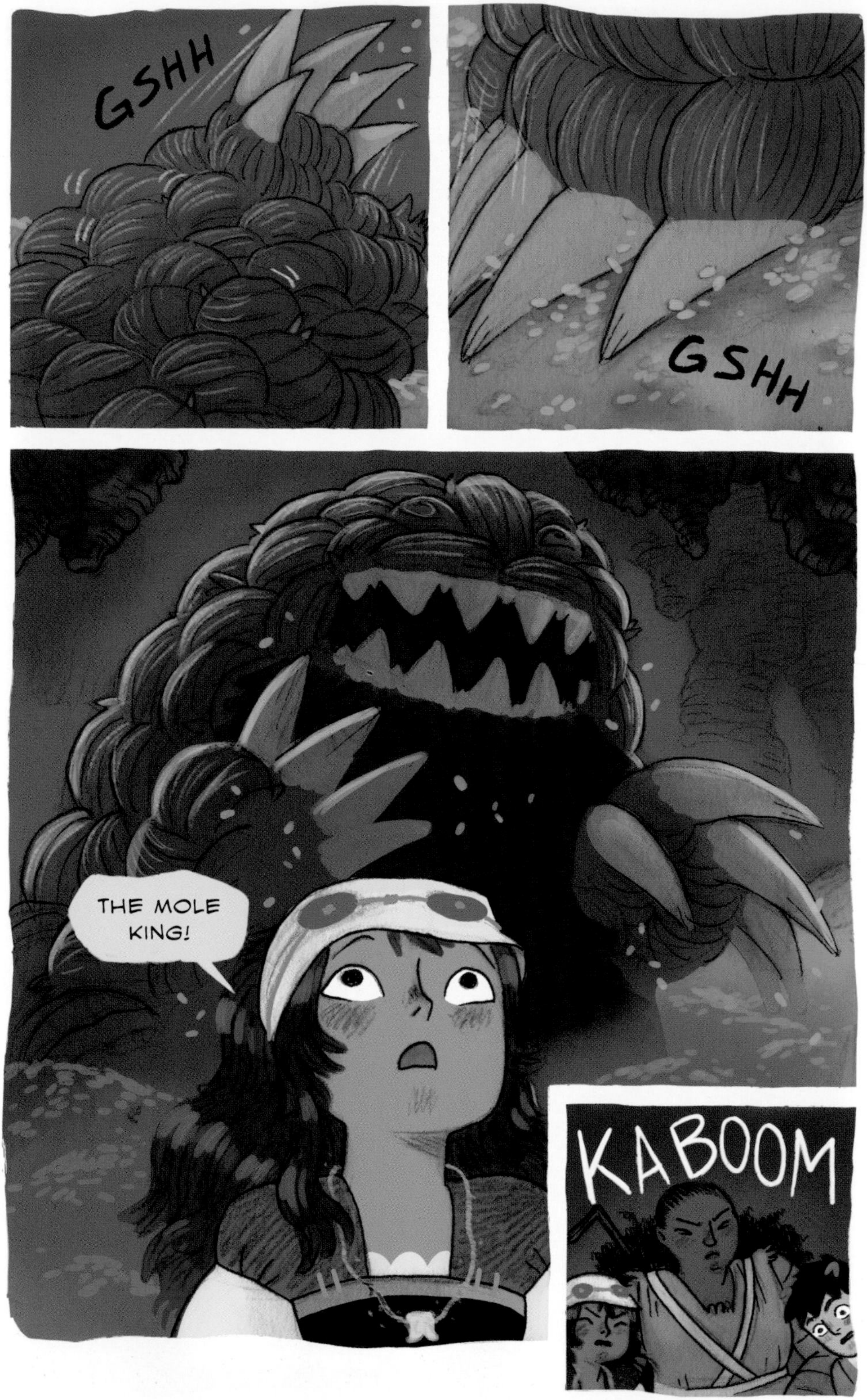
GSHH
GSHH
THE MOLE KING!
KABOOM

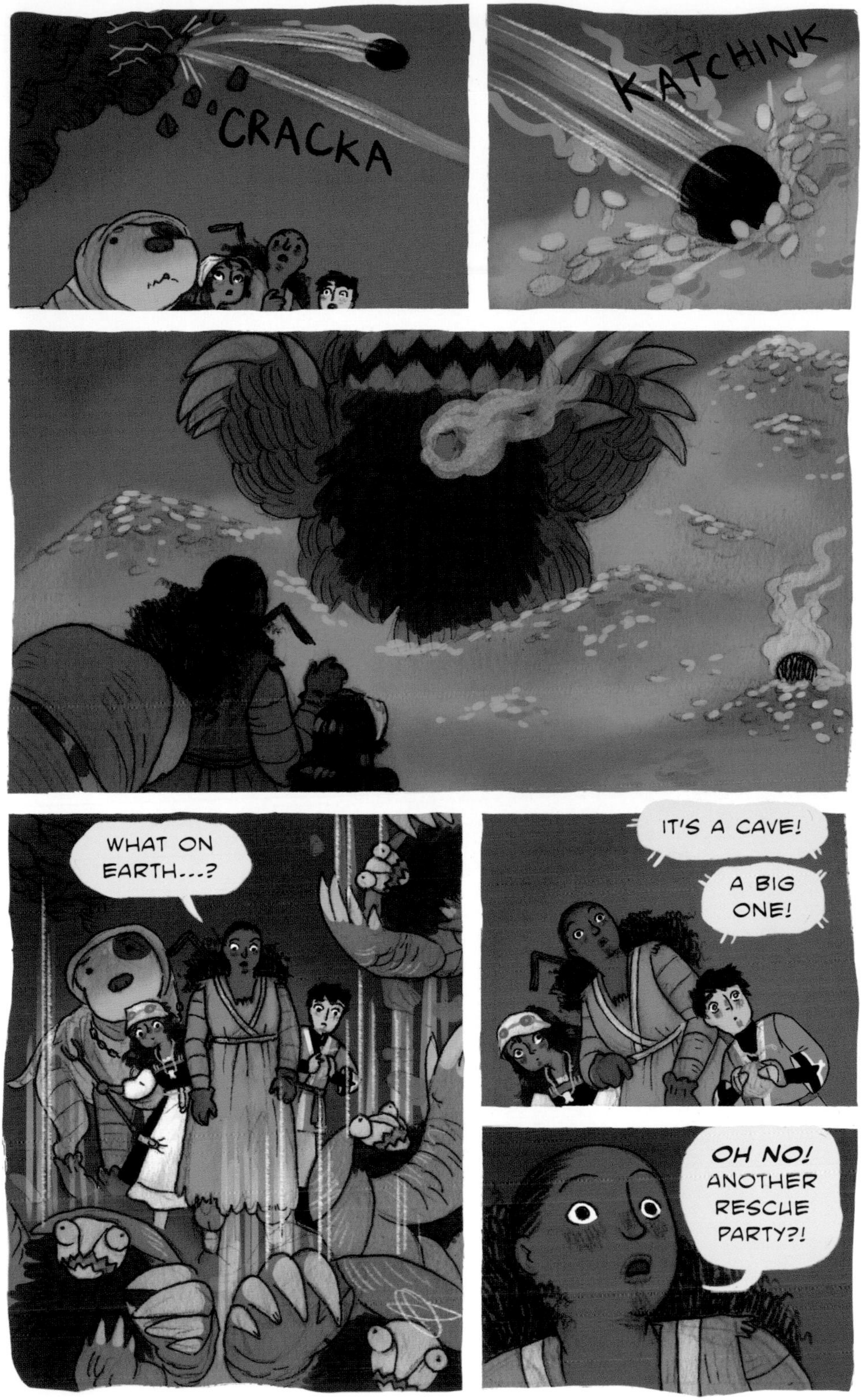
CRACKA
KATCHINK
WHAT ON EARTH...?
IT'S A CAVE!
A BIG ONE!
OH NO! ANOTHER RESCUE PARTY?!

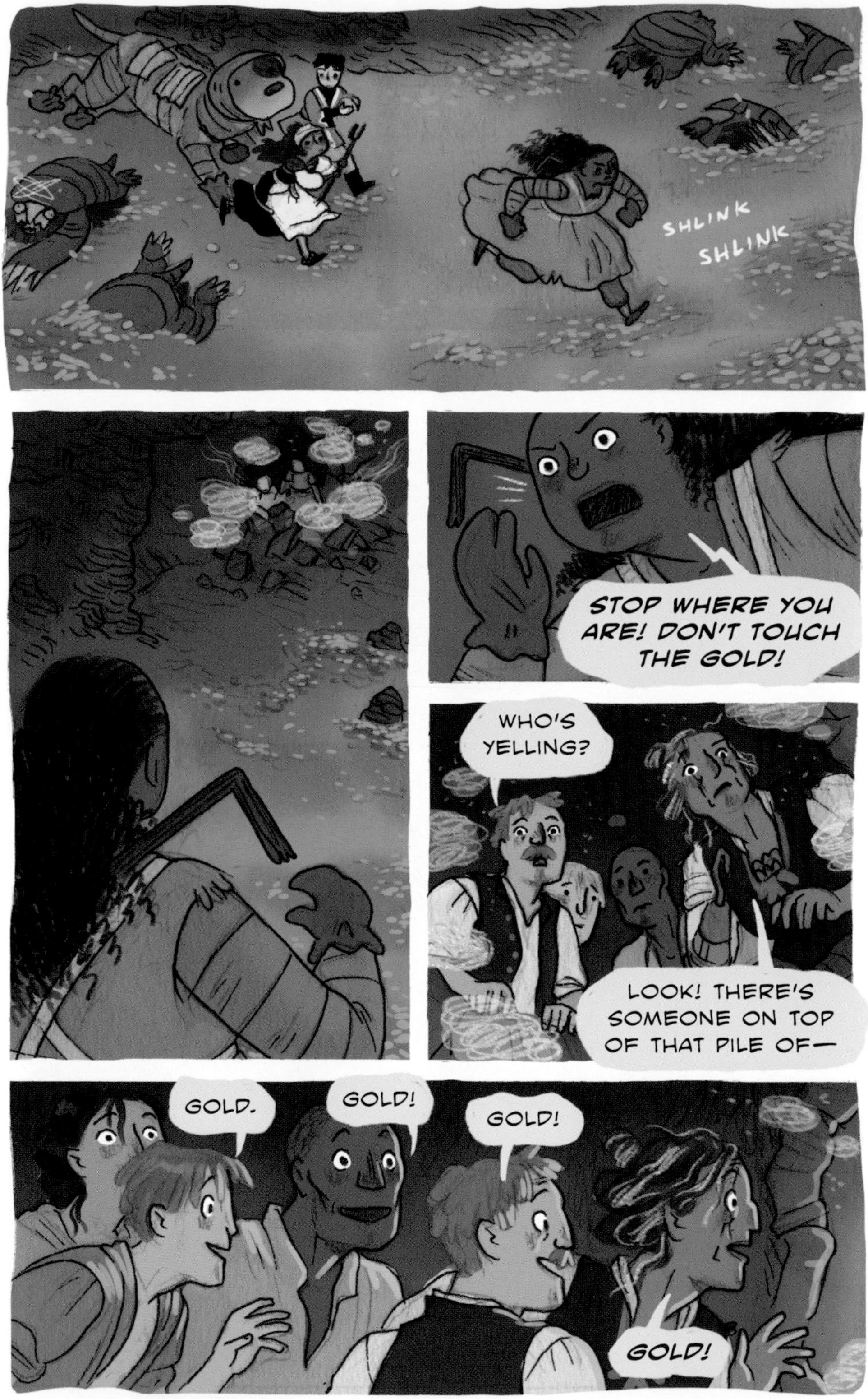
SHLINK
SHLINK
STOP WHERE YOU ARE! DON'T TOUCH THE GOLD!
WHO'S YELLING?
LOOK! THERE'S SOMEONE ON TOP OF THAT PILE OF—
GOLD.
GOLD!
GOLD!
GOLD!

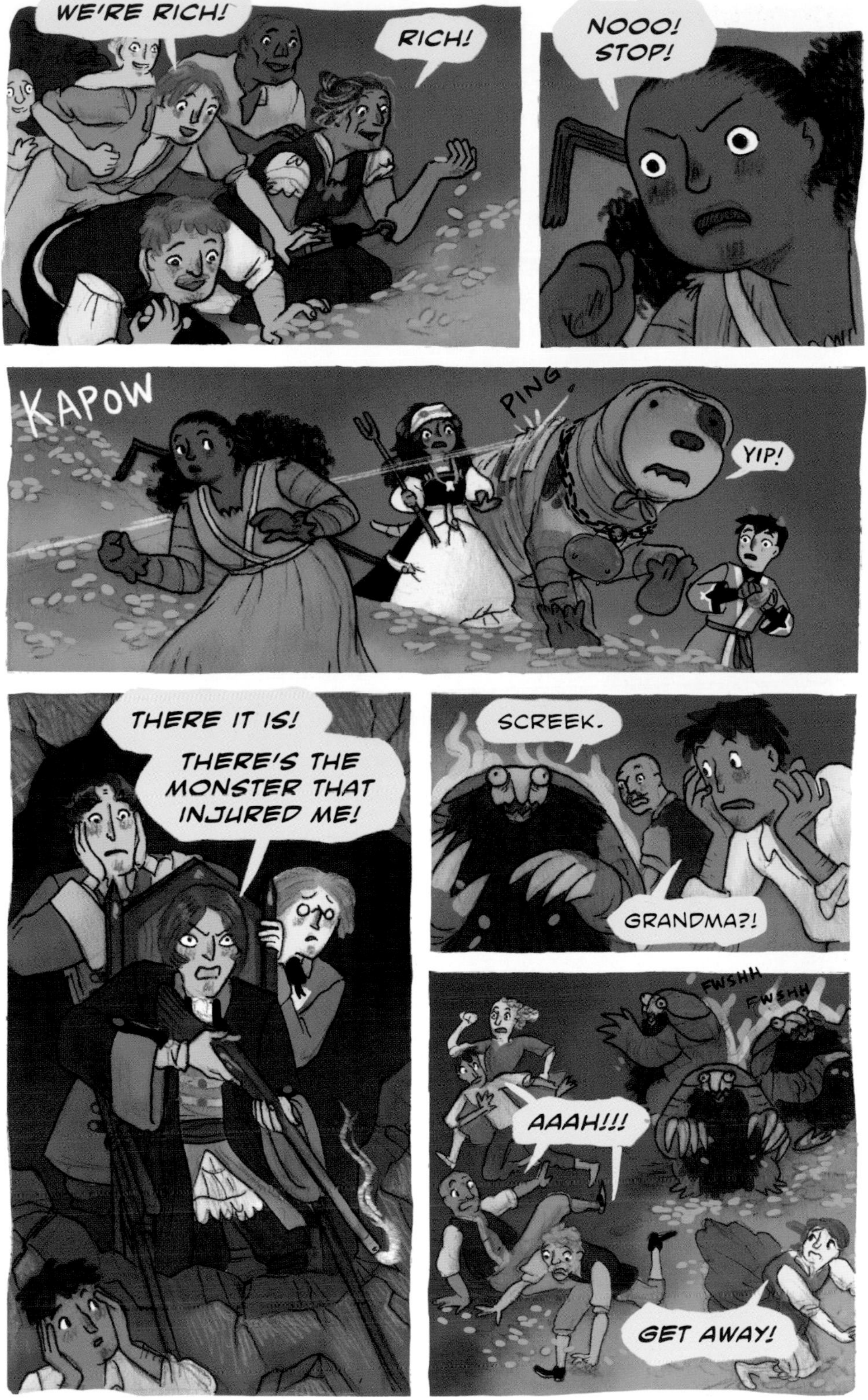
WE'RE RICH!
RICH!
NOOO! STOP!
KAPOW
PING
YIP!
THERE IT IS!
THERE'S THE MONSTER THAT INJURED ME!
SCREEK.
GRANDMA?!
FWSHH
FWSHH
AAAH!!!
GET AWAY!

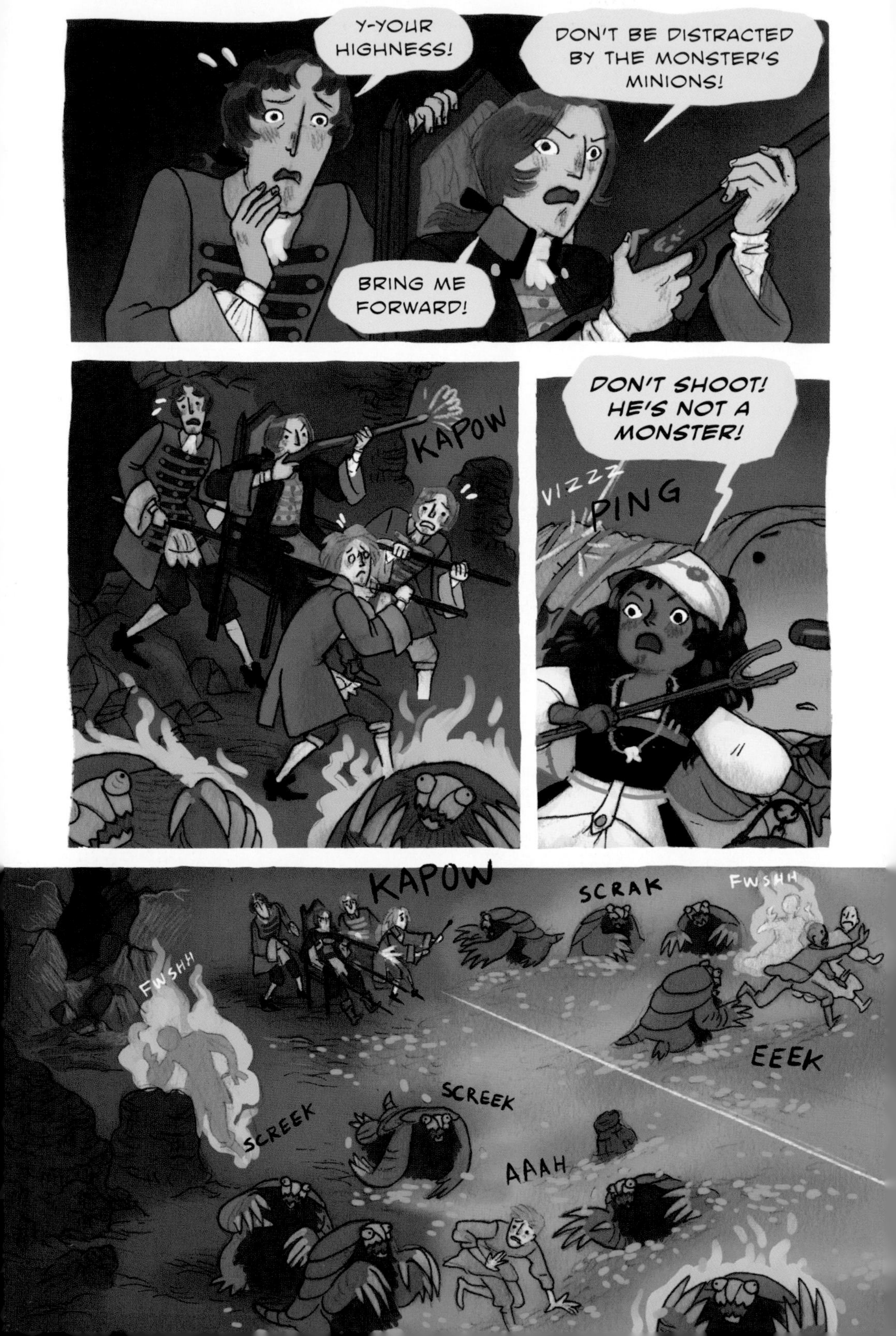
Y-YOUR HIGHNESS!
DON'T BE DISTRACTED BY THE MONSTER'S MINIONS!
BRING ME FORWARD!
KAPOW
DON'T SHOOT! HE'S NOT A MONSTER!
VIZZZ
PING
KAPOW
SCRAK
FWSHH
FWSHH
EEEK
SCREEK
SCREEK
AAAH

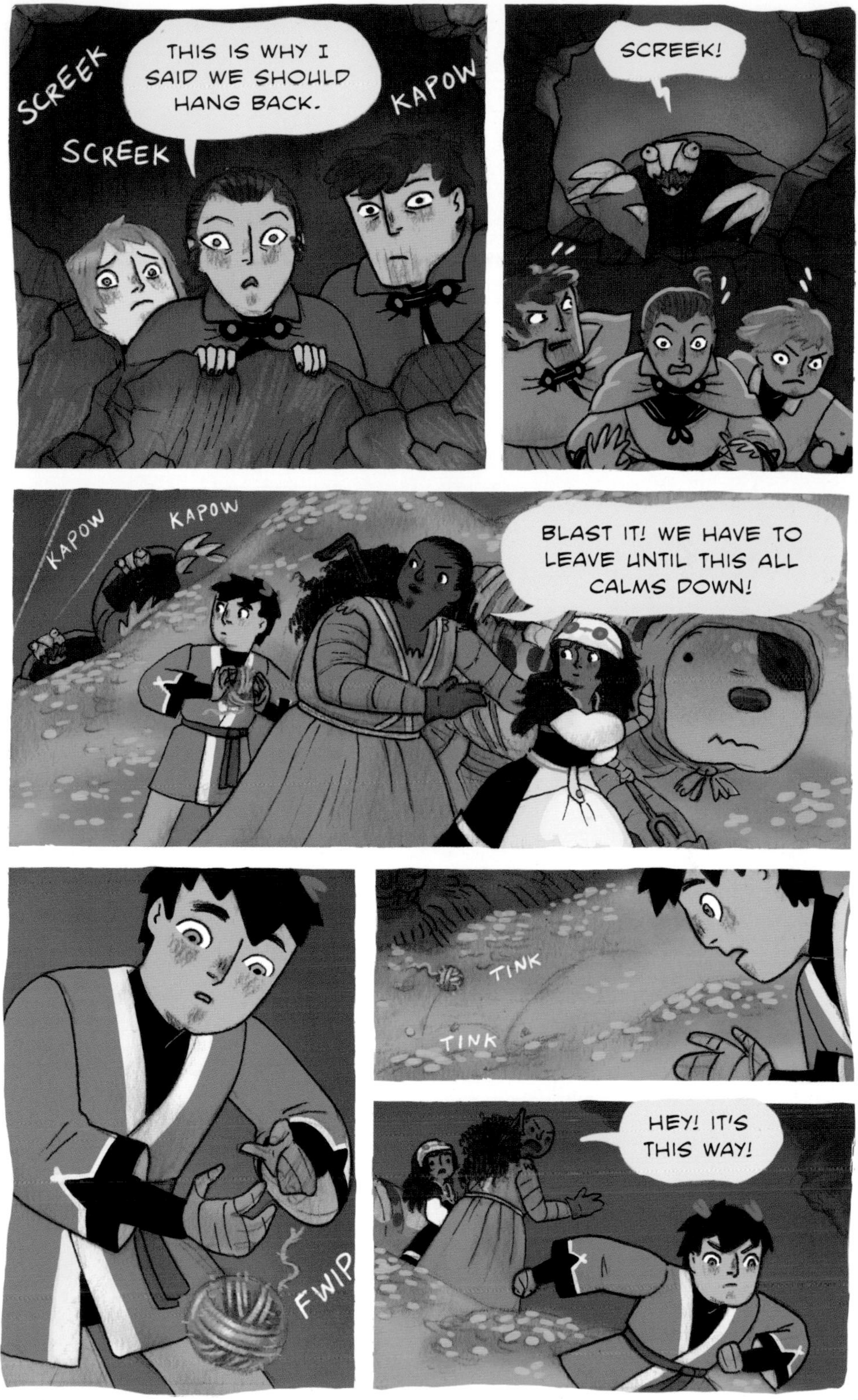
SCREEK
SCREEK
THIS IS WHY I SAID WE SHOULD HANG BACK.
KAPOW
SCREEK!
KAPOW
KAPOW
BLAST IT! WE HAVE TO LEAVE UNTIL THIS ALL CALMS DOWN!
FWIP
TINK
TINK
HEY! IT'S THIS WAY!

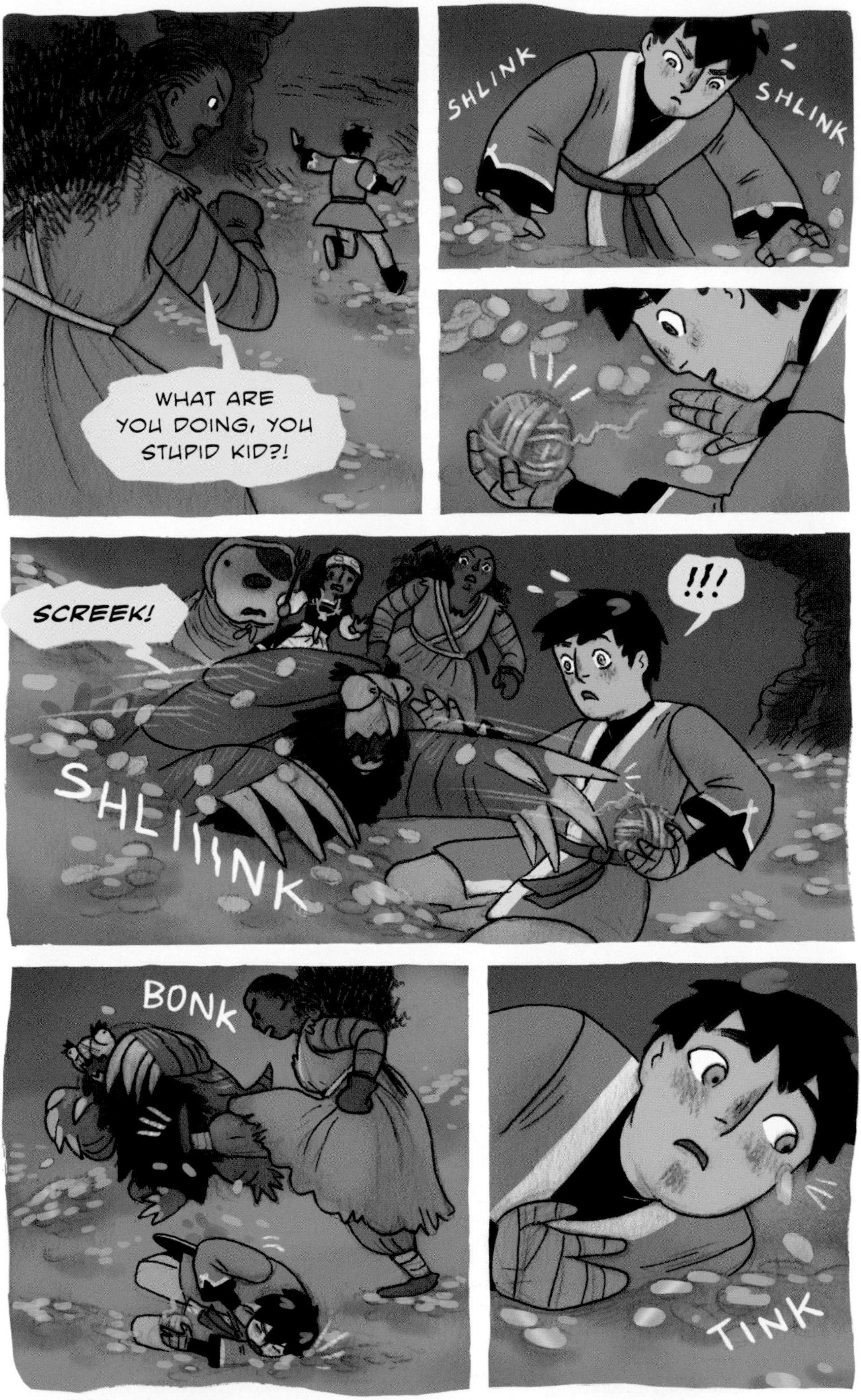
WHAT ARE YOU DOING, YOU STUPID KID?!
SHLINK
SHLINK
SCREEK!
!!!
SHLIIIINK
BONK
TINK

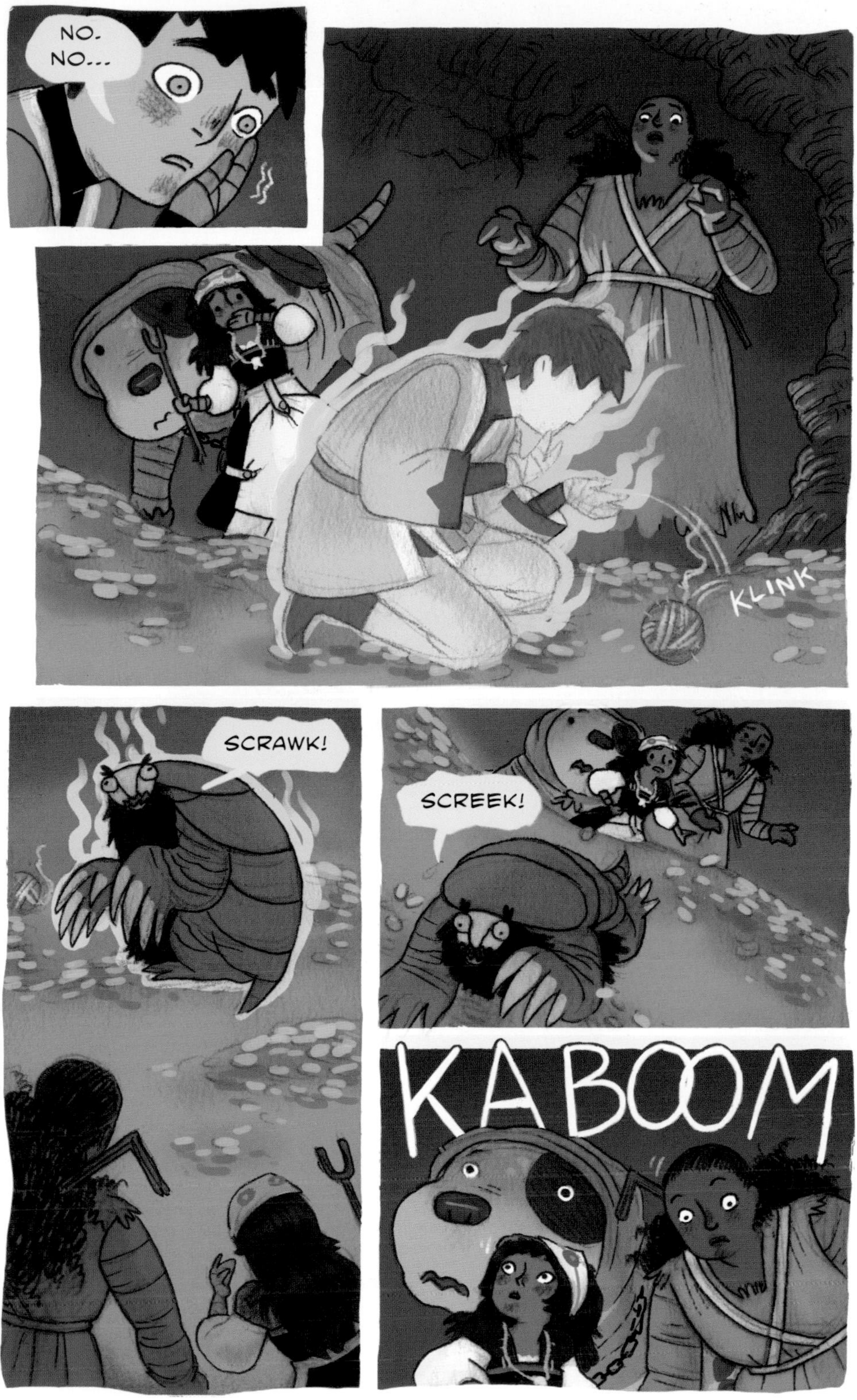
NO.
NO...
KLINK
SCRAWK!
SCREEK!
KABOOM

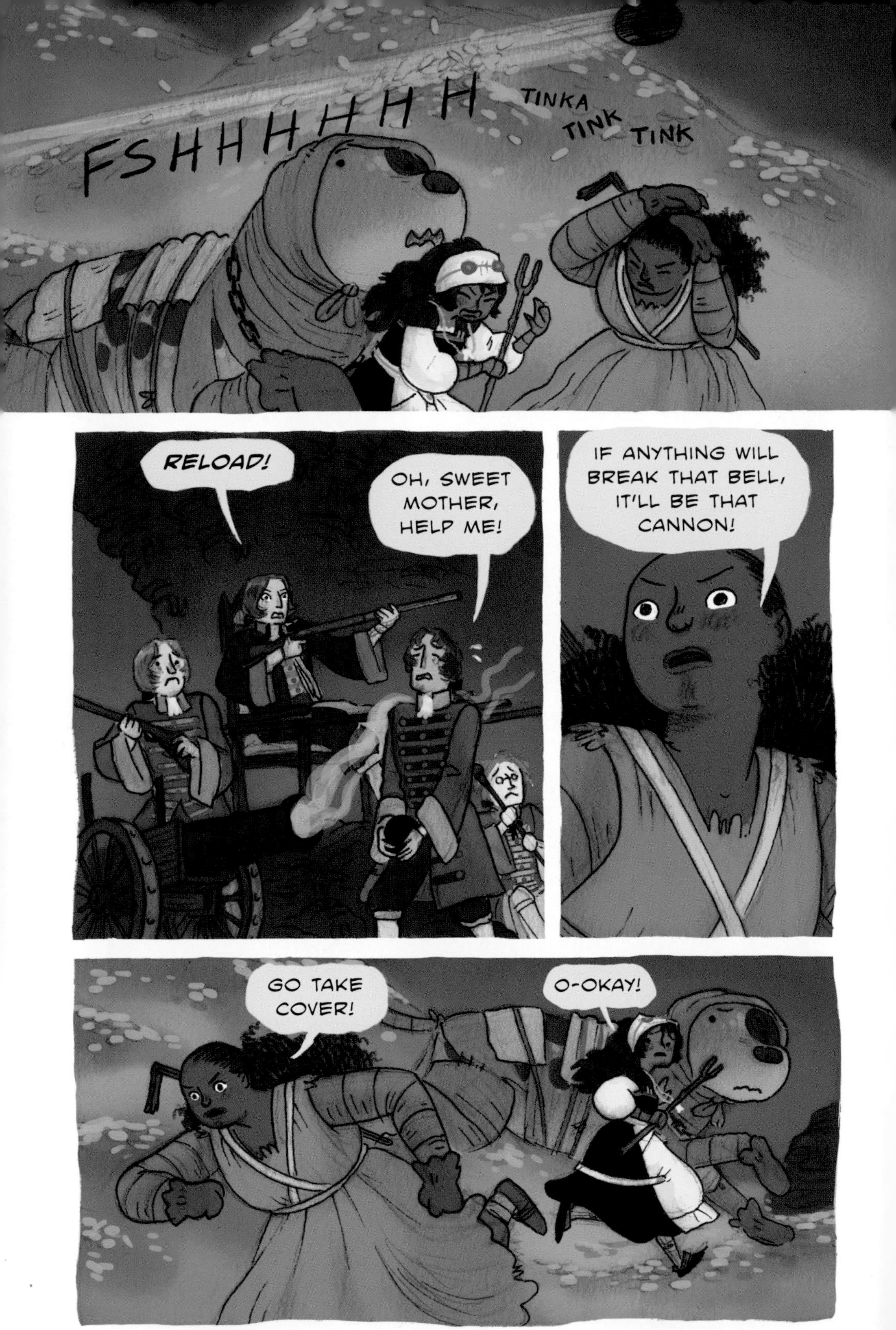
FSHHHHHH
TINKA
TINK
TINK
RELOAD!
OH, SWEET MOTHER, HELP ME!
IF ANYTHING WILL BREAK THAT BELL, IT'LL BE THAT CANNON!
GO TAKE COVER!
O-OKAY!

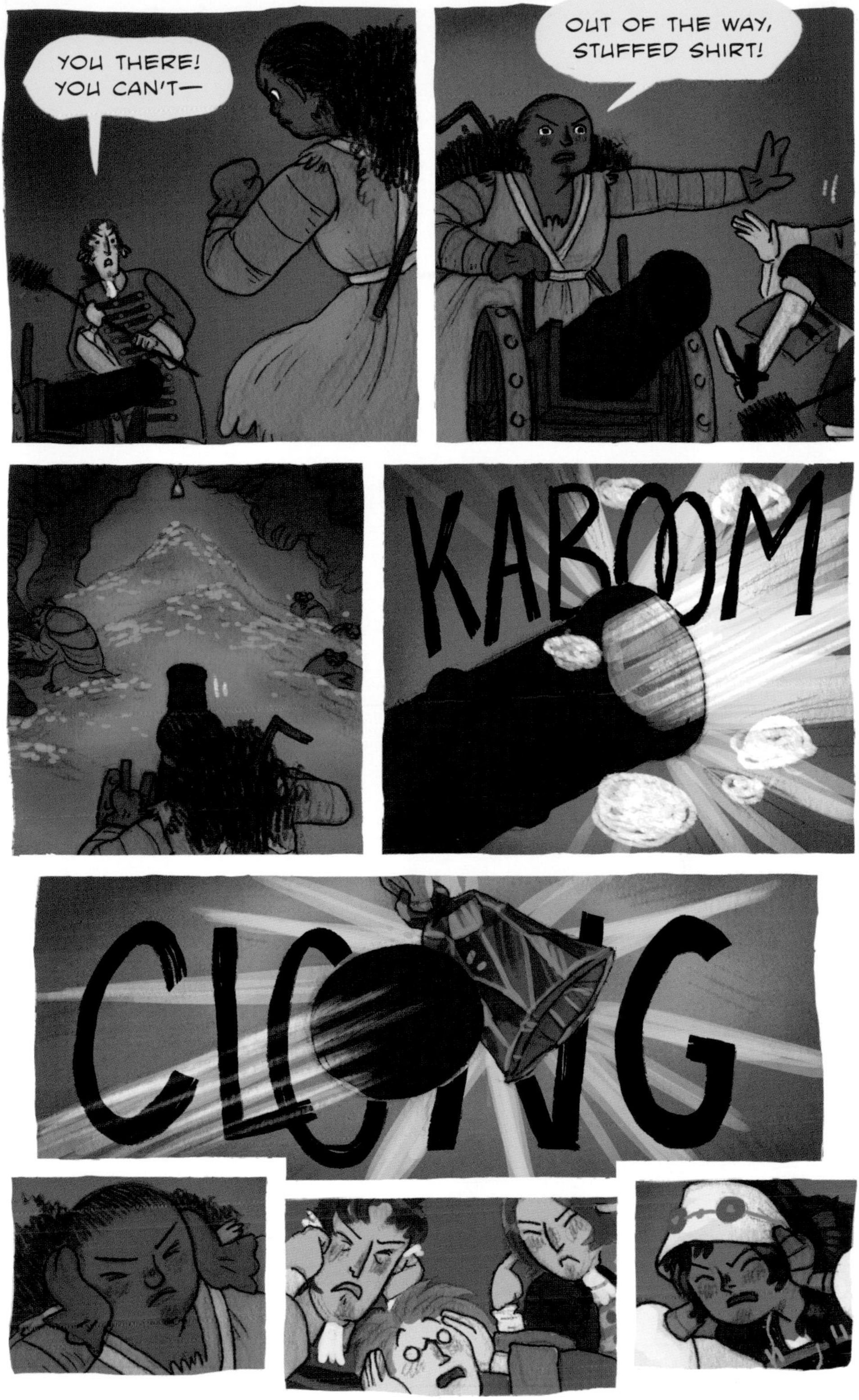
YOU THERE! YOU CAN'T—
OUT OF THE WAY, STUFFED SHIRT!
KABOOM
CLONG

IT HIT THE BELL! IT'S...

OOONNNGOOOONNNG

IT'S NOT BROKEN.

GWOOOONNOOOWONG

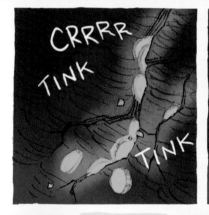

CRRRR

TINK

TINK

CRRRAAACK

TINKA

TINK

TINK

OW! WHAT'S THIS?

FSSSSHHHHH

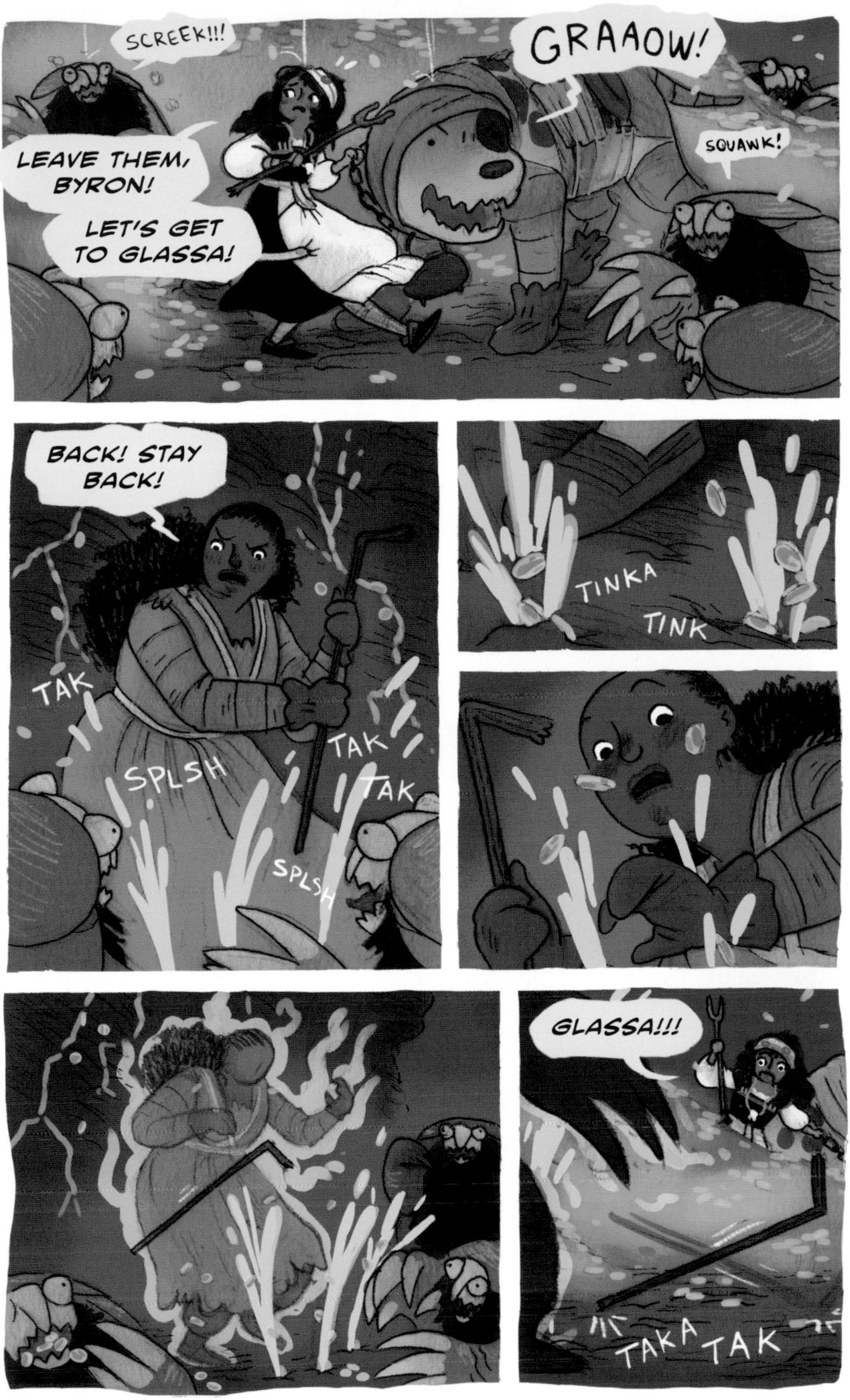
SCREEK!!!
GRAAOW!
LEAVE THEM, BYRON!
LET'S GET TO GLASSA!
SQUAWK!
BACK! STAY BACK!
TAK
SPLSH
TAK
TAK
SPLSH
TINKA
TINK
GLASSA!!!
TAKA
TAK

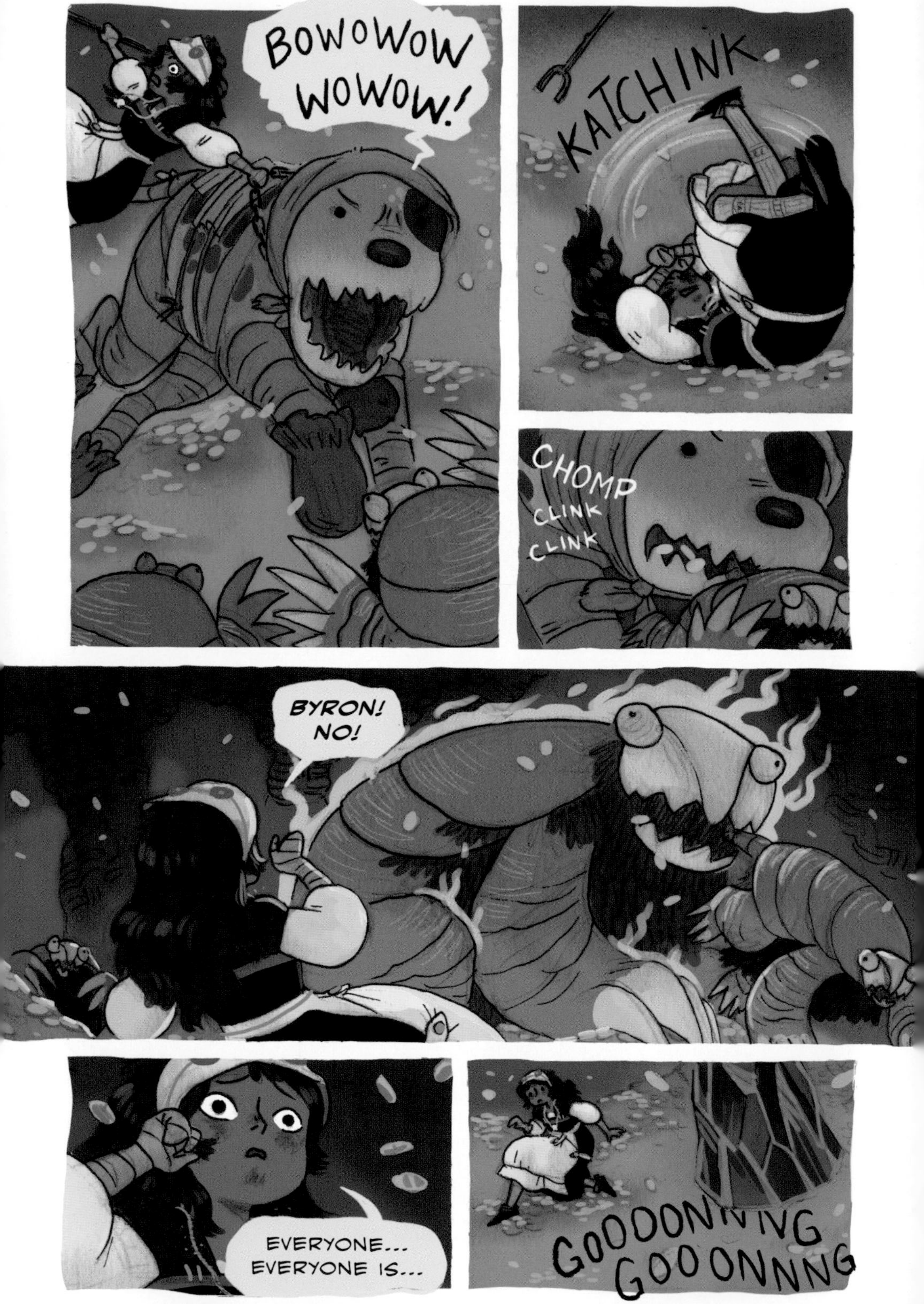
BOWOWOW WOWOW!
KATCHINK
CHOMP
CLINK
CLINK
BYRON! NO!
EVERYONE... EVERYONE IS...
GOOOONNNG
GOOONNNG

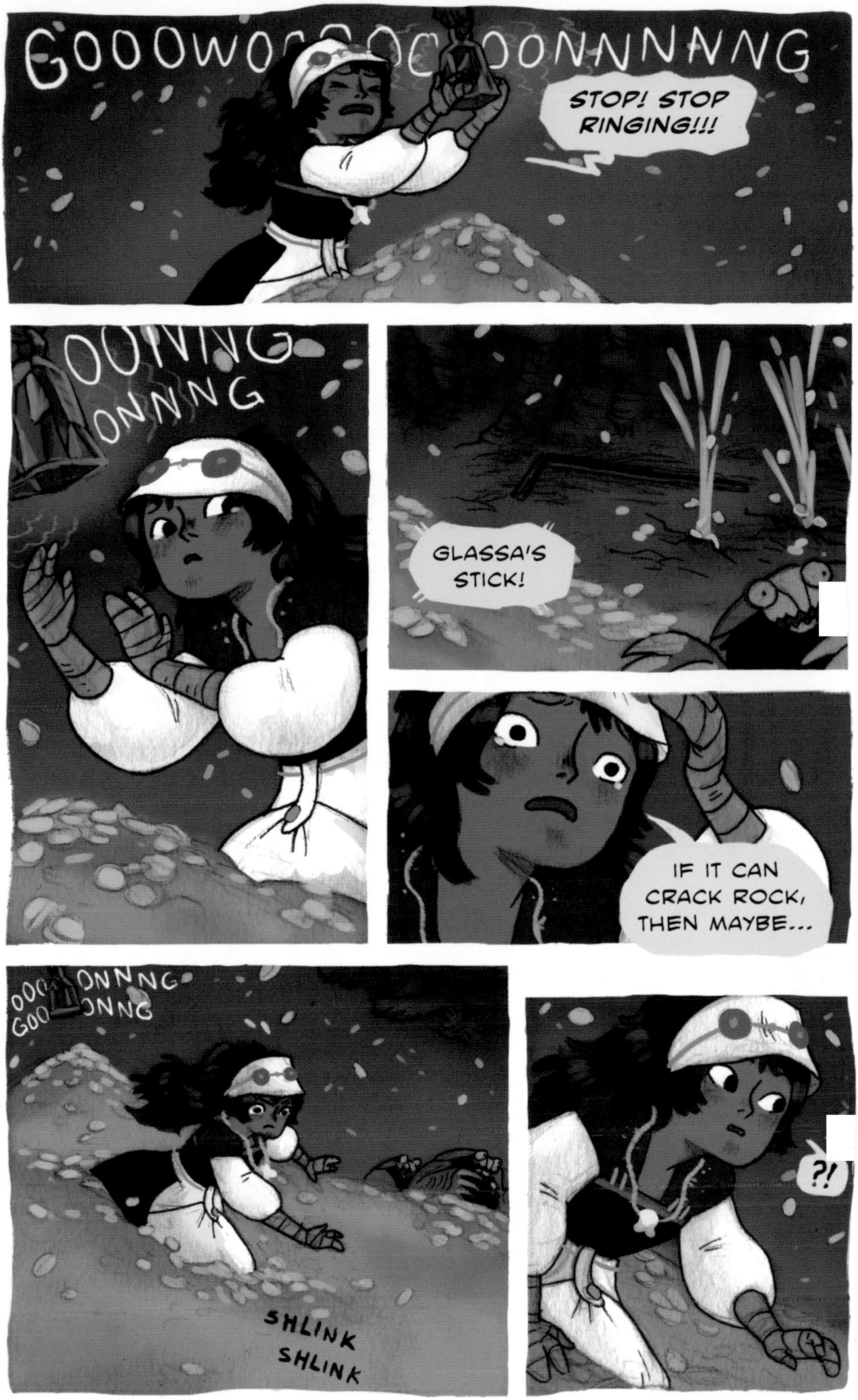
GOOOWOOOOOOONNNNNG
STOP! STOP RINGING!!!
OOONNG ONNNG
GLASSA'S STICK!
IF IT CAN CRACK ROCK, THEN MAYBE...
OOOONNNG GOOONNG
SHLINK SHLINK
?!

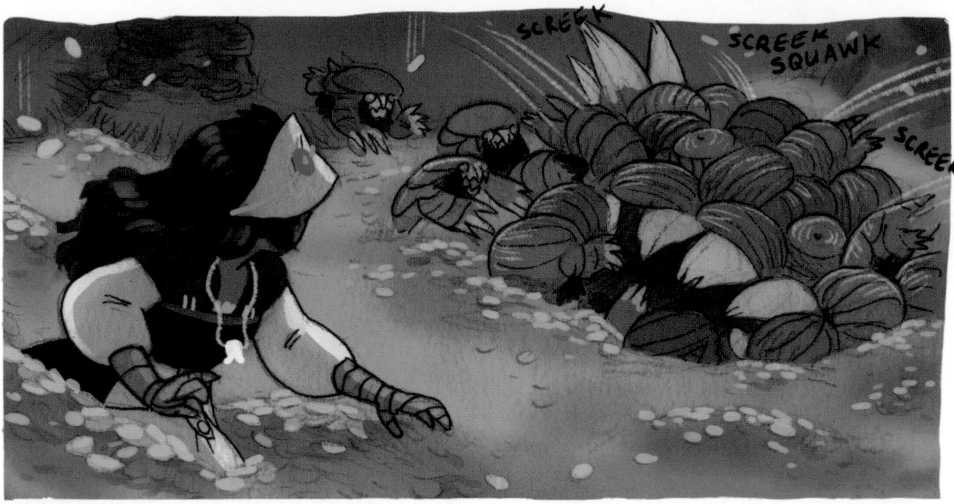
SCREEK
SCREEK
SQUAWK
SCREEK

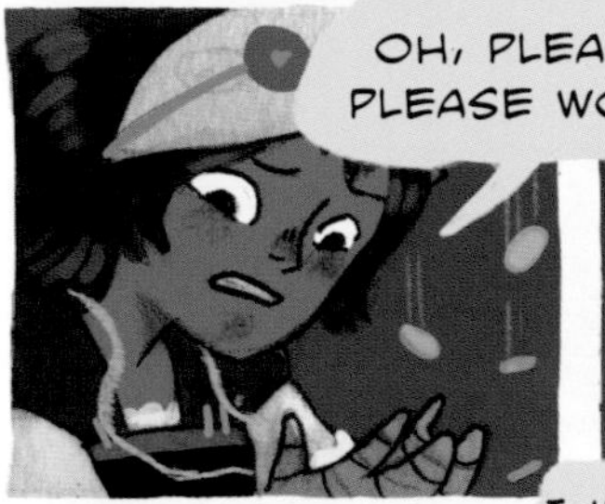
OH, PLEASE!
PLEASE WORK!

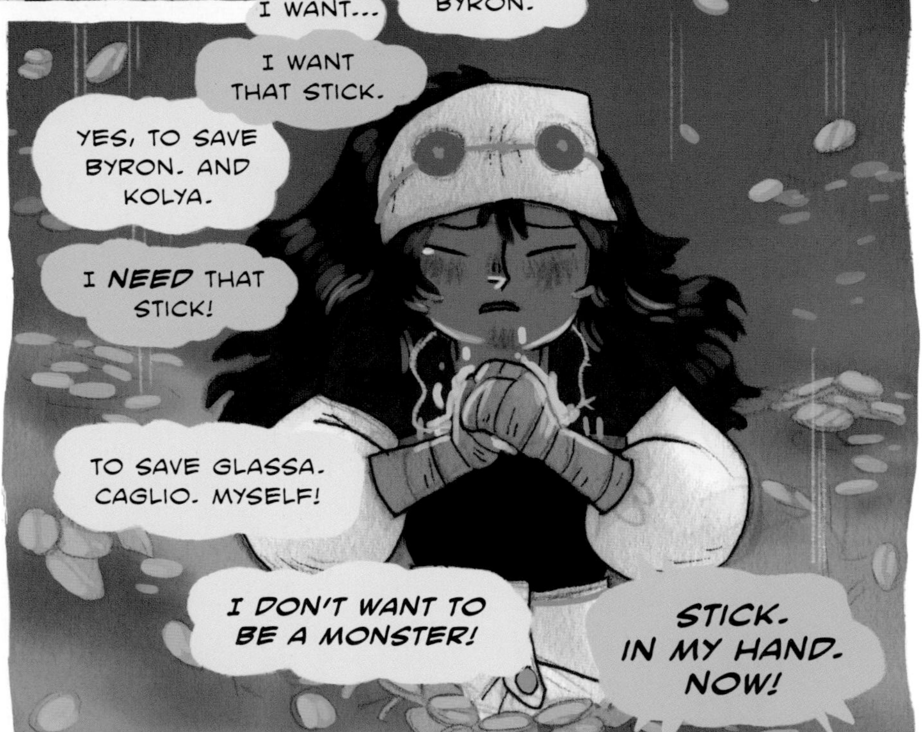
I'M SCARED.
PLEASE.
I DON'T WANT TO BE A MOLE LIKE—
OH, POOR BYRON.
I WANT...
I WANT THAT STICK.
YES, TO SAVE BYRON. AND KOLYA.
I **NEED** THAT STICK!
TO SAVE GLASSA. CAGLIO. MYSELF!
I DON'T WANT TO BE A MONSTER!
STICK. IN MY HAND. NOW!

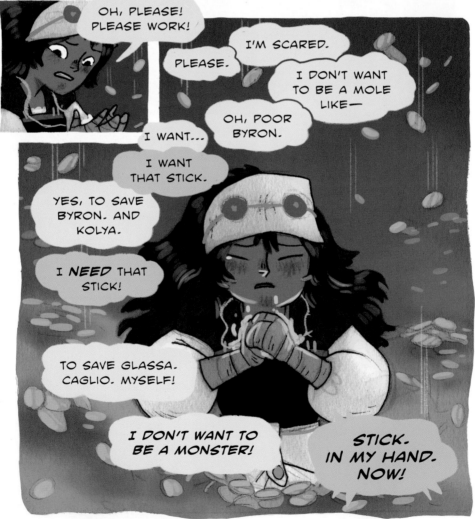

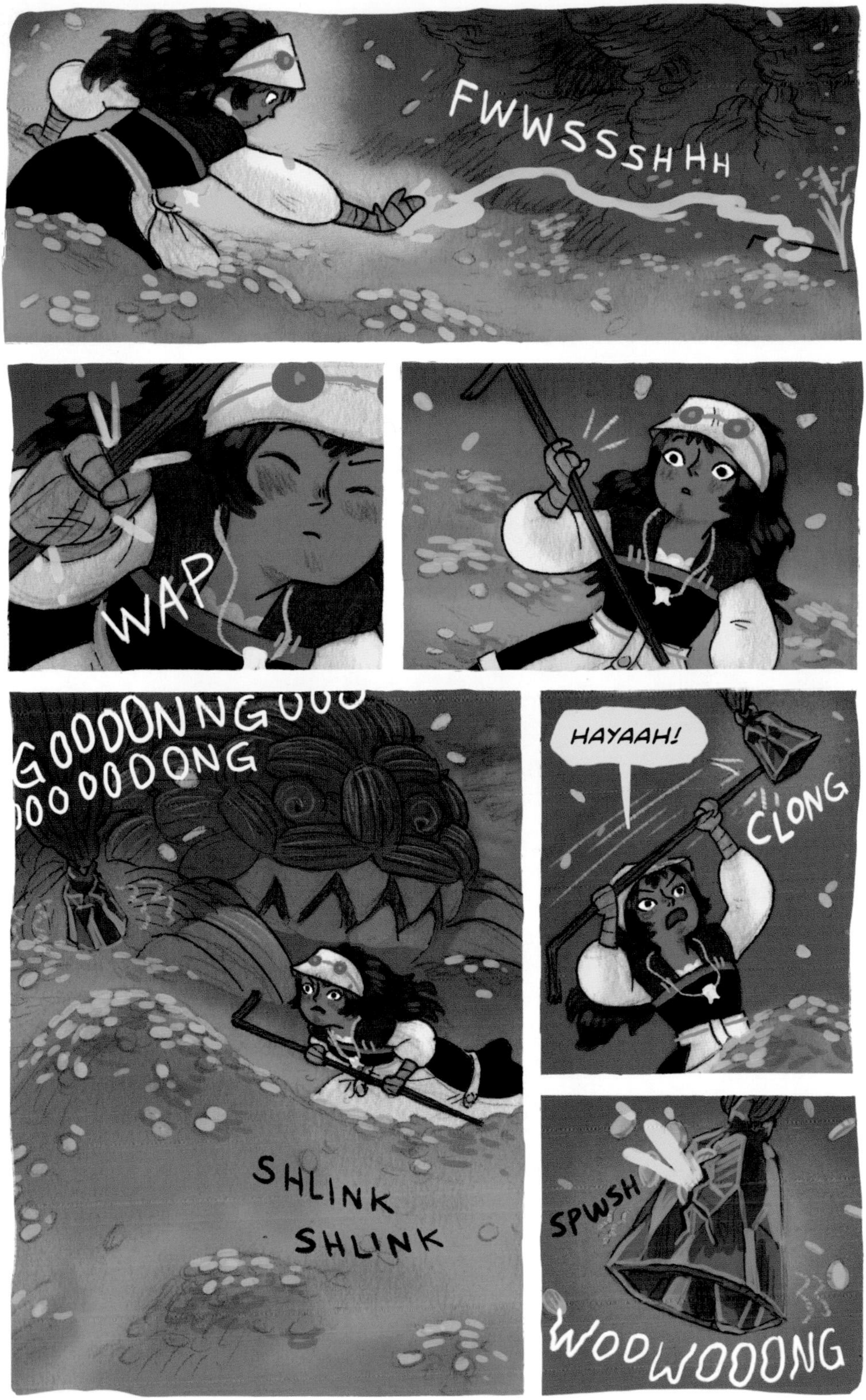
FWWSSSHHH
WAP
GOOODONNGOOO
OOOOOOONG
SHLINK
SHLINK
HAYAAH!
CLONG
SPWSH
WOOWOOONG

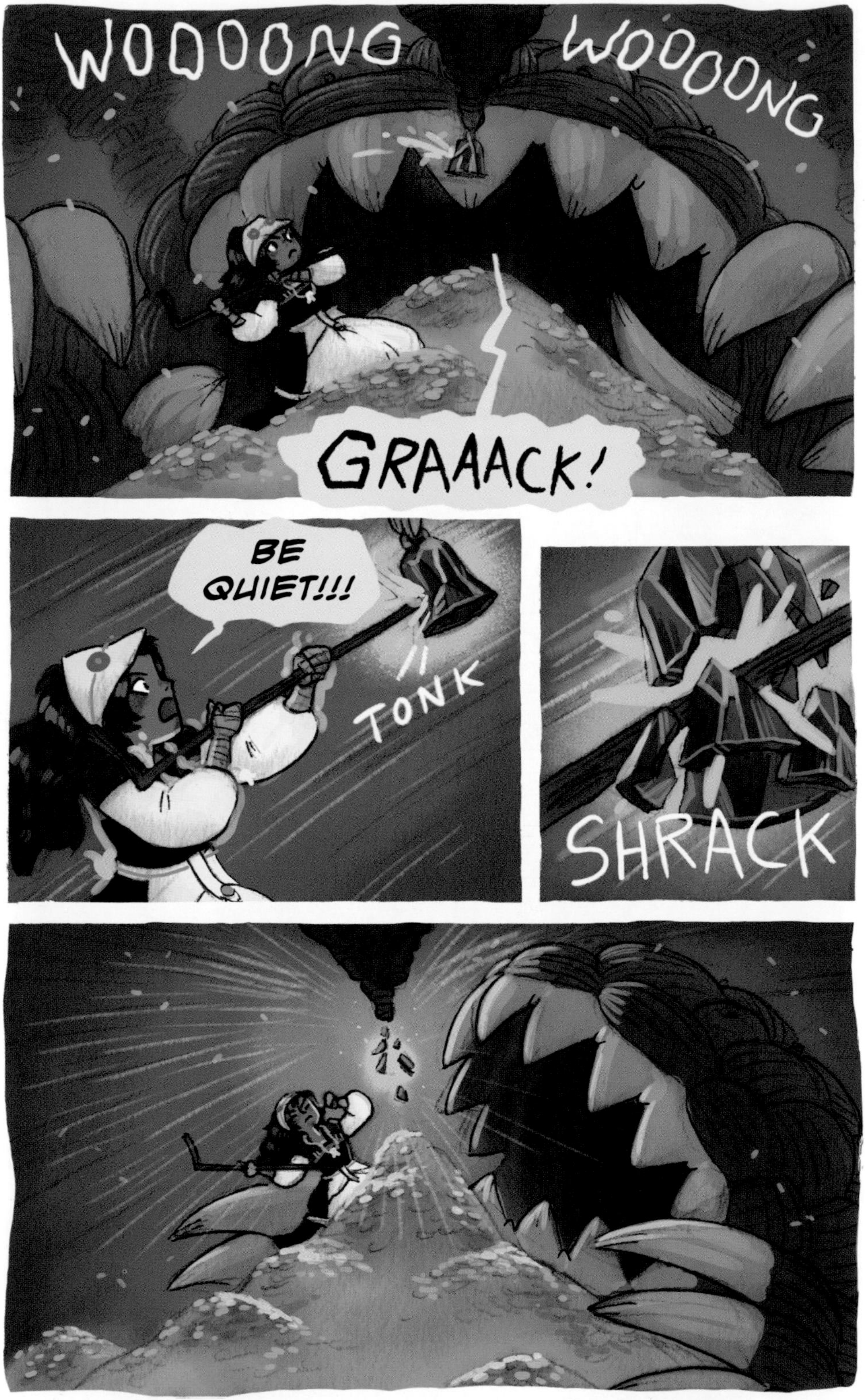
WOOOONG WOOOONG
GRAAACK!
BE QUIET!!!
TONK
SHRACK

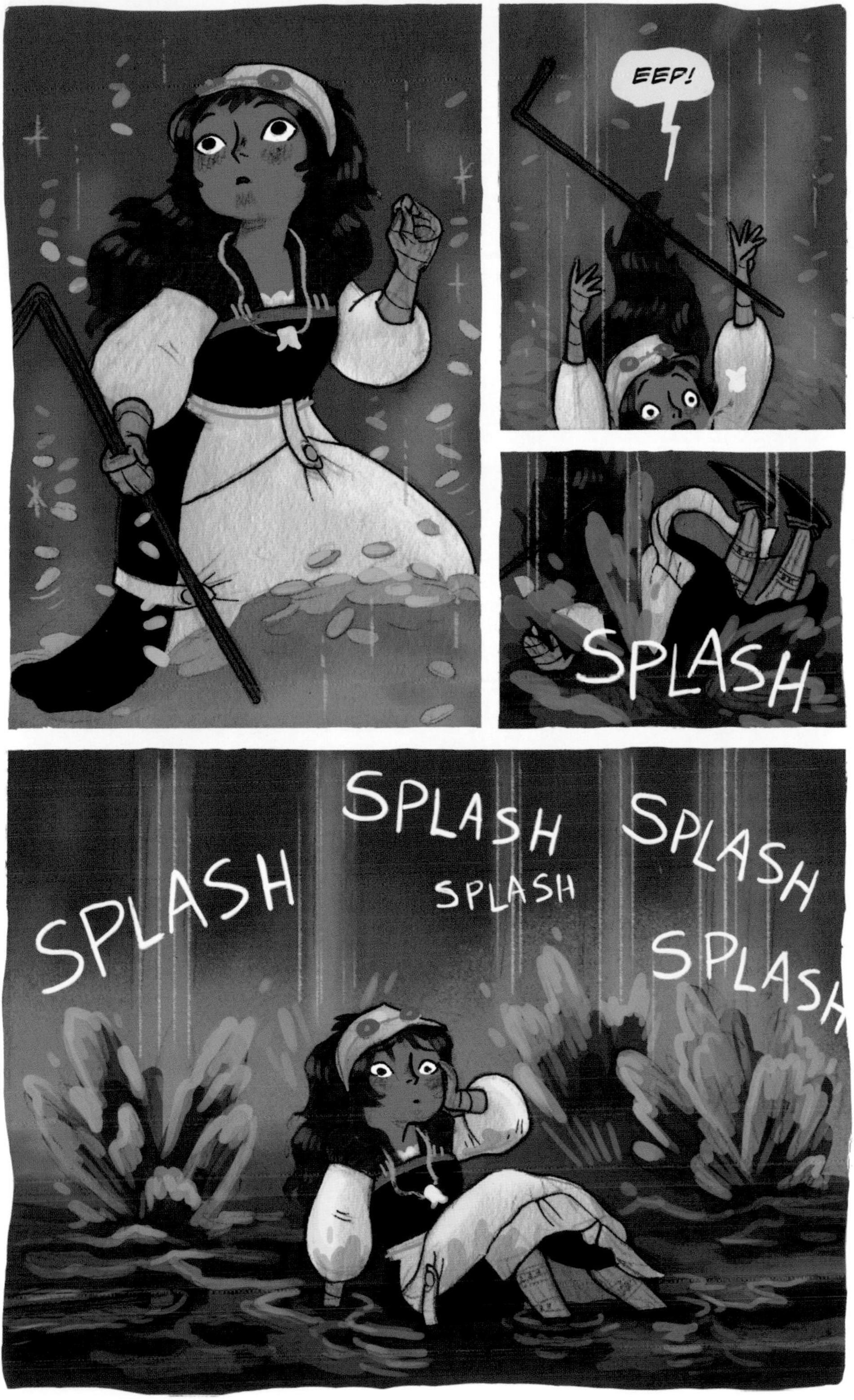
EEP!
SPLASH
SPLASH
SPLASH
SPLASH
SPLASH
SPLASH

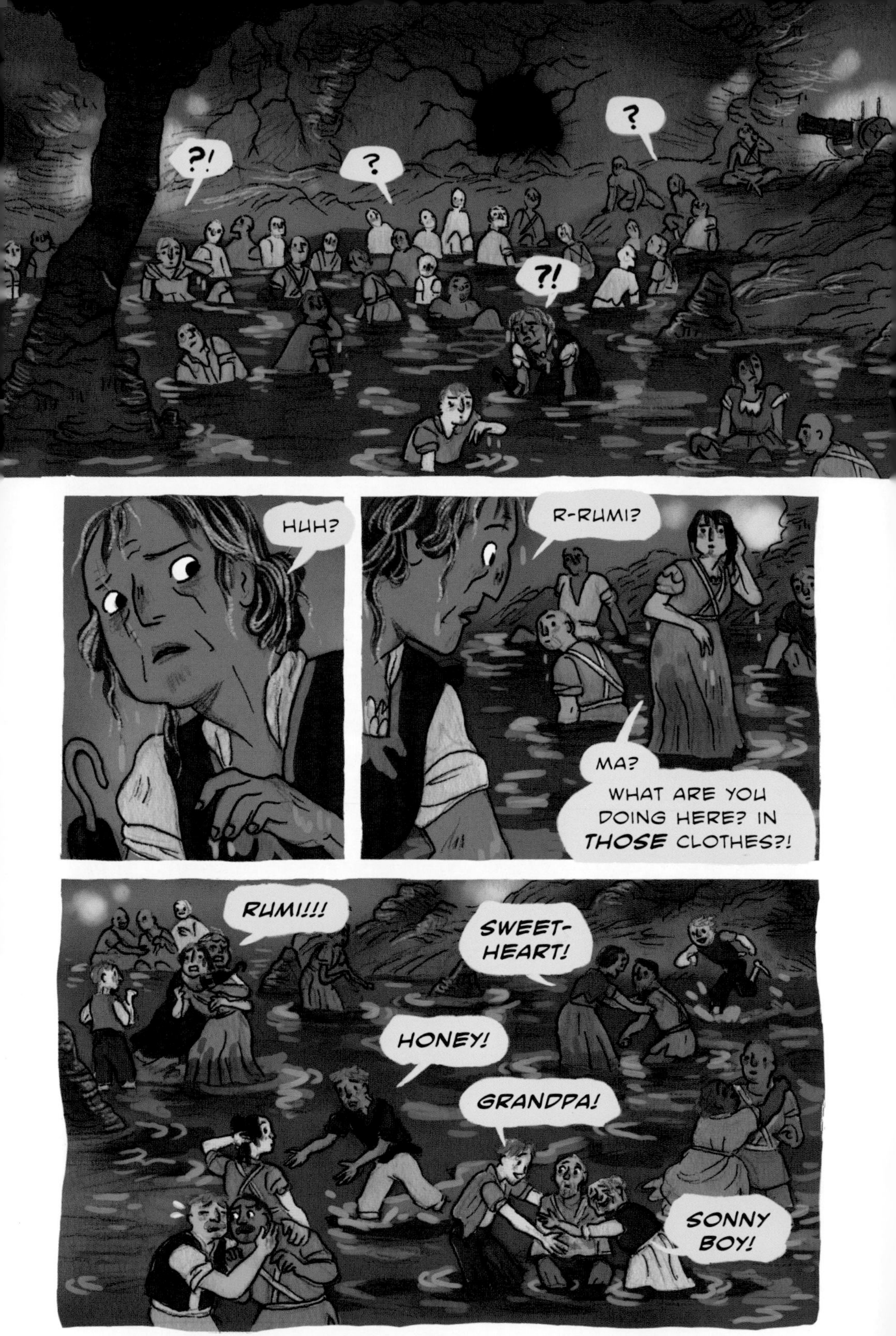
?!
?
?
?!
HUH?
R-RUMI?
MA?
WHAT ARE YOU DOING HERE? IN *THOSE* CLOTHES?!
RUMI!!!
SWEET-HEART!
HONEY!
GRANDPA!
SONNY BOY!

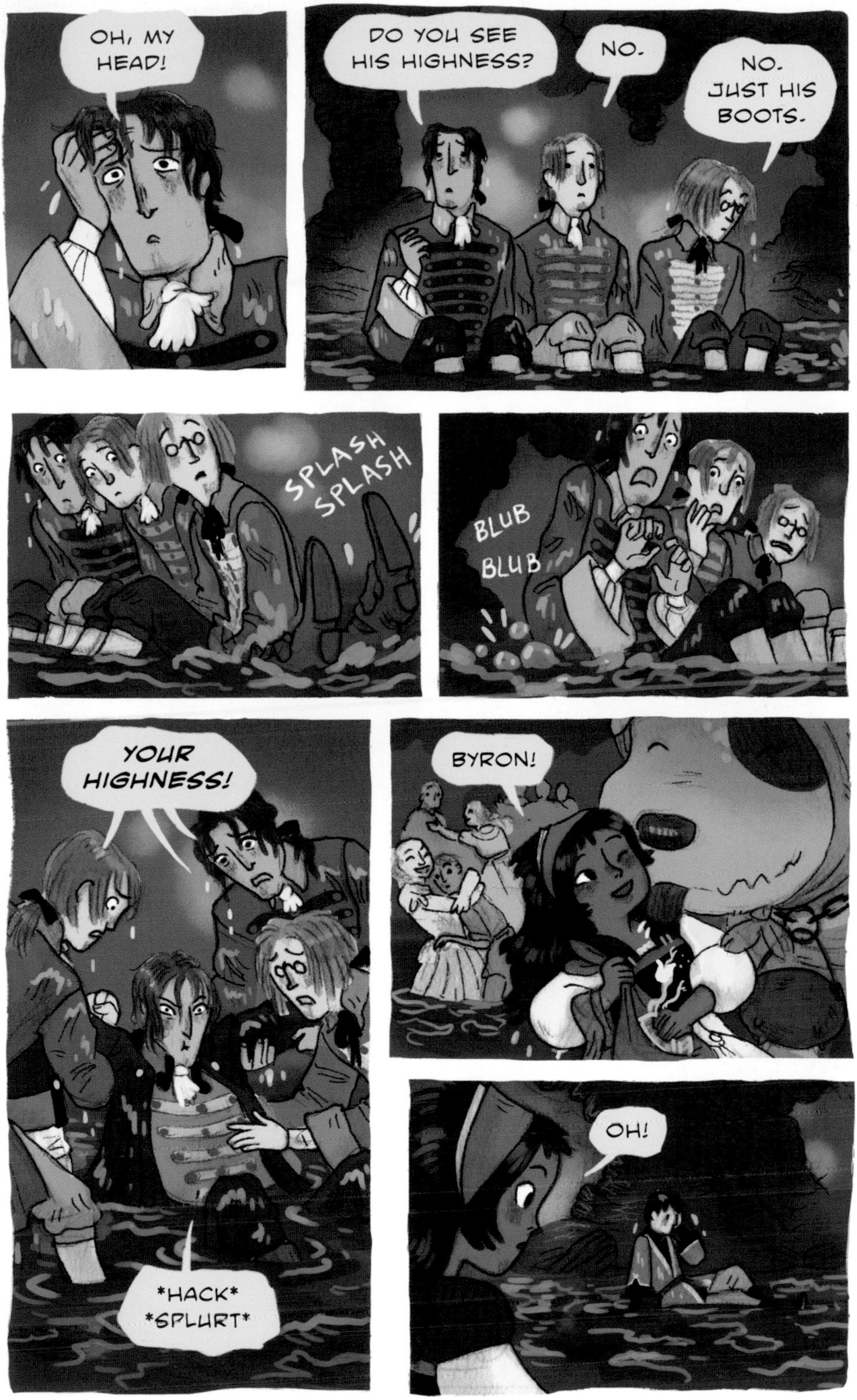
OH, MY HEAD!
DO YOU SEE HIS HIGHNESS?
NO.
NO. JUST HIS BOOTS.
SPLASH SPLASH
BLUB BLUB
YOUR HIGHNESS!
HACK *SPLURT*
BYRON!
OH!

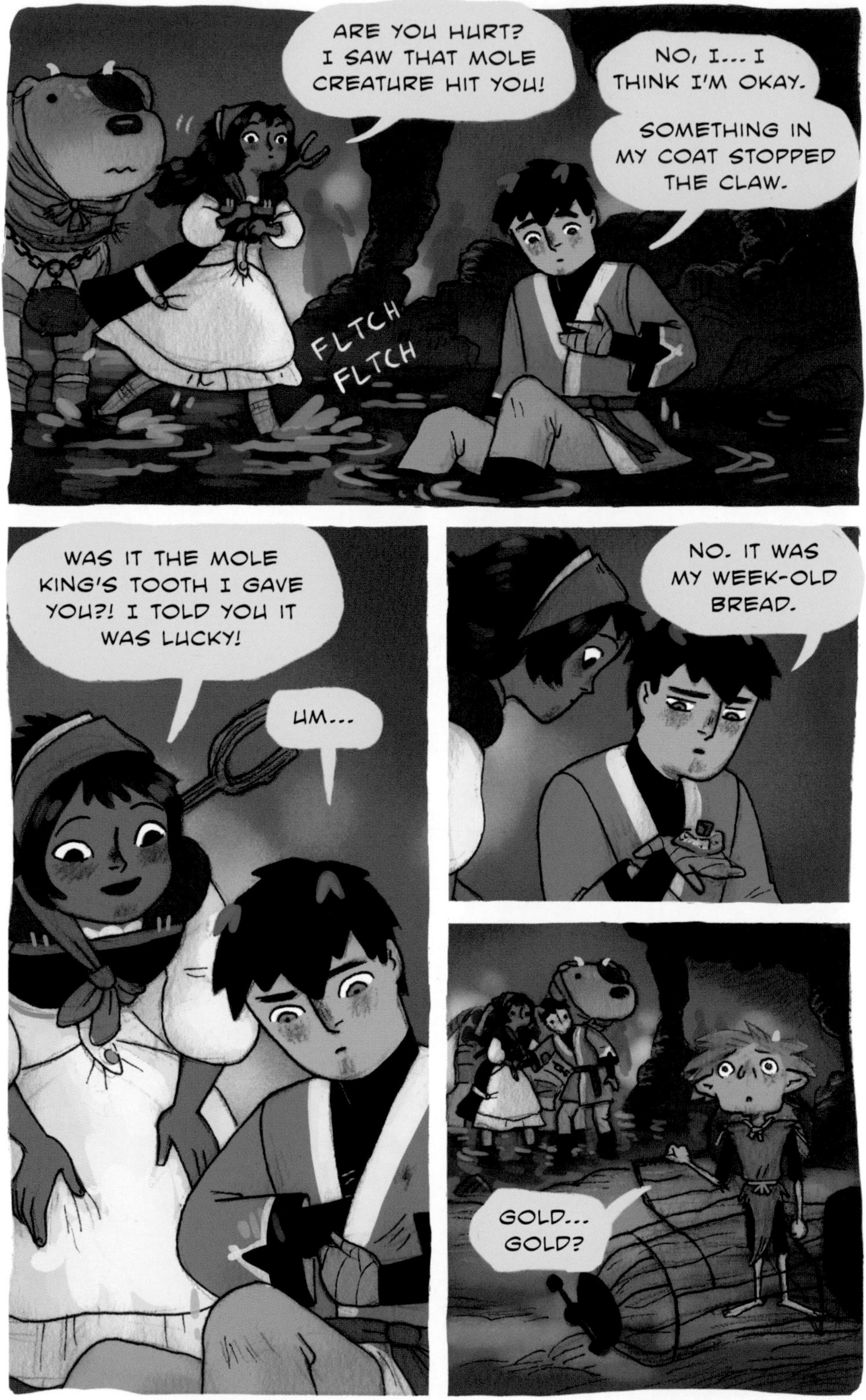
ARE YOU HURT? I SAW THAT MOLE CREATURE HIT YOU!
NO, I... I THINK I'M OKAY.
SOMETHING IN MY COAT STOPPED THE CLAW.
FLTCH FLTCH
WAS IT THE MOLE KING'S TOOTH I GAVE YOU?! I TOLD YOU IT WAS LUCKY!
UM...
NO. IT WAS MY WEEK-OLD BREAD.
GOLD... GOLD?

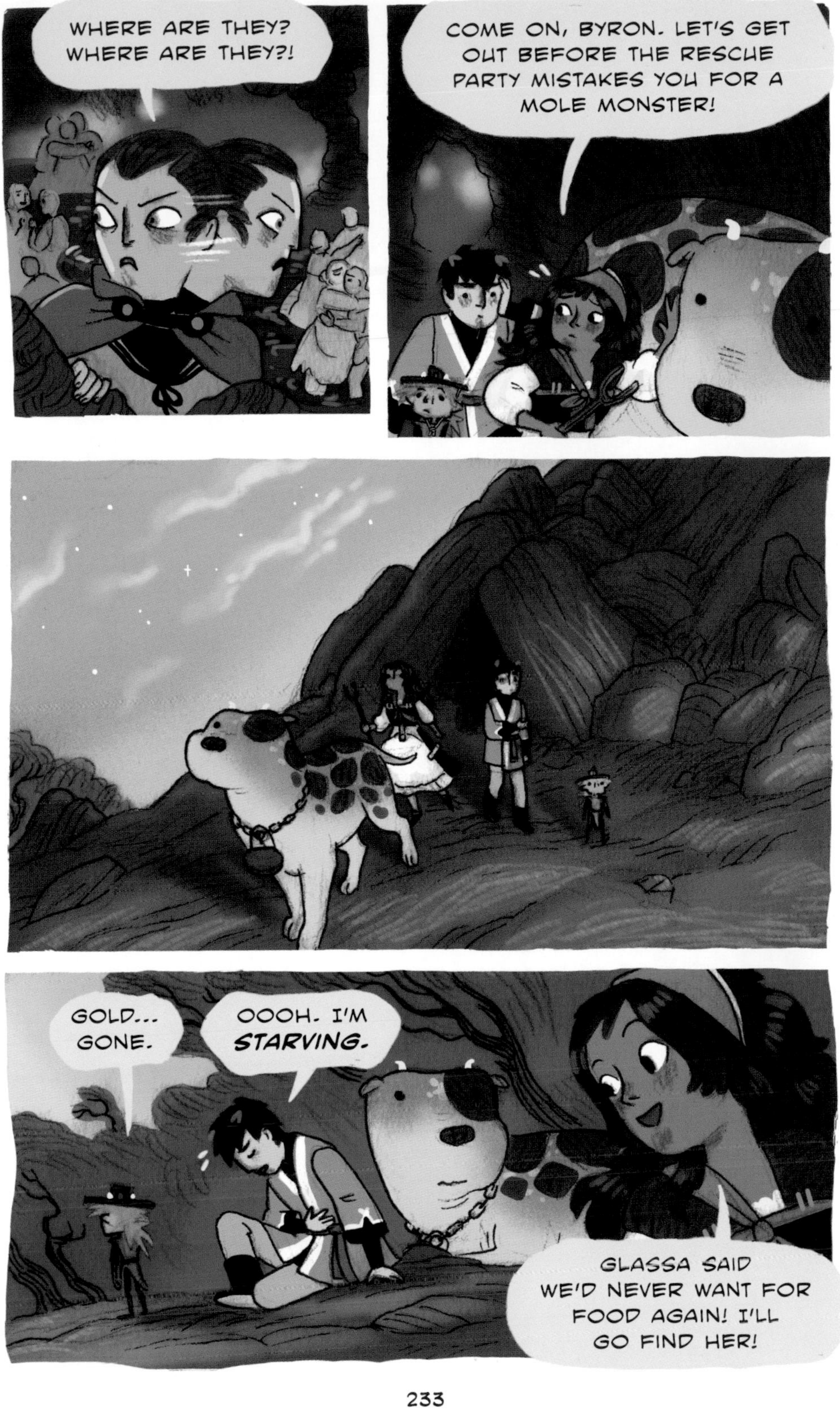
WHERE ARE THEY?
WHERE ARE THEY?!
COME ON, BYRON. LET'S GET OUT BEFORE THE RESCUE PARTY MISTAKES YOU FOR A MOLE MONSTER!
GOLD... GONE.
OOOH. I'M *STARVING.*
GLASSA SAID WE'D NEVER WANT FOR FOOD AGAIN! I'LL GO FIND HER!

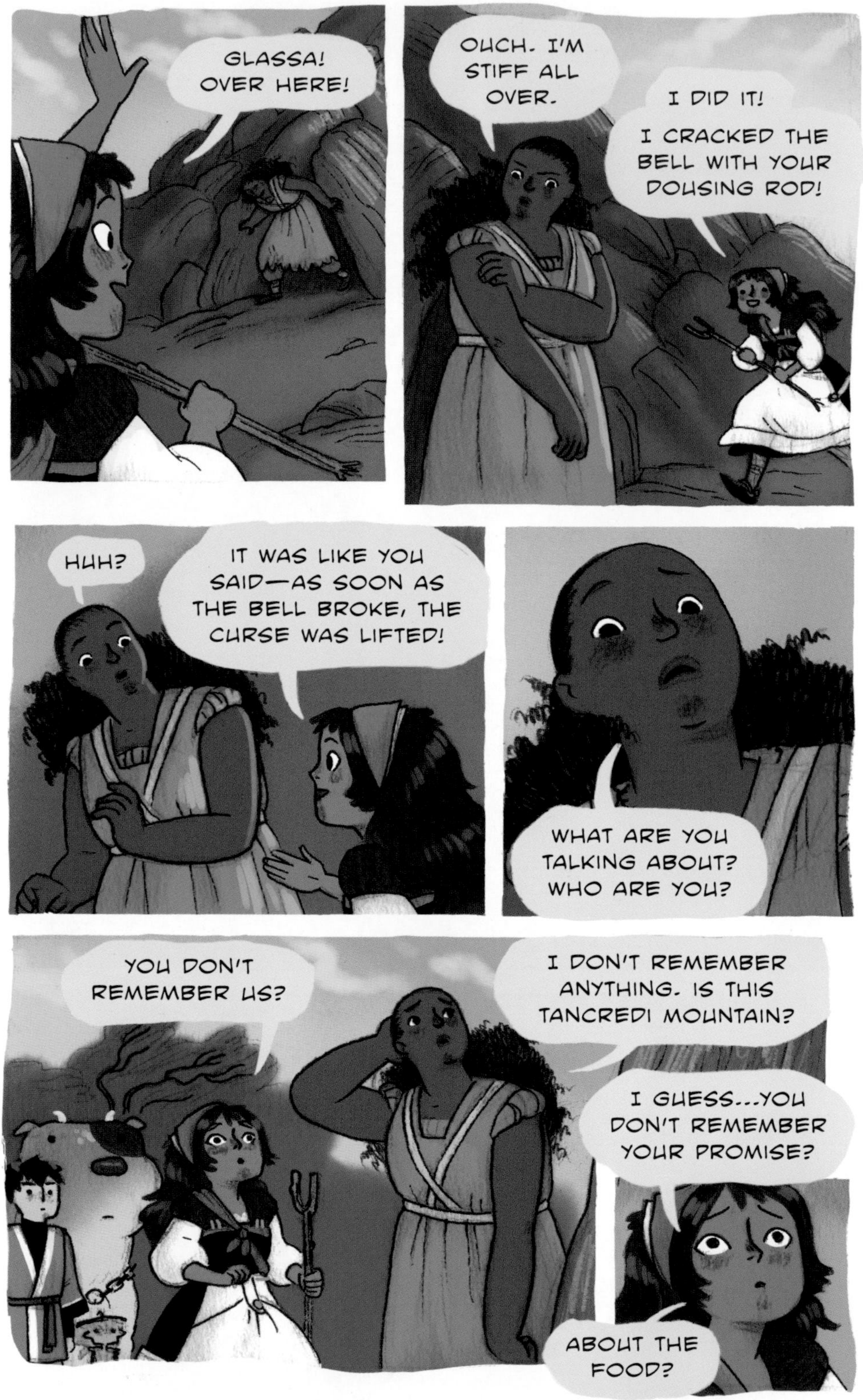
GLASSA!
OVER HERE!
OUCH. I'M
STIFF ALL
OVER.
I DID IT!
I CRACKED THE
BELL WITH YOUR
DOUSING ROD!
HUH?
IT WAS LIKE YOU
SAID—AS SOON AS
THE BELL BROKE, THE
CURSE WAS LIFTED!
WHAT ARE YOU
TALKING ABOUT?
WHO ARE YOU?
YOU DON'T
REMEMBER US?
I DON'T REMEMBER
ANYTHING. IS THIS
TANCREDI MOUNTAIN?
I GUESS...YOU
DON'T REMEMBER
YOUR PROMISE?
ABOUT THE
FOOD?

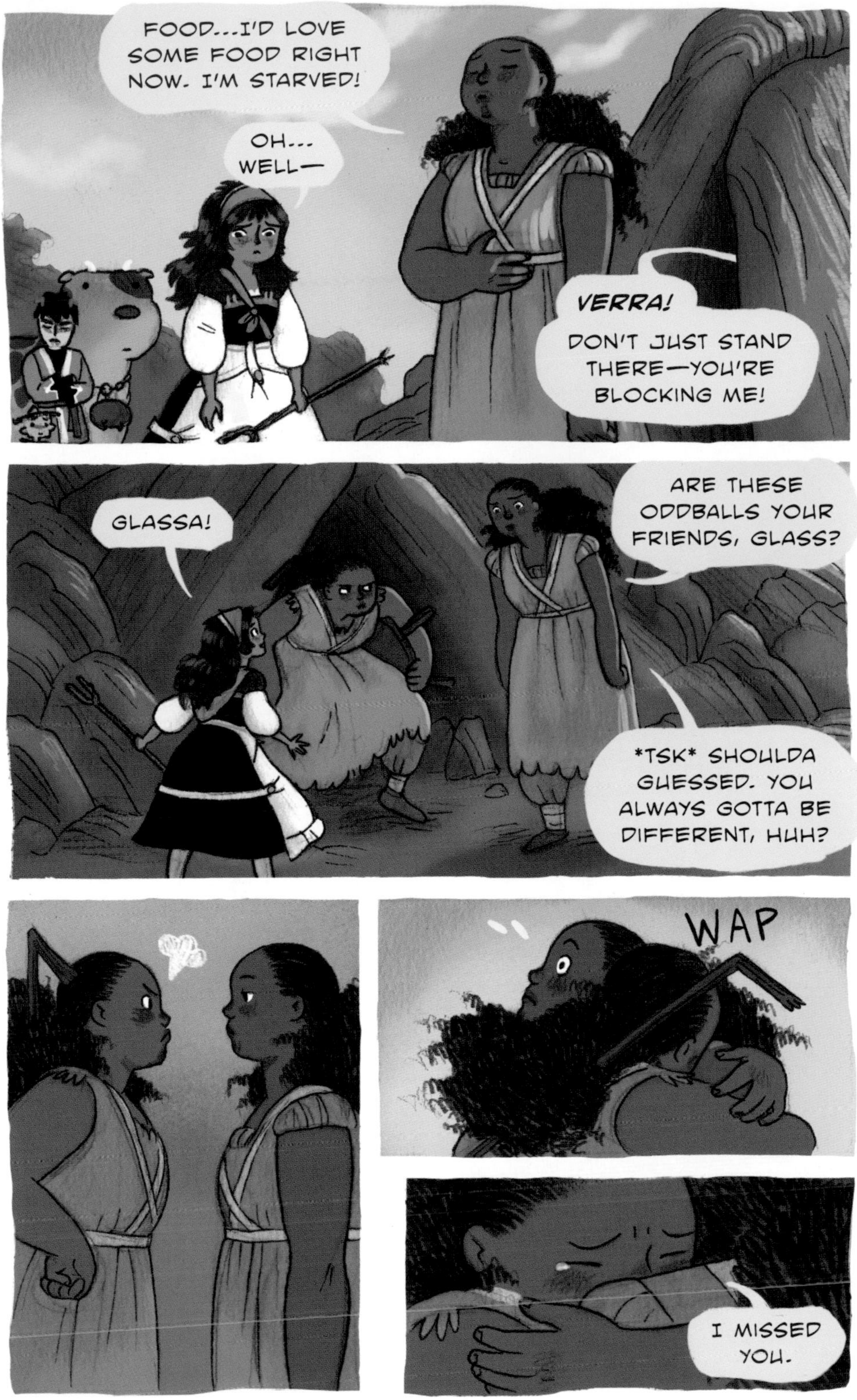
FOOD...I'D LOVE SOME FOOD RIGHT NOW. I'M STARVED!
OH... WELL—
VERRA!
DON'T JUST STAND THERE—YOU'RE BLOCKING ME!
GLASSA!
ARE THESE ODDBALLS YOUR FRIENDS, GLASS?
TSK SHOULDA GUESSED. YOU ALWAYS GOTTA BE DIFFERENT, HUH?
WAP
I MISSED YOU.

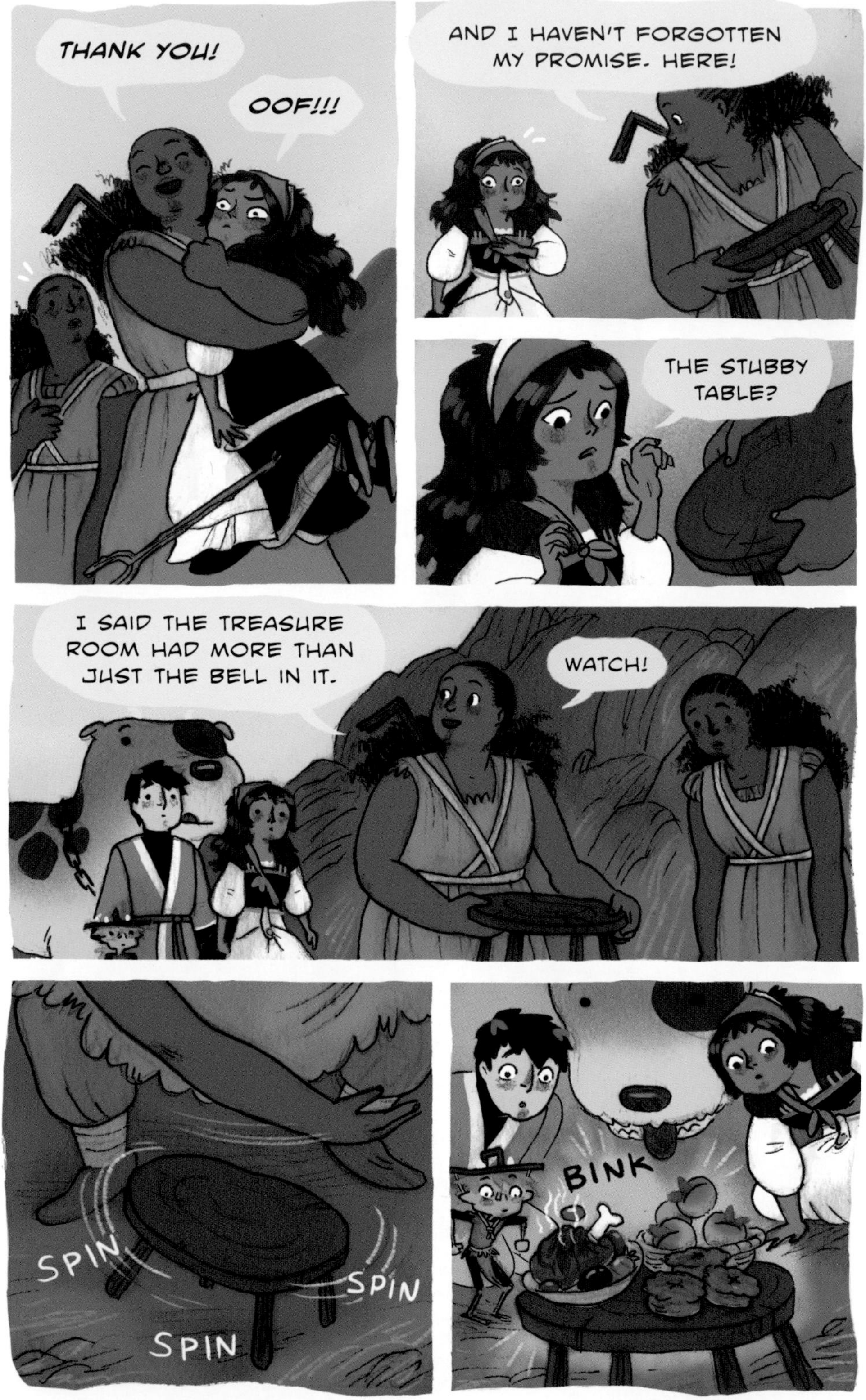
THANK YOU!
OOF!!!
AND I HAVEN'T FORGOTTEN MY PROMISE. HERE!
THE STUBBY TABLE?
I SAID THE TREASURE ROOM HAD MORE THAN JUST THE BELL IN IT.
WATCH!
SPIN
SPIN
SPIN
BINK

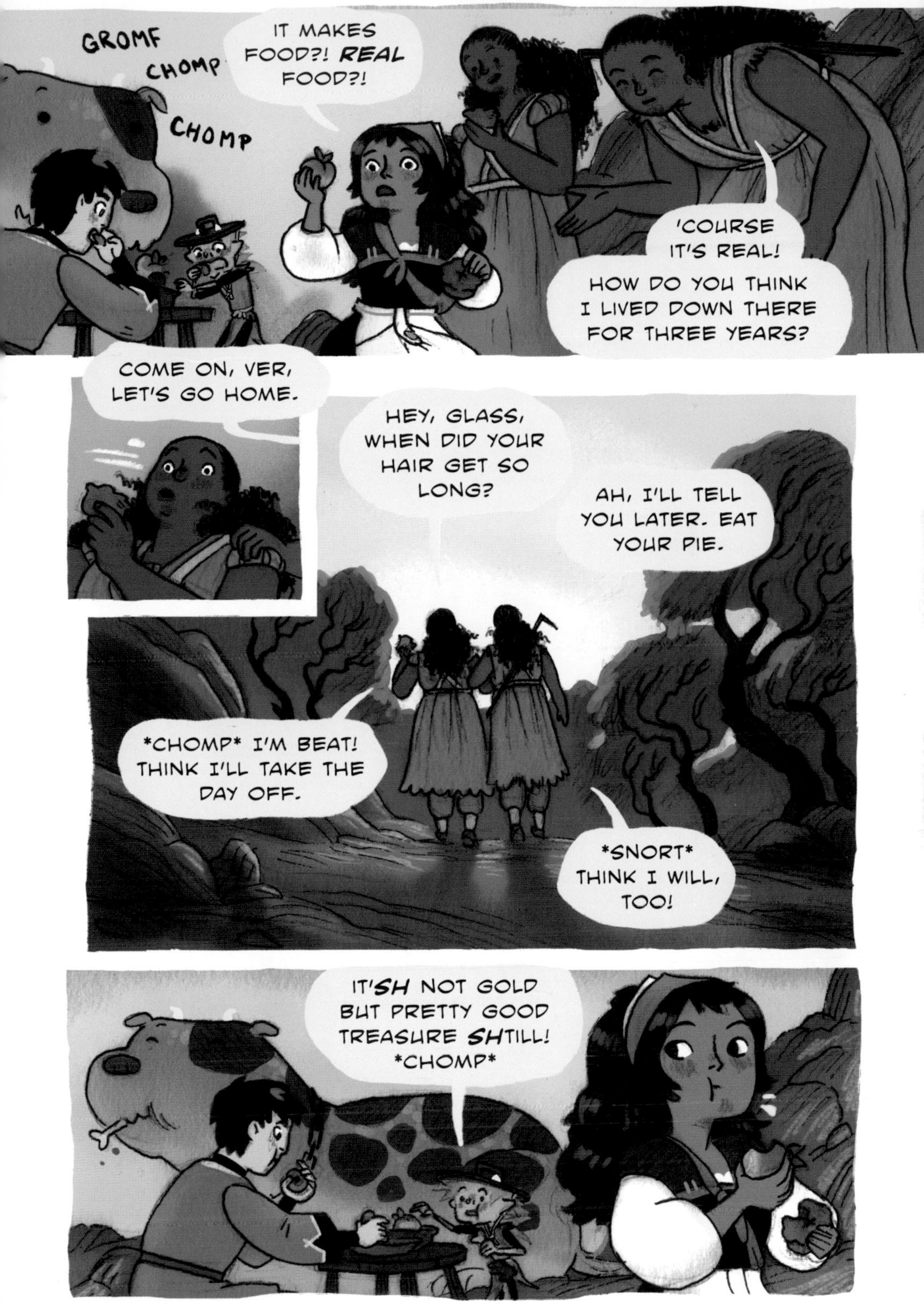
GROMF
CHOMP
CHOMP
IT MAKES FOOD?! REAL FOOD?!
'COURSE IT'S REAL!
HOW DO YOU THINK I LIVED DOWN THERE FOR THREE YEARS?
COME ON, VER, LET'S GO HOME.
HEY, GLASS, WHEN DID YOUR HAIR GET SO LONG?
AH, I'LL TELL YOU LATER. EAT YOUR PIE.
CHOMP I'M BEAT! THINK I'LL TAKE THE DAY OFF.
SNORT THINK I WILL, TOO!
IT'SH NOT GOLD BUT PRETTY GOOD TREASURE SHTILL! *CHOMP*

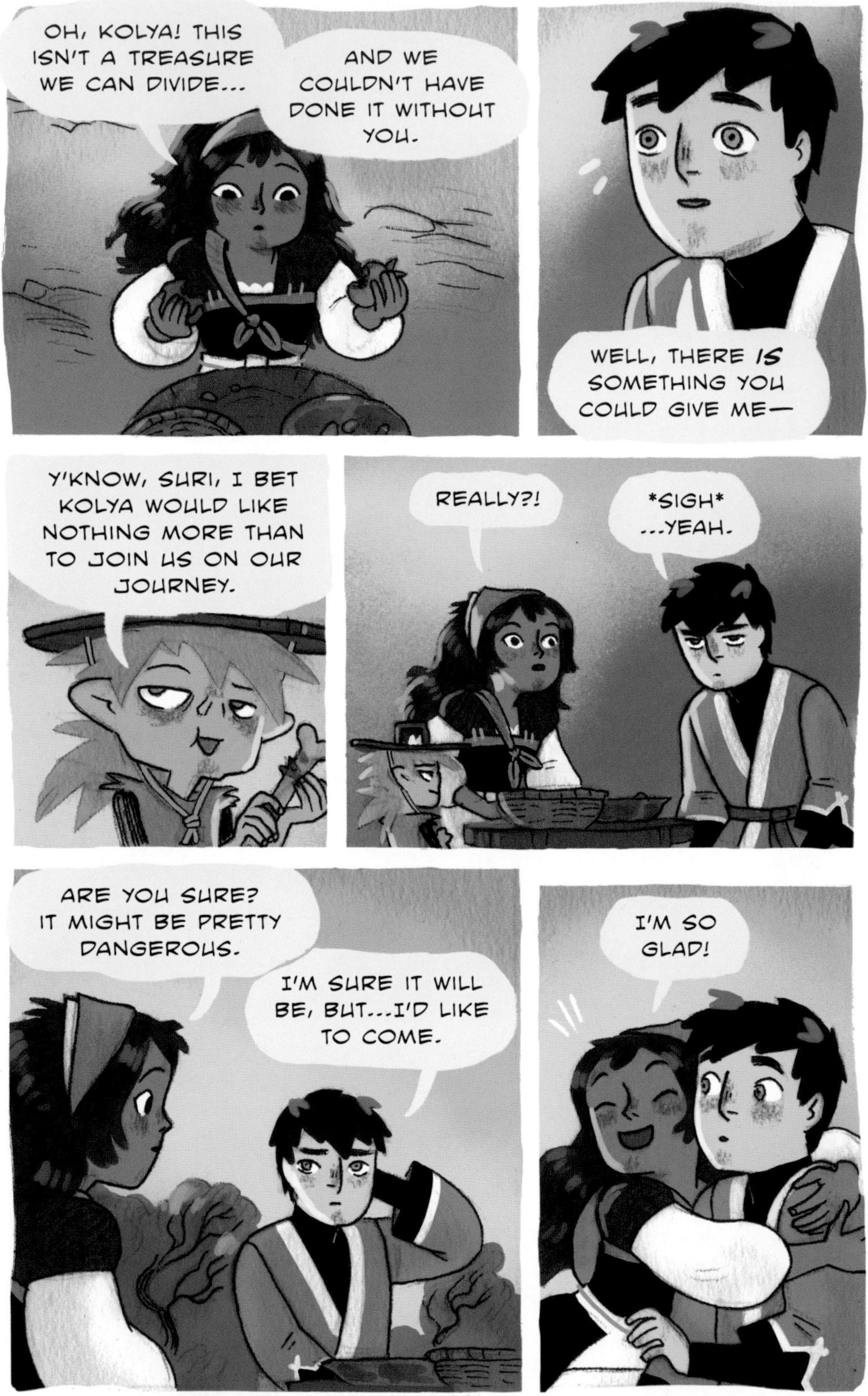
OH, KOLYA! THIS ISN'T A TREASURE WE CAN DIVIDE...
AND WE COULDN'T HAVE DONE IT WITHOUT YOU.
WELL, THERE *IS* SOMETHING YOU COULD GIVE ME—
Y'KNOW, SURI, I BET KOLYA WOULD LIKE NOTHING MORE THAN TO JOIN US ON OUR JOURNEY.
REALLY?!
SIGH ...YEAH.
ARE YOU SURE? IT MIGHT BE PRETTY DANGEROUS.
I'M SURE IT WILL BE, BUT...I'D LIKE TO COME.
I'M SO GLAD!

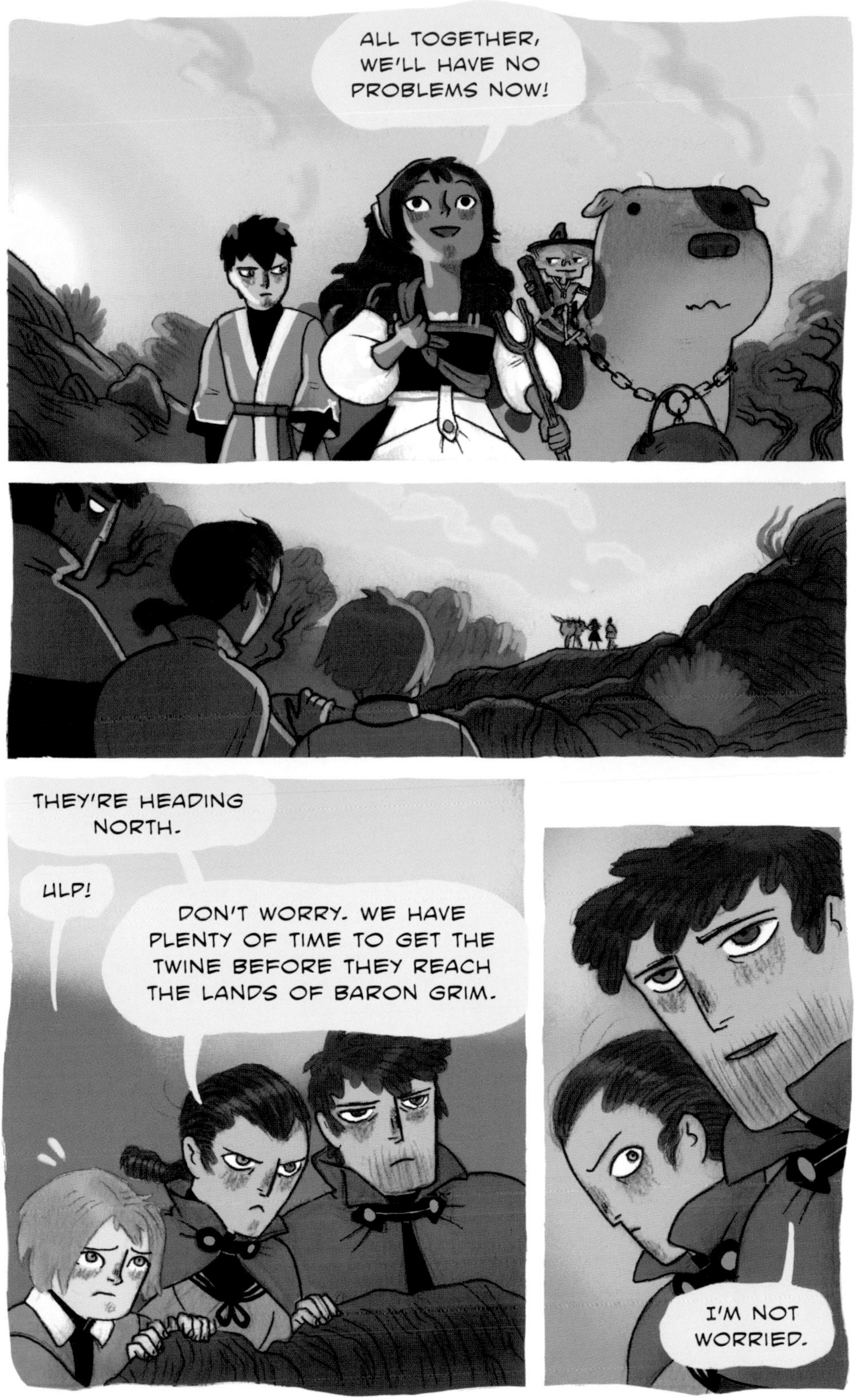
ALL TOGETHER, WE'LL HAVE NO PROBLEMS NOW!
THEY'RE HEADING NORTH.
ULP!
DON'T WORRY. WE HAVE PLENTY OF TIME TO GET THE TWINE BEFORE THEY REACH THE LANDS OF BARON GRIM.
I'M NOT WORRIED.

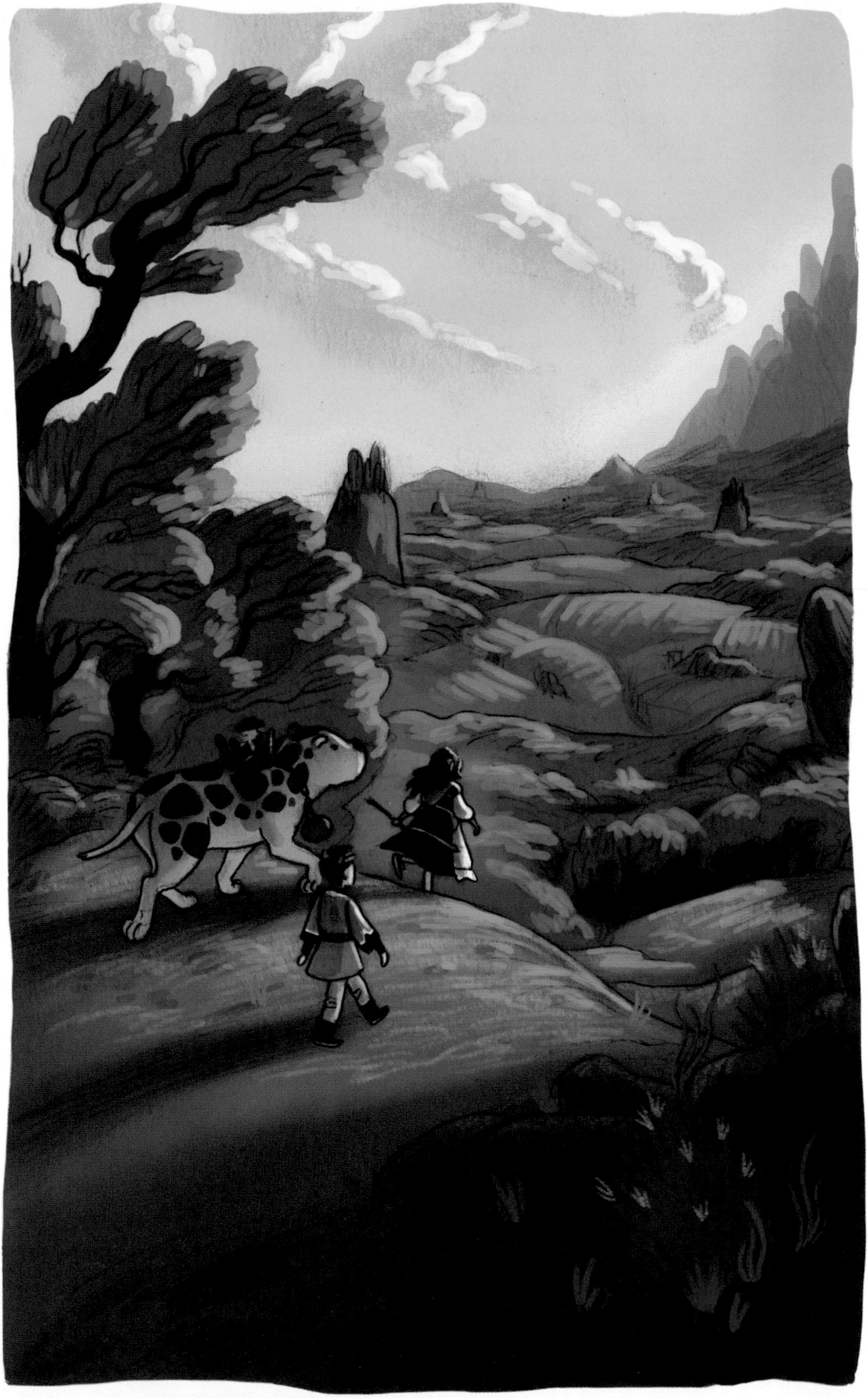

Suri's story contines in

CAT'S CRADLE
SURI'S DRAGON
JO RIOUX

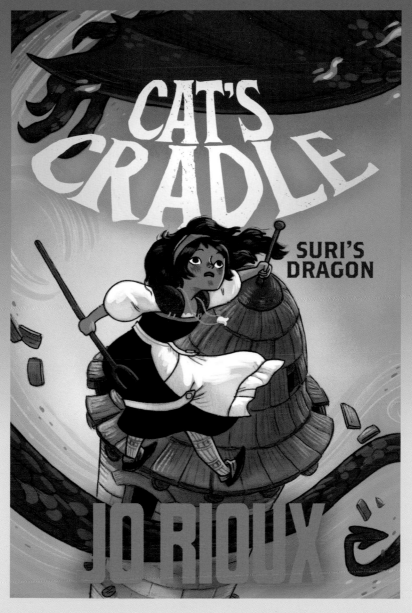

EXCERPTS FROM SURI'S JOURNAL

IMPS

TYPE: HUMAN-LIKE (WELL, BABY-LIKE)
DOMAIN: NOT SURE
NATURE: MOSTLY HARMLESS?

I'D NEVER EVEN HEARD OF IMPS BEFORE CAGLIO, SO I GUESS THEY'RE VERY RARE MONSTERS.

CAGLIO (BONE IMP)

DELUDED
CONCEITED
LIES A LOT

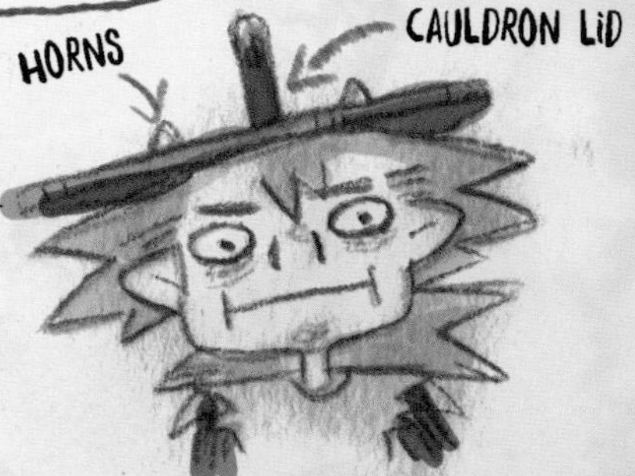

HORNS
CAULDRON LID

CAGLIO'S A BIT STRANGE—HE'S KIND OF SELF-CENTERED AND LAZY, AND HE <u>REALLY</u> LIKES MONEY AND FOOD.... WELL, MAYBE THOSE PARTS ARE NOT <u>THAT</u> DIFFERENT FROM HUMANS. BUT HE SLEEPS IN A CAULDRON AND LIKES FISH FONDUE!

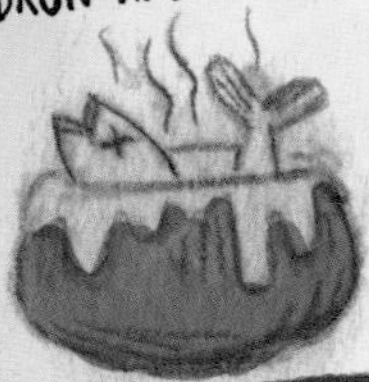

HE IS PRETTY FUNNY AND NICE TO TALK TO, THOUGH! KOLYA SAYS HE'S ONLY OUT FOR HIMSELF, BUT I GET THE IDEA KOLYA DOESN'T LIKE MANY PEOPLE.

CAITSITH (CONTINUED)

I THOUGHT CAITSITHS WERE SOLITARY, BUT NOW I KNOW THEY CAN LIVE IN GROUPS!

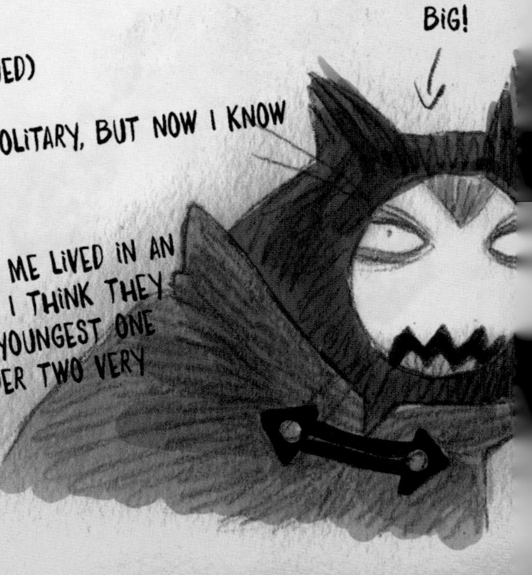

VERY BIG!

THE THREE THAT ATTACKED ME LIVED IN AN OLD HOUSE IN THE FOREST. I THINK THEY WERE SIBLINGS, BUT THE YOUNGEST ONE DIDN'T LOOK LIKE THE OLDER TWO VERY MUCH. I WONDER WHY...

POTATO iMP

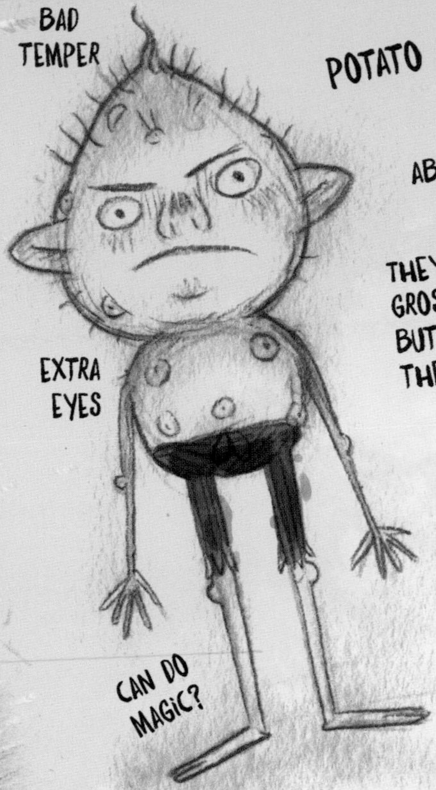
BAD TEMPER
EXTRA EYES
CAN DO MAGIC?

ABOUT 16 iNCHES TALL

THEY SPROUT (PULLULATE? UGH, SOUNDS GROSS!) FROM SPOiLED OR ROTTEN THiNGS, BUT THERE MUST BE MORE TO iT, OTHERWiSE THERE WOULD BE LOTS OF THEM AROUND!

LiVES A LONG TiME—AT LEAST 500 YEARS!

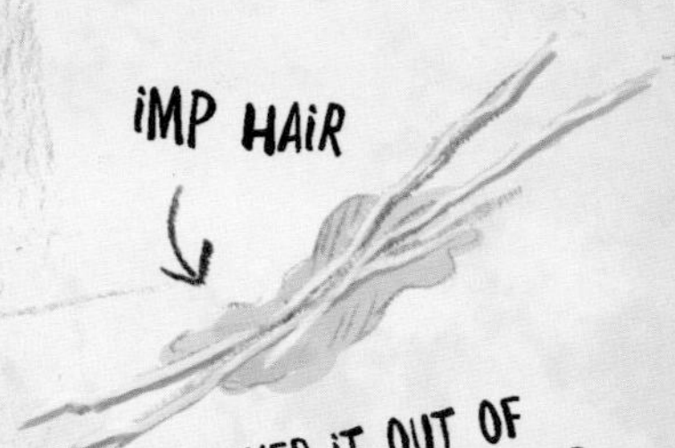
iMP HAiR

I PiCKED iT OUT OF BYRON'S TEETH AFTER HE CHEWED ON CAGLiO.

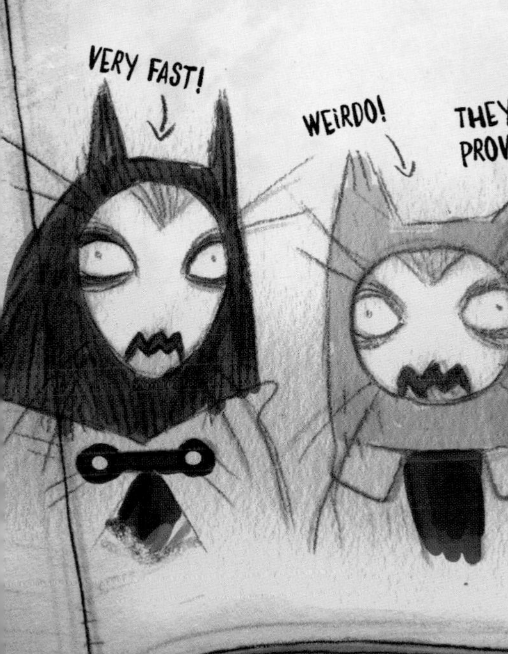
VERY FAST!
WEiRDO!

THEY TRiED TO STEAL MY DRAGON'S TOOTH. THiS PROVES iT MUST BE A REALLY POWERFUL AMULET!

WHAT'S STRANGE iS THAT I NEVER TOLD THAT WEiRDO THAT I HAD A DRAGON'S TOOTH. HOW DiD THEY FiND OUT?

I SHOULD BE ON MY GUARD FOR OTHER CAiTSiTHS ON MY JOURNEY.

MOLE KiNG

TYPE: ANiMAL MONSTER
DOMAiN: UNDERGROUND
NATURE: EViL

A CURSED CRYSTAL BELL WAS RESPONSiBLE FOR THE MOLE KiNG. GLASSA SAiD SHE FOUND iT iN A SEALED CHAMBER. I WONDER WHO PUT iT THERE...

VERY RARE. ONE OF THE OLDEST BREEDS OF MONSTERS. ORiGiNS ~~UNKNOWN~~. KNOWN!

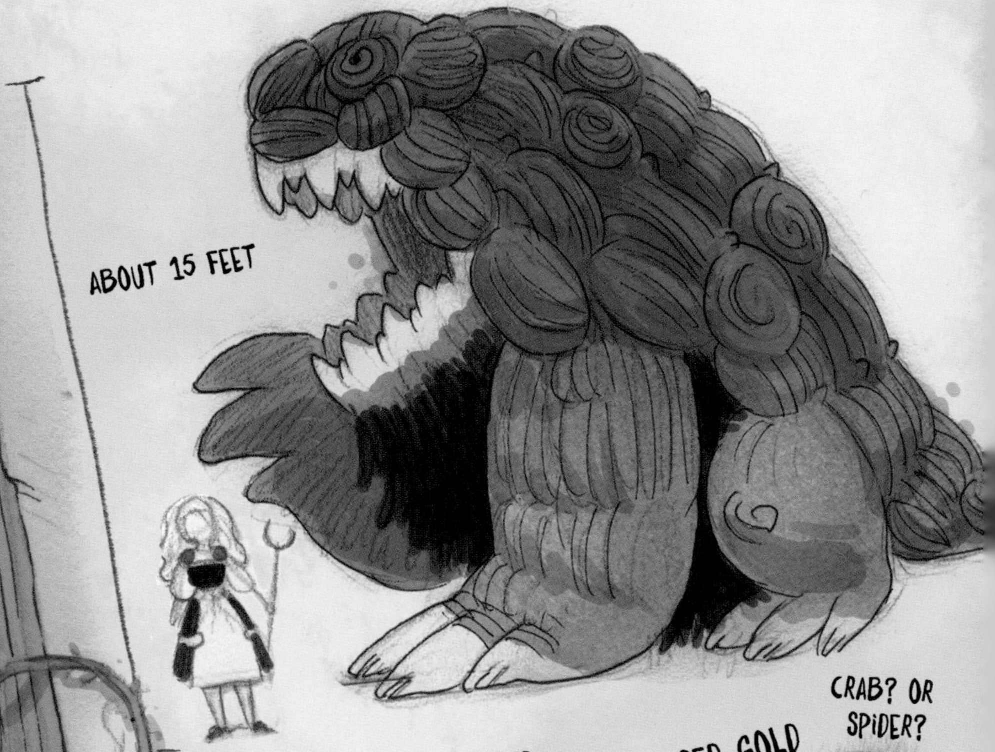
ABOUT 15 FEET

MOLE KiNGS ARE SECRETiVE AND COVETOUS. THEY RARELY LEAVE THEiR UNDERGROUND LAiRS, WHERE THEY GUARD THEiR TREASURE.

CURSED GOLD

CRAB? OR SPiDER?

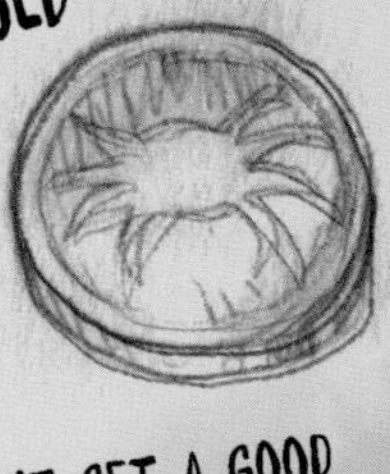

THE MOLE KiNG'S TREASURE iS A GiGANTiC PiLE OF GOLD COiNS! THEY DiG iT OUT OF CRACKS WHEN THE BELL RiNGS. TOO BAD THE GOLD iS CURSED.

I DiDN'T GET A GOOD LOOK AT THE COiNS, BUT THEY HAD THiS SYMBOL ON THEM.

MOLE CREATURES

THE MOLE KING IS NOT ONE CREATURE, BUT A COLONY OF SMALLER MOLE MONSTERS!

MOLE CREATURES ARE HUMANS THAT HAVE TOUCHED THE CURSED GOLD BROUGHT FORTH BY THE CRYSTAL BELL.

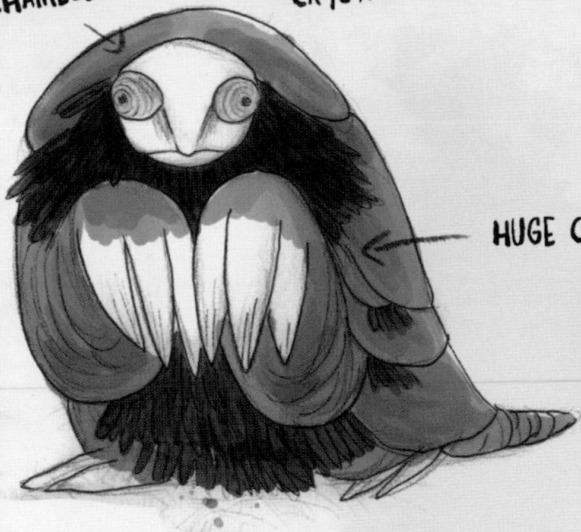
CHAMELEON EYES
HUGE CLAWS

CRYSTAL BELL

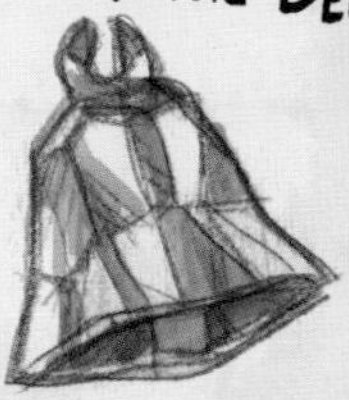

IF A MOLE CREATURE SAYS "DIG," YOU MUST ANSWER "DIG DUG" OR THEY'LL ATTACK!

BYRON

TYPE: ANIMAL MONSTER
DOMAIN: EVERYWHERE!
NATURE: GOOD BOY

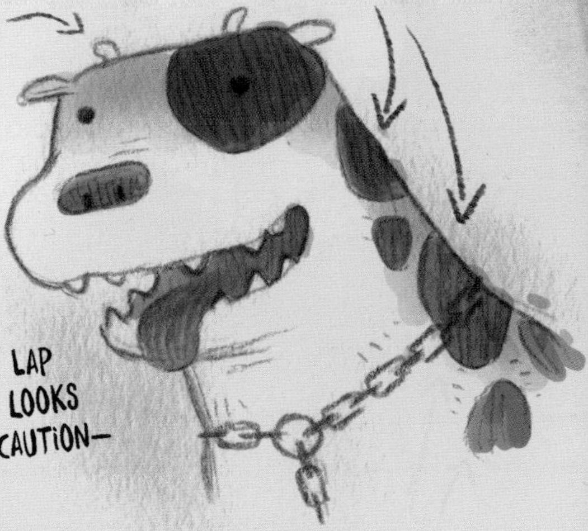
HORNS
HARD PLATES

A GIANT DOG THAT THINKS HE'S A LITTLE LAP DOG. SWEET AND LOYAL BUT A BIG BABY. LOOKS SCARY AT FIRST, BUT REALLY VERY KIND. CAUTION— MIGHT SMOTHER YOU WITH SNUGGLES!

CAGLIO SAID HE MADE BYRON WITH MAGIC.
HE THOUGHT BYRON WOULD MAKE HIS FORTUNE.
I THINK CAGLIO'S IDEAS NEED SOME WORK.

PRAISE FOR
CAT'S CRADLE: THE GOLDEN TWINE

"Jo has created a vibrant world full of magic and danger and cherry doughnuts. It's a world I'd like to live in, even with the monsters."
—**Ben Hatke**,
author of *Zita the Spacegirl* and *Mighty Jack*

"A brilliantly crafted adventure brimming with lively, lovable characters and intriguing mysteries that beg to be unraveled."
—**Matt Rockefeller**,
artist on the 5 Worlds series

"Thanks to Rioux's crackerjack pace and dramatic panel composition, *The Golden Twine* is hard to put down."
—*New York Times*

"A captivating series start that will have readers clamoring for more."
—*Kirkus*

:01 First Second

ANOTHER ADVENTURE AWAITS!

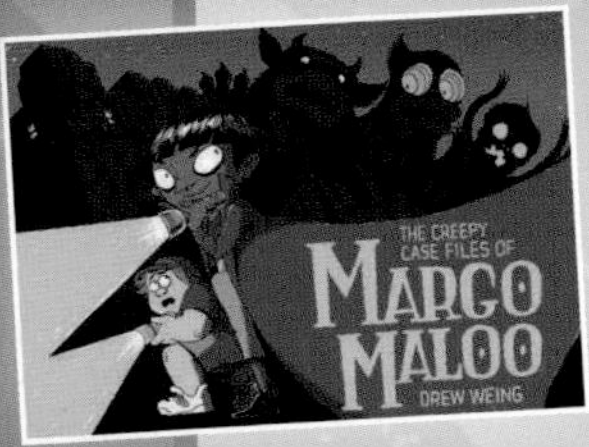
THE CREEPY CASE FILES OF
MARGO MALOO
DREW WEING

THE CREEPY CASE FILES OF MARGO MALOO BY DREW WEING

Charles just moved to Echo City, only to discover the place is teeming with monsters! Luckily, Echo City has Margo Maloo, monster mediator. She always knows exactly what to do—the neighborhood kids say monsters are afraid of *her*.

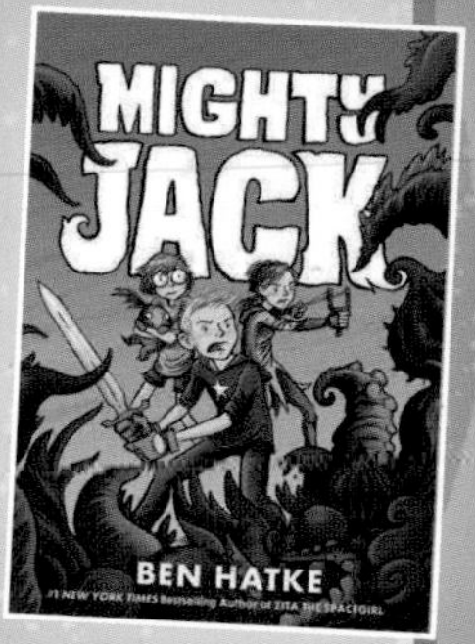
MIGHTY JACK
BEN HATKE

MIGHTY JACK BY BEN HATKE

Jack is stuck babysitting his autistic kid sister, Maddy. It can get boring because Maddy never talks. Until, one day at the flea market, when Maddy tells Jack to trade their mom's car for a box of magic beans. Jack's about to make the best mistake of his life.

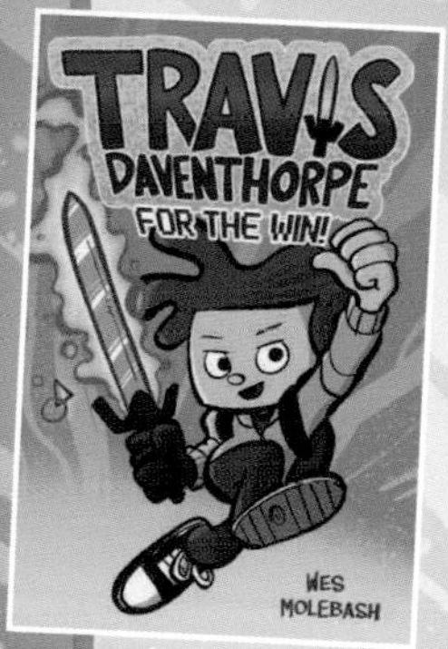
TRAVIS DAVENTHORPE
FOR THE WIN!
WES MOLEBASH

TRAVIS DAVENTHORPE FOR THE WIN! BY WES MOLEBASH

Travis is smart—really smart—but he's not exactly hero material. That is, until the day he finds a magical sword and makes a shocking discovery: He's destined to save the multiverse!

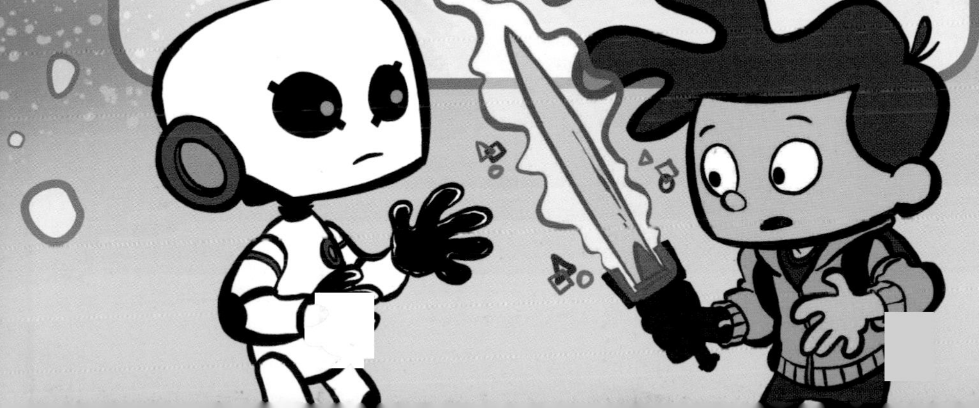

First Second

Published by First Second
First Second is an imprint of Roaring Brook Press,
a division of Holtzbrinck Publishing Holdings Limited Partnership
120 Broadway, New York, NY 10271
firstsecondbooks.com
mackids.com

Library of Congress Control Number: 2022920053

Our books may be purchased in bulk for promotional, educational, or business use.
Please contact your local bookseller or the Macmillan Corporate and Premium Sales Department
at (800) 221-7945 ext. 5442 or by email at MacmillanSpecialMarkets@macmillan.com.

First edition, 2023
Edited by Mark Siegel and Robyn Chapman
Cover design by Kirk Benshoff and Yan L. Moy
Interior book design by Molly Johanson and Yan L. Moy
Production editing by Sarah Gompper

Penciled with Prismacolor Col-Erase in terra cotta and black. Inked with
Prismacolor Premier fine line marker in black. Colored digitally with Photoshop.

Printed in China by 1010 Printing International Limited, North Point, Hong Kong.

ISBN 978-1-250-62538-0 (paperback)
10 9 8 7 6 5 4 3 2 1

ISBN 978-1-250-62537-3 (hardcover)
10 9 8 7 6 5 4 3 2 1

Don't miss your next favorite book from First Second!
For the latest updates go to firstsecondnewsletter.com
and sign up for our enewsletter.

BY ART
WE LIVE